The Wind Through the Keyhole

The Wind Through the Keyhole

A Dark Tower Novel

Stephen King

W F HOWES LTD

This large print edition published in 2012 by
W F Howes Ltd
Unit 4, Rearsby Business Park, Gaddesby Lane,
Rearsby, Leicester LE7 4YH

1 3 5 7 9 10 8 6 4 2

First published in the United Kingdom in 2012
by Hodder & Stoughton

A CIP catalogue record for this book is available
from the British Library

ISBN 978 1 47121 622 0

Typeset by Palimpsest Book Production Limited,
Falkirk, Stirlingshire
Printed and bound in Great Britain
by MPG Books Ltd, Bodmin, Cornwall

MIX
Paper from
responsible sources
FSC
www.fsc.org   FSC® C018575

This is for Robin Furth, and the gang at Marvel Comics.

CONTENTS

CONTENTS

FOREWORD

Many of the people holding this book have followed the adventures of Roland and his band – his ka-tet – for years, some of them from the very beginning. Others – and I hope there are many, newcomers and Constant Readers alike – may ask, *Can I read and enjoy this story if I haven't read the other Dark Tower books?* My answer is yes, if you keep a few things in mind.

First, Mid-World lies next to our world, and there are many overlaps. In some places there are doorways between the two worlds, and sometimes there are thin places, porous places, where the two worlds actually mingle. Three of Roland's ka-tet – Eddie, Susannah, and Jake – have been drawn separately from troubled lives in New York into Roland's Mid-World quest. Their fourth traveling companion, a billy-bumbler named Oy, is a golden-eyed creature native to Mid-World. Mid-World is very old, and falling to ruin, filled with monsters and untrustworthy magic.

Second, Roland Deschain of Gilead is a gunslinger – one of a small band that tries to keep order in an increasingly lawless world. If you think of the gunslingers of Gilead as a strange combination of knights errant and territorial marshals in the Old West, you'll be close to the mark. Most of them, although not all, are descended from the line of the old White King, known as Arthur Eld (I told you there were overlaps).

Third, Roland has lived his life under a terrible curse. He killed his mother, who was having an affair – mostly against her will, and certainly against her better judgment – with a fellow you will meet in these pages. Although it was by mistake, he holds himself accountable, and the unhappy Gabrielle Deschain's death has haunted him since his young manhood. These events are fully narrated in the Dark Tower cycle, but for our purposes here, I think it's all you have to know.

For longtime readers, this book should be shelved between *Wizard and Glass* and *Wolves of the Calla* . . . which makes it, I suppose, *Dark Tower 4.5*.

As for me, I was delighted to discover my old friends had a little more to say. It was a great gift to find them again, years after I thought their stories were told.

Stephen King
September 14, 2011

STARKBLAST

During the days after they left the Green Palace that wasn't Oz after all – but which was also the town of the unpleasant fellow Roland's ka-tet had known as the Tick-Tock Man – the boy Jake began to range farther and farther ahead of Roland, Eddie, and Susannah.

'Don't you worry about him?' Susannah asked Roland. 'Out there on his own?'

'He's got Oy with him,' Eddie said, referring to the billy-bumbler who had adopted Jake as his special friend. 'Mr Oy gets along with nice folks all right, but he's got a mouthful of sharp teeth for those who aren't so nice. As that guy Gasher found out to his sorrow.'

'Jake also has his father's gun,' Roland said. 'And he knows how to use it. That he knows very well. And he won't leave the Path of the Beam.' He pointed overhead with his reduced hand. The low-hanging sky was mostly still, but a single corridor of clouds moved steadily southeast. Toward the land of Thunderclap, if the note left behind for them by the man who styled himself RF had told the truth.

Toward the Dark Tower.

'But why—' Susannah began, and then her wheelchair hit a bump. She turned to Eddie. 'Watch where you're pushin me, sugar.'

'Sorry,' Eddie said. 'Public Works hasn't been doing any maintenance along this stretch of the turnpike lately. Must be dealing with budget cuts.'

It wasn't a turnpike, but it *was* a road . . . or had been: two ghostly ruts with an occasional tumbledown shack to mark the way. Earlier that morning they had even passed an abandoned store with a barely readable sign: TOOK'S OUTLAND MERCANTILE. They investigated inside for supplies – Jake and Oy had still been with them then – and had found nothing but dust, ancient cobwebs, and the skeleton of what had been either a large raccoon, a small dog, or a billy-bumbler. Oy had taken a cursory sniff and then pissed on the bones before leaving the store to sit on the hump in the middle of the old road with his squiggle of a tail curled around him. He faced back the way they had come, sniffing the air.

Roland had seen the bumbler do this several times lately, and although he had said nothing, he pondered it. Someone trailing them, maybe? He didn't actually believe this, but the bumbler's posture – nose lifted, ears pricked, tail curled – called up some old memory or association that he couldn't quite catch.

'Why does Jake want to be on his own?' Susannah asked.

'Do you find it worrisome, Susannah of New York?' Roland asked.

'Yes, Roland of Gilead, I find it *worrisome*.' She smiled amiably enough, but in her eyes, the old mean light sparkled. That was the Detta Walker part of her, Roland reckoned. It would never be completely gone, and he wasn't sorry. Without the strange woman she had once been still buried in her heart like a chip of ice, she would have been only a handsome black woman with no legs below the knees. With Detta onboard, she was a person to be reckoned with. A dangerous one. A gunslinger.

'He has plenty of stuff to think about,' Eddie said quietly. 'He's been through a lot. Not every kid comes back from the dead. And it's like Roland says – if someone tries to face him down, it's the someone who's apt to be sorry.' Eddie stopped pushing the wheelchair, armed sweat from his brow, and looked at Roland. '*Are* there someones in this particular suburb of nowhere, Roland? Or have they all moved on?'

'Oh, there are a few, I wot.'

He did more than wot; they had been peeked at several times as they continued their course along the Path of the Beam. Once by a frightened woman with her arms around two children and a babe hanging in a sling from her neck. Once by an old farmer, a half-mutie with a jerking tentacle that hung from one corner of his mouth. Eddie and Susannah had seen none of these people, or sensed the others that Roland felt sure had, from the safety of the woods and high grasses, marked their progress. Eddie and Susannah had a lot to learn.

But they had learned at least some of what they would need, it seemed, because Eddie now asked, 'Are they the ones Oy keeps scenting up behind us?'

'I don't know.' Roland thought of adding that he was sure something else was on Oy's strange little bumbler mind, and decided not to. The gunslinger had spent long years with no ka-tet, and keeping his own counsel had become a habit. One he would have to break, if the tet was to remain strong. But not now, not this morning.

'Let's move on,' he said. 'I'm sure we'll find Jake waiting for us up ahead.'

2

Two hours later, just shy of noon, they breasted a rise and halted, looking down at a wide, slow-moving river, gray as pewter beneath the overcast sky. On the northwestern bank – their side – was a barnlike building painted a green so bright it seemed to yell into the muted day. Its mouth jutted out over the water on pilings painted a similar green. Docked to two of these pilings by thick hawsers was a large raft, easily ninety feet by ninety, painted in alternating stripes of red and yellow. A tall wooden pole that looked like a mast jutted from the center, but there was no sign of a sail. Several wicker chairs sat in front of the pole, facing the shore on their side of the river. Jake was seated in one of these. Next to him was an old man in a vast straw hat, baggy green pants, and longboots. On his top half he wore a thin white garment – the kind of shirt Roland thought of as a slinkum. Jake and the old man appeared to be eating well-stuffed popkins. Roland's mouth sprang water at the sight of them.

Oy was beyond them, at the edge of the circus-painted raft, looking raptly down at his own reflection. Or perhaps at the reflection of the steel cable that ran overhead, spanning the river.

'Is it the Whye?' Susannah asked Roland.

'Yar.'

Eddie grinned. 'You say Whye; I say Whye Not?' He raised one hand and waved it over his head. 'Jake! Hey, Jake! Oy!'

Jake waved back, and although the river and the raft moored at its edge were still a quarter of a mile away, their eyes were uniformly sharp, and they saw the white of the boy's teeth as he grinned.

Susannah cupped her hands around her mouth. 'Oy! *Oy!* To me, sugar! Come see your mama!'

Uttering shrill yips that were the closest he could get to barks, Oy flew across the raft, disappeared into the barnlike structure, then emerged on their side. He came charging up the path with his ears

7

lowered against his skull and his gold-ringed eyes bright.

'Slow down, sug, you'll give yourself a heart attack!' Susannah shouted, laughing.

Oy seemed to take this as an order to speed up. He arrived at Susannah's wheelchair in less than two minutes, jumped up into her lap, then jumped down again and looked at them cheerfully. 'Olan! Ed! Suze!'

'Hile, Sir Throcken,' Roland said, using the ancient word for bumbler he'd first heard in a book read to him by his mother: *The Throcken and the Dragon*.

Oy lifted his leg, watered a patch of grass, then faced back the way they had come, scenting at the air, eyes on the horizon.

'Why does he keep doing that, Roland?' Eddie asked.

'I don't know.' But he *almost* knew. Was it some old story, not *The Throcken and the Dragon* but one like it? Roland thought so. For a moment he thought of green eyes, watchful in the dark, and a little shiver went through him – not of fear, exactly (although that might have been a part of it), but of remembrance. Then it was gone.

There'll be water if God wills it, he thought, and only realized he had spoken aloud when Eddie said, 'Huh?'

'Never mind,' Roland said. 'Let's have a little palaver with Jake's new friend, shall we? Perhaps he has an extra popkin or two.'

Eddie, tired of the chewy staple they called gunslinger burritos, brightened immediately. 'Hell, yeah,' he said, and looked at an imaginary watch on his tanned wrist. 'Goodness me, I see it's just gobble o'clock.'

'Shut up and push, honeybee,' Susannah said.

Eddie shut up and pushed.

3

The old man was sitting when they entered the boathouse, standing when they emerged on the river side. He saw the guns Roland and Eddie were wearing – the big irons with the sandalwood grips – and his eyes widened. He dropped to one knee. The day was still, and Roland actually heard his bones creak.

'Hile, gunslinger,' he said, and put an arthritis-swollen fist to the center of his forehead. 'I salute thee.'

'Rise up, friend,' Roland said, hoping the old man *was* a friend – Jake seemed to think so, and Roland had come to trust his instincts. Not to mention the billy-bumbler's. 'Rise up, do.'

The old man was having trouble managing it, so Eddie stepped aboard and gave him an arm.

'Thankee, son, thankee. Be you a gunslinger as well, or are you a 'prentice?'

Eddie looked at Roland. Roland gave him nothing, so Eddie looked back at the old man, shrugged, and grinned. 'Little of both, I guess. I'm Eddie Dean, of New York. This is my wife, Susannah. And this is Roland Deschain. Of Gilead.'

The riverman's eyes widened. 'Gilead that was? Do you say so?'

'Gilead that was,' Roland agreed, and felt an unaccustomed sorrow rise up from his heart. Time was a face on the water, and like the great river before them, it did nothing but flow.

'Step aboard, then. And welcome. This young man and I are already fast friends, so we are.' Oy stepped onto the big raft and the old man bent to stroke the bumbler's raised head. 'And we are, too, aren't we, fella? Does thee remember my name?'

'Bix!' Oy said promptly, then turned to the northwest again, raising his snout. His gold-ringed eyes stared raptly at the moving column of clouds that marked the Path of the Beam.

4

'Will'ee eat?' Bix asked them. 'What I have is poor and rough, but such as there is, I'd be happy to share.'

'With thanks,' Susannah said. She looked at the overhead cable that ran across the river on a diagonal. 'This is a ferry, isn't it?'

'Yeah,' Jake said. 'Bix told me there are people on the other side. Not close, but not far, either.

He thinks they're rice farmers, but they don't come this way much.'

Bix stepped off the big raft and went into the boathouse. Eddie waited until he heard the old guy rummaging around, then bent to Jake and said in a low voice, 'Is he okay?'

'He's fine,' Jake said. 'It's the way we're going, and he's happy to have someone to take across. He says it's been years.'

'I'll bet it has been,' Eddie agreed.

Bix reappeared with a wicker basket, which Roland took from him – otherwise the old man might have tumbled into the water. Soon they were all sitting in the wicker chairs, munching popkins filled with some sort of pink fish. It was seasoned and delicious.

'Eat all you like,' Bix said. 'The river's filled with shannies, and most are true-threaded. The muties I throw back. Once upon a time we were ordered to throw the bad 'uns up a-bank so they wouldn't breed more, and for a while I did, but now . . .' He shrugged. 'Live and let live is what I say. As someone who's lived long himself, I feel like I *can* say it.'

'How old are you?' Jake asked.

'I turned a hundred and twenty quite some time ago, but since then I've lost count, so I have. Time's short on this side of the door, kennit.'

On this side of the door. That memory of some old story tugged at Roland again, and then was gone.

'Do you follow that?' The old man pointed to the moving band of clouds in the sky.

'We do.'

'To the Callas, or beyond?'

'Beyond.'

'To the great darkness?' Bix looked both troubled and fascinated by the idea.

'We go our course,' Roland said. 'What fee would you take to cross us, sai ferryman?'

Bix laughed. The sound was cracked and cheerful. 'Money's no good with nothing to spend it on, you have no livestock, and it's clear as day that I have more to eat than you do. And you could always draw on me and force me to take you across.'

'Never,' Susannah said, looking shocked.

'I know that,' Bix said, waving a hand at her. 'Harriers might – and then burn my ferry for good measure once they got t'other side – but true men of the gun, never. And women too, I suppose. You don't seem armed, missus, but with women, one can never tell.'

Susannah smiled thinly at this and said nothing.

Bix turned to Roland. 'Ye come from Lud, I wot. I'd hear of Lud, and how things go there. For it was a marvelous city, so it was. Crumbling and growing strange when I knew it, but still marvelous.'

The four of them exchanged a look that was all an-tet, that peculiar telepathy they shared. It was a look that was also dark with shume, the old Mid-World term that can mean shame, but also means sorrow.

'What?' Bix asked. 'What have I said? If I've asked for something you'd not give, I cry your pardon.'

'Not at all,' Roland said, 'but Lud . . .'

'Lud is dust in the wind,' Susannah said.

'Well,' Eddie said, 'not dust, exactly.'

'Ashes,' Jake said. 'The kind that glow in the dark.'

Bix pondered this, then nodded slowly. 'I'd hear anyway, or as much as you can tell in an hour's time. That's how long the crossing takes.'

5

Bix bristled when they offered to help him with his preparations. It was his job, he said, and he could still do it – just not as quickly as once upon a time, when there had been farms and a few little trading posts on both sides of the river.

In any case, there wasn't much to do. He fetched a stool and a large ironwood ringbolt from the boathouse, mounted the stool to attach the ringbolt to the top of the post, then hooked the ringbolt to the cable. He took the stool back inside and returned with a large metal crank shaped like a block **Z**. This he laid with some ceremony by a wooden housing on the far end of the raft.

'Don't none of you kick that overboard, or I'll never get home,' he said.

Roland squatted on his hunkers to study it. He beckoned to Eddie and Jake, who joined him. He pointed to the words embossed on the long stroke of the **Z**. 'Does it say what I think it does?'

'Yep,' Eddie said. 'North Central Positronics. Our old pals.'

'When did you get that, Bix?' Susannah asked.

'Ninety year ago, or more, if I were to guess. There's an underground place over there.' He pointed vaguely in the direction of the Green Palace. 'It goes for miles, and it's full of things that belonged to the Old People, perfectly preserved. Strange music still plays from overhead, music such as you've never heard. It scrambles your thinking, like. And you don't dare stay there long, or you break out in sores and puke and start to lose your teeth. I went once. Never again. I thought for a while I was going to die.'

'Did you lose your hair as well as your chompers?' Eddie asked.

Bix looked surprised, then nodded. 'Yar, some, but it grew back. That crank, it's *still*, you know.'

Eddie pondered this a moment. Of course it was still, it was an inanimate object. Then he realized the old man was saying *steel*.

'Are'ee ready?' Bix asked them. His eyes were nearly as bright as Oy's. 'Shall I cast off?'

Eddie snapped off a crisp salute. 'Aye-aye, cap'n. We're away to the Treasure Isles, arr, so we be.'

'Come and help me with these ropes, Roland of Gilead, will ya do.'

Roland did, and gladly.

6

The raft moved slowly along the diagonal cable, pulled by the river's slow current. Fish jumped all around them as Roland's ka-tet took turns telling the old man about the city of Lud, and what had befallen them there. For a while Oy watched the fish with interest, his paws planted on the upstream edge of the raft. Then he once more sat and faced back the way they had come, snout raised.

Bix grunted when they told him how they'd left the doomed city. 'Blaine the Mono, y'say. I remember. Crack train. There was another 'un, too, although I can't remember the name—'

'Patricia,' Susannah said.

'Aye, that was it. Beautiful glass sides, she had. And you say the city's all gone?'

'All gone,' Jake agreed.

Bix lowered his head. 'Sad.'

'It is,' Susannah said, taking his hand and giving it a brief, light squeeze. 'Mid-World's a sad place, although it can be very beautiful.'

They had reached the middle of the river now, and a light breeze, surprisingly warm, ruffled their hair. They had all laid aside their heavy outer clothes and sat at ease in the wicker passenger chairs, which rolled this way and that, presumbly for the views this provided. A large fish – probably one of the kind that had fed their bellies at gobble o'clock – jumped onto the raft and lay there, flopping at Oy's feet. Although he was usually death on any small creature that crossed his path, the bumbler appeared not even to notice it. Roland kicked it back into the water with one of his scuffed boots.

'Yer throcken knows it's coming,' Bix remarked. He looked at Roland. 'You'll want to take heed, aye?'

For a moment Roland could say nothing. A clear memory rose from the back of his mind to the front, one of a dozen hand-colored woodcut illustrations in an old and well-loved book. Six bumblers sitting on a fallen tree in the forest beneath a crescent moon, all with their snouts raised. That volume, *Magic Tales of the Eld*, he had loved above all others when he had been but a sma' one, listening to his mother as she read him to sleep in his high tower bedroom, while an autumn gale sang its lonely song outside, calling down winter. 'The Wind through the Keyhole' was the name of the story that went with the picture, and it had been both terrible and wonderful.

'All my gods on the hill,' Roland said, and thumped the heel of his reduced right hand to his brow. 'I should have known right away. If only from how warm it's gotten the last few days.'

'You mean you didn't?' Bix asked. 'And you from In-World?' He made a tsking sound.

16

'Roland?' Susannah asked. 'What is it?'

Roland ignored her. He looked from Bix to Oy and back to Bix. 'The starkblast's coming.'

Bix nodded. 'Aye. Throcken say so, and about starkblast the throcken are never wrong. Other than speaking a little, it's their bright.'

'Bright what?' Eddie asked.

'He means their talent,' Roland said. 'Bix, do you know of a place on the other side where we can hide up and wait for it to pass?'

'Happens I do.' The old man pointed to the wooded hills sloping gently down to the far side of the Whye, where another dock and another boathouse – this one unpainted and far less grand – waited for them. 'Ye'll find your way forward on the other side, a little lane that used to be a road. It follows the Path of the Beam.'

'Sure it does,' Jake said. 'All things serve the Beam.'

'As you say, young man, as you say. Which do'ee ken, wheels or miles?'

'Both,' Eddie said, 'but for most of us, miles are better.'

'All right, then. Follow the old Calla road five miles . . . maybe six . . . and ye'll come to a deserted village. Most of the buildings are wood and no use to'ee, but the town meeting hall is good stone. Ye'll be fine there. I've been inside, and there's a lovely big fireplace. Ye'll want to check the chimney, accourse, as ye'll want a good draw up its throat for the day or two ye have to

17

sit out. As for wood, ye can use what's left of the houses.'

'What is this starkblast?' Susannah asked. 'Is it a storm?'

'Yes,' Roland said. 'I haven't seen one in many, many years. It's a lucky thing we had Oy with us. Even then I wouldn't have known, if not for Bix.' He squeezed the old man's shoulder. 'Thankee-sai. We all say thankee.'

7

The boathouse on the southeastern side of the river was on the verge of collapse, like so many things in Mid-World; bats roosted heads-down from the rafters and fat spiders scuttered up the walls. They were all glad to be out of it and back under the open sky. Bix tied up and joined them. They each embraced him, being careful not to hug tight and hurt his old bones.

When they'd all taken their turn, the old man wiped his eyes, then bent and stroked Oy's head. 'Keep em well, do, Sir Throcken.'

'Oy!' the bumbler replied. Then: 'Bix!'

The old man straightened, and again they heard his bones crackle. He put his hands to the small of his back and winced.

'Will you be able to get back across okay?' Eddie asked.

'Oh, aye,' Bix said. 'If it was spring, I might not – the Whye en't so placid when the snow melts and the rains come – but now? Piece o' piss. The storm's still some way off. I crank for a bit against the current, then click the bolt tight so I can rest and not slip back'ards, then I crank some more. It might take four hours instead of one, but I'll get there. I always have, anyway. I only wish I had some more food to give'ee.'

'We'll be fine,' Roland said.

'Good, then. Good.' The old man seemed reluctant to leave. He looked from face to face – seriously – then grinned, exposing toothless gums. 'We're well-met along the path, are we not?'

'So we are,' Roland agreed.

'And if you come back this way, stop and visit awhile with old Bix. Tell him of your adventures.'

'We will,' Susannah said, although she knew they would never be this way again. It was a thing they all knew.

'And mind the starkblast. It's nothing to fool with. But ye might have a day, yet, or even two. He's not turning circles yet, are ye, Oy?'

'Oy!' the bumbler agreed.

Bix fetched a sigh. 'Now you go your way,' he said, 'and I go mine. We'll both be laid up under cover soon enough.'

Roland and his tet started up the path.

'One other thing!' Bix called after them, and they turned back. 'If you see that cussed Andy, tell him I don't want no songs, and I don't want my gods-damned *horrascope* read!'

'Who's Andy?' Jake called back.

'Oh, never mind, you probably won't see him, anyway.'

That was the old man's last word on it, and none of them remembered it, although they did meet Andy, in the farming community of Calla Bryn Sturgis. But that was later, after the storm had passed.

8

It was only five miles to the deserted village, and they arrived less than an hour after they'd left the ferry. It took Roland less time than that to tell them about the starkblast.

'They used to come down on the Great Woods north of New Canaan once or twice a year, although we never had one in Gilead; they always rose away into the air before they got so far. But I remember once seeing carts loaded with frozen bodies drawn down Gilead Road. Farmers and their families, I suppose. Where their throcken had been – their billy-bumblers – I don't know. Perhaps they took sick and died. In any case, with no bumblers to warn them, those folks were unprepared. The starkblast comes suddenly, you ken. One moment you're warm as toast – because the weather always warms up before – and then it falls on you, like wolves on a ruttle of lambs. The only warning is the sound the trees make as the cold of the starkblast rolls over them. A kind of thudding sound, like grenados covered with dirt. The sound living wood makes when it contracts all at once, I suppose. And by the time they heard that, it would have been too late for those in the fields.'

'Cold,' Eddie mused. 'How cold?'

'The temperature can fall to as much as forty limbits below freezing in less than an hour,' Roland said grimly. 'Ponds freeze in an instant, with a sound like bullets breaking windowpanes. Birds turn to ice-statues in the sky and fall like rocks. Grass turns to glass.'

'You're exaggerating,' Susannah said. 'You must be.'

'Not at all. But the cold's only part of it. The wind comes, too – gale-force, snapping the frozen trees off like straws. Such storms might roll for three hundred wheels before lifting off into the sky as suddenly as they came.'

'How do the bumblers know?' Jake asked.

Roland only shook his head. The how and why of things had never interested him much.

9

They came to a broken piece of signboard lying on the path. Eddie picked it up and read the faded remains of a single word. 'It sums up Mid-World perfectly,' he said. 'Mysterious yet strangely hilarious.' He turned toward them with the piece of wood held at chest level. What it said, in large, uneven letters, was GOOK.

'A gook is a deep well,' Roland said. 'Common law says any traveler may drink from it without let or penalty.'

'Welcome to Gook,' Eddie said, tossing the sign-board into the bushes at the side of the road. 'I like it. In fact, I want a bumper sticker that says I Waited Out the Starkblast in Gook.'

Susannah laughed. Jake didn't. He only pointed at Oy, who had begun turning in tight, rapid circles, as if chasing his own tail.

'We might want to hurry a little,' the boy said.

10

The woods drew back and the path widened to what had once been a village high street. The village itself was a sad cluster of abandonment that ran on both sides for about a quarter-mile. Some of the buildings had been houses, some stores, but now it was impossible to tell which had been which. They were nothing but slumped shells staring out of dark empty sockets that might once have held glass. The only exception stood at the southern end of the town. Here the overgrown high street split around a squat blockhouse-like building constructed of gray fieldstone. It stood hip-deep in overgrown shrubbery and was partly concealed by young fir trees that must have grown up since Gook had been abandoned; the roots had already begun to work their way into the meeting hall's foundations. In the course of time they would bring it down, and time was one thing Mid-World had in abundance.

'He was right about the wood,' Eddie said. He picked up a weathered plank and laid it across the arms of Susannah's wheelchair like a make-shift table. 'We'll have plenty.' He cast an eye at Jake's furry pal, who was once more turning in brisk circles. 'If we have time to pick it up, that is.'

'We'll start gathering as soon as we make sure we've got yonder stone building to ourselves,' Roland said. 'Let's make this quick.'

11

The Gook meeting hall was chilly, and birds – what the New Yorkers thought of as swallows and Roland called bin-rusties – had gotten into the second floor, but otherwise they did indeed have the place to themselves. Once he was under a roof, Oy seemed freed of his compulsion to either face northwest or turn in circles, and he immediately reverted to his essential curious nature, bounding up the rickety stairs toward the soft flutterings and cooings above. He began his shrill yapping, and soon the members of the tet saw the bin-rusties streaking away toward less populated areas of Mid-World. Although, if Roland was right, Jake thought, the ones heading in the direction of the River Whye would all too soon be turned into birdsicles.

The first floor consisted of a single large room. Tables and benches had been stacked against the walls. Roland, Eddie, and Jake carried these to the glassless windows, which were mercifully small, and covered the openings. The ones on the north-west side they covered from the outside, so the wind from that direction would press them tighter rather than blow them over.

While they did this, Susannah rolled her wheel-chair into the mouth of the fireplace, a thing she was able to accomplish without even ducking her head. She peered up, grasped a rusty hanging ring, and pulled it. There was a hellish *skreek* sound . . . a pause . . . and then a great black cloud of soot descended on her in a flump. Her reaction was immediate, colorful, and all Detta Walker.

'*Oh, kiss my ass and go to heaven!*' she screamed. '*You cock-knocking motherfucker, just lookit this shittin mess!*'

She rolled back out, coughing and waving her hands in front of her face. The wheels of her chair left tracks in the soot. A huge pile of the stuff lay in her lap. She slapped it away in a series of hard strokes that were more like punches.

'*Filthy fucking chimbly! Dirty old cunt-tunnel! You badass, sonofa-bitching—*'

She turned and saw Jake staring at her, open-mouthed and wide-eyed. Beyond him, on the stairs, Oy was doing the same thing.

'Sorry, honey,' Susannah said. 'I got a little carried away. Mostly I'm mad at myself. I grew

24

up with stoves n fireplaces, and should have known better.'

In a tone of deepest respect, Jake said, 'You know better swears than my father. I didn't think *anyone* knew better swears than my father.'

Eddie went to Susannah and started wiping at her face and neck. She brushed his hands away. 'You're just spreadin it around. Let's go see if we can find that gook, or whatever it is. Maybe there's still water.'

'There will be if God wills it,' Roland said.

She swiveled to regard him with narrowed eyes. 'You being smart, Roland? You don't want to be smart while I'm sitting here like Missus Tarbaby.'

'No, sai, never think it,' Roland said, but there was the tiniest twitch at the left corner of his mouth. 'Eddie, see if you can find gook-water so Susannah can clean herself. Jake and I will begin gathering wood. We'll need you to help us as soon as you can. I hope our friend Bix has made it to his side of the river, because I think time is shorter than he guessed.'

12

The town well was on the other side of the meeting hall, in what Eddie thought might once have been the town common. The rope hanging from the crank-operated drum beneath the well's rotting cap was long gone, but that was no problem; they had a coil of good rope in their gunna.

'The problem,' Eddie said, 'is what we're going to tie to the end of the rope. I suppose one of Roland's old saddlebags might—'

'What's that, honeybee?' Susannah was pointing at a patch of high grass and brambles on the left side of the well.

'I don't see . . .' But then he did. A gleam of rusty metal. Taking care to be scratched by the thorns as little as possible, Eddie reached into the tangle and, with a grunt of effort, pulled out a rusty bucket with a coil of dead ivy inside. There was even a handle.

'Let me see that,' Susannah said.

He dumped out the ivy and handed it over. She tested the handle and it broke immediately, not with a snap but a soft, punky sigh. Susannah looked at him apologetically and shrugged.

''S okay,' Eddie said. 'Better to know now than when it's down in the well.' He tossed the handle aside, cut off a chunk of their rope, untwisted the outer strands to thin it, and threaded what was left through the holes that had held the old handle.

'Not bad,' Susannah said. 'You mighty handy for a white boy.' She peered over the lip of the well. 'I can see the water. Not even ten feet down. Ooo, it looks *cold*.'

'Chimney sweeps can't be choosers,' Eddie said.

The bucket splashed down, tilted, and began to fill. When it sank below the surface of the water, Eddie hauled it back up. It had sprung several leaks at spots where the rust had eaten through, but they were small ones. He took off his shirt, dipped it in the water, and began to wash her face.

'Oh my goodness!' he said. 'I see a girl!'

She took the balled-up shirt, rinsed it, wrung it out, and began to do her arms. 'At least I got the dang flue open. You can draw some more water once I get the worst of this mess cleaned off me, and when we get a fire going, I can wash in warm—'

Far to the northwest, they heard a low, thudding crump. There was a pause, then a second one. It was followed by several more, then a perfect fusillade. Coming in their direction like marching feet. Their startled eyes met.

Eddie, bare to the waist, went to the back of her wheelchair. 'I think we better speed this up.'

In the distance – but definitely moving closer – came sounds that could have been armies at war.

'I think you're right,' Susannah said.

13

When they got back, they saw Roland and Jake running toward the meeting hall with armolads of decaying lumber and splintered chunks of wood. Still well across the river but definitely closer, came those low, crumping explosions as trees in the path of the starkblast yanked themselves inward toward their tender cores. Oy was in the middle of the overgrown high street, turning and turning.

Susannah tipped herself out of her wheelchair, landed neatly on her hands, and began crawling toward the meetinghouse.

'What the hell are you doing?' Eddie asked.

'You can carry more wood in the chair. Pile it high. I'll get Roland to give me his flint and steel, get a fire going.'

'But—'

'Mind me, Eddie. Let me do what I can. And put your shirt back on. I know it's wet, but it'll keep you from getting scratched up.'

He did so, then turned the chair, tilted it on its big back wheels, and pushed it toward the nearest likely source of fuel. As he passed Roland, he gave the gunslinger Susannah's message. Roland nodded and kept running, peering over his armload of wood.

The three of them went back and forth without speaking, gathering wood against the cold on this weirdly warm afternoon. The Path of the Beam in the sky was temporarily gone, because all the clouds were in motion, rolling away to the southeast. Susannah had gotten a fire going, and it roared beastily up the chimney. The big downstairs room had a huge jumble of wood in the center, some with rusty nails poking out. So far none of them had been cut or punctured, but Eddie thought it was just a matter of time. He tried to remember when he'd last had a tetanus shot and couldn't.

As for Roland, he thought, *his blood would*

probably kill any germ the second it dared show its head inside of that leather bag he calls skin.

'What are you smiling about?' Jake asked. The words came out in little out-of-breath gasps. The arms of his shirt were filthy and covered with splinters; there was a long smutch of dirt on his forehead.

'Nothing much, little hero. Watch out for rusty nails. One more load each and we'd better call it good. It's close.'

'Okay.'

The thuds were on their side of the river now, and the air, although still warm, had taken on a queer thick quality. Eddie loaded up Susannah's wheelchair a final time and trundled it back toward the meetinghouse. Jake and Roland were ahead of him. He could feel heat baking out of the open door. *It* better *get cold,* he thought, *or we're going to fucking roast in there.*

Then, as he waited for the two ahead of him to turn sideways so they could get their loads of lumber inside, a thin and pervasive screaming joined the pops and thuds of contracting wood. It made the hair bristle on the nape of Eddie's neck. The wind coming toward them sounded alive, and in agony.

The air began to move again. First it was warm, then cool enough to dry the sweat on his face, then cold. This happened in a matter of seconds. The creepy screech of the wind was joined by a fluttering sound that made Eddie think of the plastic pennants you sometimes saw strung around used-car lots. It ramped up to a whir, and leaves began to blow off the trees, first in bundles and then in sheets. The branches thrashed against clouds that were lensing darker even as he looked at them, mouth agape.

'Oh, *shit*,' he said, and ran the wheelchair straight at the door. For the first time in ten trips, it stuck. The planks he'd stacked across the chair's arms were too wide. With any other load, the ends would have snapped off with the same soft, almost apologetic sound the bucket handle had made, but not this time. Oh no, not now that the storm was almost here. Was nothing in Mid-World ever easy? He reached over the back of the chair to shove the longest boards aside, and that was when Jake shouted.

'*Oy! Oy's still out there! Oy! To me!*'

Oy took no notice. He had stopped his turning. Now he only sat with his snout raised toward the coming storm, his gold-ringed eyes fixed and dreamy.

14

Jake didn't think, and he didn't look for the nails that were protruding from Eddie's last load of lumber. He simply scrambled up the splintery pile and jumped. He struck Eddie, sending him staggering back. Eddie tried to keep his balance but tripped on his own feet and fell on his butt. Jake went to one knee, then scrambled up, eyes wide, long hair blowing back from his head in a tangle of licks and ringlets.

'Jake, no!'

Eddie grabbed for him and got nothing but the cuff of the kid's shirt. It had been thinned by many washings in many streams, and tore away.

Roland was in the doorway. He batted the too-long boards to the right and left, as heedless of the protruding nails as Jake had been. The gunslinger yanked the wheelchair through the doorway and grunted, 'Get in here.'

'Jake—'

'Jake will either be all right or he won't.' Roland seized Eddie by the arm and hauled him to his feet. Their old bluejeans were making machine-gun noises around their legs as the wind whipped them. 'He's on his own. Get in here.'

'No! Fuck you!'

Roland didn't argue, simply yanked Eddie through the door. Eddie went sprawling. Susannah knelt in front of the fire, staring at him. Her face was streaming with sweat, and the front of her deerskin shirt was soaked.

Roland stood in the doorway, face grim, watching Jake run to his friend.

15

Jake felt the temperature of the air around him plummet. A branch broke off with a dry snap and he ducked as it whistled over his head. Oy never

31

stirred until Jake snatched him up. Then the bumbler looked around wildly, baring his teeth.

'Bite if you have to,' Jake said, 'but I won't put you down.'

Oy didn't bite and Jake might not have felt it if he had. His face was numb. He turned back toward the meetinghouse and the wind became a huge cold hand planted in the middle of his back. He began running again, aware that now he was doing so in absurd leaps, like an astronaut running on the surface of the moon in a science fiction movie. One leap . . . two . . . three . . .

But on the third one he didn't come down. He was blown straight forward with Oy cradled in his arms. There was a guttural, garumphing explosion as one of the old houses gave in to the wind and went flying southeast in a hail of shrapnel. He saw a flight of stairs, the crude plank banister still attached, spinning up toward the racing clouds. *We'll be next*, he thought, and then a hand, minus two fingers but still strong, gripped him above the elbow.

Roland turned him toward the door. For a moment the issue was in doubt as the wind bullied them away from safety. Then Roland lunged forward into the doorway with his remaining fingers sinking deep into Jake's flesh. The pressure of the wind abruptly left them, and they both landed on their backs.

'Thank God!' Susannah cried.

'Thank him later!' Roland was shouting to be

heard over the pervasive bellow of the gale. 'Push! All of you push on this damned door! Susannah, you at the bottom! All your strength! You bar it, Jake! Do you understand me? Drop the bar into the clamps! Don't hesitate!'

'Don't worry about me,' Jake snapped. Something had gashed him at one temple and a thin ribbon of blood ran down the side of his face, but his eyes were clear and sure.

'Now! Push! Push for your lives!'

The door swung slowly shut. They could not have held it for long – mere seconds – but they didn't have to. Jake dropped the thick wooden bar, and when they moved cautiously back, the rusty clamps held. They looked at each other, gasping for breath, then down at Oy. Who gave a single cheerful yap, and went to toast himself by the fire. The spell that the oncoming storm had cast on him seemed to be broken.

Away from the hearth, the big room was already growing cold.

'You should have let me grab the kid, Roland,' Eddie said. 'He could have been killed out there.'

'Oy was Jake's responsibility. He should have gotten him inside sooner. Tied him to something, if he had to. Or don't you think so, Jake?'

'Yeah, I do.' Jake sat down beside Oy, stroking the bumbler's thick fur with one hand and rubbing blood from his face with the other.

'Roland,' Susannah said, 'he's just a boy.'

'No more,' Roland said. 'Cry your pardon, but . . . no more.'

16

For the first two hours of the starkblast, they were in some doubt if even the stone meetinghouse would hold. The wind screamed and trees snapped. One slammed down on the roof and smashed it. Cold air jetted through the boards above them. Susannah and Eddie put their arms around each other. Jake shielded Oy – now lying placidly on his back with his stubby legs splayed to all points of the compass – and looked up at the swirling cloud of birdshit that had sifted through the cracks in the ceiling. Roland went on calmly laying out their little supper.

'What do you think, Roland?' Eddie asked.

'I think that if this building stands one more hour, we'll be fine. The cold will intensify, but the wind will drop a little when dark comes. It will drop still more come tomorrowlight, and by the day after tomorrow, the air will be still and much warmer. Not like it was before the coming of the storm, but that warmth was unnatural and we all knew it.'

He regarded them with a half-smile. It looked strange on his face, which was usually so still and grave.

'In the meantime, we have a good fire – not enough to heat the whole room, but fine enough if we stay close to it. And a little time to rest. We've been through much, have we not?'

'Yeah,' Jake said. '*Too* much.'

'And more ahead, I have no doubt. Danger, hard work, sorrow. Death, mayhap. So now we sit by the fire, as in the old days, and take what comfort we can.' He surveyed them, still with that little smile. The firelight cast him in strange profile, making him young on one side of his face and ancient on the other. 'We are ka-tet. We are one from many. Be grateful for warmth, shelter, and companionship against the storm. Others may not be so lucky.'

'We'll hope they are,' Susannah said. She was thinking of Bix.

'Come,' Roland said. 'Eat.'

They came, and settled themselves around their dinh, and ate what he had set out for them.

17

Susannah slept for an hour or two early that night, but her dreams – of nasty, maggoty foods she was somehow compelled to eat – woke her. Outside, the wind continued to howl, although its sound was not quite so steady now. Sometimes it seemed to drop away entirely, then rose again, uttering long, icy shrieks as it ran under the eaves in cold currents and made the stone building tremble in its old bones. The door thudded rhythmically against the bar holding it shut, but like the ceiling above them, both the bar and the rusty clamps seemed to be holding. She wondered what would have become of them if the wooden bar had been as punky and rotted as the handle of the bucket they'd found near the gook.

Roland was awake and sitting by the fire. Jake was with him. Between them, Oy was asleep with one paw over his snout. Susannah joined them. The fire had burned down a little, but this close it threw a comforting heat on her face and arms. She took a board, thought about snapping it in two, decided it might wake Eddie, and tossed it onto the fire as it was. Sparks gushed up the chimney, swirling as the draft caught them.

She could have spared the consideration, because while the sparks were still swirling, a hand caressed the back of her neck just below the hairline. She didn't have to look; she would have known that touch anywhere. Without turning, she took the hand, brought it to her mouth, and kissed the cup of the palm. The *white* palm. Even after all this time together and all the lovemaking, she could sometimes hardly believe that. Yet there it was.

At least I won't have to bring him home to meet my parents, she thought.

'Can't sleep, sugar?'

'A little. Not much. I had funny dreams.'

'The wind brings them,' Roland said. 'Anyone in Gilead would tell you the same. But I love the sound of the wind. I always have. It soothes my heart and makes me think of old times.'

He looked away, as if embarrassed to have said so much.

'None of us can sleep,' Jake said. 'So tell us a story.'

Roland looked into the fire for a while, then at Jake. The gunslinger was once more smiling, but his eyes were distant. A knot popped in the fire-place. Outside the stone walls, the wind screamed as if furious at its inability to get in. Eddie put an arm around Susannah's waist and she laid her head on his shoulder.

'What story would you hear, Jake, son of Elmer?'

'Any.' He paused. 'About the old days.'

Roland looked at Eddie and Susannah. 'And you? Would you hear?'

'Yes, please,' Susannah said.

Eddie nodded. 'Yeah. If you want to, that is.'

Roland considered. 'Mayhap I'll tell you two, since it's long until dawn and we can sleep tomorrow away, if we like. These tales nest inside each other. Yet the wind blows through both, which is a good thing. There's nothing like stories on a windy night when folks have found a warm place in a cold world.'

He took a broken piece of wood paneling, poked the glowing embers with it, then fed it to the flames. 'One I know is a true story, for I lived it along with my old ka-mate, Jamie DeCurry. The other, "The Wind through the Keyhole," is one my mother read to me when I was still sma'. Old stories can be useful, you know, and I should have thought of this one as soon as I saw Oy scenting the air as he did, but that was long ago.' He sighed. 'Gone days.'

In the dark beyond the firelight, the wind rose to a howl. Roland waited for it to die a little, then began. Eddie, Susannah, and Jake listened, rapt, all through that long and contentious night. Lud, the Tick-Tock Man, Blaine the Mono, the Green Palace – all were forgotten. Even the Dark Tower itself was forgotten for a bit. There was only Roland's voice, rising and falling.

Rising and falling like the wind.

'Not long after the death of my mother, which as you know came by my own hand . . .'

THE SKIN-MAN (PART 1)

Not long after the death of my mother, which as you know came by my own hand, my father – Steven, son of Henry the Tall – summoned me to his study in the north wing of the palace. It was a small, cold room. I remember the wind whining around the slit windows. I remember the high, frowning shelves of books – worth a fortune, they were, but never read. Not by him, anyway. And I remember the black collar of mourning he wore. It was the same as my own. Every man in Gilead wore the same collar, or a band around his shirtsleeve. The women wore black nets on their hair. This would go on until Gabrielle Deschain was six months in her tomb.

I saluted him, fist to forehead. He didn't look up from the papers on his desk, but I knew he saw it. My father saw everything, and very well. I waited. He signed his name several times while the wind whistled and the rooks cawed in the courtyard. The fireplace was a dead socket. He rarely called for it to be lit, even on the coldest days.

At last he looked up.

'How is Cort, Roland? How goes it with your teacher that was? You must know, because I've been given to understand that you spend most of your time in his hut, feeding him and such.'

'He has days when he knows me,' I said. 'Many days he doesn't. He still sees a little from one eye. The other . . .' I didn't need to finish. The other was gone. My hawk, David, had taken it from him in my test of manhood. Cort, in turn, had taken David's life, but that was to be his last kill.

'I know what happened to his other peep. Do you truly feed him?'

'Aye, Father, I do.'

'Do you clean him when he messes?'

I stood there before his desk like a chastened schoolboy called before the master, and that is how I felt. Only how many chastened schoolboys have killed their own mothers?

'Answer me, Roland. I am your dinh as well as your father and I'd have you answer.'

'Sometimes.' Which was not really a lie. Sometimes I changed his dirty clouts three and four times a day, sometimes, on the good days, only once or not at all. He could get to the jakes if I helped him. And if he remembered he had to go.

'Does he not have the white ammies who come in?'

'I sent them away,' I said.

He looked at me with real curiosity. I searched

for contempt in his face – part of me wanted to see it – but there was none that I could tell. 'Did I raise you to the gun so you could become an ammie and nurse a broken old man?'

I felt my anger flash at that. Cort had raised a moit of boys to the tradition of the Eld and the way of the gun. Those who were unworthy he had bested in combat and sent west with no weapons other than what remained of their wits. There, in Cressia and places even deeper in those anarchic kingdoms, many of those broken boys had joined with Farson, the Good Man. Who would in time overthrow everything my father's line had stood for. *Farson* had armed them, sure. He had guns, and he had plans.

'Would you throw him on the dungheap, Father? Is that to be his reward for all his years of service? Who next, then? Vannay?'

'Never in this life, as you know. But done is done, Roland, as thee also knows. And thee doesn't nurse him out of love. Thee knows that, too.'

'I nurse him out of respect!'

'If 'twas only respect, I think you'd visit him, and read to him – for you read well, your mother always said so, and about that she spoke true – but you'd not clean his shit and change his bed. You are scourging yourself for the death of your mother, which was not your fault.'

Part of me knew this was true. Part of me refused to believe it. The publishment of her death was

43

simple: 'Gabrielle Deschain, she of Arten, died while possessed of a demon which troubled her spirit.' It was always put so when someone of high blood committed suicide, and so the story of her death was given. It was accepted without question, even by those who had, either secretly or not so secretly, cast their lot with Farson. Because it became known – gods know how, not from me or my friends – that she had become the consort of Marten Broadcloak, the court magis and my father's chief advisor, and that Marten had fled west. Alone.

'Roland, hear me very well. I know you felt betrayed by your lady mother. So did I. I know that part of you hated her. Part of me hated her, too. But we both also loved her, and love her still. You were poisoned by the toy you brought back from Mejis, and you were tricked by the witch. One of those things alone might not have caused what happened, but the pink ball and the witch together . . . aye.'

'Rhea.' I could feel tears stinging my eyes, and I willed them back. I would not weep before my father. Never again. 'Rhea of the Cöos.'

'Aye, she, the black-hearted cunt. It was she who killed your mother, Roland. She turned you into a gun . . . and then pulled the trigger.'

I said nothing.

He must have seen my distress, because he resumed shuffling his papers, signing his name here and there. Finally he raised his head again.

'The ammies will have to see to Cort for a while. I'm sending you and one of your ka-mates to Debaria.'

'What? To Serenity?'

He laughed. 'The retreat where your mother stayed?'

'Yes.'

'Not there, not at all. Serenity, what a joke. Those women are the *black* ammies. They'd flay you alive if you so much as trespassed their holy doors. Most of the sisters who bide there prefer the long-stick to a man.'

I had no idea what he meant – remember I was still very young, and very innocent about many things, in spite of all I'd been through. 'I'm not sure I'm ready for another mission, Father. Let alone a quest.'

He looked at me coldly. 'I'll be the judge of what you're ready for. Besides, this is nothing like the mess you walked into in Mejis. There may be danger, it may even come to shooting, but at bottom it's just a job that needs to be done. Partly so that people who've come to doubt can see that the White is still strong and true, but mostly because what's wrong cannot be allowed to stand. Besides, as I've said, I won't be sending you alone.'

'Who'll go with me? Cuthbert or Alain?'

'Neither. I have work for Laughing Boy and Thudfoot right here. You go with Jamie DeCurry.'

I considered this and thought I would be glad

to ride with Jamie Red-Hand. Although I would have preferred either Cuthbert or Alain. As my father surely knew.

'Will you go without argument, or will you annoy me further on a day when I have much to do?'

'I'll go,' I said. In truth, it would be good to escape the palace – its shadowy rooms, its whispers of intrigue, its pervasive sense that darkness and anarchy were coming and nothing could stop them. The world would move on, but Gilead would not move on with it. That glittering, beautiful bubble would soon burst.

'Good. You're a fine son, Roland. I may never have told you that, but it's true. I hold nothing against you. Nothing.'

I lowered my head. When this meeting was finally over, I would go somewhere and let my heart free, but not just then. Not as I stood before him.

'Ten or twelve wheels beyond the hall of the women – Serenity, or whatever they call it – is the town of Debaria itself, on the edge of the alkali flats. Nothing serene about Debaria. It's a dusty, hide-smelling railhead town where cattle and block salt are shipped south, east, and north – in every direction except the one where that bastard Farson's laying his plans. There are fewer traildrive herds these days, and I expect Debaria will dry up and blow away like so many other places in Mid-World before long, but now it's still a busy place, full of saloons, whoredens, gamblers, and confidence men. Hard as it might be to believe, there are even a few good people there. One is the High Sheriff, Hugh Peavy. It's him that you and DeCurry will report to. Let him see your guns and a sigul which I will give to you. Do you ken everything I've told you so far?'

'Yes, Father,' I said. 'What's so bad there that it warrants the attention of gunslingers?' I smiled a little, a thing I had done seldom in the wake of my mother's death. 'Even baby gunslingers such as us?'

'According to the reports I have' – he lifted some of the papers and shook them at me – 'there's a skin-man at work. I have my doubts about that, but there's no doubt the folk are terrified.'

'I don't know what that is,' I said.

'Some sort of shape-changer, or so the old tales say. Go to Vannay when you leave me. He's been collecting reports.'

'All right.'

'Do the job, find this lunatic who goes around wearing animal skins – that's probably what it amounts to – but be not long about it. Matters far graver than this have begun to teeter. I'd have you back – you and all your ka-mates – before they fall.'

Two days later, Jamie and I led our horses onto the stable-car of a special two-car train that had been laid on for us. Once the Western Line ran a thousand wheels or more, all the way to the

47

Mohaine Desert, but in the years before Gilead fell, it went to Debaria and no farther. Beyond there, many tracklines had been destroyed by washouts and ground-shakers. Others had been taken up by harriers and roving bands of outlaws who called themselves land-pirates, for that part of the world had fallen into bloody confusion. We called those far western lands Out-World, and they served John Farson's purposes well. He was, after all, just a land-pirate himself. One with pretensions.

The train was little more than a steam-driven toy; Gilead folk called it Sma' Toot and laughed to see it puffing over the bridge to the west of the palace. We could have ridden faster a-horseback, but the train saved the mounts. And the dusty velveteen seats of our car folded out into beds, which we felt was a fine thing. Until we tried to sleep in them, that was. At one particularly hard jounce, Jamie was thrown right off his makeshift bed and onto the floor. Cuthbert would have laughed and Alain would have cursed, but Jamie Red-Hand only picked himself up, stretched out again, and went back to sleep.

We spoke little that first day, only looked out the wavery isinglass windows, watching as Gilead's green and forested land gave way to dirty scrub, a few struggling ranches, and herders' huts. There were a few towns where folk – many of them muties – gaped at us as Sma' Toot wheezed slowly past. A few pointed at the centers of their foreheads, as if at an invisible eye. It meant they stood for Farson, the Good Man. In Gilead, such folk would have been imprisoned for their disloyalty, but Gilead was now behind us. I was dismayed by how quickly the allegiance of these people, once taken for granted, had thinned.

On the first day of our journey, outside Beesford-on-Arten, where a few of my mother's people still lived, a fat man threw a rock at the train. It bounced off the closed stable-car door, and I heard our horses whinny in surprise. The fat man saw us looking at him. He grinned, grabbed his crotch with both hands, and waddled away.

'Someone has eaten well in a poor land,' Jamie remarked as we watched his butters jounce in the seat of his old patched pants.

The following morning, after the servant had put a cold breakfast of porridge and milk before us, Jamie said, 'I suppose you'd better tell me what it's about.'

'Will you tell me something, first? If you know, that is?'

'Of course.'

'My father said that the women at the retreat in Debaria prefer the longstick to a man. Do you know what he meant?'

Jamie regarded me in silence for a bit – as if to make sure I wasn't shaking his knee – and then his lips twitched at the corners. For Jamie this was the equivalent of holding his belly, rolling around the floor, and howling with glee. Which Cuthbert Allgood certainly would have done. 'It must be what the whores in the low town call a diddlestick. Does that help?'

'Truly? And they . . . what? Use it on each other?'

'So 'tis said, but much talk is just la-la-la. You know more of women than I do, Roland; I've never lain with one. But never mind. Given time, I suppose I will. Tell me what we're about in Debaria.'

'A skin-man is supposedly terrorizing the good folk. Probably the bad folk, as well.'

'A man who becomes some sort of animal?'

It was actually a little more complicated in this case, but he had the nub of it. The wind was blowing hard, flinging handfuls of alkali at the side of the car. After one particularly vicious gust, the little train lurched. Our empty porridge bowls slid. We caught them before they could fall. If we hadn't been able to do such things, and without even thinking of them, we would not have been fit to carry the guns we wore. Not that Jamie preferred the gun. Given a choice (and the time to make it), he would reach for either his bow or his bah.

'My father doesn't believe it,' I said. 'But Vannay does. He—'

At that moment, we were thrown forward into the seats ahead of us. The old servant, who was coming down the center aisle to retrieve our bowls and cups, was flung all the way back to the door between the car and his little kitchen. His front teeth flew out of his mouth and into his lap, which gave me a start.

Jamie ran up the aisle, which was now severely tilted, and knelt by him. As I joined him, Jamie plucked up the teeth and I saw they were made of painted wood and held together by a cunning clip almost too small to see.

'Are you all right, sai?' Jamie asked.

The old fellow got slowly to his feet, took his teeth, and filled the hole behind his upper lip with them. 'I'm fine, but this dirty bitch has derailed again. No more Debaria runs for me, I have a wife. She's an old nag, and I'm determined to outlive her. You young men had better check your horses. With luck, neither of them will have broken a leg.'

Neither had, but they were nervous and stamping, anxious to get out of confinement. We lowered the ramp and tethered them to the connecting bar between the two cars, where they stood with their heads lowered and their ears flattened against the hot and gritty wind blowing out of the west. Then we clambered back inside the passenger car and collected our gunna. The engineer, a broad-shouldered, bowlegged plug of a man, came down the side of his listing train with the old servant in tow. When he reached us, he pointed to what we could see very well.

'Yonder on that ridge be Debaria high road – see the marking-posts? You can be at the place o' the females in less than an hour, but don't bother asking nothing o' those bitches, because you won't get it.' He lowered his voice. 'They eat men, is what I've heard. Not just a way o' speakin, boys: *they . . . eat . . . the mens.*'

I found it easier to believe in the reality of the skin-man than in this, but I said nothing. It was clear that the enjie was shaken up, and one of his hands was as red as Jamie's. But the enjie's was only a little burn, and would go away. Jamie's would still be red when he was sent down in his grave. It looked as if it had been dipped in blood.

'They may call to you, or make promises. They may even show you their titties, as they know a young man can't take his eyes off such. But never mind. Turn yer ears from their promises and yer eyes from their titties. You just go on into the town. It'll be less than another hour by horse. We'll need a work crew to put this poxy whore upright. The rails are fine; I checked. Just covered with that damned alkali dust, is all. I suppose ye can't pay men to come out, but if ye can write – as I suppose such gentle fellows as yerselves surely can – you can give em a premissary note or whatever it's called—'

'We have specie,' I said. 'Enough to hire a small crew.'

The enjie's eyes widened at this. I supposed they would widen even more if I told him my father had given me twenty gold knuckles to carry in a special pocket sewn inside my vest.

'And oxes? Because we'll need oxes if they've got em. Hosses if they don't.'

'We'll go to the livery and see what they have,' I said, mounting up. Jamie tied his bow on one side of his saddle and then moved to the other, where he slid his bah into the leather boot his father had made special for it.

'Don't leave us stuck out here, young sai,' the enjie said. 'We've no horses, and no weapons.'

'We won't forget you,' I said. 'Just stay inside. If we can't get a crew out today, we'll send a bucka to take you into town.'

'Thankee. And stay away from those women! *They . . . eat . . . the mens!'*

The day was hot. We ran the horses for a bit because they wanted to stretch after being pent up, then pulled them down to a walk.

'Vannay,' Jamie said.

'Pardon?'

'Before the train derailed, you said your father didn't believe there was a skin-man, but Vannay does.'

'He said that after reading the reports High Sheriff Peavy sent along, it was hard not to believe. You know what he says at least once in every class: "When facts speak, the wise man listens." Twenty-three dead makes a moit of facts. Not shot or stabbed, mind you, but torn to pieces.'

Jamie grunted.

'Whole families, in two cases. Large ones, almost clans. The houses turned all upsy-turvy and splashed with blood. Limbs ripped off the bodies and carried away, some found – partly eaten – some not. At one of those farms, Sheriff Peavy and his deputy found the youngest boy's head stuck on a fencepole with his skull smashed in and his brains scooped out.'

'Witnesses?'

'A few. A sheepherder coming back with strays saw his partner attacked. The one who survived was on a nearby hill. The two dogs with him ran down to try and protect their other master, and were torn apart too. The thing came up the hill after the herder, but got distracted by the sheep instead, so the fellow struck lucky and got away. He said it was a wolf that ran upright, like a man. Then there was a woman with a gambler. He was caught cheating at Watch Me in one of the local pits. The two of them were given a bill of circulation and told to leave town by nightfall or be whipped. They were headed for the little town near the salt-mines when they were beset. The man fought. It gave the woman just enough time to get clear. She hid up in some rocks until the thing was gone. She's said 'twas a lion.'

'On its back legs?'

'If so, she didn't wait to see. Last, two cowpunchers. They were camped on Debaria Stream near a young Manni couple on marriage retreat, although the punchers didn't know it until they heard the couple's screams. As they rode toward the sound, they saw the killer go loping off with the woman's lower leg in its jaws. It wasn't a man, but they swore on watch and warrant that it ran upright like a man.'

Jamie leaned over the neck of his horse and spat. 'Can't be so.'

'Vannay says it can. He says there have been such before, although not for years. He believes they may be some sort of mutation that's pretty much worked its way out of the true thread.'

'All these witnesses saw different animals?'

'Aye. The cowpokes described it as a tyger. It had stripes.'

'Lions and tygers running around like trained beasts in a traveling show. And out here in the dust. Are you sure we aren't being tickled?'

I wasn't old enough to be sure of much, but I did know the times were too desperate to be sending young guns even so far west as Debaria for a prank. Not that Steven Deschain could have been described as a prankster even in the best of times.

'I'm only telling what Vannay told me. The rope-swingers who came into town with the remains of those two Manni behind them on a travois had never even *heard* of such a thing as a tyger. Yet that is what they described. The testimony's in here, green eyes and all.' I took the two creased sheets of paper I had from Vannay out of my inner vest pocket. 'Care to look?'

'I'm not much of a reader,' Jamie said. 'As thee knows.'

'Aye, fine. But take my word. Their description is just like the picture in the old story of the boy caught in the starkblast.'

'What old story is that?'

'The one about Tim Stoutheart – "The Wind through the Keyhole." Never mind. It's not important. I know the punchers may have been drunk, they usually are if they're near a town that has liquor, but if it's true testimony, Vannay says the creature is a shape-*shifter* as well as a shape-*changer*.'

'Twenty-three dead, you say. Ay-yi.'

The wind gusted, driving the alkali before it. The horses shied, and we raised our neckerchiefs over our mouths and noses.

'Boogery hot,' Jamie said. 'And this damned *dust*.'

Then, as if realizing he had been excessively chatty, he fell silent. That was fine with me, as I had much to think about.

A little less than an hour later, we breasted a hill and saw a sparkling white *haci* below us. It was the size of a barony estate. Behind it, tending down toward a narrow creek, was a large greengarden and what looked like a grape arbor. My mouth watered at the sight of it. The last time I'd had grapes, my armpits had still been smooth and hairless.

The walls of the *haci* were tall and topped with forbidding sparkles of broken glass, but the wooden gates stood open, as if in invitation. In front of them, seated on a kind of throne, was a woman in a dress of white muslin and a hood of white silk that flared around her head like gullwings. As we drew closer, I saw the throne was ironwood. Surely no other chair not made of metal could have borne her weight, for she was the biggest woman I had ever seen, a giantess who could have mated with the legendary outlaw prince David Quick.

Her lap was full of needlework. She might have been knitting a blanket, but held before that barrel of a body and breasts so big each of them could have fully shaded a baby from the sun, whatever it was looked no bigger than a handkerchief. She caught sight of us, laid her work aside, and stood up. There was six and a half feet of her, maybe a bit more. The wind was less in this dip, but there was enough to flutter her dress against her long thighs. The cloth made a sound like a sail in a running-breeze. I remembered the enjie saying *they eat the mens*, but when she put one large fist to the broad plain of her forehead and lifted the side of her dress to dip a curtsey with her free hand, I nonetheless reined up.

'Hile, gunslingers,' she called. She had a rolling voice, not quite a man's baritone. 'In the name of Serenity and the women who bide here, I salute thee. May your days be long upon the earth.'

We raised our own fists to our brows, and wished her twice the number.

'Have you come from In-World? I think so, for your duds aren't filthy enough for these parts. Although they will be, if you bide longer than a day.' And she laughed. The sound was moderate thunder.

'We do,' I said. It was clear Jamie would say nothing. Ordinarily closemouthed, he was now stunned to silence. Her shadow rose on the whitewashed wall behind her, as tall as Lord Perth.

'And have you come for the skin-man?'

'Yes,' I said. 'Have you seen him, or do you only know of him from the talk? If that's the case, we'll move on and say thankee.'

'Not a him, lad. Never think it.'

I only looked at her. Standing, she was almost tall enough to look into my eyes, although I sat on Young Joe, a fine big horse.

'An *it*,' she said. 'A monster from the Deep Cracks, as sure as you two serve the Eld and the White. It may have been a man once, but no more. Yes, I've seen it, and seen its work. Sit where you are, never move, and you shall see its work, too.'

Without waiting for any reply, she went through the open gate. In her white muslin she was like a sloop running before the wind. I looked at Jamie. He shrugged and nodded. This was what we had come for, after all, and if the enjie had to wait a bit longer for help putting Sma' Toot back on the rails, so be it.

'*ELLEN!*' she bawled. Raised to full volume, it was like listening to a woman shouting into an electric megaphone. *'CLEMMIE! BRIANNA! BRING FOOD! BRING MEAT AND BREAD AND ALE – THE LIGHT, NOT THE DARK! BRING A TABLE, AND MIND YOU DON'T FORGET THE CLOTH! SEND FORTUNA TO ME NOW! HIE TO IT! DOUBLE-QUICK!'*

With these orders delivered she returned to us, delicately lifting her hem to keep it out of the alkali that puffed around the black boats she wore on her enormous feet.

'Lady-sai, we thank you for your offer of hospitality, but we really must—'

'You must eat is what you must do,' she said. 'We'll have it out here a-roadside, so your digestion will not be discomposed. For I know what stories they tell about us in Gilead, aye, so do we all. Men tell the same about any women who dare to live on their own, I wot. It makes em doubt the worth of their hammers.'

'We heard no stories about—'

She laughed and her bosom heaved like the sea. 'Polite of you, young gunnie, aye, and very snick, but it's long since I was weaned. We'll not eat ye.' Her eyes, as black as her shoes, twinkled. 'Although ye'd make a tasty snack, I think – one or both. I am Everlynne of Serenity. The prioress, by the grace of God and the Man Jesus.'

'Roland of Gilead,' I said. 'And this is Jamie of same.'

Jamie bowed from his saddle.

She curtsied to us again, this time dropping her

head so that the wings of her silken hood closed briefly around her face like curtains. As she rose, a tiny woman glided through the open gate. Or perhaps she was of normal size, after all. Perhaps she only looked tiny next to Everlynne. Her robe was rough gray cotton instead of white muslin; her arms were crossed over her scant bosom, and her hands were buried deep in her sleeves. She wore no hood, but we could still see only half of her face. The other half was hidden beneath a thick swath of bandagement. She curtsied to us, then huddled in the considerable shade of her prioress.

'Raise your head, Fortuna, and make your manners to these young gentlemen.'

When at last she looked up, I saw why she had kept her head lowered. The bandages could not fully conceal the damage to her nose; on the right side, a good part of it was gone. Where it had been was only a raw red channel.

'Hile,' she whispered. 'May your days be long upon the earth.'

'May you have twice the number,' Jamie said, and I saw from the woeful glance she gave him with her one visible eye that she hoped this was not true.

'Tell them what happened,' Everlynne said. 'What you remember, any-ro'. I know 't isn't much.'

'Must I, Mother?'

'Yes,' she said, 'for they've come to end it.'

60

Fortuna peered doubtfully at us, just a quick snatch of a glance, and then back at Everlynne. 'Can they? They look so *young*.'

She realized what she had said must sound impolite, and a flush colored the cheek we could see. She staggered a little on her feet, and Everlynne put an arm around her. It was clear that she had been badly hurt, and her body was still far from complete recovery. The blood that had run to her face had more important work to do in other parts of her body. Chiefly beneath the bandage, I supposed, but given the voluminous robe she wore, it was impossible to tell where else she might have been wounded.

'They may still be a year or more from having to shave but once a week, but they're gunslingers, Fortie. If they can't set this cursed town right, then no one can. Besides, it will do you good. Horror's a worm that needs to be coughed out before it breeds. Now tell them.'

She told. As she did, other Sisters of Serenity came out, two carrying a table, the others carrying food and drink to fill it. Better viands than any we'd had on Sma' Toot, by the look and the smell, yet by the time Fortuna had finished her short, terrible story, I was no longer hungry. Nor, by the look of him, was Jamie.

It was dusk, a fortnight and a day gone. She and another, Dolores, had come out to close the gate and draw water for the evening chores. Fortuna

61

was the one with the bucket, and so she was the one who lived. As Dolores began to swing the gate closed, a creature knocked it wide, grabbed her, and bit her head from her shoulders with its long jaws. Fortuna said that she saw it well, for the Peddler's Moon had just risen full in the sky. Taller than a man it was, with scales instead of skin and a long tail that dragged behind it on the ground. Yellow eyes with slitted dark pupils glowed in its flat head. Its mouth was a trap filled with teeth, each as long as a man's hand. They dripped with Dolores's blood as it dropped her still-twitching body on the cobbles of the courtyard and ran on its stubby legs toward the well where Fortuna stood.

'I turned to flee . . . it caught me . . . and I remember no more.'

'I do,' Everlynne said grimly. 'I heard the screams and came running out with our gun. It's a great long thing with a bell at the end of the barrel. It's been loaded since time out of mind, but none of us has ever fired it. For all I knew, it could have blown up in my hands. But I saw it tearing at poor Fortie's face, and then something else, too. When I did, I never thought of the risk. I never even thought that I might kill her, poor thing, as well as it, should the gun fire.'

'I wish you had killed me,' Fortuna said. 'Oh, I wish you had.' She sat in one of the chairs that had been brought to the table, put her face in her hands, and began to weep. Her one remaining eye did, at least.

'Never say so,' Everlynne told her, and stroked her hair on the side of her head not covered by the bandagement. 'For 'tis blasphemy.'

'Did you hit it?' I asked.

'A little. Our old gun fires shot, and one of the pellets – or p'raps more than one – tore away some of the knobs and scales on its head. Black tarry stuff flew up. We saw it later on the cobbles, and sanded it over without touching it, for fear it might poison us right through our skin. The chary thing dropped her, and I think it had almost made up its mind to come for me. So I pointed the gun at it, though a gun like that can only be fired once, then must be recharged down its throat with powder and shot. I told it to come on. Told it I'd wait until it was good and close, so the shot wouldn't spread.' She hawked back and spat into the dust. 'It must have a brain of some sort even when it's out of its human shape, because it heard me and ran. But before I lost sight of it round the wall, it turned and looked back at me. As if marking me. Well, let it. I have no more shot for the gun, and won't unless a trader happens to have some, but I have this.'

She lifted her skirts to her knee, and we saw a butcher's knife in a rawhide scabbard strapped to the outside of her calf.

'So let it come for Everlynne, daughter of Roseanna.'

'You said you saw something else,' I said.

She considered me with her bright black eyes,

then turned to the women. 'Clemmie, Brianna, serve out. Fortuna, you will say grace, and be sure to ask God forgiveness for your blasphemy and thank Him that your heart still beats.'

Everlynne grasped me above the elbow, drew me through the gate, and walked me to the well where the unfortunate Fortuna had been attacked. There we were alone.

'I saw its prick,' she said in a low voice. 'Long and curved like a scimitar, twitching and full of the black stuff that serves it for blood . . . serves it for blood in *that* shape, any-ro'. It meant to kill her as it had Dolores, aye, right enough, but it meant to fuck her, too. It meant to fuck her as she died.'

Jamie and I ate with them – Fortuna even ate a little – and then we mounted up for town. But before we left, Everlynne stood by my horse and spoke to me again.

'When your business here is done, come and see me again. I have something for you.'

'What might that be, sai?'

She shook her head. 'Now is not the time. But when the filthy thing is dead, come here.' She took my hand, raised it to her lips, and kissed it. 'I know who you are, for does your mother not live in your face? Come to me, Roland, son of Gabrielle. Fail not.'

Then she stepped away before I could say another word, and glided in through the gate.

★   ★   ★

The Debaria high street was wide and paved, although the pavement was crumbling away to the hardpan beneath in many places and would be entirely gone before too many years passed. There was a good deal of commerce, and judging from the sound coming from the saloons, they were doing a fine business. We only saw a few horses and mules tied to the hitching-posts, though; in that part of the world, livestock was for trading and eating, not for riding.

A woman coming out of the mercantile with a basket over her arm saw us and stared. She ran back in, and several more people came out. By the time we reached the High Sheriff's office – a little wooden building attached to the much larger stone-built town jail – the streets were lined with spectators on both sides.

'Have ye come to kill the skin-man?' the lady with the basket called.

'Those two don't look old enough to kill a bottle of rye,' a man standing in front of the Cheery Fellows Saloon & Café called back. There was general laughter and murmurs of agreement at this sally.

'Town looks busy enough now,' Jamie said, dismounting and looking back at the forty or fifty men and women who'd come away from their business (and their pleasure) to have a gleep at us.

'It'll be different after sundown,' I said. 'That's when such creatures as this skin-man do their marauding. Or so Vannay says.'

We went into the office. Hugh Peavy was a big-bellied man with long white hair and a droopy mustache. His face was deeply lined and careworn. He saw our guns and looked relieved. He noted our beardless faces and looked less so. He wiped off the nib of the pen he had been writing with, stood up, and held out his hand. No forehead-knocking for this fellow.

After we'd shaken with him and introduced ourselves, he said: 'I don't mean to belittle you, young fellows, but I was hoping to see Steven Deschain himself. And perhaps Peter McVries.'

'McVries died three years ago,' I said.

Peavy looked shocked. 'Do you say so? For he was a trig hand with a gun. Very trig.'

'He died of a fever.' Very likely induced by poison, but this was nothing the High Sheriff of the Debaria Outers needed to know. 'As for Steven, he's otherwise occupied, and so he sent me. I am his son.'

'Yar, yar, I've heard your name and a bit of your exploits in Mejis, for we get some news even out here. There's the dit-dah wire, and even a jing-jang.' He pointed to a contraption on the wall. Written on the brick beneath it was a sign reading DO NOT TOUCH WITHOUT PERMIZION. 'It used to go all the way to Gilead, but these days only to Sallywood in the south, the Jefferson spread to the north, and the village in the foothills – Little Debaria, it's called. We even have a few streetlamps that still work – not gas or kerosene

66

but real sparklights, don'tcha see. Townfolk think such'll keep the creature away.' He sighed. 'I am less confident. This is a bad business, young fellows. Sometimes I feel the world has come loose of its moorings.'

'It has,' I said. 'But what comes loose can be tied tight again, Sheriff.'

'If you say so.' He cleared his throat. 'Now, don't take this as disrespect, I know ye are who ye say ye are, but I was promised a sigul. If you've brought it, I'd have it, for it means special to me.'

I opened my swag-bag and brought out what I'd been given: a small wooden box with my father's mark – the *D* with the *S* inside of it – stamped on the hinged lid. Peavy took it with the smallest of smiles dimpling the corners of his mouth beneath his mustache. To me it looked like a remembering smile, and it took years off his face.

'Do'ee know what's inside?'

'No.' I had not been asked to look.

Peavy opened the box, looked within, then returned his gaze to Jamie and me. 'Once, when I was still only a deputy, Steven Deschain led me, and the High Sheriff that was, and a posse of seven against the Crow Gang. Has your father ever spoken to you of the Crows?'

I shook my head.

'Not skin-men, no, but a nasty lot of work, all the same. They robbed what there was to rob, not just in Debaria but all along the ranchlands out this way. Trains, too, if they got word one was worth stopping. But their main business was kidnapping for ransom. A coward's crime, sure – I'm told Farson favors it – but it paid well.

'Your da' showed up in town only a day after they stole a rancher's wife – Belinda Doolin. Her husband called on the jing-jang as soon as they left and he was able to get himself untied. The Crows didn't know about the jing-jang, and that was their undoing. Accourse it helped that there was a gunslinger doing his rounds in this part of the world; in those days, they had a knack of turning up when and where they were needed.'

He eyed us. ''P'raps they still do. Any-ro', we got out t'ranch while the cirme was still fresh. There were places where any of us would have lost the trail – it's mostly hardpan out north of here, don'tcha see – but your father had eyes like you wouldn't believe. Hawks ain't even in it, dear, or eagles, either.'

I knew of my father's sharp eyes and gift for trailing. I also knew that this story probably had nothing to do with our business, and I should have told him to move along. But my father never talked about his younger days, and I wanted to hear this tale. I was *hungry* to hear it. And it turned out to have a little more to do with our business in Debaria than I at first thought.

'The trail led in the direction of the mines – what Debaria folk call the salt-houses. The workings had been abandoned in those days; it was before the new plug was found twenty year ago.'

'Plug?' Jamie asked.

'Deposit,' I said. 'He means a fresh deposit.'

'Aye, as you say. But all that were abandoned then, and made a fine hideout for such as those beastly Crows. Once the trail left the flats, it went through a place of high rocks before coming out on the Low Pure, which is to say the foothill meadows below the salt-houses. The Low is where a sheepherder was killed just recent, by something that looked like a—'

'Like a wolf,' I said. 'This we know. Go on.'

'Well-informed, are ye? Well, that's all to the good. Where was I, now? Ah, I know – those rocks that are now known in these parts as Ambush Arroyo. It's not an arroyo, but I suppose people like the sound. That's where the tracks went, but Deschain wanted to go around and come in from the east. From the High Pure. The sheriff, Pea Anderson it was back then, didn't want none o' that. Eager as a bird with its eye on a worm he was, made to press on. Said it would take em three days, and by then the woman might be dead and the Crows anywhere. He said he was going the straight way, and he'd go alone if no one wanted to go with him. "Or unless you order me in the name of Gilead to do different," he says to your da'.

'"Never think it," Deschain says, "for Debaria is your fill; I have my own."

69

'The posse went. I stayed with your da', lad. Sheriff Anderson turned to me in the saddle and said, "I hope they're hiring at one of the ranches, Hughie, because your days of wearing tin on your vest are over. I'm done with'ee."

'Those were the last words he ever said to me. They rode off. Steven of Gilead squatted on his hunkers and I hunkered with him. After half an hour of quiet – might have been longer – I says to him, "I thought we were going to hook around . . . unless you're done with me, too."

'"No," he says. "Your hire is not my business, Deputy."

'"Then what are we waitin for?"

'"Gunfire," says he, and not five minutes later we heard it. Gunfire and screams. It didn't last long. The Crows had seen us coming – probably nummore'n a glint of sun on a bootcap or bit o' saddle brightwork was enough to attract their attention, for Pa Crow was powerful trig – and doubled back. They got up in those high rocks and poured down lead on Anderson and his possemen. There were more guns in those days, and the Crows had a good share. Even a speed-shooter or two.

'So we went around, all right? Took us only two days, because Steven Deschain pushed hard. On the third day, we camped downslope and rose before dawn. Now, if ye don't know, and no reason ye should, salt-houses are just caverns in the cliff faces up there. Whole families lived in em, not just the miners themselves. The tunnels go down into the earth from the backs of em. But as I say, in those days all were deserted. Yet we saw smoke coming from the vent on top of one, and that was as good as a kinkman standing out in front of a carnival tent and pointing at the show inside, don'tcha see it.

'"This is the time," Steven says, "because they will have spent the last nights, once they were sure they were safe, deep in drink. They'll still be sleeping it off. Will you stand with me?"

'"Aye, gunslinger, that I will," I tells him.'

When Peavy said this, he unconsciously straightened his back. He looked younger.

'We snuck the last fifty or sixty yards, yer da' with his gun drawn in case they'd posted a guard. They had, but he was only a lad, and fast asleep. The Deschain holstered his gun, swotted him with a rock, and laid him out. I later saw that young fellow standing on a trapdoor with tears running out of his eyes, a mess in his pants, and a rope around his neck. He wasn't but fourteen, yet he'd taken his turn at sai Doolin – the kidnapped woman, don'tcha know, and old enough to be his grandmother – just like the rest of them, and I shed no tears when the rope shut off his cries for mercy. The salt ye take is the salt ye must pay for, as anyone from these parts will tell you.

'The gunslinger crep' inside, and I right after him. They was all lying around, snoring like dogs.

71

Hell, boys, they *were* dogs. Belinda Doolin was tied to a post. She saw us, and her eyes widened. Steven Deschain pointed to her, then to himself, then cupped his hands together, then pointed to her again. *You're safe*, he meant. I never forgot the look of gratitude in her face as she nodded to him that she understood. *You're safe* – that's the world we grew up in, young men, the one that's almost gone now.

'Then the Deschain says, "Wake up, Allan Crow, unless you'd go into the clearing at the end of the path with your eyes shut. Wake up, all."

'They did. He never meant to try and bring them all in alive – 'twould have been madness, that I'm sure you must see – but he wouldn't shoot them as they slept, either. They woke up to varying degrees, but not for long. Steven drew his guns so fast I never saw his hands move. Lightning ain't in it, dear. At one moment those revolvers with their big sandalwood grips were by his sides; at the next he was blazing away, the noise like thunder in that closed-in space. But that didn't keep me from drawing my own gun. It was just an old barrel-shooter I had from my granda', but I put two of them down with it. The first two men I ever killed. There have been plenty since, sad to say.

'The only one who survived that first fusillade was Pa Crow himself – Allan Crow. He was an old man, all snarled up and frozen on one side of his face from a stroke or summat, but he moved fast as the devil just the same. He was in his long-johns, and his gun was stuck in the top of one of his boots there at the end of his bedroll. He grabbed it up and turned toward us. Steven shot him, but the old bastard got off a single round. It went wild, but . . .'

Peavy, who could have been no older in those days than we two young men standing before him, opened the box on its cunning hinges, mused a moment at what he saw inside, then looked up at me. That little remembering smile still touched the corners of his mouth. 'Have you ever seen a scar on your father's arm, Roland? Right here?' He touched the place just above the crook of his elbow, where a man's yanks begin.

My father's body was a map of scars, but it was a map I knew well. The scar above his inner elbow was a deep dimple, almost like the ones not quite hidden by Sheriff Peavy's mustache when he smiled.

'Pa Crow's last shot hit the wall above the post where the woman was tied, and ricocheted.' He turned the box and held it out to me. Inside was a smashed slug, a big one, a hard caliber. 'I dug this out of your da's arm with my skinning knife, and gave it to him. He thanked me, and said someday I should have it back. And here it is. Ka is a wheel, sai Deschain.'

'Have you ever told this story?' I asked. 'For I have never heard it.'

'That I dug a bullet from the flesh of Arthur's

73

true descendant? Eld of the Eld? No, never until now. For who would believe it?'

'I do,' I said, 'and I thank you. It could have poisoned him.'

'Nar, nar,' Peavy said with a chuckle. 'Not him. The blood of Eld's too strong. And if I'd been laid low . . . or too squeamy . . . he would have done it himself. As it was, he let me take most of the credit for the Crow Gang, and I've been sheriff ever since. But not much longer. This skin-man business has done for me. I've seen enough blood, and have no taste for mysteries.'

'Who'll take your place?' I asked.

He seemed surprised by the question. 'Probably nobody. The mines will play out again in a few years, this time for good, and such rail lines as there are won't last much longer. The two things together will finish Debaria, which was once a fine little city in the time of yer grandfather. That holy hencoop I'm sure ye passed on the way in may go on; nothing else.'

Jamie looked troubled. 'But in the meantime?'

'Let the ranchers, drifters, whoremasters, and gamblers all go to hell in their own way. It's none o' mine, at least for much longer. But I'll not leave until this business is settled, one way or another.'

I said, 'The skin-man was at one of the women at Serenity. She's badly disfigured.'

'Been there, have ye?'

'The women are terrified.' I thought this over, and remembered a knife strapped to a calf as thick as the trunk of a young birch. 'Except for the prioress, that is.'

He chuckled. 'Everlynne. That one'd spit in the devil's face. And if he took her down to Nis, she'd be running the place in a month.'

I said, 'Do you have any idea who this skin-man might be when he's in his human shape? If you do, tell us, I beg. For, as my father told your Sheriff Anderson that was, this is not our fill.'

'I can't give ye a name, if that's what you mean, but I might be able to give ye something. Follow me.'

He led us through the archway behind his desk and into the jail, which was in the shape of a **T**. I counted eight big cells down the central aisle and a dozen small ones on the cross-corridor. All were empty except for one of the smaller ones, where a drunk was snoozing away the late afternoon on a straw pallet. The door to his cell stood open.

'Once all of these cells would have been filled on Efday and Ethday,' Peavy said. 'Loaded up with drunk cowpunchers and farmhands, don'tcha see it. Now most people stay in at night. Even on Efday and Ethday. Cowpokes in their bunkhouses, farmhands in theirs. No one wants to be staggering home drunk and meet the skin-man.'

'The salt-miners?' Jamie asked. 'Do you pen them, too?'

'Not often, for they have their own saloons up in Little Debaria. Two of em. Nasty places. When the whores down here at the Cheery Fellows or the Busted Luck or the Bider-Wee get too old or too diseased to attract custom, they end up in Little Debaria. Once they're drunk on White Blind, the salties don't much care if a whore has a nose as long as she still has her sugar-purse.'

'Nice,' Jamie muttered.

Peavy opened one of the large cells. 'Come on in here, boys. I haven't any paper, but I do have some chalk, and here's a nice smooth wall. It's private, too, as long as old Salty Sam down there doesn't wake up. And he rarely does until sundown.'

From the pocket of his twill pants the sheriff took a goodish stick of chalk, and on the wall he drew a kind of long box with jags all across the top. They looked like a row of upside-down Vs.

'Here's the whole of Debaria,' Peavy said. 'Over here's the rail line you came in on.' He drew a series of hashmarks, and as he did so I remembered the enjie and the old fellow who'd served as our butler.

'Sma' Toot is off the rails,' I said. 'Can you put together a party of men to set it right? We have money to pay for their labor, and Jamie and I would be happy to work with them.'

'Not today,' Peavy said absently. He was studying his map. 'Enjie still out there, is he?'

'Yes. Him and another.'

'I'll send Kellin and Vikka Frye out in a bucka. Kellin's my best deputy – the other two ain't worth much – and Vikka's his son. They'll pick em up and bring em back in before dark. There's time, because the days is long this time o' year. For now, just pay attention, boys. Here's the tracks and here's Serenity, where that poor girl you spoke to was mauled. On the high road, don'tcha see it.' He drew a little box for Serenity, and put an **X** in it. North of the women's retreat, up toward the jags at the top of his map, he put another **X**. 'This is where Yon Curry, the sheepherder, was killed.'

To the left of this **X** but pretty much on the same level – which is to say, below the jags – he put another.

'The Alora farm. Seven killed.'

Farther yet to the left and little higher, he chalked another **X**.

'Here's the Timbersmith farm on the High Pure. Nine killed. It's where we found the little boy's head on a pole. Tracks all around it.'

'Wolf?' I asked.

He shook his head. 'Nar, some kind o' big cat. At first. Before we lost the trail, they changed into what looked like hooves. Then . . .' He looked at us grimly. 'Footprints. First big – like a giant's, almost – but then smaller and smaller until they were the size of any man's tracks. Any-ro', we lost em in the hardpan. Mayhap your father wouldn't've, sai.'

He went on marking the map, and when he was done, stepped away so we could see it clearly.

'Such as you are supposed to have good brains as well as fast hands, I was always told. So what do you make of this?'

Jamie stepped forward between the rows of pallets (for this cell must have been for many guests, probably brought in on drunk-and-disorderly), and traced the tip of his finger over the jags at the top of the map, blurring them a little. 'Do the salt-houses run all along here? In all the foothills?'

'Yar. The Salt Rocks, those hills're called.'

'Little Debaria is where?'

Peavy made another box for the salt-miners' town. It was close to the **X** he'd made to mark the place where the woman and the gambler had been killed . . . for it was Little Debaria they'd been headed for.

Jamie studied the map a bit more, then nodded. 'Looks to me like the skin-man could be one of the miners. Is that what you think?'

'Aye, a saltie, even though a couple of them has been torn up, too. It makes sense – as much as anything in a crazy business like this *can* make sense. The new plug's a lot deeper than the old ones, and everyone knows there are demons in the earth. Mayhap one of the miners struck on one, wakened it, and was done a mischief by it.'

'There are also leftovers from the Great Old Ones in the ground,' I said. 'Not all are dangerous, but some are. Perhaps one of those old things . . . those what-do-you-callums, Jamie?'

'Artyfax,' he said.

'Yes, those. Perhaps one of those is responsible. Mayhap the fellow will be able to tell us, if we take him alive.'

'Sma' chance of that,' Peavy growled.

I thought there was a good chance. If we could identify him and close on him in the daytime, that was.

'How many of these salties are there?' I asked.

'Not s'many as in the old days, because now it's just the one plug, don'tcha see it. I sh'd say no more'n . . . two hundred.'

I met Jamie's eyes, and saw a glint of humor in them. 'No fret, Roland,' said he. 'I'm sure we can interview em all by Reaptide. If we hurry.'

He was exaggerating, but I still saw several weeks ahead of us in Debaria. We might interview the skin-man and still not be able to pick him out, either because he was a masterful liar or because he had no guilt to cover up; his day-self might truly not know what his night-self was doing. I wished for Cuthbert, who could look at things that seemed unrelated and spot the connections, and I wished for Alain, with his power to touch minds. But Jamie wasn't so bad, either. He had, after all, seen what I should have seen myself, what was right in front of my nose. On one matter I was in complete accord with Sheriff Hugh Peavy: I hated mysteries. It's a thing that has never changed in this long life of mine. I'm not good at solving them; my mind has never run that way.

When we trooped back into the office, I said, 'I have some questions I must ask you, Sheriff. The first is, will you open to us, if we open to you? The second—'

'The second is do I see you for what you are and accept what you do. The third is do I seek aid and succor. Sheriff Peavy says yar, yar, and yar. Now for gods' sake set your brains to working, fellows, for it's over two weeks since this thing showed up at Serenity, and that time it didn't get a full meal. Soon enough it'll be out there again.'

'It only prowls at night,' Jamie said. 'You're sure of that much?'

'I am.'

'Does the moon have any effect on it?' I asked. 'Because my father's advisor – and our teacher that was – says that in some of the old legends . . .'

'I've heard the legends, sai, but in that they're wrong. At least for this particular creatur' they are. Sometimes the moon's been full when it strikes – it was Full Peddler when it showed up at Serenity, all covered with scales and knobs like an alligator from the Long Salt Swamps – but it did its work at Timbersmith when the moon was dark. I'd like to tell you different, but I can't. I'd also like to end this without having to pick anyone else's guts out of the bushes or pluck some other kiddie's head off'n a fencepost. Ye've been sent here to help, and I hope like hell you can . . . although I've got my doubts.'

When I asked Peavy if there was a good hotel or boardinghouse in Debaria, he chuckled.

'The last boardinghouse was the Widow Brailley's.

80

Two year ago, a drunk saddletramp tried to rape her in her own outhouse, as she sat at business. But she was always a trig one. She'd seen the look in his eye, and went in there with a knife under her apron. Cut his throat for him, she did. Stringy Bodean, who used to be our Justice Man before he decided to try his luck at raising horses in the Crescent, declared her not guilty by reason of self-defense in about five minutes, but the lady decided she'd had enough of Debaria and trained back to Gilead, where she yet bides, I've no doubt. Two days after she left, some drunken buffoon burned the place to the ground. The hotel still stands. It's called the Delightful View. The view ain't delightful, young fellows, and the beds is full of bugs as big as toads' eyeballs. I wouldn't sleep in one without putting on a full suit of Arthur Eld's armor.'

And so we ended up spending our first night in Debaria in the large drunk-and-disorderly cell, beneath Peavy's chalked map. Salty Sam had been set free, and we had the jail to ourselves. Outside, a strong wind had begun to blow off the alkali flats to the west of town. The moaning sound it made around the eaves caused me to think again of the story my mother used to read to me when I was just a sma' toot myself – the story of Tim Stoutheart, and the starkblast Tim had to face in the Great Woods north of New Canaan. Thinking of the boy alone in those woods has always chilled my heart, just as Tim's bravery has always warmed it. The stories we hear in childhood are the ones we remember all our lives.

After one particularly strong gust – the Debaria wind was warm, not cold like the starkblast – struck the side of the jail and puffed alkali grit in through the barred window, Jamie spoke up. It was rare for him to start a conversation.

'I hate that sound, Roland. It's apt to keep me awake all night.'

I loved it myself; the sound of the wind has always made me think of good times and far places. Although I confess I could have done without the grit.

'How are we supposed to find this thing, Jamie? I hope you have some idea, because I don't.'

'We'll have to talk to the salt-miners. That's the place to start. Someone may have seen a fellow with blood on him creeping back to where the salties live. Creeping back naked. For he can't come back clothed, unless he takes them off beforehand.'

That gave me a little hope. Although if the one we were looking for knew what he was, he might take his clothes off when he felt an attack coming on, hide them, then come back to them later. But if he didn't know . . .

It was a small thread, but sometimes – if you're careful not to break it – you can pull on a small thread and unravel a whole garment.

'Goodnight, Roland.'

'Goodnight, Jamie.'

I closed my eyes and thought of my mother. I often did that year, but for once they weren't thoughts of how she had looked dead, but of how beautiful she had been in my early childhood, as she sat beside me on my bed in the room with the colored glass windows, reading to me. 'Look you, Roland,' she'd say, 'here are the billy-bumblers sitting all a-row and scenting the air. *They* know, don't they?'

'Yes,' I would say, 'the bumblers know.'

'And what is it they know?' the woman I would kill asked me. 'What is it they know, dear heart?'

'They know the starkblast is coming,' I said. My eyes would be growing heavy by then, and minutes later I would drift off to the music of her voice.

As I drifted off now, with the wind outside blowing up a strong gale.

I woke in the first thin light of morning to a harsh sound: *BRUNG! BRUNG! BRUNNNNG!*

Jamie was still flat on his back, legs splayed, snoring. I took one of my revolvers from its holster, went out through the open cell door, and shambled toward that imperious sound. It was the jing-jang Sheriff Peavy had taken so much pride in. He wasn't there to answer it; he'd gone home to bed, and the office was empty.

Standing there bare-chested, with a gun in my hand and wearing nothing but the swabbies and slinkum I'd slept in – for it was hot in the cell – I took the listening cone off the wall, put the narrow end in my ear, and leaned close to the speaking tube. 'Yes? Hello?'

'*Who the hell's this?*' a voice screamed, so loud that it sent a nail of pain into the side of my head. There were jing-jangs in Gilead, perhaps as many as a hundred that still worked, but none spoke so clear as this. I pulled the cone away, wincing, and could still hear the voice coming out of it.

'*Hello? Hello? Gods curse this fucking thing! HELLO?*'

'I hear you,' I said. 'Lower thy voice, for your father's sake.'

'Who is this?' There was just enough drop in volume for me to put the listening cone a little closer to my ear. But not in it; I would not make that mistake twice.

'A deputy.' Jamie DeCurry and I were the farthest things in the world from that, but simplest is usually best. *Always* best, I wot, when speaking with a panicky man on a jing-jang.

'Where's Sheriff Peavy?'

'At home with his wife. It isn't yet five o' the clock, I reckon. Now tell me who you are, where you're speaking from, and what's happened.'

'It's Canfield of the Jefferson. I—'

'Of the Jefferson *what*?' I heard footsteps behind me and turned, half-raising my revolver. But it was only Jamie, with his hair standing up in sleep-spikes all over his head. He was holding his own gun, and had gotten into his jeans, although his feet were yet bare.

84

'The Jefferson Ranch, ye great grotting idiot! You need to get the sheriff out here, and jin-jin. Everyone's dead. Jefferson, his fambly, the cookie, all the proddies. Blood from one end t'other.'

'How many?' I asked.

'Maybe fifteen. Maybe twenty. Who can tell?' Canfield of the Jefferson began to sob. 'They're all in pieces. Whatever it was did for em left the two dogs, Rosie and Mozie. They was in there. We had to shoot em. They was lapping up the blood and eating the brains.'

It was a ten-wheel ride, straight north toward the Salt Hills. We went with Sheriff Peavy, Kellin Frye – the good deputy – and Frye's son, Vikka. The enjie, whose name turned out to be Travis, also came along, for he'd spent the night at the Fryes' place. We pushed our mounts hard, but it was still full daylight by the time we got to the Jefferson spread. At least the wind, which was still strengthening, was at our backs.

Peavy thought Canfield was a pokie – which is to say a wandering cowboy not signed to any particular ranch. Some such turned outlaw, but most were honest enough, just men who couldn't settle down in one place. When we rode through the wide stock gate with JEFFERSON posted over it in white birch letters, two other cowboys – his mates – were with him. The three of them were bunched together by the shakepole fence of the horse corral, which stood near to the big house. A half a mile or so north, standing atop a little hill, was the bunkhouse. From this distance, only two things looked out of place: the door at the south end of the bunkie was unlatched, swinging back and forth in the alkali-wind, and the bodies of two large black dogs lay stretched on the dirt.

We dismounted and Sheriff Peavy shook with the men, who looked mightily glad to see us. 'Aye, Bill Canfield, see you very well, pokie-fella.'

The tallest of them took off his hat and held it against his shirt. 'I ain't no pokie nummore. Or maybe I am, I dunno. For a while here I was Canfield of the Jefferson, like I told whoever answered the goddam speakie, because I signed on just last month. Old man Jefferson himself oversaw my mark on the wall, but now he's dead like the rest of em.'

He swallowed hard. His Adam's apple bobbed up and down. The stubble on his face looked very black, because his skin was very white. There was drying vomit on the front of his shirt.

'His wife and daughters've gone into the clearing, too. You can tell em by their long hair and their . . . their . . . ay, ay, Man Jesus, you see a thing like that and it makes you wish you were born blind.' He raised his hat to his face to hide it and began to weep.

One of Canfield's mates said, 'Is those gunslingers, Sheriff? Mighty young to be hauling iron, ain't they?'

86

'Never mind them,' said Peavy. 'Tell me what brought you here.'

Canfield lowered his hat. His eyes were red and streaming. 'The three of us was camped out on the Pure. Roundin strays, we were, and camped for the night. Then we heard screamin start from the east. Woke us from a sound sleep, because we was that tired. Then gunshots, two or three of em. They quit and there was more screamin. And somethin – somethin *big* – roarin and snarlin.'

One of the others said, 'It sounded like a bear.'

'No, it didn't,' said the third. 'Never at all.'

Canfield said, 'Knew it was comin from the ranch, whatever it was. Had to've been four wheels from where we were, maybe six, but sound carries on the Pure, as ye know. We mounted up, but I got here way ahead of these two, because I was signed and they're yet pokies.'

'I don't understand,' I said.

Canfield turned to me. 'I had a ranch horse, didn't I? A good 'un. Snip and Arn there had nothing but mules. Put em in there, with the others.' He pointed into the corral. A big gust of wind blew through just then, driving dust before it, and all the livestock galloped away like a wave.

'They're still spooked,' Kellin Frye said.

Looking toward the bunkhouse, the enjie – Travis – said, 'They en't the only ones.'

By the time Canfield, the Jefferson Ranch's newest proddie – which is to say hired hand – reached the home place, the screaming had stopped. So had the roaring of the beast, although there was still a good deal of snarling going on. That was the two dogs, fighting over the leavings. Knowing which side of the biscuit his honey went on, Canfield bypassed the bunkhouse – and the dogs snarling within – for the big house. The front door was wide open and there were lit 'seners in both the hall and the kitchen, but no one answered his hail.

He found Jefferson's lady-sai in the kitchen with her body under the table and her half-eaten head rolled up against the pantry door. There were tracks going out the stoop door, which was banging in the wind. Some were human; some were the tracks of a monstrous great bear. The bear tracks were bloody.

'I took the 'sener off o' sink-side where it'd been left and followed the tracks outside. The two girls was a-layin in the dirt between the house and the barn. One had gotten three or four dozen running steps ahead of her sissa, but they were both just as dead, with their nightdresses tore off em and their backs carved open right down to the spines.' Canfield shook his head slowly from side to side, his large eyes – swimming with tears, they were – never leaving High Sheriff Peavy's face. 'I never want to see the claws that could do a thing like that. Never, never, never in my life. I seen what they done, and that's enough.'

'The bunkhouse?' Peavy asked.

'Aye, there I went next. You can see what's inside for yourself. The womenfolk too, for they're still where I found em. I won't take ye. Snip and Arn might—'

'Not me,' said Snip.

'Me, neither,' said Arn. 'I'll see 'un all in my dreams, and that'll do me fine.'

'I don't think we need a guide,' Peavy said. 'You three boys stay right here.'

Sheriff Peavy, closely followed by the Fryes and Travis the enjie, started toward the big house. Jamie put a hand on Peavy's shoulder, and spoke almost apologetically when the High Sheriff turned to look at him. 'Mind the tracks. They'll be important.'

Peavy nodded. 'Yar. We'll mind em very well. Especially those headed off to wherever the thing went.'

The women were as sai Canfield had told us. I had seen bloodshed before – aye, plenty of it, both in Mejis and in Gilead – but I had never seen anything like this, and neither had Jamie. He was as pale as Canfield, and I could only hope he would not discredit his father by passing out. I needn't have worried; soon he was down on his knees in the kitchen, examining several enormous blood-rimmed animal tracks.

'These really are bear tracks,' he said, 'but there was never one so big, Roland. Not even in the Endless Forest.'

'There was one here last night, cully,' Travis said.

He looked toward the body of the rancher's wife and shivered, even though she, like her unfortunate daughters, had been covered with blankets from upstairs. 'I'll be glad to get back to Gilead, where such things are just legends.'

'What do the tracks tell otherwise?' I asked Jamie. 'Anything?'

'Yes. It went to the bunkhouse first, where the most . . . the most food was. The rumpus would have wakened the four of them here in the house . . . were there only four, Sheriff?'

'Aye,' Peavy said. 'There are two sons, but Jefferson would have sent em to the auctions in Gilead, I expect. They'll find a sack of woe when they return.'

'The rancher left his womenfolk and went running for the bunkhouse. The gun Canfield and his mates heard must have been his.'

'Much good it did him,' Vikka Frye said. His father hit him on the shoulder and told him to hush.

'Then the thing came up here,' Jamie went on. 'The lady-sai Jefferson and the two girls were in the kitchen by then, I think. And I think the sai must have told her daughters to run.'

'Aye,' Peavy said. 'And she'd try to keep it from coming after them long enough for them to get away. That's how it reads. Only it didn't work. If they'd been at the front of the house – if they'd seen how big it was – she'd have known better, and we would have found all three of em out there in the dirt.' He fetched a deep sigh. 'Come on, boys, let's see what's in the bunkhouse. Waiting won't make it any prettier.'

'I think I might just stay out by the corral with those saddletramps,' Travis said. 'I've seen enough.'

Vikka Frye blurted: 'Can I do that too, Pa?'

Kellin looked at his son's haunted face and said he could. Before he let the boy go, he put a kiss on his cheek.

Ten feet or so in front of the bunkhouse, the bare earth had been scuffed into a bloody churn of bootprints and clawed animal tracks. Nearby, in a clump of jugweed, was an old short-arm four-shot with its barrel bent to one side. Jamie pointed from the confusion of tracks, to the gun, to the open bunkhouse door. Then he raised his eyebrows, silently asking me if I saw it. I saw it very well.

'This is where the thing – the skin-man wearing the shape of a bear – met the rancher,' I said. 'He got off a few rounds, then dropped the gun—'

'No,' Jamie said. 'The thing took it from him. That's why the barrel's bent. Maybe Jefferson turned to run. Maybe he stood his ground. Either way, it did no good. His tracks stop here, so the thing picked him up and threw him through that door and into the bunkhouse. It went to the big house next.'

'So we're backtracking it,' Peavy said.

Jamie nodded. 'We'll front-track it soon enough,' he said.

★   ★   ★

The thing had turned the bunkhouse into an abattoir. In the end, the butcher's bill came to eighteen: sixteen proddies, the cook – who had died beside his stove with his rent and blood-stained apron thrown over his face like a shroud – and Jefferson himself, who had been torn limbless. His severed head stared up at the rafters with a fearful grin that showed only his top teeth. The skin-man had ripped the rancher's lower jaw right out of his mouth. Kellin Frye found it under a bunk. One of the men had tried to defend himself with a saddle, using it as a shield, but it had done him no good; the thing had torn it in half with its claws. The unfortunate cowboy was still holding onto the pommel with one hand. He had no face; the thing had eaten it off his skull.

'Roland,' Jamie said. His voice was strangled, as if his throat had closed up to no more than a straw. 'We have to find this thing. We *have* to.'

'Let's see what the outward tracks say before the wind wipes them out,' I replied.

We left Peavy and the others outside the bunkhouse and circled the big house to where the covered bodies of the two girls lay. The tracks beyond them had begun to blur at the edges and around the claw-points, but they would have been hard to miss even for someone not fortunate enough to have had Cort of Gilead as a teacher. The thing that made them must have weighed upwards of eight hundred pounds.

'Look here,' Jamie said, kneeling beside one. 'See how it's deeper at the front? It was running.'

'And on its hind legs,' I said. 'Like a man.'

The tracks went past the pump house, which was in shambles, as if the thing had given it a swipe out of pure malice as it went by. They led us onto an uphill lane that headed north, toward a long unpainted outbuilding that was either a tack shed or a smithy. Beyond this, perhaps twenty wheels farther north, were the rocky badlands below the salt hills. We could see the holes that led to the worked-out mines; they gaped like empty eyesockets.

'We may as well give this up,' I said. 'We know where the tracks go – up to where the salties live.'

'Not yet,' Jamie said. 'Look here, Roland. You've never seen anything like this.'

The tracks began to change, the claws merging into the curved shapes of large unshod hooves.

'It lost its bear-shape,' I said, 'and became . . . what? A bull?'

'I think so,' Jamie said. 'Let's go a little further. I have an idea.'

As we approached the long outbuilding, the hoofprints became pawprints. The bull had become some kind of monstrous cat. These tracks were large at first, then started to grow smaller, as if the thing were shrinking from the size of a lion to that of a cougar even as it ran. When they veered off the lane and onto the dirt path leading to the tackshed, we found a large patch of jugweed grass that had been beaten down. The broken stalks were bloody.

'It fell,' Jamie said. 'I think it fell . . . and then thrashed.' He looked up from the bed of matted weed. His face was thoughtful. 'I think it was in pain.'

'Good,' I said. 'Now look there.' I pointed to the path, which was imprinted with the hooves of many horses. And other signs, as well.

Bare feet, going to the doors of the building, which were run back on rusty metal tracks.

Jamie turned to me, wide-eyed. I put my finger to my lips, and drew one of my revolvers. Jamie did likewise, and we moved toward the shed. I waved him around to the far side. He nodded and split off to the left.

I stood outside the open doors, gun held up, giving Jamie time to get to the other end of the building. I heard nothing. When I judged my pard must be in place, I bent down, picked up a good-size stone with my free hand, and tossed it inside. It thumped, then rolled across wood. There was still nothing else to hear. I swung inside, crouched low, gun at the ready.

The place seemed empty, but there were so many shadows it was at first hard to tell for sure. It was already warm, and by noonday would be an oven. I saw a pair of empty stalls on either side, a little smithy-stove next to drawers full of rusty shoes and equally rusty shoe-nails, dust-covered jugs of liniment and stinkum, branding irons in a tin sleeve, and a large pile of old tack that needed either to be mended or thrown out. Above a couple of benches hung a fair assortment of tools on pegs. Most were as rusty as the shoes and nails. There were a few wooden hitching hooks and a pedestal pump over a cement trough. The water in the trough hadn't been changed for a while; as my eyes adjusted to the dimness, I could see bits of straw floating on the surface. I kenned that this had once been more than a tack shed. It had also been a kind of hostelry where the ranch's working stock was seen to. Likely a jackleg veterinary, as well. Horses could be led in at one end, dealt with, and led out the other. But it looked in disrepair, abandoned.

The tracks of the thing that had by then been human led up the center aisle to other doors, also open, at the far end. I followed them. 'Jamie? It's me. Don't shoot me, for your father's sake.'

I stepped outside. Jamie had holstered his gun, and now pointed at a large heap of horseapples. 'He knows what he is, Roland.'

'You know this from a pile of horseshit?'

'As happens, I do.'

He didn't tell me how, but after a few seconds I saw it for myself. The hostelry had been abandoned, probably in favor of one built closer in to the main house, but the horseapples were fresh. 'If he came a-horseback, he came as a man.'

'Aye. And left as one.'

I squatted on my hunkers and thought about

95

this. Jamie rolled a smoke and let me. When I looked up, he was smiling a little.

'Do you see what it means, Roland?'

'Two hundred salties, give or take,' I said. 'I've ever been slow, but in the end I usually get there.

'Aye.'

'*Salties*, mind, not pokies or proddies. Diggers, not riders. As a rule.'

'As you say.'

'How many of em up there have horses, do you suppose? How many even know how to ride?'

His smile broadened. 'There might be twenty or thirty, I suppose.'

'It's better than two hundred,' I said. 'Better by a long stride. We'll go up as soon as—'

I never finished what I was going to say, because that's when the moaning started. It was coming from the tack shed I'd dismissed as empty. How glad I was at that moment Cort wasn't there. He would have cuffed my ear and sent me sprawling. At least in his prime, he would have.

Jamie and I looked into each other's startled eyes, then ran back inside. The moaning continued, but the place looked as empty as before. Then that big heap of old tack – busted hames, bridles, cinch straps and reins – started to heave up and down, as if it were breathing. The tangled bunches of leather began to tumble away to either side and from them a boy was born. His white-blond hair was sticking up in all directions. He wore jeans and an old shirt that hung open and unbuttoned.

He didn't look hurt, but in the shadows it was hard to tell.

'Is it gone?' he asked in a trembling voice. 'Please, sais, say it is. Say it's gone.'

'It is,' I said.

He started to wade his way out of the pile, but a strip of leather had gotten wound around one of his legs and he fell forward. I caught him and saw a pair of eyes, bright blue and utterly terrified, looking up into my face.

Then he passed out.

I carried him to the trough. Jamie pulled off his bandanna, dipped it in the water, and began to wipe the boy's dirt-streaked face with it. He might have been eleven; he might have been a year or two younger. He was so thin it was hard to tell. After a bit his eyes fluttered open. He looked from me to Jamie and then back to me again. 'Who are you?' he asked. 'You don't b'long to the ranch.'

'We're friends of the ranch,' I said. 'Who are you?'

'Bill Streeter,' he said. 'The proddies call me Young Bill.'

'Aye, do they? And is your father Old Bill?'

He sat up, took Jamie's bandanna, dipped it in the trough, and squeezed it out so the water ran down his thin chest. 'No, Old Bill's my granther, went into the clearing two years ago. My da', he's just plain Bill.' Something about speaking his father's name made his eyes widen. He grasped my arm. 'He ain't dead, is he? Say he ain't, sai!'

Jamie and I exchanged another look, and that scared him worse than ever.

'Say he ain't! Please say my daddy ain't dead!' He started to cry.

'Hush and go easy now,' I said. 'What is he, your da'? A proddie?'

'Nay, no, he's the cook. *Say he ain't dead!*'

But the boy knew he was. I saw it in his eyes as clearly I'd seen the bunkhouse cook with his bloodstained apron thrown over his face.

There was a willa-tree on one side of the big house, and that was where we questioned Young Bill Streeter – just me, Jamie, and Sheriff Peavy. The others we sent back to wait in the shade of the bunkhouse, thinking that to have too many folks around him would only upset the boy more. As it happened, he could tell us very little of what we needed to know.

'My da' said to me that it was going to be a warm night and I should go up to the graze t'other side of the corral and sleep under the stars,' Young Bill told us. 'He said it'd be cooler and I'd sleep better. But I knew why. Elrod'd got a bottle some-where – again – and he was in drink.'

'That'd be Elrod Nutter?' Sheriff Peavy asked.

'Aye, him. Foreman of the boys, he is.'

'I know him well,' Peavy said to us. 'Ain't I had him locked up half a dozen times and more?

Jefferson keeps him on because he's a helluva rider and roper, but he's one mean whoredog when he's in drink. Ain't he, Young Bill?'

Young Bill nodded earnestly and brushed his long hair, still all dusty from the tack he'd hidden in, out of his eyes. 'Yessir, and he had a way of takin after me. Which my father knew.'

'Cook's apprentice, were ye?' Peavy asked. I knew he was trying to be kind, but I wished he'd mind his mouth and stop talking in the way that says *once, but no more.*

But the boy didn't seem to notice. 'Bunkhouse boy. Not cook's boy.' He turned to Jamie and me. 'I make the bunks, coil the rope, cinch the bedrolls, polish the saddles, set the gates at the end of the day after the horses is turned in. Tiny Braddock taught me how to make a lasso, and I throw it pretty. Roscoe's teaching me the bow. Freddy Two-Step says he'll show me how to brand, come fall.'

'Do well,' I said, and tapped my throat.

That made him smile. 'They're good fellas, mostly.' The smile went away as fast as it had come, like the sun going behind a cloud. 'Except for Elrod. He's just grouchy when he's sober, but when he's in drink, he likes to tease. *Mean* teasing, if you do ken it.'

'Ken it well,' I said.

'Aye, and if you don't laugh and act like it's all a joke – even if it's twisting on your hand or yanking you around on the bunkhouse floor by

99

your hair – he gets uglier still. So when my da'
told me to sleep out, I took my blanket and my
shaddie and I went. A word to the wise is suffi-
cient, my da' says.'

'What's a shaddie?' Jamie asked the sheriff.

'Bit o' canvas,' Peavy said. 'Won't keep off rain,
but it'll keep you from getting damp after dewfall.'

'Where did you roll in?' I asked the boy.

He pointed beyond the corral, where the horses
were still skitty from the rising wind. Above us
and around us, the willa sighed and danced. Pretty
to hear, prettier still to look at. 'I guess my blanket
n shaddie must still be there.'

I looked from where he had pointed, to the tackshed hostelry where we'd found him, then to the
bunkhouse. The three places made the corners of
a triangle probably a quarter-mile on each side,
with the corral in the middle.

'How did you get from where you slept to hiding
under that pile of tack, Bill?' Sheriff Peavy asked.

The boy looked at him for a long time without
speaking. Then the tears began to fall again. He
covered them with his fingers so we wouldn't
see them. 'I don't remember,' he said. 'I don't
remember *nuffink*.' He didn't exactly lower his
hands; they seemed to drop into his lap, as if they'd
grown too heavy for him to hold up. 'I want
my da'.'

Jamie got up and walked away, with his hands
stuffed deep in his back pockets. I tried to say
what needed saying, and couldn't. You have to

remember that although Jamie and I wore guns, they weren't yet the big guns of our fathers. I'd never again be so young as before I met Susan Delgado, and loved her, and lost her, but I was still too young to tell this boy that his father had been torn to pieces by a monster. So I looked to Sheriff Peavy. I looked to the grownup.

Peavy took off his hat and laid it aside on the grass. Then he took the boy's hands. 'Son,' he said, 'I've got some very hard news for you. I want you to pull in a deep breath and be a man about it.'

But Young Bill Streeter had only nine or ten summers behind him, eleven at most, and he couldn't be a man about anything. He began to wail. When he did it, I saw my mother's pale dead face as clear as if she had been lying next to me under that willa, and I couldn't stand it. I felt like a coward, but that didn't stop me from getting up and walking away.

The lad either cried himself to sleep or into unconsciousness. Jamie carried him into the big house and put him in one of the beds upstairs. He was just the son of a bunkhouse cook, but there was no one else to sleep in them, not now. Sheriff Peavy used the jing-jang to call his office where one of the not-so-good deputies had been ordered to wait for his ring. Soon enough, Debaria's undertaker – if there was one – would organize a little convoy of wagons to come and pick up the dead.

Sheriff Peavy went into sai Jefferson's little office

and plunked himself down in a chair on rollers. 'What's next, boys?' he asked. 'The salties, I reckon . . . and I suppose you'll want to get up there before this wind blows into a simoom. Which it certainly means t'do.' He sighed. 'The boy's no good to ye, that's certain. Whatever he saw was evil enough to scrub his mind clean.'

Jamie began, 'Roland has a way of—'

'I'm not sure what's next,' I said. 'I'd like to talk it over a little with my pard. We might take a little *pasear* back up to that tack shed.'

'Tracks'll be blown away by now,' Peavy said, 'but have at it and may it do ya well.' He shook his head. 'Telling that boy was hard. Very hard.'

'You did it the right way,' I said.

'Do ya think so? Aye? Well, thankya. Poor little cullie. Reckon he can stay with me n the wife for a while. Until we figure what comes next for him. You boys go on and palaver, if it suits you. I think I'll just sit here and try to get back even wi' myself. No hurry about anything now; that damned thing ate well enough last night. It'll be a good while before it needs to go hunting again.'

Jamie and I walked two circuits around the shed and corral while we talked, the strengthening wind rippling our pantlegs and blowing back our hair.

'Is it all truly erased from his mind, Roland?'

'What do *you* think?' I asked.

'No,' he said. 'Because "Is it gone?" was the first thing he asked.'

'And he knew his father was dead. Even when he asked us, it was in his eyes.'

Jamie walked without replying for a while, his head down. We'd tied our bandannas over our mouths and noses because of the blowing grit. Jamie's was still wet from the trough. Finally he said, 'When I started to tell the sheriff you have a way of getting at things that are buried – buried in people's minds – you cut me off.'

'He doesn't need to know, because it doesn't always work.'

It had with Susan Delgado, in Mejis, but part of Susan had wanted badly to tell me what the witch, Rhea, had tried to hide from Susan's front-mind, where we hear our own thoughts very clearly. She'd wanted to tell me because we were in love.

'But will you try? You will, won't you?'

I didn't answer him until we had started our second circuit of the corral. I was still putting my thoughts in order. As I may have said, that has always been slow work for me.

'The salties don't live in the mines anymore; they have their own encampment a few wheels west of Little Debaria. Kellin Frye told me about it on the ride out here. I want you to go up there with Peavy and the Fryes. Canfield, too, if he'll go. I think he will. Those two pokies – Canfield's trail-mates – can stay here and wait for the undertaker.'

'You mean to take the boy back to town?'

103

'Yes. Alone. But I'm not sending you up there just to get you and the others away. If you travel fast enough, and they have a remuda, you may still be able to spot a horse that's been rode hard.'

Under the bandanna, he might have smiled. 'I doubt it.'

I did, too. It would have been more likely but for the wind – what Peavy had called the simoom. It would dry the sweat on a horse, even one that had been ridden hard, in short order. Jamie might spot one that was dustier than the rest, one with burdocks and bits of jugweed in its tail, but if we were right about the skin-man knowing what he was, he would have given his mount a complete rubdown and curry, from hooves to mane, as soon as he got back.

'Someone may have seen him ride in.'

'Yes . . . unless he went to Little Debaria first, cleaned up, and came back to the saltie encampment from there. A clever man might do that.'

'Even so, you and the sheriff should be able to find out how many of them own horses.'

'And how many of them can ride, even if they don't own,' Jamie said. 'Aye, we can do that.'

'Round that bunch up,' I told him, 'or as many of them as you can, and bring them back to town. Any who protests, remind them that they'll be helping to catch the monster that's been terrorizing Debaria . . . Little Debaria . . . the whole Barony. You won't have to tell them that any who still refuse will be looked at with extra suspicion; even the dumbest of them will know.'

Jamie nodded, then grabbed the fencerail as an especially strong gust of wind blasted us. I turned to face him.

'And one other thing. You're going to pull a cosy, and Kellin's son, Vikka, will be your cat's-paw. They'll believe a kid might run off at the mouth, even if he's been told not to. *Especially* if he's been told not to.'

Jamie waited, but I felt sure he knew what I was going to say, for his eyes were troubled. It was a thing he'd never have done himself, even if he thought of it. Which was why my father had put me in charge. Not because I'd done well in Mejis – I hadn't, not really – and not because I was his son, either. Although in a way, I suppose that was it. My mind was like his: cold.

'You'll tell the salties who know about horses that there was a witness to the murders at the ranch. You'll say you can't tell them who it was – naturally – but that he saw the skin-man in his human form.'

'You don't know that Young Bill actually saw him, Roland. And even if he did, he might not have seen the face. He was hiding in a pile of tack, for your father's sake.'

'That's true, but the skin-man won't know it's true. All the skin-man will know is that it *might* be true, because he was human when he left the ranch.'

I began to walk again, and Jamie walked beside me.

'Now here's where Vikka comes in. He'll get separated from you and the others a bit and whisper to someone – another kid, one his own age, would be best – that the survivor was the cook's boy. Bill Streeter by name.'

'The boy just lost his father and you want to use him as bait.'

'It may not come to that. If the story gets to the right ears, the one we're looking for may bolt on the way to town. Then you'll know. And none of it matters if we're wrong about the skin-man being a saltie. We could be, you know.'

'What if we're right, and the fellow decides to face it out?'

'Bring them all to the jail. I'll have the boy in a cell – a locked one, you ken – and you can walk the horsemen past, one by one. I'll tell Young Bill to say nothing, one way or the other, until they're gone. You're right, he may not be able to pick our man out, even if I can help him remember some of what happened last night. But our man won't know that, either.'

'It's risky,' said Jamie. 'Risky for the kid.'

'Small risk,' I said. 'It'll be daylight, with the skin-man in his human shape. And Jamie . . .' I grasped his arm. 'I'll be in the cell, too. The bastard will have to go through me if he wants to get to the boy.'

★   ★   ★

Peavy liked my plan better than Jamie had. I wasn't a bit surprised. It was his town, after all. And what was Young Bill to him? Only the son of a dead cook. Not much in the great scheme of things.

Once the little expedition to Saltie Town was on its way, I woke the boy and told him we were going to Debaria. He agreed without asking questions. He was distant and dazed. Every now and then he rubbed his eyes with his knuckles. As we walked out to the corral, he asked me again if I was sure his da' was dead. I told him I was. He fetched a deep sigh, lowered his head, and put his hands on his knees. I gave him time, then asked if he'd like me to saddle a horse for him.

'If it's all right to ride Millie, I can saddle her myself. I feed her, and she's my special friend. People say mules ain't smart, but Millie is.'

'Let's see if you can do it without getting kicked,' I said.

It turned out he could, and smartly. He mounted up and said, 'I guess I'm ready.' He even tried to give me a smile. It was awful to look at. I was sorry for the plan I'd set in motion, but all I had to do was think of the carnage we were leaving behind and Sister Fortuna's ruined face to remind myself of what the stakes were.

'Will she skit in the wind?' I asked, nodding at the trim little mule. Sitting on her back, Young Bill's feet came almost down to the ground. In another year, he'd be too big for her, but of course in another year, he'd probably be far from Debaria, just another wanderer on the face of a fading world. Millie would be a memory.

'Not Millie,' he said. 'She's as solid as a dromedary.'

'Aye, and what's a dromedary?'

'Dunno, do I? It's just something my da' says. One time I asked him, and he didn't know, either.'

'Come on, then,' I said. 'The sooner we get to town, the sooner we'll get out of this grit.' But I intended to make one stop before we got to town. I had something to show the boy while we were still alone.

About halfway between the ranch and Debaria, I spied a deserted sheepherder's lean-to, and suggested we shelter in there for a bit and have a bite. Bill Streeter agreed willingly enough. He had lost his da' and everyone else he'd known, but he was still a growing boy and he'd had nothing to eat since his dinner the night before.

We tethered our mounts away from the wind and sat on the floor inside the lean-to with our backs against the wall. I had dried beef wrapped in leaves in my saddlebag. The meat was salty, but my waterskin was full. The boy ate half a dozen chunks of the meat, tearing off big bites and washing them down with water.

A strong gust of wind shook the lean-to. Millie blatted a protest and fell silent.

'It'll be a full-going simoom by dark,' Young Bill said. 'You watch and see if it ain't.'

'I like the sound of the wind,' I said. 'It makes me think of a story my mother read to me when I was a sma' one. "The Wind through the Keyhole," it was called. Does thee know it?'

Young Bill shook his head. 'Mister, are you really a gunslinger? Say true?'

'I am.'

'Can I hold one of your guns for a minute?'

'Never in life,' I said, 'but you can look at one of these, if you'd like.' I took a shell from my belt and handed it to him.

He examined it closely, from brass base to lead tip. 'Gods, it's heavy! Long, too! I bet if you shot someone with one of these, he'd stay down.'

'Yes. A shell's a dangerous thing. But it can be pretty, too. Would you like to see a trick I can do with this one?'

'Sure.'

I took it back and began to dance it from knuckle to knuckle, my fingers rising and falling in waves. Young Bill watched, wide-eyed. 'How does thee do it?'

'The same way anyone does anything,' I said. 'Practice.'

'Will you show me the trick?'

'If you watch close, you may see it for yourself,' I said. 'Here it is . . . and here it isn't.' I palmed the shell so fast it disappeared, thinking of Susan Delgado, as I supposed I always would when I did this trick. 'Now here it is again.'

The shell danced fast . . . then slow . . . then fast again.

'Follow it with your eyes, Bill, and see if you can make out how I get it to disappear. Don't take your eyes off it.' I dropped my voice to a lulling murmur. 'Watch . . . and watch . . . and watch. Does it make you sleepy?'

'A little,' he said. His eyes slipped slowly closed, then the lids rose again. 'I didn't sleep much last night.'

'Did you not? Watch it go. Watch it slow. See it disappear and then . . . see it as it speeds up again.'

Back and forth the shell went. The wind blew, as lulling to me as my voice was to him.

'Sleep if you want, Bill. Listen to the wind and sleep. But listen to my voice, too.'

'I hear you, gunslinger.' His eyes closed again and this time didn't reopen. His hands were clasped limply in his lap. 'I hear you very well.'

'You can still see the shell, can't you? Even with your eyes closed.'

'Yes . . . but it's bigger now. It flashes like gold.'

'Do you say so?'

'Yes . . .'

'Go deeper, Bill, but hear my voice.'

'I hear.'

'I want you to turn your mind back to last night.

Your mind and your eyes and your ears. Will you do that?'

A frown creased his brow. 'I don't want to.'

'It's safe. All that's happened, and besides, I'm with you.'

'You're with me. And you have guns.'

'So I do. Nothing will happen to you as long as you can hear my voice, because we're together. I'll keep thee safe. Do you understand that?'

'Yes.'

'Your da' told you to sleep out under the stars, didn't he?'

'Aye. It was to be a warm night.'

'But that wasn't the real reason, was it?'

'No. It was because of Elrod. Once he twirled the bunkhouse cat by her tail, and she never came back. Sometimes he pulls me around by my hair and sings "The Boy Who Loved Jenny." My da' can't stop him, because Elrod's bigger. Also, he has a knife in his boot. He could cut with it. But he couldn't cut the beast, could he?' His clasped hands twitched. 'Elrod's dead and I'm glad. I'm sorry about all the others . . . and my da', I don't know what I'll do wi'out my da' . . . but I'm glad about Elrod. He won't tease me nummore. He won't scare me nummore. I seen it, aye.'

So he *did* know more than the top of his mind had let him remember.

'Now you're out on the graze.'

'On the graze.'

'Wrapped up in your blanket and shinnie.'

'*Shaddie.*'

'Your blanket and shaddie. You're awake, maybe looking up at the stars, at Old Star and Old Mother—'

'No, no, asleep,' Bill said. 'But the screams wake me up. The screams from the bunkhouse. And the sounds of fighting. Things are breaking. And something's *roaring.*'

'What do you do, Bill?'

'I go down. I'm afraid to, but my da' . . . my da's in there. I look in the window at the far end. It's greasepaper, but I can see through it well enough. More than I want to see. Because I see . . . I see . . . mister, can I wake up?'

'Not yet. Remember that I'm with you.'

'Have you drawn your guns, mister?' He was shivering.

'I have. To protect you. What do you see?'

'Blood. And a beast.'

'What kind, can you tell?'

'A bear. One so tall its head reaches the ceiling. It goes up the middle of the bunkhouse . . . between the cots, ye ken, and on its back legs . . . and its grabs the men . . . it grabs the men and pulls them to pieces with its great long claws.' Tears began to escape his closed lids and roll down his cheeks. 'The last one was Elrod. He ran for the back door . . . where the woodpile is just outside, ye ken . . . and when he understood it would have him before he could open the door and dash out,

he turned around to fight. He had his knife. He
went to stab it . . .'

Slowly, as if underwater, the boy's right hand
rose from his lap. It was curled into a first. He
made a stabbing motion with it.

'The bear grabbed his arm and tore it off his
shoulder. Elrod screamed. He sounded like a horse
I saw one time, after it stepped in a gompa hole
and broke its leg. The thing . . . it hit Elrod in the
face with 'is own arm. The blood flew. There was
gristle that flapped and wound around the skin
like strings. Elrod fell against the door and started
to slide down. The bear grabbed him and lifted
him up and bit into his neck and there was a
sound . . . mister, it bit Elrod's head right off his
neck. I want to wake up now. *Please*.'

'Soon. What did you do then?'

'I ran. I meant to go to the big house, but sai
Jefferson . . . he . . . he . . .'

'He what?'

'He *shot* at me! I don't think he meant to. I think
he just saw me out of the corner of his eye and
thought . . . I heard the bullet go by me. *Wishhh!*
That's how close it was. So I ran for the corral
instead. I went between the poles. While I was
crossing, I heard two more shots. Then there was
more screaming. I didn't look to see, but I knew
it was sai Jefferson screaming that time.'

This part we knew from the tracks and leavings:
how the thing had come charging out of the bunkhouse, how it had grabbed away the four-shot pistol

113

and bent the barrel, how it had unzipped the rancher's guts and thrown him into the bunkhouse with his proddies. The shot Jefferson had thrown at Young Bill had saved the boy's life. If not for that, he would have run straight to the big house and been slaughtered with the Jefferson womenfolk.

'You go into the old hostelry where we found you.'

'Aye, so I do. And hide under the tack. But then I hear it . . . coming.'

He had gone back to the *now* way of remembering, and his words came more slowly. They were broken by bursts of weeping. I knew it was hurting him, remembering terrible things always hurts, but I pressed on. I had to, for what happened in that abandoned hostelry was the important part, and Young Bill was the only one who had been there. Twice he tried to come back to the *then* way of remembering, the *ago*. This was a sign that he was trying to struggle free of his trance, so I took him deeper. In the end I got it all.

The terror he'd felt as the grunting, snuffling thing approached. The way the sounds had changed, blurring into the snarls of a cat. Once it had roared, Young Bill said, and when he heard that sound, he'd let loose water in his trousers. He hadn't been able to hold it. He waited for the cat to come in, knowing it would scent him where he lay – from the urine – only the cat didn't. There was silence . . . silence . . . and then more screaming.

'At first it's the cat screaming, then it changes

114

into a human screaming. High to begin with, it's like a woman, but then it starts to go down until it's a man. It screams and screams. It makes *me* want to scream. I thought—'

'Think,' I said. 'You think, Bill, because it's happening now. Only I'm here to protect you. My guns are drawn.'

'I think my head will split open. Then it stops . . . and it comes in.'

'It walks up the middle to the other door, doesn't it?'

He shook his head. 'Not walks. Shuffles. *Staggers.* Like it's hurt. It goes right past me. *He.* Now it's *he.* He almost falls down, but grabs one of the stall doors and stays up. Then he goes on. He goes on a little better now.'

'Stronger?'

'Aye.'

'Do you see his face?' I thought I already knew the answer to that.

'No, only his feet, through the tack. The moon's up, and I see them very well.'

Perhaps so, but we wouldn't be identifying the skin-man from his feet, I felt quite sure. I opened my mouth, ready to start bringing him up from his trance, when he spoke again.

'There's a ring around one of his ankles.'

I leaned forward, as if he could see me . . . and if he was deep enough, mayhap he could, even with his eyes closed. 'What kind of ring? Was it metal, like a manacle?'

115

'I don't know what that is.'

'Like a bridle-ring? You know, a hoss-clinkum?'

'No, no. Like on Elrod's arm, but that's a picture of a nekkid woman, and you can hardly make it out nummore.'

'Bill, are you talking about a tattoo?'

In his trance, the boy smiled. 'Aye, that's the word. But this one wasn't a picture, just a blue ring around his ankle. A blue ring in his skin.'

I thought, *We have you. You don't know it yet, sai skin-man, but we have you.*

'Mister, can I wake up now? I want to wake up.'

'Is there anything else?'

'The white mark?' He seemed to be asking himself.

'What white mark?'

He shook his head slowly from side to side, and I decided to let it go. He'd had enough.

'Come to the sound of my voice. As you come, you'll leave everything that happened last night behind, because it's over. Come, Bill. Come now.'

'I'm coming.' His eyes rolled back and forth behind his closed lids.

'You're safe. Everything that happened at the ranch is ago. Isn't it?'

'Yes . . .'

'Where are we?'

'On Debaria high road. We're going to town. I ain't been there but once. My da' bought me candy.'

116

'I'll buy you some, too,' I said, 'for you've done well, Young Bill of the Jefferson. Now open your eyes.'

He did, but at first he only looked through me. Then his eyes cleared and he gave an uncertain smile. 'I fell asleep.'

'You did. And now we should push for town before the wind grows too strong. Can you do that, Bill?'

'Aye,' he said, and as he got up he added, 'I was dreaming of candy.'

The two not-so-good deputies were in the sheriff's office when we got there, one of them – a fat fellow wearing a tall black hat with a gaudy rattlesnake band – taking his ease behind Peavy's desk. He eyed the guns I was wearing and got up in a hurry.

'You're the gunslinger, ain'tcha?' he said. 'Well-met, well-met, we both say so. Where's t'other one?'

I escorted Young Bill through the archway and into the jail without answering. The boy looked at the cells with interest but no fear. The drunk, Salty Sam, was long gone, but his aroma lingered.

From behind me, the other deputy asked, 'What do you think you're doing, young sai?'

'My business,' I said. 'Go back to the office and bring me the keyring to these cells. And be quick about it, if you please.'

None of the smaller cells had mattresses on their bunks, so I took Young Bill to the drunk-and-disorderly cell where Jamie and I had slept the night before. As I put the two straw pallets together to give the boy a little more comfort – after what he'd been through, I reckoned he deserved all the comfort he could get – Bill looked at the chalked map on the wall.

'What is it, sai?'

'Nothing to concern you,' I said. 'Now listen to me. I'm going to lock you in, but you're not to be afraid, for you've done nothing wrong. 'Tis but for your own safety. I have an errand that needs running, and when it's done, I'm going to come in there with you.'

'And lock us both in,' said he. 'You'd better lock us both in. In case it comes back.'

'Do you remember it now?'

'A little,' said he, looking down. 'It wasn't a man . . . then it was. It killed my da'.' He put the heels of his hands against his eyes. 'Poor Da'.'

The deputy with the black hat returned with the keys. The other was right behind him. Both were gawking at the boy as if he were a two-headed goat in a roadshow.

I took the keys. 'Good. Now back to the office, both of you.'

'Seems like you might be throwing your weight around a little, youngster,' Black Hat said, and the other – a little man with an undershot jaw – nodded vigorously.

'Go now,' I said. 'This boy needs rest.'

They looked me up and down, then went. Which

was the correct thing. The only thing, really. My mood was not good.

The boy kept his eyes covered until their bootheels faded back through the arch, then he lowered his hands. 'Will you catch him, sai?'

'Yes.'

'And will you kill him?'

'Does thee *want* me to kill him?'

He considered this, and nodded. 'Aye. For what he did to my da', and to sai Jefferson, and all the others. Even Elrod.'

I closed the door of the cell, found the right key, and turned it. The keyring I hung over my wrist, for it was too big for my pocket. 'I'll make you a promise, Young Bill,' I said. 'One I swear to on my father's name. I won't kill him, but you shall be there when he swings, and with my own hand I'll give you the bread to scatter beneath his dead feet.'

In the office, the two not-so-good deputies eyed me with caution and dislike. That was nothing to me. I hung the keyring on the peg next to the jing-jang and said, 'I'll be back in an hour, maybe a little less. In the meantime, no one goes into the jail. And that includes you two.'

'High-handed for a shaveling,' the one with the undershot jaw remarked.

'Don't fail me in this,' I said. 'It wouldn't be wise. Do you understand?'

Black Hat nodded. 'But the sheriff will hear how you done with us.'

'Then you'll want to have a mouth still capable of speech when he gets back,' I said, and went out.

The wind had continued to strengthen, blowing clouds of gritty, salt-flavored dust between the false-fronted buildings. I had Debaria high street entirely to myself except for a few hitched horses that stood with their hindquarters turned to the wind and their heads unhappily lowered. I would not leave my own so – nor Millie, the mule the boy had ridden – and led them down to the livery stable at the far end of the street. There the hostler was glad to take them, especially when I split him off half a gold knuck from the bundle I carried in my vest.

No, he said in answer to my first question, there was no jeweler in Debaria, nor ever had been in his time. But the answer to my second question was yar, and he pointed across the street to the blacksmith's shop. The smith himself was standing in the doorway, the hem of his tool-filled leather apron flapping in the wind. I walked across and he put his fist to his forehead. 'Hile.'

I hiled him in return and told him what I wanted – what Vannay had said I might need. He listened closely, then took the shell I handed him. It was the very one I'd used to entrance Young Bill. The blackie held it up to the light. 'How many grains of powder does it blow, can'ee say?'

Of course I could. 'Fifty-seven.'

'As many as that? Gods! It's a wonder the barrel

120

of your revolver don't bust when'ee pull the trigger!'

The shells in my father's guns – the ones I might someday carry – blew seventy-six, but I didn't say so. He'd likely not have believed it. 'Can you do what I ask, sai?'

'I think so.' He considered, then nodded. 'Aye. But not today. I don't like to run my smithhold hot in the wind. One loose ember and the whole town might catch ablaze. We've had no fire department since my da' was a boy.'

I took out my bag of gold knuckles and shook two into the palm of my hand. I considered, then added a third. The smith stared at them with wonder. He was looking at two years' wages.

'It has to be today,' I said.

He grinned, showing teeth of amazing whiteness within the forest of his ginger beard. 'Tempting devil, get not aside! For what you're showin me, I'd risk burning Gilead herself to her foundations. You'll have it by sundown.'

'I'll have it by three.'

'Aye, three's what I meant. To the shaved point of the minute.'

'Good. Now tell me, which restaurant cooks the best chow in town?'

'There's only two, and neither of em'll make you remember your mother's bird puddin, but neither'll poison'ee. Racey's Café is probably the better.'

That was good enough for me; I thought a growing boy like Bill Streeter would take quantity

121

over quality any day. I headed for the café, now working against the wind. *It'll be a full-going simoom by dark*, the boy had told me, and I thought he was right. He had been through a lot, and needed time to rest. Now that I knew about the ankle tattoo, I might not need him at all . . . but the skin-man wouldn't know that. And in the jail, Young Bill was safe. At least I hoped so.

It was stew, and I could have sworn it had been seasoned with alkali grit instead of salt, but the kid ate all of his and finished mine as well when I put it aside. One of the not-so-good deputies had made coffee, and we drank that from tin cups. We made our meal right there in the cell, sitting cross-legged on the floor. I listened for the jing-jang, but it stayed quiet. I wasn't surprised. Even if Jamie and the High Sheriff came near one at their end, the wind had probably taken the wires down.

'I guess you know all about these storms you call simooms,' I said to Young Bill.

'Oh, yes,' he said. 'This is the season for em. The proddies hate em and the pokies hate em even more, because if they're out on the range, they have to sleep rough. And they can't have a fire at night, accourse, because of—'

'Because of the embers,' I said, remembering the blacksmith.

'Just as you say. Stew all gone, is it?'

'So it is, but there's one more thing.'

I handed over a little sack. He looked inside it

and lit up. 'Candy! Rollers and chocker-twists!'
He extended the bag. 'Here, you have the first.'

I took one of the little chocolate twists, then
pushed the bag back to him. 'You have the rest.
If it won't make your belly sick, that is.'

'It won't!' And he dived in. It did me good to
see him. After the third roller went into his gob,
he cheeked it – which made him look like a squirrel
with a nut – and said, 'What'll happen to me, sai?
Now that my da's gone?'

'I don't know, but there'll be water if God wills
it.' I already had an idea where that water might
be. If we could put paid to the skin-man, a certain
large lady named Everlynne would owe us a good
turn, and I doubt if Bill Streeter would be the first
stray she'd taken in.

I returned to the subject of the simoom. 'How
much will it strengthen?'

'It'll blow a gale tonight. Probably after midnight.
And by noon tomorrow, it'll be gone.'

'Does thee know where the salties live?'

'Aye, I've even been there. Once with my da',
to see the races they sometimes have up there,
and once with some proddies looking for strays.
The salties take em in, and we pay with hard
biscuit for the ones that have the Jefferson brand.'

'My trailmate's gone there with Sheriff Peavy
and a couple of others. Think they have any chance
of getting back before nightfall?'

I felt sure he would say no, but he surprised me.
'Being as it's all downhill from Salt Village – which

is on this side of Little Debaria – I'd say they could. If they rode hard.'

That made me glad I'd told the blacksmith to hurry, although I knew better than to trust the reckoning of a mere boy.

'Listen to me, Young Bill. When they come back, I expect they'll have some of the salties with em. Maybe a dozen, maybe as many as twenty. Jamie and I may have to walk em through the jail for you to look at, but you needn't be afraid, because the door of this cell will be locked. And you don't have to say anything, just look.'

'If you're thinking I can tell which one killed my da', I can't. I don't even remember if I saw him.'

'You probably won't have to see them at all,' I said. This I truly believed. We'd have them into the sheriff's office by threes, and have them hike their pants. When we found the one with the blue ring tattooed around his ankle, we'd have our man. Not that he *was* a man. Not anymore. Not really.

'Wouldn't you like another chocker, sai? There's three left, and I can't eat nummore.'

'Save them for later,' I said, and got up.

His face clouded. 'Will you come back? I don't want to be in here on my own.'

'Aye, I'll come back.' I stepped out, locked the cell door, then tossed the keys to him through the bars. 'Let me in when I do.'

★   ★   ★

124

The fat deputy with the black hat was Strother. The one with the undershot jaw was Pickens. They looked at me with care and mistrust, which I thought a good combination, coming from the likes of them. I could work with care and mistrust.

'If I asked you fellows about a man with a blue ring tattooed on his ankle, would it mean anything to you?'

They exchanged a glance and then Black Hat – Strother – said, 'The stockade.'

'What stockade would that be?' Already I didn't like the sound of it.

'Beelie Stockade,' Pickens said, looking at me as if I were the utterest of utter idiots. 'Does thee not know of it? And thee a gunslinger?'

'Beelie Town's west of here, isn't it?' I asked.

'Was,' Strother said. 'It's Beelie Ghost Town now. Harriers tore through it five year ago. Some say John Farson's men, but I don't believe that. Never in life. 'Twas plain old garden-variety outlaws. Once there was a militia outpost – back in the days when there *was* a militia – and Beelie Stockade was their place o' business. It was where the circuit judge sent thieves and murderers and card cheats.'

'Witches n warlocks, too,' Pickens volunteered. He wore the face of a man remembering the good old days, when the railroad trains ran on time and the jing-jang no doubt rang more often, with calls from more places. 'Practicers of the dark arts.'

'Once they took a cannibal,' Strother said. 'He ate his wife.' This caused him to give out with a

125

foolish giggle, although whether it was the eating or the relationship that struck him funny I couldn't say.

'He was hung, that fellow,' Pickens said. He bit off a chunk of chew and worked it with his peculiar jaw. He still looked like a man remembering a better, rosier past. 'There was lots of hangings at Beelie Stockade in those days. I went several times wi' my da' and my marmar to see em. Marmar allus packed a lunch.' He nodded slowly and thoughtfully. 'Aye, many and many-a. Lots o' folks came. There was booths and clever people doing clever things such as juggling. Sometimes there was dogfights in a pit, but accourse it was the hangins that was the real show.' He chuckled. 'I remember this one fella who kicked a regular commala when the drop didn't break 'is—'

'What's this to do with blue ankle tattoos?'

'Oh,' Strother said, recalled to the initial subject. 'Anyone who ever did time in Beelie had one of those put on, y'see. Although I disremember if it was for punishment or just identification in case they ran off from one o' the work gangs. All that stopped ten year ago, when the stockade closed. That's why the harriers was able to have their way with the town, you know – because the militia left and the stockade closed. Now we have to deal with all the bad element and riffraff ourselves.' He eyed me up and down in the most insolent way. 'We don't get much help from Gilead these days. Nawp. Apt to get more from John Farson, and there's some that'd send a parlay-party west to ask him.' Perhaps he saw something in my eyes, because he sat up a little straighter in his chair and said, 'Not me, accourse. Never. I believe in the straight law and the Line of Eld.'

'So do we all,' Pickens said, nodding vigorously.

'Would you want to guess if some of the salt-miners did time in Beelie Stockade before it was decommissioned?' I asked.

Strother appeared to consider, then said: 'Oh, probably a few. Nummore'n four in every ten, I should say.'

In later years I learned to control my face, but those were early times, and he must have seen my dismay. It made him smile. I doubt if he knew how close that smile brought him to suffering. I'd had a difficult two days, and the boy weighed heavily on my mind.

'Who did'ee think would take a job digging salt blocks out of a miserable hole in the ground for penny wages?' Strother asked. 'Model citizens?'

It seemed that Young Bill would have to look at a few of the salties, after all. We'd just have to hope the fellow we wanted didn't know the ring tattoo was the only part of him the kid had seen.

When I went back to the cell, Young Bill was lying on the pallets, and I thought he'd gone to sleep, but at the sound of my bootheels he sat up. His eyes were red, his cheeks wet. Not sleeping, then, but mourning. I let myself in, sat down beside

127

him, and put an arm around his shoulders. This didn't come naturally to me – I know what comfort and sympathy are, but I've never been much good at giving such. I knew what it was to lose a parent, though. Young Bill and Young Roland had that much in common.

'Did you finish your candy?' I asked.

'Don't want the rest,' he said, and sighed.

Outside the wind boomed hard enough to shake the building, then subsided.

'I hate that sound,' he said – just what Jamie DeCurry had said. It made me smile a little. 'And I hate being in here. It's like *I* did something wrong.'

'You didn't,' I said.

'Maybe not, but it already seems like I've been here forever. Cooped up. And if they don't get back before nightfall, I'll have to stay longer. Won't I?'

'I'll keep you company,' I said. 'If those deputies have a deck of cards, we can play Jacks Pop Up.'

'For babies,' said he, morosely.

'Then Watch Me or poker. Can thee play those?'

He shook his head, then brushed at his cheeks. The tears were flowing again.

'I'll teach thee. We'll play for matchsticks.'

'I'd rather hear the story you talked about when we stopped in the sheppie's lay-by. I don't remember the name.'

'"The Wind through the Keyhole,"' I said. 'But it's a long one, Bill.'

'We have time, don't we?'

I couldn't argue that. 'There are scary bits in it, too. Those things are all right for a boy such as I was – sitting up in his bed with his mother beside him – but after what you've been through . . .'

'Don't care,' he said. 'Stories take a person away. If they're good ones, that is. It is a good one?'

'Yes. I always thought so, anyway.'

'Then tell it.' He smiled a little. 'I'll even let you have two of the last three chockers.'

'Those are yours, but I might roll a smoke.' I thought about how to begin. 'Do you know stories that start, "Once upon a bye, before your grandfather's grandfather was born"?'

'They all start that way. At least, the ones my da' told me. Before he said I was too old for stories.'

'A person's never too old for stories, Bill. Man and boy, girl and woman, never too old. We live for them.'

'Do you say so?'

'I do.'

I took out my tobacco and papers. I rolled slowly, for in those days it was a skill yet new to me. When I had a smoke just to my liking – one with the draw end tapered to a pinhole – I struck a match on the wall. Bill sat cross-legged on the straw pallets. He took one of the chockers, rolled it between his fingers much as I'd rolled my smoke, then tucked it into his cheek.

I started slowly and awkwardly, because story-telling was another thing that didn't come naturally to me in those days . . . although it was a thing I learned to do well in time. I had to. All gunslingers have to. And as I went along, I began to speak more naturally and easily. Because I began hearing my mother's voice. It began to speak through my own mouth: every rise, dip, and pause.

I could see him fall into the tale, and that pleased me – it was like hypnotizing him again, but in a better way. A more honest way. The best part, though, was hearing my mother's voice. It was like having her again, coming out from far inside me. It hurt, of course, but more often than not the best things do, I've found. You wouldn't think it could be so, but – as the oldtimers used to say – the world's tilted, and there's an end to it.

'Once upon a bye, before your grandfather's grandfather was born, on the edge of an unexplored wilderness called the Endless Forest, there lived a boy named Tim with his mother, Nell, and his father, Big Ross. For a time, the three of them lived happily enough, although they owned little . . .'

THE WIND THROUGH
THE KEYHOLE

Once upon a bye, long before your grandfather's grandfather was born, on the edge of an unexplored wilderness called the Endless Forest, there lived a boy named Tim with his mother, Nell, and his father, Big Ross. For a time the three of them lived happily enough, although they owned little.

'I have only four things to pass on to you,' Big Ross told his son, 'but four's enough. Can you say them to me, young boy?'

Tim had said them to him many and many-a, but never tired of it. 'Thy ax, thy lucky coin, thy plot, and thy place, which is as good as the place of any king or gunslinger in Mid-World.' He would then pause and add, 'My mama, too. That makes five.'

Big Ross would laugh and kiss the boy's brow as he lay in his bed, for this catechism usually came at the end of the day. Behind them, in the doorway, Nell waited to put her kiss on top of her husband's. 'Aye,' Big Ross would say, 'we must never forget Mama, for wi'out her, all's for naught.'

So Tim would go off to sleep, knowing he was

loved, and knowing he had a place in the world, and listening to the night wind slip its strange breath over the cottage: sweet with the scent of the blossiewood at the edge of the Endless Forest, and faintly sour – but still pleasant – with the smell of the ironwood trees deeper in, where only brave men dared go.

Those were good years, but as we know – from stories and from life – the good years never last long.

One day, when Tim was eleven, Big Ross and his partner, Big Kells, drove their wagons down Main Road to where the Ironwood Trail entered the forest, as they did every morning save the seventh, when all in the village of Tree rested. On this day, however, only Big Kells came back. His skin was sooty and his jerkin charred. There was a hole in the left leg of his homespun pants. Red and blistered flesh peeped through it. He slumped on the seat of his wagon, as if too weary to sit up straight.

Nell Ross came to the door of her house and cried, 'Where is Big Ross? Where is my husband?'

Big Kells shook his head slowly from side to side. Ash sifted out of his hair and onto his shoulders. He spoke only a single word, but one was enough to turn Tim's knees to water. His mother began to shriek.

The word was *dragon*.

★   ★   ★

No one living today has ever seen the like of the Endless Forest, for the world has moved on. It was dark and full of dangers. The woodsmen of Tree Village knew it better than anyone in Mid-World, and even they knew nothing of what might live or grow ten wheels beyond the place where the blossie groves ended and the ironwood trees – those tall, brooding sentinels – began. The great depths were a mystery filled with strange plants, stranger animals, stinking weirdmarshes, and – so 'twas said – leavings of the Old People that were often deadly.

The folken of Tree feared the Endless Forest, and rightly so; Big Ross wasn't the first woodsman who went down Ironwood Trail and did not come back. Yet they loved it, too, for 'twas ironwood fed and clothed their families. They understood (though none would have said so aloud) that the forest was alive. And, like all living things, it needed to eat.

Imagine that you were a bird flying above that great tract of wildland. From up there it might look like a giant dress of a green so dark it was almost black. Along the bottom of the dress was a hem of lighter green. These were the blossiewood groves. Just below the blossies, at the farthest edge of North'rd Barony, was the village of Tree. It was the last town in what was then a civilized country. Once Tim asked his father what *civilized* meant.

'Taxes,' Big Ross said, and laughed – but not in a funny way.

Most of the woodsmen went no farther than the blossie groves. Even there, sudden dangers could arise. Snakes were the worst, but there were also poisonous rodents called wervels that were the size of dogs. Many men had been lost in the blossies over the years, but on the whole, blossie was worth the risk. It was a lovely fine-grained wood, golden in color and almost light enough to float on air. It made fine lake and rivercraft, but was no good for sea travel; even a moderate gale would tear apart a boat made of blossie.

For sea travel ironwood was wanted, and ironwood brought a high price from Hodiak, the barony buyer who came twice a year to the Tree sawmill. It was ironwood that gave the Endless Forest its green-black hue, and only the bravest woodsmen dared go after it, for there were dangers along the Ironwood Trail – which barely pierced the skin of the Endless Forest, remember – that made the snakes, wervels, and mutie bees of the blossie groves seem mild by comparison.

Dragons, for instance.

So it was that in his twelfth year, Tim Ross lost his da'. Now there was no ax and no lucky coin hanging around Big Ross's burly neck on its fine silver chain. Soon there might be no plot in the village or place in the world, either. For in those days, when the time of Wide Earth came around, the Barony Covenanter came with it. He carried a scroll of parchment paper, and the name of every family in Tree was writ upon it, along with a number. That number was the amount of tax. If you could pay it – four or six or eight silver knucks, even a gold one for the largest of the freeholds – all was well. If you couldn't, the Barony took your plot and you were turned out on the land. There was no appeal.

Tim went half-days to the cottage of the Widow Smack, who kept school and was paid in food – usually vegetables, sometimes a bit of meat. Long ago, before the bloodsores had come on her and eaten off half her face (so the children whispered, although none had actually seen it), she had been a great lady in the barony estates far away (or so the children's elders claimed, although none actually knew). Now she wore a veil and taught likely lads, and even a few lassies, how to read and practice the slightly questionable art known as *mathmatica*.

She was a fearsomely smart woman who took no guff, and most days she was tireless. Her pupils usually came to love her in spite of her veil, and the horrors they imagined might lie beneath it. But on occasion she would begin to tremble all over, and cry that her poor head was splitting, and that she must lie down. On these days she would send the children home, sometimes commanding them to tell their parents that she regretted nothing, least of all her beautiful prince.

Sai Smack had one of her fugues about a month after the dragon burned Big Ross to ashes, and when Tim came back to his cottage, which was called Goodview, he looked in the kitchen window and saw his mother crying with her head on the table.

He dropped the slate with his *mathmatica* problems on it (long division, which he had feared but turned out to be only backwards multiplication) and rushed to her side. She looked up at him and tried to smile. The contrast between her upturned lips and her streaming eyes made Tim feel like crying himself. It was the look of a woman at the end of her tether.

'What is it, Mama? What's wrong?'

'Just thinking of your father. Sometimes I miss him so. Why are you home early?'

He began to tell her, but stopped when he saw the leather purse with the drawstring top. She had put one of her arms over it, as if to hide it from him, and when she saw him looking, she swept it off the table and into her lap.

Now Tim was far from a stupid boy, so he made tea before saying anything else. When she had drunk some – with sugar, which he insisted she take, although there was little enough left in the pot – and had calmed, he asked her what else was wrong.

'I don't know what you mean.'

'Why were you counting our money?'

'What little there is to count,' said she. 'Covenant Man will be here once Reaptide's gone – aye, while the embers of the bonfire are still hot, if I know his ways – and what then? He'll want six silver knuckles this year, p'raps as many as eight, for taxes have gone up, so they do say, probably another of their stupid wars somewhere far from here, soldiers with their banners flying, aye, very fine.'

'How much do we have?'

'Four and a scrap of a fifth. We have no livestock to sell, nor a single round of ironwood since your father died. What shall we do?' She began to cry again. 'What shall we *do*?'

Tim was as frightened as she was, but since there was no man to comfort her, he held his own tears back and put his arms around her and soothed her as best he could.

'If we had his ax and his coin, I'd sell them to Destry,' she said at last.

Tim was horrified even though the ax and lucky coin were gone, burned in the same fiery blast that had taken their cheerful, goodhearted owner. 'You never would!'

'Aye. To keep his plot and his place, I would. Those were the things he truly cared about, and thee, and me. Could he speak he'd say "Do it, Nell, and welcome, for Destry has hard coin."' She sighed. 'But then would come old Barony Covenant Man next year . . . and the year after that . . .' She put her hands over her face. 'Oh, Tim, we shall be turned out on the land, and there's not one thing I can think to change it. Can you?'

Tim would have given everything he owned (which was very little) to be able to give her an answer, but he could not. He could only ask how long it would be before the Covenant Man would appear in Tree on his tall black horse, sitting astride a saddle worth more than Big Ross had made in twenty-five years of risking his life on that narrow track known as the Ironwood Trail.

She held up four fingers. 'This many weeks if the weather is fair.' She held up four more. 'This many if it's foul, and he's held up in the farming villages of the Middles. Eight is the most we can hope for, I think. And then . . .'

'Something will happen before he comes,' Tim said. 'Da' always said that the forest gives to them that love it.'

'All I've ever seen it do is take,' said Nell, and covered her face again. When he tried to put an arm around her, she shook her head.

Tim trudged out to get his slate. He had never felt so sad and frightened. *Something will happen to change it,* he thought. *Please let something happen to change it.*

The worst thing about wishes is that sometimes they come true.

That was a rich Full Earth in Tree; even Nell knew it, although the ripe land was bitter in her eye. The following year she and Tim might be following the crops with burlap rucksacks on their backs, farther and farther from the Endless Forest, and that made summer's beauty hard to look at. The forest was a terrible place, and it had taken her man, but it was the only place she had ever known. At night, when the wind blew from the north, it stole to her bed through her open window like a lover, bringing its own special smell, one both bitter and sweet, like blood and strawberries. Sometimes when she slept, she dreamed of its deep tilts and secret corridors, and of sunshine so diffuse that it glowed like old green brass.

The smell of the forest when the wind's out of the north brings visions, the old folken said. Nell didn't know if this was true or just chimneycorner blather, but she knew the smell of the Endless Forest was the smell of life as well as death. And she knew that Tim loved it as his father had. As she herself had (although often against her will).

She had secretly feared the day when the boy would grow tall enough and strong enough to go down that dangerous trail with his da', but now she found herself sorry that day would never come. Sai Smack and her *mathmatica* were all very well, but Nell knew what her son truly wanted, and she hated the dragon that had stolen it from him. Probably it had been a she-dragon, and only protecting her egg, but Nell hated it just the same. She hoped the plated yellow-eyed bitch would swallow her own fire, as the old stories said they sometimes did, and explode.

★   ★   ★

One day not so many after Tim had arrived home early and found her in tears, Big Kells came calling on Nell. Tim had gotten two weeks' work helping farmer Destry with the hay-cutting, so she was by her onesome in her garden, weeding on her knees. When she saw her late husband's friend and partner, she got to her feet and wiped her dirty hands on the burlap apron she called her weddiken.

A single look at his clean hands and carefully trimmed beard was enough to tell her why he'd come. Once upon a bye, Nell Robertson, Jack Ross, and Bern Kells had been children together, and great pals. *Littermates from different litters*, people of the village sometimes said when they saw the three together; in those days they were inseparable.

When they grew to young manhood, both boys fancied her. And while she loved them both, it was Big Ross she burned for, Big Ross she'd wed and taken to bed (although whether that was the order of it no one knew, nor really cared). Big Kells had taken it as well as any man can. He stood beside Ross at the wedding, and slipped the silk around them for their walk back down the aisle when the preacher was done. When Kells took it off them at the door (although it never *really* comes off, so they do say), he kissed them both and wished them a lifetime of long days and pleasant nights.

Although the afternoon Kells came to her in the

142

garden was hot, he was wearing a broadcloth jacket. From the pocket he took a loosely knotted length of silk rope, as she knew he would. A woman knows. Even if she's long married, a woman knows, and Kells's heart had never changed.

'Will'ee?' he asked. 'If'ee will, I'll sell my place to Old Destry – he wants it, for it sits next to his east field – and keep this'un. Covenant Man's coming, Nellie, and he'll have his hand out. With no man, how'll'ee fill it?'

'I cannot, as thee knows,' said she.

'Then tell me – shall we slip the rope?'

She wiped her hands nervously on her weddiken, although they were already as clean as they'd be without water from the creek. 'I . . . I need to think about it.'

'What's to think about?' He took his bandanna – neatly folded in his pocket instead of tied loosely, woodsman-style, around his neck – and mopped his forehead with it. 'Either'ee do and we go on in Tree as we always have – I'll find the boy something to work at that'll bring in a little, although he's far too wee for the woods – or ye and he'll go on the land. I can share, but I can't give, much as I might like to. I have only one place to sell, kennit.'

She thought, *He's trying to buy me to fill the empty side of the bed that Millicent left behind.* But that seemed an unworthy thought for a man she'd known long before he *was* a man, and one who had worked for years by her beloved husband's side in the dark and dangerous trees near the end of the Ironwood Trail. *One to watch and one to work*, the oldtimers said. *Pull together and never apart*. Now that Jack Ross was gone, Bern Kells was asking her to pull with him. It was natural.

Yet she hesitated.

'Come tomorrow at this same time, if you still have a mind,' Nell told him. 'I'll give thee an answer then.'

He didn't like it; she saw he didn't like it; she saw something in his eyes that she had occasionally glimpsed when she had been a green girl sparked by two likely lads and the envy of all her friends. That look was what caused her to hesitate, even though he had appeared like an angel, offering her – and Tim, of course – a way out of the terrible dilemma that had come with Big Ross's death.

Perhaps he saw her seeing it, for he dropped his gaze. He studied his feet for a bit, and when he looked up again, he was smiling. It made him almost as handsome as he'd been as a youth . . . but never so handsome as Jack Ross.

'Tomorrow, then. But no longer. They have a saying in the West'rds, my dear. "Look not long at what's offered, for every precious thing has wings and may fly away."'

She washed at the edge of the creek, stood smelling the sweet-sour aroma of the forest for a bit, then went inside and lay down upon her bed.

It was unheard of for Nell Ross to be horizontal while the sun was still in the sky, but she had much to think of and much to remember from those days when two young woodsmen had vied for her kisses.

Even if her blood had called toward Bern Kells (not yet Big Kells in those days, although his father was dead, slain in the woods by a vurt or some such nightmare) instead of Jack Ross, she wasn't sure she would have slipped the rope with him. Kells was good-humored and laughing when he was sober, and as steady as sand through a glass, but he could be angry and quick with his fists when he was drunk. And he was drunk often in those days. His binges grew longer and more frequent after Ross and Nell were wed, and on many occasions he woke up in jail.

Jack had borne it awhile, but after a binge where Kells had destroyed most of the furniture in the saloon before passing out, Nell told her husband something had to be done. Big Ross reluctantly agreed. He got his partner and old friend out of jail – as he had many times before – but this time he spoke to him frankly instead of just telling Kells to go jump in the creek and stay there until his head was clear.

'Listen to me, Bern, and with both ears. You've been my friend since I could toddle, and my pard since we were old enough to go past the blossie and into the ironwood on our own. You've watched my back and I've watched yours. There's not a

145

man I trust more, when you're sober. But once you pour the redeye down your throat, you're no more reliable than quickmud. I can't *go* into the forest alone, and everything I have – everything we *both* have – is at risk if I can't depend on'ee. I'd hate to cast about for a new pard, but fair warning: I have a wife and a kiddy on the way, and I'll do what I have to do.'

Kells continued his drinking, brawling, and bawding for a few more months, as if to spite his old friend (and his old friend's new wife). Big Ross was on the verge of severing their partnership when the miracle happened. It was a small miracle, hardly more than five feet from toes to crown, and her name was Millicent Redhouse. What Bern Kells would not do for Big Ross, he did for Milly. When she died in childbirth six seasons later (and the babby soon after – even before the flush of labor had faded from the poor woman's dead cheek, the midwife confided to Nell), Ross was gloomy.

'He'll go back for the drink now, and gods know what will become of him.'

But Big Kells stayed sober, and when his business happened to bring him into the vicinity of Gitty's Saloon, he crossed to the other side of the street. He said it had been Milly's dying request, and to do otherwise would be an insult to her memory. 'I'll die before I take another drink,' he said.

He had kept this promise . . . but Nell sometimes

felt his eyes upon her. Often, even. He had never touched her in a way that could be called intimate, or even forward, had never stolen so much as a Reaptide kiss, but she felt his eyes. Not as a man looks at a friend, or at a friend's wife, but as a man looks at a woman.

Tim came home an hour before sunset with hay stuck to every visible inch of his sweaty skin, but happy. Farmer Destry had paid him in scrip for the town store, a fairish sum, and his good-wife had added a sack of her sweet peppers and busturd tomatoes. Nell took the scrip and the sack, thanked him, kissed him, gave him a well-stuffed popkin, and sent him down to the spring to bathe.

Ahead of him, as he stood in the cold water, ran the dreaming, mist-banded fields toward the Inners and Gilead. To his left bulked the forest, which began less than a wheel away. In there it was twilight even at noonday, his father had said. At the thought of his father, his happiness at being paid a man's wages (or almost) for a day's work ran out of him like grain from a sack with a hole in it. This sorrow came often, but it always surprised him. He sat for a while on a big rock with his knees drawn up to his chest and his head cradled in his arms. To be taken by a dragon so close to the edge of the forest was unlikely and terribly unfair, but it had happened before. His father wasn't the first and wouldn't be the last.

147

His mother's voice came floating to him over the fields, calling him to come in and have some real supper. Tim called cheerily back to her, then knelt on the rock to splash cold water on his eyes, which felt swollen, although he had shed no tears. He dressed quickly and trotted up the slope. His mother had lit the lamps, for the gloaming had come, and they cast long rectangles of light across her neat little garden. Tired but happy again – for boys turn like weathercocks, so they do – Tim hurried into the welcoming glow of home.

When the meal was done and the few dishes ridded between them, Nell said: 'I'd talk to you mother to son, Tim . . . and a bit more. You're old enough to work a little now, you'll soon be leaving your childhood behind – sooner than I'd like – and you deserve a say in what happens.'

'Is it about the Covenant Man, Mama?'

'In a way, but I . . . I think more than that.' She came close to saying *I fear* instead of *I think*, but why would she? There was a hard decision to be made, an important decision, but what was there to fear?

She led the way into their sitting room – so cozy Big Ross had almost been able to touch the opposing walls when he stood in the middle with his arms outstretched – and there, as they sat before the cold hearth (for it was a warm Full Earth night), she told him all that had passed between Big Kells and herself. Tim listened with surprise and mounting unease.

'So,' Nell said when she had finished. 'What does thee think?' But before he could answer – perhaps she saw in his face the worry she felt in her own heart – she rushed on. 'He's a good man, and was more brother than mate to your da'. I believe he cares for me, and cares for thee.'

No, thought Tim, *I'm just what comes in the same saddlebag. He never even looks at me. Unless I happened to be with Da', that is. Or with you.*

'Mama, I don't know.' The thought of Big Kells in the house – lying next to Mama in his da's place – made him feel light in his stomach, as if his supper had not set well. In truth, it no longer *was* sitting well.

'He's quit the drink,' she said. Now she seemed to be talking to herself instead of to him. 'Years ago. He could be wild as a youth, but your da' tamed him. And Millicent, of course.'

'Maybe, but neither of them is here anymore,' Tim pointed out. 'And Ma, he hasn't found anyone yet to partner him on the Ironwood. He goes a-cutting on his own, and that's dead risky.'

'It's early days yet,' she said. 'He'll find someone to partner up with, for he's strong and he knows where the good stands are. Your father showed him how to find them when they were both fresh to the work, and they have fine stakeouts near the place where the trail ends.'

Tim knew this was so, but was less sure Kells

would find someone to partner with. He thought the other woodcutters kept clear of him. They seemed to do it without knowing they were doing it, the way a seasoned woodsman would detour around a poisonthorn bush, even if he only saw it from the corner of his eye.

Maybe I'm only making that up, he thought.

'I don't know,' he said again. 'A rope that's slipped in church can't be unslipped.'

Nell laughed nervously. 'Where in Full Earth did thee hear that?'

'From you,' Tim said.

She smiled. 'Yar, p'raps thee did, for my mouth's hung in the middle and runs at both ends. We'll sleep on it, and see clearer in the morning.'

But neither of them slept much. Tim lay wondering what it would be like to have Big Kells as a steppa. Would he be good to them? Would he take Tim into the forest with him to begin learning the woodsman's life? That would be fine, he thought, but would his mother want him going into the line of work that had killed her husband? Or would she want him to stay south of the Endless Forest? To be a farmer?

I like Destry well enough, he thought, *but I'd never in life be a farmer. Not with the Endless Forest so close, and so much of the world to see.*

Nell lay a wall away, with her own uncomfortable thoughts. Mostly she wondered what their lives would be like if she refused Kells's offer and they were turned out on the land, away from the

150

only place they'd ever known. What their lives would be like if the Barony Covenanter rode up on his tall black horse and they had nothing to give him.

The next day was even hotter, but Big Kells came wearing the same broadcloth coat. His face was red and shining. Nell told herself she didn't smell graf on his breath, and if she did, what of it? 'Twas only hard cider, and any man might take a drink or two before going to hear a woman's decision. Besides, her mind was made up. Or almost.

Before he could ask his question, she spoke boldly. As boldly as she was able, anyhap. 'My boy reminds me that a rope slipped in church can't be unslipped.'

Big Kells frowned, although whether it was the mention of the boy or the marriage-loop that fashed him, she could not tell. 'Aye, and what of that?'

'Only will you be good to Tim and me?'

'Aye, good as I can be.' His frown deepened. She couldn't tell if it was anger or puzzlement. She hoped for puzzlement. Men who could cut and chop and dare beasts in the deep wood often found themselves lost in affairs like this, she knew, and at the thought of Big Kells lost, her heart opened to him.

'Set your word on it?' she asked.

The frown eased. White flashed in his neatly

151

trimmed black beard as he smiled. 'Aye, by watch and by warrant.'

'Then I say yes.'

And so they were wed. That is where many stories end; it's where this one – sad to say – really begins.

There was graf at the wedding reception, and for a man who no longer drank spirits, Big Kells tossed a goodly amount down his gullet. Tim viewed this with unease, but his mother appeared not to notice. Another thing that made Tim uneasy was how few of the other woodsmen showed up, although it was Ethday. If he had been a girl instead of a boy, he might have noticed something else. Several of the women whom Nell counted among her friends were looking at her with expressions of guarded pity.

That night, long after midnight, he was awakened by a thump and a cry that might have been part of a dream, but it seemed to come through the wall from the room his mother now shared (true, but not yet possible to believe) with Big Kells. Tim lay listening, and had almost dropped off to sleep again when he heard quiet weeping. This was followed by the voice of his new steppa, low and gruff: 'Shut it, can't you? You ain't a bit hurt, there's no blood, and I have to be up with the birdies.'

The sounds of crying stopped. Tim listened, but there was no more talk. Shortly after Big Kells's snores began, he fell asleep. The next morning, while she was at the stove frying eggs, Tim saw a bruise on his mother's arm above the inside of her elbow.

'It's nothing,' Nell said when she saw him looking. 'I had to get up in the night to do the necessary, and bumped it on the bedpost. I'll have to get used to finding my way in the dark again, now that I'm not alone.'

Tim thought, *Yar – that's what I'm afraid of.*

When the second Ethday of his married life came round, Big Kells took Tim with him to the house that now belonged to Baldy Anderson, Tree's other big farmer. They went in Kells's wood-wagon. The mules stepped lightly with no rounds or strakes of ironwood to haul; today there were only a few little piles of sawdust in the back of the wagon. And that lingering sweet-sour smell, of course, the smell of the deep woods. Kells's old place looked sad and abandoned with its shutters closed and the tall, unscythed grass growing up to the splintery porch slats.

'Once I get my gunna out'n it, let Baldy take it all for kindling, do it please 'im,' Kells grunted. 'Fine wi' me.'

As it turned out, there were only two things he wanted from the house – a dirty old footrest and a large leather trunk with straps and a brass lock. This was in the bedroom, and Kells stroked it as if it were a pet. 'Can't leave this,' he said. 'Never this. 'Twas my father's.'

Tim helped him get it outside, but Kells had to do most of the work. The trunk was very heavy. When it was in the wagonbed, Big Kells leaned over with his hands on the knees of his newly (and neatly) mended trousers. At last, when the purple patches began to fade from his cheeks, he stroked the trunk again, and with a gentleness Tim had as yet not seen applied to his mother. 'All I own stowed in one trunk. As for the house, did Baldy pay the price I should have had?' He looked at Tim challengingly, as if expecting an argument on this subject.

'I don't know,' Tim said cautiously. 'Folk say sai Anderson's close.'

Kells laughed harshly. 'Close? *Close?* Tight as a virgin's cootchie is what he is. Nar, nar, I got crumbs instead of a slice, for he knew I couldn't afford to wait. Help me tie up this tailboard, boy, and be not sluggardly.'

Tim was not sluggardly. He had his side of the tailboard roped tight before Kells had finished tying his in a sloppy ollie-knot that would have made his father laugh. When he was finally done, Big Kells gave his trunk another of those queerly affectionate caresses.

'All in here now, all I have. Baldy knew I had to have silver before Wide Earth, didn't he? Old You Know Who is coming, and he'll have his hand out.' He spat between his old scuffed boots. 'This is all your ma's fault.'

'*Ma's* fault? Why? Didn't you want to marry her?'

'Watch your mouth, boy.' Kells looked down, seemed surprised to see a fist where his hand had been, and opened his fingers. 'You're too young to understand. When you're older, you'll find out how women can get the good of a man. Let's go on back.'

Halfway to the driving seat, he stopped and looked across the stowed trunk at the boy. 'I love yer ma, and that's enough for you to be going on with.'

And as the mules trotted up the village high street, Big Kells sighed and added, 'I loved yer da', too, and how I miss 'im. 'Tain't the same wi'out him beside me in the woods, or seein Misty and Bitsy up the trail ahead of me.'

At this Tim's heart opened a little to the big, slump-shouldered man with the reins in his hands – in spite of himself, really – but before the feeling had any chance to grow, Big Kells spoke again.

'Ye've had enough of books and numbers and that weirdy Smack woman. She with her veils and shakes – how she manages to wipe her arse after she shits is more than I'll ever know.'

Tim's heart seemed to clap shut in his chest. He loved learning things, and he loved the Widow Smack – veil, shakes, and all. It dismayed him to hear her spoken of with such crude cruelty. 'What would I do, then? Go into the woods with you?' He could see himself on Da's wagon, behind Misty and Bitsy. That would not be so bad. No, not so bad at all.

155

Kells barked a laugh. '*You?* In the woods? And not yet twelve?'

'I'll be twelve next m—'

'You won't be big enough to lumber on the Ironwood Trail at twice that age, for'ee take after yer ma's side of things, and will be Sma' Ross all yer life.' That bark of laughter again. Tim felt his face grow hot at the sound of it. 'No, lad, I've spoke a place for'ee at the sawmill. You ain't too sma' to stack boards. Ye'll start after harvest's done, and before first snow.'

'What does Mama say?' Tim tried to keep the dismay out of his voice and failed.

'She don't get aye, no, or maybe in the matter. I'm her husband, and that makes me the one to decide.' He snapped the reins across the backs of the plodding mules. '*Hup!*'

Tim went down to Tree Sawmill three days later, with one of the Destry boys – Straw Willem, so called for his nearly colorless hair. Both were hired on to stack, but they would not be needed for yet awhile, and only part-time, at least to begin with. Tim had brought his father's mules, which needed the exercise, and the boys rode back side by side.

'Thought you said your new step-poppa didn't drink,' Willem said, as they passed Gitty's – which at midday was shuttered tight, its barrelhouse piano silent.

'He doesn't,' Tim said, but he remembered the wedding reception.

'Do you say so? I guess the fella my big brother seed rollin out of yonder redeye last night must've been some other orphing-boy's steppa, because Randy said he was as sloshed as a shindybug and heavin up over the hitchin-rail.' Having said this, Willem snapped his suspenders, as he always did when he felt he'd gotten off a good one.

Should have let you walk back to town, you stupid git, Tim thought.

That night, his mother woke him again. Tim sat bolt upright in bed and swung his feet out onto the floor, then froze. Kells's voice was soft, but the wall between the two rooms was thin.

'Shut it, woman. If you wake the boy and get him in here, I'll give you double.'

Her crying ceased.

'It was a slip, is all – a mistake. I went in with Mellon just to have a ginger-beer and hear about his new stake, and someone put a glass of jack-aroe in front of me. It was down my throat before I knew what I was drinking, and then I was off. 'Twon't happen again. Ye have my word on it.'

Tim lay back down again, hoping that was true.

He looked up at a ceiling he could not see, and listened to an owl, and waited for either sleep or the first light of morning. It seemed to him that if the wrong man stepped into the marriage-loop with a woman, it was a noose instead of a ring. He prayed that wasn't the case here. He already knew he couldn't like his mother's new husband,

157

let alone love him, but perhaps his mother could do both. Women were different. They had larger hearts.

Tim was still thinking these long thoughts as dawn tinted the sky and he finally fell asleep. That day there were bruises on both of his mother's arms. The bedpost in the room she now shared with Big Kells had grown very lively, it seemed.

Full Earth gave way to Wide Earth, as it always must. Tim and Straw Willem went to work stacking at the sawmill, but only three days a week. The foreman, a decent sai named Rupert Venn, told them they might get more time if that season's snowfall was light and the winter haul was good – meaning the ironwood rounds that cutters such as Kells brought back from the forest.

Nell's bruises faded and her smile came back. Tim thought it a more cautious smile than before, but it was better than no smile at all. Kells hitched his mules and went down the Ironwood Trail, and although the stakes he and Big Ross had claimed were good ones, he still had no one to partner him. He consequently brought back less haul, but ironwood was ironwood, and ironwood always sold for a good price, one paid in shards of silver rather than scrip.

Sometimes Tim wondered – usually as he was wheeling boards into one of the sawmill's long covered sheds – if life might be better were his new step-poppa to fall afoul a snake or a wervel. Perhaps even a vurt, those nasty flying things sometimes known as bullet-birds. One such had done for Bern Kells's father, boring a hole right through him with its stony beak.

Tim pushed these thoughts away with horror, amazed to find that some room in his heart – some *black* room – could hold such things. His father, Tim was sure, would be ashamed. Perhaps *was* ashamed, for some said that those in the clearing at the end of the path knew all the secrets the living kept from each other.

At least he no longer smelled *graf* on his step-father's breath, and there were no more stories – from Straw Willem or anyone else – of Big Kells reeling out of the redeye when Old Gitty shut and locked the doors.

He promised and he's keeping his promise, Tim thought. *And the bedpost has stopped moving around in Mama's room, because she doesn't have those bruises. Life's begun to come right. That's the thing to remember.*

When he got home from the sawmill on the days he had work, his mother would have supper on the stove. Big Kells would come in later, first stopping to wash the sawdust from his hands, arms, and neck at the spring between the house and the barn, then gobbling his own supper. He ate prodigious amounts, calling for seconds and thirds that Nell brought promptly. She didn't speak when she did this; if she did, her new husband would only growl a response. Afterward, he would go into the back hall, sit on his trunk, and smoke.

Sometimes Tim would look up from his slate, where he was working the *mathmatica* problems the Widow Smack still gave him, and see Kells staring at him through his pipe-smoke. There was something disconcerting about that gaze, and Tim began to take his slate outside, even though it was growing chilly in Tree, and dark came earlier each day.

Once his mother came out, sat beside him on the porch step, and put her arm around his shoulders. 'You'll be back to school with sai Smack next year, Tim. It's a promise. I'll bring him round.'

Tim smiled at her and said thankee, but he knew better. Next year he'd still be at the sawmill, only by then he'd be big enough to carry boards as well as stack them, and there would be less time to do problems, because he'd have work five days a week instead of three. Mayhap even six. The year after that, he'd be planing as well as carrying, then using the swing-saw like a man. In a few more years he'd *be* a man, coming home too tired to think about reading the Widow Smack's books even if she still wanted to lend them out, the orderly ways of the *mathmatica* fading in his mind. That grown Tim Ross might want no more than to fall into bed after meat and bread. He would begin to smoke a pipe and perhaps get a taste for *graf* or beer. He would watch his mother's smile grow pale; he would watch her eyes lose their sparkle.

And for these things he would have Bern Kells to thank.

Reaping was gone by; Huntress Moon grew pale, waxed again, and pulled her bow; the first gales of Wide Earth came howling in from the west. And just when it seemed he might not come after all, the Barony Covenanter blew into the village of Tree on one of those cold winds, astride his tall black horse and as thin as Tom Scrawny Death. His heavy black cloak flapped around him like a batwing. Beneath his wide hat (as black as his cloak), the pale lamp of his face turned ceaselessly from side to side, marking a new fence here, a cow or three added to a herd there. The villagers would grumble but pay, and if they couldn't pay, their land would be taken in the name of Gilead. Perhaps even then, in those olden days, some were whispering it wasn't fair, the taxes were too much, that Arthur Eld was long dead (if he had ever existed at all), and the Covenant had been paid a dozen times over, in blood as well as silver. Perhaps some of them were already waiting for a Good Man to appear, and make them strong enough to say *No more, enough's enough, the world has moved on.*

Perhaps, but not that year, and not for many and many-a to come.

Late in the afternoon, while the swag-bellied clouds tumbled across the sky and the yellow cornstalks clattered in Nell's garden like teeth in a loose jaw, sai Covenanter nudged his tall black horse between gateposts Big Ross had set up himself (with Tim looking on and helping when asked). The horse paced slowly and solemnly up to the front steps. There it halted, nodding and blowing. Big Kells stood on the porch and still had to look up to see the visitor's pallid face. Kells held his hat crushed to his breast. His thinning black hair (now showing the first streaks of gray, for he was nearing forty and would soon be old) flew around his head. Behind him in the doorway stood Nell and Tim. She had an arm around her boy's shoulders and was clutching him tightly, as if afraid (maybe 'twas a mother's intuition) that the Covenant Man might steal him away.

For a moment there was silence save for the flapping of the unwelcome visitor's cloak, and the wind, which sang an eerie tune beneath the eaves. Then the Barony Covenanter bent forward, regarding Kells with wide dark eyes that did not seem to blink. His lips, Tim saw, were as red as a woman's when she paints them with fresh madder. From somewhere inside his cloak he produced not a book of slates but a roll of real parchment paper, and pulled it down so 'twas long. He studied it, made it short again, and replaced it in whatever inner pocket it had come from. Then he returned

162

his gaze to Big Kells, who flinched and looked at his feet.

'Kells, isn't it?' He had a rough, husky voice that made Tim's skin pucker into hard points of goose-flesh. He had seen the Covenant Man before, but only from a distance; his da' had made shift to keep Tim away from the house when the barony's tax-man came calling on his annual rounds. Now Tim understood why. He thought he would have bad dreams tonight.

'Kells, aye.' His step-poppa's voice was shakily cheerful. He managed to raise his eyes again. 'Welcome, sai. Long days and pleasant—'

'Yar, all that, all that,' the Covenant Man said with a dismissive wave of one hand. His dark eyes were now looking over Kells's shoulder. 'And . . . Ross, isn't it? Now two instead of three, they tell me, Big Ross having fallen to unfortunate happenstance.' His voice was low, little more than a monotone. *Like listening to a deaf man try to sing a lullabye*, Tim thought.

'Just so,' Big Kells said. He swallowed hard enough for Tim to hear the gulping sound, then began to babble. 'He n me were in the forest, ye ken, in one of our little stakes off the Ironwood Path – we have four or five, all marked proper wi' our names, so they are, and I haven't changed em, because in my mind he's still my partner and always will be – and we got separated a bit. Then I heard a hissin. You know that sound when you hear it, there's no sound on earth like the

163

hiss of a bitch dragon drawrin in breath before she—'

'Hush,' the Covenant Man said. 'When I want to hear a story, I like it to begin with "Once upon a bye."'

Kells began to say something else – perhaps only to cry pardon – and thought better of it. The Covenant Man leaned an arm on the horn of his saddle and stared at him. 'I understand you sold your house to Rupert Anderson, sai Kells.'

'Yar, and he cozened me, but I—'

The visitor overrode him. 'The tax is nine knuckles of silver or one of rhodite, which I know you don't have in these parts, but I'm bound to tell you, as it's in the original Covenant. One knuck for the transaction, and eight for the house where you now sit your ass at sundown and no doubt hide your tallywhacker after moonrise.'

'Nine?' Big Kells gasped. '*Nine?* That's—'

'It's what?' the Covenant Man said in his rough, crooning voice. 'Be careful how you answer, Bern Kells, son of Mathias, grandson of Limping Peter. Be ever so careful, because, although your neck is thick, I believe it would stretch thin. Aye, so I do.'

Big Kells turned pale . . . although not as pale as the Barony Covenanter. 'It's very fair. That's all I meant to say. I'll get it.'

He went into the house and came back with a deerskin purse. It was Big Ross's moneysack, the one over which Tim's mother had been crying on

164

a day early on in Full Earth. A day when life had seemed fairer, even though Big Ross was dead. Kells handed the sack to Nell and let her count the precious knuckles of silver into his cupped hands.

All during this, the visitor sat silent on his tall black horse, but when Big Kells made to come down the steps and hand him the tax – almost all they had, even with Tim's little bit of wages added into the common pot – the Covenant Man shook his head.

'Keep your place. I'd have the boy bring it to me, for he's fair, and in his countenance I see his father's face. Aye, I see it very well.'

Tim took the double handful of knucks – so heavy! – from Big Kells, barely hearing the whisper in his ear: 'Have a care and don't drop em, ye gormless boy.'

Tim walked down the porch steps like a boy in a dream. He held up his cupped hands, and before he knew what was happening, the Covenant Man had seized him by the wrists and hauled him up onto his horse. Tim saw that bow and pommel were decorated with a cascade of silver runes: moons and stars and comets and cups pouring cold fire. At the same time, he realized his double handful of knucks was gone. The Covenant Man had taken them, although Tim couldn't remember exactly when it had happened.

Nell screamed and ran forward.

'Catch her and hold her!' the Covenant Man

thundered, so close by Tim's ear that he was near deafened on that side.

Kells grabbed his wife by the shoulders and jerked her roughly backwards. She tripped and tumbled to the porch boards, long skirts flying up around her ankles.

'*Mama!*' Tim shouted. He tried to jump from the saddle, but the Covenant Man restrained him easily. He smelled of campfire meat and old cold sweat. 'Sit easy, young Tim Ross, she's not hurt a mite. See how spry she rises.' Then, to Nell – who had indeed regained her feet: 'Be not fashed, sai, I'd only have a word with him. Would I harm a future taxpayer of the realm?'

'If you harm him, I'll kill you, you devil,' said she.

Kells raised a fist to her. 'Shut yer stupid mouth, woman!' Nell did not shrink from the fist. She had eyes only for Tim, sitting on the high black horse in front of the Covenant Man, whose arms were banded across her son's chest.

The Covenant Man smiled down at the two on the porch, one with his fist still upraised to strike, the other with tears coursing down her cheeks. 'Nell and Kells!' he proclaimed. 'The happy couple!'

He kneed his mount in a circle and slow-walked it as far as the gate, his arms still firmly around Tim's chest, his rank breath puffing against Tim's cheek. At the gate he squeezed his knees again and the horse halted. In Tim's ear – which was still ringing – he whispered: 'How does thee like thy new steppa, young Tim? Speak the truth, but speak it low. This is our palaver, and they have no part in it.'

Tim didn't want to turn, didn't want the Covenant Man's pallid face any closer than it already was, but he had a secret that had been poisoning him. So he did turn, and in the tax-man's ear he whispered, 'When he's in drink, he beats my ma.'

'Does he, now? Ah, well, does that surprise me? For did not his da' beat his own ma? And what we learn as children sets as a habit, so it does.'

A gloved hand threw one wing of the heavy black cloak over them like a blanket, and Tim felt the other gloved hand slither something small and hard into his pants pocket. 'A gift for you, young Tim. It's a key. Does thee know what makes it special?'

Tim shook his head.

''Tis a magic key. It will open anything, but only a single time. After that, 'tis as useless as dirt, so be careful how you use it!' He laughed as if this were the funniest joke he'd ever heard. His breath made Tim's stomach churn.

'I . . .' He swallowed. 'I have nothing to open. There's no locks in Tree, 'cept at the redeye and the jail.'

'Oh, I think thee knows of another. Does thee not?'

167

Tim looked into the Covenant Man's blackly merry eyes and said nothing. That worthy nodded, however, as if he had.

'*What are you telling my son?*' Nell screamed from the porch. '*Pour not poison in his ears, devil!*'

'Pay her no mind, young Tim, she'll know soon enough. She'll know much but see little.' He snickered. His teeth were very large and very white. 'A riddle for you! Can you solve it? No? Never mind, the answer will come in time.'

'Sometimes he opens it,' Tim said, speaking in the slow voice of one who talks in his sleep. 'He takes out his honing bar. For the blade of his ax. But then he locks it again. At night he sits on it to smoke, like it was a chair.'

The Covenant Man didn't ask what *it* was. 'And does he touch it each time he passes by, young Tim? As a man would touch a favorite old dog?'

He did, of course, but Tim didn't say so. He didn't need to say so. He felt there wasn't a secret he could keep from the mind ticking away behind that long white face. Not one.

He's playing with me, Tim thought. *I'm just a bit of amusement on a dreary day in a dreary town he'll soon leave behind. But he breaks his toys. You only have to look at his smile to know that.*

'I'll camp a wheel or two down the Ironwood Trail the next night or two,' the Covenant Man said in his rusty, tuneless voice. 'It's been a long ride, and I'm weary of all the quack I have to

168

listen to. There are vurts and wervels and snakes in the forest, but they don't *quack*.'

You're never weary, Tim thought. *Not you.*

'Come and see me if you care to.' No snicker this time; this time he tittered like a naughty girl. 'And if you *dare* to, of course. But come at night, for this jilly's son likes to sleep in the day when he gets the chance. Or stay here if you're timid. It's naught to me. *Hup!*'

This was to the horse, which paced slowly back to the porch steps, where Nell stood wringing her hands and Big Kells stood glowering beside her. The Covenant Man's thin strong fingers closed over Tim's wrists again – like handcuffs – and lifted him. A moment later he was on the ground, staring up at the white face and smiling red lips. The key burned in the depths of his pocket. From above the house came a peal of thunder, and it began to rain.

'The Barony thanks you,' the Covenant Man said, touching one gloved finger to the side of his wide-brimmed hat. Then he wheeled his black horse around and was gone into the rain. The last thing Tim saw was passing odd: when the heavy black cloak belled out, he spied a large metal object tied to the top of the Covenant Man's gunna. It looked like a washbasin.

Big Kells came striding down the steps, seized Tim by the shoulders, and commenced shaking him. Rain matted Kells's thinning hair to the sides of his face and streamed from his beard. Black when he had slipped into the silk rope with Nell, that beard was now heavily streaked with gray.

'What did he tell'ee? Was it about me? What lies did'ee speak? *Tell!*'

Tim could tell him nothing. His head snapped back and forth hard enough to make his teeth clack together.

Nell rushed down the steps. 'Stop it! Let him alone! You promised you'd never—'

'Get out of what don't concern you, woman,' he said, and struck her with the side of his fist. Tim's mama fell into the mud, where the teeming rain was now filling the tracks left by the Covenant Man's horse.

'*You bastard!*' Tim screamed. 'You can't hit my mama, you can't *ever*!'

He felt no immediate pain when Kells dealt him a similar sidehand blow, but white light sheared across his vision. When it lifted, he found himself lying in the mud next to his mother. He was dazed, his ears were ringing, and still the key burned in his pocket like a live coal.

'Nis take both of you,' Kells said, and strode away into the rain. Beyond the gate he turned right, in the direction of Tree's little length of high street. Headed for Gitty's, Tim had no doubt. He had stayed away from drink all of that Wide Earth – as far as Tim knew, anyway – but he would not stay away from it this night. Tim saw from his mother's sorrowful face – wet with rain, her hair hanging limp against her reddening muck-splattered cheek – that she knew it, too.

Tim put his arm around her waist, she put hers about his shoulders. They made their way slowly up the steps and into the house.

She didn't so much sit in her chair at the kitchen table as collapse into it. Tim poured water from the jug into the basin, wetted a cloth, and put it gently on the side of her face, which had begun to swell. She held it there for a bit, then extended it wordlessly to him. To please her, he took it and put it on his own face. It was cool and good against the throbbing heat.

'This is a pretty business, wouldn't you say?' she asked, with an attempt at brightness. 'Woman beaten, boy slugged, new husband off t'boozer.'

Tim had no idea what to say to this, so said nothing.

Nell lowered her head to the heel of her hand and stared at the table. 'I've made such a mess of things. I was frightened and at my wits' end, but that's no excuse. We would have been better on the land, I think.'

Turned off the place? Away from the plot? Wasn't it enough that his da's ax and lucky coin were gone? She was right about one thing, though: it was a mess.

But I have a key, Tim thought, and his fingers stole down to his pants to feel the shape of it.

'Where has he gone?' Nell asked, and Tim knew that it wasn't Bern Kells she was speaking of.

171

*A wheel or two down the Ironwood. Where he'll
wait for me.*

'I don't know, Mama.' So far as he could
remember, it was the first time he had ever lied
to her.

'But we know where Bern's gone, don't we?' She
laughed, then winced because it hurt her face. 'He
promised Milly Redhouse he was done with the
drink, and he promised me, but he's weak. Or . . .
is it me? Did I drive him to it, do you think?'

'No, Mama.' But Tim wondered if it might not
be true. Not in the way she meant – by being a
nag, or keeping a dirty house, or refusing him
what men and women did in bed after dark – but
in some other way. There was a mystery here, and
he wondered if the key in his pocket might solve
it. To keep from touching it again, he got up and
went to the pantry. 'What would you like to eat?
Eggs? I'll scramble them, if you do.'

She smiled wanly. 'Thankee, son, but I'm not
hungry. I think I'll lie down.' She rose a bit shakily.

Tim helped her into the bedroom. There he
pretended to look at interesting things out the
window while she took off her mud-stained day
dress and put on her nightgown. When Tim turned
around again, she was under the covers. She patted
the place beside her, as she had sometimes done
when he was sma'. In those days his da' might
have been in bed beside her, wearing his long
woodsman's underwear and smoking one of his
roll-ups.

'I can't turn him out,' she said. 'I would if I could, but now that the rope's slipped, the place is more his than mine. The law can be cruel to a woman. I never had cause to think about that before, but now . . . now . . .' Her eyes had gone glassy and distant. She would sleep soon, and that was probably a good thing.

He kissed her unbruised cheek and made to get up, but she stayed him. 'What did the Covenant Man say to thee?'

'Asked me how I liked my new step-da'. I can't remember how I answered him. I was scared.'

'When he covered thee with his cloak, I was, too. I thought he meant to ride away with thee, like the Red King in the old story.' She closed her eyes, then opened them again, very slowly. There was something in them now that could have been horror. 'I remember him coming to my da's when I was but a wee girl not long out of clouts – the black horse, the black gloves and cape, the saddle with the silver siguls on it. His white face gave me nightmares – it's so *long*. And do you know what, Tim?'

He shook his head slowly from side to side.

'He even carries the same silver basin roped on behind, for I saw it then, too. That's twenty years a-gone – aye, twenty and a doubleton-deucy more – but he looks the same. *He hasn't aged a day.*'

Her eyes closed again. This time they didn't reopen, and Tim stole from the room.

★　　★　　★

173

When he was sure his mother was asleep, Tim went down the little bit of back hall to where Big Kells's trunk, a squarish shape under an old remnant of blanket, stood just outside the mudroom. When he'd told the Covenant Man he knew of only two locks in Tree, the Covenant Man had replied, *Oh, I think thee knows of another.*

He stripped off the blanket and looked at his step-da's trunk. The trunk he sometimes caressed like a well-loved pet and often sat upon at night, puffing at his pipe with the back door cracked open to let out the smoke.

Tim hurried back to the front of the house – in his stocking feet, so as not to risk waking his mother – and peered out the front window. The yard was empty, and there was no sign of Big Kells on the rainy road. Tim had expected nothing else. Kells would be at Gitty's by now, getting through as much of what he had left as he could before falling down unconscious.

I hope somebody beats him up and gives him a taste of his own medicine. I'd do it myself, were I big enough.

He went back to the trunk, padding noiselessly in his stockings, knelt in front of it, and took the key from his pocket. It was a tiny silver thing the size of half a knuck, and strangely warm in his fingers, as if it were alive. The keyhole in the brass facing on the front of the trunk was much bigger. *The key he gave me will never work in that,* Tim thought. Then he remembered the Covenant Man

174

saying *'Tis a magic key. It will open anything, but only a single time.*

Tim put the key in the lock, where it clicked smoothly home, as if it had been meant for just that place all along. When he applied pressure, it turned smoothly, but the warmth left it as soon as it did. Now there was nothing between his fingers but cold dead metal.

'After that, 'tis as useless as dirt,' Tim whispered, then looked around, half convinced he'd see Big Kells standing there with a scowl on his face and his hands rolled into fists. There was no one, so he unbuckled the straps and raised the lid. He cringed at the screak of the hinges and looked over his shoulder again. His heart was beating hard, and although that rainy evening was chilly, he could feel a dew of sweat on his forehead.

There were shirts and pants on top, stuffed in any whichway, most of them ragged. Tim thought (with a bitter resentment that was entirely new to him), *It's my Mama who'll wash them and mend them and fold them neat when he tells her to. And will he thank her with a blow to the arm or a punch to her neck or face?*

He pulled the clothes out, and beneath them found what made the trunk heavy. Kells's father had been a carpenter, and here were his tools. Tim didn't need a grownup to tell him they were valuable, for they were of made metal. *He could have sold these to pay the tax, he never uses them nor even knows how, I warrant. He could have sold them to someone who does – Haggerty the Nail, for instance – and paid the tax with a good sum left over.*

There was a word for that sort of behavior, and thanks to the Widow Smack's teaching, Tim knew it. The word was *miser*.

He tried to lift the toolbox out, and at first couldn't. It was too heavy for him. Tim laid the hammers and screwdrivers and honing bar aside on the clothes. Then he could manage. Beneath were five ax-heads that would have made Big Ross slap his forehead in disgusted amazement. The precious steel was speckled with rust, and Tim didn't have to test with his thumb to see that the blades were dull. Nell's new husband occasionally honed his current ax, but hadn't bothered with these spare heads for a long time. By the time he needed them, they would probably be useless.

Tucked into one corner of the trunk were a small deerskin bag and an object wrapped in fine chamois cloth. Tim took this latter up, unwrapped it, and beheld the likeness of a woman with a sweetly smiling face. Masses of dark hair tumbled over her shoulders. Tim didn't remember Millicent Kells – he would have been no more than three or four when she passed into the clearing where we must all eventually gather – but he knew it was she.

He rewrapped it, replaced it, and picked up the little bag. From the feel there was only a single object inside, small but quite heavy. Tim pulled the drawstring with his fingers and tipped the bag. More thunder boomed, Tim jerked with surprise, and the object which had been hidden at the very bottom of Kells's trunk fell out into Tim's hand.

It was his father's lucky coin.

Tim put everything but his father's property back into the trunk, loading the toolbox in, returning the tools he'd removed to lighten it, and then piling in the clothes. He refastened the straps. All well enough, but when he tried the silver key, it turned without engaging the tumblers.

Useless as dirt.

Tim gave up and covered the trunk with the old piece of blanket again, fussing with it until it looked more or less as it had. It might serve. He'd often seen his new steppa pat the trunk and sit on the trunk, but only infrequently did he *open* the trunk, and then just to get his honing bar. Tim's burglary might go undiscovered for a little while, but he knew better than to believe it would go undiscovered forever. There would come a day – maybe not until next month, but more likely next week (or even tomorrow!), when Big Kells would decide to get his bar, or remember that he had more clothes than the ones he'd brought in his kick-bag. He would discover the trunk was unlocked, he'd dive for the deerskin bag, and find the coin it had contained was gone. And then? Then his new wife and new stepson would take a beating. Probably a fearsome one.

Tim was afraid of that, but as he stared at the familiar reddish-gold coin on its length of silver chain, he was also truly angry for the first time in his life. It was not a boy's impotent fury but a man's rage.

He had asked Old Destry about dragons, and what they might do to a fellow. Did it hurt? Would there be . . . well . . . *parts* left? The farmer had seen Tim's distress and put a kindly arm around his shoulders. 'Nar to both, son. Dragon's fire is the hottest fire there is – as hot as the liquid rock that sometimes drools from cracks in the earth far south of here. So all the stories say. A man caught in dragonblast is burned to finest ash in but a second – clothes, boots, buckle and all. So if you're asking did yer da' suffer, set yer mind at rest. 'Twas over for him in an instant.'

Clothes, boots, buckle and all. But Da's lucky coin wasn't even smudged, and every link of the silver chain was intact. Yet he didn't take it off even to sleep. So what had happened to Big Jack Ross? And why was the coin in Kells's trunk? Tim had a terrible idea, and he thought he knew someone who could tell him if the terrible idea was right. If Tim were brave enough, that was.

Come at night, for this jilly's son likes to sleep in the day when he gets the chance.

It was night now, or almost.

His mother was still sleeping. By her hand Tim left his slate. On it he had written: I WILL BE BACK. DON'T WORRY ABOUT ME.

Of course, no boy who ever lived can comprehend how useless such a command must be when addressed to a mother.

Tim wanted nothing to do with either of Kells's mules, for they were ill-tempered. The two his father had raised from guffins were just the opposite. Misty and Bitsy were mollies, unsterilized females theoretically capable of bearing offspring, but Ross had kept them so for sweetness of temper rather than for breeding. 'Perish the thought,' he had told Tim when Tim was old enough to ask about such things. 'Animals like Misty and Bitsy weren't meant to breed, and almost never give birth to true-threaded offspring when they do.'

Tim chose Bitsy, who had ever been his favorite, leading her down the lane by her bridle and then mounting her bareback. His feet, which had ended halfway down the mule's sides when his da' had first lifted him onto her back, now came almost to the ground.

At first Bitsy plodded with her ears lopped dispiritedly down, but when the thunder faded and the rain slackened to a drizzle, she perked up. She wasn't used to being out at night, but she and Misty had been cooped up all too much since Big Ross had died, and she seemed eager enough to—

Maybe he's not dead.

This thought burst into Tim's mind like a

179

skyrocket and for a moment dazzled him with hope. Maybe Big Ross was still alive and wandering somewhere in the Endless Forest—

Yar, and maybe the moon's made of green cheese, like Mama used to tell me when I was wee.

Dead. His heart knew it, just as he was sure his heart would have known if Big Ross were still alive. *Mama's heart would have known, too. She would have known and never married that . . . that . . .*

'That bastard.'

Bitsy's ears pricked. They had passed the Widow Smack's house now, which was at the end of the high street, and the woodland scents were stronger: the light and spicy aroma of blossiewood and, overlaying that, the stronger, graver smell of ironwood. For a boy to go up the trail alone, with not so much as an ax to defend himself with, was madness. Tim knew it and went on just the same.

'That hitting *bastard*.'

This time he spoke in a voice so low it was almost a growl.

Bitsy knew the way, and didn't hesitate when Tree Road narrowed at the edge of the blossies. Nor did she when it narrowed again at the edge of the ironwood. But when Tim understood he was truly in the Endless Forest, he halted her long enough to rummage in his pack and bring out a gaslight he'd filched from the barn. The little tin bulb at the base was heavy with fuel, and he

180

thought it would give at least an hour's light. Two, if he used it sparingly.

He popped a sulphur match with a thumbnail (a trick his da' had taught him), turned the knob where the bulb met the gaslight's long, narrow neck, and stuck the match through the little slot known as the marygate. The lamp bloomed with a blue-white glow. Tim raised it and gasped.

He had been this far up the Ironwood several times with his father, but never at night, and what he saw was awesome enough to make him consider going back. This close to civilization the best irons had been cut to stumps, but the ones that remained towered high above the boy on his little mule. Tall and straight and as solemn as Manni elders at a funeral (Tim had seen a picture of this in one of the Widow's books), they rose far beyond the light thrown by his puny lamp. They were completely smooth for the first forty feet or so. Above that, the branches leaped skyward like upraised arms, tangling the narrow trail with a cobweb of shadows. Because they were little more than thick black stakes at ground level, it would be possible to walk among them. Of course it would also be possible to cut your throat with a sharp stone. Anyone foolish enough to wander off the Ironwood Trail – or go beyond it – would quickly be lost in a maze, where he might well starve. If he were not eaten first, that was. As if to underline this idea, somewhere in the darkness a creature that sounded big uttered a hoarse chuckling sound.

Tim asked himself what he was doing here when he had a warm bed with clean sheets in the cottage where he had grown up. Then he touched his father's lucky coin (now hanging around his own neck), and his resolve hardened. Bitsy was looking around as if to ask, *Well? Which way? Forward or back? You're the boss, you know.*

Tim wasn't sure he had the courage to extinguish the gaslight until it was done and he was in darkness again. Although he could no longer see the ironwoods, he could feel them crowding in.

Still: forward.

He squeezed Bitsy's flanks with his knees, clucked his tongue against the roof of his mouth, and Bitsy got moving again. The smoothness of her gait told him she was keeping to the right-hand wheelrut. The placidity of it told him she did not sense danger. At least not yet, and honestly, what did a mule know of danger? From that *he* was supposed to protect *her*. He was, after all, the boss.

Oh, Bitsy, he thought. *If thee only knew.*

How far had he come? How far did he still have to go? How far *would* he go before he gave this madness up? He was the only thing in the world his mother had left to love and depend on, so how far?

It felt like he'd ridden ten wheels or more since leaving the fragrant aroma of the blossies behind, but he knew better. As he knew that the rustling he heard was the Wide Earth wind in the high

182

branches, and not some nameless beast padding along behind him with its jaws opening and closing in anticipation of a small evening snack. He knew this very well, so why did that wind sound so much like breathing?

I'll count to a hundred and then turn Bitsy around, he told himself, but when he reached a hundred and there was still nothing in the pitch black save for him and his brave little mollie-mule (*plus whatever beast treads behind us, closer and closer,* his traitorous mind insisted on adding), he decided he would go on to two hundred. When he reached one hundred and eighty-seven, he heard a branch snap. He lit the gaslight and whirled around, holding it high. The grim shadows seemed first to rear up, then leap forward to clutch him. And did something retreat from the light? Did he see the glitter of a red eye?

Surely not, but—

Tim hissed air through his teeth, turned the knob to shut off the gas, and clucked his tongue. He had to do it twice. Bitsy, formerly placid, now seemed uneasy about going forward. But, good and obedient thing that she was, she gave in to his command and once more began walking. Tim resumed his count, and reaching two hundred didn't take long.

I'll count back down to ought, and if I see no sign of him, I really will go back.

He had reached nineteen in this reverse count when he saw an orange-red flicker ahead and to his left. It was a campfire, and Tim was in no doubt of who had built it.

The beast stalking me was never behind, he thought. *It's ahead. Yon flicker may be a campfire, but it's also the eye I saw. The red eye. I should go back while there's still time.*

Then he touched the lucky coin lying against his breast and pushed on.

He lit his lamp again and lifted it. There were many short side-trails, called stubs, shooting off from either side of the main way. Just ahead, nailed to a humble birch, was a wooden board marking one of these. Daubed on it in black paint was *COSINGTON-MARCHLY*. Tim knew these men. Peter Cosington (who had suffered his own ill luck that year) and Ernest Marchly were cutters who had come to supper at the Ross cottage on many occasions, and the Ross family had many times eaten at one or the other of theirs.

'Fine fellows, but they won't go deep,' Big Ross told his son after one of these meals. 'There's plenty of good ironwood left in close to the blossie, but the true treasure – the densest, purest wood – is in deep, close to where the trail ends at the edge of the Fagonard.'

So perhaps I only did *come a wheel or two, but the dark changes everything.*

He turned Bitsy up the Cosington-Marchly stub, and less than a minute later entered a clearing where the Covenant Man sat on a log before a cheery campfire. 'Why, here's young Tim,' he said. 'You've got balls, even if there won't be hair on em for another year or three. Come, sit, have some stew.'

Tim wasn't entirely sure he wanted to share whatever this strange fellow ate for his supper, but he'd had none of his own, and the smell wafting from the pot hung over the fire was savory.

Reading the cast of his young visitor's thoughts with an accuracy that was unsettling, the Covenant Man said: 'It'll not poison thee, young Tim.'

'I'm sure not,' Tim said . . . but now that poison had been mentioned, he wasn't sure at all. Nevertheless, he let the Covenant Man ladle a goodly helping onto a tin plate, and took the offered tin spoon, which was battered but clean.

There was nothing magical about the meal; the stew was beef, taters, carrots, and onions swimming in a flavorsome gravy. While he squatted on his hunkers and ate, Tim watched Bitsy cautiously approach his host's black horse. The stallion briefly touched the humble mule's nose, then turned away (rather disdainfully, Tim thought) to where the Covenant Man had spread a moit of oats on ground which had been carefully cleared of splinters – the leavings of sais Cosington and Marchly.

The tax collector made no conversation while Tim ate, only kicked repeatedly into the ground with one bootheel, making a small hole. Beside it was the basin that had been tied on top of the stranger's gunna. It was hard for Tim to believe his mother had been right about it – a basin made of silver would be worth a fortune – but it certainly *looked* like silver. How many knucks would have to be melted and smelted to make such a thing?

The Covenant Man's bootheel encountered a root. From beneath his cloak he produced a knife almost as long as Tim's forearm and slit it at a stroke. Then he resumed with his heel: *thud* and *thud* and *thud*.

'Why does thee dig?' asked Tim.

The Covenant Man looked up long enough to flash the boy a thin smile. 'Perhaps you'll find out. Perhaps you won't. I think you will. Have you finished your meal?'

'Aye, and say thankya.' Tim tapped his throat three times. 'It was fine.'

'Good. Kissin don't last, cookin do. So say the Manni-folk. I see you admiring my basin. It's fine, isn't it? A relic of Garlan that was. In Garlan there really were dragons, and bonfires of them still live deep in the Endless Forest, I feel sure. There, young Tim, you've learned something. Many lions is a pride; many crows is a murder; many bumblers is a throcket; many dragons is a bonfire.'

'A bonfire of dragons,' Tim said, tasting it. Then the full sense of what the Covenant Man had said came home to him. 'If the dragons of the Endless Forest are in deep—'

But the Covenant Man interrupted before Tim could finish his thought. 'Ta-ta, sha-sha, na-na. Save thy imaginings. For now, take the basin and fetch me water. You'll find it at the edge of the clearing. You'll want your little lamp, for the glow of the fire doesn't reach so far, and there's a pooky in one of the trees. He's fair swole, which means he's eaten not long ago, but I still wouldn't draw water from beneath him.' He flashed another smile. Tim thought it a cruel one, but this was no surprise. 'Although a boy brave enough to come into the Endless Forest with only one of his father's mules for company must do as he likes.'

The basin *was* silver; it was too heavy to be anything else. Tim carried it clumsily beneath one arm. In his free hand he held up the gaslight. As he approached the far end of the clearing, he began to smell something brackish and unpleasant, and to hear a low smacking sound, like many small mouths. He stopped.

'You don't want this water, sai, it's stagnant.'

'Don't tell me what I do or don't want, young Tim, just fill the basin. And mind the pooky, do ya, I beg.'

The boy knelt, set the basin down in front of him, and looked at the sluggish little stream. The water teemed with fat white bugs. Their oversize heads were black, their eyes on stalks. They looked like waterborne maggots and appeared to be at war. After a moment's study, Tim realized they

187

were eating each other. His stew lurched in his stomach.

From above him came a sound like a hand gliding down a long length of sandpaper. He raised his gaslight. In the lowest branch of an ironwood tree to his left, a huge reddish snake hung down in coils. Its spade-shaped head, bigger than his mama's largest cooking pot, was pointed at Tim. Amber eyes with black slit pupils regarded him sleepily. A ribbon of tongue, split into a fork, appeared, danced, then snapped back, making a liquid *sloooop* sound.

Tim filled the basin with the stinking water as fast as he could, but with most of his attention fixed on the creature looking at him from above, several of the bugs got on his hands, where they immediately began to bite. He brushed them off with a low cry of pain and disgust, then carried the basin back to the campfire. He did this slowly and carefully, determined not to spill a drop on himself, because the foul water squirmed with life.

'If this is to drink or to wash . . .'

The Covenant Man looked at him with his head cocked to one side, waiting for him to finish, but Tim couldn't. He just put the basin down beside the Covenant Man, who seemed to have done with his pointless hole.

'Not to drink, not to wash, although we could do either, if we wanted to.'

'You're joking, sai! It's *foul*!'

'The *world* is foul, young Tim, but we build up a resistance, don't we? We breathe its air, eat its food, do its doings. Yes. Yes, we do. Never mind. Hunker.'

The Covenant Man pointed to a spot, then rummaged in his gunna. Tim watched the bugs eating each other, revolted but fascinated. Would they go on until only one – the strongest – was left?

'Ah, here we are!' His host produced a steel rod with a white tip that looked like ivory, and squatted so the two of them faced each other above the lively brew in the basin.

Tim stared at the steel rod in the gloved hand. 'Is that a magic wand?'

The Covenant Man appeared to consider. 'I suppose so. Although it started life as the gearshift of a Dodge Dart. America's economy car, young Tim.'

'What's America?'

'A kingdom filled with toy-loving idiots. It has no part in our palaver. But know this, and tell your children, should you ever be so unfortunate as to have any: in the proper hand, any object can be magic. Now watch!'

The Covenant Man threw back his cloak to fully free his arm, and passed the wand over the basin of murky, infested water. Before Tim's wide eyes, the bugs fell still . . . floated on the surface . . . disappeared. The Covenant Man made a second pass and the murk disappeared, as well. The water did indeed now look drinkable. In it, Tim found himself staring down at his own amazed face.

'Gods! How did—'

'Hush, stupid boy! Disturb the water even the slightest bit and thee'll see nothing!'

The Covenant Man passed his makeshift wand over the basin yet a third time, and Tim's reflection disappeared just as the bugs and the murk had. What replaced it was a shivery vision of Tim's own cottage. He saw his mother, and he saw Bern Kells. Kells was walking unsteadily into the kitchen from the back hall where he kept his trunk. Nell was standing between the stove and the table, wearing the nightgown she'd had on when Tim last saw her. Kells's eyes were red-rimmed and bulging in their sockets. His hair was plastered to his forehead. Tim knew that, if he had been in that room instead of only watching it, he would have smelled redeye jackaroe around the man like a fog. His mouth moved, and Tim could read the words as they came from his lips: *How did you open my trunk?*

No! Tim wanted to cry. *Not her, me!* But his throat was locked shut.

'Like it?' the Covenant Man whispered. 'Enjoying the show, are you?'

Nell first shrank back against the pantry door, then turned to run. Kells seized her before she could, one hand gripping her shoulder, the other wrapped in her hair. He shook her back and forth like a Rag Sally, then threw her against the wall. He swayed back and forth in front of her, as if about to collapse. But he didn't fall, and when Nell once more tried to run, he seized the heavy ceramic jug that stood by the sink – the same water-jug Tim had poured from earlier to ease her hurt – and brought it crashing into the center of her forehead. It shattered, leaving him holding nothing but the handle. Kells dropped it, grabbed his new wife, and began to rain blows upon her.

'*No!*' Tim screamed.

His breath ruffled the water and the vision was gone.

Tim sprang to his feet and lunged toward Bitsy, who was looking at him in surprise. In his mind, the son of Jack Ross was already riding back down the Ironwood Trail, urging Bitsy with his heels until she was running full-out. In reality, the Covenant Man seized him before he could manage three steps, and hauled him back to the campfire.

'Ta-ta, na-na, young Tim, be not so speedy! Our palaver's well begun but far from done.'

'Let me loose! She's dying, if he ain't killed her already! Unless . . . was it a glam? Your little joke?' If so, Tim thought, it was the meanest joke ever played on a boy who loved his mother. Yet he hoped it was. He hoped the Covenant Man would laugh and say *I really pulled your snout that time, didn't I, young Tim?*

The Covenant Man was shaking his head. 'No joke and no glammer, for the basin never lies. It's already happened, I fear. Terrible what a man in drink may do to a woman, isn't it? Yet look again. This time thee may find some comfort.'

Tim fell on his knees in front of the basin. The Covenant Man flicked his steel stick over the water. A vague mist seemed to pass above it . . . or perhaps it was only a trick of Tim's eyes, which were filled with tears. Whichever it was, the obscurity faded. Now in the shallow pool he saw the porch of their cottage, and a woman who seemed to have no face bending over Nell. Slowly, slowly, with the newcomer's help, Nell was able to get to her feet. The woman with no face turned her toward the front door, and Nell began taking shuffling, painful steps in that direction.

'She's alive!' Tim shouted. 'My mama's alive!'

'So she is, young Tim. Bloody but unbowed. Well . . . a *bit* bowed, p'raps.' He chuckled.

This time Tim had shouted across the basin rather than into it, and the vision remained. He realized that the woman helping his mother appeared to have no face because she was wearing a veil, and the little burro he could see at the very edge of the wavering picture was Sunshine. He had fed, watered, and walked Sunshine many times. So had the other pupils at the little Tree school; it was part of what the headmistress called their 'tuition,' but Tim had never seen her actually ride him. If asked, he would have said she was probably unable. Because of her shakes.

'That's the Widow Smack! What's *she* doing at our house?'

'Perhaps you'll ask her, young Tim.'

'Did you send her, somehow?'

Smiling, the Covenant Man shook his head. 'I have many hobbies, but rescuing damsels in distress isn't one of them.' He bent close to the basin, the brim of his hat shading his face. 'Oh, dearie me. I believe she's *still* in distress. Which is no surprise; it was a terrible beating she took. People say the truth can be read in a person's eyes, but look at the hands, I always say. Look at your mama's, young Tim!'

Tim bent close to the water. Supported by the Widow, Nell crossed the porch with her spread hands held out before her, and she was walking toward the wall instead of the door, although the porch was not wide and the door right in front of her. The Widow gently corrected her course, and the two women went inside together.

The Covenant Man used his tongue to make a *tch-tch* sound against the roof of his mouth. 'Doesn't look good, young Tim. Blows to the head can be very nasty things. Even when they don't kill, they can do terrible damage. *Lasting* damage.' His words were grave, but his eyes twinkled with unspeakable merriment.

Tim barely noticed. 'I have to go. My mother needs me.'

Once again he started for Bitsy. This time he got almost half a dozen steps before the Covenant Man laid hold of him. His fingers were like rods of steel. 'Before you go, Tim – and with my blessing, of course – you have one more thing to do.'

Tim felt as if he might be going mad. *Maybe,* he thought, *I'm in bed with tick fever and dreaming all this.*

'Take my basin. Take it back to the stream and dump it. But not where you got it, because yon pooky has begun to look far too interested in his surroundings.'

The Covenant Man picked up Tim's gaslight, twisted the feed-knob fully open, and held it up. The snake now hung down for most of its length. The last three feet, however – the part ending in the pooky's spade-shaped head – was raised and weaving from side to side. Amber eyes stared raptly into Tim's blue ones. Its tongue lashed out – *slooooop* – and for a moment Tim saw two long curved fangs. They sparkled in the glow cast by the gaslight.

'Go to the left of him,' the Covenant Man advised. 'I shall accompany you and stand watch.'

'Can't you just dump it yourself? I want to go to my mother. I *need* to—'

'Your mother isn't why I brought you here, young Tim.' The Convenant Man seemed to grow taller. '*Now do as I say.*'

Tim picked up the basin and cut across the

clearing to his left. The Covenant Man, still holding up the gaslight, kept between him and the snake. The pooky had swiveled to follow their course but made no attempt to follow, although the ironwoods were so close and their lowest branches so intertwined, it could have done so with ease.

'This stub is part of the Cosington-Marchly stake,' the Covenant Man said chattily. 'Perhaps thee read the sign.'

'Aye.'

'A boy who can read is a treasure to the Barony.' The Covenant Man was now treading so close to Tim that it made the boy's skin prickle. 'You will pay great taxes some day – always assuming you don't die in the Endless Forest this night . . . or the next . . . or the night after that. But why look for storms that are still over the horizon, eh?

'You know whose stake this is, but I know a little more. Discovered it when I made my rounds, along with news of Frankie Simons's broken leg, the Wyland baby's milk-sick, the Riverlys' dead cows – about which they're lying through their few remaining teeth, if I know my business, and I do – and all sorts of other interesting fiddle-de-dum. How people talk! But here's the point, young Tim. I discovered that, early on in Full Earth, Peter Cosington was caught under a tree that fell wrong. Trees will do that from time to time, especially ironwood. I believe that ironwood trees actually *think*, which is where the tradition of

195

crying their pardon before each day's chopping comes from.'

'I know about sai Cosington's accident,' Tim said. In spite of his anxiety, he was curious about this turn of the conversation. 'My mama sent them a soup, even though she was in mourning for my da' at the time. The tree fell across his back, but not *square* across. That would have killed him. What of it? He's better these days.'

They were near the water now, but the smell here was less strong and Tim heard none of those smacking bugs. That was good, but the pooky was still watching them with hungry interest. Bad.

'Yar, Square Fella Cosie's back to work and we all say thankya. But while he was laid up – for two weeks before your da' met his dragon and for six weeks after – this stub and all the others in the Cosington-Marchly stake were empty, because Ernie Marchly's not like your steppa. Which is to say, he won't come cutting in the Endless Forest without a pard. But of course – *also* not like your steppa – Slow Ernie actually *has* a pard.'

Tim remembered the coin lying against his skin, and why he'd come on this mad errand in the first place. 'There *was* no dragon! If there'd been a dragon, it would have burned up my da's lucky coin with the rest of him! And why was it in Kells's trunk?'

'Dump out my basin, young Tim. I think you'll find there are no bugs in the water to trouble thee. No, not here.'

196

'But I want to know—'

'Close thy clam and dump my basin, for you'll not leave this clearing while it's full.'

Tim knelt to do as he was told, wanting only to complete the chore and be gone. He cared nothing about Peter 'Square Fella' Cosington, and didn't believe the man in the black cloak did, either. *He's teasing me, or torturing me. Maybe he doesn't even know the difference. But as soon as this damn basin is empty, I'll mount Bitsy and ride back as fast as I can. Let him try to stop me. Just let him tr—*

Tim's thoughts broke as cleanly as a dry stick under a bootheel. He lost his hold on the basin and it fell upsy-turvy in the matted underbrush. There were no bugs in the water here, the Covenant Man was right about that; the stream was as clear as the water that flowed from the spring near their cottage. Lying six or eight inches below the surface was a human body. The clothes were only rags that floated in the current. The eyelids were gone, and so was most of the hair. The face and arms, once deeply tanned, were now as pale as alabaster. But otherwise, the body of Big Jack Ross was perfectly preserved. If not for the emptiness in those lidless, lashless eyes, Tim could have believed his father might rise, dripping, and fold him into an embrace.

The pooky made its hungry *sloooop*.

Something broke inside of Tim at the sound, and he began to scream.

★   ★   ★

The Covenant Man was forcing something into Tim's mouth. Tim tried to fend him off, but it did no good. The Covenant Man simply seized Tim's hair at the back of his head, and when Tim yelled, the mouth of a flask was shoved between his teeth. Some fiery liquid gushed down his throat. Not redeye, for instead of making him drunk, it calmed him. More – it made him feel like an icy visitor in his own head.

'That will wear off in ten minutes, and then I'll let you go your course,' the Covenant Man said. His jocularity was gone. He no longer called the boy young Tim; he no longer called him anything. 'Now dig out thy ears and listen. I began to hear stories in Tavares, forty wheels east of here, of a woodsman who'd been cooked by a dragon. It was on everyone's lips. A bitch dragon as big as a house, they said. I knew it was bullshit. I believe there might still be a tyger somewhere in the forest –'

At that the Covenant Man's lips twitched in a rictus of a grin, there and gone almost too quickly to see.

'– but a dragon? Never. There hasn't been one this close to civilization for years ten times ten, and never one as a big as a house. My curiosity was aroused. Not because Big Ross is a taxpayer – or *was* – although that's what I'd've told the toothless multitude, were any member of it trig enough – and brave enough – to ask. No, it was curiosity for its own sake, because wanting to know secrets has always been my besetting vice. Someday 'twill be the death of me, I have no doubt.

'I was camped on the Ironwood Trail last night, too – before I started my rounds. Only last night I went all the way to the trail's end. The signs on the last few stubs before the Fagonard Swamp say Ross and Kells. There I filled my basin at the last clear stream before the swamp begins, and what did I see in the water? Why, a sign reading Cosington-Marchly. I packed up my gunna, mounted Blackie, and rode him back here, just to see what I might see. There was no need to consult the basin again; I saw where yon pooky would not venture and where the bugs hadn't polluted the stream. The bugs are voracious flesh-eaters, but according to the old wives, they'll not eat the flesh of a virtuous man. The old wives are often wrong, but not about that, it seems. The chill of the water has preserved him, and he appears to be unmarked, because the man who murdered him struck from behind. I saw the riven skull when I turned him over, and have put him back as you see him now to spare you that sight.' The Covenant Man paused, then added: 'And so he'd see you, I suppose, if his essence lingers near his corse. On that, the old wives reach no consensus. Still all right, or would you like another small dose of nen?'

'I'm all right.' Never had he told such a lie.

'I felt quite sure of who the culprit was – as you

do, I reckon – but any remaining doubts were put to rest at Gitty's Saloon, my first stop in Tree. The local boozer's always good for a dozen knucks come tax time, if not more. There I found out that Bern Kells had slipped the rope with his dead partner's widow.'

'Because of *you*,' Tim said in a monotone that didn't sound like his own voice at all. 'Because of your gods-damned *taxes*.'

The Covenant Man laid a hand on his breast and spoke in wounded tones. 'You wrong me! 'Twasn't *taxes* that kept Big Kells burning in his bed all these years, aye, even when he still had a woman next to him to quench his torch.'

He went on, but the stuff he called nen was wearing off, and Tim lost the sense of the words. Suddenly he was no longer cold but hot, burning up, and his stomach was a churning bag. He staggered toward the remains of the campfire, fell on his knees, and vomited his supper into the hole the Covenant Man had been digging with his bootheel.

'There!' the man in the black cloak said in a tone of hearty self-congratulation. 'I *thought* that might come in handy.'

'You'll want to go and see your mother now,' said the Covenant Man when Tim had finished puking and was sitting beside the dying campfire with his head down and his hair hanging in his eyes. 'Good son that you are. But I have something you may want. One more minute. It'll make no difference to Nell Kells; she is as she is.'

'Don't call her so!' Tim spat.

'How can I not? Is she not wed? Marry in haste, repent at leisure, the old folken say.' The Covenant Man squatted once more in front of his heaped gunna, his cloak billowing around him like the wings of an awful bird. 'They also say what's slipped cannot be unslipped, and they say true. An amusing concept called *divorce* exists on some levels of the Tower, but not in our charming little corner of Mid-World. Now let me see . . . it's here somewhere . . .'

'I don't understand why Square Peter and Slow Ernie didn't find him,' Tim said dully. He felt deflated, empty. Some emotion still pulsed deep in his heart, but he didn't know what it was. 'This is their plot . . . their stake . . . and they've been back cutting ever since Cosington was well enough to work again.'

'Aye, they cut the iron, but not here. They've plenty of other stubs. They've left this one fallow for a bit. Does thee not know why?'

Tim supposed he did. Square Peter and Slow Ernie were good and kindly, but not the bravest men ever to log the iron, which was why they didn't go much deeper into the forest than this. 'They've been waiting for the pooky to move on, I wot.'

'It's a wise child,' the Covenant Man said approvingly. 'He wots well. And how does thee think thy steppa felt, knowing yon treeworm might move on at any time, and those two come back? Come back and find his crime, unless he screws up enough gut to come himself and move the body deeper into the woods?'

The new emotion in Tim's heart was pulsing more strongly now. He was glad. Anything was better than the helpless terror he felt for his mother. 'I hope he feels bad. I hope he can't sleep.' And then, with dawning understanding: 'It's why he went back to the drink.'

'A wise child indeed, wise beyond his— Ah! Here it is!'

The Covenant Man turned toward Tim, who was now untying Bitsy and preparing to mount up. He approached the boy, holding something beneath his cloak. 'He did it on impulse, sure, and afterward he must have been in a panic. Why else would he concoct such a ridiculous story? The other woodsmen doubt it, of that you may be sure. He built a fire and leaned into it as far as he dared and for as long as he could take it, scorching his clothes and blistering his skin. I know, because I built my fire on the bones of his. But first he threw his dead pard's gunna across yon stream, as far into the woods as his strength would allow. Did it with your da's blood not yet dry on his hands, I warrant. I waded across and found it. Most of it's useless mickle, but I saved thee one thing. It was rusty, but my pumice stone and honing bar have cleaned it up very well.'

From beneath his cloak he produced Big Ross's hand-ax. Its freshly sharpened edge glittered. Tim, now astride Bitsy, took it, brought it to his lips, and kissed the cold steel. Then he shoved the handle into his belt, blade turned out from his body, just as Big Ross had taught him, once upon a bye.

'I see you wear a rhodite double around your neck. Was it your da's?'

Mounted, Tim was almost eye-to-eye with the Covenant Man. 'It was in that murdering bastard's trunk.'

'You have his coin; now you have his ax, as well. Where will you put it, I wonder, if ka offers you the chance?'

'In his head.' The emotion – pure rage – had broken free of his heart like a bird with its wings on fire. 'Back or front, either will do me fine.'

'Admirable! I like a boy with a plan! Go with all the gods you know, and the Man Jesus for good measure.' Then, having wound the boy to his fullest stop, he turned to build up his fire. 'I may bide along the Iron for another night or two. I find Tree strangely interesting this Wide Earth. Watch for the green sighe, my boy! She glows, so she does!'

Tim made no reply, but the Covenant Man felt sure he had heard.

Once they were wound to the fullest stop, they always did.

* * *

The Widow Smack must have been watching from the window, for Tim had just led a footsore Bitsy up to the porch (in spite of his growing anxiety he had walked the last half-mile to spare her) when she came rushing out.

'Thank gods, thank gods. Your mother was three quarters to believing you were dead. Come in. Hurry. Let her hear and touch you.'

The import of these words didn't strike Tim fully until later. He tied Bitsy beside Sunshine and hurried up the steps. 'How did you know to come to her, sai?'

The Widow turned her face to him (which, given her veil, was hardly a face at all). 'Has thee gone soft in the head, Timothy? You rode past my house, pushing that mule for all she was worth. I couldn't think why you'd be out so late, and headed in the direction of the forest, so I came here to ask your mother. But come, come. And keep a cheery voice, if you love her.'

The Widow led him across the living room, where two 'seners burned low. In his mother's room another 'sener burned on the bed table, and by its light he saw Nell lying in bed with much of her face wrapped in bandages and another – this one badly bloodstained – around her neck like a collar.

At the sound of their footsteps, she sat up with a wild look upon her face. 'If it's Kells, stay away! You've done enough!'

'It's Tim, Mama.'

She turned toward him and held out her arms. 'Tim! To me, to me!'

He knelt beside the bed, and the part of her face not covered by bandages he covered with kisses, crying as he did so. She was still wearing her nightgown, but now the neck and bosom were stiff with rusty blood. Tim had seen his steppa fetch her a terrible lick with the ceramic jug, and then commence with his fists. How many blows had he seen? He didn't know. And how many had fallen on his hapless mother after the vision in the silver basin had disappeared? Enough so he knew she was very fortunate to be alive, but one of those blows – likely the one dealt with the ceramic jug – had struck his mother blind.

'Twas a concussive blow,' the Widow Smack said. She sat in Nell's bedroom rocker; Tim sat on the bed, holding his mother's left hand. Two fingers of the right were broken. The Widow, who must have been very busy since her fortuitous arrival, had splinted them with pieces of kindling and flannel strips torn from another of Nell's nightgowns. 'I've seen it before. There's swelling to the brain. When it goes down, her sight may return.'

'May,' Tim said bleakly.

'There will be water if God wills it, Timothy.'

Our water is poisoned now, Tim thought, *and it was none of any god's doing.* He opened his mouth to say just that, but the Widow shook her head.

'She's asleep. I gave her an herb drink – not strong, I didn't dare give her strong after he cuffed her so around the head – but it's taken hold. I wasn't sure 'twould.'

Tim looked down at his mother's face – terribly pale, with freckles of blood still drying on the little exposed skin the Widow's bandagements had left – and then back up at his teacher. 'She'll wake again, won't she?'

The Widow repeated, 'There will be water if God wills it.' Then the ghost-mouth beneath the veil lifted in what might have been a smile. 'In this case, I think there will be. She's strong, your ma.'

'Can I talk to you, sai? For if I don't talk to someone, I'll explode.'

'Of course. Come out on the porch. I'll stay here tonight, by your leave. Will you have me? And will you stable Sunshine, if so?'

'Aye,' Tim said. In his relief, he actually managed a smile. 'And say thankya.'

The air was even warmer. Sitting in the rocker that had been Big Ross's favorite roost on summer nights, the Widow said, 'It feels like starkblast weather. Call me crazy – you wouldn't be the first – but so it does.'

'What's that, sai?'

'Never mind, it's probably nothing . . . unless you see Sir Throcken dancing in the starlight or looking north with his muzzle upraised, that is. There hasn't been a starkblast in these parts since

I was a weebee, and that's many and many-a year a-gone. We've other things to talk about. Is it only what that beast did to your mother that troubles you so, or is there more?'

Tim sighed, not sure how to start.

'I see a coin around your neck that I believe I've seen around your father's. Perhaps that's where you'll begin. But there's one other thing we have to speak of first, and that's protecting your ma. I'd send you to Constable Howard's, no matter it's late, but his house is dark and shuttered. I saw that for myself on my way here. No surprise, either. Everyone knows that when the Covenant Man comes to Tree, Howard Tasley finds some reason to make himself scarce. I'm an old woman and you're but a child. What will we do if Bern Kells comes back to finish what he started?'

Tim, who no longer felt like a child, reached down to his belt. 'My father's coin isn't all I found tonight.' He pulled Big Ross's hand-ax and showed it to her. 'This was also my da's, and if he dares to come back, I'll put it in his head, where it belongs.'

The Widow Smack began to remonstrate, but saw a look in his eyes that made her change direction. 'Tell me your tale,' said she. 'Leave out not a word.'

When Tim had finished – minding the Widow's command to leave nothing out, he made sure to tell what his mother had said about the peculiar changelessness of the man with the silver basin

207

– his old teacher sat quietly for a moment . . . although the night breeze caused her veil to flutter eerily and made her look as though she were nodding.

'She's right, you know,' she said at last. 'You chary man hasn't aged a day. And tax collecting's not his job. I think it's his hobby. He's a man with *hobbies*, aye. He has his little *pastimes*.' She raised her fingers in front of her veil, appeared to study them, then returned them to her lap.

'You're not shaking,' Tim ventured.

'No, not tonight, and that's a good thing if I'm to sit vigil at your mother's bedside. Which I mean to do. You, Tim, will make yourself a pallet behind the door. 'Twill be uncomfortable, but if your steppa comes back, and if you're to have a chance against him, you'll have to come at him from behind. Not much like Brave Bill in the stories, is it?'

Tim's hands rolled shut, the fingernails digging into his palms. 'It's how the bastard did for my da', and all he deserves.'

She took one of his hands in her own and soothed it open. 'He'll probably not come back, anyway. Certainly not if he thinks he's done for her, and he may. There was so much blood.'

'*Bastard*,' Tim said in a low and choking voice.

'He's probably lying up drunk somewhere. Tomorrow you must go to Square Peter Cosington and Slow Ernie Marchly, for it's their patch where your da' now lies. Show them the coin you wear, and tell how you found it in Kells's trunk. They can round up a posse and search until Kells is found and locked up tight in the jailhouse. It won't take them long to run him down, I warrant, and when he comes back sober, he'll claim he has no idea of what he's done. He may even be telling the truth, for when it gets in some men, strong drink draws down a curtain.'

'I'll go with them.'

'Nay, it's no work for a boy. Bad enough you have to watch for him tonight with your da's hand-ax. Tonight you need to be a man. Tomorrow you can be a boy again, and a boy's place when his mother has been badly hurt is by her side.'

'The Covenant Man said he might bide along the Ironwood Trail for another night or two. Maybe I should—'

The hand that had soothed moments before now grasped Tim's wrist where the flesh was thin, and hard enough to hurt. 'Never think it! Hasn't he done damage enough?'

'What are you saying? That he made all this happen? It was Kells who killed my da', and it was Kells who beat my mama!'

'But 'twas the Covenant Man who gave you the key, and there's no telling what else he may have done. Or *will* do, if he gets the chance, for he leaves ruin and weeping in his wake, and has for time out of mind. Do you think people only fear him because he has the power to turn them out on the land if they can't pay the barony taxes? No, Tim, no.'

'Do you know his name?'

'Nay, nor need to, for I know what he *is* – pestilence with a heartbeat. Once upon a bye, after he'd done a foul business here I'd not talk about to a boy, I determined to find out what I could. I wrote a letter to a great lady I knew long ago in Gilead – a woman of discretion as well as beauty, a rare combination – and paid good silver for a messenger to take it and bring a reply . . . which my correspondent in the great city begged me to burn. She said that when Gilead's Covenant Man is not at his *hobby* of collecting taxes – a job that comes down to licking the tears from the faces of poor working folk – he's an advisor to the palace lords who call themselves the Council of Eld. Although it's only themselves who claim they have any blood connection to the Eld. 'Tis said he's a great mage, and there may be at least some truth in that, for you've seen his magic at work.'

'So I have,' Tim said, thinking of the basin. And of the way sai Covenant Man seemed to grow taller when he was wroth.

'My correspondent said there are even some who claim he's Maerlyn, he who was court mage to Arthur Eld himself, for Maerlyn was said to be eternal, a creature who lives backward in time.' From behind the veil came a snorting sound. 'Just thinking of it makes my head hurt, for such an idea makes no earthly sense.'

'But Maerlyn was a white magician, or so the stories do say.'

'Those who claim the Covenant Man's Maerlyn in disguise say he was turned evil by the glam of the Wizard's Rainbow, for he was given the keeping of it in the days before the Elden Kingdom fell. Others say that, during his wanderings after the fall, he discovered certain artyfax of the Old People, became fascinated by them, and was blackened by them to the bottom of his soul. This happened in the Endless Forest, they say, where he still keeps in a magic house where time stands still.'

'Doesn't seem too likely,' Tim said . . . although he was fascinated by the idea of a magic house where clock hands never moved and sand never fell in the glass.

'Bullshit is what it is!' And, noting his shocked look: 'Cry your pardon, but sometimes only vulgarity will serve. Even Maerlyn couldn't be two places at the same time, mooning around the Endless Forest at one end of the North'rd Barony and serving the lords and gunslingers of Gilead at the other. Nay, the tax-man's no Maerlyn, but he is a magician – a black one. So said the lady I once taught, and so I believe. That's why you must never go near him again. Any good he offers to do you will be a lie.'

Tim considered this, then asked: 'Do you know what a sighe is, sai?'

'Of course. The sighe are the fairy-folk, who

supposedly live in the deep woods. Did the dark man speak of them?'

'No, 'twas just some story Straw Willem told me one day at the sawmill.'

Now why did I lie?

But deep in his heart, Tim knew.

Bern Kells didn't come back that night, which was for the best. Tim meant to stay on guard, but he was just a boy, and exhausted. *I'll close my eyes for a few seconds, to rest them* was what he told himself when he lay down on the straw pallet he made for himself behind the door, and it *felt* like no more than a few seconds, but when he opened them again, the cottage was filled with morning light. His father's ax lay on the floor beside him, where his relaxing hand had dropped it. He picked it up, put it back in his belt, and hurried into the bedroom to see his mother.

The Widow Smack was fast asleep in the Tavares rocker, which she had drawn up close to Nell's bed, her veil fluttering with her snores. Nell's eyes were wide open, and they turned toward the sound of Tim's steps. 'Who comes?'

'Tim, Mama.' He sat beside her on the bed. 'Has your sight come back? Even a little?'

She tried to smile, but her swollen mouth could do little more than twitch. 'Still dark, I'm afraid.'

'It's all right.' He raised the hand that wasn't splinted and kissed the back of it. 'Probably still too early.'

212

Their voices had roused the Widow. 'He says true, Nell.'

'Blind or not, next year we'll be turned out for sure, and then what?'

Nell turned her face to the wall and began to cry. Tim looked at the Widow, not sure what to do. She motioned for him to leave. 'I'll give her something to calm her – 'tis in my bag. You have men to see, Tim. Go at once, or they'll be off to the woods.'

He might have missed Peter Cosington and Ernie Marchly anyway, if Baldy Anderson, one of Tree's big farmers, hadn't stopped by the pair's storing shed to chat as they hitched their mules and prepared for the day. The three men listened to his story in grim silence, and when Tim finally stumbled to a halt, telling them his mother was still blind this morning, Square Peter gripped Tim by the upper arms and said, 'Count on us, boy. We'll rouse every ax-man in town, those who work the blossies as well as those who go up the Ironwood. There'll be no cutting in the forest today.'

Anderson said, 'And I'll send my boys around to the farmers. To Destry and to the sawmill, as well.'

'What about the constable?' Slow Ernie asked, a trifle nervously.

Anderson dipped his head, spat between his boots, and wiped his chin with the heel of his hand. 'Gone up Tavares way, I hear, either looking for poachers or visiting the woman he keeps up there. Makes no difference. Howard Tasley en't never been worth a fart in a high wind. We'll do the job ourselves, and have Kells jugged by the time he comes back.'

'With a pair of broken arms, if he kicks up rough,' Cosington added. 'He's never been able to hold his drink or his temper. He was all right when he had Jack Ross to rein 'im in, but look what it's come to! Nell Ross beaten blind! Big Kells always kept a warm eye for her, and the only one who didn't know it was—'

Anderson hushed him with an elbow, then turned to Tim, bending forward with his hands on his knees, for he was tallish. ''Twas the Covenant Man who found your da's corse?'

'Aye.'

'And you saw the body yourself.'

Tim's eyes filled, but his voice was steady enough. 'Aye, so I did.'

'On our stake,' Slow Ernie said. 'T'back of one of our stubs. The one where the pooky's set up housekeeping.'

'Aye.'

'I could kill him just for that,' Cosington said, 'but we'll bring him alive if we can. Ernie, you n me'd best ride up there and bring back the . . . you know, remains . . . before we get in on the search. Baldy, can you get the word around on your own?'

'Aye. We'll gather at the mercantile. Keep a good eye out along the Ironwood Trail as you go, boys, but my best guess is that we'll find the booger in town, laid up drunk.' And, more to himself than to the others: 'I *never* believed that dragon story.'

'Start behind Gitty's,' Slow Ernie said. 'He's slept it off there more than once.'

'So we will.' Baldy Anderson looked up at the sky. 'I don't care much for this weather, tell ya true. It's too warm for Wide Earth. I hope it don't bring a storm, and I hope to gods it don't bring a starkblast. That'd cap everything. Wouldn't be none of us able to pay the Covenant Man when he comes next year. Although if it's true what the boy says, he's turned a bad apple out of the basket and done us a service.'

He didn't do my mama one, Tim thought. *If he hadn't given me that key, and if I hadn't used it, she'd still have her sight.*

'Go on home now,' Marchly said to Tim. He spoke kindly, but in a tone that brooked no argument. 'Stop by my house on the way, do ya, and tell my wife there's ladies wanted at yours. Widow Smack must need to go home and rest, for she's neither young nor well. Also . . .' He sighed. 'Tell her they'll be wanted at Stokes's burying parlor later on.'

This time Tim had taken Misty, and she was the one who had to stop and nibble at every bush. By the time he got home, two wagons and a pony-

215

trap had passed him, each carrying a pair of women eager to help his mother in her time of hurt and trouble.

He had no more than stabled Misty next to Bitsy before Ada Cosington was on the porch, telling him he was needed to drive the Widow Smack home. 'You can use my pony-trap. Go gentle where there's ruts, for the poor woman's fair done up.'

'Has she got her shakes, sai?'

'Nay, I think the poor thing's too tired to shake. She was here when she was most needed, and may have saved your mama's life. Never forget that.'

'Can my mother see again? Even a little?'

Tim knew the answer from sai Cosington's face before she opened her mouth. 'Not yet, son. You must pray.'

Tim thought of telling her what his father had sometimes said: *Pray for rain all you like, but dig a well as you do it.* In the end, he kept silent.

It was a slow trip to the Widow's house with her little burro tied to the back of Ada Cosington's pony-trap. The unseasonable heat continued, and the sweet-sour breezes that usually blew from the Endless Forest had fallen still. The Widow tried to say cheerful things about Nell, but soon gave up; Tim supposed they sounded as false to her ears as they did to his own. Halfway up the high street, he heard a thick gurgling sound from his right. He looked around, startled, then relaxed. The Widow had fallen asleep with her chin resting on her birdlike chest. The hem of her veil lay in her lap.

When they reached her house on the outskirts of the village, he offered to see her inside. 'Nay, only help me up the steps and after that I'll be fine-o. I want tea with honey and then my bed, for I'm that tired. You need to be with your mother now, Tim. I know half the ladies in town will be there by the time you get back, but it's you she needs.'

For the first time in the five years he'd had her as a schoolteacher, she gave Tim a hug. It was dry and fierce. He could feel her body thrumming beneath her dress. She wasn't too tired to shake after all, it seemed. Nor too tired to give comfort to a boy – a tired, angry, deeply confused boy – who badly needed it.

'Go to her. And stay away from that dark man, should he appear to thee. He's made of lies from boots to crown, and his gospels bring nothing but tears.'

On his way back down the high street, he encountered Straw Willem and his brother, Hunter (known as Spot Hunter for his freckles), riding to meet the posse, which had gone out Tree Road. 'They mean to search every stake and stub on the Ironwood,' Spot Hunter said excitedly. 'We'll find him.'

The posse hadn't found Kells in town after all, it seemed. Tim had a feeling they'd not find him along the Iron, either. There was no basis for the feeling, but it was strong. So was his feeling that the Covenant Man hadn't finished with him yet. The man in the black cloak had had some of his fun . . . but not *all* of it.

His mother was sleeping but woke when Ada Cosington ushered him in. The other ladies sat about in the main room, but they had not been idle while Tim was away. The pantry had been mysteriously stocked – every shelf groaned with bottles and sacks – and although Nell was a fine country housekeeper, Tim had never seen the place looking so snick. Even the overhead beams had been scrubbed clean of woodsmoke.

Every trace of Bern Kells had been removed. The awful trunk had been banished to beneath the back porch stoop, to keep company with the spiders, fieldmice, and moortoads.

'Tim?' And when he put his hands in Nell's, which were reaching out, she sighed with relief. 'All right?'

'Aye, Mama, passing fine.' This was a lie, and they both knew it.

'We knew he was dead, didn't we? But it's no comfort. It's as if he's been killed all over again.' Tears began to spill from her sightless eyes. Tim cried, himself, but managed to do it silently. Hearing him sob would do her no good. 'They'll bring him to the little burying parlor Stokes keeps out behind his smithy. Most of these kind ladies will go to him there, to do the fitting things, but will you go to him first, Timmy? Will you take him your love and all of mine? For I can't. The man I was fool enough to marry has lamed me so badly I can hardly walk . . . and of course I can't see anything. What a ka-mai I turned out to be, and what a price we've paid!'

'Hush. I love you, Mama. Of course I'll go.'

But because there was time, he went first to the barn (there were far too many women in the cottage for his taste) and made a jackleg bed with hay and an old mule blanket. He fell asleep almost at once. He was awakened around three of the clock by Square Peter, who held his hat clasped to his breast and wore an expression of sad solemnity.

Tim sat up, rubbing his eyes. 'Have you found Kells?'

'Nay, lad, but we've found your father, and brought him back to town. Your mother says you'll pay respects for the both of you. Does she say true?'

'Aye, yes.' Tim stood up, brushing hay from his pants and shirt. He felt ashamed to have been caught sleeping, but his rest the previous night had been thin, and haunted by bad dreams.

'Come, then. We'll take my wagon.'

★   ★   ★

The burying parlor behind the smithy was the closest thing the town had to a mortuary in a time when most country folk preferred to see to their own dead, interring them on their own land with a wooden cross or a slab of roughly carved stone to mark the grave. Dustin Stokes – inevitably known as Hot Stokes – stood outside the door, wearing white cotton pants instead of his usual leathers. Over them billowed a vast white shirt, falling all the way to the knees so it looked almost like a dress.

Looking at him, Tim remembered it was customary to wear white for the dead. He understood everything in that moment, realizing the truth in a way that not even looking at his father's open-eyed corse in running water had been able to make him realize it, and his knees loosened.

Square Peter bore him up with a strong hand. 'Can'ee do it, lad? If'ee can't, there's no shame. He was your da', and I know you loved him well. We all did.'

'I'll be all right,' Tim said. He couldn't seem to get enough air into his lungs, and the words came out in a whisper.

Hot Stokes put a fist to his forehead and bowed. It was the first time in his life that Tim had been saluted as a man. 'Hile, Tim, son of Jack. His ka's gone into the clearing, but what's left is here. Will'ee come and see?'

'Yes, please.'

Square Peter stayed behind, and now it was Stokes who took Tim's arm, Stokes not dressed in his leather breeches and cursing as he fanned an open furnance-hole with his bellows, but clad in ceremonial white; Stokes who led him into the little room with forest scenes painted on the walls all around; Stokes who took him to the ironwood bier in the center – that open space that had ever represented the clearing at the end of the path.

Big Jack Ross also wore white, although his was a fine linen shroud. His lidless eyes stared raptly at the ceiling. Against one painted wall leaned his coffin, and the room was filled with the sour yet somehow pleasant smell of it, for the coffin was also of ironwood, and would keep this poor remnant very well for a thousand years and more.

Stokes let go of his arm, and Tim went forward on his own. He knelt. He slipped one hand into the linen shroud's overlap and found his da's hand. It was cold, but Tim did not hesitate to entwine his warm and living fingers with the dead ones. This was the way the two of them had held hands when Tim was only a sma' one, and barely able to toddle. In those days, the man walking beside him had seemed twelve feet tall, and immortal.

Tim knelt by the bier and beheld the face of his father.

★   ★   ★

221

When he came out, Tim was startled by the declining angle of the sun, which told him more than an hour had passed. Cosington and Stokes stood near the man-high ash heap at the rear of the smithy, smoking roll-ups. There was no news of Big Kells.

'P'raps he's thow'd hisself in the river and drownded,' Stokes speculated.

'Hop up in the wagon, son,' Cosington said. 'I'll drive'ee back to yer ma's.'

But Tim shook his head. 'Thankee, I'll walk, if it's all the same to you.'

'Need time to think, is it? Well, that's fine. I'll go on to my own place. It'll be a cold dinner, but I'll eat it gladly. No one begrudges your ma at a time like this, Tim. Never in life.'

Tim smiled wanly.

Cosington put his feet on the splashboard of his wagon, seized the reins, then had a thought and bent down to Tim. 'Have an eye out for Kells as ye walk, is all. Not that I think ye'll see 'im, not in daylight. And there'll be two or three strong fellas posted around yer homeplace tonight.'

'Thankee-sai.'

'Nar, none of that. Call me Peter, lad. You're old enough, and I'd have it.' He reached down and gave Tim's hand a brief squeeze. 'So sorry about yer da'. *Dreadful* sorry.'

Tim set out along Tree Road with the sun declining red on his right side. He felt hollow, scooped out, and perhaps it was better so, at least for the time being. With his mother blind and no man in the house to bring a living, what future was there for them? Big Ross's fellow woodcutters would help as much as they could, and for as long as they could, but they had their own burdens. His da' had always called the homeplace a freehold, but Tim now saw that no cottage, farm, or bit of land in Tree Village was truly free. Not when the Covenant Man would come again next year, and all the years after that, with his scroll of names. Suddenly Tim hated far-off Gilead, which for him had always seemed (when he thought of it at all, which was seldom) a place of wonders and dreams. If there were no Gilead, there would be no taxes. Then they would be truly free.

He saw a cloud of dust rising in the south. The lowering sun turned it into a bloody mist. He knew it was the women who had been at the cottage. They were bound in their wagons and traps for the burying parlor Tim had just left. There they would wash the body that had already been washed by the stream into which it had been cast. They would anoint it with oils. They would put birch bark inscribed with the names of his wife and son in the dead man's right hand. They would put the blue spot on his forehead and place him in his coffin. This Hot Stokes would nail shut with short blows of his hammer, each blow terrible in its finality.

The women would offer Tim their condolences with the best will in the world, but Tim didn't want them. Didn't know if he could bear them without breaking down once again. He was so *tired* of crying. With that in mind, he left the road and walked overland to the little chuckling rivulet known as Stape Brook, which would in short order bring him to its source-point: the clear spring between the Ross cottage and barn.

He trudged in a half-dream, thinking first of the Covenant Man, then of the key that would work only once, then of the pooky, then of his mother's hands reaching toward the sound of his voice . . .

Tim was so preoccupied that he almost passed the object jutting up from the path that followed the course of the stream. It was a steel rod with a white tip that looked like ivory. He hunkered, staring at it with wide eyes. He remembered asking the Covenant Man if it was a magic wand, and heard the enigmatic reply: *It started life as the gearshift of a Dodge Dart.*

It had been jammed to half its length in the hardpan, something that must have taken great strength. Tim reached for it, hesitated, then told himself not to be a fool, it was no pooky that would paralyze him with its bite and then eat him alive. He pulled it free and examined it closely. Steel it was, fine-forged steel of the sort only the Old Ones had known how to make. Very valuable, for sure, but was it really magic? To him it felt like any other metal thing, which was to say cold and dead.

In the proper hand, the Covenant Man whispered, *any object can be magic.*

Tim spied a frog hopping along a rotted birch on the far side of the stream. He pointed the ivory tip at it and said the only magic word he knew: *abba-ka-dabba*. He half-expected the frog to fall over dead or change into . . . well, *something*. It didn't die and it didn't change. What it did was hop off the log and disappear into the high green grass at the edge of the brook. Yet this had been left for him, he was sure of it. The Covenant Man had somehow known he'd come this way. And when.

Tim turned south again, and saw a flash of red light. It came from between their cottage and the barn. For a moment Tim only stood looking at that bright scarlet reflection. Then he broke into a run. The Covenant Man had left him the key; the Covenant Man had left him his wand; and beside the spring where they drew their water, he had left his silver basin.

The one he used in order to see.

Only it wasn't the basin, just a battered tin pail. Tim's shoulders slumped and he started for the barn, thinking he would give the mules a good feed before he went in. Then he stopped and turned around.

A pail, but not *their* pail. Theirs was smaller,

225

made of ironwood, and equipped with a blossie handle. Tim returned to the spring and picked it up. He tapped the ivory knob of the Covenant Man's wand against the side. The pail gave back a deep and ringing note that made Tim leap back a step. No piece of tin had ever produced such a resonant sound. Now that he thought of it, no old tin pail could reflect the declining sun as perfectly as this one had, either.

Did you think I'd give up my silver basin to a half-grown sprat like you, Tim, son of Jack? Why would I, when any object can be magic? And, speaking of magic, haven't I given you my very own wand?

Tim understood that this was but his imagination making the Covenant Man's voice, but he believed the man in the black cloak would have said much the same, if he had been there.

Then another voice spoke in his head. *He's made of lies from boots to crown, and his gospels bring nothing but tears.*

This voice he pushed away and stooped to fill the pail that had been left for him. When it was full, doubt set in again. He tried to remember if the Covenant Man had made any particular series of passes over the water – weren't mystic passes part of magic? – and couldn't. All Tim could remember was the man in black telling him that if he disturbed the water, he would see nothing.

Doubtful not so much of the magic wand as of his ability to use it, Tim waved the rod aimlessly back and forth above the water. For a moment there was nothing. He was about to give up when a mist clouded the surface, blotting out his reflection. It cleared, and he saw the Covenant Man looking up at him. It was dark wherever the Covenant Man was, but a strange green light, no bigger than a thumbnail, hovered over his head. It rose higher, and by its light Tim saw a board nailed to the trunk of an ironwood tree. **ROSS-KELLS** had been painted on it.

The bit of green light spiraled up until it was just below the surface of the water in the pail, and Tim gasped. There was a *person* embedded in that green light – a tiny green woman with transparent wings on her back.

It's a sighe – one of the fairy-folk!

Seemingly satisfied that she had his attention, the sighe spun away, lighted briefly on the Covenant Man's shoulder, then seemed to leap from it. Now she hovered between two posts holding up a crossbar. From this there hung another sign, and, as was the case with the lettering on the sign marking out the Ross-Kells stake, Tim recognized his father's careful printing. IRONWOOD TRAIL ENDS HERE, the sign read. BEYOND LIES FAGONARD. And below this, in larger, darker letters: **TRAVELER, BEWARE!**

The sighe darted back to the Covenant Man, made two airy circles around him that seemed to leave spectral, fading trails of greenglow behind, then rose and hovered demurely beside his cheek.

The Covenant Man looked directly at Tim; a figure that shimmered (as Tim's own father had when Tim beheld the corse in the water) and yet was perfectly real, perfectly *there*. He raised one hand in a semicircle above his head, scissoring the first two fingers as he did so. This was sign language Tim knew well, for everyone in Tree used it from time to time: *Make haste, make haste.*

The Covenant Man and his fairy consort faded to nothing, leaving Tim staring at his own wide-eyed face. He passed the wand over the pail again, barely noticing that the steel rod was now vibrating in his fist. The thin caul of mist reappeared, seeming to rise from nowhere. It swirled and disappeared. Now Tim saw a tall house with many gables and many chimneys. It stood in a clearing surrounded by ironwoods of such great girth and height that they made the ones along the trail look small. *Surely*, Tim thought, *their tops must pierce the very clouds*. He understood this was deep in the Endless Forest, deeper than even the bravest ax-man of Tree had ever gone, and by far. The many windows of the house were decorated with cabalistic designs, and from these Tim knew he was looking at the home of Maerlyn Eld, where time stood still or perhaps even ran backward.

A small, wavering Tim appeared in the pail. He approached the door and knocked. It was opened. Out came a smiling old man whose white waist-length beard sparkled with gems. Upon his head was a conical cap as yellow as the Full Earth sun. Water-Tim spoke earnestly to Water-Maerlyn. Water-Maerlyn bowed and went back inside his house . . . which seemed to be constantly changing shape (although that might have been the water). The mage returned, now holding a black cloth that looked like silk. He lifted it to his eyes, demonstrating its use: a blindfold. He handed it toward Water-Tim, but before that other Tim could take it, the mist reappeared. When it cleared, Tim saw nothing but his own face and a bird passing overhead, no doubt wanting to get home to its nest before sunset.

Tim passed the rod across the top of the pail a third time, now aware of the steel rod's thrumming in spite of his fascination. When the mist cleared, he saw Water-Tim sitting at Water-Nell's bedside. The blindfold was over his mother's eyes. Water-Tim removed it, and an expression of unbelieving joy lit Water-Nell's face. She clasped him to her, laughing. Water-Tim was laughing, too.

The mist overspread this vision as it had the other two, but the vibration in the steel rod ceased. *Useless as dirt*, Tim thought, and it was true. When the mist melted away, the water in the tin pail showed him nothing more miraculous than the dying light in the sky. He passed the Covenant Man's wand over the water several more times, but nothing happened. That was all right. He knew what he had to do.

Tim got to his feet, looked toward the house, and saw no one. The men who had volunteered to stand watch would be here soon, though. He would have to move fast.

In the barn, he asked Bitsy if she would like to go for another evening ride.

The Widow Smack was exhausted by her unaccustomed labors on Nell Ross's behalf, but she was also old, and sick, and more disturbed by the queerly unseasonable weather than her conscious mind would admit. So it was that, although Tim did not dare knock loudly on her door (knocking at all after sunset took most of his resolve), she woke at once.

She took a lamp, and when by its light she saw who stood there, her heart sank. If the degenerative disease that afflicted her had not taken the ability of her remaining eye to make tears, she would have wept at the sight of that young face so full of foolish resolve and lethal determination.

'You mean to go back to the forest,' said she.

'Aye.' Tim spoke low, but firmly.

'In spite of all I told thee.'

'Aye.'

'He's fascinated you. And why? For gain? Nay, not him. He saw a bright light in the darkness of this forgotten backwater, that's all, and nothing will do for him but to put it out.'

'Sai Smack, he showed me—'

'Something to do with your mother, I wot. He knows what levers move folk; aye, none better. He has magic keys to unlock their hearts. I know I can't stop thee with words, for one eye is enough to read your face. And I know I can't restrain thee with force, and so do you. Why else was it me you came to for whatever it is you want?'

At this Tim showed embarrassment but no flagging of resolve, and by this she understood he was truly lost to her. Worse, he was likely lost to himself.

'What *is* it you want?'

'Only to send word to my mother, will it please ya. Tell her I've gone to the forest, and will return with something to cure her sight.'

Sai Smack said nothing to this for several seconds, only looked at him through her veil. By the light of her raised lamp, Tim could see the ruined geography of her face far better than he wanted to. At last she said, 'Wait here. Don't skitter away wi'out taking leave, lest you'd have me think thee a coward. Be not impatient, either, for thee knows I'm slow.'

Although he was in a fever to be off, Tim waited as she asked. The seconds seemed like minutes, the minutes like hours, but she returned at last. 'I made sure you were gone,' said she, and the old woman could not have wounded Tim more if she had whipped his face with a quirt.

She handed him the lamp she had brought to the door. 'To light your way, for I see you have none.'

It was true. In his fever to be off, he had forgotten.

'Thankee-sai.'

In her other hand she held a cotton sack. 'There's a loaf of bread in here. 'Tisn't much, and two days old, but for provender 'tis the best I can do.'

Tim's throat was temporarily too full for speech, so he only tapped his throat three times, then held out his hand for the bag. But she held it a moment longer.

'There's something else in here, Tim. It belonged to my brother, who died in the Endless Forest almost twenty years ago now. He bought it from a roving peddler, and when I chafed him about it and called him a fool easily cozened, he took me out to the fields west of town and showed me it worked. Ay, gods, such a noise it made! My ears rang for hours!'

From the bag she brought a gun.

Tim stared at it, wide-eyed. He had seen pictures of them in the Widow's books, and Old Destry had on the wall of his parlor a framed drawing of a kind called a rifle, but he had never expected to see the real thing. It was about a foot long, the gripping handle of wood, the trigger and barrels of dull metal. The barrels numbered four, bound together by bands of what looked like brass. The holes at the end, where whatever it shot came out, were square.

'He fired it twice before showing me, and it's never been fired since the day he did, because he died soon after. I don't know if it still *will* fire, but I've kept it dry, and once every year – on his birthday – I oil it as he showed me. Each chamber is loaded, and there are five more projectiles. They're called bullets.'

'Pullets?' Tim asked, frowning.

'Nay, nay, *bullets*. Look you.'

She handed him the bag to free both of her gnarled hands, then turned to one side in the doorway. 'Joshua said a gun must never be pointed at a person unless you want to hurt or kill him. For, he said, guns have eager hearts. Or perhaps he said evil hearts? After all these years, I no longer remember. There's a little lever on the side . . . just here . . .'

There was a click, and the gun broke open between the handle and the barrels. She showed him four square brass plates. When she pulled one from the hole where it rested, Tim saw that the plate was actually the base of a projectile – a *bullet*.

'The brass bottom remains after you fire,' said she. 'You must pull it out before you can load in another. Do you see?'

'Aye.' He longed to handle the bullets himself. More; he longed to hold the gun in his hand, and pull the trigger, and hear the explosion.

The Widow closed the gun (again it made that perfect little click) and then showed him the handle end. He saw four small cocking devices meant to be pulled back with the thumb. 'These are the hammers. Each one fires a different barrel . . . if the cursed thing still fires at all. Do you see?'

'Aye.'

'It's called a four-shot. Joshua said it was safe as long as none of the hammers were drawn.' She reeled a bit on her feet, as if she had come over lightheaded. 'Giving a gun to a child! One who means to go into the Endless Forest at night, to meet a devil! Yet what else can I do?' And then, not to Tim: 'But he won't expect a child to have a gun, will he? Mayhap there's White in the world yet, and one of these old bullets will end up in his black heart. Put it in the bag, do ya.'

She held the gun out to him, handle first. Tim almost dropped it. That such a small thing could be so heavy seemed astounding. And, like the Covenant Man's magic wand when it had passed over the water in the pail, it seemed to *thrum*.

'The extra bullets are wrapped in cotton batting. With the four in the gun, you have nine. May they do you well, and may I not find myself cursed in the clearing for giving them to you.'

'Thank . . . *thankee*-sai!' It was all Tim could manage. He slipped the gun into the bag.

She put her hands to the sides of her head and uttered a bitter laugh. 'You're a fool, and I'm another. Instead of bringing you my brother's four-shot, I should have brought my broom and hit you over the head wi' it.' She voiced that bitter, despairing laugh again. 'Yet 'twould do no good, with my old woman's strength.'

'Will you take word to my mama in the morning? For it won't be just a little way down the Ironwood Trail I'll be going this time, but all the way to the end.'

'Aye, and break her heart, likely.' She bent toward him, the hem of her veil swinging. 'Has thee thought of that? I see by your face thee has. Why do you do this when you know the news of it will harrow her soul?'

Tim flushed from chin to hairline, but held his ground. In that moment he looked very much like his gone-on father. 'I mean to save her eyesight. He has left me enough of his magic to show me how it's to be done.'

'*Black* magic! In support of lies! Of *lies*, Tim Ross!'

'So you say.' Now his jaw jutted, and that was also very like Jack Ross. 'But he didn't lie about the key – it worked. He didn't lie about the beating – it happened. He didn't lie about my mama being blind – she is. As for my da' . . . thee knows.'

'Yar,' she said, now speaking in a harsh country accent Tim had never heard before. 'Yar, and each o' his truths has worked two ways: they hurt'ee, and they've baited his trap for'ee.'

He said nothing to this at first, only lowered his head and studied the toes of his scuffed shor'boots. The Widow had almost allowed herself to hope when he raised his head, met her eyes, and said, 'I'll leave Bitsy tethered uptrail from the Cosington-Marchly stake. I don't want to leave her at the stub where I found my da', because there's a pooky in the trees. When you go to see Mama, will you ask sai Cosington to fetch Bitsy home?'

A younger woman might have continued to argue, perhaps even to plead – but the Widow was not that woman. 'Anything else?'

'Two things.'

'Speak.'

'Will you give my mama a kiss for me?'

'Aye, and gladly. What's the other?'

'Will you set me on with a blessing?'

She considered this, then shook her head. 'As for blessings, my brother's four-shot is the best I can do.'

'Then it will have to be enough.' He made a leg and brought his fist to his forehead in salute; then he turned and went down the steps to where the faithful little mollie mule was tethered.

In a voice almost – but not quite – too low to hear, the Widow Smack said, 'In Gan's name, I bless thee. Now let ka work.'

The moon was down when Tim dismounted Bitsy and tethered her to a bush at the side of the Ironwood Trail. He had filled his pockets with oats ere leaving the barn, and he now spread them before her as he'd seen the Covenant Man do for his horse the previous night.

236

'Be easy, and sai Cosington will come for thee in the morning,' Tim said. An image of Square Peter finding Bitsy dead, with a gaping hole in her belly made by one of the predators of the forest (perhaps the very one he'd sensed behind him on his *pasear* down the Ironwood the night before) lit up his mind. Yet what else could he do? Bitsy was sweet, but not smart enough to find her way home on her own, no matter how many times she'd been up and down this same trail.

'Thee'll be passing fine,' he said, stroking her smooth nose . . . but would she? The idea that the Widow had been right about everything and this was just the first evidence of it came to his mind, and Tim pushed it aside.

He told me the truth about the rest; surely he told the truth about this, too.

By the time he was three wheels farther up the Ironwood Trail, he had begun to believe this.

You must remember he was only eleven.

He spied no campfire that night. Instead of the welcoming orange glow of burning wood, Tim glimpsed a cold green light as he approached the end of the Ironwood Trail. It flickered and sometimes disappeared, but it always came back, strong enough to cast shadows that seemed to slither around his feet like snakes.

The trail – faint now, because the only ruts were those made by the wagons of Big Ross and Big

237

Kells – swept left to skirt an ancient ironwood with a trunk bigger than the largest house in Tree. A hundred paces beyond this curve, the way forward ended in a clearing. There was the crossbar, and there the sign. Tim could read every word, for above it, suspended in midair by virtue of wings beating so rapidly they were all but invisible, was the sighe.

He stepped closer, all else forgotten in the wonder of this exotic vision. The sighe was no more than four inches tall. She was naked and beautiful. It was impossible to tell if her body was as green as the glow it gave off, for the light around her was fierce. Yet he could see her welcoming smile, and knew she was seeing him very well even though her upturned, almond-shaped eyes were pupilless. Her wings made a steady low purring sound.

Of the Covenant Man there was no sign.

The sighe spun in a playful circle, then dived into the branches of a bush. Tim felt a tingle of alarm, imagining those gauzy wings torn apart by thorns, but she emerged unharmed, rising in a dizzy spiral to a height of fifty feet or more – as high as the first upreaching ironwood branches – before plunging back down, right at him. Tim saw her shapely arms cast out behind her, making her look like a girl who dives into a pool. He ducked, and as she passed over his head close enough to stir his hair, he heard laughter. It sounded like bells coming from a great distance.

He straightened up cautiously and saw her returning, now somersaulting over and over in the air. His heart was beating fiercely in his chest. He thought he had never seen anything so lovely.

She flew above the crossbar, and by her firefly light he saw a faint and mostly overgrown path leading into the Endless Forest. She raised one arm. The hand at the end of it, glowing with green fire, beckoned to him. Enchanted by her other-worldly beauty and welcoming smile, Tim did not hesitate but at once ducked beneath the crossbar with never a look at the last two words on his dead father's sign: **TRAVELER, BEWARE**.

The sighe hovered until he was almost close enough to reach out and touch her, then whisked away, down the remnant of path. There she hovered, smiling and beckoning. Her hair tumbled over her shoulders, sometimes concealing her tiny breasts, sometimes fluttering upward in the breeze of her wings to reveal them.

The second time he drew close, Tim called out . . . but low, afraid that if he hailed her in a voice too loud, it might burst her tiny eardrums. 'Where is the Covenant Man?'

Another silvery tinkle of laughter was her reply. She barrel-rolled twice, knees drawn all the way up to the hollows of her shoulders, then was off, pausing only to look back and make sure Tim was following before darting onward. So it was that she led the captivated boy deeper and deeper into the Endless Forest. Tim didn't notice when the poor remnant of path disappeared and his course took him between tall ironwood trees that had been seen by the eyes of only a few men, and that long ago. Nor did he notice when the grave, sweet-sour smell of the ironwoods was replaced by the far less pleasant aroma of stagnant water and rotting vegetation. The ironwood trees had fallen away. There would be more up ahead, countless leagues of them, but not here. Tim had come to the edge of the great swamp known as the Fagonard.

The sighe, once more flashing her teasing smile, flew on. Now her glow was reflected up at her from murky water. Something – not a fish – broke the scummy surface, stared at the airy interloper with a glabrous eye, and slid back below the surface.

Tim didn't notice. What he saw was the tussock above which she was now hovering. It would be a long stride, but there was no question of not going. She was waiting. He jumped just to be safe and still barely made it; that greenglow was deceptive, making things look closer than they actually were. He tottered, pinwheeling his arms. The sighe made things worse (unintentionally, Tim was sure; she was just playing) by spinning rapid circles around his head, blinding him with her aura and filling his ears with the bells of her laughter.

The issue was in doubt (and he never saw the scaly head that surfaced behind him, the protruding eyes, or the yawning jaws filled with triangular teeth), but Tim was young and agile. He caught his balance and was soon standing on top of the tussock.

'What's thy name?' he asked the glowing sprite, who was now hovering just beyond the tussock.

He wasn't sure, in spite of her tinkling laughter, that she could speak, or that she would respond in either the low speech or the High if she could. But she answered, and Tim thought it was the loveliest name he'd ever heard, a perfect match for her ethereal beauty.

'Armaneeta!' she called, and then was off again, laughing and looking flirtatiously back at him.

He followed her deeper and deeper into the Fagonard. Sometimes the tussocks were close enough for him to step from one to the next, but as they progressed onward, he found that more and more frequently he had to jump, and these leaps grew longer and longer. Yet Tim wasn't frightened. On the contrary, he was dazzled and euphoric, laughing each time he tottered. He did not see the V-shapes that followed him, cutting through the black water as smoothly as a seamstress's needle through silk; first one, then three, then half a dozen. He was bitten by suckerbugs and brushed them off without feeling their sting, leaving bloody splats on his skin. Nor did he see the slumped but more or less upright shapes that paced him on one side, staring with eyes that gleamed in the dark.

He reached for Armaneeta several times, calling, 'Come to me, I won't hurt thee!' She always eluded him, once flying between his closing fingers and tickling his skin with her wings.

She circled a tussock that was larger than the others. There were no weeds growing on it, and Tim surmised it was actually a rock – the first one he'd seen in this part of the world, where things seemed more liquid than solid.

'That's too far!' Tim called to Armaneeta. He looked for another stepping-stone, but there was none. If he wanted to reach the next tussock, he would have to leap onto the rock first. And she was beckoning.

Maybe I can make it, he thought. *Certainly she thinks I can; why else would she beckon me on?*

There was no space on his current tussock to back up and get a running start, so Tim flexed his knees and broad-jumped, putting every ounce of his strength into it. He flew over the water, saw he wasn't going to make the rock – almost, but not quite – and stretched out his arms. He landed on his chest and chin, the latter connecting hard enough to send bright dots flocking in front of eyes already dazzled by fairy-glow. There was a moment to realize it wasn't a rock he was clutching – not unless rocks breathed – and then there was a vast and filthy grunt from behind him. This was followed by a great splash that

242

spattered Tim's back and neck with warm, bug-infested water.

He scrambled up on the rock that was not a rock, aware that he had lost the Widow's lamp but still had the bag. Had he not knotted the neck of it tightly around one wrist, he would have lost that, too. The cotton was damp but not actually soaked. At least not yet.

Then, just as he sensed the thing behind him closing in, the 'rock' began to rise. He was standing on the head of some creature that had been taking its ease in the mud and silt. Now it was fully awake and not happy. It let out a roar, and green-orange fire belched from its mouth, sizzling the reeds poking up from the water just ahead.

Not as big as a house, no, probably not, but it's a dragon, all right, and oh, gods, I'm standing on its head!

The creature's exhalation lit this part of the Fagonard brightly. Tim saw the reeds bending this way and that as the critters that had been following him made away from the dragon's fire as fast as they could. Tim also saw one more tussock. It was a little bigger than the ones he had hopscotched across to arrive at his current – and very perilous – location.

There was no time to worry about being eaten by an oversize cannibal fish if he landed short, or being turned into a charcoal boy by the dragon's next breath if he actually reached the tussock. With an inarticulate cry, Tim leaped. It was by far his longest jump, and almost too long. He had to grab at handfuls of sawgrass to keep from tumbling off the other side and into the water. The grass was sharp, cutting into his fingers. Some bunches were also hot and smoking from the irritated dragon's broadside, but Tim held on. He didn't want to think about what might be waiting for him if he tumbled off this tiny island.

Not that his position here was safe. He rose onto his knees and looked back the way he had come. The dragon – 'twas a bitch, for he could see the pink maiden's-comb on her head – had risen from the water, standing on her back legs. Not the size of a house, but bigger than Blackie, the Covenant Man's stallion. She fanned her wings twice, sending droplets in every direction and creating a breeze that blew Tim's sweat-clotted hair off his forehead. The sound was like his mother's sheets on the clothesline, snapping in a brisk wind.

She was looking at him from beady, red-veined eyes. Ropes of burning saliva dropped from her jaws and hissed out when they struck the water. Tim could see the gill high up between her plated breasts fluttering as she pulled in air to stoke the furnace in her guts. He had time to think how strange it was – also a bit funny – that what his steppa had lied about would now become the truth. Only Tim would be the one cooked alive.

The gods must be laughing, Tim thought. And if they weren't, the Covenant Man probably was.

With no rational consideration, Tim fell to his knees and held his hands out to the dragon, the cotton sack still swinging from his right wrist. 'Please, my lady!' he cried. 'Please don't burn me, for I was led astray and cry your pardon!'

For several moments the dragon continued to regard him, and her gill continued to pulse; her fiery spittle went on dripping and hissing. Then, slowly – to Tim it seemed like inches at a time – she began to submerge again. Finally there was nothing left but the top of her head . . . and those awful, staring eyes. They seemed to promise that she would not be merciful, should he choose to disturb her repose a second time. Then they were gone, too, and once more all that Tim could see was something that might have been a rock.

'Armaneeta?' He turned around, looking for her greenglow, knowing he would not see it. She had led him deep into the Fagonard, to a place where there were no more tussocks ahead and a dragon behind. Her job was done.

'Nothing but lies,' Tim whispered.

The Widow Smack had been right all along.

He sat down on the hummock, thinking he would cry, but there were no tears. That was fine with Tim. What good would crying do? He had been made a fool of, and that was an end to it. He promised himself he would know better next time . . . if there *was* a next time. Sitting here alone in the gloom, with the hidden moon casting an ashy glow through the overgrowth, that didn't seem likely. The submerged things that had fled were back. They avoided the dragon's watery boudoir, but that still left them plenty of room to maneuver, and there could be no doubt that the sole object of their interest was the tiny island where Tim sat. He could only hope they were fish of some kind, unable to leave the water without dying. He knew, however, that large creatures living in water this thick and shallow were very likely air-breathers as well as water-breathers.

He watched them circle and thought, *They're getting up their courage to attack.*

He was looking at death and knew it, but he was still eleven, and hungry in spite of everything. He took out the loaf, saw that only one end was damp, and had a few bites. Then he set it aside to examine the four-shot as well as he could by the chancy moonlight and the faint phosphorescent glow of the swampwater. It looked and felt dry enough. So did the extra shells, and Tim thought he knew a way to make sure they stayed that way. He tore a hole in the dry half of the loaf, poked the spare bullets deep inside, plugged the cache, and put the loaf beside the bag. He hoped the bag would dry, but he didn't know. The air was very damp, and—

And here they came, two of them, arrowing straight for Tim's island. He jumped to his feet and shouted the first thing to come into his head. 'You better not! You better not, cullies! There's a gunslinger here, a true son of Gilead and the Eld, so you better not!'

He doubted if such beasts with their pea brains had the slightest idea what he was shouting – or would care if they did – but the sound of his voice startled them, and they sheared off.

'Ware you don't wake yon fire-maiden, Tim thought. *She's apt to rise up and crisp you just to stop the noise.*

But what choice did he have?

The next time those living underwater boats came charging at him, the boy clapped his hands as well as shouted. He would have pounded on a hollow log if he'd had a log to pound on, and Na'ar take the dragon. Tim thought that, should it come to the push, her burning death would be more merciful than what he would suffer in the jaws of the swimming things. Certainly it would be quicker.

He wondered if the Covenant Man was somewhere close, watching this and enjoying it. Tim decided that was half-right. Watching, yes, but the Covenant Man wouldn't dirty his boots in this stinking swamp. He was somewhere dry and pleasant, watching the show in his silver basin with Armaneeta circling close. Perhaps even sitting on his shoulder, her chin propped on her tiny hands.

★   ★   ★

By the time a dirty dawnlight began to creep through the overhanging trees (gnarled, moss-hung monstrosities of a sort Tim had never seen before), his tussock was surrounded by two dozen of the circling shapes. The shortest looked to be about ten feet in length, but most were far longer. Shouting and clapping no longer drove them away. They were going to come for him.

If that wasn't bad enough, there was now enough light coming through the greenroof for him to see that his death and ingestion would have an audience. It wasn't yet bright enough for him to make out the faces of the watchers, and for this Tim was miserably glad. Their slumped, semihuman shapes were bad enough. They stood on the nearest bank, seventy or eighty yards away. He could make out half a dozen, but thought there were more. The dim and misty light made it hard to tell for sure. Their shoulders were rounded, their shaggy heads thrust forward. The tatters hanging from their indistinct bodies might have been remnants of clothing or ribbons of moss like those hanging from the branches. To Tim they looked like a small tribe of mudmen who had risen from the watery floor of the swamp just to watch the swimmers first tease and then take their prey.

What does it matter? I'm a goner whether they watch or not.

One of the circling reptiles broke from the pack and drove at the tussock, tail lashing the water, prehistoric head raised, jaws split in a grin that looked longer than Tim's whole body. It struck below the place where Tim stood, and hard enough to make the tussock shiver like jelly. On the bank, several of the watching mudmen hooted. Tim thought they were like spectators at a Saturday-afternoon Points match.

The idea was so infuriating that it drove his fear out. What rushed in to fill the place where it had been was fury. Would the water-beasts have him? He saw no way they would not. Yet if the four-shot the Widow had given him hadn't taken too much of a wetting, he might be able to make at least one of them pay for its breakfast.

And if it doesn't fire, I'll turn it around and club the beast with the butt end until it tears my arm off my shoulder.

The thing was crawling out of the water now, the claws at the ends of its stubby front legs tearing away clumps of reed and weed, leaving black gashes that quickly filled up with water. Its tail – blackish-green on top, white as a dead man's belly beneath – drove it ever forward and upward, slapping at the water and throwing fans of muddy filth in all directions. Above its snout was a nest of eyes that pulsed and bulged, pulsed and bulged. They never left Tim's face. The long jaws gnashed; the teeth sounded like stones driven together.

On the shore – seventy yards or a thousand wheels, it made no difference – the mudmen called again, seeming to cheer the monster on.

Tim opened the cotton sack. His hands were steady and his fingers sure, although the thing had hauled half its length onto the little island and there was now only three feet between Tim's sodden boots and those clicking teeth.

He pulled back one of the hammers as the Widow had shown him, curled his finger around the trigger, and dropped to one knee. Now he and the approaching horror were on the same level. Tim could smell its rich carrion breath and see deep into its pulsing pink gullet. Yet Tim was smiling. He felt it stretching his lips, and he was glad. It was good to smile in one's final moments, so it was. He only wished it was the barony tax collector crawling up the bank, with his treacherous green familiar on his shoulder.

'Let's see how'ee like this, cully,' Tim murmured, and pulled the trigger.

There was such a huge bang that Tim at first believed the four-shot had exploded in his hand. Yet it wasn't the gun that exploded, but the reptile's hideous nest of eyes. They splattered blackish-red ichor. The creature uttered an agonized roar and curled backward on its tail. Its short forelegs pawed the air. It fell into the water, thrashed, then rolled over, displaying its belly. A red cloud began to grow around its partially submerged head. Its hungry ancient grin had become a death rictus. In the trees, rudely awakened birds flapped and chattered and screamed down abuse.

Still wrapped in that coldness (and still smiling, although he wasn't aware of it), Tim broke open the four-shot and removed the spent casing. It was smoking and warm to the touch. He grabbed the half-loaf, stuck the bread-plug in his mouth, and thumbed one of the spare loads into the empty chamber. He snapped the pistol closed, then spat out the plug, which now had an oily taste.

'*Come on!*' he shouted to the reptiles that were now swimming back and forth in agitated fashion (the hump marking the top of the submerged dragon had disappeared). '*Come have some more!*'

Nor was this bravado. Tim discovered he actually *wanted* them to come. Nothing – not even his father's ax, which he still carried in his belt – had ever felt so divinely right to him as did the heavy weight of the four-shot in his left hand.

From the shore came a sound Tim could not at first identify, not because it was strange but because it ran counter to all the assumptions he had made about those watching. The mudmen were clapping.

When he turned to face them, the smoking gun still in his hand, they dropped to their knees, fisted their foreheads, and spoke the only word of which they seemed capable. That word was *hile*, one of the few which is exactly the same in both low and High Speech, the one the Manni called fin-Gan, or the first word; the one that set the world spinning.

Is it possible . . .

Tim Ross, son of Jack, looked from the kneeling mudmen on the bank to the antique (but very effective) weapon he still held.

Is it possible they think . . .

It *was* possible. More than possible, in fact.

These people of the Fagonard believed he was a gunslinger.

For several moments he was too stunned to move. He stared at them from the tussock where he had fought for his life (and might yet lose it); they knelt in high green reeds and oozy mud seventy yards away, fisted hands to their shaggy heads, and stared back.

Finally some semblance of reason began to reassert itself, and Tim understood that he must use their belief while he still could. He groped for the stories his mama and his da' had told him, and those the Widow Smack had read to her pupils from her precious books. Nothing quite seemed to fit the situation, however, until he recalled a fragment of an old story he'd heard from Splinter Harry, one of the codgers who worked part-time at the sawmill. Half-foolish was Old Splint, apt to point a finger-gun at you and pretend to pull the trigger, also prone to babbling nonsense in what he claimed was the High Speech. He loved nothing better than talking about the men from Gilead who carried the big irons and went forth on quests.

Oh, Harry, I only hope it was ka that put me in earshot on that particular noonrest.

'Hile, bondsmen!' he cried to the mudmen on the bank. 'I see you very well! Rise in love and service!'

For a long moment, nothing happened. Then they rose and stood staring at him from deep-socketed and fundamentally exhausted eyes. Their sloping jaws hung almost to their breastbones in identical expressions of wonder. Tim saw that some carried primitive bows; others had bludgeons strapped to their sunken chests with woven vines.

What do I say now?

Sometimes, Tim thought, only the bald truth would do.

'*Get me off this fucking island!*' he shouted.

At first the mudmen only gaped at him. Then they drew together and palavered in a mixture of grunts, clicks, and unsettling growls. Just when Tim was begining to believe the conference would go on forever, several of the tribesmen turned and sprinted off. Another, the tallest, turned to Tim and held out both of his hands. They *were* hands, although there were too many fingers on them and the palms were green with some mossy substance. The gesture they made was clear and emphatic: *Stay put.*

Tim nodded, then sat down on the tussock (*like Sma' Lady Muffin on her tuffin*, he thought) and began munching the rest of his bread. He cocked an eye for the wakes of returning swimmers as he ate, and kept the four-shot in one hand. Flies and small bugs settled on his skin long enough to sip his sweat before flying off again. Tim thought that if something didn't happen soon, he'd have to jump in the water just to get away from the irritating things, which were too quick to catch with a slap. Only who knew what else might be hiding in that murk, or creeping along the bottom?

As he swallowed the last bite of bread, a rhythmic thudding began to pulse across the morning-misty swamp, startling more birds into flight. Some of these were surprisingly large, with pink plumage and long, thin legs that paddled the water as they fought their way into the air. They made high, ululating cries that sounded to Tim like the laughter of children who had lost their minds.

Someone's beating on the hollow log I wished for, not so long ago. The thought raised a tired grin.

The pounding went on for five minutes or so, then ceased. The cullies on the bank were staring in the direction from which Tim had come – a much younger Tim that had been, foolishly laughing and following a bad fairy named Armaneeta. The mudmen shaded their eyes against the sun, now shining fiercely through the overhanging foliage and burning off the mist. It was shaping to be another unnaturally hot day.

Tim heard splashing, and it was not long before a queer, misshapen boat emerged from the unraveling mists. It had been cobbled together of wood-scraps gleaned from gods knew where and rode low in the water, trailing long tangles of moss and waterweed. There was a mast but no sail; at the top, acting as lookout, was a boar's head surrounded by a shifting skein of flies. Four of the swamp-dwellers rowed with paddles of some orange wood Tim did not recognize. A fifth stood at the prow, wearing a black silk top hat decorated with a red ribbon that trailed down over one bare shoulder. He peered ahead, sometimes waving left, sometimes right. The oarsmen followed his wigwagging with the efficiency of long practice, the boat swooping neatly between the tussocks that had led Tim into his present difficulty.

When the boat approached the black stretch of still water where the dragon had been, the helmsman bent, then stood up with a grunt of effort. In his arms he held a dripping chunk of carcass that Tim assumed had not long ago been attached to the head decorating the mast. The helmsman cradled it, never minding the blood that smeared his shaggy chest and arms, peering down into the water. He uttered a sharp, hooting cry, followed by several rapid clicks. The crew shipped their oars. The boat maintained a little headway toward the tussock where Tim waited, but Helmsman paid no attention; he was still peering raptly into the water.

With a quiet more shocking than the noisiest splash, a giant claw rose up, the talons half-clenched. Sai Helmsman laid the bloody chunk of boar into that demanding palm as gently as a mother lays her sleeping babe into its crib. The talons closed around the meat, squeezing out droplets of blood that pattered into the water. Then, as quietly as it had come, the claw disappeared, bearing its tribute.

Now you know how to appease a dragon, Tim thought. It occurred to him that he was amassing a wonderful store of tales, ones that would hold not just Old Splint but the whole village of Tree in thrall. He wondered if he would ever live to tell them.

The scow bumped the tussock. The oarsmen bent their heads and fisted their brows. Helmsman did the same. When he gestured to Tim from the boat, indicating that he should board, long strands of green and brown swung back and forth from his scrawny arm. More of this growth hung on his cheeks and straggled from his chin. Even his nostrils seemed plugged with vegetable matter, so that he had to breathe through his mouth.

Not mudmen at all, Tim thought as he climbed into the boat. *They're plantmen. Muties who are becoming a part of the swamp they live in.*

'I say thankee,' Tim told Helmsman, and touched the side of his fist to his own forehead.

'Hile!' Helmsman replied. His lips spread in a grin. The few teeth thus revealed were green, but the grin was no less charming for that.

Fines, fees and charges
1st April 2012

	Standard	Young person (15 – 17)	Child (0 – 14)	Maximum
Overdue items				
Books, music recordings	25p	5p	none	£10.00
DVDs	As applicable			
Overdue notices				
Any item by letter	£1.00	40p	40p	
Any item by email/text	none	none	none	
Lost or damaged				
Membership cards	£3.00	£1.00	£1.00	
Any other items	Full replacement cost			

	Standard	MyWestminster ResCard Staff card	Concessions	Concession with Rescard
Subscriptions				
Monthly visitor subscription membership 2 items borrowed at any one time	£10.00			
Music recording subscriptions				
8 items annually	£25.00	£20.00	£12.50	£10.00
8 items quarterly	£8.00	£6.40	£4.00	£3.20
Quarterly DVD subscription 2 items at any one time	£30.00	£24.00	£15.00	£12.00

of
LI

	Standard	MyWestminster ResCard Staff card	Concessions	Concession with Rescard
Requests*				
Self service reservations	£1.00	80p	50p	40p
Reservations processed by staff	£1.50	£1.20	75p	60p
Items sourced from the British Library or University Libraries	An additional £13.00			

*Customers with disabilities that prevent them using computer terminals are entitled to requests at the self-service concessionary rate.

Pay as you go				
Music recording				
1 item on 3 week loan	80p	60p	40p	30p
DVD				
New release for two nights	£2.50	£2.00		
Features per week	£2.00	£1.60		
TV series 1- 4 disc per 2 weeks	£2.50	£2.00		
TV series 5+ disc per 2 weeks	£4.00	£3.20		
Children's release per week	£1.00	80p		
Instruction/education release	£1.00	80p		
Foreign language course	£2.20	£1.80	£1.20	£1.00
English language course	Free			
Audio book				
1 item	£1.00	80p	50p	40p

There is no charge for audio books for older residents (60+) or the visually impaired

	Standard	ResCard	Concessions
Computer games			
1 item	£2.00	£1.60	£1.00
Computer charging			
	First hour free Additional time £1.00 per hour pro rata		

'We are well-met,' Tim said.

'Hile,' Helmsman repeated, and then they all took it up, making the swamp ring: *Hile! Hile! Hile!*

Onshore (if ground that trembled and oozed at every step could be called shore), the tribe gathered around Tim. Their smell was earthy and enormous. Tim kept the four-shot in his hand, not because he intended to shoot or even threaten them with it, but because they so clearly wanted to see it. If any had reached out to actually touch it, he would have put it back in the bag, but none did. They grunted, they gestured, they made those chittering bird cries, but none of them spoke a word other than *hile* that Tim could understand. Yet when Tim spoke to them, he had no doubt that *he* was understood.

He counted at least sixteen, all men and all muties. As well as plant life, most were supporting fungoid growths that looked like the shelf mushrooms Tim sometimes saw growing on the blossiewood he'd hauled at the sawmill. They were also afflicted with boils and festering sores. A near-certainty grew in Tim: somewhere there might be women – a few – but there would be no children. This was a dying tribe. Soon the Fagonard would take them just as the bitch dragon had taken her sacrificial chunk of boar. In the meantime, though, they were looking at him in a way he also recognized from his days in the sawmill. It was the way he and the rest of the boys looked at the foreman when the last job had been done and the next not yet assigned.

The Fagonard tribe thought he was a gunslinger – ridiculous, he was only a kid, but there it was – and they were, at least for the time being, his to command. Easy enough for them, but Tim had never been a boss nor dreamed of being one. What did he want? If he asked them to take him back to the south end of the swamp, they would; he was sure of it. From there he believed he could find his way to the Ironwood Trail, which would in turn take him back to Tree Village.

Back home.

That was the reasonable thing, and Tim knew it. But when he got back, his mother would still be blind. Even Big Kells's capture would not change that. He, Tim Ross, would have dared much to no gain. Even worse, the Covenant Man might use his silver basin to watch him slink south, beaten. He'd laugh. Probably with his wretched pixie sitting on his shoulder, laughing right along with him.

As he considered this, he minded something the Widow Smack used to say in happier days, when he was just a schoolboy whose biggest concern was to finish his chores before his da' came back from the woods: *The only stupid question, my cullies, is the one you don't ask.*

Speaking slowly (and without much hope), Tim said: 'I'm on a quest to find Maerlyn, who is a great magician. I was told he has a house in the

Endless Forest, but the man who told me so was . . .' Was a bastard. Was a liar. Was a cruel trickster who passed the time cozening children. '. . . was untrustworthy,' he finished. 'Have you of the Fagonard ever heard of this Maerlyn? He may wear a tall cap the color of the sun.'

He expected headshakes or incomprehension. Instead, the members of the tribe moved away from him and formed a tight, jabbering circle. This went on for at least ten minutes, and on several occasions the discussion grew quite warm. At last they returned to where Tim waited. Crooked hands with sore-raddled fingers pushed the erstwhile helmsman forward. This worthy was broad-shouldered and sturdily built. Had he not grown up in the waterlogged poison-bowl that was the Fagonard, he might have been considered handsome. His eyes were bright with intelligence. On his chest, above his right nipple, an enormous infected sore bulged and trembled.

He raised a finger in a way Tim recognized: it was the Widow Smack's *attend me* gesture. Tim nodded and pointed the first two fingers of his right hand – the one not holding the gun – at his eyes, as the Widow had taught them.

Helmsman – the tribe's best play-actor, Tim surmised – nodded back, then stroked the air below the straggly growth of intermixed stubble and weed on his chin.

Tim felt a stab of excitement. 'A beard? Yes, he has a beard!'

Helmsman next stroked the air above his head, closing his fist as he did so, indicating not just a tall cap but a tall *conical* cap.

'That's him!' Tim actually laughed.

Helmsman smiled, but Tim thought it a troubled smile. Several of the others jabbered and twittered. Helmsman motioned them quiet, then turned back to Tim. Before he could continue his dumb-show, however, the sore above his nipple burst open in a spray of pus and blood. From it crawled a spider the size of a robin's egg. Helmsman grabbed it, crushed it, and tossed it aside. Then, as Tim watched with horrified fascination, he used one hand to push the wound wide. When the sides gaped like lips, he used his other hand to reach in and scoop out a slick mass of faintly throbbing eggs. He slatted these casually aside, ridding himself of them as a man might rid himself of a palmful of snot he has blown out of his nose on a cold morning. None of the others paid this any particular attention. They were waiting for the show to continue.

With his sore attended to, Helmsman dropped to his hands and knees and began to make a series of predatory lunges this way and that, growling as he did so. He stopped and looked up at Tim, who shook his head. He was also struggling with his stomach. These people had just saved his life, and he reckoned it would be very impolite to puke in front of them.

'I don't understand that one, sai. Say sorry.'

Helmsman shrugged and got to his feet. The matted weeds growing from his chest were now beaded with blood. Again he made the beard and the tall conical cap. Again he dropped to the ground, snarling and making lunges. This time all the others joined him. The tribe briefly became a pack of dangerous animals, their laughter and obvious good cheer somewhat spoiling the illusion.

Tim once more shook his head, feeling quite stupid.

Helmsman did not look cheerful; he looked worried. He stood for a moment, hands on hips, thinking, then beckoned one of his fellow tribesmen forward. This one was tall, bald, and toothless. The two of them palavered at length. Then the tall man ran off, making great speed even though his legs were so severely bent that he rocked from side to side like a skiff in a swell. Helmsman beckoned two others forward and spoke to them. They also ran off.

Helmsman then dropped to his hands and knees and recommenced his fierce-animal imitation. When he was done, he looked up at Tim with an expression that was close to pleading.

'Is it a dog?' Tim ventured.

At this, the remaining tribesmen laughed heartily.

Helmsman got up and patted Tim on the shoulder with a six-fingered hand, as if to tell him not to take it to heart.

'Just tell me one thing,' Tim said. 'Maerlyn . . . sai, is he real?'

Helmsman considered this, then flung his arms skyward in an exaggerated *delah* gesture. It was body language any Tree villager would have recognized: *Who knows?*

The two tribesmen who had run off together came back carrying a basket of woven reeds and a hemp shoulder strap to carry it with. They deposited it at Helmsman's feet, turned to Tim, saluted him, then stood back, grinning. Helmsman hunkered and motioned for Tim to do the same.

The boy knew what the basket held even before Helmsman opened it. He could smell fresh-cooked meat and had to wipe his mouth on his sleeve to keep from drooling. The two men (or perhaps their women) had packed the Fagonard equivalent of a woodsman's lunch. Sliced pork had been layered with rounds of some orange vegetable that looked like squash. These were wrapped in thin green leaves to make breadless popkins. There were also strawberries and blueberries, fruits long gone by for the season in Tree.

'Thankee-sai!' Tim tapped his throat three times. This made them all laugh and tap their own throats.

The tall tribesman returned. From one shoulder hung a waterskin. In his hand he carried a small purse of the finest, smoothest leather Tim had ever seen. The purse he gave to Helmsman. The waterskin he held out to the boy.

Tim wasn't aware of how thirsty he was until he felt the skin's weight and pressed his palms against its plump, gently yielding sides. He pulled the plug with his teeth, raised it on his elbow as did the men of his village, and drank deep. He expected it to be brackish (and perhaps buggy), but it was as cool and sweet as that which came from their own spring between the house and the barn.

The tribesmen laughed and applauded. Tim saw a sore on the shoulder of Tallman getting ready to give birth, and was relieved when Helmsman tapped him on the shoulder, wanting him to look at something.

It was the purse. There was some sort of metal seam running across the middle of it. When Helmsman pulled a tab attached to this seam, the purse opened like magic.

Inside was a brushed metal disc the size of a small plate. There was writing on the top side that Tim couldn't read. Below the writing were three buttons. Helmsman pushed one of these, and a short stick emerged from the plate with a low whining sound. The tribesmen, who had gathered round in a loose semicircle, laughed and applauded some more. They were clearly having a wonderful time. Tim, with his thirst slaked and his feet on solid (*semi*solid, at least) ground, decided he was having a pretty good time himself.

'Is that from the Old People, sai?'

Helmsman nodded.

'Such things are held to be dangerous where I come from.'

Helmsman at first didn't seem to understand this, and from their puzzled expressions, none of the other plant-fellas did, either. Then he laughed and made a sweeping gesture that took in everything: the sky, the water, the oozing land upon which they stood. As if to say *everything* was dangerous.

And in this place, Tim thought, *everything probably is*.

Helmsman poked Tim's chest, then gave an apologetic little shrug: *Sorry, but you must pay attention.*

'All right,' Tim said. 'I'm watching.' And forked two fingers at his eyes, which made them all chuckle and elbow each other, as if he had gotten off an especially good one.

Helmsman pushed a second button. The disc beeped, which made the watchers murmur appreciatively. A red light came on below the buttons. Helmsman began to turn in a slow circle, holding the metal device out before him like an offering. Three quarters of the way around the circle, the device beeped again and the red light turned green. Helmsman pointed one overgrown finger in the direction the device was now pointing. As well as Tim could ken from the mostly hidden sun, this was north. Helmsman looked to see if Tim understood. Tim thought he did, but there was a problem.

'There's water that way. I can swim, but . . .' He bared his teeth and chomped them together, pointing toward the tussock where he had almost become some scaly thing's breakfast. They all laughed hard at this, none harder than Helmsman, who actually had to bend and grip his mossy knees to keep from falling over.

Yar, Tim thought, *very funny, I almost got eaten alive.*

When his throe had passed and Helmsman was able to stand up straight again, he pointed at the rickety boat.

'Oh,' Tim said. 'I forgot about that.'

He was thinking that he made a very stupid gunslinger.

Helmsman saw Tim onboard, then took his accustomed place beneath the pole where decaying boar's head had been. The crew took theirs. The food and water were handed in; the little leather case with the compass (if that was what it was) Tim had stowed in the Widow's cotton sack. The four-shot went into his belt on his left hip, where it made a rough balance for the hand-ax on his right side.

There was a good deal of *hile*-ing back and forth, then Tallman – who Tim believed was probably Headman, although Helmsman had done most of the communicating – approached. He stood on the bank and looked solemnly at Tim in the boat. He forked two fingers at his eyes: *Attend me.*

'I see you very well.' And he did, although his eyes were growing heavy. He couldn't remember when he had last slept. Not last night, certainly.

Headman shook his head, made the forked-finger gesture again – with more emphasis this time – and deep in the recesses of Tim's mind (perhaps even in his soul, that tiny shining splinter of ka), he seemed to hear a whisper. For the first time it occurred to him that it might not be his *words* that these swampfolk understood.

'Watch?'

Headman nodded; the others muttered agreement. There was no laughter or merriment in their faces now; they looked sorrowful and strangely childlike.

'Watch for what?'

Headman got down on his hands and knees and began turning in rapid circles. This time instead of growls, he made a series of doglike yipping sounds. Every now and then he stopped and raised his head in the northerly direction the device had pointed out, flaring his green-crusted nostrils, as if scenting the air. At last he rose and looked at Tim questioningly.

'All right,' Tim said. He didn't know what Headman was trying to convey – or why all of them now looked so downcast – but he would remember. And he would know what Headman was trying so hard to show him, if he saw it. If he saw it, he might understand it.

'Sai, do you hear my thoughts?'

Headman nodded. They all nodded.

'Then thee knows I am no gunslinger. I was but trying to spark my courage.'

Headman shook his head and smiled, as if this were of no account. He made the *attend me* gesture again, then clapped his arms around his sore-ridden torso and began an exaggerated shivering. The others – even the seated crewmembers on the boat – copied him. After a little of this, Headman fell over on the ground (which squelched under his weight). The others copied this, too. Tim stared at this litter of bodies, astonished. At last, Headman stood up. Looked into Tim's eyes. The look asked if Tim understood, and Tim was terribly afraid he did.

'Are you saying—'

He found he couldn't finish, at least not aloud. It was too terrible.

(*Are you saying you're all going to die*)

Slowly, while looking gravely into his eyes – yet smiling a little, just the same – Headman nodded. Then Tim proved conclusively that he was no gunslinger. He began to cry.

Helmsman pushed off with a long stick. The oarsmen on the left side turned the boat, and when it had reached open water, Helmsman gestured with both hands for them to row. Tim sat in the back and opened the food hamper. He ate a little because his belly was still hungry, but only a little, because the rest of him now wasn't.

When he offered to pass the basket around, the oarsmen grinned their thanks but declined. The water was smooth, the steady rhythm of the oars lulling, and Tim's eyes soon closed. He dreamed that his mother was shaking him and telling him it was morning, that if he stayed slugabed, he'd be too late to help his da' saddle the mollies.

Is he alive, then? Tim asked, and the question was so absurd that Nell laughed.

He was shaken awake, that much *did* happen, but not by his mother. It was Helmsman who was bending over him when he opened his eyes, the man smelling so powerfully of sweat and decaying vegetable matter that Tim had to stifle a sneeze. Nor was it morning. Quite the opposite: the sun had crossed the sky and shone redly through stands of strange, gnarled trees that grew right out of the water. Those trees Tim could not have named, but he knew the ones growing on the slope beyond the place where the swamp boat had come to ground. They were ironwoods, and real giants. Deep drifts of orange and gold flowers grew around their bases. Tim thought his mother would swoon at their beauty, then remembered she would no longer be able to see them.

They had come to the end of the Fagonard. Ahead were the true forest deeps.

Helmsman helped Tim over the side of the boat, and two of the oarsmen handed out the basket of food and the waterskin. When his gunna was at Tim's feet – this time on ground that didn't ooze or quake – Helmsman motioned for Tim to open the Widow's cotton sack. When Tim did, Helmsman made a beeping sound that brought an appreciative chuckle from his crew.

Tim took out the leather case that held the metal disc and tried to hand it over. Helmsman shook his head and pointed at Tim. The meaning was clear enough. Tim pulled the tab that opened the seam and took out the device. It was surprisingly heavy for something so thin, and eerily smooth.

Mustn't drop it, he told himself. *I'll come back this way and return it as I'd return any borrowed dish or tool, back in the village. Which is to say, as it was when it was given to me. If I do that, I'll find them alive and well.*

They were watching to see if he remembered how to use it. Tim pushed the button that brought up the short stick, then the one that made the beep and the red light. There was no laughter or hooting this time; now it was serious business, perhaps even a matter of life and death. Tim began to turn slowly, and when he was facing a rising lane in the trees – what might once have been a path – the red light changed to green and there was a second beep.

'Still north,' Tim said. 'It shows the way even after sundown, does it? And if the trees are too thick to see Old Star and Old Mother?'

Helmsman nodded, patted Tim on the shoulder . . . then bent and kissed him swiftly and gently on the cheek. He stepped back, looking alarmed at his own temerity.

'It's all right,' Tim said. 'It's fine.'

Helmsman dropped to one knee. The others had gotten out of the boat, and they did the same. They fisted their foreheads and cried *Hile!*.

Tim felt more tears rise and fought them back. He said: 'Rise, bondsmen . . . if that's what you think you are. Rise in love and thanks.'

They rose and scrambled back into their boat.

Tim raised the metal disc with the writing on it. 'I'll bring this back! Good as I found it! I will!'

Slowly – but still smiling, and that was somehow terrible – Helmsman shook his head. He gave the boy a last fond and lingering look, then poled the ramshackle boat away from solid ground and into the unsteady part of the world that was their home. Tim stood watching it make its slow and stately turn south. When the crew raised their dripping paddles in salute, he waved. He watched them go until the boat was nothing but a phantom waver on the belt of fire laid down by the setting sun. He dashed warm tears from his eyes and restrained (barely) an urge to call them back.

When the boat was gone, he slung his gunna about his slender body, turned in the direction the device had indicated, and began to walk deeper into the forest.

★   ★   ★

270

Dark came. At first there was a moon, but its glow was only an untrustworthy glimmer by the time it reached the ground . . . and then that too was gone. There *was* a path, he was sure of it, but it was easy to wander to one side or the other. The first two times this happened he managed to avoid running into a tree, but not the third. He was thinking of Maerlyn, and how likely it was there was no such person, and smacked chest-first into the bole of an ironwood. He held onto the silver disc, but the basket of food tumbled to the ground and spilled.

Now I'll have to grope around on my hands and knees, and unless I stay here until morning, I'll still probably miss some of the—

'Would you like a light, traveler?' a woman's voice asked.

Tim would later tell himself he shouted in surprise – for don't we all have a tendency to massage our memories so they reflect our better selves? – but the truth was a little balder: he screamed in terror, dropped the disc, bolted to his feet, and was on the verge of taking to his heels (and never mind the trees he might crash into) when the part of him dedicated to survival intervened. If he ran, he would likely never be able to find the food scattered at the edge of the path. Or the disc, which he had promised to protect and bring back undamaged.

It was the disc that spoke.

A ridiculous idea, even a fairy the size of

Armaneeta couldn't fit inside that thin plate of metal . . . but was it any more ridiculous than a boy on his own in the Endless Forest, searching for a mage who had to be long centuries dead? Who, even if alive, was likely thousands of wheels north of here, in that part of the world where the snow never melted?

He looked for the greenglow and didn't see it. With his heart still hammering in his chest, Tim got down on his knees and felt around, touching a litter of leaf-wrapped pork popkins, discovering a small basket of berries (most spilled on the ground), discovering the hamper itself . . . but no silver disc.

In despair, he cried: 'Where in Nis are you?'

'Here, traveler,' the woman's voice said. Perfectly composed. Coming from his left. Still on his hands and knees, he turned in that direction.

'Where?'

'Here, traveler.'

'Keep talking, will ya do.'

The voice was obliging. 'Here, traveler. Here, traveler, here, traveler.'

He reached toward the voice; his hand closed on the precious artifact. When he turned it over in his hand, he saw the green light. He cradled it to his chest, sweating. He thought he had never been so terrified, not even when he realized he was standing on the head of a dragon, nor so relieved.

'Here, traveler. Here, traveler. Here—'

'I've got you,' Tim said, feeling simultaneously foolish and not foolish at all. 'You can, um, be quiet now.'

Silence from the silver disc. Tim sat still for perhaps five minutes, listening to the night-noises of the forest – not so threatening as those in the swamp, at least so far – and getting himself under control. Then he said, 'Yes, sai, I'd like a light.'

The disc commenced the same low whining noise it made when it brought forth the stick, and suddenly a white light, so brilliant it made Tim temporarily blind, shone out. The trees leaped into being all around him, and some creature that had crept close without making a sound leaped back with a startled *yark* sound. Tim's eyes were still too dazzled for him to get a good look, but he had an impression of a smooth-furred body and – perhaps – a squiggle of tail.

A second stick had emerged from the plate. At the top, a small hooded bulge was producing that furious glare. It was like burning phosphorous, but unlike phosphorous, it did not burn out. Tim had no idea how sticks and lights could hide in a metal plate so thin, and didn't care. One thing he did care about.

'How long will it last, my lady?'

'Your question is nonspecific, traveler. Rephrase.'

'How long will the light last?'

'Battery power is eighty-eight percent. Projected life is seventy years, plus or minus two.'

Seventy years, Tim thought. *That should be enough.*

He began picking up and repacking his gunna.

With the bright glare to guide him, the path he was following was even clearer than it had been on the edge of the swamp, but it sloped steadily upward, and by midnight (if it *was* midnight; he had no way of telling), Tim was tired out in spite of his long sleep in the boat. The oppressive and unnatural heat continued, and that didn't help. Neither did the weight of the hamper and the waterskin. At last he sat, put the disc down beside him, opened the hamper, and munched one of the popkins. It was delicious. He considered a second, then reminded himself that he didn't know how long he would have to make these rations last. It also crossed his mind that the brilliant light shining from the disc could be seen by anything that happened to be in the vicinity, and some of those things might not be friendly.

'Would you turn the light off, lady?'

He wasn't sure she would respond – he had tried several conversational gambits in the last four or five hours, with no result – but the light went off, plunging him into utter darkness. At once Tim seemed to sense living things all around him – boars, woods-wolves, vurts, mayhap a pooky or two – and he had to restrain an urge to ask for the light again.

These ironwoods seemed to know it was Wide Earth in spite of the unnatural heat, and had sprinkled down plenty of year-end duff, mostly on the flowers that surrounded their bases, but also beyond them. Tim gathered up enough to make a jackleg bed and lay down upon it.

I've gone jippa, he thought – the unpleasant Tree term for people who lost their minds. But he didn't *feel* jippa. What he felt was full and content, although he missed the Fagonarders and worried about them.

'I'm going to sleep,' he said. 'Will you wake me if something comes, sai?'

She responded, but not in a way Tim understood: 'Directive Nineteen.'

That's the one after eighteen and before twenty, Tim thought, and closed his eyes. He began to drift at once. He thought to ask the disembodied female voice another question: *Did thee speak to the swamp people?* But by then he was gone.

In the deepest crease of the night, Tim Ross's part of the Endless Forest came alive with small, creeping forms. Within the sophisticated device marked North Central Positronics Portable Guidance Module DARIA, NCP-1436345-AN, the ghost in the machine marked the approach of these creatures but remained silent, sensing no danger. Tim slept on.

The throcken – six in all – gathered around the slumbering boy in a loose semicircle. For a while they watched him with their strange gold-ringed eyes, but then they turned north and raised their snouts in the air.

Above the northernmost reaches of Mid-World, where the snows never end and New Earth never comes, a great funnel had begun to form, turning in air lately arrived from the south that was far too warm. As it began to breathe like a lung, it sucked up a moit of frigid air from below and began to turn faster, creating a self-sustaining energy pump. Soon the outer edges found the Path of the Beam, which Guidance Module DARIA read electronically and which Tim Ross saw as a faint path through the woods.

The Beam tasted the storm, found it good, and sucked it in. The starkblast began to move south, slowly at first, then faster.

Tim awoke to birdsong and sat up, rubbing his eyes. For a moment he didn't know where he was, but the sight of the hamper and the greenish shafts of sunlight falling through the high tops of the ironwood trees soon set him in place. He stood up, started to step off the path to do his morning necessary, then paused. He saw several tight little bundles of scat around the place where he had slept, and wondered what had come to investigate him in the night.

Something smaller than wolves, he thought. *Let that be enough.*

He unbuttoned his flies and took care of his business. When he was finished, he repacked the hamper (a little surprised that his visitors hadn't raided it), had a drink from the waterskin, and picked up the silver disc. His eye fell on the third button. The Widow Smack spoke up inside his head, telling him not to push it, to leave well enough alone, but Tim decided this was advice he would disregard. If he had paid attention to well-meaning advice, he wouldn't be here. Of course, his mother might also have her sight . . . but Big Kells would still be his steppa. He supposed all of life was full of similar trades.

Hoping the damned thing wouldn't explode, Tim pushed the button.

'Hello, traveler!' the woman's voice said.

Tim began to hello her back, but she went on without acknowledging him. 'Welcome to DARIA, a guidance service of North Central Positronics. You are on the Beam of the Cat, sometimes known as the Beam of the Lion or of the Tyger. You are also on the Way of the Bird, known variously as the Way of the Eagle, the Way of the Hawk, and the Way of the Vulturine. All things serve the Beam!'

'So they do say,' Tim agreed, so wonderstruck he was hardly aware he was speaking. 'Although no one knows what it means.'

'You have left Waypoint Nine, in Fagonard Swamp. There is no Dogan in Fagonard Swamp, but there is a charging station. If you need a charging station, say *yes* and I will compute your course. If you do not need a charging station, say *continue*.'

'Continue,' Tim said. 'Lady . . . Daria . . . I seek Maerlyn—'

She overrode him. 'The next Dogan on the current course is on the North Forest Kinnock, also known as the Northern Aerie. The charging station at the North Forest Kinnock Dogan is off-line. Disturbance in the Beam suggests magic at that location. There may also be Changed Life at that location. Detour is recommended. If you would like to detour, say *detour* and I will compute the necessary changes. If you would like to visit the North Forest Kinnock Dogan, also known as the Northern Aerie, say *continue.*'

Tim considered the choices. If the Daria-thing was suggesting a detour, this Dogan-place was probably dangerous. On the other hand, wasn't magic exactly what he had come in search of? Magic, or a miracle? And he'd already stood on the head of a dragon. How much more dangerous could the North Forest Kinnock Dogan be?

Maybe a lot, he admitted to himself . . . but he had his father's ax, he had his father's lucky coin, and he had a four-shot. One that worked, and had already drawn blood.

'Continue,' he said.

'The distance to the North Forest Kinnock Dogan is fifty miles, or forty-five-point-forty-five wheels. The terrain is moderate. Weather conditions . . .'

Daria paused. There was a loud click. Then: 'Directive Nineteen.'

'What is Directive Nineteen, Daria?'

'To bypass Directive Nineteen, speak your password. You may be asked to spell.'

'I don't know what that means.'

'Are you sure you would not like me to plot a detour, traveler? I am detecting a strong disturbance in the Beam, indicating deep magic.'

'Is it white magic or black?' It was as close as Tim could come to asking a question the voice from the plate probably wouldn't understand: *Is it Maerlyn or is it the man who got Mama and me into this mess?*

When there was no answer for ten seconds, Tim began to believe there would be no answer at all . . . or another repetition of *Directive Nineteen*, which really amounted to the same thing. But an answer came back, although it did him little good.

'Both,' said Daria.

His way continued upward, and the heat continued, as well. By noon, Tim was too tired and hungry to go on. He had tried several times to engage Daria in conversation, but she had once again gone silent. Pushing the third button did not help, although her navigation function seemed unimpaired; when he deliberately turned to the right or left of the discernible path leading ever deeper into the woods (and ever upward), the green light turned red. When he turned back, the green reappeared.

He ate from the hamper, then settled in for a nap. When he awoke, it was late afternoon and a little cooler. He reslung the hamper on his back (it was lighter now), shouldered the waterskin, and pushed ahead. The afternoon was short and the twilight even shorter. The night held fewer terrors for him, partly because he had already survived one, but mostly because, when he called for the light, Daria provided it. And after the heat of the day, the cool of evening was refreshing.

Tim went on for a good many hours before he began to tire again. He was gathering some duff to sleep on until daylight when Daria spoke up. 'There is a scenic opportunity ahead, traveler. If you wish to take advantage of this scenic opportunity, say *continue*. If you do not wish to observe, say *no*.'

Tim had been in the act of putting the hamper on the ground. Now he picked it up again, intrigued. 'Continue,' he said.

The disc's bright light went out, but after Tim's eyes had a chance to adjust, he saw light up ahead. Only moonlight, but far brighter than that which filtered through the trees overhanging the path.

'Use the green navigation sensor,' Daria said. 'Move quietly. The scenic opportunity is one mile, or point-eight wheels, north of your current location.'

With that, she clicked off.

Tim moved as quietly as he could, but to himself he sounded very loud. In the end, it probably made no difference. The path opened into the first large clearing he had come to since entering the forest, and the beings occupying it took no notice of him at all.

There were six billy-bumblers sitting on a fallen ironwood tree, with their snouts raised to the crescent moon. Their eyes gleamed like jewels. Throcken were hardly ever seen in Tree these days, and to see even one was considered extremely lucky. Tim never had. Several of his friends claimed to have glimpsed them at play in the fields, or in the blossie groves, but he suspected they were fibbing. And now . . . to see a full half-dozen . . .

They were, he thought, far more beautiful than the treacherous Armaneeta, because the only magic about them was the plain magic of living things. *These were the creatures that surrounded me last night – I know they were.*

He approached them as in a dream, knowing he would probably frighten them away, but helpless to stay where he was. They did not move. He stretched his hand out to one, ignoring the doleful voice in his head (it sounded like the Widow's) telling him he would certainly be bitten.

The bumbler did not bite, but when it felt Tim's fingers in the dense fur below the shelf of its jaw, it seemed to awake. It leaped from the log. The others did the same. They began to chase around his feet and between his legs, nipping at each other and uttering high-pitched barks that made Tim laugh.

One looked over its shoulder at him . . . and seemed to laugh back.

They left him and raced to the center of the clearing. There they made a moving ring in the moonlight, their faint shadows dancing and weaving. They all stopped at once and rose on their hind legs with their paws outstretched, looking for all the world like little furry men. Beneath the cold smile of the crescent moon, they all faced north, along the Path of the Beam.

'You're wonderful!' Tim called.

They turned to him, concentration broken. 'Wunnerful!' one of them said . . . and then they all raced into the trees. It happened so quickly that Tim could almost believe he had imagined the whole thing.

Almost.

He made camp in the clearing that night, hoping they might return. And, as he drifted toward sleep, he remembered something the Widow Smack had said about the unseasonably warm weather. *It's probably nothing . . . unless you see Sir Throcken dancing in the starlight or looking north with his muzzle upraised.*

He had seen not just one bumbler but a full half-dozen doing both.

Tim sat up. The Widow had said those things were a sign of something – what? A stunblast? That was close, but not quite—

'Starkblast,' he said. 'That was it.'

'Starkblast,' Daria said, startling him more wide awake than ever. 'A fast-moving storm of great power. Its features include steep and sudden drops in temperature accompanied by strong winds. It has been known to cause major destruction and loss of life in civilized portions of the world. In primitive areas, entire tribes have been wiped out. This definition of *starkblast* has been a service of North Central Positronics.'

Tim lay down again on his bed of duff, arms crossed behind his head, looking up at the circle of stars this clearing made visible. A service of North Central Positronics, was it? Well . . . maybe. He had an idea it might really have been a service of Daria. She was a marvelous machine (although he wasn't sure a machine was *all* she was), but there were things she wasn't allowed to tell him. He had an idea she might be *hinting* at some things, though. Was she leading him on, as the Covenant Man and Armaneeta had done? Tim had to admit it was a possibility, but he didn't really believe it. He thought – possibly because he was just a stupid kid, ready to believe anything – that maybe she hadn't had anyone to talk to for a long time, and had taken a shine to him. One thing he knew for sure:

283

if there was a terrible storm coming, he would do well to finish his business quickly, and then get undercover. But where would be safe?

This led his musings back to the Fagonard tribe. They weren't a bit safe . . . as they knew, for hadn't they already imitated the bumblers for him? He had promised himself he would recognize what they were trying to show him if it was put before him, and he had. The storm was coming – the starkblast. They knew it, probably from the bumblers, and they expected it to kill them.

With such thoughts in his mind, Tim guessed it would be a long time before he could get to sleep, but five minutes later he was lost to the world.

He dreamed of throcken dancing in the moonlight.

He began to think of Daria as his companion, although she didn't speak much, and when she did, Tim didn't always understand why (or what in Na'ar she was talking about). Once it was a series of numbers. Once she told him she would be 'off-line' because she was 'searching for satellite' and suggested he stop. He did, and for half an hour the plate seemed completely dead – no lights, no voice. Just when he'd begun to believe she really had died, the green light came back on, the little stick reappeared, and Daria announced, 'I have reestablished satellite link.'

'Wish you joy of it,' Tim replied.

Several times, she offered to calculate a detour. This Tim continued to decline. And once, near the end of the second day after leaving the Fagonard, she recited a bit of verse:

> *See the Eagle's brilliant eye,*
> *And wings on which he holds the sky!*
> *He spies the land and spies the sea*
> *And even spies a child like me.*

If he lived to be a hundred (which, given his current mad errand, Tim doubted was in the cards), he thought he would never forget the things he saw on the three days he and Daria trudged ever upward in the continuing heat. The path, once vague, became a clear lane, one that for several wheels was bordered by crumbling rock walls. Once, for a space of almost an hour, the corridor in the sky above that lane was filled with thousands of huge red birds flying south, as if in migration. *But surely,* Tim thought, *they must come to rest in the Endless Forest.* For no birds like that had ever been seen above the village of Tree. Once four blue deer less than two feet high crossed the path ahead of him, seeming to take no notice of the thunderstruck boy who stood staring at these mutie dwarfs. And once they came to a field filled with giant yellow mushrooms standing four feet high, with caps the size of umbrellas.

'Are they good to eat, Daria?' Tim asked, for he was reaching the end of the goods in the hamper. 'Does thee know?'

'No, traveler,' Daria replied. 'They are poison. If you even brush their dust on your skin, you will die of seizures. I advise extreme caution.'

This was advice Tim took, even holding his breath until he was past that deadly grove filled with treacherous, sunshiny death.

Near the end of the third day, he emerged on the edge of a narrow chasm that fell away for a thousand feet or more. He could not see the bottom, for it was filled with a drift of white flowers. They were so thick that he at first mistook them for a cloud that had fallen to earth. The smell that wafted up to him was fantastically sweet. A rock bridge spanned this gorge, on the other side passing through a waterfall that glowed blood-red in the reflected light of the setting sun.

'Am I meant to cross that?' Tim asked faintly. It looked not much wider than a barn-beam . . . and, in the middle, not much thicker.

No answer from Daria, but the steadily glowing green light was answer enough.

'Maybe in the morning,' Tim said, knowing he would not sleep for thinking about it, but also not wanting to chance it so close to day's end. The idea of having to negotiate the last part of that lofty causeway in the dark was terrifying.

'I advise you to cross now,' Daria told him,

'and continue to the North Forest Kinnock Dogan with all possible speed. Detour is no longer possible.'

Looking at the gorge with its chancy bridge, Tim hardly needed the voice from the plate to tell him that a detour was no longer possible. But still . . .

'Why can't I wait until morning? Surely it would be safer.'

'Directive Nineteen.' A click louder than any he had heard before came from the plate and then Daria added, 'But I advise speed, Tim.'

He had several times asked her to call him by name rather than as *traveler*. This was the first time she had done so, and it convinced him. He left the Fagonard tribe's basket – not without some regret – because he thought it might unbalance him. He tucked the last two popkins into his shirt, slung the waterskin over his back, then checked to make sure both the four-shot and his father's hand-ax were firmly in place on either hip. He approached the stone causeway, looked down into the banks of white flowers, and saw the first shadows of evening beginning to pool there. He imagined himself making that one you-can-never-take-it-back misstep; saw himself whirling his arms in a fruitless effort to keep his balance; felt his feet first losing the rock and then running on air; heard his scream as the fall began. There would be a few moments to regret all the life he might have lived, and then—

'Daria,' he said in a small, sick voice, 'do I have to?'

No answer, which was answer enough. Tim stepped out over the drop.

The sound of his bootheels on rock was very loud. He didn't want to look down, but had no choice; if he didn't mind where he was going, he would be doomed for sure. The rock bridge was as wide as a village path when he began, but by the time he got to the middle – as he had feared, although he had hoped it was just his eyes playing tricks – it was only the width of his shor'boots. He tried walking with his arms outstretched, but a breeze came blowing down the gorge, billowing his shirt and making him feel like a kite about to lift off. He lowered them and walked on, heel-to-toe and heel-to-toe, wavering from side to side. He became convinced his heart was beating its last frenzied beats, his mind thinking its last random thoughts.

Mama will never know what happened to me.

Halfway across, the bridge was at its narrowest, also its thinnest. Tim could feel its fragility through his feet, and could hear the wind playing its pitch pipe along its eroded underside. Now each time he took a step, he had to swing a boot out over the drop.

Don't freeze, he told himself, but he knew that if he hesitated, he might do just that. Then, from the corner of his eye, he saw movement below, and he *did* hesitate.

Long, leathery tentacles were emerging from the flowers. They were slate-gray on top and as pink as burned skin underneath. They rose toward him in a wavery dance – first two, then four, then eight, then a forest of them.

Daria again said, 'I advise speed, Tim.'

He forced himself to start walking again. Slowly at first, but faster as the tentacles continued to close in. Surely no beast had a thousand-foot reach, no matter how monstrous the body hiding down there in the flowers, but when Tim saw the tentacles thinning out and stretching to reach even higher, he began to hurry. And when the longest of them reached the underside of the bridge and began to fumble its way along it, he broke into a run.

The waterfall – no longer red, now a fading pinkish-orange – thundered ahead of him. Cold spray spattered his hot face. Tim felt something caress his boot, seeking purchase, and threw himself forward at the water with an inarticulate yell. There was one moment of freezing cold – it encased his body like a glove – and then he was on the other side of the falls and back on solid ground.

One of the tentacles came through. It reared up like a snake, dripping . . . and then withdrew.

'Daria! Are you all right?'

'I'm waterproof,' Daria replied with something that sounded suspiciously like smugness.

Tim picked himself up and looked around. He was in a little rock cave. Written on one wall, in paint that once might have been red but had over the years (or perhaps centuries) faded to a dull rust, was this cryptic notation:

JOHN 3:16
FEER HELL HOPE FOR HEVEN
MAN JESUS

Ahead of him was a short stone staircase filled with fading sunset light. To one side of it was a litter of tin cans and bits of broken machinery – springs, wires, broken glass, and chunks of green board covered with squiggles of metal. On the other side of the stairs was a grinning skeleton with what looked like an ancient canteen draped over its rib cage. *Hello, Tim!* that grin seemed to say. *Welcome to the far side of the world! Want a drink of dust? I have plenty!*

Tim climbed the stairs, skittering past the relic. He knew perfectly well it wouldn't come to life and try to snare him by the boot, as the tentacles from the flowers had tried to do; dead was dead. Still, it seemed safer to skitter.

When he emerged, he saw that the path once more entered the woods, but he wouldn't be there for long. Not far ahead, the great old trees pulled back and the long, long upslope he had been climbing ended in a clearing far larger than the one where the bumblers had danced. There an enormous tower made of metal girders rose into the sky. At the top was a blinking red light.

'You have almost reached your destination,' Daria said. 'The North Forest Kinnock Dogan is three wheels ahead.' That click came again, even louder than before. 'You really must hurry, Tim.'

As Tim stood looking at the tower with its blinking light, the breeze that had so frightened him while crossing the rock bridge came again, only this time its breath was chilly. He looked up into the sky and saw the clouds that had been lazing toward the south were now racing.

'It's the starkblast, Daria, isn't it? The starkblast is coming.'

Daria didn't reply, but Tim didn't need her to.

He began to run.

By the time he reached the Dogan clearing, he was out of breath and only able to trot, in spite of his sense of urgency. The wind continued to rise, pushing against him, and the high branches of the ironwood trees had begun to whisper. The air was still warm, but Tim didn't think it would stay that way for long. He needed to get under cover, and he hoped to do so in this Dogan-thing.

But when he entered the clearing, he barely spared a glance for the round, metal-roofed building which stood at the base of the skeletal tower with its blinking light. He had seen something else that took all his attention, and stole his breath.

Am I seeing that? Am I really seeing that?

'Gods,' he whispered.

The path, as it crossed the clearing, was paved in some smooth dark material, so bright that it reflected both the trees dancing in the rising wind and the sunset-tinged clouds flowing overhead. It ended at a rock precipice. The whole world seemed to end there, and to begin again a hundred wheels or more distant. In between was a great chasm of rushing air in which leaves danced and swirled. There were bin-rusties as well. They rose and twisted helplessly in the eddies and currents. Some were obviously dead, the wings ripped from their bodies.

Tim hardly noticed the great chasm and the dying birds, either. To the left of the metal road, about three yards from the place where the world dropped off into nothingness, there stood a round cage made of steel bars. Overturned in front of it was a battered tin bucket he knew all too well.

In the cage, pacing slowly around a hole in the center, was an enormous tyger.

It saw the staring, gapemouthed boy and approached the bars. Its eyes were as large as Points balls, but a brilliant green instead of blue. On its hide, stripes of dark orange alternated with those of richest midnight black. Its ears were cocked. Its snout wrinkled back from long white teeth. It growled. The sound was low, like a silk garment being ripped slowly up a seam. It could have been a greeting . . . but Tim somehow doubted it.

Around its neck was a silver collar. From this hung two objects. One looked like a playing card. The other was a key with a strange twisted shape.

Tim had no idea how long he stood captured by those fabulous emerald eyes, or how long he might have remained so, but the extreme peril of his situation announced itself in a series of low, thudding explosions.

'What's that?'

'Trees on the far side of the Great Canyon,' Daria said. 'Extreme rapid temperature change is causing them to implode. Seek shelter, Tim.'

The starkblast – what else? 'How long before it gets here?'

'Less than an hour.' There was another of those loud clicks. 'I may have to shut down.'

'No!'

'I have violated Directive Nineteen. All I can say in my defense is that it's been a very long time since I have had anyone to talk to.' *Click!* Then – more worrisome, more ominous – *Clunk!*

'What about the tyger? Is it the Guardian of the Beam?' As soon as he articulated the idea, Tim was filled with horror. 'I can't leave a Guardian of the Beam out here to die in the starkblast!'

'The Guardian of the Beam at this end is Aslan,'

Daria said. 'Aslan is a lion, and if he still lives, he is far from here, in the land of endless snows. This tyger is . . . *Directive Nineteen!*' Then an even louder clunk as she overrode the directive, at what cost Tim did not know. 'This tyger is the magic of which I spoke. Never mind it. *Seek shelter!* Good luck, Tim. You have been my fr—'

Not a click this time, nor a clunk, but an awful crunch. Smoke drifted up from the plate and the green light went out.

'Daria!'

Nothing.

'*Daria, come back!*'

But Daria was gone.

The artillery sounds made by the dying trees were still far across that cloudy gap in the world, but there could be no doubt that they were approaching. The wind continued to strengthen, growing ever colder. High above, a final batch of clouds was boiling past. Behind them was an awful violet clarity in which the first stars had begun to appear. The whisper of the wind in the high branches of the surrounding trees had risen to an unhappy chorus of sighs. It was as if the ironwoods knew their long, long lives were coming to an end. A great woodsman was on the way, swinging an ax made of wind.

Tim took another look at the tyger (it had resumed its slow and stately pacing, as if Tim had been worth only momentary consideration), then hurried to the Dogan. Small round windows of real glass – very thick, from the look – marched around its circumference at the height of Tim's head. The door was also metal. There was no knob or latch, only a slot like a narrow mouth. Above the slot, on a rusting steel plate, was this:

NORTH CENTRAL POSITRONICS, LTD.
North Forest Kinnock
Bend Quadrant

OUTPOST 9

Low Security
USE KEYCARD

These words were hard for him to make out, because they were in a weird mixture of High and low speech. What had been scrawled below them, however, was easy. **All here are dead.**

At the base of the door was a box that looked like the one Tim's mother had for her little trinkets and keepsakes, only of metal instead of wood. He tried to open it, but it was locked. Engraved upon it were letters Tim couldn't read. There was a keyhole of odd shape – like the letter ∜* – but no key. He tried to lift the box and couldn't. It might have been anchored to the ground at the top of a buried stone post.

A dead bin-rusty smacked the side of Tim's face. More feathered corpses flew past, turning over

---

* Which sounds *S*, in the low speech.

295

and over in the increasingly lively air. Some struck the side of the Dogan and fell around him.

Tim read the last words on the steel plate again: USE KEYCARD. If he had any doubt about what such a thing might be, he had only to look at the slot just below the words. He thought he even knew what a 'keycard' looked like, for he believed he had just seen it, along with a more recognizable key that might fit the ⸀-shaped keyhole of the metal box. Two keys – and possible salvation – hanging around the neck of a tyger that could probably swallow him down in three bites. And, since there had been no food that Tim could see in the cage, it might only take two.

This was smelling more and more like a practical joke, although only a very cruel man would find such a joke amusing. The sort of fellow who might use a bad fairy to lure a boy into a dangerous swamp, perhaps.

What to do? Was there anything he *could* do? Tim would have liked to ask Daria, but he was terribly afraid his friend in the plate – a good fairy to match the Covenant Man's bad one – was dead, killed by Directive Nineteen.

Slowly, he approached the cage, now having to lean against the wind. The tyger saw him and came padding around the hole in the middle to stand by the door of the cage. It lowered its great head and stared at him with its lambent eyes. The wind rippled its thick coat, making the stripes waver and seem to change places.

The tin bucket should have rolled away in the wind, but it didn't. Like the steel box, it seemed anchored in place.

The bucket he left for me back home, so I could see his lies and believe them.

The whole thing had been a joke, and under this bucket he would find the point of it, that final clever line – like *I can't fork hay with a spoon!* or *So then I turned her over and warmed the other side* – that was supposed to make folks roar with laughter. But since it was the end, why not? He could use a laugh.

Tim grasped the bucket and lifted it. He expected to find the Covenant Man's magic wand beneath, but no. The joke was better than that. It was another key, this one large and ornately carved. Like the Covenant Man's seeing-basin and the tyger's collar, it was made of silver. A note had been attached to the key's head with a bit of twine.

Across the gorge, the trees cracked and boomed. Now dust came rolling up from the chasm in giant clouds that were whipped away in ribbons like smoke.

The Covenant Man's note was brief:

Greetings, Brave and Resourceful Boy!
Welcome to the North Forest Kinnock,
which was once known as the Gateway

of Out-World. Here I have left you a troublesome Tyger. He is VERY hungry! But as you may have guessed, the Key to SHELTER hangs about his Neck. As you may have also guessed, this Key opens the Cage. Use it if you dare! With all regards to your Mother (whose New Husband will visit her SOON), I remain your Faithful Servant!

RF/MB

The man – if he was a man – who left Tim that note was surprised by very little, but he might have been surprised by the smile on the boy's face as he rose to his feet with the key in his hand and booted away the tin bucket. It rose and flew off on the rising wind, which had now almost reached gale-force. Its purpose had been served, and all the magic was out of it.

Tim looked at the tyger. The tyger looked at Tim. It seemed completely unaware of the rising storm. Its tail swished slowly back and forth.

'He thinks I'd rather be blown away or die of the cold than face your claws and teeth. Perhaps he didn't see this.' Tim drew the four-shot from his belt. 'It did for the fish-thing in the swamp, and I'm sure it would do for you, Sai Tyger.'

Tim was once more amazed by how right the gun felt. Its function was so simple, so clear. All it wanted to do was shoot. And when Tim held it, shooting was all he wanted to do.

But.

'Oh, he saw it,' Tim said, and smiled more widely. He could hardly feel the corners of his mouth drawing up, because the skin on his face had begun to grow numb from the cold. 'Yar, he saw it very well. Did he think I would get so far as this? Perhaps not. Did he think that if I did, I'd shoot you to live? Why not? *He* would. But why send a boy? Why, when he's probably hung a thousand men and cut a hundred throats and turned who knows how many poor widows like my mama out on the land? Can you answer that, Sai Tyger?'

The tyger only stared, head lowered and tail swishing slowly from side to side.

Tim put the four-shot back into his belt with one hand; with the other he slid the ornate silver key into the lock on the cage's curved door. 'Sai Tyger, I offer a bargain. Let me use the key around your neck to open yon shelter and we'll both live. But if you tear me to shreds, we'll both die. Does thee kennit? Give me a sign if thee does.'

The tyger gave no sign. It only stared at him.

Tim really hadn't expected one, and perhaps he didn't need one. There would be water if God willed it.

'I love you, Mama,' he said, and turned the key. There was a thud as the ancient tumblers turned. Tim grasped the door and pulled it open on hinges that uttered a thin screaming sound. Then he stood back with his hands at his sides.

For a moment the tyger stood where it was, as if suspicious. Then it padded out of the cage. He and Tim regarded each other beneath the deepening purple sky while the wind howled and the marching explosions neared. They regarded each other like gunslingers. The tyger began to walk forward. Tim took one step back, but understood if he took another his nerve would break and he would take to his heels. So he stood where he was.

'Come, thee. Here is Tim, son of Big Jack Ross.'

Instead of tearing out Tim's throat, the tyger sat down and raised its head to expose its collar and the keys that hung from it.

Tim did not hesitate. Later he might be able to afford the luxury of amazement, but not now. The wind was growing stronger by the second, and if he didn't act fast, he'd be lifted and blown into the trees, where he would probably be impaled. The tyger was heavier, but it would follow soon enough.

The key that looked like a card and the key that looked like an ¶ were welded to the silver collar, but the collar's clasp was easy enough. Tim squeezed its sides at the indentations and the collar dropped off. He had a moment to register the fact that the tyger was still wearing a collar – this one made of pink hide where the fur had been rubbed away – and then he was hurrying to the Dogan's metal door.

He lifted the keycard and inserted it. Nothing

300

happened. He turned it around and tried it the other way. Still nothing. The wind gusted, a cold dead hand that slammed him into the door and started his nose bleeding. He pushed back from it, turned the card upside down, and tried again. Still nothing. Tim suddenly remembered something Daria had said – had it only been three days ago? *North Forest Kinnock Dogan is off-line.* Tim guessed he now knew what that meant. The flasher on the tower of metal girders might still be working, but down here the sparkpower that had run the place was out. He had dared the tyger, and the tyger had responded by not eating him, but the Dogan was locked. They were going to die out here just the same.

It was the end of the joke, and somewhere the man in black was laughing.

He turned and saw the tyger pushing its nose against the metal box with the engraving on top. The beast looked up, then nuzzled the box again.

'All right,' Tim said. 'Why not?'

He knelt close enough to the tyger's lowered head to feel its warm breath puffing against his cold cheek. He tried the ¶-key. It fit the lock perfectly. For a moment he had a clear memory of using the key the Covenant Man had given him to open Kells's trunk. Then he turned this one, heard the click, and lifted the lid. Hoping for salvation.

Instead of that, he saw three items that seemed of no earthly use to him: a large white feather, a

301

small brown bottle, and a plain cotton napkin of the sort that were laid out on the long tables behind the Tree meeting hall before each year's Reaptide dinner.

The wind had passed gale-force; a ghostly screaming had begun as it blew through the criss-crossing girders of the metal tower. The feather whirled out of the box, but before it could fly away, the tyger stretched out its neck and snatched it in its teeth. It turned to the boy, holding it out. Tim took it and stuck it in his belt beside his father's hand-ax, not really thinking about it. He began to creep away from the Dogan on his hands and knees. Flying into the trees and being struck through by a branch would not be a pleasant way to die, but it might be better – quicker – than having the life crushed out of him against the Dogan while that deadly wind crept through his skin and into his vitals, freezing them.

The tyger growled; that sound of slowly ripping silk. Tim started to turn his head and was slammed into the Dogan. He fought to catch another breath, but the wind kept trying to rip it out of his mouth and nose.

Now it was the napkin the tyger was holding out, and as Tim finally whooped air into his lungs (it numbed his throat as it went down), he saw a surprising thing. Sai Tyger had picked the napkin up by the corner, and it had unfolded to four times its former size.

That's impossible.

Except he was seeing it. Unless his eyes – now gushing water that froze on his cheeks – were deceiving him, the napkin in the tyger's jaws had grown to the size of a towel. Tim reached out for it. The tyger held on until it saw the thing firmly clutched in Tim's numb fist, then let go. The gale was howling around them, now hard enough to make even a six-hundred-pound tyger brace against it, but the napkin that was now a towel hung limply from Tim's hand, as if in a dead calm.

Tim stared at the tyger. It stared back, seemingly at complete ease with itself and the howling world around it. The boy found himself thinking of the tin bucket, which had done as well for seeing as the Covenant Man's silver basin. *In the proper hand,* he had said, *any object can be magic.*

Mayhap even a humble swatch of cotton.

It was still doubled – at least doubled. Tim unfolded it again, and the towel became a tablecloth. He held it up in front of him, and although the rising gale continued to storm past on both sides, the air between his face and the hanging cloth was dead calm.

And *warm*.

Tim grabbed the tablecloth that had been a napkin in both hands, shook it, and it opened once again. Now it was a sheet, and it lay easily on the ground even though a storm of dust, twigs, and dead bin-rusties flew past it and on either side.

303

The sound of all that loose gunna striking the curved side of the Dogan was like hail. Tim started to crawl beneath the sheet, then hesitated, looking into the tyger's brilliant green eyes. He also looked at the thick spikes of its teeth, which its muzzle did not quite cover, before raising the corner of the magic cloth.

'Come on. Get under here. There's no wind or cold.'

But you knew that, Sai Tyger. Didn't you?

The tyger crouched, extended its admirable claws, and crawled forward on its belly until it was beneath the sheet. Tim felt something like a nest of wires brush down his arm as the tyger made itself comfortable: whiskers. He shivered. Then the long furred length of the beast was lying against the side of his body.

It was very large, and half its body still lay outside the thin white covering. Tim half rose, fighting the wind that buffeted his head and shoulders as they emerged into the open air, and shook the sheet again. There was a rippling sound as it once more unfolded, this time becoming the size of a lakeboat's mainsail. Now its hem lay almost at the base of the tyger's cage.

The world roared and the air raged, but beneath the sheet, all was still. Except, that was, for Tim's pounding heart. When that began to settle, he felt another heart pounding slowly against his ribcage. And heard a low, rough rumble. The tyger was purring.

'We're safe, aren't we?' Tim asked it.

The tyger looked at him for a moment, then closed its eyes. It seemed to Tim answer enough.

Night came, and the full fury of the starkblast came with it. Beyond the strong magic that had at first looked to be no more than a humble napkin, the cold grew apace, driven by a wind that was soon blowing at well over one hundred wheels an hour. The windows of the Dogan grew inch-thick cataracts of frost. The ironwood tres behind it first imploded inward, then toppled backward, then blew southward in a deadly cloud of branches, splinters, and entire treetrunks. Beside Tim, his bedmate snoozed on, oblivious. Its body relaxed and spread as its sleep deepened, pushing Tim toward the edge of their covering. At one point he found himself actually elbowing the tyger, the way one might elbow any fellow sleeper who is trying to steal all the covers. The tyger made a furry growling sound and flexed its claws, but moved away a bit.

'Thankee-sai,' Tim whispered.

An hour after sunset – or perhaps it was two; Tim's sense of time had gotten lost – a ghastly screeching sound joined the howl of the wind. The tyger opened its eyes. Tim cautiously pulled down the top edge of the sheet and looked out. The tower above the Dogan had begun to bend. He watched, fascinated, as the bend became a lean. Then, almost too fast to see, the tower disintegrated. At one moment it was there; at the next it was flying bars and spears of steel thrown by the wind into a wide lane of what had been, only that day, a forest of ironwood trees.

The Dogan will go next, Tim thought, but it didn't.

The Dogan stayed, as it had for a thousand years.

It was a night he never forgot, but one so fabulously strange that he could never describe it . . . or even remember rationally, as we remember the mundane events of our lives. Full understanding only returned to him in his dreams, and he dreamed of the starkblast until the end of his life. Nor were they nightmares. These were good dreams. They were dreams of safety.

It was warm beneath the sheet, and the sleeping bulk of his bunkmate made it even warmer. At some point he slipped down their covering enough to see a trillion stars sprawled across the dome of the sky, more than he had ever seen in his life. It was as if the storm had blown tiny holes in the world above the world, and turned it into a sieve. Shining through was all the brilliant mystery of creation. Perhaps such things were not meant for human eyes, but Tim felt sure he had been granted a special dispensation to look, for he was under a blanket of magic, and lying next to a creature even the most credulous villagers in Tree would have dismissed as mythical.

He felt awe as he looked up at those stars, but also a deep and abiding contentment, such as he had felt as a child, awakening in the night, safe and warm beneath his quilt, drowsing half in and half out of sleep, listening to the wind sing its lonely song of other places and other lives.

Time is a keyhole, he thought as he looked up at the stars. *Yes, I think so. We sometimes bend and peer through it. And the wind we feel on our cheeks when we do – the wind that blows through the keyhole – is the breath of all the living universe.*

The wind roared across the empty sky, the cold deepened, but Tim Ross lay safe and warm, with a tyger sleeping beside him. At some point he slipped away himself, into a rest that was deep and satisfying and untroubled by dreams. As he went, he felt that he was very wee, and flying on the wind that blew through time's keyhole. Away from the edge of the Great Canyon, over the Endless Forest and the Fagonard, above the Ironwood Trail, past Tree – just a brave little nestle of lights from where he rode the wind – and farther, farther, oh, very much farther, across the entire reach of Mid-World to where a huge ebony Tower reared itself into the heavens.

I will go there! Someday I will!

It was his last thought before sleep took him.

In the morning, the steady shriek of the wind had lowered to a drone. Tim's bladder was full. He pushed back the sheet, crawled out onto

307

ground that had been swept clean all the way to the bone of underlying rock, and hurried around the Dogan with his breath emerging from his mouth in bursts of white vapor that were immediately yanked away by the wind. The other side of the Dogan was in the lee of that wind, but it was cold, cold. His urine steamed, and by the time he finished, the puddle on the ground was starting to freeze.

He hurried back, fighting the wind for every step and shivering all over. By the time he crawled back beneath the magic sheet and into the blessed warmth, his teeth were chattering. He wrapped his arms around the tyger's heavily muscled body without even thinking, and had only a moment's fright when its eyes and mouth opened. A tongue that looked as long as a rug runner and as pink as a New Earth rose emerged. It licked the side of his face and Tim shivered again, not from fright but from memory: his father rubbing his cheek against Tim's early in the morning, before Big Ross filled the basin and scraped his face smooth. He said he would never grow a beard like his partner's, said 'twouldn't suit him.

The tyger lowered its head and began to sniff at the collar of his shirt. Tim laughed as its whiskers tickled his neck. Then he remembered the last two popkins. 'I'll share,' he said, 'although we know thee could have both if thee wanted.'

He gave one of the popkins to the tyger. It disappeared at once, but the beast only watched as Tim went to work on the other one. He ate it as fast as he could, just in case Sai Tyger changed its mind. Then he pulled the sheet over his head and drowsed off again.

When he woke the second time, he guessed it might be noon. The wind had dropped still more, and when he poked his head out, the air was a trifle warmer. Still, he guessed the false summer the Widow Smack had been so right to distrust was now gone for good. As was the last of his food.

'What did thee eat in there?' Tim asked the tyger. This question led naturally to another. 'And how long was thee caged?'

The tyger rose to its feet, walked a little distance toward the cage, and then stretched: first one rear leg and then the other. It walked farther toward the edge of the Great Canyon, where it did its own necessary. When it had finished, it sniffed the bars of its prison, then turned from the cage as though it were of no interest, and came back to where Tim lay propped on his elbows, watching.

It regarded him somberly – so it seemed to Tim – with its green eyes, then lowered its head and nosed back the magic sheet that had sheltered them from the starkblast. The metal box lay beneath. Tim couldn't remember picking it up, but he must have; if it had been left where it was, it would have blown away. That made him think of the feather. It was still safely tucked in his belt. He took it out and examined it closely, running his fingers over its rich thickness. It might have been a hawk feather . . . if, that was, it had been half the size. Or if he had ever seen a white hawk, which he had not.

'This came from an eagle, didn't it?' Tim asked. 'Gan's blood, it *did.*'

The tyger seemed uninterested in the feather, although it had been eager enough to snatch it from the breath of the rising storm last evening. The long, yellow-fuzzed snout lowered and pushed the box at Tim's hip. Then it looked at him.

Tim opened the box. The only thing left inside was the brown bottle, which looked like the sort that might contain medicine. Tim picked it up and immediately felt a tingle in his fingertips, very like the one he'd felt in the Covenant Man's magic wand when he passed it back and forth over the tin bucket.

'Shall I open it? For it's certain thee can't.'

The tyger sat, its green eyes fixed unwaveringly on the tiny bottle. Those eyes seemed to glow from within, as if its very brain burned with magic. Carefully, Tim unscrewed the top. When he took it off, he saw a small transparent dropper fixed beneath.

The tyger opened its mouth. The meaning was clear enough, but . . .

'How much?' Tim asked. 'I'd not poison thee for the world.'

The tyger only sat with its head slightly uptilted and its mouth open, looking like a baby bird waiting to receive a worm.

After a little experimentation – he'd never used a dropper before, although he'd seen a larger, cruder version that Destry called a bull-squirter – Tim got some of the fluid into the little tube. It sucked up almost all the liquid in the bottle, for there was only a bit. He held it over the tyger's mouth, heart beating hard. He thought he knew what was going to happen, for he had heard many legends of skin-men, but it was impossible to be sure the tyger was an enchanted human.

'I'll put it in drop by drop,' he told the tyger. 'If you want me to stop before it's gone, close thy mouth. Give me a sign if you understand.'

But, as before, the tyger gave no sign. It only sat, waiting.

One drop . . . two . . . three . . . the little tube half-empty now . . . four . . . fi—

Suddenly the tyger's skin began to ripple and bulge, as if creatures were trapped beneath and struggling to get out. The snout melted away to reveal its cage of teeth, then reknit itself so completely that its mouth was sealed over. Then it gave a muffled roar of either pain or outrage, seeming to shake the clearing.

Tim scooted away on his bottom, terrified.

The green eyes began to bulge in and out, as if on springs. The lashing tail was yanked inward,

311

reappeared, was yanked inward again. The tyger staggered away, this time toward the precipice at the edge of the Great Canyon.

'*Stop!*' Tim screamed. '*Thee'll fall over!*'

The tyger lurched drunkenly along the edge, one paw actually going over and dislodging a spall of pebbles. It walked behind the cage that had held it, the stripes first blurring, then fading. Its head was changing shape. White emerged, and then, above it, a brilliant yellow where its snout had been. Tim could hear a grinding sound as the very bones inside its body rearranged themselves.

On the far side of the cage, the tyger roared again, but halfway through, the roar became a very human cry. The blurring, changing creature reared up on its back legs, and where there had been paws, Tim now saw a pair of ancient black boots. The claws became silver siguls: moons, crosses, spirals.

The yellow top of the tyger's head continued to grow until it became the conical hat Tim had seen in the tin pail. The white below it, where the tyger's bib had been, turned into a beard that sparkled in the cold and windy sunshine. It sparkled because it was full of rubies, emeralds, sapphires, and diamonds.

Then the tyger was gone, and Maerlyn of the Eld stood revealed before the wondering boy.

He was not smiling, as he had been in Tim's vision of him . . . but of course that had never been *his* vision at all. It had been the Covenant

Man's glammer, meant to lead him on to destruction. The real Maerlyn looked at Tim with kindness, but also with gravity. The wind blew his robe of white silk around a body so thin it could have been little more than a skeleton.

Tim got on one knee, bowed his head, and raised a trembling fist to his brow. He tried to say *Hile, Maerlyn,* but his voice had deserted him, and he could manage nothing but a dusty croak.

'Rise, Tim, son of Jack,' the mage said. 'But before you do, put the cap back on the bottle. There's a few drops left, I wot, and you'll want them.'

Tim raised his head and looked questioningly at the tall figure standing beside the cage that had held him.

'For thy mother,' said Maerlyn. 'For thy mother's eyes.'

'Say true?' Tim whispered.

'True as the Turtle that holds up the world. You've come a goodly way, you've shown great bravery – and not a little foolishness, but we'll pass that, since they often go together, especially in the young – and you've freed me from a shape I've been caught in for many and many-a. For that you must be rewarded. Now cap the bottle and get on your feet.'

'Thankee,' Tim said. His hands were trembling and his eyes were blurred with tears, but he managed to get the cap on the bottle without spilling what was left. 'I thought you were a

Guardian of the Beam, so I did, but Daria told me different.'

'And who is Daria?'

'A prisoner, like you. Locked in a little machine the people of the Fagonard gave me. I think she's dead.'

'Sorry for your loss, son.'

'She was my friend,' Tim said simply.

Maerlyn nodded. 'It's a sad world, Tim Ross. As for me, since this is the Beam of the Lion, 'twas his little joke to put me in the shape of a great cat. Although not in the shape of Aslan, for that's magic not even he can do . . . although he'd like to, aye. Or slay Aslan and all the other Guardians, so the Beams collapse.'

'The Covenant Man,' Tim whispered.

Maerlyn threw back his head and laughed. His conical cap stayed on, which Tim thought magical in itself. 'Nay, nay, not he. Little magic and long life's all *he's* capable of. No, Tim, there's one far greater than he of the broad cloak. When the Great One points his finger from where he bides, the Broad Cloak scurries. But sending you was none of the Red King's bidding, and the one you call the Covenant Man will pay for his foolery, I'm sure. He's too valuable to kill, but to hurt? To *punish*? Aye, I think so.'

'What will he do to him? This Red King?'

'Best not to know, but of one thing you can be sure: no one in Tree will ever see him again. His tax-collecting days are finally over.'

'And will my mother . . . will she really be able to see again?'

'Aye, for you have done me fine. Nor will I be the last you'll serve in your life.' He pointed at Tim's belt. 'That's only the first gun you'll wear, and the lightest.'

Tim looked at the four-shot, but it was his father's ax he took from his belt. 'Guns are not for such as me, sai. I'm just a village boy. I'll be a woodcutter, like my father. Tree's my place, and I'll stay there.'

The old mage looked at him shrewdly. 'You say so with the ax in your hand, but would you say so if 'twas the gun? Would your *heart* say so? Don't answer, for I see the truth in your eyes. Ka will take you far from Tree Village.'

'But I love it,' Tim whispered.

'Thee'll bide there yet awhile, so be not fashed. But hear me well, and obey.'

He put his hands on his knees and leaned his tall, scrawny body toward Tim. His beard lashed in the dying wind, and the jewels caught in it flickered like fire. His face was gaunt, like the Covenant Man's, but illuminated by gravity instead of malicious humor, and by kindness rather than cruelty.

'When you return to your cottage – a trip that will be much faster than the one you made to get here, and far less risky – you will go to your mother and put the last drops from the bottle in her eyes. Then you must give thy father's ax to

315

her. Do you understand me? His coin you'll wear all your life – you'll be buried with it yet around your neck – *but give the ax to thy mother.* Do it at once.'

'W-Why?'

The wild tangle of Maerlyn's brows drew together; his mouth turned down at the corners; suddenly the kindness was gone, replaced by a frightening obduracy. 'Not yours to ask, boy. When ka comes, it comes like the wind – like the starkblast. Will you obey?'

'Yes,' Tim said, frightened. 'I'll give it to her as you say.'

'Good.'

The mage turned to the sheet beneath which they had slept and raised his hands over it. The end near the cage flipped up with a brisk ruffling sound, folded over, and was suddenly half the size it had been. It flipped up again and became the size of a tablecloth. Tim thought the women of Tree would much like to have magic like that when beds needed to be made, and wondered if such an idea were blasphemy.

'No, no, I'm sure you're right,' Maerlyn said absently. 'But 'twould go wrong and cause hijinks. Magic's full of tricks, even for an old fellow like me.'

'Sai . . . is it true you live backwards in time?'

Maerlyn raised his hands in amused irritation; the sleeves of his robe slipped back, revealing arms as thin and white as birch branches. 'Everyone thinks so, and if I said different, they'd still think it, wouldn't they? I live as I live, Tim, and the truth is, I'm mostly retired these days. Have you also heard of my magical house in the woods?'

'Aye!'

'And if I told you I lived in a cave with nothing but a single table and a pallet on the floor, and if you told others that, would they believe you?'

Tim considered this, and shook his head. 'No. They wouldn't. I doubt folk will believe I met you at all.'

'That's their business. As for yours . . . are you ready to go back?'

'May I ask one more question?'

The mage raised a single finger. '*Only* one. For I've been here many long years in yon cage – which you see keeps its place to the very inch, in spite of how hard the wind blew – and I'm tired of shitting in that hole. Living monk-simple is all very fine, but there's a limit. Ask your question.'

'How did the Red King catch thee?'

'He can't catch anyone, Tim – he's himself caught, pent at the top of the Dark Tower. But he has his powers, and he has his emissaries. The one you met is far from the greatest of them. A man came to my cave. I was fooled into believing he was a wandering peddler, for his magic was strong. Magic lent to him by the King, as you must ken.'

Tim risked another question. 'Magic stronger than yours?'

'Nay, but . . .' Maerlyn sighed and looked up

at the morning sky. Tim was astounded to realize that the magician was embarrassed. 'I was drunk.'

'Oh,' Tim said in a small voice. He could think of nothing else to say.

'Enough palaver,' said the mage 'Sit on the dibbin.'

'The—?'

Maerlyn gestured at what was sometimes a napkin, sometimes a sheet, and was now a table-cloth. 'That. And don't worry about dirtying it with your boots. It's been used by many far more travel-stained than thee.'

Tim had been worried about exactly that, but he stepped onto the tablecloth and then sat down.

'Now the feather. Take it in your hands. It's from the tail of Garuda, the eagle who guards the other end of this Beam. Or so I was told, although as a wee one myself – yes, I was once wee, Tim, son of Jack – I was also told that babies were found under cabbages in the garden.'

Tim barely heard this. He took the feather which the tyger had saved from flying away into the wind, and held it.

Maerlyn regarded him from beneath his tall yellow cap. 'When thee gets home, what's the first thing thee'll do?'

'Put the drops in Mama's eyes.'

'Good, and the second?'

'Give her my da's ax.'

'Don't forget.' The old man leaned forward and

kissed Tim's brow. For a moment the whole world flared as brilliantly in the boy's eyes as the stars at the height of the starkblast. For a moment it was all *there*. 'Thee's a brave boy with a stout heart – as others will see and come to call you. Now go with my thanks, and fly away home.'

'F-F-Fly? *How?*'

'How does thee walk? Just think of it. Think of home.' A thousand wrinkles flowed from the corners of the old man's eyes as he broke into a radiant grin. 'For, as someone or other famous once said, there's no place like home. See it! See it very well!'

So Tim thought of the cottage where he had grown up, and the room where he had all his life fallen asleep listening to the wind outside, telling its stories of other places and other lives. He thought of the barn where Misty and Bitsy were stabled, and hoped someone was feeding them. Straw Willem, perhaps. He thought of the spring where he had drawn so many buckets of water. He thought most of all of his mother: her sturdy body with its wide shoulders, her chestnut hair, her eyes when they had been full of laughter instead of worry and woe.

He thought, *How I miss you, Mama . . .* and when he did, the tablecloth rose from the rocky ground and hovered over its shadow.

Tim gasped. The cloth rocked, then turned. Now he was higher than Maerlyn's cap, and the magician had to look up at him.

'What if I fall?' Tim cried.

Maerlyn laughed. 'Sooner or later, we all do. For now, hold tight to the feather! The dibbin won't spill thee, so just hold tight to the feather and think of home!'

Tim clutched it before him and thought of Tree: the high street, the smithy with the burial parlor between it and the cemetery, the farms, the sawmill by the river, the Widow's cottage, and – most of all – his own plot and place. The dibbin rose higher, floated above the Dogan for several moments (as if deciding), then headed south along the track of the starkblast. It moved slowly at first, but when its shadow fell over the tangled, frost-rimed deadfalls that had lately been a million acres of virgin forest, it began to go faster.

A terrible thought came to Tim: what if the starkblast had rolled over Tree, freezing it solid and killing everyone, including Nell Ross? He turned to call his question back to Maerlyn, but Maerlyn was already gone. Tim saw him once more, but when that happened, Tim was an old man himself. And that is a story for another day.

The dibbin rose until the world below was spread out like a map. Yet the magic that had protected Tim and his furry bedmate from the storm still held, and although he could hear the last of the starkblast's cold breath whooshing all around him, he was perfectly warm. He sat cross-legged on his transport like a young prince of the

Mohaine on an elephaunt, the Feather of Garuda held out before him. He *felt* like Garuda, soaring above a great tract of wildland that looked like a giant dress of a green so dark it was almost black. Yet a gray scar ran through it, as if the dress had been slashed to reveal a dirty underskirt beneath. The starkblast had ruined everything it had touched, although the forest as a whole was very little hurt. The lane of destruction was no more than forty wheels wide.

Yet forty wheels wide had been enough to lay waste to the Fagonard. The black swampwater had become yellowish-white cataracts of ice. The gray, knotted trees that had grown out of that water had all been knocked over. The tussocks were no longer green; now they looked like tangles of milky glass.

Run aground on one of them and lying on its side was the tribe's boat. Tim thought of Helmsman and Headman and all the others, and burst into bitter tears. If not for them, he would be lying frozen on one of those tussocks five hundred feet below. The people of the swamp had fed him, and they had gifted him with Daria, his good fairy. It was not fair, it was not fair, it was not fair. So cried his child's heart, and then his child's heart died a little. For that is also the way of the world.

Before leaving the swamp behind, he saw something else that hurt his heart: a large blackened patch where the ice had been melted. Sooty chunks of ice floated around a vast, plated corse lying on its side like the beached boat. It was the dragon that had spared him. Tim could imagine – aye, all too well – how she must have fought the cold with blasts of her fiery breath, but in the end the starkblast had taken her, as it had everything else in the Fagonard. It was now a place of frozen death.

Above the Ironwood Trail, the dibbin began to descend. Down and down it glided, and when it came to the Cosington-Marchly stub, it touched down. But before the wider sweep of the world was lost, Tim had observed the path of the starkblast, formerly dead south, bending to a course more westerly. And the damage seemed less, as if the storm had been starting to lift off. It gave him hope that the village had been spared.

He studied the dibbin thoughtfully, and then waved his hands over it. 'Fold!' he said (feeling a trifle foolish). The dibbin did not, but when he bent to do the job himself, it flipped over once, then twice, then thrice, becoming smaller each time – but no thicker. In a matter of seconds it once more appeared to be nothing but a cotton napkin lying on the path. Not one you'd want to spread on your lap at dinner, though, for it had a bootprint square in the middle of it.

Tim put it in his pocket and began walking. And, when he reached the blossie groves (where most of the trees were still standing), he began to run.

He skirted the town, for he didn't want to waste even minutes answering questions. Few people would have had time for him, anyway. The starkblast *had* largely spared Tree, but he saw folk tending to livestock they'd managed to pull from flattened barns, and inspecting their fields for damage. The sawmill had been blown into Tree River. The pieces had floated away downstream, and nothing was left but the stone foundation.

He followed Stape Brook, as he had on the day when he had found the Covenant Man's magic wand. Their spring, which had been frozen, was already beginning to thaw, and although some of the blossie shingles had been ripped from the roof of the cottage, the building itself stood as firm as ever. It looked as though his mother had been left alone, for there were no wagons or mules out front. Tim understood that people would want to see to their own plots with such a storm as a starkblast coming, but it still made him angry. To leave a woman who was blind and beaten to the whims of a storm . . . that wasn't right. And it wasn't the way folk in Tree neighbored.

Someone took her to safety, he told himself. *To the Gathering Hall, most likely.*

Then he heard a bleat from the barn that didn't sound like either of their mules. Tim poked his head in, and smiled. The Widow Smack's little burro, Sunshine, was tethered to a post, munching hay.

Tim reached into his pocket and felt a moment's panic when he couldn't find the precious bottle. Then he discovered it hiding under the dibbin, and his heart eased. He climbed to the porch (the familiar creak of the third step making him feel like a boy in a dream), and eased the door open. The cottage was warm, for the Widow had made a good fire in the hearth, which was only now burning down to a thick bed of gray ash and rosy embers. She sat sleeping in his da's chair with her back to him and her face to the fire. Although he was wild to go to his mother, he paused long enough to slip off his boots. The Widow had come when there was no one else; she had built a fire to keep the cottage warm; even with the prospect of what looked like ruin for the whole village, she had not forgotten how to neighbor. Tim wouldn't have wakened her for anything.

He tiptoed to the bedroom door, which stood open. There in bed lay his mother, her hands clasped on the counterpane, her eyes staring sightlessly up at the ceiling.

'Mama?' Tim whispered.

For a moment she didn't stir, and Tim felt a cold shaft of fear. He thought, *I'm too late. She's a-lying there dead.*

Then Nell rose on her elbows, her hair cascading in a flood to the down pillow behind her, and looked toward him. Her face was wild with hope. 'Tim? Is it you, or am I dreaming?'

'You're awake,' he said.

And rushed to her.

Her arms enfolded him in a strong grip, and she covered his face with the heartfelt kisses that are only a mother's to give. 'I thought you were killed! Oh, Tim! And when the storm came, I made sure of it, and I wanted to die myself. Where have you been? How could you break my heart so, you bad boy?' And then the kissing began again.

Tim gave himself over to it, smiling and rejoicing in the familiar clean smell of her, but then he remembered what Maerlyn had said: *When thee gets home, what's the first thing thee'll do?*

'Where have you been? Tell me!'

'I'll tell you everything, Mama, but first lie back and open your eyes wide. As wide as you can.'

'Why?' Her hands kept fluttering over his eyes and nose and mouth, as if to reassure herself that he was really here. The eyes Tim hoped to cure stared at him . . . and through him. They had begun to take on a milky look. 'Why, Tim?'

He didn't want to say, in case the promised cure didn't work. He didn't believe Maerlyn would have lied – it was the Covenant Man who made lies his hobby – but he might have been mistaken.

Oh please, don't let him have been mistaken.

'Never mind. I've brought medicine, but there's only a little, so you must lie very still.'

'I don't understand.'

In her darkness, Nell thought what he said next might have come from the dead father rather than the living son. 'Just know I've been far and dared much for what I hold. Now lie still!'

She did as he bade, looking up at him with her blind eyes. Her lips were trembling.

Tim's hands were, too. He commanded them to grow still, and for a wonder, they did. He took a deep breath, held it, and unscrewed the top of the precious bottle. He drew all there was into the dropper, which was little enough. The liquid didn't even fill half of the short, thin tube. He leaned over Nell.

'Still, Mama! Promise me, for it may burn.'

'Still as can be,' she whispered.

One drop in the left eye. 'Does it?' he asked. 'Does it burn?'

'No,' said she. 'Cool as a blessing. Put some in the other, will ya please.'

Tim put a drop into the right eye, then sat back, biting his lip. Was the milkiness a little less, or was that only wishing?

'Can you see anything, Mama?'

'No, but . . .' Her breath caught. 'There's light! *Tim, there's light!*'

She started to rise up on her elbows again, but Tim pressed her back. He put another drop in each eye. It would have to be enough, for the dropper was empty. A good thing, too, for when Nell shrieked, Tim dropped it on the floor.

'Mama? *Mama!* What is it?'

'*I see thy face!*' she cried, and put her hands on his cheeks. Now her eyes were filling with tears, but that did Tim very well, because now they were looking at him instead of through him. And they were as bright as they ever had been. 'Oh, Tim, oh my dear, *I see thy face, I see it very well!*'

Next came a bit of time which needs no telling – a good thing, too, for some moments of joy are beyond description.

You must give thy father's ax to her.

Tim fumbled in his belt, brought the hand-ax from it, and placed it beside her on the bed. She looked at it – and saw it, a thing still marvelous to both of them – then touched the handle, which had been worn smooth by long years and much use. She raised her face to him questioningly.

Tim could only shake his head, smiling. 'The man who gave me the drops told me to give it to you. That's all I know.'

'Who, Tim? What man?'

'That's a long story, and one that would go better with some breakfast.'

'Eggs!' she said, starting to rise. 'At least a dozen! And the pork side from the cold pantry!'

Still smiling, Tim gripped her shoulders and pushed her gently back to the pillow. 'I can scramble eggs and fry meat. I'll even bring it to you.' A thought occurred to him. 'Sai Smack can eat with us. It's a wonder all the shouting didn't wake her.'

'She came when the wind began to blow, and was up all through the storm, feeding the fire,' Nell said. 'We thought the house would blow over, but it stood. She must be so tired. Wake her, Tim, but be gentle about it.'

Tim kissed his mother's cheek again and left the room. The Widow slept on in the dead man's chair by the fire, her chin upon her breast, too tired even to snore. Tim shook her gently by the shoulder. Her head jiggled and rolled, then fell back to its original position.

Filled with a horrid certainty, Tim went around to the front of the chair. What he saw stole the strength from his legs and he collapsed to his knees. Her veil had been torn away. The ruin of a face once beautiful hung slack and dead. Her once remaining eye stared blankly at Tim. The bosom of her black dress was rusty with dried blood, for her throat had been cut from ear to ear.

He drew in breath to scream, but was unable to let it out, for strong hands had closed around his throat.

Bern Kells had stolen into the main room from the mudroom, where he had been sitting on his trunk and trying to remember why he had killed the old woman. He thought it was the fire.

He had spent two nights shivering under a pile of hay in Deaf Rincon's barn, and this old kitty, she who had put all sorts of useless learning into his stepson's head, had been warm as toast the whole time. 'Twasn't right.

He had watched the boy go into his mother's room. He had heard Nell's cries of joy, and each one was like a nail in his vitals. She had no right to cry out with anything but pain. She was the author of all his misery; had bewitched him with her high breasts, slim waist, long hair, and laughing eyes. He had believed her hold on his mind would lessen over the years, but it never had. Finally he simply had to have her. Why else would he have murdered his best and oldest friend?

Now came the boy who had turned him into a hunted man. The bitch was bad and the whelp was worse. And what was that jammed into his belt? Was it a gun, by gods? Where had he gotten such a thing?

Kells choked Tim until the boy's struggles began to weaken and he simply hung from the woodsman's strong hands, rasping. Then he plucked the gun from Tim's belt and tossed it aside.

'A bullet's too good for a meddler such as you,' Kells said. His mouth was against Tim's ear. Distantly – as if all sensation were retreating deep into his body – Tim felt his steppa's beard tickling his skin. 'So's the knife I used to cut the diseased old bitch's throat. It's the fire for you, whelp.

There's plenty of coals yet. Enough to fry your eyeballs and boil the skin from your—'

There was a low, meaty sound, and suddenly the choking hands were gone. Tim turned, gasping in air that burned like fire.

Kells stood beside Big Ross's chair, looking unbelievingly over Tim's head at the gray field-stone chimney. Blood pattered down on the right sleeve of his flannel woodsman's shirt, which was still speckled with hay from his fugitive nights in Deaf Rincon's barn. Above his right ear, his head had grown an ax-handle. Nell Ross stood behind him, the front of her nightgown spattered with blood.

Slowly, slowly, Big Kells shuffled around to face her. He touched the buried blade of the ax, and held his hand out to her, the palm full of blood.

'I cut the rope so, chary man!' Nell screamed into his face, and as if the words rather than the ax had done it, Bern Kells collapsed dead on the floor.

Tim put his hands to his face, as if to blot from sight and memory the thing he had just seen . . . although he knew even then it would be with him the rest of his life.

Nell put her arms around him and led him out onto the porch. The morning was bright, the frost on the fields beginning to melt, a misty haze rising in the air.

330

'Are you all right, Tim?' she asked.

He drew in a deep breath. The air in his throat was still warm, but no longer burning. 'Yes. Are you?'

'I'll be fine,' said she. '*We'll* be fine. It's a beautiful morning, and we're alive to see it.'

'But the Widow . . .' Tim began to cry.

They sat down on the porch steps and looked out on the yard where not long ago, the Barony Covenanter had sat astride his tall black horse. *Black horse, black heart*, Tim thought.

'We'll pray for Ardelia Smack,' Nell said, 'and all of Tree will come to her burying. I'll not say Kells did her a favor – murder's never a favor – but she suffered terribly for the last three years, and her life would not have been long, in any case. I think we should go to town, and see if the constable's back from Taveres. On the way, you can tell me everything. Can thee help me hitch Misty and Bitsy to the wagon?'

'Yes, Mama. But I have to get something, first. Something she gave me.'

'All right. Try not to look at what's left in there, Tim.'

Nor did he. But he picked up the gun, and put it in his belt . . .

331

THE SKIN-MAN (PART 2)

'She told him not to look at what was left inside – the body of his steppa, you ken – and he said he wouldn't. Nor did he, but he picked up the gun, and put it in his belt—'

'The four-shot the widow-woman gave him,' Young Bill Streeter said. He was sitting against the cell wall below the chalked map of Debaria with his chin on his chest; he had said little, and in truth, I thought the lad had fallen asleep and I was telling the tale only to myself. But he had been listening all along, it seemed. Outside, the rising wind of the simoom rose to a brief shriek, then settled back to a low and steady moan.

'Aye, Young Bill. He picked up the gun, put it in his belt on the left side, and carried it there for the next ten years of his life. After that he carried bigger ones – six-shooters.' That was the story, and I ended it just as my mother had ended all the stories she read me when I was but a sma' one in my tower room. It made me sad to hear those words from my own mouth. 'And so it happened, once upon a bye, long before your grandfather's grandfather was born.'

Outside, the light was beginning to fail. I thought it would be tomorrow after all before the deputation that had gone up to the foothills would return with the salties who could sit a horse. And really, did it matter so much? For an uncomfortable thought had come to me while I was telling Young Bill the story of Young Tim. If I were the skin-man, and if the sheriff and a bunch of deputies (not to mention a young gunslinger all the way from Gilead) came asking if I could saddle, mount, and ride, would I admit it? Not likely. Jamie and I should have seen this right away, but of course we were still new to the lawman's way of thinking.

'Sai?'

'Yes, Bill.'

'Did Tim ever become a real gunslinger? He did, didn't he?'

'When he was twenty-one, three men carrying hard calibers came through Tree. They were bound for Tavares and hoping to raise a posse, but Tim was the only one who would go with them. They called him "the lefthanded gun," for that was the way he drew.

'He rode with them, and acquitted himself well, for he was both fearless and a dead shot. They called him tet-fa, or friend of the tet. But there came a day when he became *ka*-tet, one

336

of the very, very few gunslingers not from the proven line of Eld. Although who knows? Don't they say that Arthur had many sons from three wives, and moity-more born on the dark side of the blanket?'

'I dunno what that means.'

With that I could sympathize; until two days before, I hadn't known what was meant by 'the longstick.'

'Never mind. He was known first as Lefty Ross, then – after a great battle on the shores of Lake Cawn – as Tim Stoutheart. His mother finished her days in Gilead as a great lady, or so my mother said. But all those things are—'

'—a tale for another day,' Bill finished. 'That's what my da' always says when I ask for more.' His face drew in on itself and his mouth trembled at the corners as he remembered the bloody bunkhouse and the cook who had died with his apron over his face. 'What he *said*.'

I put my arm around his shoulders again, a thing that felt a little more natural this time. I'd made my mind up to take him back to Gilead with us if Everlynne of Serenity refused to take him in . . . but I thought she would not refuse. He was a good boy.

Outside the wind whined and howled. I kept an ear out for the jing-jang, but it stayed silent. The lines were surely down somewhere.

'Sai, how long was Maerlyn caged as a tyger?'

'I don't know, but a very long time, surely.'

'What did he *eat*?'

Cuthbert would have made something up on the spot, but I was stumped.

'If he was shitting in the hole, he must have eaten,' Bill said, and reasonably enough. 'If you don't eat, you can't shit.'

'I don't know what he ate, Bill.'

'P'raps he had enough magic left – even as a tyger – to make his own dinner. Out of thin air, like.'

'Yes, that's probably it.'

'Did Tim ever reach the Tower? For there are stories about that, too, aren't there?'

Before I could answer, Strother – the fat deputy with the rattlesnake hatband – came into the jail. When he saw me sitting with my arm around the boy, he gave a smirk. I considered wiping it off his face – it wouldn't have taken long – but forgot the idea when I heard what he had to say.

'Riders comin. Must be a moit, and wagons, because we can hear em even over the damn beastly wind. People is steppin out into the grit to see.'

I got up and let myself out of the cell.

'Can I come?' Bill asked.

'Better that you bide here yet awhile,' I said, and locked him in. 'I won't be long.'

'I hate it here, sai!'

'I know,' I told him. 'It'll be over soon enough.'

I hoped I was right about that.

★ ★ ★

When I stepped out of the sheriff's office, the wind made me stagger and alkali grit stung my cheeks. In spite of the rising gale, both boardwalks of the high street were lined with spectators. The men had pulled their bandannas over their mouths and noses; the women were using their kerchiefs. I saw one lady-sai wearing her bonnet backwards, which looked strange but was probably quite useful against the dust.

To my left, horses began to emerge from the whitish clouds of alkali. Sheriff Peavy and Canfield of the Jefferson were in the van, with their hats yanked low and their neckcloths pulled high, so only their eyes showed. Behind them came three long flatbed wagons, open to the wind. They were painted blue, but their sides and decks were rimed white with salt. On the side of each of the words DEBARIA SALT COMBYNE had been daubed in yellow paint. On each deck sat six or eight fellow in overalls and the straw workingmen's hats known as clobbers (or clumpets, I disremember which). On one side of this caravan rode Jamie DeCurry, Kellin Frye, and Kellin's son, Vikka. On the other were Snip and Arn from the Jefferson spread and a big fellow with a sand-colored handlebar mustache and a yellow duster to match. This turned out to be the man who served as constable in Little Debaria . . . at least when he wasn't otherwise occupied at the faro or Watch Me tables.

None of the new arrivals looked happy, but the

salties looked least happy of all. It was easy to regard them with suspicion and dislike; I had to remind myself that only one was a monster (assuming, that was, the skin-man hadn't slipped our net entirely). Most of the others had probably come of their own free will when told they could help put an end to the scourge by doing so.

I stepped into the street and raised my hands over my head. Sheriff Peavy reined up in front of me, but I ignored him for the time being, looking instead at the huddled miners in the flatbed wagons. A swift count made their number twenty-one. That was twenty more suspects than I wanted, but far fewer than I had feared.

I shouted to make myself heard over the wind. *'You men have come to help us, and on behalf of Gilead, I say thankya!'*

They were easier to hear, because the wind was blowing toward me. 'Balls to your Gilead,' said one. 'Snot-nosed brat,' said another. 'Lick my johnny on behalf of Gilead,' said a third.

'I can smarten em up anytime you'd like,' said the man with the handlebar mustache. 'Say the word, young'un, for I'm constable of the shithole they come from, and that makes em my fill. Will Wegg.' He put a perfunctory fist to his brow.

'Never in life,' I said, and raised my voice again. *'How many of you men want a drink?'*

That stopped their grumbling in its tracks, and they raised a cheer instead.

'*Then climb down and line up!*' I shouted. '*By twos, if you will!*' I grinned at them. '*And if you won't, go to hell and go there thirsty!*'

That made most of them laugh.

'Sai Deschain,' Wegg said, 'puttin drink in these fellers ain't a good idea.'

But I thought it was. I motioned Kellin Frye to me and dropped two gold knucks into his hand. His eyes widened.

'You're the trail-boss of this herd,' I told him. 'What you've got there should buy them two whiskeys apiece, if they're short shots, and that's all I want them to have. Take Canfield with you, and that one there.' I pointed to one of the pokies. 'Is it Arn?'

'Snip,' the fellow said. 'T'other one's Arn.'

'Aye, good. Snip, you at one end of the bar, Canfield at the other. Frye, you stand behind them at the door and watch their backs.'

'I won't be taking my son into the Busted Luck,' Kellin Frye said. 'It's a whore-hole, so it is.'

'You won't need to. Soh Vikka goes around back with the other pokie.' I cocked my thumb at Arn. 'All you two fellows need to do is watch for any saltie trying to sneak out the back door. If you do, let loose a yell and then scat, because he'll probably be our man. Understand?'

'Yep,' Arn said. 'Come on, kid, off we go. Maybe if I get out of this wind, I can get a smoke to stay lit.'

'Not just yet,' I said, and beckoned to the boy.

'Hey, gunbunny!' one of the miners yelled. 'You gonna let us out of this wind before nightfall? I'm fuckin thirsty!'

The others agreed.

'Hold your gabber,' I said. 'Do that, and you get to wet your throat. Run your gums at me while I'm doing my job and you'll sit out here in the back of a wagon and lick salt.'

That quieted them, and I bent to Vikka Frye. 'You were to tell someone something while you were up there at the Salt Rocks. Did you do it?'

'Yar, I—' His father elbowed him almost hard enough to knock him over. The boy remembered his manners and started again, this time with a fist to his brow. 'Yes, sai, do it please you.'

'Who did you speak to?'

'Puck DeLong. He's a boy I know from Reap Fairday. He's just a miner's kid, but we palled around some, and did the three-leg race together. His da's foreman of the nightwork crew. That's what Puck says, anyways.'

'And what did you tell him?'

'That it was Billy Streeter who seen the skin-man in his human shape. I said how Billy hid under a pile of old tack, and that was what saved him. Puck knew who I was talking about, because Billy was at Reap Fairday, too. It was Billy who won the Goose Dash. Do you know the Goose Dash, sai gunslinger?'

'Yes,' I said. I had run it myself on more

than one Reap Fairday, and not that long ago, either.

Vikka Frye swallowed hard, and his eyes filled with tears. 'Billy's da' cheered like to bust his throat when Billy come in first,' he whispered.

'I'm sure he did. Did this Puck DeLong put the story on its way, do you think?'

'Dunno, do I? But I would've, if it'd been me.'

I thought that was good enough, and clapped Vikka on the shoulder. 'Go on, now. And if anyone tries to take it on the sneak, raise a shout. A good loud one, so to be heard over the wind.'

He and Arn struck off for the alley that would take them behind the Busted Luck. The salties paid them no mind; they only had eyes for the batwing doors and thoughts for the rotgut waiting behind them.

'*Men!*' I shouted. And when they turned to me: '*Wet thy whistles!*'

That brought another cheer, and they set off for the saloon. But walking, not running, and still two by two. They had been well trained. I guessed that their lives as miners were little more than slavery, and I was thankful ka had pointed me along a different path . . . although, when I look back on it, I wonder how much difference there might be between the slavery of the mine and the slavery of the gun. Perhaps one: I've always had the sky to look at, and for that I tell Gan, the Man Jesus, and all the other gods that may be, thankya.

*   *   *

343

I motioned Jamie, Sheriff Peavy, and the new one – Wegg – to the far side of the street. We stood beneath the overhang that shielded the sheriff's office. Strother and Pickens, the not-so-good deputies, were crowded into the doorway, fair goggling.

'Go inside, you two,' I told them.

'We don't take orders from you,' Pickens said, just as haughty as Mary Dame, now that the boss was back.

'Go inside and shut the door,' Peavy said. 'Have you thudbrains not kenned even yet who's in charge of this raree?'

They drew back, Pickens glaring at me and Strother glaring at Jamie. The door slammed hard enough to rattle the glass. For a moment the four of us stood there, watching the great clouds of alkali dust blow up the high street, some of them so thick they made the saltwagons disappear. But there was little time for contemplation; it would be night all too soon, and then one of the salties now drinking in the Busted Luck might be a man no longer.

'I think we have a problem,' I said. I was speaking to all of them, but it was Jamie I was looking at. 'It seems to me that a skin-turner who knows what he is would hardly admit to being able to ride.'

'Thought of that,' Jamie said, and tilted his head to Constable Wegg.

'We've got all of em who can sit a horse,' Wegg said. 'Depend on it, sai. Ain't I seen em myself?'

'I doubt if you've seen all of them,' I said.

'I think he has,' Jamie said. 'Listen, Roland.'

'There's one rich fella up in Little Debaria, name of Sam Shunt,' Wegg said. 'The miners call him Shunt the Cunt, which ain't surprising, since he's got most of em where the hair grows short. He don't own the Combyne – it's big bugs in Gilead who've got that – but he owns most of the rest: the bars, the whores, the skiddums—'

I looked at Sheriff Peavy.

'Shacks in Little Debaria where some of the miners sleep,' he said. 'Skiddums ain't much, but they ain't underground.'

I looked back at Wegg, who had hold of his duster's lapels and was looking pleased with himself.

'Sammy Shunt owns the company store. Which means he owns the miners.' He grinned. When I didn't grin back, he took his hands from his lapels and flipped them skyward. 'It's the way of the world, young sai – I didn't make it, and neither did you.

'Now Sammy's a great one for fun n games . . . always assumin he can turn a few pennies on em, that is. Four times a year, he sets up races for the miners. Some are footraces, and some are obstacle-course races, where they have to jump over wooden barrycades, or leap gullies filled up with mud. It's pretty comical when they fall in. The whores always come to watch, and that makes em laugh like loons.'

345

'Hurry it up,' Peavy growled. 'Those fellas won't take long to get through two drinks.'

'He has hoss-races, too,' said Wegg, 'although he won't provide nothing but old nags, in case one of them ponies breaks a leg and has to be shot.'

'If a miner breaks a leg, is *he* shot?' I asked.

Wegg laughed and slapped his thigh as if I'd gotten off a good one. Cuthbert could have told him I don't joke, but of course Cuthbert wasn't there. And Jamie rarely says anything, if he doesn't have to.

'Trig, young gunslinger, very trig ye are! Nay, they're mended right enough, if they can be mended; there's a couple of whores that make a little extra coin working as ammies after Sammy Shunt's little competitions. They don't mind; it's servicin em either way, ain't it?

'There's an entry fee, accourse, taken out of wages. That pays Sammy's expenses. As for the miners, the winner of whatever the particular competition happens to be – dash, obstacle-course, hoss-race – gets a year's worth of debt forgiven at the company store. Sammy keeps the in'drest s'high on the others that he never loses by it. You see how it works? Quite snick, wouldn't you say?'

'Snick as the devil,' I said.

'Yar! So when it comes to racing those nags around the little track he had made, any miner who *can* ride, *does* ride. It's powerful comical to

346

watch em smashin their nutsacks up n down, set my watch and warrant on that. And I'm allus there to keep order. I've seen every race for the last seven years, and every diggerboy who's ever run in em. For riders, those boys over there are it. There was one more, but in the race Sammy put on this New Earth, that pertic'ler salt-mole fell off his mount and got his guts squashed. Lived a day or two, then goozled. So I don't think he's your skin-man, do you?'

At this, Wegg laughed heartily. Peavy looked at him with resignation, Jamie with a mixture of contempt and wonder.

Did I believe this man when he said they'd rounded up every saltie who could sit a horse? I would, I decided, if he could answer one question in the affirmative.

'Do you bet on these horse-races yourself, Wegg?'

'Made a goodish heap last year,' he said proudly. 'Course Shunt only pays in scrip – he's tight – but it keeps me in whores and whiskey. I like the whores young and the whiskey old.'

Peavy looked at me over Wegg's shoulder and shrugged his shoulders as if to say, *He's what they have up there, so don't blame me for it.*

Nor did I. 'Wegg, go on in the office and wait for us. Jamie and Sheriff Peavy, come with me.'

I explained as we crossed the street. It didn't take long.

★   ★   ★

'You tell them what we want,' I said to Peavy as we stood outside the batwings. I kept it low because we were still being watched by the whole town, although the ones clustered outside the saloon had drawn away from us, as if we might have something that was catching. 'They know you.'

'Not as well as they know Wegg,' he said.

'Why do you think I wanted him to stay across the street?'

He grunted a laugh at that, and pushed his way through the batwings. Jamie and I followed.

The regular patrons had drawn back to the gaming tables, giving the bar over to the salties. Snip and Canfield flanked them; Kellin Frye stood with his back leaning against the barnboard wall and his arms folded over his sheepskin vest. There was a second floor – given over to bump-cribs, I assumed – and the balcony up there was loaded with less-than-charming ladies, looking down at the miners.

'You men!' Peavy said. 'Turn around and face me!'

They did as he said, and promptly. What was he to them but just another foreman? A few held onto the remains of their short whiskeys, but most had already finished. They looked livelier now, their cheeks flushed with alcohol rather than the scouring wind that had chased them down from the foothills.

'Now here's what,' Peavy said. 'You're going to

348

sit up on the bar, every mother's son of you, and take off your boots so we can see your feet.'

A muttering of discontent greeted this. 'If you want to know who's spent time in Beelie Stockade, why not just ask?' a graybeard called. 'I was there, and I en't ashamed. I stole a loaf for my old woman and our two babbies. Not that it did the babbies any good; they both died.'

'What if we won't?' a younger one asked. 'Them gunnies shoot us? Not sure I'd mind. At least I wouldn't have to go down in the plug nummore.'

A rumble of agreement met this. Someone said something that sounded like *green light*.

Peavy took hold of my arm and pulled me forward. 'It was this gunny got you out of a day's work, then bought you drinks. And unless you're the man we're looking for, what the hell are you afraid of?'

The one that answered this couldn't have been more than my age. 'Sai Sheriff, we're *always* afraid.'

This was truth a little balder than they were used to, and complete silence dropped over the Busted Luck. Outside, the wind moaned. The grit hitting the thin board walls sounded like hail.

'Boys, listen to me,' Peavy said, now speaking in a lower and more respectful tone of voice. 'These gunslingers could draw and make you do what has to be done, but I don't want that, and you shouldn't need it. Counting what happened at the Jefferson spread, there's over three dozen dead in Debaria.

Three at the Jefferson was women.' He paused. 'Nar, I tell a lie. One was a woman, the other two mere girls. I know you've got hard lives and nothing to gain by doing a good turn, but I'm asking you, anyway. And why not? There's only one of you with something to hide.'

'Well, what the fuck,' said the graybeard.

He reached behind him to the bar and boosted himself up so he was sitting on it. He must have been the Old Fella of the crew, for all the others followed suit. I watched for anyone showing reluctance, but to my eye there was none. Once it was started, they took it as a kind of joke. Soon there were twenty-one overalled salties sitting on the bar, and the boots rained down on the sawdusty floor in a series of thuds. Ay, gods, I can smell the reek of their feet to this day.

'Oogh, that's enough for me,' one of the whores said, and when I looked up, I saw our audience vacating the balcony in a storm of feathers and a swirl of pettislips. The bartender joined the others by the gaming tables, holding his nose pinched shut. I'll bet they didn't sell many steak dinners in Racey's Café at suppertime; that smell was an appetite-killer if ever there was one.

'Yank up your cuffs,' Peavy said. 'Let me gleep yer ankles.'

Now that the thing was begun, they complied without argument. I stepped forward. 'If I point to you,' I said, 'get down off the bar and go stand against the wall. You can take your boots, but don't bother putting them on. You'll only be walking across the street, and you can do that barefooty.'

I walked down the line of extended feet, most pitifully skinny and all but those belonging to the youngest miners clogged with bulging purple veins.

'You . . . you . . . and you . . .'

In all, there were ten of them with blue rings around their ankles that meant time in the Beelie Stockade. Jamie drifted over to them. He didn't draw, but he hooked his thumbs in his crossed gunbelts, with his palms near enough to the butts of his six-shooters to make the point.

'Barkeep,' I said. 'Pour these men who are left another short shot.'

The miners without stockade tattoos cheered at this and began putting on their boots again.

'What about us?' the graybeard asked. The tattooed ring above his ankle was faded to a blue ghost. His bare feet were as gnarled as old tree-stumps. How he could walk on them – let alone *work* on them – was more than I could understand.

'Nine of you will get *long* shots,' I said, and that wiped the gloom from their faces. 'The tenth will get something else.'

'A yank of rope,' Canfield of the Jefferson said in a low voice. 'And after what I seen out t'ranch, I hope he dances at the end of it a long time.'

★   ★   ★

351

We left Snip and Canfield to watch the eleven salties drinking at the bar, and marched the other ten across the street. The graybeard led the way and walked briskly on his tree-stump feet. That day's light had drained to a weird yellow I had never seen before, and it would be dark all too soon. The wind blew and the dust flew. I was watching for one of them to make a break – hoping for it, if only to spare the child waiting in the jail – but none did.

Jamie fell in beside me. 'If he's here, he's hoping the kiddo didn't see any higher than his ankles. He means to face it out, Roland.'

'I know,' I said. 'And since that's all the kiddo *did* see, he'll probably ride the bluff.'

'What then?'

'Lock em all up, I suppose, and wait for one of em to change his skin.'

'What if it's not just something that comes over him? What if he can keep it from happening?'

'Then I don't know,' I said.

Wegg had started a penny-in, three-to-stay Watch Me game with Pickens and Strother. I thumped the table with one hand, scattering the matchsticks they were using as counters. 'Wegg, you'll accompany these men into the jail with the sheriff. It'll be a few minutes yet. There's a few more things to attend to.'

'What's in the jail?' Wegg asked, looking at the scattered matchsticks with some regret. I guessed he'd been winning. 'The boy, I suppose?'

'The boy and the end of this sorry business,' I said with more confidence than I felt.

I took the graybeard by the elbow – gently – and pulled him aside. 'What's your name, sai?'

'Steg Luka. What's it to you? You think I'm the one?'

'No,' I said, and I didn't. No reason; just a feeling. 'But if you know which one it is – if you even think you know – you ought to tell me. There's a frightened boy in there, locked in a cell for his own good. He saw something that looked like a giant bear kill his father, and I'd spare him any more pain if I could. He's a good boy.'

He considered, then it was him who took my elbow . . . and with a hand that felt like iron. He drew me into the corner. 'I can't say, gunslinger, for we've all been down there, deep in the new plug, and we all saw it.'

'Saw what?'

'A crack in the salt with a green light shining through. Bright, then dim. Bright, then dim. Like a heartbeat. And . . . it speaks to your face.'

'I don't understand you.'

'I don't understand myself. The only thing I know is we've all seen it, and we've all felt it. It speaks to your face and tells you to come in. It's bitter.'

'The light, or the voice?'

'Both. It's of the Old People, I've no doubt of that. We told Banderly – him that's the bull foreman – and he went down himself. Saw it for himself. *Felt* it for himself. But was he going to close the plug for that? Balls he was. He's got his own bosses to answer to, and they know there's a moit of salt left down there. So he ordered a crew to close it up with rocks, which they did. I know, because I was one of em. But rocks that are put in can be pulled out. And they have been, I'd swear to it. They were one way then, now they're another. Someone went in there, gunslinger, and whatever's on the other side . . . it changed him.'

'But you don't know who.'

Luka shook his head. 'All I can say is it must've been between twelve o' the clock and six in the morning, for then all's quiet.'

'Go on back to your mates, and say thankee. You'll be drinking soon enough, and welcome.' But sai Luka's drinking days were over. We never know, do we?

He went back and I surveyed them. Luka was the oldest by far. Most of the others were middle-aged, and a couple were still young. They looked interested and excited rather than afraid, and I could understand that; they'd had a couple of drinks to perk them up, and this made a change in the drudgery of their ordinary days. None of them looked shifty or guilty. None looked like anything more or less than what they were: salties in a dying mining town where the rails ended.

'Jamie,' I said. 'A word with you.'

I walked him to the door, and spoke directly into his ear. I gave him an errand, and told him to do it as fast as ever he could. He nodded and slipped out into the stormy afternoon. Or perhaps by then it was early evening.

'Where's *he* off to?' Wegg asked.

'That's nonnies to you,' I said, and turned to the men with the blue tattoos on their ankles. 'Line up, if you please. Oldest to youngest.'

'I dunno how old I am, do I?' said a balding man wearing a wrist-clock with a rusty string-mended band. Some of the others laughed and nodded.

'Just do the best you can,' I said.

I had no interest in their ages, but the discussion and argument took up some time, which was the main object. If the blacksmith had fulfilled his commission, all would be well. If not, I would improvise. A gunslinger who can't do that dies early.

The miners shuffled around like kids playing When the Music Stops, swapping spots until they were in some rough approximation of age. The line started at the door to the jail and ended at the door to the street. Luka was first; Wrist-Clock was in the middle; the one who looked about my age – the one who'd said they were always afraid – was last.

'Sheriff, will you get their names?' I asked. 'I want to speak to the Streeter boy.'

★   ★   ★

Billy was standing at the bars of the drunk-and-disorderly cell. He'd heard our palaver, and looked frightened. 'Is it here?' he asked. 'The skin-man?'

'I think so,' I said, 'but there's no way to be sure.'

'Sai, I'm ascairt.'

'I don't blame you. But the cell's locked and the bars are good steel. He can't get at you, Billy.'

'You ain't seen him when he's a bear,' Billy whispered. His eyes were huge and shiny, fixed in place. I've seen men with eyes like that after they've been punched hard on the jaw. It's the look that comes over them just before their knees go soft. Outside, the wind gave a thin shriek along the underside of the jail roof.

'Tim Stoutheart was afraid, too,' I said. 'But he went on. I expect you to do the same.'

'Will you be here?'

'Aye. My mate, Jamie, too.'

As if I had summoned him, the door to the office opened and Jamie hurried in, slapping alkali dust from his shirt. The sight of him gladdened me. The smell of dirty feet that accompanied him was less welcome.

'Did you get it?' I asked.

'Yes. It's a pretty enough thing. And here's the list of names.'

He handed both over.

'Are you ready, son?' Jamie asked Billy.

'I guess so,' Billy said. 'I'm going to pretend I'm Tim Stoutheart.'

Jamie nodded gravely. 'That's a fine idea. May you do well.'

A particularly strong gust of wind blew past. Bitter dust puffed in through the barred window of the drunk-and-disorderly cell. Again came that eerie shriek along the eaves. The light was fading, fading. It crossed my mind that it might be better – safer – to jail the waiting salties and leave this part for tomorrow, but nine of them had done nothing. Neither had the boy. Best to have it done. If it *could* be done, that was.

'Hear me, Billy,' I said. 'I'm going to walk them through nice and slow. Maybe nothing will happen.'

'A-All right.' His voice was faint.

'Do you need a drink of water first? Or to have a piss?'

'I'm fine,' he said, but of course he didn't look fine; he looked terrified. 'Sai? How many of them have blue rings on their ankles?'

'All,' I said.

'Then how—'

'They don't know how much you saw. Just look at each one as he passes. And stand back a little, doya.' Out of reaching-distance was what I meant, but I didn't want to say it out loud.

'What should I say?'

'Nothing. Unless you see something that sets off a recollection, that is.' I had little hope of that. 'Bring them in, Jamie. Sheriff Peavy at the head of the line and Wegg at the end.'

He nodded and left. Billy reached through the bars. For a second I didn't know what he wanted, then I did. I gave his hand a brief squeeze. 'Stand back now, Billy. And remember the face of your father. He watches you from the clearing.'

He obeyed. I glanced at the list, running over names (probably misspelled) that meant nothing to me, with my hand on the butt of my righthand gun. That one now contained a very special load. According to Vannay, there was only one sure way to kill a skin-man: with a piercing object of the holy metal. I had paid the blacksmith in gold, but the bullet he'd made me – the one that would roll under the hammer at first cock – was pure silver. Perhaps it would work.

If not, I would follow with lead.

The door opened. In came Sheriff Peavy. He had a two-foot ironwood headknocker in his right hand, the rawhide drop cord looped around his wrist. He was patting the business end gently against his left palm as he stepped through the door. His eyes found the white-faced lad in the cell, and he smiled.

'Hey-up, Billy, son of Bill,' he said. 'We're with ye, and all's fine. Fear nothing.'

Billy tried to smile, but looked like he feared much.

Steg Luka came next, rocking from side to side on those tree-stump feet of his. After him came a man nearly as old, with a mangy white mustache, dirty gray hair falling to his shoulders, and a sinister, squinted look in his eyes. Or perhaps he was only nearsighted. The list named him as Bobby Frane.

'Come slow,' I said, 'and give this boy a good look at you.'

They came. As each one passed, Bill Streeter looked anxiously into his face.

'G'd eve'n to'ee, boy,' Luka said as he went by. Bobby Frane tipped an invisible cap. One of the younger ones – Jake Marsh, according to the list – stuck out a tongue yellow from bingo-weed tobacco. The others just shuffled past. A couple kept their heads lowered until Wegg barked at them to raise up and look the kiddo in the eye.

There was no dawning recognition on Bill Streeter's face, only a mixture of fright and perplexity. I kept my own face blank, but I was losing hope. Why, after all, would the skin-man break? He had nothing to lose by playing out his string, and he must know it.

Now there were only four left . . . then two . . . then only the kid who in the Busted Luck had spoken of being afraid. I saw a change on Billy's face as that one went by, and for a moment I thought we had something, then realized it was nothing more than the recognition of one young person for another.

Last came Wegg, who had put away his head-knocker and donned brass knuckledusters on each hand. He gave Billy Streeter a not very pleasant smile. 'Don't see no merchandise you want to buy, younker? Well, I'm sorry, but I can't say I'm surpri—'

'Gunslinger!' Billy said to me. 'Sai Deschain!'

'Yes, Billy.' I shouldered Wegg aside and stood in front of the cell.

Billy touched his tongue to his upper lip. 'Walk them by again, if it please you. Only this time have them hold up their pants. I can't see the rings.'

'Billy, the rings are all the same.'

'No,' he said. 'They ain't.'

The wind was in a lull, and Sheriff Peavy heard him. 'Turn around, my cullies, and back you march. Only this time hike up your trousers.'

'Ain't enough enough?' the man with the old wrist-clock grumbled. The list called him Ollie Ang. 'We was promised shots. *Long* ones.'

'What's it to you, honey?' Wegg asked. 'Ain't you got to go back that way any-ro'? Did yer marmar drop'ee on your head?'

They grumbled about it, but started back down the corridor toward the office, this time from youngest to oldest, and holding up their pants. All the tattoos looked about the same to me. I at first thought they must to the boy, as well. Then I saw his eyes widen, and he took another step away from the bars. Yet he said nothing.

'Sheriff, hold them right there for a moment, if you will,' I said.

Peavy moved in front of the door to the office.

I stepped to the cell and spoke low. 'Billy? See something?'

'The mark,' he said. 'I seen the mark. It's the man with the broken ring.'

I didn't understand . . . then I did. I thought of all the times Cort had called me a slowkins from the eyebrows up. He called the others those things and worse – of course he did, it was his job – but standing in the corridor of that Debaria jail with the simoom blowing outside, I thought he had been right about me. I *was* a slowkins. Only minutes ago I'd thought that if there had been more than the memory of the tattoo, I'd have gotten it from Billy when he was hypnotized. Now, I realized, I *had* gotten it.

Is there anything else? I'd asked him, already sure that there wasn't, only wanting to raise him from the trance that was so obviously upsetting him. And when he'd said *the white mark* – but dubiously, as if asking himself – foolish Roland had let it pass.

The salties were getting restless. Ollie Ang, the one with the rusty wrist-clock, was saying they'd done as asked and he wanted to go back to the Busted to get his drink and his damn boots.

'Which one?' I asked Billy.

He leaned forward and whispered.

I nodded, then turned to the knot of men at the end of the corridor. Jamie was watching them closely, hands resting on the butts of his revolvers. The men must have seen something in my face, because they ceased their grumbling and just stared. The only sound was the wind and the constant gritty slosh of dust against the building.

As to what happened next, I've thought it over many times since, and I don't think we could have prevented it. We didn't know how fast the change happened, you see; I don't think Vannay did, either, or he would have warned us. Even my father said as much when I finished making my report and stood, with all those books frowning down upon me, waiting for him to pass judgment on my actions in Debaria – not as my father, but as my dinh.

For one thing I was and am grateful. I almost told Peavy to bring forward the man Billy had named, but then I changed my mind. Not because Peavy had helped my father once upon a bye, but because Little Debaria and the salt-houses were not his fill.

'Wegg,' I said. 'Ollie Ang to me, do it please ya.'

'Which?'

'The one with the clock on his wrist.'

'Here, now!' Ollie Ang squawked as Constable Wegg laid hold of him. He was slight for a miner, almost bookish, but his arms were slabbed with muscle and I could see more muscle lifting the shoulders of his chambray workshirt. 'Here, now, I ain't done nothing! It ain't fair to single me out just because this here kid wants to show off!'

'Shut your hole,' Wegg said, and pulled him through the little clot of miners.

'Huck up your pants again,' I told him.

'Fuck you, brat! And the horse you rode in on!'

'Huck up or I'll do it for you.'

He raised his hands and balled them into fists. 'Try! Just you t—'

Jamie strolled up behind him, drew one of his guns, tossed it lightly into the air, caught it by the barrel, and brought the butt down on Ang's head. A smartly calculated blow: it didn't knock the man out, but he dropped his fists, and Wegg caught him under the armpit when his knees loosened. I pulled up the right leg of his overalls, and there it was: a blue Beelie Stockade tattoo that had been cut – *broken*, to use Billy Streeter's word – by a thick white scar that ran all the way to his knee.

'That's what I saw,' Billy breathed. 'That's what I saw when I was a-layin under that pile of tack.'

'He's making it up,' Ang said. He looked dazed and his words were muzzy. A thin rill of blood ran down the side of his face from where Jamie's blow had opened his scalp a little.

I knew better. Billy had mentioned the white mark long before he'd set eyes on Ollie Ang in the jail. I opened my mouth, meaning to tell Wegg to throw him in a cell, but that was when the Old Man of the crew burst forward. In his eyes was a look of belated realization. Nor was that all. He was furious.

Before I or Jamie or Wegg could stop him, Steg Luka grabbed Ang by the shoulders and bore him back against the bars across the aisle from the drunk-and-disorderly cell. *'I should have known!'* he shouted. *'I should have known weeks ago, ye great growit shifty asshole! Ye murderin trullock!'* He seized the arm bearing the old watch. *'Where'd ye get this, if not in the crack the green light comes from? Where else? Oh, ye murderin skin-changin* bastard!'

Luka spit into Ang's dazed face, then turned to Jamie and me, still holding up the miner's arm. 'Said he found it in a hole outside one of the old foothill plugs! Said it was probably leftover outlaw booty from the Crow Gang, and like fools we believed him! Even went diggin around for more on our days off, didn't we!'

He turned back to the dazed Ollie Ang. Dazed was how he looked to us, anyway, but who knows what was going on behind those eyes?

'And you laughin up your fuckin sleeve at us while we did it, I've no doubt. You found it in a hole, all right, but it wasn't in one of the old plugs. You went into the crack! Into the green light! It was you! It was you! It was—'

Ang twisted from the chin up. I don't mean he grimaced; his entire head *twisted*. It was like watching a cloth being wrung by invisible hands. His eyes rose up until one was almost above the other, and they turned from blue to jet-black. His skin paled first to white, then to green. It rose as if pushed by fists from beneath, and cracked into scales. His clothes dropped from his body, because his body was no longer that of a man. Nor was it a bear, or a wolf, or a lion. Those things we might have been prepared for. We might even have been prepared for an ally-gator, such as the thing that had assaulted the unfortunate Fortuna at Serenity. Although it was closer to an ally-gator than anything else.

In a space of three seconds, Ollie Ang turned into a man-high snake. A pooky.

Luka, still holding onto an arm that was shrinking toward that fat green body, gave out a yell that was muffled when the snake – still with a flopping tonsure of human hair around its elongating head – jammed itself into the old man's mouth. There was a wet popping sound as Luka's lower jaw was torn from the joints and tendons holding it to the upper. I saw his wattled neck swell and grow smooth as that thing – still changing, still standing on the dwindling remnants of human legs – bored into his throat like a drill.

There were yells and screams of horror from the head of the aisle as the other salties stampeded. I paid them no notice. I saw Jamie wrap his arms around the snake's growing, swelling body in a fruitless attempt to pull it out of the dying Steg Luka's throat, and I saw the enormous reptilian head when it tore its way through the nape of Luka's neck, its red tongue flicking, its scaly head painted with beads of blood and bits of flesh.

Wegg threw one of his brass-knuckle-decorated

fists at it. The snake dodged easily, then struck forward, exposing enormous, still-growing fangs: two on top, two on bottom, all dripping with clear liquid. It battened on Wegg's arm and he shrieked.

'*Burns! Dear gods, it BURNS!*'

Luka, impaled at the head, seemed to dance as the snake dug its fangs into the struggling constable. Blood and gobbets of flesh spattered everywhere.

Jamie looked at me wildly. His guns were drawn, but where to shoot? The pooky was writhing between two dying men. Its lower body, now legless, flipped free of the heaped clothes, wound itself around Luka's waist in fat coils, drew tight. The part behind the head was slithering out through the widening hole at the nape of Luka's neck.

I stepped forward, seized Wegg, and dragged him backward by the scruff of his vest. His bitten arm had already turned black and swelled to twice its normal size. His eyes were bulging from their sockets as he stared at me, and white foam began to drizzle from his lips.

Somewhere, Billy Streeter was screaming.

The fangs tore free. 'Burns,' Wegg said in a low voice, and then he could say no more. His throat swelled, and his tongue shot out of his mouth. He collapsed, shuddering in his death-throes. The snake stared at me, its forked tongue licking in and out. They were black snake-eyes, but they were filled with human understanding. I lifted the revolver holding the special load. I had only one silver shell and the head was weaving erratically from side to side, but I never doubted I could make the shot; it's what such as I was made for. It lunged, fangs flashing, and I pulled the trigger. The shot was true, and the silver bullet went right into that yawning mouth. The head blew away in a splatter of red that had begun to turn white even before it hit the bars and the floor of the corridor. I'd seen such mealy white flesh before. It was brains. *Human* brains.

Suddenly it was Ollie Ang's ruined face peering at me from the ragged hole in the back of Luka's neck – peering from atop a snake's body. Shaggy black fur sprang from between the scales on its body as whatever force dying inside lost all control of the shapes it made. In the moment before it collapsed, the remaining blue eye turned yellow and became a wolf's eye. Then it went down, bearing the unfortunate Steg Luka with it. In the corridor, the dying body of the skin-man shimmered and burned, wavered and changed. I heard the pop of muscles and the grind of shifting bones. A naked foot shot out, turned into a furry paw, then became a man's foot again. The remains of Ollie Ang shuddered all over, then grew still.

The boy was still screaming.

'Go to yon pallet and lie down,' I said to him. My voice was not quite steady. 'Close your eyes and tell yourself it's over, for now it is.'

'I want you,' Billy sobbed as he went to the pallet. His cheeks were speckled with blood. I was drenched with it, but this he didn't see. His eyes were already closed. 'I want you with me! Please, sai, please!'

'I'll come to you as soon as I can,' I said. And I did.

Three of us spent the night on pushed-together pallets in the drunk-and-disorderly cell: Jamie on the left, me on the right, Young Bill Streeter in the middle. The simoom had begun to die, and until late, we heard the sound of revels on the high street as Debaria celebrated the death of the skin-man.

'What will happen to me, sai?' Billy asked just before he finally fell asleep.

'Good things,' I said, and hoped Everlynne of Serenity would not prove me wrong about that.

'Is it dead? Really dead, sai Deschain?'

'Really.'

But on that score I meant to take no chance. After midnight, when the wind was down to a bare breeze and Bill Streeter lay in an exhausted sleep so deep even bad dreams couldn't reach him, Jamie and I joined Sheriff Peavy on the waste ground behind the jail. There we doused the body of Ollie Ang with coal oil. Before setting match to it, I asked if either of them wanted the wrist-clock as a souvenir. Somehow it hadn't been broken in

368

the struggle, and the cunning little second hand still turned.

Jamie shook his head.

'Not I,' said Peavy, 'for it might be haunted. Go on, Roland. If I may call ye so.'

'And welcome,' I said. I struck the sulphur and dropped it. We stood watching until the remains of Debaria's skin-man were nothing but black bones. The wrist-clock was a charred lump in the ash.

The following morning, Jamie and I rounded up a crew of men – more than willing, they were – to go out to the rail line. Once they were there, it was a matter of two hours to put Sma' Toot back on the double-steel. Travis, the enjie, directed the operation, and I made many friends by telling them I'd arranged for everyone in the crew to eat free at Racey's at top o' day and drink free at the Busted Luck that afternoon.

There was to be a town celebration that night, at which Jamie and I would be guests of honor. It was the sort of thing I could happily do without – I was anxious to get home, and as a rule, company doesn't suit me – but such events are often part of the job. One good thing: there would be women, some of them no doubt pretty. That part I wouldn't mind, and suspected Jamie wouldn't, either. He had much to learn about women, and Debaria was as good a place to begin his studies as any.

He and I watched Sma' Toot puff slowly up to the roundway and then make its way toward us again, pointed in the right direction: toward Gilead.

'Will we stop at Serenity on the way back to town?' Jamie asked. 'To ask if they'll take the boy in?'

'Aye. And the prioress said she had something for me.'

'Do you know what?'

I shook my head.

Everlynne, that mountain of a woman, swept toward us across the courtyard of Serenity, her arms spread wide. I was almost tempted to run; it was like standing in the path of one of the vast trucks that used to run at the oil-fields near Kuna.

Instead of running us down, she swept us into a vast and bosomy double hug. Her aroma was sweet: a mixture of cinnamon and thyme and baked goods. She kissed Jamie on the cheek – he blushed. Then she kissed me full on the lips. For a moment we were enveloped by her complicated and billowing garments and shaded by her winged silk hood. Then she drew back, her face shining.

'What a service you have done this town! And how we say thankya!'

I smiled. 'Sai Everlynne, you are too kind.'

'Not kind enough! You'll have noonies with us,

370

yes? And meadow wine, although only a little. Ye'll have more to drink tonight, I have no doubt.' She gave Jamie a roguish side-glance. 'But ye'll want to be careful when the toasts go around; too much drink can make a man less a man later on, and blur memories he might otherwise want to keep.' She paused, then broke into a knowing grin that went oddly with her robes. 'Or . . . p'raps not.'

Jamie blushed harder than ever, but said nothing.

'We saw you coming,' Everlynne said, 'and there's someone else who'd like to give you her thanks.'

She moved aside and there stood the tiny Sister of Serenity named Fortuna. She was still swathed in bandagement, but she looked less wraithlike today, and the side of the face we could see was shining with happiness and relief. She stepped forward shyly.

'I can sleep again. And in time, I may even be able to sleep wi'out nightmares.'

She twitched up the skirt of her gray robe, and – to my deep discomfort – fell on her knees before us. 'Sister Fortuna, Annie Clay that was, says thank you. So do we all, but this comes from my own heart.'

I took her gently by the shoulders. 'Rise, bondswoman. Kneel not before such as us.'

She looked at me with shining eyes, and kissed me on the cheek with the side of her mouth that could still kiss. Then she fled back across the courtyard toward what I assumed was their kitchen. Wonderful smells were already arising from that part of the *haci*.

Everlynne watched her go with a fond smile, then turned back to me.

'There's a boy—' I began.

She nodded. 'Bill Streeter. I know his name and his story. We don't go to town, but sometimes the town comes to us. Friendly birds twitter news in our ears, if you take my meaning.'

'I take it well,' I said.

'Bring him tomorrow, after your heads have shrunk back to their normal size,' said she. 'We're a company of women, but we're happy to take an orphan boy . . . at least until he grows enough hair on his upper lip to shave. After that, women trouble a boy, and it might not be so well for him to stay here. In the meantime, we can set him about his letters and numbers . . . if he's trig enough to learn, that is. Would you say he's trig enough, Roland, son of Gabrielle?'

It was odd to be called from my mother's side rather than my father's, but strangely pleasant. 'I'd say he's very trig.'

'That's well, then. And we'll find a place for him when it's time for him to go.'

'A plot and a place,' I said.

Everlynne laughed. 'Aye, just so, like in the story of Tim Stoutheart. And now we'll break bread

372

together, shall we? And with meadow wine we'll toast the prowess of young men.'

We ate, we drank, and all in all, it was a very merry meeting. When the sisters began to clear the trestle tables, Prioress Everlynne took me to her private quarters, which consisted of a bedroom and a much larger office where a cat slept in a bar of sun on a huge oaken desk heaped high with papers.

'Few men have been here, Roland,' she said. 'One was a fellow you might know. He had a white face and black clothes. Do you know the man of whom I speak?'

'Marten Broadcloak,' I said. The good food in my stomach was suddenly sour with hate. And jealousy, I suppose – nor just on behalf of my father, whom Gabrielle of Arten had decorated with cuckold's horns. 'Did he see her?'

'He demanded to, but I refused and sent him hence. At first he declined to go, but I showed him my knife and told him there were other weapons in Serenity, aye, and women who knew how to use them. One, I said, was a gun. I reminded him he was deep inside the *haci*, and suggested that, unless he could fly, he had better take heed. He did, but before he went he cursed me, and he cursed this place.' She hesitated, stroked the cat, then looked up at me. 'There was a time when I thought perhaps the skin-man was his work.'

'I don't think so,' I said.

'Nor I, but neither of us will ever be entirely sure, will we?' The cat tried to climb into the vast playground of her lap, and Everlynne shooed it away. 'Of one thing I *am* sure: he spoke to her anyway, although whether through the window of her cell late at night or only in her troubled dreams, no one will ever know. That secret she took with her into the clearing, poor woman.'

To this I did not reply. When one is amazed and heartsick, it's usually best to say nothing, for in that state, any word will be the wrong word.

'Your lady-mother quit her retirement with us shortly after we turned this Broadcloak fellow around. She said she had a duty to perform, and much to atone for. She said her son would come here. I asked her how she knew and she said, "Because ka is a wheel and it always turns." She left this for you.'

Everlynne opened one of the many drawers of her desk, and removed an envelope. Written on the front was my name, in a hand I knew well. Only my father would have known it better. That hand had once turned the pages of a fine old book as she read me 'The Wind through the Keyhole.' Aye, and many others. I loved all the stories held in the pages that hand turned, but never so much as I loved the hand itself. Even more, I loved the sound of the voice that told them as the wind blew outside. Those were the days before she was mazed and fell into the sad bitchery that brought her under a gun in another hand. My gun, my hand.

Everlynne rose, smoothing her large apron. 'I must go and see how things are advancing in other parts of my little kingdom. I'll bid you goodbye now, Roland, son of Gabrielle, only asking that you pull the door shut when you go. It will lock itself.'

'You trust me with your things?' I asked.

She laughed, came around the desk, and kissed me again. 'Gunslinger, I'd trust you with my life,' said she, and left. She was so tall she had to duck her head when she went through the door.

I sat looking at Gabrielle Deschain's last missive for a long time. My heart was full of hate and love and regret – all those things that have haunted me ever since. I considered burning it, unread, but at last I tore the envelope open. Inside was a single sheet of paper. The lines were uneven, and the pigeon-ink in which they had been written was blotted in many places. I believe the woman who wrote those lines was struggling to hold onto a few last shreds of sanity. I'm not sure many would have understood her words, but I did. I'm sure my father would have, as well, but I never showed it to him or told him of it.

The feast I ate was rotten
  what I thought was a palace was a dungeon
    how it burns Roland

I thought of Wegg, dying of snakebite.

  If I go back and tell what I know
    what I overheard
Gilead may yet be saved a few years
      you may be saved a few years
        your father little that he ever cared
        for me

The words 'little that he ever cared for me' had
been crossed out with a series of heavy lines, but
I could read them, anyway.

    he says I dare not
      he says 'Bide at Serenity until death finds you.'
    he says 'If you go back death will find you early.'
      he says 'Your death will destroy the only one
        in the world for whom you care.'
          he says 'Would you die at your brat's
          hand and see
    every goodness
    every kindness
    every loving thought
        poured out of him like water from a
        dipper?
        for Gilead that cared for you little
        and will die anyway?'

*But I must go back. I have prayed on it
and meditated on it
and the voice I hear always speaks the
same words:
THIS IS WHAT KA DEMANDS*

There was a little more, words I traced over and over during my wandering years after the disastrous battle at Jericho Hill and the fall of Gilead. I traced them until the paper fell apart and I let the wind take it – the wind that blows through time's keyhole, ye ken. In the end, the wind takes everything, doesn't it? And why not? Why other? If the sweetness of our lives did not depart, there would be no sweetness at all.

I stayed in Everlynne's office until I had myself under control. Then I put my mother's last word – her dead-letter – in my purse and left, making sure the door locked behind me. I found Jamie and we rode to town. That night there were lights and music and dancing; many good things to eat and plenty of liquor to wash it down with. There were women, too, and that night Silent Jamie left his virginity behind him. The next morning . . .

STORM'S OVER

'That night,' Roland said, 'there were lights and music and dancing; many good things to eat and plenty of liquor to wash it down with.'

'Booze,' Eddie said, and heaved a seriocomic sigh. 'I remember it well.'

It was the first thing any of them had said in a very long time, and it broke the spell that had held them through that long and windy night. They stirred like people awaking from a deep dream. All except Oy, who still lay on his back in front of the fireplace with his short paws splayed and the tip of his tongue lolling comically from the side of his mouth.

Roland nodded. 'There were women, too, and that night Silent Jamie left his virginity behind him. The next morning we reboarded Sma' Toot, and made our way back to Gilead. And so it happened, once upon a bye.'

'Long before my grandfather's grandfather was born,' Jake said in a low voice.

'Of that I can't say,' Roland said with a slight smile, and then took a long drink of water. His throat was very dry.

For a moment there was silence among them. Then Eddie said, 'Thank you, Roland. That was boss.'

The gunslinger raised an eyebrow.

'He means it was wonderful,' Jake said. 'It was, too.'

'I see light around the boards we put over the windows,' Susannah said. 'Just a little, but it's there. You talked down the dark, Roland. I guess you're not the strong silent Gary Cooper type after all, are you?'

'I don't know who that is.'

She took his hand and gave it a brief hard squeeze. 'Ne'mine, sugar.'

'Wind's dropped, but it's still blowing pretty hard,' Jake observed.

'We'll build up the fire, then sleep,' the gunslinger said. 'This afternoon it should be warm enough for us to go out and gather more wood. And tomorrowday . . .'

'Back on the road,' Eddie finished.

'As you say, Eddie.'

Roland put the last of their fuel on the guttering fire, watched as it sprang up again, then lay down and closed his eyes. Seconds later, he was asleep.

Eddie gathered Susannah into his arms, then looked over her shoulder at Jake, who was sitting cross-legged and looking into the fire. 'Time to catch forty winks, little trailhand.'

'Don't call me that. You know I hate it.'

'Okay, buckaroo.'

Jake gave him the finger. Eddie smiled and closed his eyes.

The boy gathered his blanket around him. *My shaddie*, he thought, and smiled. Beyond the walls, the wind still moaned – a voice without a body. Jake thought, *It's on the other side of the keyhole. And over there, where the wind comes from? All of eternity. And the Dark Tower.*

He thought of the boy Roland Deschain had been an unknown number of years ago, lying in a circular bedroom at the top of a stone tower. Tucked up cozy and listening to his mother read the old tales while the wind blew across the dark land. As he drifted, Jake saw the woman's face and thought it kind as well as beautiful. His own mother had never read him stories. In his plot and place, that had been the housekeeper's job.

He closed his eyes and saw billy-bumblers on their hind legs, dancing in the moonlight.

He slept.

2

When Roland woke in the early afternoon, the wind was down to a whisper and the room was much brighter. Eddie and Jake were still deeply asleep, but Susannah had awakened, boosted herself into her wheelchair, and removed the boards blocking one of the windows. Now she sat there with her chin propped on her hand, looking out. Roland went to her and put his own hand on her shoulder. Susannah reached up and patted it without turning around.

'Storm's over, sugar.'

'Yes. Let's hope we never see another like it.'

'And if we do, let's hope there's a shelter as good as this one close by. As for the rest of Gook village . . .' She shook her head.

Roland bent a little to look out. What he saw didn't surprise him, but it was what Eddie would have called *awesome*. The high street was still there, but it was full of branches and shattered trees. The buildings that had lined it were gone. Only the stone meeting hall remained.

'We were lucky, weren't we?'

'Luck's the word those with poor hearts use for ka, Susannah of New York.'

She considered this without speaking. The last breezes of the dying starkblast came through the hole where the window had been and stirred the tight cap of her hair, as if some invisible hand were stroking it. Then she turned to him. 'She left Serenity and went back to Gilead – your lady-mother.'

'Yes.'

'Even though the sonofabitch told her she'd die at her own son's hand?'

'I doubt if he put it just that way, but . . . yes.'

'It's no wonder she was half-crazy when she wrote that letter.'

Roland was silent, looking out the window at the destruction the storm had brought. Yet they had found shelter. Good shelter from the storm.

She took his three-fingered right hand in both of hers. 'What did she say at the end? What were the words you traced over and over until her letter fell apart? Can you tell me?'

He didn't answer for a long time. Just when she was sure he wouldn't, he did. In his voice – almost undetectable, but most certainly there – was a tremor Susannah had never heard before. 'She wrote in the low speech until the last line. That she wrote in the High, each character beautifully drawn: *I forgive you everything*. And: *Can you forgive me?*'

Susannah felt a single tear, warm and perfectly human, run down her cheek. 'And could you, Roland? Did you?'

Still looking out the window, Roland of Gilead – son of Steven and Gabrielle, she of Arten that was – smiled. It broke upon his face like the first glow of sunrise on a rocky landscape. He spoke a single word before going back to his gunna to build them an afternoon breakfast.

The word was *yes*.

3

They spent one more night in the meeting hall. There was fellowship and palaver, but no stories. The following morning they gathered their gunna and continued along the Path of the Beam – to Calla Bryn Sturgis, and the borderlands, and Thunderclap, and the Dark Tower beyond. These are things that happened, once upon a bye.

AFTERWORD

In the High Speech, Gabrielle Deschain's final message to her son looks like this:

⊙ ⅄ⓒⒺ⅄⊙☙⅃ Ⓔⅽ ⅄☙⅃ⅽ ⅄⊙⅃⅄ ℰ⅃⊙ Ⓒⅽ ⅄ⓒⒺ⅄⊙☙⅃ Ⓒⅽ⅄

The two most beautiful words in any language are ⊙ ⅄ⓒⒺ⅄⊙☙⅃: *I forgive.*

Please return or renew this item by the last date shown. There may be a charge if you fail to do so. Items can be returned to any Westminster library.

Telephone: Enquiries 020 764_____
Renewals (24 hour service) 020 7641 1400
Online renewal service av_____
Web site: www.westmi_____.uk

QUE

KT-420-393

City of Westminster

3011780356240 0

No Spin

No Spin

SHANE WARNE
MY AUTOBIOGRAPHY

With Mark Nicholas

3 5 7 9 10 8 6 4 2

EBURY
PRESS

This edition published in 2019 by Ebury Press, an imprint of Ebury
Publishing

20 Vauxhall Bridge Road
London SW1V 2SA

Ebury Press is part of the Penguin Random House group of companies
whose addresses can be found at global.penguinrandomhouse.com

Penguin
Random House
UK

First published by Ebury Press in 2018

www.penguin.co.uk

A CIP catalogue record for this book is available from the British Library

ISBN 9781785037856

Printed and bound in Great Britain by Clays Ltd, Elcograf S.p.A.

For Mum and Dad
And for Brooke, Jackson and Summer

Contents

Author's Note

I MET SHANE IN 1993 outside my girlfriend's house in London, having driven at the speed of light from a county game in Nottingham, nerves on edge, to ask her to marry me. I parked in the road, took a deep breath, and climbed out of the car, only to see the blond leg-spinner who had bowled the Gatting ball a couple of weeks earlier emerge from her front door. Okay, I thought, this boy is good!

Charm was written all over him. He explained that a mate of his knew her sister and that the four of them had whacked back a bottle or two of rosé in the next-door pub, before attacking another on the tiny back patio of the girls' terraced cottage. He said he was sorry to rush but he had a commitment for which he was already late. No worries, I said, and that was that. The next time I saw him was on telly, knocking over England again. I didn't propose that night, the adrenalin had disappeared into the ether. I was not to know that he had only recently popped the question himself, on a boat in the Lake District somewhere, a question that received an enthusiastic response.

Women have been both his fun and his folly. Cricket, of course, has been his fulfilment. He is, in the truest sense, a great cricketer. He has touched the game in all its genres and formats, and in myriad ways. Mainly, he has ridden roughshod over any opponent who has stood in his way. Only in Test matches in India has the local talent held sway, though there were mitigating circumstances. Richie Benaud called him not just the greatest leg-spinner of all time but the greatest bowler he had seen, full stop. Richie's judgement will do for me.

He is a challenging and rewarding personality, and about as strong a character as the sport has seen. He is a loyal friend and, thankfully, after more than a year on the project of this book, I find him just as engaging as I ever did. The pace of his life can be overwhelming, for the dull moments are few and far between; with Warney, it's all or nothing.

The book is written mainly in his vocabulary, as a stream of consciousness. I could see no other way, since it is Shane's story not mine. After 35 hours of recorded conversation there were expletives to delete and, necessarily I think, a few worth keeping. Given there have been at least 12 books written about him by other people, it has been fun hearing his own version of a life less than ordinary.

The songs at the heading of most chapters reflect his great love of contemporary music, as well as his general sense of a good time. The choices come mostly from favourites in his own collection and they attempt, at least in some way, to reflect the chapter of his life to come. The saying goes that singing makes you happy; well, he sings a great deal.

Whatever conclusions you may make, most of all I hope that you hear his voice, for it continues to echo with the game he so loves.

Mark Nicholas, August 2018

Introduction

I STARTED OUT IN the Melbourne suburbs and I remain happily there to this day. Though London has called for a lot of the time over the past few years, Brighton, just a few miles out of Melbourne's city centre, is my patch. I've traded houses there like I don't know what home is, but I do; I know what's in my heart.

I've only ever had two serious relationships. Yep, two: the first with my wife of 10 years, Simone, and the second – much more recently – with my ex-fiancée, Elizabeth Hurley. Believe it or not, I'd take the quiet life over the red carpet any day. The trouble is I haven't often portrayed myself as anything but a good-time boy, hunting down something different every week of the year. Kerry Packer once told me, 'Sell the blue Ferrari, son, and lie low for a while,' so I did as I was told, and bought a silver one. Lying low hasn't been my thing.

I have lived in the moment and ignored the consequences. This has served me both well and painfully, depending on which moment. I've tried to live up to the legend, or the myth in my view, which has been a mistake because I've let life off the field become as public as life on it. In my defence, I've never pretended to be someone or something I'm not.

I'm a little older now and often wish I was wiser. I'm sick of taking up space in tabloid newspapers and plan to work on that with a bit more conviction than previously in my life. Yes, I've been silly at times but, equally, I like to think I've done justice to my talent, openly shared it with the world and provided plenty of entertainment. Regrets? A few but not as many as you might think. I can't change anything so what's the point of regret? I've tried to do the best by Brooke, Jackson and Summer, my beautiful kids, but the space in those tabloid papers has at times embarrassed and hurt them. Right there is a regret.

Now that's off my chest, we can get down to business. Other than 'Would you sign this, please?' and 'Can I have a selfie?', the question I'm asked most is 'How did you do it?' By that I think people are referring to the Gatting ball, the World Cup semi-final, Amazing Adelaide, the MCG 700th, the IPL and so on. I might be wrong, of course, but probably not, so as my life unfolds over the coming pages, I hope to answer the question. Yes, the search for fame, love, admiration and lifestyle are in the make-up some-where. Ultimately, though, it's about the leg-break, and the strategy, instinct and burning desire to win that came with it.

The stories on the pages that follow are the result of many recorded conversations with a longtime friend, Mark Nicholas. Mark's job has been to make sense of it all – his magic trick, if you like – and he's pulled more than a few rabbits out of the hat. Mine is more mysterious and has been worth a bunch of wickets and a few trophies along the way. Best of all, it has been a whole lot of fun. You gotta remember football was my thing, not cricket . . .

1

Satisfaction

I ANNOUNCED MY RETIREMENT from international cricket soon after midday on 21 December 2006, almost exactly 15 years after first appearing for Australia against India at the Sydney Cricket Ground. I probably wasn't ready back then in January 1992, but now I knew for sure that the time was right to wave it goodbye. As Ian Chappell said to me, 'It's better they ask "Why are you?" than "Why don't you?"' I was done, physically and mentally, and had the feeling that I'd run out of arse anyway. You can't play at that level without it. I don't care who you are!

The timing of the announcement meant that I'd play a final Boxing Day Test against England on my home ground five days later, and then finish with the New Year Test in Sydney, where it all started. Nice symmetry.

The build-up to that Boxing Day Test was manic – understandably, I guess. By the time Christmas Day came I was cooked, so it was a relief to have a few hours of nothing with my family and children.

I had a few chuckles to myself about how my life in the game had panned out. I mean, going into the occasion I valued above all others with 699 Test match wickets under my belt, and gunning for number 700 at the Melbourne Cricket Ground, of all places – well, it doesn't get any better than that. I knew there'd be sadness too, partly because I still loved playing Test match cricket and partly because I was saying goodbye (or thought I was!) to the mighty 'G.

✧

I'd set the phone at full volume, and I remember how the suddenness of the 5 am alarm makes for that feeling of shock when it wakes you up from a deep sleep. There was no time for the usual snooze buttons and then the last-minute panic to get ready: I had to move right then. *Urrgghh*.

It had been a bad night. I'd last checked the time at 3.30 am and then fallen into the kind of heavy sleep that knocks you about a bit. It took a while to get my head round where I was and what I was doing. I rolled over, stiff and sore as usual, lit the first cigarette of the day and checked out texts and emails. There were hundreds of 'em. Then I pulled myself together – shower, suit, tie, R. M. Williams black suede boots. I had a juice and, yep, another dart.

I was hosting a Boxing Day breakfast event for the Shane Warne Foundation, the charity I'd started to help seriously ill and under-privileged children. Today was different in so many ways. It wasn't like I hadn't played a Boxing Day Test before – I'd played nine of them – but this was the last one, which is a totally different thing. At that stage the foundation had raised three million dollars for various children's causes and this brekkie was a big deal for us as we looked to push forward to even greater things. And then, of course, there was the Ashes, which gives everything an extra kick.

The MCG was a second home and being a Victorian playing in a Boxing Day Test is extra special. The crowd is so passionate, so unconditionally on your side, and that feeling of being wanted and loved – well, there's no pretending you don't like that, I don't care who you are. So to play my last-ever game there was big, really big.

I had this absolute certainty that we'd bowl first. Driving to the Crown Towers ballroom for the brekkie, I began imagining the moment when Ricky Ponting would throw me the ball in front of nearly 90,000 people. Bring it on.

My phone was hot. There were a million tickets to sort out for friends and family; a thousand people coming to the breakfast wanting value for money; Michael Clarke and Kevin Pietersen, the star guests, to check on; cars for them (I was so grateful to them for giving up their time on game day); auction items; last-minute changes to the seating plan – just so much stuff. I had a full-time PA, as well as some volunteers working on the event, but in the end the thing came down to me and I wanted to get it right. Then there was the Test match to play.

During breakfast, I made a speech and we gave out significant cheques to our chosen charities, all of which made me feel great. Then I hung around for a while, mingled with the happy faces in the crowd, did some photos and signatures with the Barmy Army and shook a lot of hands. Above all, I wanted to thank everyone for their support. I left about 8.30 am, determined to be at the ground before the rest of the guys. I was first there.

Victoria's Australian players are recognised with photographs on the dressing-room wall. I sat under mine, the furthest away from everyone else's lockers so I could smoke in my own little corner. Usually I sleep well, really well, and I'm hardly ever nervous. I do remember shitting myself in my first Test match but was generally alright after that. But on Boxing Day morning 2006, I felt uneasy, and was pleased to have a few minutes to myself.

All alone, with not a single distraction, I looked around the dressing-room and thought about 17 years of first-class cricket whizzing by me. I had arrived as a kid and would leave a little less of one. It hit me how much I'd miss it: the changing-room banter; 90,000 people in the crowd; the heat of the battle. What an amazing ride it had been. Proudly, emotionally, I smiled to myself and thought, 'Wow, that was fun.'

I thought about Allan Border, Merv Hughes, Mark Taylor, Mark Waugh – all the guys I started out with – and the great days of 'Babsie' Boon's hat-trick catch and the Richie Richardson flipper in the seven-for in my first Boxing Day Test. I thought right back to 'AB' and Jeff Thomson's last-wicket partnership against the Poms in 1982/83, with us kids in the stands willing them over the line, but how Ian Botham had won the game at the last gasp – great Ashes cricket, inspiring wonderful memories. Then I started to imagine how it could be me today. I kind of hoped we might bat so I could have an afternoon nap but, deep down, I just knew we'd be bowling. Destiny was loud that day.

Then the guys arrived in twos and threes and the room took on a new life. All the Christmas wishes and nervous energy wrapped up in a group of egos thrown together to play cricket for Australia. We could hardly wait. It was like it was bursting out of us. We'd regained the Ashes in Perth the week before, speedy revenge for 2005 in England. Now we had our feet on the Poms' throats, we wanted 5–0.

Destiny had its say. We lost the toss and we would bowl first.

It had suddenly got very cold. Hard rain swept over the 'G and play was delayed for half an hour. It had been so hot leading up to the game and the change caught everyone off guard. In fact, everything felt weird, almost eerie. We were on edge, as was the crowd, all of us keen to get going.

When the rain stopped and the umpires announced the start time, I remember everyone wishing me the best. 'Good luck, mate', 'Yeah good luck, Warney', 'Go well, King', 'Have a great day, mate' etc, and I was like, 'Yep, thanks, guys'. To be honest, it felt terrific that the players were excited for me at this moment – they understood what it meant to me. They also knew that a 700th wicket would create history.

As the minutes ticked by to the start, I began thinking, 'Geez, the guy who writes these scripts, he's good. This is another beauty!' And then I wondered if I'd do it justice. Suddenly I was over-thinking everything. 'What if they're 0/100 and smashing me, what then?' Little demons I had hardly ever known before were now my enemy. 'Stop it, mate! Just get out there and bowl and it'll be fine,' I thought, as I had my last dart.

So, eventually we ran out there to 90,000 people screaming and yelling and again I thought, *'Bring this on!'* It was like someone had shut the negative-energy door and opened the positive one. White-line fever, I suppose. Ah yes, I thought, this is my place . . .

✧

England were 2/82 when Ricky Ponting threw me the ball. Andrew Strauss, on 48, and Paul Collingwood on 11, looked set. It's always harder to come on when batsmen are 'in'. Their feet are going, usually their timing is right, and they're obviously comfortable and increasingly confident. It's especially difficult for a spinner, so the trick is to find a way to stay on. First thing for me was to peel off the long-sleeve jumper that most of us were wearing and to somehow warm up the fingers that were a little older than when they'd first got to work in the late 1980s.

As I mentioned, I was unusually nervous before the toss but I was excited too. How could I not be: my last-ever game at the MCG, friends, family and my three children watching their dad – all of it special. All the talk amongst family and friends was around who would be number 700 and how would you like to get him out, etc, etc. I just thought, 'I really don't care. Just let me get it sooner rather than later!'

I started okay, slowly but surely finding some rhythm. On the first day of a Test match there's rarely much spin on offer, so bowling is all about changes of pace, angles on the crease and deception. I sensed Collingwood and Strauss had decided not to let me settle. I remember Collingwood running down a couple of times, but he went a bit early so I had time to adjust. I think he got me once down the ground but I didn't mind that because I was starting to hit my straps.

I was encouraged to take a few more risks by slowing the ball up and giving it more of a rip. I beat the bat a couple of times and could feel in my bones that both batsmen were surprised by the spin. Usually, the response to this is to turn the bat into a broom, and sweep. Strauss timed a couple of sweeps well, so at the end of the over I suggested to Ricky Ponting that we block his area behind square on the leg-side and try to force him to drive off the front foot straight down the ground. 'Punter' liked it. We moved mid-wicket into square leg and put in a 45-degree sweeper behind square for the top edge. We made a show of these changes, talking loudly to each other from distance and pretty much telling Strauss the plan.

Whenever I walked onto the cricket field, it was like someone had shut a door behind me. I could block out everything else in my life and focus directly on what had to be done in that moment. I'm the first to admit that I have weaknesses but getting into the 'zone' was a definite strength. You hear commentators in all sports say, 'He or she is in the zone today,' but exactly what is the zone? To me it's the state of total concentration; a place of calm and awareness that allows you to control and direct events as you see them. It's also the ability to switch on and off, so you don't become tight under pressure and make unnecessary mistakes. When you get it right, you feel pretty good. In fact, you feel everything happens slowly and so clearly.

The morning nerves had gone soon after play got underway. Now, I was in the zone. Throughout my career, I backed myself to knock anyone over. So much of sport is in the mind and the more aggressive you think, the more things will go in your favour. Equally, the more defensive you think, the more they won't. Even when guys like Lara and Tendulkar were smacking me around, I wanted the ball in my hand and the chance to get them out. I loved the tactical and strategic challenges, and the contest.

This was one of them: England on Boxing Day with Strauss and Collingwood building a partnership. My idea was to bowl slower, higher and wider of off-stump and to keep encouraging Strauss to drive. Away I went with the plan.

I worked him wide of the crease, too wide to sweep, and could feel his frustration at not being able to score. For two overs it was cat and mouse and then, instinctively, I knew it was time to go for the kill.

I threw up a top-spinning leggie and, as soon as it left my hand, it felt good. I spun it right up, high into the cold air, which suckered Strauss into going for the big drive. Then it dipped.

He kind of got stuck on the crease, playing a half-shot aiming to drive the ball through mid-on. He missed. The ball hit the top of middle stump.

Seven hundred.

You little ripper!

I started running. I've got no idea why – I just did. The crowd went *berserk* – just nuts. In 23 years in the game, I've never heard a louder roar. (The only one that comes close was also at the MCG when Mitchell Starc bowled Brendon McCullum in the first over of the 2015 World Cup final.) I'll treasure that moment forever more.

I hadn't planned what I was going to do – you can't really because the game situation dictates the celebration. For example, it might be cruising time in the middle of the afternoon and it's 'Oh yeah, I got a wicket', or it might be 'Hey, we badly need a wicket' and then you go off a bit. So I don't know why I started running around, sort of demented. My team-mates were all over me, which meant a lot as they were genuinely happy for me, which I see as a sign of a good team – the enjoyment of each other's success. The guys still say the same thing over a beer now, 'Do you remember Boxing Day when the crowd erupted and you got the 700? How bloody loud was that!'

We went through them after that. I got 5/33 and we knocked them over for 159 – from 2/101! It was an emotional and hugely special moment walking off with nearly 90,000 people standing, cheering and chanting your name.

I don't think it was so much about the overall achievement of 700 wickets – though being the first to get there was pretty cool – it was more about that precise moment. It's hard to explain but the only way I can try is to say that I sensed everyone in Australia wanted me to take the 700th *that* day – cricket lovers or non-cricket lovers – like it was a celebration of my career over a long period. Cricket fans had stuck with me, forgiven me and still supported me, and at that unforgettable moment it was like we were all together, along with family and friends, in the city I love most, at the stadium I love most. The 700th wicket was a bonus; in all honesty it could have been the 100th. The point was that I think Australians were happy to share it, on Boxing Day of all days. I've since realised that it brought a lot of joy to people who've lived my life with me from when I started out as a naive 22-year-old, through all the madness and a bit of the magic, to the final throw of the dice here in my own backyard.

Looking back I've often thought my life has been a bit like *The Truman Show* – after all, I turned from boy into man on people's televisions. As a kid I made plenty of mistakes, and still make a few to this day, but I've achieved things that have brought smiles and happiness. The public grew up with me, just as they did on *The Truman Show*, sort of living and breathing it all. I think they could relate to me, as I've never pretended to be something I'm not. Australians love the Australian cricket team and they tune in for the next instalment with the players whose stories they share. It's like 'Hey, Warney's about to bowl', and they come in from the backyard to have a look. I've tried to repay their enthusiasm by being an entertainer with a sense of fun. I want to do well for the team, for my country and for everyone who watches us. And I like to entertain. Perhaps it's as simple, or as complicated, as that.

2

Heroes

My Mother

MUM IS ONE OF the funniest people I've ever met, and most of the time she's not even trying to be funny – the same as Mark Waugh! She's not academic but she is street smart. What's more, she has the best shit detector I know. I promise you, she could meet any of my friends and when they've gone she'll say, 'Great guy, you want him on your side,' or 'Lovely person but watch out for . . .' I don't know what it is but she just picks up on things – she has second, third, fourth, fifth *and* sixth senses. It's weird, but extremely useful! She's virtually never wrong either. It's uncanny, as if she's got a crystal ball. She's like a witch but a good one, a spiritual one, if that makes any sense. Probably not, but I'd go to Mum about anyone.

When I was a kid, Mum went to work. She was hardly ever sick, never complained and brought us up great. We weren't lovey-dovey in our house but we respected and loved each other deeply. She was born right after the war in 1946 in Germany. Her father was a Polish refugee who, when he was still a teenager, ended up in Germany on her grandparents' cabbage farm. His name was Joey and he worked his nuts off on their property just outside Wesselburen. It was there he met Lotte. They were married and had their first child – my mum, Brigitte. A couple of years back, Mum and Dad went to find Wessel-buren and, would you believe, they discovered that not only does it produce the most cabbages in Europe, it also has a cabbage museum, a cabbage festival and every year somebody is crowned Miss Cabbage – fact. Hence, Mum says she was born under a cabbage.

It wasn't long before my grandfather Joey, my grandmother Lotte, Mum and her sister, Regina, had enough of living as cabbage-farm refugees and did a runner all the way to Rome, where they hoped to find a ship to America. Instead, they had to go further south to Naples. They found a ship there alright but the wrong one, and they all ended up coming to Australia. Apparently, the ships to the States were full, so rather than wait for months they bought into Australia's land of opportunity. None of us are complaining – Australia has been a wonderful place for our family and I'd have been a pretty ordinary baseballer.

Dad has a copy of the register list from the ship, the SS *Castel Bianco*. It shows passengers from a heap of Eastern European coun-tries that left Naples on 29 November 1949 and arrived in Geelong on 29 December, and there are the names of the family that reared me: Wladyslaw Szczepiak and Lotte Szczepiak, Regina Szczepiak and Brigitte Szczepiak.

Wladyslaw (aka Joey) got a job in a lime factory in Geelong but his wife and children were taken hundreds of kilometres away to Bonegilla Army Camp, out Wagga Wagga way. Joey worked for six months or so without seeing them and pleaded for time off to go and find his family. They said, 'If you leave here, Joey, you don't have a job.' So he quit. Then he made his way to Bonegilla and brought them back – how the hell he found them I don't know, because he didn't speak English. Then he and another Polish family rented a garage and the four parents worked shifts – at the Ford factory mainly – so there was always someone home for the kids.

Joey was a tough bastard. Mum didn't like him much, but he worked hard – real hard, they say – and managed to save enough money to build a house in Geelong, fill it with brand new furni-ture and buy a new Vauxhall car. He was sitting pretty, but then some very dodgy Aussie, knowing Joey loved to work the land, sold him a farm in Apollo Bay, about 130 kilometres away on the Great Ocean Road. The bloke did a crook deal – convincing Joey that the farm was a phenomenal business opportunity and more than worth the value of the house in Geelong.

Joey did the deal and, much to the dismay of the rest of the family, they left a home they liked and made the journey to Apollo Bay. The farm was badly run-down – a really shitty place, apparently – but the land had a bit of potential. Somehow, they scraped a living from it and soon enough had upgraded to a dairy farm in Skenes Creek, a few kilometres east of Apollo Bay, which Joey said had potential to be something big. Unbelievable courage and determination in that man!

At 13 years of age, Mum got dragged out of school and was made to help work the land, clear the rocks, pick and shovel stuff and tear down the thistle. The property was about 550 acres – a lot of it unusable – but Joey, Lotte and Mum managed to clear around 175 acres of it. You have to hand it to them because in the years since then the land has become really valuable.

Mum had a gift as a runner. For sure the manual work had developed her, both physically and mentally. She trained quietly when the opportunity arose and began to surprise people in competitive races, but her ambitions of Olympic glory – a dreamer, like her son! – were shattered when she got glandular fever. How unlucky is that? It knocked her about for a long time after. She'd missed her moment and didn't run competitively again. And she never, ever complained. Mum is as tough as they come and probably the most honest person I know.

She left the farm when she was about 14 to work at the Apollo Bay Hotel, and a couple of years later, having made a success of the dairy farm, Joey bought the girls a house in Melbourne, in Moonee Ponds, for them to go to school and work there.

In the mid-1970s, Joey went inland to Gerangamete, about 35 kilometres out of Colac. The beef market was up, and he wanted to get out of dairy and into beef. But just as he did, world beef prices collapsed and the US Government put a tariff on Australian beef. There wasn't money in beef anymore, so he went back to dairy!

By this time, Joey was easing up a little on the hard yards and decided he'd win Tattslotto, the local lottery. He got really passionate about it. Joey had a book and he used to write down every single Tattslotto draw number because he thought he'd found a system. He claimed the third and fourth division prizes plenty of times – they were never huge sums of money, though.

Dad reckons Joey was a difficult bloke with a bad temper. He used to get in fits of rage. For instance, he'd knock out a cow if it crapped on him while he was milking – he would be like BANG! He was strong and wide but only about five feet five inches tall. A tough little character, like a tank. We knew he was a good farmer, because he was on the front of one of the country magazines in Apollo Bay for ploughing an unploughable field. It was like a moonscape and he ploughed it like he was on a mission. It was dangerous work. The plough would only have to hit a rock and jump out and there was no way you wouldn't end up in the creek, which my dad did once. Joey got the best out of his crops: that's what he knew.

Then, out of nowhere, in the early 1980s a massive heart attack killed him. He just caved in, and about three years later my grandmother passed, both of them in their mid-to-late 50s. The trauma of their lives probably finally got to them. Like a lot of first-generation immigrants, they worked hard and died young.

My grandmother was a big lady and nice. Jase and I never really spent that much time with Nan and Pop – as we knew them – although I remember Nan best for the white chocolate bars she gave us off the top shelf at her place. We must have been seven or eight back then.

Nan worked as hard as Joey, if not harder – she was the silent type who just got on with it. It was terrible when she got cancer. The doctors operated but didn't hold out any hope and sent her home with three months to live. Mum and Dad chased around and found this guy called Milan Brych in the Cook Islands, who said he could bring cancer patients to remission. He used unorthodox methods, alternative medicine and he made outrageous claims about easing the pain and adding precious years to people's lives, so the medical profession and pharma companies hated him.

I think Dad said he was jailed in three different countries, under suspicion of false medical practice. But Brych never said he could cure cancer, only delay the inevitable. Twenty-five per cent of his treatment was a mixture of apple seeds and other concoctions, 75 per cent of it was him getting people to believe that it worked. Brych needed all patients to bring medical records with them but the authorities wouldn't release Nan's. Dad said, 'You've got me on your doorstop until you give me those documents.' Eventually they sent him to another surgery that did hand them over. Mum then took Nan to the Cook Islands, Brych treated her and, incredibly, as promised, he gave her three more years of life than the doctors told her she had. She died at 57. It was sad because she was such a positive, uncomplaining person.

The immigrant families were hard people, they never gave in. I guess that's what making a new life in someone else's country does to you. They had good manners and kept a clean slate. Mum always shoved good manners down our throat. She said manners were free, and she harped on about being clean and tidy, picking stuff off the floor – that sort of thing. She's round at my place most days, organising washing, cleaning and all that. She loves it. I've tried to follow her example by instilling good manners into my own kids and thankfully my children are wonderfully mannered.

We had so many laughs, and we still do. She calls me and my best mate, Aaron Hamill, the former Aussie Rules football star, the two 'Rockafellas'. 'Where are you Rockafellas off to then?' That was where the diuretic pill came from. 'Rockafella, you're looking heavy, try one of my fluid tablets. Look good, feel good, Shane,' she said. 'Yeah,' I thought, 'give us one of them.' Oh my God! Little did I know. More of that later. What I will say now is that nothing hurt me more than the way the Cricket Australia lawyer, Andrew Thwaites, bullied her in the courtroom during his cross-examination. Like it was her fault.

Mum and Dad would welcome everyone to our home, it was an open-door policy. They also drove me and my brother Jason to and from all sports and made sure we were smart and ready for each day of our lives. Mum worked the canteen at the sports club – she was always giving back to people. Neither of them ever interfered, they only encouraged. Mum is a *very* special person – a strong parent with a keen eye for detail and an amazing ability to stand up for me when things get tough. I guess Mum is the tough one who just gets going.

My Father

My dad, Keith, is my other hero. A bit like Mum, he has a tough story to tell. His own father, Malcolm, was born in Condobolin, a town with a strong Indigenous background in the middle of New South Wales. 'Mac', or 'Boy', as he was also known, was brought up on the hard side of the track by my great-grandfather, Norman, who was a big noise in the town and ruled with an iron fist. He would tie Mac and his brother to the bed and whip them if they did anything wrong. In his late teens Mac fell in love with a local Catholic girl called Anne, but Norman, a committed Protestant, wouldn't let him marry her. That was Australia back then, like the Catholics Jack Fingleton and Bill O'Reilly against the Protestant Bradman and all that stuff in the 1930s.

Mac got nowhere in his pleas to his old man, so he left home to join the Air Force. One leave – and I've no idea when or where – he met, and quickly married, Dorothy. They had four kids, one of which, of course, was Dad. Jumping years ahead, Dorothy died and Mac was on his own – he was about 65 or 66 at this stage – forlorn and lonely. One ANZAC Day, with nothing else to do, he drove back to Condobolin, still very much a country town, and the news got out that 'Boy' Warne was back in town.

'Tell him to go round to Walter's place,' they said. So Mac went round, knocked on the door, and there was this grey-haired old lady, Anne. She lived in Albury, but by coincidence was in Condobolin visiting friends – obviously, one of them was this Walter. Seeing Anne again, it was as if Grandpa had turned the clock back 50 years. He saw her as he'd always seen her and she saw him the same way. They struck up a relationship again.

Anne had had a terrible life – an abusive husband and a son who committed suicide – but now she and Grandpa were picking up where they left off when they were teenagers. He brought her down to meet the family. She was a lovely lady, Dad says, and without Norman around to stop them, they were planning to get married.

Six months later, though, Pa died and poor Anne went back to Albury on her own. It was incredibly sad. Dad had got a call from him one night, but when Pa heard the background noise of some folks having a good time at a social occasion, he said he'd call back in a day or two and quickly put down the phone. Three days later, they found him dead beside the phone in a chair.

He used to wear a mask that helped him breathe, and the enquiry into his death reckoned he must have been trying to put it on but couldn't, so he rang for help, didn't get it and panicked. He'd been dead for those three days and all his bits and pieces – the mask and other stuff – were around the chair. Dad and Pa didn't get on that great, but Dad said he should have known something was up because Pa hardly ever rang. I was 14 when he passed. The Warnes were a complicated family in those days!

My father and his sister were born in Elsternwick, near Brighton of all places, where I've lived so much of my adult life. When Pa returned from the Second World War, houses were scarce and the owner of the place he'd been renting kicked him out. The four of them out on the street, no money and nowhere. Thank God he qualified for a War Service loan and bought a house in Boronia, up near Ferntree Gully at the foot of the Dandenongs.

Dad started at Ferntree Gully Tech but wanted to move to Ringwood High for fifth and sixth form, to complete his education. The problem was he needed a uniform and the old man couldn't afford one. Pa owned a service station out at Coburg, so he said, 'Why not come and work there and I'll pay you. That way you can save up, buy a uniform and go to Ringwood.' So he did.

But Pa had other ideas. A bloke called Smedley, a customer at the gas station, was CEO of a company called Motor Credits, a car dealership finance company. Pa fixed a job for Dad with him – just an errand boy to start with – and told Dad to forget the uniform and Ringwood High and go and buy a suit instead, because he was starting with Motor Credits on Monday. Dad was around 15 at the time.

He stayed two years and then went to Payne's Bon Marche, the department store, to work in the accounting department. Dad is brilliant with numbers – he looks at lists of figures and has them sorted in seconds. He ended up managing that store but had enough of living with Pa and decided to make a clean break. He headed up to Queensland where he picked fruit, cut cane and worked on the railways. But after a couple of years, his mother, Dorothy, rang to say the council had half closed Sydney Road where Pa had the garage. He was losing a lot of business and couldn't afford to hire anyone. Dad's soft heart got the better of him and back he went to help out his old man.

Well, how about this: award after award came their way for being the best service station operators in Melbourne: you know, how they serviced the cars, looked after clients, treated customers and all that. Dad got really good at it until one evening a teenage couple pulled in and told him to clean their windscreen. There was a bit of drizzle on it, that's all.

'Err, okay,' said Dad, and when he'd finished he said, 'Now can I fill you up?'

They said, 'Nah, we just wanted our windscreen cleaned because we're going to the drive-in,' and they started laughing.

Dad said, 'Are you really?', and then picked up a handful of dirt and chucked it across the whole windscreen before saying, 'Now piss off.'

He turned around and there was his old man standing in the doorway with steam coming out of his ears. As far as he was concerned the couple could have been set up by his rivals to catch them out. Dad left that day, resigned on the spot, never to return.

He then went into white goods at H. G. Palmer's, but that didn't suit him much. He used to have to go to places to repossess fridges, amongst other things. A woman might come to the door, kids hanging off her skirt who hadn't eaten for a day, and he'd have to say, 'You haven't paid for your fridge.' She'd reply, 'I haven't got the money, I'm sorry.' The kids looked hungry, she looked desperate, so he'd pay their monthly bill for them – and even give them money for fish and chips.

It's no surprise he wasn't successful at repossession work but his heart won many a day. Not least, the day when he met Brigitte Szczepiak. Lotte said that one day she picked up Brigitte after work, and when Mum got into the car she looked across the road and said to old Lotte, 'You see that man over there? Well, I haven't met him yet but I'm going to marry him.'

She was right. They were married at St Paul's Church in Essendon three years later, on Mum's 21st birthday.

It took a bit of doing. Dad was just short of *his* 21st birthday, he had a second-hand car that he owed 600 bucks on and not another dime to bless himself with. Joey, who was very protective of Mum, figured Dad must have had it easy – you know, a milk and honey life – because he'd finished up at H. G. Palmer's and was out of a job, but seemed to have successful parents who carried him along. Not so, of course, but a hard one for Dad to explain. 'So what ya got to be worth my daughter?' he asked.

Dad didn't have the answer but told Joey he'd prove himself more than worthy of his daughter, even without his blessing. Joey kind of relented but then said the wedding would have to take place in a Catholic church. Dad said no way: 'I'll pay for my own wedding in my own place and you're welcome to come, Joey.'

They always clashed, though as I remember it Joey might have been tricky and liked to play hard ball, but he wasn't unreasonable. I must be right because to Dad's amazement, Joey said, 'Okay, I'll give you a start. I'll give you the house in Moonee Ponds as a wedding present.' Incredibly, Dad told him to stick the house up his arse. *Dad!* Mum almost reneged on the marriage! So Joey was a generous guy after all, but Dad wanted to make his own way – like Joey had, I suppose. As a thank you for his offer, Dad did Joey's books for him for nothing and saved him some mighty tax bills.

Joey was good to me and Jason. He and Mum's brother-in-law, Uncle Chris, used to take us for rides on their farm motorbikes and we'd feed the calves and mess around in the hay barn. I remember us kicking a football around with him and even setting up games of cricket. We did that in Mornington too, in the park opposite Mac and Dorothy's place. Sadly, both sets of grandparents had gone by the time I was 15. I sometimes wonder what they'd think of the way things have turned out. I don't suppose a living out of cricket was on their radar.

After Keith and Brigitte got married, they rented a unit on St Kilda Road, lived the high life for six months and then suddenly realised they weren't saving a penny. While Mum was pregnant with me, they went to live with Nan and Pa. Dad knuckled down with house re-blocking and pest control and then, on 13 September 1969, Shane Keith Warne was born at William Angliss Hospital in Upper Ferntree Gully. Keith had promised Brigitte that they'd have a house when she came out of hospital, so he flogged his car, borrowed a load from the bank, arranged a mortgage, and bought a $13,000 home in Hampton. When Mum came out of hospital with little me, she went straight to 229 Thomas Street.

3

Growin' Up

The 'Hood

OUR FIRST FAMILY HOME was a small Edwardian-style weatherboard, built on a large block on the corner of Bronte Court and Thomas Street, Hampton – a leafy middle-class suburb in the south-east of Melbourne. I used my little feet to scoot around the place, crashing my plastic motorbike into anything that came my way. It took a while to learn to steer. I was just 14 months when I gashed my forehead, smashing into a concrete step by the back door, but that had nothing on the busted legs a couple of years later. Some kid at nursery jumped off a mound and landed on my legs – *snap*.

I was three-and-a-half years old and was in traction for a few days at the Royal Children's Hospital. Mum and Dad weren't allowed to sleep over in those days and I pleaded with them every evening not to leave, often screaming in fear of what might happen next. They reckon it was pretty traumatic. When I got out of hospital I was plastered from neck to knee. It was a spiral fracture and nothing was supposed to move for months during the healing period, so I lay flat on a trolley and scooted round the house on that too.

Life wasn't easy for my folks. Not having a specific professional qualification, Dad did all sorts of work – cane cutting, house re-blocking and office and sales jobs, as I've mentioned, including a spell at Pink Pages. He landed a good one with Prudential Insurance and the two of them further subsidised family costs by taking on after-hours contract cleaning. Dad washed and polished the floors at the blood bank in the city and Mum looked after offices in nearby Sandringham. She took me and my brother, Jason – who had been born, like me, in Ferntree Gully, 21 months after his elder bro – with her, and we helped by emptying bins and tidying up. At least, we thought we did. We probably just got in the way.

Don't ask me how it came about, but Mum also worked for Bob Hawke's wife, Hazel, cleaning the house and helping out when Bob had meetings or events at home in Royal Avenue, Sandringham. We used to have a hit on Bob's tennis court and, as we grew up, he used to come and play with us, often introducing us to visiting heavies – politicians and celebrities – who played too. We loved Bob, still do: Australia's best-ever Prime Minister in my opinion.

We had beautiful neighbours in Thomas Street. The mother of the family was a friendly lady called Marge Lucas, who used to keep an eye out for me on my bike or walking home from school and leave out a pint of silver-top milk in the old bottles. Sometimes she'd make me a Blue Heaven milkshake and, right to this day, I pass shops – like the old-fashioned fish-and-chip places – and nip in to see if they've got 'em. It's like a sort of bubble-gum vanilla ice-cream – amazing. My daughter Brooke, who works in a local cafe, surprises me with one sometimes. Good girl, Brookie!

It was in this neighbourhood, often in the park across the road, that I was an AFL champion and an Aussie cricketer, a dreamer, a rock star and budding petrol head. Dad loved cars; Jase and I used to help him clean them at weekends. He had a Ford GT Phase III prototype – only a few were ever made. At different times, he also had a Corvette Stingray, a Holden Monaro GTS and a Brock Group A and Group 3 Holden Commodore (named after the legendary Australian driver Peter Brock). When I was about 17, I remember saying to myself while we were washing the Group A Commodore,

'One day I'm going to have a car like this.' It was a blue Brock Commodore and I'd sit in the driver's seat, take hold of the steering wheel and imagine cruising round the 'hood.

By now, Dad was working in the pest-control business and he was away a lot, but when he was home I badgered him to play ball or to wash the car together – stuff sons and fathers do. Then I started to travel everywhere with him, in the back of the Ford GT.

That Ford was something. It was a prototype that was put together at the factory in Geelong for the big Phase IIIs. A guy called Al Turner, I think, who was a Ford team manager at the time, tested it down Conrod Straight at Bathurst. It did an astonishing 164 miles per hour (264 kilometres per hour) and then it came up for sale after testing. Dad borrowed some money and bought it at Preston Ford in Essendon – how they got hold of it, I don't know. Anyway, Dad had it and I loved it. It was just a brutal car and magnificent. He wrote it off eventually, which gave the insurance company a shock.

I've had a few great cars myself: Ferrari 355, Ferrari 360, Lamborghini Superleggera (probably the best I've ever had, an unbelievable car), Lamborghini Murcielago, Mercedes, BMW, and wait for it – yep, a blue Brock Commodore of my own. Boom! When I'm away, Dad takes the cars of the moment round the block, or further – 'to make sure everything is okay', he says. 'Yeah, Dad, right, just make sure you fill 'em up when you're done!' I love that he does that.

I think I was seven when we moved to Beach Road in Black Rock, a few kilometres from Hampton. The day we arrived, we found a cat that had been hit by a car and was badly beaten – battered, actually – but it was still alive. We nursed it back to health and called it Rocky, because at that stage the Rocky movies were out. And like the cat, Rocky didn't give up. I loved that cat. I had two other pets, both dogs – one a tiny white fluffy poodle that I was too young to remember much about and a terrier called Bronte, after our home at Bronte Court. Bronte and I got on really well and he followed me to school most days – me on my bike, him jogging along behind. Then, one day, Bronte was hit by a car and killed. I was devastated and never wanted a dog again. I suppose it was my first emotional hit and I didn't like it one bit.

The best of the guys out on the street was David Beck. As kids, we were inseparable and he had a hot sister called Sarah, who kept us all interested. Life was simple then – you know, from hide and seek to sport, music, cars and girls. We all worshipped the Fonz from the TV show *Happy Days* and the top footy players – they were our heroes.

Becky saved my life once. We lived right opposite Half Moon Bay, where the HMAS *Cerberus*, which was used as a guard ship and munitions store in the First World War, had been sold for scrap and sunk as a breakwater off the bay in the 1920s. Jase, Becky and I used to swim out there and in and out of the hull. One day a group of us were diving off the painted railings on the pier, and I lost my footing on the new gloss paint Dad had warned me about. As if you listen at 13! So I was trying to dive out and over the jetty but, well, got it wrong. My head hit the edge of the pier and it knocked me out.

I was floating face down when Becky saw me, went for the leap, made it and turned me over. Some of the other lads helped to drag me out, while another one ran to the house and called Dad. He fixed me up. I ended up with a small scar near my eye, that's all. Lucky boy. Unfortunately, I've lost contact with Becky. Pity, because he was a great bloke and as good an all-round sportsman as I've ever seen.

Anyway, here's a story. Mum used to cook up a storm and we'd all eat everything. One day, Jason was diagnosed with a nasty infected ear. Mum had read an old wives' tale about treating ear infections with warm onion juice – apparently, it would reduce swelling and relieve the pain. So she heated up an onion, extracted the juice and syringed a few drops into Jason's ear. It worked – eureka! – but apparently all this attention on Jason, and these onions, put me off my food, so much so that one night I refused to eat. The next night too, and the next. I just ran out of interest in food and have never recovered it. Not until I met Elizabeth Hurley anyway, who improved my diet from nachos, pizza, cheese toasties and spaghetti bolognese to the healthier stuff. I haven't stuck with it enough. Blame Mum and the onions.

By the way, I must explain 'Harry' as well. It used to be a running joke in my family and it started out with Jason and me calling Dad 'Harry'. I don't know why, we just did. I think it was because he looked like Clint Eastwood – Dirty Harry. Then for some reason Mum became Harry as well. Then they both started calling me Harry. So I called Jase Harry. Imagine what that was like round the house! Someone would shout 'Harry' and everyone would answer. Nuts. But funny.

I'd started school life at Sandringham Primary and pretty quickly was riding my bike to get there. We played a lot of football and cricket in the street and tennis behind the Country Women's Association flats, which were a couple of doors up from us. Dad looked after the maintenance of the courts and in return we got to use them for free.

We had 10 cents a week pocket money and could supplement it with 20 cent jobs like washing the car, putting the bins out, clearing the leaves, cutting the edges of the lawn real neat. Then I'd buy 10 cents worth of chips for the bike ride to school, stuff them in my backpack and get into them at the first traffic lights. Actually, a 10 cent bag of lollies was the best value – a banana stick, a chocman, spearmint leaf, strawberry cream, the lot. After the 'Oniongate' scene at home, I didn't eat much, except toast with vegemite, and pizza maybe. I was skinny like you wouldn't believe, until I went to England in 1989 and discovered pints.

It was a 25-minute bike ride from our place to school and you picked up mates along the way, forming a gang. The girls were in too: Lisa Tregenza, who I had the hots for; Carmel Finlay, who was a great girl, really easy-going; and Pauline Vaughan and Michelle Scott, who I had crushes on at different stages of school life. In my head, I was going to marry Michelle. I haven't seen or heard of any of them since! Lisa was the first girl to make me nervous. She was a bit older than the rest of us and I'd leave home early in the hope of catching some time with her on our own before the other guys turned up. That didn't work out much, though! I've often wondered what happened to Lisa, and especially to Michelle.

Jase and I were right into 'Little Athletics' too: getting fit, meeting a lot of good mates, learning about competition and setting goals for improvement. On Saturdays we were always at the East Sandringham Boys Club. There were matches for the Under 10s in both footy and cricket but I was slow on the take for cricket, preferring tennis back then. Dad, Jason and I played a lot of tennis and kicked a footy all day long – park, side streets, yard, wherever.

We were all about sport – if you didn't play you were on the outer. We did the drive-in sometimes, when you'd hook up your car radio to an AM station with the speaker on and watch movies with Mum and Dad. But never on Fridays. It was always early to bed on Friday to be good for Saturday sport.

✧

We finally caught on to cricket during Kerry Packer's unbelievable World Series Cricket era, a kind of fever in the late '70s. I went with Jase to the first game out at Waverley. WSC came out of nowhere and captured our imagination like the sport hadn't done before. It's hard to exaggerate the impact it had on all of Australia, not to mention the rest of the cricketing world. It was the rock and roll of the moment, both sexy and cool. Previously when we watched a Test match, there were players we didn't know, all in the same white gear, with only one camera behind the bowler's arm – and the wicketkeeper's arse every second over – filming them and low-key commentary talking about it all. The kids of the day couldn't understand what was going on, and there was no-one to ignite their interest, so they didn't much care about it.

The second year of World Series Cricket, 1978/79, was when I have my first recollections of playing the sport in the backyard. Jason's favourite player was the South African fast bowler Garth Le Roux, so Jase bowled for the World XI and I batted for Australia – the Chappells mainly and Rod Marsh. The back gate was the wicket and we played these elaborate games mimicking all those guys. We could all do a Viv Richards and a pretty good Chappelli, with his shirt unbuttoned, collar up, chewing gum, looking like he was at war.

We'd imitate Dennis Lillee too, with his shirt unbuttoned as well, all the way down to his navel, his appeals, the way he wiped the sweat from his forehead with a flick of his right forefinger; Greg Chappell, upright and elegant and so determined; David Hookes, so exciting. All of them in the backyard against guys like Le Roux, Barry Richards and Clive Rice – the South Africans we missed.

Of all the players in WSC, the stand-out was Viv. Even today, he's the best batsman I've ever seen. From when I was 10, Viv stood alongside Peter Knights from Hawthorn footy club and Trevor Barker of St Kilda – they were both spectacular, flamboyant players – as a sporting god in my eyes. It was Trevor who christened me 'Hollywood', by the way.

I'll talk later on in the book about *Wisden*'s five players of the century, but my men of that century were Kerry Packer, Austin Robertson, John Cornell, Richie Benaud, Tony Greig and Ian Chappell – those guys changed cricket forever and made it better and more lucrative for those of us who followed. In fact, every player since should say a huge thank you to them every day! To me World Series Cricket was the best cricket ever played. I've watched hours of it on film and haven't seen anything better. I really wish the stats from those matches counted in the career averages of the players.

Anyway, I played footy all winter at East Sandy and then Dad suggested I start playing cricket at the club in summer as well. But even though I was into the WSC thing, I still hadn't found the passion for cricket that was to eventually consume my life. Living over the road from the beach and with all my friends hanging out there, I was like, 'Damn, I'm standing in a field for six hours – I'd rather be down the beach!' I was alright, though, a batsman mainly. I tried wicket-keeping and fast bowling, anything to keep interested. I was about 10 or 11 when I started to bowl a few leg-breaks for the first time.

It wasn't until I was 11, though, training in the nets, that I tried mimicking Kim Pitt, who was the club's first-team spinner. It came out great and I kept doing it. Everyone at the club paid some attention then. So did I, as I could spin it, albeit inconsistently.

✧

I should say a few extra words about Dad. He sacrificed everything for me and Jason, working all hours to put a roof over our head. He's a popular guy and a smart guy but, as I've mentioned, he was brought up the hard way and, on occasions, he wasn't afraid to let us know. He's spot on with all his advice, although unfortunately I don't listen to it as much as I should. Why? Because he's my dad. Duh! If he was my financial adviser, I'd probably say, 'Yeah that's a great idea,' but because it's my dad, it's like, 'Yeah, okay, Dad,' and I miss out.

One Christmas I wanted a new bike but money was tight so Dad built me one from scratch himself – it was a super-cool bike too. He saved money on that so he could buy me the new blue-coloured footy boots that all the guys were using. How thoughtful is that!

He was strict, though. I remember a few times arguing with him in the car before slamming the door and walking off, and he'd jump out and grab me and say, 'Respect the car. This is my car – treat it with respect or there's trouble.' I remember Jase came home drunk one night when he was 16 or 17 and threw up everywhere. Dad wasn't happy. He said, 'You do whatever you want in your house but this is the family home – you don't vomit in the family home,' and he made him get down on his hands and knees and clean it up with a spoon and an empty milk carton. Jase never came home drunk again – neither did I.

As I've said, it wasn't tender loving care in our house. At times I resented how strict it was – when we were younger, we had dinner at 6 pm and bed at eight (we couldn't even watch *Prisoner*!) – which is why I'm more lenient with my own kids. I sure learnt a lot from Mum and Dad but definitely didn't adopt enough of what I learnt. For example, my grandfather on Dad's side died of emphysema but Dad stayed a smoker for 27 years until, guess what, his lung collapsed. I was 16 when he finally stopped and it was about then that I started full on. Mum was really disappointed: 'I've just got rid of a bloke who smoked for 27 years, now you start, Harry. You're stupid.'

I'd started smoking a few years before that, though. Jase smoked a bit too. We used to hide cigarettes under the fire hydrant in the street around the corner in a plastic cover – Peter Jackson 10-packs that cost about 30 cents. Mum and Dad knew where they were, of course, and the next time we went back it was like, 'Jesus, someone has taken our smokes again.' We used to rub berries on our hands so you couldn't smell it but they knew.

When Jase and I were 11 or 12, Dad locked us in a closet. He said, 'If you guys want to smoke, here's a pack each. You're not coming out until you've smoked the lot.' I was violently ill after a couple of smokes, coughing and spluttering, shouting, 'Dad, let me out!' But Jase stayed in there for hours, smoked the lot and then came out and said, 'Any more, Dad? How many more you got?' That was Jase.

Dad was not a cricketer but he decided he wanted to play with his boys. I reckon I was about 16 by then, and he'd watch us in matches in the morning and then come and field in the arvo when we were playing in the seniors. He was no cricketer – he batted at 11 and didn't bowl – but he had a great throw and caught pretty well. Then after a Saturday afternoon game, he'd take us down to the bottle store and buy us a beer. At least we thought he did. It was alcohol-free but Jase and I thought we were such dudes having a beer every Saturday with Dad. It was so cool, a lovely thing for him to do.

We shared a lot, as boys and their fathers do – sport and music, family mates. We all got on. During my playing career, if Dad was anywhere near the dressing-room the Vics guys and Aussie guys would always say, 'Hey, Keith, come on in for a beer,' and he'd hang out there with Boon and Marsh, AB, Merv and Mark Taylor. They all loved having him around. He's a good talker, a kind man and no ego.

✧

Year on year I was doing great at footy, and at 16 years old, after kicking 16 goals in one match and eight in the next, I was picked in a representative side to go down to Tasmania. There was this guy, Peter Hudson, who was one of the best full-forwards in the history of the sport. He'd retired by now and owned a pub in Tassie. He watched me kick those goals and wanted me billeted at the pub but they wouldn't let minors in, so I missed out. They say he kept an eye on me – 'Who is this kid: he must be a talent' – but unfortunately I never met him. He was right in a way, but not how he expected!

I was locked between football and tennis. The next summer, still 16, up at Tulip Street I played Section 1 men's tennis and had daily lessons, but I was still playing cricket – and I was liking it more with each day. The tennis even impacted on footy training and I remember going to my coach, Les Burkwood, who said I was a pussy for playing the sport. I mean, in those days Borg and McEnroe were cool – and I liked Jimmy Connors' passion too – but Aussie Rules was king.

I still remember Dad saying, 'If you're not playing football, you have to tell the coach.' I was terrified of the bloke. Les told me I was taking a soft option, but anyway, that was that and I had a year off footy – and cricket too – and played tennis non-stop all year round. I was super fit and ranked three in Victoria in my age group.

All that came to an abrupt end at the start of the next summer. I was in Year 9 and playing for Hampton High, when I was chosen for a combined High Schools cricket match against Mentone Grammar. I got six wickets and made a quick 60. Then I played football for the same combined High Schools team – again against Mentone Grammar – and kicked 10. The people there said, 'Hang on, this bloke has just taken six wickets and made 60, and now he's kicked 10 against us in the footy. He's pretty good – he needs to be at our school.'

They approached Dad and offered me a scholarship, which was pretty cool at the time. Dad wanted Jason there too but couldn't afford full fees, so he cleverly negotiated a discount! So the tennis stopped, and from then on I was focused totally on the football and cricket.

Out of nowhere, there we were at Mentone Grammar and suddenly had these unbelievable cricket facilities – turf pitches, all sorts. I had two wonderful South African coaches – John Mason, who had something wrong with his leg and sat on a shooting-stick running practice sessions, and Barry Irons, who had a big moustache and really knew the game.

I was a number four batsman and part-time leg-spinner. I just wasn't consistent enough, though, bowling a good one here and there, then two shockers, and trying a flipper that was just a fast seamer. Anyway, in my first year, the summer of 1985, I went on a trip down to Gippsland, in south-east Victoria, to a first XI tournament. Being just a new kid I wasn't expecting to play, but I was picked for the second game and broke the teeth of the wicketkeeper with a big leg-break that fizzed and bounced and whacked him full in the mouth, messing up his teeth. People were thinking, 'Who is this bloke?!' I slogged a few with the bat too. We won the tournament and I ended up captain of the cricket side and of the Associated Grammar Schools team, batting at four and ripping out some liquorice-allsort leg-spinners, but breaking all sorts of records. That was really the start of the cricket thing.

School's Out

Of course, it wasn't just sport at Mentone Grammar, and it wasn't all fun and games. When I was in Year 12, I remember one teacher smashing me across the face with a text book. Those old Year 12 text books were big. I got up and was looking for something to throw at him and saw a hard-backed duster. It hit him straight in the balls. There was a big white outline of the duster on his pants and everyone in the class was laughing.

Predictably, he sent me to the principal, Keith Jones, who was a decent bloke. I admitted that I was being a smart arse in class, disruptive and disinterested, but I also said that the teacher couldn't belt me across the face and get away with it.

Jones said that what I'd done was no good – 'You know the routine, Warne, pull your blazer up, pull your pants down, I'm going to practise my golf swing on you.' Then, not for the first time, he gave me six of the best – six smashings on the arse with a cane. I got it in exactly the same spot, not six different spots, and I knew about it.

A few of us used to get caned a bit by Jones and in the end we worked out a plan. Sometimes we'd wear four or five pairs of jocks because we figured that if we got sent out of class we were going to get the cane. The extra padding was just in case we got hammered.

I seemed to get a lot of those smashings – more than most. They started in Year 11 and they happened about once a fortnight; a combination between Jones and this bloke Sergeant Evans, who took a real disliking to me.

Our school had a cadet program, where kids would be kitted out in army uniform and get taught some of the basics of army training – marching and all that. We had to wear the khaki green stuff – big black boots, belt, etc – and you had to be able to see your reflection in everything. You had to get the Brasso and shine up the buckle of the belt and polish up the leather as well. You had to polish your shoes too and if anything wasn't perfect, it was, 'Right, into my office.' That wasn't the only reason Sergeant Evans didn't like me that much, though. It was the usual stuff – my lippy backchat and unwillingness to conform, as well as smoking on the bus or at school.

He used to sneak onto the Cromer Road bus that went from my place in Black Rock, down Beach Road, left up Balcombe, then down Cromer, dropping the girls off first at Mentone Girls Grammar and then the boys. We used to have a few smokes up the back of the bus and he'd appear out of nowhere, catching us out. He nailed me all the time – whether it was smoking or whatever. 'WARNE!!!!'

I hated the bloke and in the end I was doing this stuff on purpose just to piss him off. One night, Mum saw the stripes on my bum – welts actually. She reckoned I was a bit of a mongrel at the time and probably deserved most of what I was getting, but, she said to them, do you have to smash him that bad? There was something about sportsmen and the army, I reckon, as if Sergeant Evans figured we had a sense of entitlement – us blokes with a bit of flair and personality, a bit of spunk – and that it needed taking down a peg or two. He might have had a point.

Everyone liked the principal, even though he used to belt us. He was respected for running a fantastic school. There was another wonderful teacher called Tony Drinan, a legend – everyone loved Tony. Me and my mates from school used to bump into him at the footy, watching St Kilda play at Moorabbin; he was always on the piss. We'd shout 'Tony!!' and he'd give us a thumbs up, hammering down those beer cans. See, he loved St Kilda – he was passionate about the club – and he sat there in the outer never missing a minute. Sometimes he'd say to me, 'What have you done to upset Sergeant Evans this time, mate?' I'd tell him and he'd say, 'Hang on in there, keep your cool, don't wind him up anymore.' And then we'd go back to talking footy while he knocked back the beer.

I'm writing about this because school is so different today. In the mid-1980s, that kind of stuff was the norm – not just at our school, but all schools. If you went to a private school, you'd get the cane. At a public school, like Hampton High, it was more likely the ruler across the hand. That hurt too.

I think it bred tougher kids. These guys now, they get it easy and they're so spoilt. I'm the worst – I spoil my kids rotten but it's on the back of school discipline, which is soft. If they backchat a teacher, they get detention. Who cares about half an hour detention? I'm not advocating 25 beatings a year but I think there's a line somewhere in the middle of the two extremes. I think you could have some old school standards within the new age values, like life everything is about a balance.

So, as you can probably tell, I was no academic. I couldn't concentrate and hated geography and economics in particular, but I got by and have mainly happy memories of a simple school life that will be a part of me forever. I would never say that school shaped me – Mum and Dad did that – but I think it made me see that there were options in life and that they needed attention and commitment if you were going to make them work for you. Some I pulled off, others I didn't. I guess most kids are the same.

✧

All the AFL clubs had talent scouts and obviously St Kilda had heard about this kid at Mentone Grammar, which is just a few kilometres down the Nepean Highway from the Saints' base at Moorabbin. They invited me to train with their Under 19s. I was a massive Hawthorn fan, but that didn't matter. In Year 11 and 12, I played a few games for the Saints, which was pretty exciting, but I was only allowed to turn out for the club when the school team didn't have a match.

After I left school, I played a full season for the Saints. I was going okay and in one game I kicked seven goals against Hawthorn, in front of the legendary Allan Jeans. Jeans was the Hawthorn seniors' coach, but back in 1966 he'd coached St Kilda to their one and only premiership. Although I'd been a Hawks supporter, now that I was playing for the Saints, and getting to know some of the blokes who were in the senior team, I thought, 'I can't barrack for Hawthorn any more – I've got to barrack for St Kilda now.'

I have to tell you about 'the wall'. We'd been taking some beatings, and our Under 19s coach, Darryl Nisbet, told us, 'From now on, however many points you lose by, we're gonna do "the wall" that many times.'

It went like this. We all started in the centre of the ground at Moorabbin, ran out to the outside of the ground, jumped a wire fence, and then ran up a hill. At the top of the hill, there was this huge wall – maybe eight or 10 feet high. You had to grab the top of the wall, pull yourself up, then jump down onto the ground. Then you had to do the same thing again, from the other side of the wall, then run down the hill, jump the wire fence again and run back out to the centre. That was 'one'. When we got hammered, we were there till all hours!

Another night, we got to the club, ready to go, and Darryl said, 'Rightio, guys, no training tonight. We're all going to run down to the Moorabbin pub and we're going to drink six pots (that's about three pints) and run straight back. We'll see which of you guys throws up, which of you guys is tough, which of you guys can handle it.'

So we ran about 1.5 k's to the pub, drank the beers as fast as we could, and then sprinted back. That was our session. Then Darryl said, 'Rightio, boys, come back tomorrow with a better attitude.'

In 1988 I trained with the seniors a couple of times a week for three months. It was fantastic, training alongside players who've become greats of the game – Trevor Barker, Nicky Winmar and Tony Lockett, who in my opinion was the best player to ever play the game.

I finished the year as leading goal-kicker in the Under 19s. It was an amazing time and my footy dreams were shaping up pretty well.

Jason

Jason is nearly two years younger than me and an outstanding all-round sportsman who had a lot of bad luck with injuries. He is a true mate and I love him. We did everything together growing up. Jase could bat and to this day he claims I never got him out in the nets. I'm beginning to think it might be true. He was 'Mr Puniverse' until he had his growth spurt quite late – 17, I think – and *whoosh*, he was suddenly six foot three. This was a great moment in our house because Jase could really play football and this was the boost he needed to make the most of his ability.

He played in the seniors for St Kilda against Hawthorn in a pre-season game and, by half-time, had kicked five goals. They took him off because they didn't want anyone else drafting him. He was told he was making the senior list, but then the club negotiated this unbelievable deal where they got three players they wanted for the following season and only had to trade one. Since you could only have 40 on the list, though, Jase missed out. It was a disgrace.

He went down to Sandringham in the VFA – the Victorian Football Association – which is the level down from the AFL. It killed him to be honest and then he picked up glandular fever, missed most of the year and was never quite the same again. It's ridiculous how glandular fever hurt both him and Mum when they were on the brink of breaking through. He tried to make a comeback, but he shattered his leg during a match at Sandringham and didn't think he'd ever play footy again.

Jase had the shits with everything then and went to England for 12 months to drive trucks with his mates. When he came home, the Brisbane Bears had joined the AFL and he was recruited for Southport, which, to put it in context, is like being picked for St Kilda Cricket Club before going on to play for Victoria. It was a good standard of club footy and he kicked 90-odd goals in 12 games. But he was in pain. The medics found two bulging discs in his back, and that was his sporting career over. Jase gave it everything, but it just wasn't meant to be.

Over the years I haven't spoken to him about it much – I think it still hurts. I know how proud of me he is, but I reckon he might resent the fact that I got all the lucky breaks. There's no doubt that, without injury, he'd have played in the AFL. He was also a good cricketer, and he played in the Under 17s for Victoria when I was nowhere near – batting at five and bowling off-spin. I was a better footballer than him as a kid, but after the growth spurt he became seriously good. We kind of reversed out.

Of course, Jase and I used to fight – like brothers do. I remember two instances vividly. As I've said, he was Mr Puniverse, the little weed that I picked up and threw around. I always used to say to him, 'I'm gonna time you to run to the shop and back – I bet you can't do it in a minute and a half each way.' He'd be like, 'Urrrgghh, okay.' As he got older and stronger, though, he'd say, 'Bloody hell, mate, *you* go to the shop,' and I'd tell him, 'No, mate, I'm the older brother, you go to the shop,' and we'd get into a biffo. One day, he really had the shits and trapped and twisted my left arm pretty badly. I completely lost the plot and went hard at him. He just said, 'Piss off, mate,' and loaded up a spear gun, took aim from five metres and missed me by a foot. It hit the fence behind me. *Thud!* Jesus! A spear gun – I'd have been dead. Then I knew he'd had enough of me, so I left him alone for a while. (Yes, we had a spear gun at home but I've no idea where it came from. I promise you that's true. If you ever meet Dad or Jason, ask them about it.)

The second time I remember fighting was after he got bigger, when he started doing weights and became massive. I mean like *huge*. One day he picked me up and threw me into the pool – and I was 18 years old! I climbed out and said, 'You want some action, baby brother, let's go.' We got right into each other. He pinned me down with his legs, had his hands up, and I said, 'Yeah, go on then, you haven't got the balls,' and *bang*, he smacked me in the face just as Mum walked in the house. She kicked up hell, saying, 'You guys are brothers – grow up and sort it out,' and she stormed off. There was blood everywhere. Jase said 'Leave me alone' and I did . . . this time forever.

Yeah, I love my brother. It might not always have been harmonious but we did everything together and had a ball. He was best man at my wedding. There was always friendly competition in the early days, but there's only friendship and trust now. He was my agent/ manager for two years, then ran my foundation for a couple more. He worked for IMG, the sports management company, and TWI, its television arm, for a while, drove trucks over here and over there, worked in real estate, and nowadays designs and sells office space, which is going great. He's been married to Shay for 18 years and they've got two super kids – Tyla and Sebastian. As I say, he's my mate and my bro and blood is thicker than water.

That's it, the Warnes, all those years back. Let's see what happened next.

4

A Head Full of Dreams

Home and Away

IN THE EARLY PART of 1989 I opened a letter from St Kilda Football Club that shattered my dreams. The long and short of it was 'Your services are no longer required'.

Dad says that my final 'trial' went against me. I'd been playing for the St Kilda Under 19s, doing okay, and I'd been on stand-by for the next step up – to the senior division – for six weeks in a row. Then, the day they called, I'd been sick in bed all week, really weak, and I hadn't been to training. Dad remembers that I'd climbed out of bed to ring Gary Colling, the coach of the Under 19s, to pull out of the match, but Gary beat me to it and said I was needed to play in the senior reserves match the next day. On the day I was offered my big chance, I was as sick as a dog. Strange how life turns out – sliding doors and all that. Anyway, instead of saying I was too crook to play, I said, 'Wow, yeah, alright, I'll be there.'

It was a disaster. Playing against Carlton, I was up against Milham Hanna, one of the fastest men in the league – a couple of years later, he'd be selected in the All-Australian team – and I had nothing.

I was white as a sheet. The people who matter just figured I wasn't up to it and dropped me back down to the Under 19s.

But although Dad says I was ill and should never have played in that match, the truth is that I wasn't good enough – not a mile off, but in the end not good enough. That's hard to take. It went deep, like my soul had been ripped out. I was in love with AFL football but the game was not in love with me.

What the hell was I going to do? I had passed Year 12 exams but wasn't qualified for anything that would make me a few bucks. I had sport on the brain, but I needed some money and didn't want to be dependent on my parents. So the first thing was to get a job. I drove trucks for Forty Winks, setting up new beds in people's homes. I even delivered waterbeds, though they never appealed to me – honest! From seven o'clock on Friday evenings, through the weekend, I delivered pizzas, which was worth an extra 20 bucks a night. The only problem was that I love pizza, so when I knocked off at midnight I'd smash a large ham and pineapple – that I had to pay for myself – which only left me with 12 bucks profit on the night.

Then I found a job with one of Mum's friends at Paterson's jewellers, handling signet rings, engagement rings, wedding rings, necklaces, bracelets – stuff like that – but it wasn't for me. The more I searched for the right thing, the more my shattered dream kept reappearing. I was circling, waiting, wondering about the next thing in my life – not impatiently but, then again, not too patiently either. There had to be something beyond footy that was better than delivering beds and pizzas.

It was late in the summer of 1989 – February, March time – that I saw the first sign of it. I'd just got into the first XI at St Kilda Cricket Club and then, very soon after, into the Victorian state squad. I'd started to think about cricket a lot. As I've said, it didn't have a place in my heart like footy, but it was taking over my head. I asked myself questions. Who are the great players? Which of them should I emulate? Who should I listen to? How do I improve? Where does all that start?

Later that March, a mate of mine, Ricky Gough, said he was heading over to play club cricket in England and suggested I give footy a miss for the winter and go over with him to play the leagues in the West Country. I thought, 'To hell with it. Why not?'

So, in the late English spring of 1989, I joined up with the Imperial Club in Bristol. I was 19 years old and began to hang out with a bunch of great guys who loved a beer and taught me how to drink a pint. We're talking truckloads of them. I was 79 kilograms on the scales when I left Oz and I came back 99 kilos. I learned to drink, play cricket and, well, a few other things about life too! Ricky and I slept in the cricket pavilion for the first few weeks and crashed out there.

A season in England introduces you to the game in a really interesting way. There's a lot of cricket – like three, four, sometimes even five games a week, many of them social and only one, the Saturday league game, seriously competitive – which allows you to bowl so many overs in such different conditions and circumstances. You learn about yourself and your game. It's a terrific experience.

We went all over the West Country: Devon, Torquay, Exeter, Exmouth, St Ives. I remember playing against the New Zealand Test batsman Mark Greatbatch down there somewhere and he was equally amazed at how much cricket there was if you went looking for it. The responsibility of being the overseas pro was good for me: batting at three, four or five, depending on the make-up of the team each week, and bowling on soft pitches. I played as a batting all-rounder and was surprised at how driven I was: (a) to learn and (b) to succeed.

It wasn't anywhere near county cricket level – more like second or third grade in Melbourne, to be honest – but it was competitive enough for me to have to pull a finger out or be the Aussie pro who made a goose of himself. I was there for six months and played 70 or 80 games. In Australia it would take you four or five years to play that many games, so I fast-tracked my learning and – as well as unravelling how to drink 10 pints and jump the counter at Miss Millie's, the local KFC-type place – I got to understand my craft a little more.

I took a lot of wickets, made plenty of runs and began to think, 'Right, you can play this game. You'd better start paying attention, mate.' I also picked up on how competitive I was. The norm in Australia was not the norm in Bristol and the stand-out difference between me and most others was my desire to win. Not that I'd yet perfected the art of any sort of gamesmanship – like staring down an opponent, intimidation, sledging, or creating the aura that made each ball appear to have the potential of a hand grenade. There was none of that – just overs and concentration. It was the start of the 10,000 hours theory, the simple principle that to become world-class in your field, you have to put in 10,000 hours of practice. If you include net practice, I must have bowled 2000 overs, working on leg-breaks, wrong 'uns and flippers. I kept knocking people over, which gave me confidence, and by the end of that English summer those dreams of mine began to change. Although footy still held its place in my heart, I was beginning to properly appreciate cricket's appeal.

A couple of years later, in early 1991, the maverick character Terry Jenner, who had bowled leg-breaks for Australia in the 1970s – and more of TJ in a while – introduced me to Neil Hawke, the former Australian swing bowler. Hawke teed me up with Accrington in the Lancashire League as the overseas pro. I kind of wanted to go back to Bristol but I was on a fiver a week there for painting the fences. At Accrington I was offered between £1500 and £2000 – plus car, airfare and accommodation. I thought, 'Wow, I've gotta do this.' So I used to drive miles up and down the motorway to get on the piss with the boys in Bristol through the night and then, too often, arrive back at Accy the next morning worse for wear.

I had an okay house, a little terraced place with a lounge room and a couple of bedrooms. It was clean and close to the cricket club. Fine. The ground itself was good and the locals loved the cricket, brought their kids along and generally got behind their blokes. (I later discovered that a young Jimmy Anderson had operated the scoreboard when we played at Burnley; a talented lad from the first day they saw him, apparently.) I hadn't realised how important this Lancashire League cricket was – it was more important than Test cricket in their world. The supporters got there really early and I remember arriving for the first game and thinking, 'Whoa, look at this lot!' In Bristol a few blokes came along for a beer but in Accy there were loads of people setting up their barbecues and stuff – there were people everywhere.

Anyway, the first game, batting at four, I got run out. The committee called me in and said, 'Listen, the pro never gets run out. You have to learn to turn your back on the bloke and burn him.' I argued back, saying the run out was just one of those things and that I wasn't going to be burning anyone. 'No way,' they said, 'the pro doesn't get run out.' End of story. Oh, okay. I was thrown by this and didn't bowl great. The opposition hammered me. Not a great start!

Anyway, in the next game at home to Ramsbottom, Rudi Bryson, the South African quick – and he *was* quick – who was playing as their pro was straining at the leash to nail me. He never had the chance. I came in at 2/113, nicely placed on a good deck, while Rudi was having a breather. But this bloke Stephen 'Dasher' Dearden just tore in and knocked my off-stump out of the ground first ball. I watched that stump cartwheel all the way back to the keeper, and as I walked off I heard, 'Go home, pro, you're roobbish.' I didn't bowl too good that game either. We got smashed and I started to think, 'Jeeeesus, I should have stuck with footy this winter.'

I woke up on Monday morning and gave myself a good hard look in the mirror. 'Grow up, stop larking about and *have a crack*.' On the Tuesday, I turned up at training on time, rolled up my sleeves and got into it, bowling full-on, fielding like I meant it, working with the youngsters, and talking the game to everyone at the club who'd listen. I managed to turn things around a bit and finished with 12 four-wicket bags – eight of which became five-fers – out of a total of 73 wickets that summer, and made 329 runs too. So I did alright.

We weren't the best team. Billy, the keeper, couldn't pick anything I bowled except an orthodox leg-break, so we had all sorts of coded signals for each different ball. It never worked – it was the summer of four byes! No-one could pick my flipper: no-one. It became a bit of a laugh. Most of them were as bad at it as Daryll Cullinan.

In general, though, the standard of cricket was good; better than in Bristol and equivalent to second grade in Melbourne, except for the international pro in each team. The pros in Lancashire that year were Paul Reiffel, Chris Mack, Rod Tucker, Roger Harper and some lively West Indian batters and quicks. As I say, it was funny too. Billy the Keeper was one of a number of blokes who tried hard but weren't turning pro anytime soon. There was a guy called Ian Birtwistle, who ran in almost 40 yards and bowled so slowly that I had him covered with my leg-breaks. But Birtwistle lobbed them on a length and no-one could hit them anywhere. It was hilarious to watch.

No, we weren't much good but the responsibility improved me, as it does if you sign to play county cricket. The pressure to perform is something we all have to learn. And the rules were simple: if you didn't perform they bagged you! Or worse, they didn't even bother to talk to you.

I was still drinking beer then. It wasn't until Sri Lanka 1992 that I woke up and got off it. At Accy we had collections for the pro if he scored 50 or took a 'Michelle', a five-fer. They usually amounted to something between 20 and 40 quid and I'd always say, 'Let's put it on the bar.' I was told that the pros previous to me had kept the money in their pockets and headed back to their digs at the first opportunity, and they loved that I hung around with them and spent it.

I can't stress enough how important it is to play in the UK if the chance arises. It was an invaluable experience for me. I batted up the order, bowled every over from one end and learnt a great deal about myself and the game.

That was the Accrington season. I made some good mates up there, but not quite the lifelong friendships that I'd forged in Bristol. That didn't matter. The learning curve mattered, and I was thankful to the club for the opportunity.

I watched England on the TV in the 1989 Ashes series when Border's side crushed them. It was a big surprise because Botham, Gower, Gooch, Gatting, Lamb, Emburey and Edmonds had kind of dominated the earlier stuff I'd watched in Australia in 1986/87. I liked watching Robin Smith that summer – all the Bristol guys used to talk about him in the pub. His big heart came over loud and clear. We never thought England were soft; I mean, they weren't the

West Indies but they were pretty good. And the more I watched, the more I started to analyse. How would I get Gooch out? Where would I bowl to Gatting and Gower? I still hadn't grasped a passion for the game of cricket but I now had a genuine interest in it and an appetite to know more.

Back at home, in the summer of 1989/90 – between my two stints in the UK – St Kilda had as good a club side as was going around in our part of the world. Grade cricket was very strong and guys like Dean Jones, Fleming, Reiffel, Hughes, O'Donnell – all Australian Test cricketers – appeared regularly. We also had guys like Andrew Lynch and Ivan Wingreen, who would have played state cricket during a weaker period in Victoria and a strong captain in Shaun Graf.

I remember a game against Dandenong, Rodney Hogg's side, when I did well. I'd bowled to Hoggy, who at the time had a column in the *Truth* newspaper. He wrote that there was this kid called Warne playing for St Kilda, who would end up taking 400 Test wickets. Everyone laughed. It wasn't funny for Hoggy, who got the sack. Ridiculous. Anyway, he uses the gag in his stand-up routine now, admitting that the paper was right and he should have known better. As the punchline goes, the kid didn't get 400 after all, he got 700!

So, the standard of grade cricket was high and the intensity extreme. The impact on youngsters was amazing – all of us wide-eyed kids who never said a word, we just listened and watched in awe. I'll tell you something: I never got a grade five-fer. I made a couple of hundreds but never, ever took a five-wicket haul. The guys could play and we weren't often in the field for a whole day so I'd bowl about 15 overs, not many more. My gift had always been to spin the ball. At East Sandy, we'd played on matting and that really exaggerated the turn and bounce, so we all tried to spin it miles. I was skinny back then and didn't have the strength to keep repeating it, but when I did spin it, the thing did go miles. It was bloody exciting to see it go so far.

Yeah, I guess the talent was there, but I still wasn't taking it seriously enough. I expected something for nothing and was on the beer way too much and larking about with the game. The fact is, I was a bogan. I still am deep down, really. And, thanks to Dad, a bit of a petrol head too. I had this TC Cortina, a beige/creamy colour, winding sunroof, big mags, three on the floor. I loved it, and loved the huge stereo. The car was worth about $1500 and the stereo almost a grand of that! The speakers came from Strathfield Car Radios and were fitted with extra bass. I cranked it up, super loud and listened to Big Pig, Rod Stewart, The Stones, Kiss, Fleetwood Mac, ELO, Neil Diamond and Bruce Springsteen's *Born to Run*. Oh, and Aussie Crawl, Mondo Rock and Cold Chisel. I was killing it in grade cricket and training with the state side, and yet I knew – I could *feel* – that the senior Victorian players were feeling me out and knew I could spin the ball but thought, 'He's out on the piss every night and not really taking this seriously. He turns up on time, he's a nice fella with lots of ability, but hell, what do we do with him?!'

I was thinking and breathing the game but I couldn't settle down with the game – I think it was the passion thing, or lack of it. I was still on the outside looking in, not quite ready to be inside and part of it all. Cricket is definitely not a game you can be half-hearted about, as the guys were about to tell me.

◇

Before I got into the state side, I was 12th man against New South Wales. Bill Lawry was the team manager and I remember sitting down after a day's play and a guy called Gary Watts, who had his feet up on the esky with the beers in it, said, 'Twelfy, get us a beer.' I was like, 'What?! The beers are under your feet, mate.' He said, 'I want a beer, youngster, so get me an effing beer.' I was like, 'Okay, mate, lift your feet up. I'll hold onto them and get out a beer.' So I did, and then he said, 'Open it for me, son.' So I did and only just stopped myself from chucking the whole damn thing over him.

The 12th man wasn't allowed to shower either, at least not until everyone else had. It was pathetic, but back then, in the late '80s and early '90s, that's how it was. I thought it was a joke and to some degree it put me off playing.

I didn't think the bullying culture was right back then, but I don't think the culture is right now either. It's all too easy these days, young blokes walking in and thinking they're part of the furniture. They make a couple of hundreds in grade cricket and get picked for the state team. Suddenly they expect a million-dollar contract, and an Australian cap. That's bullshit. The opportunities in the three forms of the game in the modern era mean a lot of the young players out there don't know how hard international cricket can be. Everyone – except Bradman, I suppose, although even he was dropped after his first Test match – goes through a form slump and the challenge is to fight back from that and earn your place the second time, along with the respect that comes with that fightback. I believe in all sports if you struggle at the start of your career, you appreciate the success and how hard that level is. If it comes too easy at the start, then when you have a form slump you have nothing to fall back on. That's when you see so many sportspeople in all sports being a flash in the pan.

The early Shield games I played were tougher cricket than a lot of Test matches – Victoria vs New South Wales back then was basically the Aussie batters against the Aussie bowlers. So New South Wales was Michael Slater, Mark Taylor, Steve Waugh, Mark Waugh, Michael Bevan, Greg Matthews, Phil Emery, Geoff Lawson, Wayne Holdsworth, Adrian Tucker and Glenn McGrath. We had Wayne Phillips, Matthew Elliott, Dean Jones, Jamie Siddons, Brad Hodge, Simon O'Donnell, Tony Dodemaide, Darren Berry, me, Damien Fleming, Merv Hughes and Paul Reiffel.

It was unbelievable cricket and we were at each other from the first ball till the last. I used to say to Taylor, 'Tubs, you can't pick me, mate, and soon enough, I'm knocking you over.' And he would bounce back with 'No chance, I'm going to smash you, Warne.' Harmless banter but fun. I got along really well with Tubs and we were always winding each other up. I remember a game at North Sydney Oval when I said to him, 'I could lob up an off-break and get you out, Tubby.' Right after the drinks break, I did lob up an off-break and he top-edged it straight into the hands of short square-leg. 'Yesss. Thanks, Tubby!' Then we sat in the rooms with a beer and had a yarn. We talked a lot of cricket, all of us. The more I listened, the more I learnt. Tubby is the best captain I played under and one of my closest friends in cricket. He's a ripping bloke – honest and fair. And I wish he was running Australian cricket.

The Academy

What is now called Australia's Centre of Excellence used to be called the Cricket Academy. I much preferred 'Academy' because it's a place to improve and develop – 'Centre of Excellence' sounds full of itself and arrogant. The old Cricket Academy in Adelaide, set up by the Australian Institute of Sport in conjunction with the ACB, was fantastic. I don't like what they've done to it now.

It used to be a 12-month program. Over time it got shortened which is fine, but it still needs an element of time to improve your skills and to be under expert tutelage to make sure you're on the right track – from a technical point of view, a thinking point of view and in particular a mindset/strategy point of view.

I think what they're doing now is trying to cram too much into a short space of time. These days, they have a bowling week, a captain's week, spin bowling week etc, but for some people that can be information overload – it should be spread out over a period of time.

Cricket has evolved since I was at the Academy and there's more sports science nowadays. I'm happy to move with the times with all the technology and computers – anything that can give you an edge or an advantage is going to help you. But I think it's gone too far in that direction. I think the Academy should concentrate on improving your basic cricket skills – fielding, batting, bowling – and help you to understand what's going wrong in a game, so you can self-improve during a game. There's nothing worse than someone saying, 'It just wasn't my day' – it's a pet hate of mine. You have to find a way to get into the game, and that comes from knowing yourself – one of the best pieces of advice I got early from Ian Chappell.

Anyway, as I understood it, in those days the state selectors nominated players of their own and the Aussie selectors put the seal on the final intake. That year there was me and a guy called Stephen Cottrell from Victoria; Justin Langer and Damien Martyn from

Western Australia; David Castle and Stuart Oliver from Tasmania; Greg Blewett, who was local to Adelaide, and Scott Moody and Daryl Conroy from Darwin. We were the second intake and I accepted the offer not really knowing what to expect but figuring it was sure better than delivering pizza.

Jack Potter and Peter Spence were running the Academy then. I was considered a surprise choice in that 1990/91 draft. I remember driving the TC Cortina over to Adelaide from Melbourne. I was immediately struck by the level of investment in young talent the Institute was making. We were expected to work bloody hard at our game and accept the kind of discipline and commitment that might, or might not, help us to get to the top.

Jack Potter was a bloody good cricketer and coach; Peter Spence was more an early-day version of John Buchanan. I've always bumped heads with coaches who try to reinvent the wheel. It's a simple game – don't over-complicate it! It's no surprise really that me and Spence didn't get along so well.

I'm pretty sure the guys in the year before us lived in a building that we used a lot for training and lectures and stuff in Henley. Our group was billeted out to the Alberton Hotel in Port Adelaide, which was run by a good bloke called Peter 'Beans' O'Brien and his wife. Me, billeted to a pub! So there we all were – barely out of our teens – sent across to Adelaide to improve our cricket, and we were living upstairs in a pub. Not promising. Meanwhile, back at base in Henley, Jack and Peter always seemed to be at each other's throats. We never knew why but we could see they didn't agree on much. Suddenly one day they had gone. The battle between them had been no good for us and the end result of it was that we ended up at nets and at training on our own. Jack was a cool guy, a good man, great on cricket, great brain. He knew a bit about leg-spin too. I missed him when he left – we all did. He gave us direction and confidence.

Back at the pub, Pete poured the beers and his wife cooked for us. We played a lot of pool – Justin Langer still owes me a thousand bucks. I'm unlikely to see it now! My room was three metres by three with a stunning picture of Elle Macpherson on the wall. (She's a friend now and pretty much as hot as she was then too.)

We were up each morning at 6 am. I had a dart or two out of the window, shared communal showers with other paying guests of the pub, and allowed myself about 15 minutes for anything on toast – egg, beans, vegemite or sometimes spaghetti – before the sprint into Adelaide. JL, Steve C and me, the three of us with cars, would race the 35-minute drive down the Port Road to Adelaide Number 2 Oval. JL was a terrible driver but his family owned a car yard, and over the year he had three or four cars and smashed them all.

I got along great with JL and respected him. He was a very, very hard worker. I saw a lot of people who had a lot more talent than Justin Langer but they weren't as successful because they didn't have his determination or discipline. But it's no secret that I didn't like the baggy-green worship rubbish that he liked so much. Steve Waugh brought it in when he was captain and tried to force it on the rest of us. Steve, JL, Gilly, Matthew Hayden – they loved it but, to be honest, they made me want to puke with it half the time. I mean, wearing it at Wimbledon! Who wears a green cricket cap to Wimbledon? It was just embarrassing! Mark Waugh felt the same. I don't need a baggy green to prove what playing for Australia means to me or to the people who watch us. A sunhat will do. The proof is in how you play the game.

But even that gushing about the baggy green didn't get in the way of my admiration for JL's attitude to cricket. He never gave up, was super disciplined and worked his arse off to become a very good Test player. He and Haydos had a great record together. Some verbal diarrhoea with it – there often was with Haydos – but they could really bat.

Blewy, in contrast to JL, was a fluent and elegant player. Maybe he didn't quite have the focus and discipline that JL had, but he had a beautiful drive, hooked and pulled the short stuff easily, bowled nicely, fielded great. He was a bloody good player who should have played more for Australia.

Marto was one of my best friends in cricket. We were at the Academy together, made our first-class debuts at the same time and were the first two young guys inducted into the old-school Aussie team – Border, Marsh, Reid, McDermott, Hughes, Jones, all those guys. I was 22, still a kid in so many ways. Then Marto came in at 19 or 20 and he was the same. But what a talent he was – wow. We went to Sri Lanka together in 1992 and used to run the drinks in some of the one-day games. It was like school, looking up to the big guys.

Marto could really play – he was in a different class. After Mark Waugh, he was the most gifted I'd seen up close. No-one timed the ball better or had more time to play. It was like everything was in slow motion when he batted. And he could bowl alright too – he had that happy knack of getting top players out. And he fielded naturally, brilliantly.

Unfortunately as it turned out, I set him up with his first fiancée, Simone, through an evening out with me and my own Simone. The four of us met at Bobby McGee's, a bar in Melbourne. We had a ball and he fell in love that night, proposed soon after and they immediately moved in together. He was 20, I think, maybe 21! A year later, he came back from a tour and she locked him out of his own house. My God, they used to go hard at each other. The lock-out worked in his favour, actually. It was like: end of relationship!

For a long while I felt I owed Marto one, because that night in Bobby McGee's ended up causing him all sorts of grief. Thankfully he was later to marry very happily and I'm pleased to say that Elizabeth Hurley and I had a hand in it. He was staying with us in the Cotswolds in England and kept saying to Elizabeth, 'You must have a friend for me. Come on, all the women you know!' So we set him up with Lucy, a lovely Aussie girl who was living in England and working on a part-time basis for Elizabeth in PR. Two months later he called to say they were engaged!

'I'm getting married to Lucy.'

'Marto,' I said, 'not again. Please, mate! I can't go through it all *again*.'

'No, no, this is it, the real deal,' he insisted.

I thought, 'Oh my God.' I mean, Lucy is a great chick, but come on, guys, you've only just got it together. He's very impulsive, that Damien Martyn. Anyway, they're still together six years on and I've never seen him so happy, so I suppose Elizabeth and I can say we set it right!

Back to his cricket for a minute. I've talked about the talent but not yet about his instinct for the game, which was a reason he was the second youngest-ever Western Australia captain, just past his 23rd birthday. He was a good choice for his tactical nous but it was too early otherwise. There was still an arrogance in him that needed ironing out. I'd argue that he was picked for Australia too soon as well. Some guys, for whatever reason, just aren't quite ready.

Mind you, he was unfairly binned after we lost to South Africa at the SCG in January 1994. It was a small run chase, just 117, and the senior batsmen got out playing big shots. We lost by five. Marto hung in there tough with the tail — 59 balls across an hour and 45 minutes for six runs — and then, with only a few needed, he drove a length ball into the hands of cover. The press made him the scapegoat and the selectors dropped him for — wait for it — six years! Some experienced guys played rubbish shots and stayed in the team. Also, South Africa were outstanding. When you lose, you always know you could have done better, but remember, the opposition is trying just as hard as you are! Marto took it to the wire and got the bullet. That was very harsh; in fact, just straight unfair. Maybe that arrogance in him rubbed too many people up the wrong way.

In hindsight, I think being dropped was the best thing for him. He came back a wonderful player. Geez, he was good. Mark Waugh was the better all-round batsman but Marto was his equal as an artist.

Martyn, Blewett, Langer — three ways to skin a cat. Each of them a lesson to others, especially youngsters, but in very different ways. The message is that it takes all sorts and it don't come easy. You have to treat the game well to get the most from your talent. Ask JL — he's proof of the right way. Treat it badly, or lightly, and it bites you hard. Cricket offers no hiding place.

I was about to find that out for myself.

One of the replacements for Potter and Spence was Andrew Sincock, who was still blow-drying his hair long after Ian Chappell said about him, 'No quick bowler of mine who blow-dries his hair gets the new ball,' so Chappelli opened up in a Shield game with off-spinner Ashley Mallett instead — love that! The other was Barry

Causby, a bank teller who'd played a bit of first-class cricket for South Australia in the Chappell days too. Neither of them were Jack Potter, not close. It was chaos and, increasingly, a waste of time in my view. As much as I hadn't liked Peter Spence, he was strong on discipline and I trained my arse off under him. Peter cared about us and about the game – I'll give him that. Just because you don't agree with a person, you must respect the position – unless the guy is a total imbecile – especially if he's good at what he does. And Jack? Well, Jack just knew the game and understood us youngsters who were trying to make it big. Without Jack and Peter, trouble loomed. We had no direction.

We went to Darwin for some games. It was stinking hot and Blewy was with me in the pool. There were a couple of girls up on a balcony and, as boys do, we tried to get their attention by yelling up, 'Hey, girls, check this out!' and I started flashing brown eyes out of the pool. 'Come on, girls, jump in the pool with us!' Stupid, really, but harmless fun in my view. Anyway, they *did* invite us to their room but it never went any further. We had a drink, a laugh and then left. End of story, or so I thought.

Next day, we got called into a meeting saying that a couple of guys had been out of order yesterday and the incident had been reported.

I was thinking, 'Geez, what's happened – who's done something?'

'We're talking about the pool yesterday,' said Sincock, before asking the culprits to own up.

'No problem,' I said, 'that's me,' and I told them exactly what happened. Then we went to a private room for a chat.

'We think you're a liability,' one of them said, 'and we've decided to send you back to Adelaide.'

'Okay, that's a bit harsh but I'll take it on the chin, guys. When do I leave?'

'Now. By bus.'

'Whaaat? Are you for real?'

They were. I caught the bus from Darwin to Adelaide that afternoon and, let me tell you, the scenery ain't that great. It's red dirt and red rock, one road, all the way for about 3000 kilometres. Every hour or two the bus would stop and little old ladies or groups of foreign tourists would buy souvenirs – tea towels, mugs and spoons – from old dry towns that none of them would ever see again. My hair was big and blond, a spiky mullet – the Rod Stewart type of thing. I'd changed out of my Academy tracksuit into an acid-wash t-shirt and acid-wash flared jeans with a high waist. Alongside these people I was a freak. I travelled through the middle of Australia, across desert mainly, squashed up against a bus window, thinking, *'What am I doing here?'* By the time we pulled in to Adelaide I was pretty much done with the Academy and not so far from done with cricket.

Picture it. My mates were in Darwin playing and practising – I was back in Adelaide. I'd been reprimanded and told to go to the swimming pool every morning at 6 am, then to the gym for cardio, followed by weights, and then to long afternoon sessions bowling at the South Australian state squad.

I was living in a pub, at 19, on my own. There was temptation around me and demons in my head. As I swam along doing lengths, the chlorine invaded my throat and stung my eyes. In a stuffy gym, I was half-hearted – no-one around me, no motivation. *'What am I doing here?'* I kept asking myself. I did the wrong thing, yes, and I was being punished, but how was this improving my cricket? I was thinking, 'I may as well be back in Melbourne.' I sat tight for a few days, festering in the pub, playing pool, having a few beers, not much else. Inside, I was burning.

When the other guys got back from Darwin, Rob de Castella – one of Australia's great athletes who was now running the Australian Institute of Sport – came to see me.

'Shane,' he said, like a head teacher, 'I am very disappointed in what happened up at Darwin. I need to get to the bottom of it.'

'Okay,' I replied, 'here it is. I flashed a brown eye to these girls in the pool, said some stupid things and they invited us up to their room where nothing happened and we left. Then they reported it.'

'Yeah, I heard that, but I'm going to get to the bottom of what exactly happened.'

'That's exactly what happened.'

'No, no, Shane, there's more to it than that.'

'No, there isn't. I can make stuff up, if you like. What do you want to hear? Why won't you accept what I'm telling you, which is the truth? Ask anyone who was there, ask the girls, anyone – that *is* what happened.'

'Right, well, I'll be in touch.'

'Okay, lovely to meet you. Thanks for coming along, Rob.'

This charade went on for another week and then, suddenly, Marto got pulled out of the Academy to play for Western Australia. The combination of Marto's promotion and my demotion, because that's what it was in effect, really got to me. I thought, 'Hmm, my best mate has gone, I'm being treated like a schoolkid – I think I'll go too.'

I rang Jim Higgs, who was a Victorian selector, and he assured me that I had a good chance of getting in the state side soon. That was the clincher. I wrote a letter to Brendan Flynn, the guy who ran the administration of the Academy, thanking him for the opportunity and saying how sorry I was that things hadn't worked as we both hoped. But I accepted this opportunity to improve my cricket. I told him I was heading home to Melbourne with a view to getting into the state team. Then I left. He didn't argue, and I didn't have any regrets. So when people say I was kicked out of the Academy, it's a lie. I decided to leave for myself.

When I was chosen to play my first Test against India the next season, the Academy changed their tune. They tried to claim me as one of theirs, saying I was the first Academy-trained player to be picked for Australia. It was only half true. They even hung a picture of me on the wall there – classic! The same guys who were treating me like a kid put me up on their pedestal. Move on, Warney, I thought, move on.

✧

I'm often asked how I got together with Terry Jenner. Well, the cricket world is pretty small and the game looks after its own. TJ had been in prison for embezzlement of funds, and now that he'd served his time, he needed something to get his teeth into. He was told there was a kid at the Academy he should go and have a look at.

I'd been having a rough time, but my rough time had nothing on his and we instantly hit it off, like peas from the same pod. I had some private sessions with him that fascinated me – he knew the art of leg-spin like no-one else. I'd begun talking cricket to someone who understood *me*.

Without Terry, I wouldn't have been the cricketer that I became. He helped me through life stuff as well as cricket. I owe him a lot. He gave me belief and direction after arriving in my life at exactly the right moment for us both. I'll talk about TJ at length in a minute, but first, what else did I learn at the Academy?

For some reason, I was obsessed with the flipper. Jack Potter taught me his version and Jim Higgs, Bob Paulsen, Richie Benaud, David Emerson and TJ all had their methods, which shows how hard it is. I remember the first time I tried it was at the Junction Oval nets at St Kilda, and it hit the top-right hand corner on the full. It went way over the batsman's head and pinged back to him off the pole. I thought, '*Wow*, I'm not bowling that again, that's just toooo hard.' But of course I was fascinated and couldn't let go. I kept at it every day, more obsessed than before. I'd go off on my own, or with my brother, up to the Tulip Street nets on the malthoid surface – a concrete base with black-painted rubber on it – and bowl leg-breaks, wrong 'uns and then hundreds of flippers.

I experimented with all the versions but settled on Jack's with a modification of my own, positioning the ball between third finger and thumb and squeezing it out of the front of my hand. I started to land it pretty well and celebrated like a lunatic in a grade game when I got the Aussie Test batsman Julien Wiener – we called him 'Schnitzel' – with a beauty. It was my first wicket with the flipper actually – so I was very happy! A similar ball knocked over Alec Stewart at the Gabba four years later. From such moments . . .

(Speaking of nicknames, Aussies come up with some very good ones. Schnitzel was one, but my favourite is 'Ferfuck' for David Saker. You'll work it out.)

Learning at Last

Academy resignation accepted, I went back to Melbourne and within a few weeks was making my first-class debut at the Junction Oval for

Victoria against Western Australia. Guess what, Marto was in the WA side. Simon O'Donnell was Victorian captain and Les Stillman coach, and they took me out for dinner at the Marine Hotel. I ordered two white rolls and a bowl of hot chips. O'Donnell said, 'Are you serious?' I said yep, before stuffing the chips between the rolls and adding loads of sauce, salt and vinegar.

O'Donnell, or 'Scuba' as he was called, was great with me. Patient, thoughtful and firm. I respect him for the role he played in me staying with the Vics when I was approached by New South Wales around that time. He was straight with me, no bullshit, and he made me truly believe in my skills and spirit, while always looking to help me get the best out of them. Mind you, he grassed a simple catch when Graeme Wood got a leading edge to a decent leg-break in one of my first overs on debut and just threw it back, saying, 'Well bowled, mate, bad luck.' 'Oh okay,' I thought. 'No worries. I've only been working on that moment for two years. Thanks, Scube!' Pretty laidback guy, the Scube. Woody went on to smash us all over the park. In the end, it was big Tom Moody who had the dubious honour of being my first wicket in first-class cricket.

(Dennis Lillee was the team manager for Western Australia at the time. I'd never met Lillee – who is such an absolute legend. At tea on the second day I asked Marto if I could meet him, but Marto said he slept from tea to stumps so he'd be right for the night ahead. 'He drinks hard,' said Marto, 'has fun with the guys and tells incredible stories, so we give him one session off a day.' And little starstruck me thought, 'Yes, he *is* a legend!')

In August 1990 I was picked to go to the West Indies with the Australian Young Cricketers, which was a great experience if no great success story. Then, in September 1991, I was chosen to go to Zimbabwe on an Australia B tour that Mark Taylor captained.

Zimbabwe was a great country, ruined by its president, Robert Mugabe, but thankfully it's making a comeback now that he's out of the way. The Zimbos could play alright. They were hugely competitive blokes and magnificent hosts after hours. We took a strong team and all of us made good mates over there.

I kept nailing their big-hitting all-rounder, Iain Butchart, with the flipper. He was as hopeless at reading it as Daryll Cullinan. He kind of smiled at me in his stance before I came in, then I let it go and knocked him over. Simple! We called it the 'Butchy ball' for a while but it didn't stick.

Tubby was a top-class captain and it was obvious that he'd lead Australia soon enough. I picked up 7/49 in the second first-class game, the first time I'd done anything on the international stage. It gave me a huge sense of satisfaction. The pitches in both Bulawayo and Harare suited me well and I certainly got more from that trip than from the West Indies a year earlier. Although one or two of the guys had already played Test cricket, that Zimbabwe trip saw the foundation of the new Australian team – Taylor, Steve Waugh, Tom Moody, Michael Bevan, Paul Reiffel and me. Our liaison officer was a guy called Russell Tiffin. I drank 'soapies' with him most nights – cane, lime, soda and Robinson's lemon barley to wash it down real quick. He was a great bloke who later became an international umpire, and whenever I hit a batsman on the pads and it was anything like close, I was up, and Russell, more often than not, raised that finger of his. I reckon those happy nights at the Harare Sports Club had given me a better than even chance!

John Benaud, Richie's brother, was the manager of the tour, an absolute beauty of a guy. We heard that he came up with the word 'sledging', as applied to cricket, in a Shield game in the early 1970s when he was having a real go at a player he disliked in the opposition. They came off at the lunch break and one of his team-mates said, 'Hey, JB, did you get out of bed the wrong side this morning, mate? You're about as subtle as a sledgehammer.' Hence the word sledging. He was pretty shy when we asked him about it, so we were never certain how true it was. Ripper bloke, JB.

After the Zimbabwe tour, my confidence started to grow. The bad experience of the Academy could be weighed against a better than average start to state cricket and backing from the Aussie selectors. The incentives were clear. Keep at it, keep believing in yourself and all things are possible. I noticed that cricket was beginning to match footy in those dreams of mine.

One thing I'd picked up during the days of World Series Cricket was how exciting the game could be for anyone with the personality to break the mould and give the crowd something for their buck. My own playing experiences had allowed me to sense the hidden elements of cricket, subtleties that don't immediately come over on television. I loved the intense competition that made up the conflict between bat and ball and the showmanship that came with it. That's what started to do it for me – the head-to-heads, the one-on-ones. We all need our boat rocked and this question about who out-thinks and outlasts who is the crux of the game and the bit that most interests me.

Though I was angry at the way I'd been treated at the Academy, I'd learnt enough to realise that I could make more of my talent. In a way, that long bus journey from Darwin gave me time to work out what I really wanted. Hell, I was playing state cricket a few weeks later, so no-one could say I gave up: far from it, I got stuck in. My dreams were changing. My appetite for cricket increased and my ambition went up – not one level but about five.

I'd been in the state squad for a couple of years, been to the Academy, toured the West Indies and Zimbabwe, won the flag in grade cricket and played four Shield games. I'd done okay, showing glimpses of what I could do – but not better than that, to be honest.

Then the lightning bolt.

It was Christmas 1991. I was at the Boxing Day Test with my mate Dean Waugh – watching his brother Mark – and bumped into Ian McDonald, the Australian team manager. He saw the three pies under my right arm and the beer under my left and said, 'Go easy, mate, you might be playing in Sydney.' Yeah, right, Macca, nice one. What happened the next morning shocked the life out of me. Macca called and said the selectors had picked me in the squad for the New Year Test against India. Oh my God!

Yes, that was the ambition. But not yet! Not nearly.

Straya

Imagine it for a moment. The kid with the football dream, the bogan at heart, told he was going to play cricket for Australia. Not much floors me, but that call did. I felt like I was out of my league. Talk about daunting. I didn't know many of my team-mates – I mean, I'd been copying most of them in the backyard the week before. You know, doing impressions and commentating their performances. Now I was shaking their hand and changing alongside them. I felt awkward, disorientated, exposed.

Ravi Shastri smashed me all over the park; it was sort of embarrassing. I didn't bowl long hops or full tosses, not many anyway. I bowled mainly pretty good balls, but got hammered everywhere. At that stage I didn't really have a plan – I just bowled and waited for the batsman to make a mistake. The art of spin bowling is the real key – more on that later.

I dropped Ravi – a caught and bowled chance when he had 66 – which might have made a huge difference. Instead, he got a double hundred. It went from bad to worse, as Sachin got 140-odd as well. He was about 12 years old, looked eight and smashed me.

My figures were 1/150. I felt stupid and wanted a hole to disappear into, but that's the thing about Test cricket – there is no hole. You're stuck with it for up to five days and every bastard is watching and has something to say. We had to fight to save the game and no-one does that better than Allan Border. I was in with him at the end, facing seven balls to survive, so at least I contributed to something. I was really struck by Border's authority and determination. He seemed to embody much of what Australia stands for and, immediately, I felt comfortable around him. AB was a great leader, as I was to find out soon enough.

I played the next Test in Adelaide too, another horror, and yet I had immediately liked the taste of Test match cricket and seen the attraction of its unique and very special appeal. In short, my imagination had been fired. 'Dream, baby, dream,' as the song goes.

There was definitely something in the air and I wanted to know more about it. I needed a kindred spirit, someone like-minded to guide my journey. So I found a teacher, and he helped to change my life. As I said, I had a taste and now I was hungry for knowledge.

5

Something in the Air

TJ's Place – March 1992

I STOPPED OFF AT some Adelaide drive-through bottle store and bought a slab of beer, having driven fast from Melbourne, on a whim, and been done by the cops for speeding in a small town called Keith, 220 kilometres short of Adelaide. I'd traded in the TC Cortina for a Nissan Vector with a few bucks from my various jobs and an early contract with the Australian Cricket Board worth three grand.

There was no plan for a new car but I'd been on the Nepean Highway driving home one afternoon and on the corner of the big junction near Brighton was a showroom with this gleaming Pulsar Vector, white with white wheels. It was up on a shiny steel rack and looked very cool. I wanted that car! I got 1200 bucks for the Cortina and Dad lent me a grand. The rest was me. I bought a mobile phone, the big brick that somehow fitted in the car in those days, hooked it all up and took off for Adelaide, music on loud and calling all my mates. The long road to South Australia flew by, until that flashing light in the mirror, the inquisition, the fine and the demerit points.

I knew the address and, mid-afternoon on a hot late-summer day, I knocked on Terry Jenner's door. He looked pretty shocked. I told him that the idea of a life in football had truly passed me by and that cricket was now the dream. The taste of Test cricket, the thrill of state cricket and the challenge of finding a new path forward in my life had got hold of me. 'I want to learn. The passion is bubbling and I'll do whatever it takes.'

TJ gave it to me. He just ripped into me like you wouldn't believe. 'What the hell?' he said. 'You're overweight – fat, actually. You've got no discipline and you think you're better than you are. You didn't deserve to play for Australia. Some guys used to dominate Shield cricket and never got picked. Others – me for one – would get a game here and there, and get binned. You've got some amazing talent, but I question your commitment. You got a game for Australia because there's no-one else out there right now. You're a lucky boy alright, but you're not that good. Not yet, anyway, although you could be. So let's get serious. Put the beers back in the car, all two dozen of them, and tomorrow take 'em back to the bottle store. While you work with me, there are no beers. Actually, put them in my fridge for another time.'

And that was the point when I thought, 'Right, no-one has ever spoken to me like that before. I'm in.' Mind you, Simon O'Donnell had come close. Initially, in the summer of 1991/92 I hadn't secured a regular place in the Victorian state side and received an offer from New South Wales via Steve Waugh, who was keen for me to join the Blues. I thought about it very seriously but was put in my place, first by Darren 'Chuck' Berry who walked me round the Albert Ground – where the Victorian team trained – and told me to get my act together, and then Scuba, who went a stage further. In short, he had me up against a wall and called me a weak bastard for not backing myself in Victoria. He said, 'You can piss off to NSW if you like, but you're going for the wrong reasons, and, mark my words, mate, you'll regret it.' Mum and Dad helped convince me to stay too, so that was that. Four people I rated highly all making it clear!

So, I backed myself to be better than the others in Victoria – better than blokes like Peter McIntyre and Paul Jackson. 'Toughen up,' I thought, 'and get into this Victorian cricket team.' Which I did, but that was no longer my limit: I suddenly wanted more in a way I had never, ever felt before. This was more than my goal, or an ambition now, it was even more than a desire – it had become a form of desperation and I was determined to do whatever it took to make it and not fail. The thing was that I didn't know how to manage it. Thankfully, Terry Jenner did. Bring on the instigator.

'Okay, mate, can we start tomorrow?' I asked him.

He said, 'No way, Shane – we start now, here. Let's talk.'

That's what we did until midnight – about everything that had happened to me so far, from club cricket and the Academy to playing for Australia, and everything we needed to do going forward. About the history of the game, about the greats and their achievements, about pitches and places and umpires and the laws and captaincy and fielding positions. Then we crashed out and slept till the sun came up and my new life started.

I climbed off the couch and, for the first time since I'd started smoking full-on when I was 16, I didn't light a cigarette that morning. Then I went for a long, hard run. Well, sort of. It didn't turn out that long or that far. Geez, I was unfit. When I got back TJ was awake and he said, 'Oh, right, you've been for a run – that's progress already.'

Then we sat down and he listed a bunch of former players, most I hadn't heard of and the rest I didn't know much about. He asked me a heap of questions about them. I was clueless. So TJ made me watch old footage of a lot of the greats – people like Arthur Mailey and Clarrie Grimmett. He said, 'Test cricket didn't start in 1991/92 when you got a game, mate, we've got 120 years to catch up on.'

I'd driven from Melbourne to Terry Jenner's house in Adelaide with the idea of surprising him and spending a couple of days picking his brains. I stayed for six weeks. The gist of our first conversations and practical experiments was this.

'Shane, you bowl nicely and rip your leg-spinners, you bowl your wrong 'uns and your straight ones and you've got an unbelievable flipper. You can also catch well and bat too. You've got the toys, mate, but you don't know how to use them. In other words, you don't know how to get people out.'

I said, 'What do you mean?'

'You need to learn what, when and why.'

'I don't understand.'

'*What* you are bowling, *when* you are bowling it and *why* you are bowling it.'

'Yes, I sort of get that.'

'You don't just bowl a wrong 'un because you haven't bowled one for 10 balls, and you don't bowl a wrong 'un because a new batsman comes in and you want to make him look a fool. You don't bowl a flipper because you haven't bowled one for two overs. For a flipper to really work, you have to plan its disguise, and to do that you have to set up the batsman with a faster leg-break. The idea is to push the batsman back and then strike, for LBW or bowled. You want them looking to cut or pull. In other words you want them back in the crease and it takes time, patience and strategy to push them back. Big leg-break, small leg-break, any of the varieties – think tactics and strategy.'

There was more, much more. 'At the moment, there are a few things you haven't got. Like you haven't really got a top-spinner, which is an over-spinner that people mistake for a wrong 'un. You haven't got a high-bouncing leggie. You haven't got the mastery of side-spin and over-spin yet. You've got a great natural leggie, although it needs to be more consistent; you have a decent wrong 'un and an outstanding flipper, but you need that over-spinner and a slider, and you need to conquer the various types of delivery and levels of spin. Above all, you'll need to learn patience in order to execute these plans.'

I was salivating now, with a ball in my hand, ripping it from one hand to the other. 'How, how, how, TJ?' I was thinking. 'I wanna know!' I realised we had lots to do. I asked Terry to tell me a bit more about what, when and why.

'I'll repeat the earlier question,' he said. 'Ask yourself what you're bowling, when you're going to bowl it and why.'

'Okay,' I said, 'let's start with a "what". Let's say I'm trying to nick them off, caught keeper or slip.'

'Right,' he said, 'are you bowling wide of the crease or tight to the stumps? How are you setting the guy up? How does he grip the bat? Where is he most likely to attack you?'

'I don't know,' I admitted.

'Good, that's a start – you don't think you know it all. So let's go to work on why you bowl certain deliveries, when you're going to bowl them and how we can disguise them. And let's work out an over-spinner. That's a month of education and then years of practice. Okay with you?'

'Yep. Cool,' I said.

First up, I figured I better get fitter, so I got up and ran every morning, like Forrest Gump. Just ran and ran. I never once had a fag before I went on a run. And I completely gave up alcohol. When I first knocked on Terry's door, I was 93 kilograms; a month later I was less than 85. I went to Merv Hughes' wedding during that time, drank water and left earlyish.

Two days later I was back. Terry taught me how to bowl close to the stumps and wide of the crease; how to bowl one middle and leg, then middle stump, then off-stump; how to bowl outside off-stump, straight and sucker wide too; how to drag them across the crease and how to get them stuck where they were on the crease. How to repeat the leg-break, ball after ball, from these different angles, and how and when to use the wrong 'un, or googly as it's usually known overseas. I then thought about what to put in my armoury regarding what worked for me. That's the thing with advice. Listen to it all, and work out for yourself whether it's good for you or not.

I actually learnt how to bowl different wrong 'uns – Richie Benaud showed me one with an orange in an airport lounge. It was a beauty. My wrong 'un was good until 1998 when I did my shoulder. I never really got it back so good after that.

Above all, I worked on a plan. You have to have a plan for every batsman, Terry insisted, to quickly work out where his strengths and weaknesses are. There was no real technology for analysis in those days, so you had to watch and listen and use your brain. After computers came in, I still liked instinct and working out the mental state of a player. No computer can tell you that.

One day, Terry blindfolded me and I bowled without the distraction of a target but in search of rhythm and feel. Then, straight after removing the blindfold, I'd bowl at a target – a handkerchief, say – and expect to hit it more often than not.

Man, I was in the zone: so, so focused. I've never been that focused in my life. I was committed to learning, I was disciplined, I hardly smoked, I slept great and was overwhelmed by determination. Getting seriously fit felt fantastic. I wanted to be the best I could ever imagine being and never again wanted to hear the words that had haunted me: '*You're not good enough.*'

We spent a lot of time back at the Academy, where Rod Marsh was now in charge. A year on, it was a totally different place. Rod was terrific, giving me a lot of his time even though he had other responsibilities. He allowed me all the Academy facilities and all the time in the world. Terry and I bowled for three to four hours a day, maybe more. The routine was run, eat, morning net session, train, lunch, and back for an afternoon session every day. I was completing the beep test at 13.5, pool sessions, weights, the lot. I trained my arse off. I've never trained harder before or since and climbed on the scales one day to read 79 kilos. Awesome!

Soon after, I was picked to tour Sri Lanka in August with the Australian team. We had precious little time to get it right. Terry said, 'They've basically gifted you this tour – you don't deserve it yet.' And then he added, 'But when you get there, Allan Border and the guys are going to go, "Wow, this guy is really up for it."'

I said, 'TJ, I'm not going to fail at cricket. I failed at footy and had to read a letter that left me completely shattered. I've delivered beds and pizzas and didn't like it much. I'm going to make this happen, I promise you.'

The Sri Lankan Miracle – August 1992

Sri Lanka was exciting for me. It was the chance to prove to myself and to others how far I'd come. From when the guys had last seen me in early January, when I was 99 kilograms and generally down in the dumps, to Sri Lanka in August when I was 79 kilos and ripping them, I'd become a very different cricketer. Better than that, I'd begun to understand what I was doing.

Sri Lanka is a beautiful country but, at the time, was torn apart by civil war. This was their first home Test series since a horrific bomb blast in Colombo in 1987. Security was tight, but to be honest I hardly noticed. I was like a kid on Christmas Eve – so excited. I bowled for hours in the nets on days so hot and humid that Tony Dodemaide, a surprise selection ahead of Merv Hughes, lost 5 kilograms in a morning session. Sweat soaked through his socks and poured out of a hole he'd cut in his boots to relieve pressure on an injured big toe.

I bowled for hours to AB because he was one guy who always treated a net like a game. 'What's your field?' he'd say, and off we'd go. These sessions became mini-Tests between us. He was like, 'You're not getting me out,' and I'm not sure I ever did. The trick at a net session or practice is to recreate, as near as possible, the intensity of a match and work daily on an improvement in your game, however small. It isn't easy, but if your team can do that more often than not, that's when the magic happens – along with laughter and fun afterwards. I did exactly that and showed AB that I was bowling well. Occasionally the ball slipped out of my hand because of the sweat pouring down my forearms and AB suggested gripping it with the seam up, like a quick bowler, to get some purchase. He figured if I didn't know what would happen to it, well, the same might apply to the batsman. I tried. It didn't work.

So we got to the first Test match and I was picked. Though Australia had beaten Sri Lanka in a Test in Kandy in 1983, it was the only game we'd won anywhere in Asia since 1969 – Bill Lawry's successful tour of India. It was an intense match in many ways. We didn't get enough first up – 256, thanks to Ian Healy, who dragged us back into it. Then Romesh Kaluwitharana smashed 132 not out on debut. They all hammered us, making 8/547 declared. We responded well in the second innings with well over 400 and left them 181 to win. Not a difficult target, but not dead easy either.

You have to start well in a low chase. They did. 0/76; 2/127, and then Aravinda de Silva ran down to smack Craig McDermott over his head. It was a high ball, really high. AB sprinted back, whipped his sunnies and hat off, dived horizontally and took this unbelievable running catch. 3/127 – Aravinda gone. Now they needed 54 with seven wickets in the shed. Asanka Gurusinha was playing really well in a heated contest with Greg Matthews, who was bowling beautifully.

At the other end, I bowled a rubbish over and went for nine. Aarrgghh!

In the first innings, Arjuna Ranatunga had got into me, while making a typically resilient hundred. Arjuna had a habit of doing my head in. He was cocky and confrontational and we never saw eye to eye – can't imagine why!

I'd finished that innings with 0/107 in 22 overs. 'Help me, Lord,' I thought, '0/107 is no better than Sydney or Adelaide against India.' So, at tea, during the second innings, I retreated into myself. 'Jesus, I've done all this work, trained my arse off and I'm still getting hammered. Maybe cricket isn't my go.' It sounds stupid, I know, but the game gets to you pretty quick. I was totally disheartened.

Allan Border sensed something, saw me on the balcony having a smoke, and came and sat next to me. 'Mate, you're bowling bloody well,' he said. 'You've done the hard yards so keep believing, stay patient – trust me, it will happen.' I was like, 'Yeah, thanks, AB.' I couldn't help but wonder if he was just saying that. I doubted he truly believed what he was telling me. One thing, though, I respected him for trying and at least I knew he cared.

Anyway, 'Mo' Matthews chipped away and the Sri Lankans were six down, still needing 34 to win, when my cricket career took a dramatic turn. AB signalled down to fine leg and shouted, 'Next over, Warney!'

'Oh no, no, no, no, you can't be serious,' I thought. 'This could be done and dusted in a couple of overs, AB. You can't do this to me, not now, not with so much at stake. I could cost us the match.' But I kept my outward emotions in check and began to convince myself that, actually, now was as good a time as any.

I bowled a maiden – I'd never concentrated so hard in my life. I thought, 'We're still in this. We haven't lost yet. No way.' Then Mo took his fourth wicket, an LBW that we were long overdue. Seven down, 34 to win.

What you don't fully appreciate, until you've played a bit, is that your opponents are under severe pressure too. Aravinda had played a shocking shot – the one caught by AB – having played the same shot an over before and got away with it by an inch or two – a finger-tipper, again to AB. Yes, the guys waiting in the rooms to bat are nervous, or worse, and when they see their star players make mistakes, they begin to imagine hand-grenades themselves. You learn to trade on that and to back yourself to handle the pressure better than the other bloke. And you can only think like that once you've done it a few times when the game is there to be won. It's amazing that when you reach that point, the opposition starts to think you'll do it when the game is in the balance. That's how you create an aura out on the ground and off the pitch too – it's an inner-confidence. It's also that *something* that some players have that you can't put your finger on. But back then . . .

Mo, who was always supportive and good to me, was shouting, 'C'mon, Suicide' (his nickname for me, after the INXS song, 'Suicide Blonde'). AB was, like, possessed – you almost didn't dare let him down – and it was in situations like this that he demanded courage and concentration.

Oh Jeeeesus . . . I was nervous, but I just tried to stay focused. Then, a breakthrough. Mark Waugh took a catch off me to dismiss Pramodya Wickramasinghe. My second Test wicket. Yes! Dean Jones came up to me and said, 'Well done, mate, your average just came down to 160.' I think it was meant to be a joke, at least I hope it was. Good one, Deano.

The match was so tight now. The wicket gave us the scent of victory and that's the point when it got even more intense out there. I was thinking, 'Holy shit!' Honestly, I could hardly talk. I was elsewhere, gasping. Then 'Junior' caught another – Don Anurasiri. Sri Lanka were nine down and imploding. End of over.

Next one, Mo went for two boundaries – strong sweeps by the Guru. Seventeen to win. One ball of Mo's over left and the Guru wanted to steal the strike, but Ranjith Madurasinghe turned him down at the non-striker's end.

Me to bowl. Madurasinghe looked terrified and couldn't help himself: he wound up, mishitting the leg-break high but nowhere.

Mo circled underneath it and hung on. Australia win! By 16. The guys go crazy. Me too.

I'd taken 3/11 – the last three – without conceding a run. There was joy everywhere, not least on AB's face. In the dressing-room, led by David Boon, we belted out 'Underneath the Southern Cross', our victory song. We were later to hear that next door, in the Sri Lanka room, it was like someone had died. 'Kalu' was quoted as saying he felt stabbed in the chest with a knife over and over again. In our dressing-room, AB called it 'The greatest heist since the Great Train Robbery'. Sri Lanka had lost eight wickets for 37. If it had been on TV in Australia it would be remembered as one of the great Test matches.

That team was Mark Taylor, Tom Moody, David Boon, Mark Waugh, Dean Jones, Allan Border, Greg Matthews, Ian Healy, Shane Warne, Craig McDermott and Mike Whitney. I contributed to the win and sensed the relief. It's hard to explain exactly how good it was to feel I belonged; or if not quite belonged, that I didn't let anyone down.

I'm indebted to AB for having the confidence to throw me the ball. I'll never forget that. It was also great captaincy and leadership. God I love that man. He did so much for me over the years, and he was a great leader for sure, who is nowadays regarded as the grandad of Australian cricket. All of us who played under him listened and learnt. He toughened us up and set us on a straight road. The part AB has played in our game has been truly exceptional.

I missed the second Test match with a weird foot thing called Plantar fasciitis. It was unbelievably painful – I couldn't walk. I played the third Test but most of it was a washout. So that was the series over.

I felt pretty good about my game right then and started the 1992/93 summer in Australia smashing it in Shield cricket with both bat and ball. However, I wasn't picked for the first Test against West Indies in Brisbane. We should have won the game but couldn't bowl them out on the last day. At the press conference, Allan Border said we'd have won if Shane Warne had played. So, after making 69 with the bat and taking six-for against WA at the Junction I got picked Boxing Day!

Boxing Day for the First Time – December 1992

In the Boxing Day Test, I took 1/65 in the first innings. That got people talking: 'This Warne isn't much good.' Remember Australians had only seen me in Sydney and Adelaide against India previously. Sri Lanka hadn't been televised. The frustration that my home town wasn't seeing the best of me turned into motivation. I came out second innings and took 7/52 – against Haynes, Hooper, Lara, Richardson; all those guys in the team that was still rated number one in the world. I knocked them over with my flipper – the one to Richie Richardson was about the best I ever bowled. Everything clicked, it felt like magic. Richie had come down to a wrong 'un and said afterwards, 'Hey, man, was that the wrong one?!' I said, 'Yeah, watch out for it, Richie,' and then knocked him over with the flipper next ball! Merv took the last catch and the party began.

When I'd finished my days with TJ and Rod Marsh in Adelaide, I'd given them both a bottle of red wine to thank them for their help. They said they'd open them at an appropriate time, like after Warne took some wickets! Rod rang the MCG dressing-room after that victory and said he was at home drinking the red I'd given him. It was wonderful of him to call. I called TJ to see if he'd opened one too. 'Still not the time, mate,' he said, 'but great job, well done.' I said 'Okay, no worries.'

I remember Greg Matthews running out to get my dad to cele-brate with us in the rooms and I got a fun picture of him and me having a beer with Merv, who threw most of it all over us. Ian 'Molly' Meldrum came in too. He'd been the host of the TV music show *Countdown* and was a legend in Australia – as big as Michael Parkinson in England. He loved his sport. 'Mate, that was one of the best days,' he said. 'I've never seen a leg-spinner bowl like that, and against the West Indies – can you believe it? It was unreal. Love ya, Warney.'

Boony sang the team song with unbelievable passion and we all just went berserk. It was an awesome night. I woke up the next day thinking, 'If I bowl like that, I'm good enough. Yes, I'm ready to go and watch me fucking go.'

That was my first night back on the beer proper. I'd worked so hard – I'd drunk water at Merv's wedding, trained, practised, starved myself. So I got flying drunk and was nothing more than a statistic the next day. But from then on – certainly for the rest of that series – I was okay with it and took things easy. The booze didn't matter, the performances did.

We drew in Sydney over the New Year, the match that Brian Lara played his great innings of 277. I've said it before and I'll say it again: if we hadn't run him out, we'd have never got him out. Our 500 played their 600 – a batting deck! He tells a good story about naming his daughter Sydney after that innings. Then he pauses and adds, 'Lucky I didn't make 277 in Lahore!'

All of this meant we were one up going into Adelaide in late January. It's perhaps the biggest disappointment of my cricket life that we lost that incredible Test match by one run. 2006 against England became known as 'Amazing Adelaide', but 1993 came close to claiming that title. We were the ones chasing this time, just 186 to win. It was our dressing-room's turn to be so nervous, to feel that pressure I talked about, and we could barely watch as Curtly Ambrose, Courtney Walsh and Ian Bishop got stuck into us. What a match it was! In the end those great fast bowlers were just too good.

I only bowled eight overs in the whole game; Tim May bowled 22 and took seven wickets. 'Maysey' was a ripper – top bloke, top bowler. We loved operating together – he was my favourite spinner to bowl with – and we certainly complemented each other. I'd bet our record re wickets taken and Test matches won is as good as anyone's.

He came within a whisker of getting us over the line with the bat, finishing unbeaten on 42 when Craig McDermott was caught at the wicket off Courtney Walsh. The margin was one run! That's all, one. So near, so far. Some game, this Test cricket. We all remember the television footage of our viewing gallery when McDermott was given out. Border and his boys were not happy. Just a scratch on the glove of a steepling ball at 'Billy's head. Cruel. But it was brilliant by Walsh, who was a hugely respected cricketer. And a brave and great decision by the umpire Darrell Hair.

We went to Perth with the series to play for, and Curtly Ambrose took 7/1 on a minefield. From 0/24 with the new nut, he finished with 7/25 – the most lethal spell of fast bowling I've ever seen. The game was over in two days basically. The pitch was green and rock hard; good-length balls flew past and over our heads. They'd replaced Kenny Benjamin with Anderson Cummins – so it was Ambrose, Bishop, Walsh and this guy Cummins, who was no slouch. I mean, please. We had . . . no chance, as the scores prove. We lost the match by an innings and the series 2–1. The legend of the modern-day West Indians lived on.

By now, I really felt I belonged. After the West Indies tour, we went straight to New Zealand, where I took 17 wickets in three matches at an average of 15 each. It had been an extraordinary year. From setting off to TJ's place in Adelaide to the final Test of the 1992/93 summer in Auckland, my life had changed beyond all recognition. There had been something in the air alright.

By this point, some important and influential people had placed a lot of faith in me. First up was TJ, for the detailed technical stuff, the mental side and the tactics – plus his unwavering belief that I had it in me to be something special. TJ treated me like a son and I responded like we were family. Nothing was left uncovered.

Rod Marsh was a big influence too, and because Rod, TJ and Ian Chappell were great mates, the four of us spent a lot of time together. Rod was good on discipline and cricket common-sense. He helped me think clearly.

Chappelli has this amazing cricket brain and I reckon he must be one of the two or three greatest captains of all time. Who are the candidates? Douglas Jardine, of course, for what he achieved against Bradman and having the courage to change the game's parameters; Sir Frank Worrell, definitely, for the image he gave cricket and the flair with which his team played the game; Richie Benaud, for imagination, flair and style, and . . . Ian Chappell, in my view.

I've listened to him talking cricket for a long time now and he makes more sense than anyone. He taught me so much about the tactical side of the game, about strategy, about getting the best out of players and about loyalty to them – the aspects of the job that matter most. He sees inside the game and inside the minds of all of us who play it, even from 150 metres away in the commentary box, and he continues to push for the things that matter most – attacking cricket and good pitches that give an equal chance to batsman and bowler. I've spoken to a lot of former captains over these past 30 years and I've learnt more from Chappelli than anyone.

I remember having breakfast with him around the time I was at the Academy and thinking, 'Wow, this guy is good.' One particular thing he said has always stuck with me: 'Know yourself.' When people ask me about their own game these days, I add to that, 'Never pretend to be something you're not. Be straight up and you'll be respected for it.'

Chappelli introduced me to Bill O'Reilly in a bar in Perth. I had a couple of minutes with him, in passing. He had a hat on – I particularly remember that – and he said it was nice to meet me and that I should keep up the good work. We didn't talk for long, but he was full of encouragement. Next day I read an article by him saying he'd watched a young leg-spinner who was going to have a huge future. Stick with him, the article said, because it was fantastic to see leg-spin back in the game. Chappelli says he was a brilliant observer of the game. I have to agree!

There have been a few other important influences. Dad, of course, who always encouraged me and was there every day; Shaun Graf, who did a lot for me at St Kilda and for the Vics; and Simon O'Donnell, who shoved me up against that wall. Good job, Scuba! Then there are Jack Potter, Jimmy Higgs, Bob Paulsen – all good leggies – and Laurie Sawle, the chairman of selectors who backed me without much to go on.

Growing up, I followed Abdul Qadir. I played and trained with Peter Sleep. I watched Bob Holland take five wickets at Lord's. I remember Kerry O'Keeffe's hop and I can picture Jim Higgs, who had a big drag, with a nice wrong 'un and a big-spinning leggie. There was no-one, though, that I specifically emulated or copied. For sure, me and Jason would impersonate Qadir in the backyard, at the top of his mark, giving it the arm twirls and then the leap and bound. Magic bowler, that guy, but I didn't copy his approach or action. In fact, I tried to slow my whole process down: to measure it and time it, to create drama, precision, power and aggression.

We were all captivated by Richie Benaud presenting the cricket on television and with TJ I'd watched film of him bowling. He passed on to me what O'Reilly had told him: learn to land six leg-breaks perfectly. It'll take you three years to do it, Richie said. Apparently, he later said that I did it in two, which was why I was better than the other guys. I don't know if that's true or not, but let's say it is. Thanks, Rich.

After my first finger operation in 1996, I lost the feel for the leg-break, and though TJ was sure it was coming out right I knew I had more to do than we first realised. The feeling of the ball coming out of the hand – the use of the fourth finger on the right hand, next to the little finger – that's the key to the whole thing. I used to spin off that knuckle, fizzing the ball in a way that alarmed most batsmen. To be honest, I didn't get that back for a while, and I got by through experience and a bit of bluff and bling.

Richie had commentated on the last game of the summer before we left for the World Cup on the subcontinent and he'd rung Austin Robertson – my manager at the time – to tell 'Ocker' that he'd seen something in my action that he wanted to talk to me about. Ock gave me a number to call Richie in France.

I'd been lucky enough to go out to dinner with Richie and his wife, Daphne, a couple of times, so we got to know each other well enough. Remember, Richie was like the messiah, the conscience for all things cricket, and we loved him. If he wanted a chat it was cool by me.

That night, I dialled the number and a familiar voice said 'Hello, Benaud residence.'

'Oh, g'day, Richie, it's Shane Warne here, mate. Ock said to ring you.'

The voice said, 'No, this isn't Richie but I'll get him for you.'

I said 'Really? Okay, thanks.'

And it was like three, two, one – 'Hello, who's calling?'

'It's Shane Warne, Richie. Ock said to call.'

'Oh, g'day, Shane . . .'

It was like Richie had pretended to be the butler! Anyway, he couldn't help re the finger injury – he just said bowl as many balls as you can and the feel will come. Then he talked about the gather, just before the final delivery stride. He said, 'You haven't got a full arc on your gather. You're sort of going from shoulder height, which limits the arc and puts pressure on the follow-through. Get a fuller arc going again, like you used to. It'll give you better shape on the ball, allowing you to bowl it "up" more.'

It made great sense. I said, 'Thanks very much, Richie, I really appreciate your input.'

He said, 'Anytime,' and added, 'I won't come and trouble you, Shane, but if you ever have a question, don't be afraid to ask.' Then it was 'Goodbye and go well' and the phone hung up. Brilliant. I wondered if the butler then served breakfast to Daphne.

Richie was spot on. The advice worked well and I soon got a rhythm going. The best way I can explain it is to say that it's like a golfer not making a full shoulder turn and take-away of the club. Once I got a full arc, everything slotted into place.

I bowled a lot in the nets, got my feel back soon enough and had a good World Cup, especially in the semi-final against the West Indies. We were gone for all money until I knocked over two or three guys in the middle-order – the flipper was coming out great – and we were back in the game. Damien Fleming came on at the end and bowled superbly under pressure. West Indies had been 2/165 chasing 208 and bombed – all out 202. We won by five. A place in the final was ours (not that we made much of it).

Again, thanks, Rich. What a man!

6

The Rising

No-One Teaches You This Bit

I WAS A BOY from Bayside in Melbourne, who'd had a simple upbringing. Summer was the beach, tennis and a bit of cricket now and again; winter was footy. Warne family holidays were mainly in September when we'd drive to Surfers Paradise in Queensland. There was a place there that had these cool, thrill-a-minute water-slides. We were either on the slides or hanging out at the beach for a week or two a year, and then we drove home. Jase and me led a pretty sheltered life, and by the time of my 18th birthday I'd been down the pub a bit with mates and chased a few girls, but I'll bet I wouldn't have been to more than half-a-dozen parties.

I've talked about my dreams – the AFL one shot down and the cricket one brought to life. Almost from nowhere I'd gone from working in factories, driving trucks, flogging pizzas and delivering beds to travelling the world and playing international cricket. It had been a pretty amazing journey; little did I know what was to come.

Old Trafford in England in 1993 changed everything. I bowled the best ball that anyone had ever seen – or so they told me. 'The Ball of the Century', they said, as if it was an all-time classic song, y'know, 'Honky Tonk Women' or 'Bohemian Rhapsody'. There were photographers and newsos everywhere, following me close – too close – and I was thinking, 'Hey, whoa, what's going on?' I had no idea about this stuff and it was massive. I was 23 years old and wherever I went it suddenly felt like there was a kid with zinc cream on his nose, trying to bowl leg-spin. A cult had appeared from nothing in the UK and I was it.

No-one teaches you this bit. There is no school – you just have to trust your gut, be yourself and get a bit lucky. There are plenty of sharks out there, in it for themselves. The trick I quickly learnt was to surround myself with good people. I didn't see myself as this new global superstar who'd bowled a miracle delivery that had everyone out of their seats, but the families and kids in the streets – or at hotels, restaurants, bars and, of course, at cricket grounds – well, they did. I didn't want all the other stuff and I sure didn't see it coming. It's been an ongoing problem of mine. I don't see the big-shot sportsman, I see the guy from Bayside, cruising with his mates, happy with a pizza and a beer.

Everywhere I went, there'd be someone who wanted a piece of me. Though it was flattering at first, it soon became hard to deal with. I'd be out with mates and people would come up and say hi, then pause, just standing there, launching into a bunch of questions about cricket. I got it, and tried to stay polite, but I wanted to relax not engage. Occasionally, I'd get ratty so they'd turn on me – 'Big head' or 'Rude bastard'. I felt on show, exposed and, at times, threatened. I was beginning to see how fame was double-edged. There were even articles about the clothes I wore. 'Warne was seen out,' didn't matter where, 'dressed in ripped denim jeans.' Really? Who cares?

At home in Melbourne, Mum and Dad's house was the escape. In England, it was my hotel room or 'Help, guys, stick with me tonight!' to my team-mates. This took some digesting. I'd wanted sporting success but never considered the implications and responsibilities that came with it. People stop you for an autograph or photo and they're meeting the headline, not the person. It's confusing and potentially derailing.

During the two or three years that followed, I was on a roller-coaster. I took 200 wickets in that time and broke a bunch of records. The Australian team pretty much smashed everyone and life was good.

I was in glossy mags and meeting rock stars. Guys like the Rolling Stones' tour manager would say, 'Hey, Shane, I'm a big fan – love you, mate.' I'd hang out backstage, before watching the show from the mixing desk, posing for a million pics and signing another million autographs. It was nuts and, though I didn't pick up on it immediately, I was starting to feel as if I was in a pressure cooker that was increasingly close to exploding. I felt I was getting away from who I was.

It was like it wasn't me, like I was two different people – Shane Warne the cricketer and Shane Warne the person. A lot of people spend their life trying to be in the newspaper or magazines. I've spent most of my life trying not to be in them. It might sound ridiculous, but that's the way I see it.

Anyway, let's do *that* ball first.

The Gatting Ball

1993 Ashes. I remember sitting on the plane to England next to Merv. I said I'd watched a lot of the '89 series when the Aussies, as underdogs, hammered the Poms. He said, 'Mate, these are great tours: no flights, you travel round the place in a bus together drinking free beer from XXXX, the sponsors. The county games are no sweat and the Test matches have rest days on Sunday! Best of all, England are crap.' He said it was the best tour, full stop.

I thought that sounded pretty good. We landed in England and basically went straight to Lord's, did a press conference, had a jog, and over the next few days got rid of the cobwebs – bat, bowl, catch, throw, and then repeat it. The facilities were great and before we knew it we were off – three one-day warm-ups before the first county game at Worcestershire.

New Road, Worcester is a beautiful ground but with very short boundaries. On the outfield before the start of play, Allan Border pulled me aside and said, 'Mate, these guys over here haven't seen much of you, so there's a surprise element we can exploit. I want you to bowl leg-breaks and nothing else – no top-spinners, no flippers, no wrong 'uns, just leggies.'

AB added that Graeme Hick – who played for Worcestershire – had the ability to play a major part in the Test series. 'Now is not the moment to show him your box of tricks. Switch over and round the wicket a bit if you want – not too much – and just bowl leggies to him, nothing else for now. Keep the magic up your sleeve.'

In the second innings, Hick made 187. He hit me for eight sixes. There were so many times I wanted to bowl a flipper or a wrong 'un, to show him something, but, well, AB was the boss. Geez, Hicky played well. I was bowling the leg-breaks properly, trying to fizz them, but he just kept smashing me. (Warne 23-6-122-1 in that innings!)

To be honest, I'd thought the leg-break might have been good enough for the Poms anyway, but now I was thinking this bloke Hick wasn't a bad player, and I already knew about guys like Gooch and Gatting, so a few doubts suddenly crept in.

I was very low key through the other county matches – actually quite down in the dumps 'These are only county games, Warney, she'll be right on the night,' said the other bowlers, but it sounded hollow. I felt vulnerable.

By the time we got to Old Trafford for the first Test, I was like a caged animal, ripping them in the nets – leggies, wrong 'uns, flippers – and bowling for hours on end just to get back on track mentally as much as anything. As the hours and minutes ticked by to the Test, I started to overthink it. I was wondering if they'd pick Tim May instead of me because I'd been smashed by Hick at Worcester.

But AB came up to me the day before the Test and said, 'Mate, you're going great. They're coming out well – you're fizzing them.'

I said, 'Yeah, I feel good.'

'Great,' AB replied, 'because we're unleashing you tomorrow and we are going to hammer them.'

'Phew, okay, I'm ready to go, mate,' I told him. 'I'm ready.'

I really needed that. I was learning that confidence was at the heart of performance and that you couldn't take it for granted. I had a spring in my step.

When AB walked out to toss the coin, it was like, 'How awesome is this! The huge crowd and the legend of the Ashes – love it!' Yes, I was nervous but part of that was just wanting to get on with it, to burst out of the blocks and rip some massive leggies and show Hick and company there was more than a leg-break in this bag of tricks.

England won the toss, put us in and bowled us out on a damp pitch for 289. Mark Taylor made a fantastic hundred (he got 124) and then it was our turn to bowl.

Craig McDermott was having a horror tour, he'd hardly taken a wicket, and Mike Atherton and Gooch got off to a great start – 0/70. Just before one of the breaks, Merv knocked over Atherton, which opened the door. Gatting came in and started well. Then AB signalled for me to bowl, saying he didn't want Gatt to settle.

I was fighting off those demons in my head. 'To hell with it,' I thought. 'Get a grip, go for it, fizz these things out like you've never fizzed them before.' Peter Such had taken six for England in the first innings so we knew there was plenty of spin in the pitch. All I had to do was make use of it.

I clearly remember standing at the top of my mark and taking in deep breaths. It was chilly, which seemed to add to my nerves, and I kind of shivered in anticipation of this first Ashes moment. Gatt was on strike with Goochie at the non-striker's end.

Goochie just stared at me the whole time, watching everything I did, trying to unsettle me. I was almost too pumped now, so I turned away from him and tried to rein back the emotion and find that – how can I say – fired-up sense of calm that served me best. It sounds daft, I know, but it's a state that is in there somewhere, a perfect state of concentration. I can only find it if I blank out everything else. It's hard when you're that nervous, so I took the deep breaths and slowed everything down, which settled the shivering.

Then the perfect state kicked in, like I was in a trance.

'Right, mate, just rip this leg-break and send the England dressing-room a message that I can spin it big!'

I sensed the crowd's excitement. More deep breaths.

Then something inside me said, 'You gotta go. Come on, go, mate, pull the trigger, let's rip this.'

I remember letting go of the ball and it felt great. It couldn't have come out any better.

Now, of course, what it does after that I can never be sure. A lot depends on how the batsman wants to play the ball and his thought process/mindset.

It happens in half a second but seems to take forever. It floats and swerves and dips. I like it, really like it.

It pitches outside leg-stump and spins. Boy, does it spin! I like it more.

Gatt plays half-forward, down the line of leg-stump, and misses.

The ball hits the top of off.

Momentarily the world stood still. Everyone, it seemed, was frozen in shock.

Gatt looked at the pitch in suspicion, like it had conned him. Then he turned for the pavilion with a bemused look and a shake of the head.

We all went berserk. I was thinking, 'You beauty – what a cherry!' Not a bad way to start.

It was the first time that those huge Citroen replay screens (I even remember the sponsor!) were at Test grounds and we all looked up together. Heals said, 'Mate, that is as good a ball as you will ever bowl. That is an *unbelievable* delivery.'

In the change-rooms at the close of play, the BBC were televising a wrap of the day and we sat there watching. Heals was still all over it: 'Hey, boys, have a look at this, watch this . . .' They replayed it 10 times from every different angle and it wasn't until then that we realised – *I* realised – that it was out there, something way beyond even my expectation. As time went on, I figured that to have done that with my first ball, with the nerves and the cold – well, I'd call it a fluke. I guess it was meant to be. I never, ever did it again in my career.

(On reflection, I did take a wicket with the first ball of a spell one other time – Marcus Trescothick, Trent Bridge 2005, caught at bat-pad. I strongly felt Punter should have opened the bowling with me that day. It was the fourth innings of the pivotal fourth Test. England had made us follow on and then left themselves just 129 to win. Trescothick got off to a flyer against the new nut but

I should have been landing into the rough outside his off-stump straight away.)

Back to the middle, where we were buzzing in a way that doesn't happen often. It was like the ante had been upped. We dispersed and got ready for the next bloke.

Robin Smith came out. I spun a couple past his outside edge before he played a beautiful drive down the ground for four off the last ball of the over. No worries. I was feeling real good, I'd got a wicket with my first ball in England, broken the partnership, and was champing for Merv to bowl his half-dozen quickly so I could have another go.

Next over, Smith was still on strike and I thought, 'If he fancies driving me, I'll get it full around leg-stump, the Gatting line, and might nick him off.'

I did. I bowled another one, first ball, bang, he tried to drive, nicked it to Tubby, gone, out! Almost as good as the Gatting ball. This time it was Smith on his bike.

I had 2/4 from seven balls and I just kept going. It was overcast, cold, and as good as I ever bowled in a Test match. I loved the pitch because the ball gathered pace and turned quickly. Merv knocked Hick over for 34 and 22 and then, in the next Test match, took it upon himself to barrage him – verbally and physically. After a couple of games, Hick was dropped; Gatting too. Gooch lost the captaincy. It turned square again in the fifth Test at Edgbaston, where me and Maysey picked up five each. The pitches played into our hands. We swarmed all over the Poms.

Captaincy is everything. Get it right and you release your players; get it wrong and you shackle them. AB released me in Sri Lanka and then in England in 1993. The rest became a little piece of cricketing history.

'Simmo' and the Work Ethic

I've talked a lot about Allan Border but not much about Bob Simpson and the role he played in my development. Simmo formed an outstanding opening partnership for Australia with Bill Lawry in the 1960s, was the best slip fielder anyone around back then had seen, bailed out the ACB during World Series Cricket by coming out of retirement to play his first Test in a decade, and became the Australian coach in 1986. That's a good CV. In my view, he was the best coach Australia ever had and I had too.

I was always a hard worker when it came to cricket training. The failed footy audition inspired that. In hindsight, I didn't train hard enough at footy. I was a good mark and had a good kick, but my fitness wasn't great. I was just lazy. I relied on my talent in the junior age groups, but after the switch to play at senior level I just didn't work hard enough to be stronger, fitter and improve. That's the key to any player in any sport – you must improve as your career goes on! It means you care. When I latched onto cricket, I put in the hard yards. I listened, watched and learnt. I'm perceptive when it comes to sport and those who play it, and I learn quickly. I can fast-track. I accept I have plenty of weaknesses but this isn't one of them. I wasn't going to fail twice.

Ian Chappell told me to watch captains, so I never took my eye off Allan Border or, later, Mark Taylor. Chappelli said, 'Always put yourself in the captain's shoes and think what you would do next.' I was bowling for hours and hours in the nets to different players and in different conditions. The more games I played, the more experience I was getting and the more I was getting a feel for captaincy. Once your place is secure, you play with a greater freedom. It's a great feeling that you know you're going to play the next game. You are more prepared to take a risk or experiment, try the impossible – in real terms you lose the fear of failure. We sometimes forget what it's like – and how hard it is – for younger players playing for their spot. I soon learnt how the game worked and how I could influence it. I took on board Terry Jenner's stuff about how a batsman walks to the crease, how he grips his bat, how he takes guard and studies the field – those detailed things that you start to build a kind of mental dossier from. Is this bloke really so confident? Or is it bravado? I wanted to know what he had deep down and whether it was enough to cope with the moment and with me.

I found these intricacies really made me tick. I absorbed the way they affected the battle, which I loved, and felt how the challenges pumped electricity through my veins. I tried to change the tempo of matches, accelerating momentum or, at times, slowing it right down. And I always looked to do the very thing the opposition didn't want me to do.

Simmo pushed me even harder than I was pushing myself. Bowl, bowl, bowl; bat, bat, bat – hour upon hour. Then with Tubby, AB and 'Junior' – Mark Waugh – he'd make us catch, catch, catch, and then catch, catch, catch again. It's like anything: once you see the improvement, you want more. The worst thing is to put in the hours and not see any improvement – like if you go to the gym, sweat your balls off, and at the end of it your muscles look the same. So what happens? You don't go to the gym no more!

But I was showing results. I was getting better, and better still. I was taking plenty of wickets, making a few useful runs and holding on to catches. (Here's a couple of stats for the people who are into them. I have the most Test runs without a hundred and there are only two players ever, of which I'm one, to take 300 or more wickets, make 3000 or more runs and have 100 catches or more – the other is Ian Botham.) I ensured my fitness stayed good, my physio was disciplined and my shoulders and arm stayed strong. I was doing cricket-specific training, getting massages most days and even eating healthier. I was enjoying success. Remember, a few years earlier I'd been told I wasn't good enough so my whole drive was 'Yes, I am good enough and I'll prove it to myself and to the world.' I was like a steam train, nothing was going to stop me.

I've departed a bit from Simmo here and I'll be back to him in just a minute. First, I want to give you an example of the fever that had overtaken me. The early problems any leg-spinner faces are accuracy and consistency: it's complex and it's hard work. That's why so many kids have a crack and give it up; that, and the coaches and captains who don't get it. I came to it relatively late which might have helped, actually. I knew a bit more and figured, 'Right, I've got to be more accurate than anyone, ever.' Hard graft can achieve that, which means hours, days, months.

In the nets I put an old ball, or a handkerchief, on the spot where a good leg-break should pitch and then I bowled at it until I hit it more often than not. Most sessions I would tell myself I had to hit the ball x times before I can go! That was as much a mental thing, as well as improving my skill. That's not easy, I promise you. After a while, I hit it lots. So then I moved the ball, or the handkerchief, a fraction left or right or fuller or shorter and started again. Then I'd position it for a left-hander and do the same. And that was just the leg-break. There was the slider, the wrong 'un and the flipper too. The process could take 40 minutes or four hours. If I achieved my target in 40 minutes, I'd go home. If not, I'd keep going until I did. I was mainly on my own, often bowling two to three hundred balls per session, but I never left a session beaten.

Back to Simmo, and once I got into the Australian side, he helped me out – fielding balls and making suggestions. He respected my work ethic and began to relate his own experience to the match situations I'd be facing.

It was Simmo who taught me that bowling round the wicket could be a weapon to both left and right-handers. I was 12th man for a Test in Perth and he asked if I'd ever thought of bowling round the wicket. I said it was bloody hard around there, because of the lines, angles and body shape at delivery. Nah, he said, it was easy, and that I'd take a heap of wickets from round there once I understood the basics.

I said, 'Why go through all that? I'm doing okay from over the wicket, aren't I?'

'You have to change the angles to right-handers,' he said, 'especially when it's not turning much. And, of course, it's perfect against left-handers once the pitch starts to deteriorate.'

I thought about it a bit and then said that if someone bowled round the wicket to me, I'd smash them miles.

He said, 'Oh, is that right?'

Anyway, the day went on and at the close of play, I fixed all the drinks for the guys. Out of nowhere, Bob said, 'Shane, put your pads on, we're going to the nets and I'm going to bowl at you from round the wicket.'

Simmo was pretty good by the way. He knocked me over about five times, easy, so then I got curious. 'Tell me more,' I said. We talked about the angles, not just to attack the batsmen, but more importantly the angles that I needed to align myself at delivery: so, my approach to the crease, shoulder position and hip drive.

I did okay. I asked TJ about it, and he said, 'Yeah, it could be good but be careful of getting too round-arm in delivery or of just "putting it there". You've still got to *bowl* it.'

I was really curious now and started to practise it a lot. The rough outside the right-hander's off-stump came into play big time and the options gave me opportunities I'd never considered. I could play tricks with batsmen's minds. If you're batting and you see a ball explode out of the rough – even if you're just kicking it away – it stays in your head. I thought, 'I can work with this – thanks, Bob.' Not that it's as easy as it might sound to get right. Murali never felt comfortable bowling round the wicket; quite a few spinners I know didn't.

Bob Simpson was so good because he challenged us to get better every day. During the 1993 Ashes tour, we dropped a few catches in the slips in an early county game. Practice had got a bit lazy, I reckon. Me, Mark Taylor, Mark Waugh and AB were just sort of catching, without concentrating on a result from the session. Junior was trying to take them one handed and that sort of stuff, like only he could. Simmo was real angry. 'Right, you blokes aren't catching too well and you're not taking it seriously either, so you're going to nick some to me and I'm going to show you how to do it.' He threw his bat down and came into the slips.

'You've got to get your weight right. Go on, throw full on and nick it to me,' he said. He caught everything, every one, anywhere, and we went, '*Wow*.' We'd heard about him but we hadn't seen it for ourselves. He reinforced some tips like the weight on the inside of the feet. Then he explained how the head and body should move with the line of the ball and how opening up the left or right foot a touch allowed that to happen. 'In turn,' he said, 'this will allow you to ride the pace of the ball and give with your hands, keeping them soft. Too many people just reach to the line of the ball and their hands snatch at it, or they stay static with hard hands and expect hand/eye instinct to take over. If you get the footwork right and go with this flowing motion it becomes a whole lot easier.' Brilliant. We listened and we learnt.

So Bob could catch in the slips and bowl leg-spin pretty well. He could bat, of course, was brilliant on the philosophies of building an innings, combating an opponent and even more brilliant on running between the wickets. His knowledge of the game was not only very good but very simply explained and easy to understand. He could show us stuff, not lecture us like a school teacher, and he improved our thinking and our skills. It was proper cricket coaching, and for us young kids, he was a game-changer. We'd talk about the game for hours with him; we were very lucky to have Simmo.

7

Unguarded Moment

John

WHEN I ARRIVED IN Sri Lanka for the Singer series one-day tournament in September 1994, I was just 10 days or so short of my 25th birthday. All-up, I was earning about $25,000 a year from Cricket Australia – a figure made up of the retainer contract fee and match payments. The bigger bucks started to roll in that following Ashes summer at home, from the exciting sponsorship deals I signed with Nike and Just Jeans.

I love a punt. It never mattered whether I had money or not, it was the buzz that got me. A couple of hundred metres from the hotel in Colombo was a casino, and I love a casino – blackjack, roulette, poker, I love them all. Best of all, like in most casinos, if you gamble you get free drinks. On the first night, I lost five grand. *Ouch*, that hurt. So I needed a drink.

I was pretty shitty about my loss when I went over to join Mark Waugh and a Sri Lankan mate of his at the bar – at least I've always assumed he was Sri Lankan. He was from the subcontinent, that much I know. The guy introduced himself as John. I said, 'G'day, John, how are ya?' He said, 'Good, mate, good.' It was a five or

10 minute conversation, nothing more than general chat – how's the cricket, are you looking forward to the tour, blah blah blah.

At the end of the conversation, he said, 'I see you like a punt on the roulette.'

'Yep, I love it,' I told him, 'but I lost all my money.'

'Oh, right,' he said. 'Well, look, I've won a lot of money on Australia winning games of cricket over the years. Here's a five-grand chip to cover you for the money you lost tonight.'

I said, 'Mate, I've got my own money. I'm fine, thanks.'

He said, 'No worries,' and that was that. I went back to the hotel.

You have to remember that back then there was no talk of bookies or spot-fixing and match-fixing. It wasn't on the game's radar, not at all – no whispers, nothing. As a youngster, I wouldn't have known a thing. Actually none of us would, I reckon. This was 24 years ago! There was no clue of what we know now.

The next day we finished training and went back to the hotel. The phone rang in my room – there were no mobiles then – and a bloke asked for Shane.

'Yes,' I said, 'this is Shane.'

'Hello, it's John, I met you last night with Mark. I just wanted to come by, say g'day and have some lunch.'

I said, 'Yeah, sure, I'm not doing anything. Any friend of Mark's is a friend of mine.'

So we had a sandwich in the hotel lobby and he said he'd been thinking about last night. I remember his words pretty clearly.

'Five thousand dollars is a lot of money. I want to give you back the $5000. No strings attached, no nothing – here is five grand, please take it. I love the way you play your cricket and I'm a wealthy man.'

I thought, 'Hmmm.' I said, 'Mate, it's very generous of you. I repeat, any friend of Mark's is a friend of mine, but I don't need it, so no problem and thank you, I'm fine.'

He said, 'I insist, take it, no strings attached, from a friend to a friend.' He kept arguing the case, in the end persuasively.

I took it.

Then I went down the casino that night and lost it again. I thought, 'Shit, lost another five grand.'

So we did the tour and I never heard from or spoke to John again.

Anyway, having missed the start of the series against the West Indies that summer I got back into the side for the Boxing Day Test. We were staying at the Hilton just across the park from the MCG and on Christmas morning the hotel phone rang.

'Hello.'

'Merry Christmas, mate.'

'Who's this?'

'John.'

'John who?'

'I met you in Sri Lanka with Mark.'

'Oh right, how are you, mate, what are you doing?'

'I'm great, thanks. I thought I would just ring you to wish you a merry Christmas and congratulate you on getting back into the side.'

I thought, 'How nice is that?'

'Yeah, yeah, and I'm looking forward to the Test match against West Indies,' he added.

'Yeah, should be a cracker,' I replied. 'I'm looking forward to it too. It's great being back in the side – I'm feeling in good form.'

We had a general chat about cricket. There were no alarm bells when he asked how the weather was in Melbourne. I said, 'Fine, bit overcast but should be fine, good forecast for the five days, pitch looks good.' I kind of chatted as you would to a journo if doing an interview – dry pitch, might spin towards the end of the match, should be good for me, blah blah blah.

'Yeah cool, thanks,' he said. 'I am catching up with Junior soon, so I might see you around.'

'Sure, mate, look forward to it. Have a good Christmas and all the best for the new year.'

That was that.

Until six months later.

We were in New Zealand for a one-day competition to mark the centenary of the New Zealand Cricket Council when the tour manager, Ian McDonald, took me aside. He asked if I knew anything about players taking money from outsiders for providing information on teams, pitches and weather. I didn't, simple as that.

What I could tell him, however, was that I'd been given five grand by a mate of Mark Waugh's in Colombo back in September, in lieu of the five grand I'd lost at the roulette table. Macca listened to the story, and the more of it he heard, the trickier his position became. In a knowing way, he said that John was the same guy who had a business deal with Mark to provide this sort of information. I remember a bit of a sinking feeling, like, what had I got into?

We were on the way to the West Indies a few weeks later and stopped off in London for a night or two to break up the journey. Bob Simpson and Jack Edwards, a St Kilda guy and the new team manager, pulled me in and asked about my dealings with a Sri Lankan bookmaker. I said I didn't know any Sri Lankan bookmakers.

Jack said, 'Mark Waugh reckons he introduced you in Sri Lanka.'

I said, 'Oh, John, Junior's mate. Yeah, I've spoken to him a couple of times.'

As I was telling Jack that John had given me five grand in the casino, his face changed colour. '*He did what?!*'

Jack said, 'The bloke is a dodgy bookmaker who bets on cricket.'

I said, 'Okay, that's not good news but I didn't know that when I spoke with him.' As far as I was concerned he was a mate of Junior's who gave me five grand after I'd lost five grand one night. 'I've spoken to him a couple of times on the phone and that's it. I've had no other dealings with him at all.'

Jack was in a state, saying, 'This is trouble, real trouble.'

I said, 'What do you mean? I haven't done anything wrong here. If someone wants to give me five grand because I lost five grand in the casino, I'll take the five grand. If he gives me 20 grand, I'll take 20 if I choose to.'

Jack and Bob said, 'No way, mate. This bloke is a bookmaker who bets on the cricket and Junior told us he has a business deal with him.'

'Well, I didn't,' I told them. 'I had some general chats about cricket with him, like I would with any journo at any time.'

They just said again, 'Oh no, mate, this is bad.'

So this time I started shitting myself, thinking, 'What have I done? I didn't know the guy bets on cricket.'

I'd figured he was a gambler and he told me he won lots of money on Australian cricket, but I didn't know anything about that world. I was 24, for Christ's sake! *Arghhhh!* This was not funny. I didn't understand but equally I began to wonder how I could have been so naive.

Jack said the board had decided to fine us both – me $8000 and Junior $10,000 – which left a very bad taste. He said it was as a warning signal to us and that the fines wouldn't be made public. Then everything went quiet, as if it was understood that our fault was naivety and nothing worse, and, thankfully, it seemed as if the ACB had decided to move on.

But let's go back a step, because when I was called in to Jack's room I also told him about something else.

Salim Malik

We were playing Pakistan in Karachi, the opening Test of the 1994 tour. It was Mark Taylor's first as captain and the pitch was a road. When play finished on the fourth day, Pakistan were 3/155, needing 314 to win. I was rooming with Tim May and that evening the phone rang.

'Hello, Shane, it's Salim Malik.' The Pakistan captain, by the way.

'G'day, mate, how are you?'

'Not bad, not bad. Look, please, can I have a chat?'

'Sure, what's up?'

'No, can you come to my room, please?'

'Um, what for? Just talk, mate, I'm sitting here with Maysey.'

'No, no, this is very important – you have got to come to my room.'

I thought, 'This sounds serious. I hope all's okay – maybe I should go, maybe I shouldn't.' What does he want, I wondered.

I hung up the phone and Maysey asked who it was. 'The Rat,' I said. It was his nickname because we thought he looked like a rat, not because he *was* a rat. Not at that stage, anyway.

I went to his room. He was dressed in a kurtha, the white robe style clothing the locals wear.

'Thanks for coming up.'

'Sure, mate, how can I help? You sounded very serious on the phone.'

'We can't lose tomorrow.'

'Er, well, I'm sure you're going to try and win and we're going to try and win too. Should be a good game.'

'No, no, you don't understand. We can't lose tomorrow.'

'What do you mean you can't lose?'

'We can't lose tomorrow. It would be devastation for Pakistan and for the players. People will have their houses burnt down.'

'Well that's unfortunate, mate,' I told him, 'but I'm here to win. We're in good shape, the wicket is turning, I think I'm going to bowl alright tomorrow, so your hands are pretty full and I think we'll probably win.'

'Listen to what I'm saying to you,' Malik said. 'We *cannot* lose tomorrow and it's down to you.'

I wondered what exactly he was getting at. 'Right, so what is it that you're saying to me?'

Then he dropped the bomb.

'I am prepared to give you and Tim May $US200,000 each to bowl wide of off-stump tomorrow. It can be delivered to your room in half an hour.'

'*Whaat?* Sorry? Mate, please, you have to be kidding.'

'We can't lose tomorrow, please just make it a draw. Bowl wide of off-stump all day, we let the ball go and it's a draw.'

I was thinking, 'Fuck, $US200,000 each,' and at first I was kind of laughing, but then I began to realise he was serious. Man, he had this look in him.

'Yes, I'm serious. Cash, in half an hour, in your room.'

I said, 'Jesus Christ, mate, I don't know what to say other than no, and that we're going to beat you tomorrow.'

'So you don't want the money.'

'Of course I want $200,000 but not from you. We're going to win the Test match and so I've gotta say no.'

'Don't rush. There's no hurry. Think about it and let me know before tomorrow morning.'

'There's nothing to think about. We're going to win tomorrow. Good luck. See ya.'

I ran down the corridor, heart racing and thinking, 'What the hell just happened there?' I stopped outside the door of my room. 'Come on, Shane, be clear. You've just been offered $200,000 to bowl wide of off-stump. Yes, that *is* what happened.'

I went in and said to Maysey, 'You'll never guess what the Rat wanted.'

'Tell me.'

'He offered you and me $US200,000 each, cash in here in half an hour, to bowl some shit wide of off-stump tomorrow.'

Maysey laughed. 'I don't need 200K to bowl shit!' Pause. He looked at me again. For a moment there was silence. Then he said, 'You serious?'

'Yep.'

'Shit.'

We started laughing, nervous laughing. Jeeesus, is he serious? What are we going to do? We quickly agreed the first thing was to tell Mark Taylor and Bob Simpson what had just happened. So I called their rooms and arranged a meeting. We told them the story. It was Tubby's first Test match as captain, remember, which obviously he was pretty keen to win. Also, he'd already got a pair, so he hadn't had a great match personally. To sum up, he had a lot on his mind. Then his two key bowlers for the conditions turn up and tell him Salim Malik has offered them $US200,000 each to bowl shit the next day.

You should have seen their faces! It was like, 'Wow, what's that about? Two hundred thousand dollars? Where does he get that from?' I can't emphasise enough how hard it was to comprehend. It was that new to us. We took a deep breath and then sort of all had a bit of a laugh about it, but it was another nervous laugh because we instinctively realised how dangerous it was.

In 1994, as I've mentioned, the match-fixing stuff just wasn't on the radar. No-one had ever thought a match was fixed, no-one had ever heard of spot-fixing or spread-betting – nothing. Honestly, we had a nervous giggle about it, resolved to brush it aside and win the match the next day. Then we went for a beer.

Bob Simpson wrote a report of our conversation and gave it to the match referee, John Reid, the former New Zealand player. 'Holy shit,' John said, 'this is big. Leave it with me.' We assume that John reported it to the ICC but we didn't hear.

The Test had got to the last day with all results possible and no clear favourite. The way things turned out was incredible: this would be one of the most famous Test matches of all time.

I'd taken one of three wickets to fall on the fourth afternoon and I then took four more on the final day. It had begun with Pakistan requiring a further 159 with those seven wickets in hand. There was plenty of spin in the pitch and my confidence was high. I bowled almost unchanged. We chipped away all day, as did they with the bat. It was seriously good Test cricket that became increasingly tense with both teams in the hunt.

When the ninth wicket fell, 56 runs were still needed and we felt sure we had it covered. Big Jo Angel was playing his second Test – the first had been a while back, by the way – and was running in with tremendous heart and belief. Inzamam-ul-Haq was still there, looking to farm the strike with Mushtaq Ahmed – 'Mushy' – at the other end. The target was creeping down, so too the overs in the final hour, when Jo ripped a perfect reversed in-swinger into Inzy's pads – smack dead LBW, thanks very much, game over.

Except that one of the umpires gave it not out. We were like, '*What*, you're kidding, aren't you?! That's just out, stuck on the crease. Just plum, out.'

Geez, things were at fever pitch now. Both teams on the edge and the atmosphere electric out there.

'Right,' we thought, 'we're going to have to take more than one wicket here. Come on, boys.' We then had more appeals turned down for catches and LBWs but, to be fair, nothing conclusively out. Inzy nicked and nudged and, in between, hit some really good shots. Mushy mainly blocked, played and missed, but then suddenly slogged the odd one for four. There was a point – with about 20 needed – when Inzy stepped up a gear, taking us on more aggressively, like he suddenly felt the pressure might get to Mushy.

It got down to three to win, that single wicket still in hand, and I was bowling. Imagine the scene. The night before I'd been offered

$200,000 to throw the game. We had a report to the ICC hanging around and the opposing captain's offer of money was its subject. It was bound to be hugely controversial. It was Tub's first Test as captain and he'd got a pair. Pakistan needed three to win, nine wickets down. Some drama.

I was at the top of my mark. Tub came over and said, 'Right, mate, how are we getting Inzy out?'

I said, 'Driving or trying to whip it through mid-wicket. Do you like this plan, Tubs? I'll bowl a big spinning leg-break at the stumps – let's leave a big gap leg-side. If Inzy nails it, fair enough; if not, let's hope he nicks it or falls out of his crease – stumped.'

'Okay, like it,' said Tub. 'Let's do that.'

So we had a bat-pad fielder on the on-side, a sweeper at straight-ish mid-wicket on the boundary and a man at 45 behind square for the top-edged sweep. We had just three men on the leg-side – no mid-on or mid-wicket, no-one in front of square except the sweeper. Well, I said I liked a gamble! My plan was to bowl wide of the crease and a fraction wide of leg-stump. We had two slips, bat-pad off-side, short cover, mid-off and point just behind square.

Standing there, spinning the ball from hand to hand, I thought, 'Come on, after everything they don't deserve this. I'm going to rip this leg-break to Inzy, *rip it.*'

And rip it, I did. It came out perfect. Inzy took a step or two down the pitch and tried to whip it through mid-wicket, overbalancing as it missed his outside edge. He was out of his ground.

Heals missed it too. It went through his legs for four byes.

We stood there, rooted to the spot. The shock delayed our reaction. The game was over, the Test was lost. It took a moment to sink in. Pakistan had won the bloody Test. From nowhere, it felt like, from nowhere. We had 'em. But we'd lost.

At the presentation ceremony I was announced as man of the match. So I'd got wickets, runs and then a gong. But I – we – had taken a beating, in more ways than one.

On the way to the podium I passed Salim Malik. 'You should have taken the cash, shouldn't you?' he said.

I was ropeable. I should have turned round and knocked him out, but somehow resisted. I will never, ever forget that moment or that feeling. The massive contradictions everywhere and Salim Malik's taunt.

Yes, that was a pretty famous Test match and, later, Salim Malik got rubbed out. So it became even more famous. To my knowledge at least, the can of worms that is match-fixing was opened there, in Karachi in 1994. Eventually, he was banned, initially for life. In the Pakistan courtroom that convicted him, he called me a liar, saying it never happened, that the meeting never took place. In my absence, he told them I was making it all up. He had tried the same thing on Mark Waugh, as it turned out. Junior went to Pakistan to give his testimony and the Rat called him a liar too. Basically, we dobbed on Salim Malik and got him rubbed out for life. Good thing.

'Match-fixers'

Out of the blue, in 1998 I got called into Graham Halbish's office – Graham was then CEO of the ACB. It was nearly four years after the incident with 'John' and I don't know why it came to light at this particular point, but he said the board were under pressure to now make public the fines Junior and I had received in 1995. They still accepted I was pretty innocent in the whole thing, but said they had to be seen to have done something. I guess match-fixing was increasingly an issue for the game and, given that people were understanding better what was involved, they didn't want to hide anything that had happened previously, however innocent it may have been at the time.

It was just after that meeting that the papers broke the story – a sensational story too – that Shane Warne and Mark Waugh had been fined for selling information about Test matches to a bookmaker. The *Herald Sun* put the two of us on the front page with the heading 'Match-Fixers'. The press conference was a nightmare and Junior was booed onto the field in Adelaide.

We immediately went down the legal route to sue the *Herald Sun* but ended up doing a deal to write for them instead. John Hartigan was the big boss at News Limited and a huge Australian media figure. The day before the court case he rang to say, 'You don't want to do this and we don't want to do this, so let's find a deal that hires you as a News Limited columnist.' And that was that.

I copped the punishment, learning my lesson the hard way. The facts are that I took $5000 off a stranger who was a mate of Mark Waugh's. I didn't know he was a bookmaker. I'll always say we got a rough deal but I accept I was naive. Looking back, what stranger gives you five grand unless there's something in it for him?

I trust people, I always have. Call it a character flaw if you like, but I'll always say g'day to people, I'll accept most interview requests and chat about cricket to pretty much anyone.

There were no mobiles back then. On tour we watched telly in the hotel room or played table tennis, billiards and darts. If not, we just hung out by the pool, talking cricket. We'd chat about the game, the opposition, about where to bowl to them and all that stuff. Plenty of people were on the fringe of those conversations and plenty of others wanted to be. John was a nice enough guy. I only met him twice, for a maximum 30 minutes in total. I liked him, no problem. So when he rang me on Christmas Day, I was happy enough to chat to him. I doubt the conversation lasted 10 minutes.

I was hurt that the ACB didn't stand up for us more than they did but, equally, I understand that I did the wrong thing. I never knew why the board held it back for so long – for four years after I first told them. My guess is that some journo got a sniff of it and though the board wanted to keep it under wraps they couldn't do so any longer. It would have been better if they'd come clean at the time.

There was no code of conduct back then and no anti-corruption units and/or advice to the players of the dangers around them. I never, ever thought about fixing games, bowling rubbish on purpose or whatever. When people called us match-fixers and said we'd sold out on Australian cricket, it was hard. But I understand how big it was and I'm glad that people saw the facts in the end. Salim Malik was banned, that's what matters.

Hansie

I had no idea that Hansie Cronje was fixing games and was totally blown away when it all came out. I actually felt sorry for him. He was such a competitive player. I really enjoyed and respected him and would never have imagined he was involved, even among the rumours that were rife in cricket in the late 1990s and into the new millennium. Big names and unknowns – it didn't seem to matter, suddenly match-fixing was the talk of the game. Unfortunately, Hansie got involved in something he probably started relatively innocently and then became addicted to. For sure, he got in too far. From the point of view of an outsider looking in, he got trapped and later deeply regretted doing what he did, particularly coercing guys like Herschelle Gibbs and Henry Williams. That was almost the worst part of it.

There was no sympathy for Hansie but there wasn't any great hatred either. We liked Hansie and respected him. When he died in the plane crash, it was so so sad. The whole thing made us second guess everyone and everything. You start thinking back to games and go, 'Well hang on, I remember some bloke couldn't hit it off the square,' and you ask yourself, 'Was he trying?' We never once thought Hansie wasn't trying.

IPL

I was captain/coach of the Rajasthan Royals in the IPL for four years. Everyone in our side was 100 per cent committed and honest in their effort for us, but there were whispers, even before the tournament began in 2008, of some big names on the take. The anti-corruption people gave us lectures, and were pretty conspicuous wherever we went, but I wanted to be sure our guys were clean, so I came up with a plan.

Darren Berry was assistant coach and Jeremy Snape was performance director/psychologist. In a meeting with them, I said I wanted to nip any idea of corruption in the bud. My plan was to tell the players that my own phone had been tapped and that I'd been called in to see IPL Chairman and Commissioner Lalit Modi and the IPL heavies because an investigation had been launched into a conversation that had taken place on it. They said, 'Great idea.'

We had a training camp organised in the build-up to the first game. Each day we practised and talked. We planned set plays for the first and last ball of overs, for example; trained the minds of go-to bowlers in certain pressure situations; decided on, and then drilled, specific fielding positions for everyone; divided the 20 overs into three sections of six and one of two and established each person's role in those periods. We worked in private groups where the players would represent their own views and then offer views on others. Then we arrived at a collective agreement on team style of play. The three of us in management sold the vision, the players bought into it.

After one intense group session, I called everyone in and dramatically changed the subject. I said, 'Guys, something very serious has happened to me overnight. I want you to know that I had a cricket conversation with a friend in Australia a couple of days ago and that I've been hauled into the IPL offices, where I was told my phone had been tapped during the conversation and that I'm now under suspicion. In other words, the conversation I had was recorded and I'm being investigated.

'Don't worry, it's all good. I've done nothing wrong but Lalit Modi and his offsiders are on the case. It's a warning and a lesson to us all. If any of you try to fix games, throw games and the like, you will be banned. You may never get an opportunity like the IPL again so I leave it to you as to how you handle it, but while you're with the Royals and under my captaincy, there is zero tolerance for any form of fixing. Be warned that your mobiles and your hotel-room phones are being tapped. I'm in trouble right now but I'm going to be fine. You won't be if you put a foot out of line.'

Well, you could have heard a pin drop. Graeme Smith, Shane Watson, Dimi Mascarenhas, Kamran Akmal, Younis Khan, Sohail Tanvir and all the Indians in our squad of 20 – silence. Job done.

Hopefully one day the bad guys will be weeded out. It's almost impossible to police the game and the only way is for the players to come clean on everything they know, which is a tough thing for anyone to do. Match-fixing is like a cancer. Terrible. Cricket is too great a game to be destroyed by a greedy few.

8

Changes

I FIRST MET SIMONE when she was working as a promo model for Foster's at the Vics annual golf day in 1992. We kind of caught each other's eye – she was such a beautiful girl. I thought, 'This is a really cool chick, sexy and funny.' She gave me her number and I lost it. I put it in my cigarette packet and never saw it again. I tried to track her down over the next week or two but with no luck.

A few months later I was at a St Kilda Football Club function and she was working there too.

'Oh my God, I'm so sorry,' I said to her. 'I lost your number.'

'Yeah, whatever,' she said.

'No I'm serious. I put it in a cigarette packet and threw it out when I finished them.'

'No way,' she said, and wouldn't give me her number. I gave her mine, of course, but heard nothing. Not at first.

Then, out of nowhere a couple of months later, she called to say merry Christmas. She didn't know much about me, so I told her I was playing in the Boxing Day Test for Australia and asked her to meet me for a drink after play on the first day.

'I don't know,' she said. 'I don't think it's for me.'

I said, 'I'll bring a mate, you bring a mate,' and after a bit of persuasion she agreed. So, as I mentioned in an earlier chapter, myself and Damien Martyn went out to Bobby McGee's with Simone and her friend . . . Simone. Yep, she was also called Simone – bizarre, but true. Even more bizarre, Simone 2 and Marto hit it off and a few months later were engaged.

Anyway, I kept in touch with Simone 1 this time and we began to hang out more and more. I talked her into coming to Perth for the Test against West Indies. That was the match in which Curtly Ambrose took 7/1 and we got hammered. She wasn't impressed. Next thing, I was back in Melbourne having dinner with her parents, Bryan and Coral, and things just developed.

She came to England in 1993 and hung out with Sue Hughes, Merv's wife. They stayed at bed and breakfasts – nothing flash, because, back then, we weren't allowed wives or girlfriends in the hotel at all, not even in the bar. We paid for their flights and hotels and were expected to sneak over to their joint! Simone and Sue went to Santorini in Greece for some mid-tour sunshine and loved it there, so we really didn't see much of them. The players shared rooms in those days – in my case mainly with Merv and Mark Waugh, or sometimes with Boony. Me and Boony smoked a lot of cigarettes together, we were like Cheech and Chong. It was hardly a place for your girl.

By the way, half the side either smoked regularly or had the odd dart. We were sponsored by Benson & Hedges, remember. Boony, Geoff Marsh, Bruce Reid, Greg Matthews, AB when he was having a drink, me and the physio Errol Alcott were smokers. Mark Taylor, Mark Waugh, Dean Jones, Ian Healy, Craig McDermott and Merv all used to give us a hard time. Six smokers in the rooms. It was partly the culture at the time and partly the sponsors making the fags so available – the dressing-rooms stank of cigarettes! So much of life was so different back then. On the smoking front, everyone just lit up – in restaurants, trains, cars and planes. I used to bag a non-smoking seat on flights and then hibernate in the back corner of the plane with my fags.

I remember one funny moment. India were touring, and on a flight to Perth, Venkatapathy Raju, the left-arm spinner, snuck into the back with us, chain-smoked and got completely pissed on two cans of Swan Light. I think he was more terrified of his captain, Mohammad Azharuddin, finding out about the darts than the beers, so we gave him a bunch of mints and told him to crash out for an hour. I'm not sure it worked, to be honest. He was sheepish for days.

For all the rules about wives and girlfriends at the hotel, Simone and I were seeing more of each other than most. A few days after the Gatting ball in early June, we took some time off together in the Lake District. On the second day we hired a rowing boat but I just couldn't get the rhythm of rowing the damn thing and we kept going round in circles. The longer it went on, the funnier it got.

The truth was, though Simone didn't know it, I was nervous. I really felt something strong with her and, right then, out on the water, after the Gatting ball, a win in the first Test on my first tour of England, the man-of-the-match award, and all the excitement and attention that was around us . . . I proposed. I didn't go there to propose but, I dunno, everything was so cool in our world and I just came out with it.

'We're getting along really well – so what do you reckon?'

'What do you mean, "reckon"?'

'I mean, what do you reckon . . . like, how about we go for it?'

'What do you mean, "go for it"?' (Perhaps she was thinking, 'Shane, you can start by rowing in a straight line.')

I said, 'Well, let's get married. What do you think? Do you want to spend the rest of your life with me?'

And without missing a beat, she said, 'Yes.'

'Great! That's amazing. Let's do it then . . . we'll have so much fun together. Awesome.'

Simple as that. It wasn't the most romantic proposal ever, but, gee, it was sure a romantic place. Except for the boat still going around in circles.

Our next game was in Bristol and I asked Mum and Dad down to meet some of the great people I'd played with and met during my time in club cricket there – Mike Gerrish, or 'Biggsy' as everyone knew him, and Merv, Maureen and Pat, who all ran the George pub. I told everyone not to say a word because I still had to call Simone's dad. A bunch of us were in Biggsy's car and Mum and Dad pulled up alongside us. I couldn't help myself and just blurted out, 'Hey, guess what, I got engaged,' and they were like *'Whaaat?!'* And we just kept driving to the pub.

Once there I rang her dad, Bryan, from a call box, shoving the coins in and getting a shitty line. I asked for his permission and he answered 'Go for it!' He never complained, and was delighted.

Mum and Dad really liked Simone but weren't sure if I was doing the right thing at that stage of my life – just 23 and with so much suddenly going on. She was my first proper girlfriend. I had kissed at 15 and gone a step or two further over the next couple of years. But not until I was 17 did I . . . well, you know. Then I had the crush on Michelle Scott at school and later Pauline Vaughan – when I was touring Europe with mates straight out of school – the girls I talked about in Chapter 3. I liked Melissa Judd too but her dad didn't approve of me! Only in England in 1989 did I start to get it together with girls.

Anyway, the point is that Simone was my first full-time *proper* girlfriend and I loved being with her. It was a time of 'firsts'. In February 1994 I bought my first house in Tuxen Court in East Brighton for $240,000 – I put down 50K and borrowed the rest. Simone moved in and we did it up together, put in a pool – all the gear – and then it became the regular spot for the Australian team's Christmas Eve parties.

I started earning $3000 a year from my Cricket Board contract, which shot up to 10K after the Ashes tour in '93. There were match payments on top of that for both Test and one-day cricket – $1500 and $500 respectively, I think. In Shield cricket, I got a couple of hundred bucks per match and an extra 50 if I wore Kookaburra protective gear. The Australian Cricket Board contract went up to 30K a year or so later, but we were hardly turning into millionaires. The game-changer was sponsorship.

My managers Austin 'Ocker' Robertson and John Cornell were really big in those days. They'd both played a major part in the establishment of World Series Cricket with Kerry Packer, and John teamed up with Paul Hogan to make the *Crocodile Dundee* movies.

With John by his and my side, Ocker did a huge deal with Nike – $1.25 million over five years. It was unheard of at the time. Then Just Jeans came in at 250K a year for three years. Suddenly I could pay off the house.

The deals came on the back of the fact that I was getting a lot of air time. On one Valentine's Day, a newspaper ran a poll asking parents – mums actually – who they would most like their daughter to come home with as a Valentine date. I won! I was on TV shows, doing ads for various products, and my face led the Nike campaign in Oz, which was huge. I won a couple of cars too – international player of the summer for both Test and one-day cricket against South Africa and New Zealand. I drove these two Toyotas round the Adelaide Oval. It was mad back then. Oh, and I was voted Australian sportsperson of the year in 1994. It was like someone had their finger on the fast-forward button.

Nike

As part of the arrangement with Nike, I did some TV commercials for them, and got to hang out in Portland, Oregon with Nike founder Phil Knight, the great American NFL and Major League Baseball player Bo Jackson and Michael Jordan. Nike had me designing a new range of footwear for the global cricket market and sold it as the best cricket shoe ever made. The batting one was called Air Century; then there was Air Oval, Air Flipper and the Max trainer – 'The Nike Collection by Shane Warne'. I don't mind admitting that this felt pretty cool!

Guys like Brian Lara were on the phone saying, 'Send me those shoes,' and once the best players started wearing them, they flew out of the door. Knight would stand up at events and introduce me as this amazing cricketer from 'Orrstralia', and everyone was gushing. In the States, in the UK and at home I was invited to everything – concerts, Grand Prix, exhibitions.

Just Jeans

I also did the catwalk with Helena Christensen and Claudia Schiffer at a Just Jeans show in Melbourne. I walked out with Helena and said, 'How cool is this!' and she went 'Ssshhhh!' Oh, okay. I kept going to the end of the catwalk, spun round with my best 'blue steel' look in an effort not to giggle, and headed back to where we'd come from and through to backstage.

The next thing I knew, she had all her clothes off, tits out. I thought, 'Oh shit.' Then she had the next outfit on before I'd barely had time to blink, never mind have a look. At which point she turned to me and said, 'Listen, you do not talk when we walk out there, you just walk, stare straight ahead at whoever or whatever you want, get to the end, turn around, walk back and do it all over again. Just concentrate on what you're doing.' Oh, right.

That was about it with her and I can't say I had much of a chat with Claudia either. Helena was dating Michael Hutchence of INXS at the time. I met Michael in Perth after one of their concerts. We had a beer backstage and I told him the story. He had a laugh about it and then called Helena over. I didn't know she was there! Anyway, she had a giggle about it too and said, 'Sorry, but I do that stuff every day – must have got out of bed the wrong side that morning!' I've got a big picture in my house of Helena and me walking down the catwalk.

I was in good shape through most of the '90s – certainly from 1992 with TJ up to 1998 when my shoulder went. After the operation – a SLAP lesion that surgeons usually perform on javelin throwers – I had it in a sling for six weeks, so I didn't train at all and ate rubbish food. Then there was the second spinning-finger op, wire and all that, and I was down on myself for a while. I got heavy, back up to 95 kilograms, and lost motivation for training and other stuff. Operations and rehabilitation are a hidden side of sporting life. The surgery can be frightening and the trauma sucks oxygen out of you.

So, yeah, 1998 to 2001 I was overweight. Then I was fit again from 2002 till 2006/07. I think the idea that I was always a fat bastard comes from first impressions. Those first two Tests against

India, before I went and hung out with TJ in Adelaide, yep, I wasn't in very good shape. But after that, well, I wouldn't have been in blue jeans on the catwalk with Helena if I was still a fat bastard.

The funny thing is that, as I've mentioned, I've never been into food and never will be. I reckon sitting in a restaurant is a waste of time, the same as cooking. I'd rather have a pizza on the couch than, say, go out to a fancy restaurant and discuss the quality of the meat. I hate those flash restaurants with tiny portions that already tell you to head for the McDonald's drive-through on the way home, as you're still hungry. Food gets in the way of a good time. Eat, go, party. I'm all about atmosphere and vibe. And music.

As I see it, a steak is a steak: what's the big deal? Spaghetti bolognese is about as far as it goes with me, unless we have people round and then I'll do a barbecue chicken, burgers or sausages. I'll eat if I'm hungry, and I won't if I'm not. I like hot chips, pasta, pizza, white-bread cheese sandwiches and apples – everything else I can take or leave, mainly leave. I do like ribs and roast pork too. But if there's an opposite to a foodie, I'm it.

I'm not a heavy daily drinker either, by the way. I used to do a lot of beers but gave that up when I was getting fit with TJ. Now I like a glass of wine, red mainly – I did a wine course a few years back actually – and if I'm out at night I'll drink vodka and Red Bull. But that's more a binge thing. I can go weeks without a drink, I don't even think about it, and then when I hit the clubs I might be on the vodka till four in the morning. And, by the way, I'm no slouch. I can drink most people under the table.

I just put on weight, that's all. Blame the diet, or lack of it. When I want to lose weight, I can do that too. I'm one thing or the other, nothing in the middle. I did like one cold beer after a bowling day.

11,660 Balls Already

We'd drawn 1–1 with South Africa over three Tests at home either side of the 1993/94 Christmas and New Year period, then headed to South Africa in late February for the second leg of three more Tests, along with eight one-dayers.

I hadn't had a proper break from the game since starting out in Test cricket and, frankly, I was a bit of a wreck by the end of the 1993/94 home season. I'd bowled 8843 balls (1473.5 overs) in first-class cricket in 32 matches in the 1993 calendar year alone – the most of any bowler in a calendar year since Bishan Bedi in 1976 and not beaten by anyone since! (The most ever was another leg-break bowler, Tich Freeman of Kent, who bowled 2378.2 overs in 1928. Bet he was tired.)

In fact, from Boxing Day 1992 to the end of the South Africa tour in April 1994, I played 40 first-class matches for Australia and Victoria – the most of any player in the world. I bowled 11,660 balls (1943.2 overs) – many more than anyone else – taking 191 wickets (the most again) at 22.21 – 4143 more balls in that period than Tim May, who was second on the list. In that period I played 22 Tests, five Sheffield Shield matches, another first-class game in New Zealand prior to the series there, 10 first-class games in England against counties and universities, and two first-class games against South African provincial sides. And I got engaged. See what I mean, *exhausted*! Something had to give.

When we arrived in South Africa, AB gave me the first two weeks off. He said, 'Miss the warm-up games and just come to the nets if you fancy a bowl, bat, catch, or whatever. Otherwise have daily physio, do some light training and take it easy – we want you to be right for the first Test.'

The long and short of those instructions was that I had two free weeks in Joburg. There was temptation everywhere, in its many faces. I was out every night, back just before sun up, crashing out in the change-room. Warne was on fire . . .

But this was extremely bad preparation for a Test series against a good side and, deep down, I knew it. I'd lost focus on the disciplines that had brought me a great couple of years. Things had spiralled, almost out of control.

With the recent series in Australia, this was the return leg in what was effectively a six-match showdown. We were the first Aussie touring side since 1969/70 and thousands of people met us at the airport and interest followed us wherever we went. We even met

Nelson Mandela and South African President FW de Klerk. They were hazy, crazy days and cricket was king. Part of the excitement came from South Africa's return to the international stage after the apartheid years, and part of it the quality of the teams and players around the world at that time. Every series had real edge.

The first Test was at the Wanderers, a ground where Hansie Cronje's guys fancied themselves and where the crowd got very aggressive, driving their boys on. The Wanderers wasn't called the Bull Ring for nothing. The whole situation felt very hostile. During Australia's last Test series in South Africa, under Bill Lawry's captaincy, they'd smashed us 4–0, and it was pretty obvious the locals had missed the smell of Aussie blood.

The two first innings were almost dead even – 251 played 248 in their favour. I'd been off the pace in general, and my bowling had been ordinary, so I could see why AB didn't bring me on immediately in the second innings. After a while, though, I was ticking because we weren't looking like taking a pole and the crowd were getting into us. Hansie Cronje and Andrew Hudson developed a second-wicket partnership, and the longer it continued the more I was tearing at the leash to bowl.

Then, out of the blue, after 43 overs, AB said, 'Come on, Warney, we need a wicket.'

I remember saying to myself, 'Why didn't you bowl me earlier then!'

In my first over I bowled Hudson round his legs, sweeping. I've got no idea how or why but I completely lost the plot. I look at the footage now and think, 'That's not me, is it? Is that me?'

I can see a kind of rage in my eyes and anger in my body language. In short, I told him to fuck off and then I chased him, still shouting, louder and louder. I had a goatee, which is kind of a mean look anyway, and I had this irrational anger pouring out of me. Looking back, it was definitely the build-up of everything over the previous 18 months, not just that moment. I snapped and I'm not proud of it.

After the day's play, I went to Jonty Rhodes, who I knew pretty well, and asked if I could have a word with Hudson because I wanted to apologise to him. 'Come on in, mate,' he said, 'we're all having a laugh about it.' I went into the dressing-room and they were all giggling. I said, 'Look, it wasn't funny, I'm sorry,' and Andrew was like, 'Hey, no problem.' We shook hands and all had a beer and that was that. (Oh, for the good old days when we could have a laugh, share a beer, break down barriers and form lifelong friendships with the opposition.)

That wasn't the end of it, though. The ICC fined me, the Australian Cricket Board fined me my match fee, there was talk of a ban – all sorts. Apparently, the radio journalist Tim Lane had walked onto the middle of the MCG back home and done a piece saying he was embarrassed to be an Australian. It was an unbelievable overreaction. Allan Border was steaming.

Merv was fined too. He'd walked up the player's race – which has a cage around it at the Wanderers – after playing a rubbish shot and being dismissed, and some idiot shouted abuse, so Merv threatened him with his bat. To be honest, it didn't look great and Merv later said he regretted it. I said, 'Really? That doesn't sound like you, mate.' He said, 'No, no, mate, my regret was that I should've smacked the prick in the head. At least the fine would have been worth it.'

I've never experienced a crowd like that one in 1994: everywhere we went, the streets, the hotels, the ground, the Joburg people were so hostile. By the time you walked down that race and on to the Bull Ring, you were ready to go 10 rounds with Rocky. They were throwing things at us, smashing stuff around us, grabbing our hats through the wire of the cage as we walked on and off, bad-mouthing us, so when it came time to bat and bowl we were raring. In a way, I love that passion and, anyway, I can hardly complain because the Aussie crowds can be OTT too.

I love South Africa. I've been back a million times since and have many friends there. But I never fully understood the reaction to us in 1994. Maybe we'd got too cocky and the crowds picked up on that. Or maybe, we hadn't been back for so long that the chance to get one over us was a nationwide thing, not just a cricket thing. We were the best team in the world and what was clear was that anyone and everyone wanted to knock us off our perch. I guess it was as simple as that.

We ended up drawing the series 1–1. It was the same result as their tour to Australia and an accurate reflection of the contest between us. In general, the South Africans were a very good side – tough and smart. Kepler Wessels was a tough leader and South Africa had some good variety in their attack. The one-day series was a ripper as well: it finished 4–4 after we won the unbelievably tense final game by one run.

Incidentally, the Daryll Cullinan thing really caught on in Australia. Everyone played up to it, including the crowds. I just kept knocking him over and the harder he tried to give it back to me, the worse it got for him. The press heard that he was seeing a sports psychologist to learn how to cope with me. The next time he took guard, I asked him what colour the couch was and knocked him over again.

I always thought Daryll should have come in with a beer after a day's play and said 'I missed another straight one, hey, Warney' or 'I didn't pick it *again*!' Then we'd have laughed about it and I might not have been quite so killer in my desire to knock him over every time!

Anyway, after that crazy start of mine, it turned out a great tour. The South African players themselves and the people who looked after us were fantastic. Hotels, security, officials – everyone was great, so welcoming, and we made a lot of good friends that remain to this day. Sure, the crowds got to us and, no, I'm not on Daryll's Christmas card list. But South Africa 1994 was fun.

We're Going to the Como, But First, We're . . . Going To Get Married

It finally happened on 1 September 1995, in a beautiful Melbourne park, the one on the left as you drive down Williams Road in South Yarra. No church or chapel, just the park and a marquee for the after party, along with the Victorian cricket chaplain for the vows, of course.

While we were waiting for Simone to rock up, AB came up to me and said, 'You okay, mate, you don't look great. You sure you want to go through with this? You can still pull out, you know.'

I said, 'Simone's a wonderful girl, mate – let's get it done.'

It felt great on the surface but deep down I'd begun to feel I shouldn't be doing this. Or maybe I should. Or shouldn't? Perhaps it's the way everyone feels in the days before they get married, I thought. Who knows? It was nothing to do with Simone. She looked so beautiful on the day, and in the year and a bit since we'd got engaged she'd easily become my best friend. We were good together, she understood me and me her. But I could feel my life changing at frightening speed and I just wasn't sure it was the right time.

Shaun Graf, my Victorian mentor and team-mate, was MC in the marquee. We had 200 people and Simone did a great job, decking it out magnificently and making sure the detail was spot on. Everyone got plastered. We stayed at the Como Hotel – a fantastic place. My brother was best man, with the groomsmen being Merv Hughes and a good mate from my Academy days, Stephen Cottrell. Simone had her sister, Lisa, and best friend, Sharon, and her cousin Tanya.

A guy called Tuffy, who used to play guitar in a Hawaiian shirt at a place called City Rowers in Brisbane, did the entertainment – he was better than brilliant, playing all the great covers, many of them with Steve Waugh and Mark Taylor on stage. 'Tugga' loved 'Khe Sanh' and Tubby loved 'Bow River', the two Cold Chisel classics. We all had such a happy night. I remember thinking it had been the best day of my life. What was all the worry about?!

On a slightly different subject, I can hear the question, 'Steve Waugh was at your wedding?' Well, he was. I was close with Tugga back then. We toured Zimbabwe together in 1991 and he asked me to come and play club cricket with him at Bankstown – he even spoke to the club about getting me a job behind the bar. We hung out a lot in those days and I did consider going to play in Sydney to try to get into the New South Wales team but, as I've mentioned, Simon O'Donnell set me straight on that one! Tugga wasn't in the Test side when we got to know each other well; he'd been left out for a while but came back against West Indies in 1992/93, batting at number three. Then he settled into the middle order, which suited him best.

He became a completely different person when he took over as captain. All that worship of the baggy green – some of the guys went with it, like Lang, Haydos and Gilly, but it wasn't for me. I think he turned into a more selfish player when he had his second run in the Test team, which changed him. My philosophies on the game were more aligned with Tubby than with Steve; though, in fairness, Steve was a successful cricketer – if in a very different way to AB and Tubs, whose style and direction I much preferred. It's no secret that Tugga and I don't see eye to eye these days.

Simone

Simone and I have three amazing children. We spent 13 great years together, created a beautiful home in Middle Crescent, and even though we went through a few dramas, we look back now and can have a laugh.

My relationship with her is fantastic. We have brought up Brooke, Jackson and Summer together. We think differently about parenthood – I'm a lot stricter in many ways – which has been a good thing for them as they've seen different points of view. She understands me, I understand her and we get along fine and are friends.

There's a perception out there that every relationship is driven by the same rules – society's white picket fence, if you like. Mum, Dad, wife and kids, good job, solid home – and above all loyalty to your partner. But reality isn't like that. Simone and I made our marriage work. The intimate details of how are not for the public domain. Do people really think we'd still be such good friends if it was all as bad as people make out?

As I've said, my life was going nuts. I think maybe we were more sister and brother – we loved going to the movies, playing pool, seeing concerts, hanging out at the pub, but perhaps we didn't have that emotional lock-in. My respect for her remains to this day.

In the early years together we were really happy, enjoyed creating homes and sharing day-to-day life with friends and family – all the normal stuff that young couples do as they grow together. The trouble with cricket is that it invades your space, occupying everything from conversation to consistency in a relationship.

Friends looking to catch up start by wanting to know the gossip about the cricket, so the blokes hang out at one end of the room and the girls the other. When that's done and you're back at home together the next morning, planning a movie or night out or something, more often than not you're planning it while packing a bag or suitcase. International cricketers are always on the move. The amount of time away is ridiculous, months on end, and it's unfair on wives and children. Then, when you come back from four months in England or 12 weeks in Pakistan, you have to get to know your partner again. Dressing-room habits die hard: in-jokes, language, untidiness and all that stuff that is natural on tour. It spills over into home life and creates an edgy environment that needs ironing out. I was lucky that Simone understood this and the sacrifices that came with it. Success at the highest level comes with a price but she always supported me, no matter what – which I'm thankful for.

Sport is, or was, a man's world and that has the potential to overrun family life in a way that a sportsman might not realise because everything – the whole rhythm of how families live their life together – revolves around him, or me in this case. It's a huge sacrifice your partner makes so that everything revolves around the sport. This might not always be a conscious thing, but it is a fact.

We bought a house out near Portsea on the Mornington Peninsula, at Arthur's Seat, with great views across the countryside and down to the bay. We had happy holidays there when we weren't travelling abroad: tennis court, pool, barbecues – the kids loved it. At Christmas, our parents, Jase and his family and Simone and all her family would come and join us there for one great big family party. Most years Simone would do the whole turkey thing and, as Dad or Bryan carved, I'd be pulling my lunch out of the pizza oven I'd installed on the back deck. There was lots of laughter at our place but, of course, we were interrupted by the incidents, or 'scandals', that the media turned into long-running shows. That was the test – the tough times when everything was so public.

The worst of these was probably in 2000 when I was having my first stint at Hampshire and the *Daily Mirror* in the UK got hold of a series of drunken texts I'd sent to a girl I met at a club in Leicester, Donna Wright. I'd spoken to her for about half an hour – that's all, half an hour – but we swapped numbers. It became a binge-drinking night – vodka/Red Bull – and I sent the texts when I got back to my room. They were pretty full-on. She sent plenty too. A million jokes have come from them but they weren't funny, and neither was the situation I created. The whole thing was just plain dumb of me.

In England, the story soon blew over, but in Australia, oh my God, it had legs, arms, fingers and toes. It was everywhere – talkback radio, TV, newspapers and magazines. I ended up being interviewed by Mike Munro on *A Current Affair*, apologising for the texts. That was stupid of me too, publicly apologising for a private matter.

I said something like 'I didn't think it would become public. Now that it has, it's a mistake. If it hadn't become public, it wouldn't be a mistake.' That comment just made things worse and, in hindsight, I accept that I explained myself badly. I should have just admitted to a mistake and accepted it. From there it seemed like all Australia was on my case. I wanted to say, 'What it's got to do with anyone else except Simone and me?', but by now, nothing I could have said would have helped.

After a few more girls had come out and exaggerated a consensual night of fun, Simone asked a clever question – are there any more that could come out? I thought about it and said, 'I don't think so.' That was humiliating for Simone, for sure. I was certainly testing her loyalty, along with the things we still held valuable between us. In the years that followed, the pressure became more and more intense for both of us. We just grew apart.

The split came in early 2005. We decided to sell the house in Middle Crescent – the house I still love the most and was to buy back for a high price 10 years later – and I agreed to buy a new one for Simone just down the road. Meantime, Dad was on the lookout for me while I was playing in the Ashes series in England and found something pretty good in Park Street, less than 100 metres from Simone.

The divorce time was difficult. She was hurt and angry, and the way the press focused on it seemed to magnify every tiny detail. Why did she ever marry him? Should have left him years ago. That stuff.

She'd put up with everything previously and now still stayed by my side, because she knew we had something going together that the outside world couldn't see. Sadly, we were on a different wavelength; I was lost in cricket and all that it brings.

At the time, as news of the split and the inevitable divorce got out, I felt deeply sorry for the children. They were too young to fully understand but I knew I'd let them down.

In private I was as upset as I ever remember being about anything. In hotel rooms on tour, I'd look at photos of them and wonder how the hell I had got it so wrong and how it would all work out. Michael Clarke spent hours with me – sometimes over a pizza in the room, other times in the corner of a bar – just keeping me going. Thanks, Pup – it meant the world to me.

I hadn't seen it getting worse, however, but it did. Simone, Brooke, Jackson and Summer flew to London together for the start of the Ashes in July 2005, and on the day of their arrival a graphic story broke in the British tabloids about another girl. It was horrendous and there was no way back. After three days, they flew home. That was basically that. Did I feel sorry for Simone? Of course, yes, it was another humiliation for her. As I say, I was embarrassed, and also distraught to see the kids in such a mess. Look, there was anger on my side too. Certain things had broken down in the marriage that weren't all my fault. But in the end, the blame lay at my door and I take full responsibility.

The truth is that we shouldn't have married so young. She might well agree with that – I don't know. I accept that I let down the people closest to me. The road back to a harmonious and meaningful relationship was all but impossible. But in the end we have three amazing children who came from our relationship.

Simone soon started finding fame of her own – *Dancing with the Stars*, TV commercials, a slot on Channel Seven at the spring racing carnival, columns in magazines. I didn't believe she should have used me as the weekly subject for her columns but, in general, I was happy for her that some identity of her own had won through.

As time went on, the anger subsided and we began to rebuild our friendship. Neither of us found anyone else and we started to see more of each other again through the kids. We were alternating Christmases and in 2009, I think it was, we said, 'This is ridiculous. How about we move back in together and make all this stuff so much easier and so much better for Brooke, Jackson and Summer?'

So we had a crack, just to see how it would work out. The answer was not so well. Our reasons for getting back together were admirable, as we tried for the kids, but they could sense that their mum and dad weren't happy. It soon became obvious enough to us all that the basics of a strong relationship had broken down.

The fact is, we'd grown too far apart. A lot has happened to us since 1992 but the bottom line, and the truth, is that we changed. The other truth is that I hurt my family and that is something I have to live with. I hold my hands up and hope Brooke, Jackson and Summer can forgive me. I know those memories still hurt my children, but the wonderful relationship we have now is enough to heal.

The Ashes of 2005 was a strange time for me. On the one hand there was the divorce and all the angst that creates; on the other was the business of a good England team staring us in the face and saying, 'What have you got?' I'm lucky in that I've always been a good sleeper and the only thing that mattered, cricket wise, in this period, was to arrive at the ground fresh and relaxed. I didn't go out much that series anyway, to be honest; the paparazzi were hunting me down. So I hung out in my room with the guys, Pup mainly, and bunkered down.

I was also able to throw myself into the Test matches with complete focus. When I cross the white line, everything is left behind. I love what I do and am good at it, so I had something important and consuming to fall back on. My attitude was, you've let down the people you love; you'd better not let down the game you love too. Most of the time, fame is not that much fun, anyway;

it had sure contributed to the breakdown of my marriage. The fame thing came from bowling a decent leg-break but was not the reason behind it. Maybe the Ashes of 2005 underlines that better than any other cricket I played.

Birth

Until you have children, I don't think you can understand what being in love with someone really means. When I first saw Brooke, I thought, 'Wow, that's it, that's love!' The connection was intense and now Simone and I were 'Mum and Dad' ourselves. I used to see people with kids and think, 'What are they doing with their lives?' In that moment, I got it.

On 27 June 1997 we were playing in Oxford against the Universities when Simone went into labour. The game was washed out and me and Tubs were smoking cigars over a beer in the pavilion in anticipation of the birth of my first child. Then Simone's sister, Lisa, rang with a sense of panic in her voice. She said Simone had been rushed to hospital for an emergency C-section and then said, 'I've gotta go – I'll phone you back.' Oh my God!

After the 14-week scan, we'd wanted to know if we were going to have a girl or boy. Simone was up for a pink room, me for blue. It was to be pink. I was disappointed as hell but now, nervously sitting in that little Oxford pavilion, I was praying for a 100 per cent healthy child – that's all, nothing more. I guess everyone does. As far as Shane Warne, Oxford University 1997, was concerned, a healthy, happy little girl had suddenly become a damn cool idea. Then Lisa rang back. Great news, all good, Simone well, baby healthy. I said, 'Thank God.' *Yes!*

Then I said, 'Boy or girl?' Can you believe that? How weird. It shows the state I was in. Lisa said, 'Are you serious? Your first child is a girl, Shane, you've even chosen the name for her!' We'd decided on the name – Brooke – straight away, easy. I asked Lisa to send some pictures super quick, like right then! What a day.

At the lunch break, first day of the Old Trafford Test, there was a parcel sitting at my spot in the changing-room and I thought, 'What's this?' I lit a dart, opened the parcel, and there were photographs of my first daughter. I was shocked. Oh my God, that can't be my child, what is that?! So I didn't show anyone – I hid them in my bag.

After play, I caught up with Mum and Dad. They said, 'Have you got any pictures?' I said, 'No, haven't got any yet.' I was just too embarrassed to show them the photos – she looked like a smashed tomato. That can't be my child, surely. The next day, I'd got over the shock and did show Mum and Dad. They said, 'Jesus, what a mess.' Normally everyone says how beautiful your baby is, but mine . . . mine did not look beautiful at all. (Later, Lisa explained the photographs were taken before Brooke was even bathed and cleaned. Silly me!)

After the Test match I begged not to play in the two tour games against counties and to fly home instead. I just *had* to see my child. The management were cool, so I flew back via Hong Kong with Gilly, who was injured and heading home. He was so upset at missing out on the tour that I spent half the flight counselling him. And there was me, trying to get some sleep to be ready to see my newborn child.

I landed, jumped in a cab, sped home and Simone came to the door – glowing. She took me to the cot and there, wrapped in blankets, was our baby girl. She was so beautiful. What were those pictures about?! I was blown away by Brooke, and I couldn't take my eyes off her. I just cuddled her, held her, and fell asleep on the couch with her on my chest. It was tough to leave two days later but I did so knowing that something unique and awesomely special had happened to my life.

Jackson was born two years later – 20 May 1999. We were playing an early World Cup game in Cardiff against New Zealand and lost. I hung a banner over the change-room balcony saying, 'Welcome to the world, Jackson – lots of love Shane, Simone and Brooke,' but some officials came and told me to take it down because it was hanging over a sponsor's board. I was so angry they did that.

We were all in a filthy mood. The Kiwis beat us pretty easy and a bit of siege mentality had set in early, so we got on the piss that night, like we'd lost the World Cup and the Ashes on the same day.

Actually, my mood changed fast and the night out became a celebration for me – having a son was like, you little beauty! By the way, I didn't dare have any pictures sent(!) and there was no gap in the schedule to fly home. I was fine about it. I had a great vibe about Jacko. I think it was a boy thing

Then, on 12 October 2001, Summer was born and, finally, I was there at the birth. My respect for women went through the roof that day. Us guys think we're tough! Geez, I saw Simone go through real pain. It was an unbelievable experience to witness that. Being a mother might be the hardest job in the world, but if it's not, giving birth is.

I immediately had a new respect for my parents when we had Brooke. I realised that I would never, ever stop caring. My kids have been no trouble and put up with a lot of crap. I so admire them for that. We now have three well-respected, well-rounded people as our children. Sure, social media has placed the spotlight on them. There's no hiding place.

And yes, I've been embarrassed by some of the stuff they have seen and read. Often enough, they pull me in and say, 'Dad, you can't be serious!' Kids can be pretty cruel at school and mine copped a lot for a while. I know they always stuck up for me, which was amazing. These days they're the first to admit that there are upsides to the lifestyle they have known; like their friends can come over to hang out with Chris Martin, who is a great mate, or hang out backstage with Ed Sheeran – pretty cool.

As kids, you always see your dad as this old guy, so when they see me caught on camera kissing a younger girl, Brooke is like, 'Oh no, Dad, what are you thinking about? She's my age, isn't she?'

'No, she's not your age, Brooke, she's not 20.'

'Dad, she's 26.'

But we talk about it – that's the good thing with us four. In fact, we're always in communication with each other. That's the key to any issue – communication. If they ask, 'Dad, what the hell happened last night?', I'll tell them.

'I met this girl, we got along great, we went out for dinner, had a few drinks or whatever.'

'Yeah, we don't need to know the rest!'

Their message is: you're a single guy, go for it, but pleeese, hang out with someone your own age. Good advice.

I call them most days and text every morning and night without fail, no matter where I am in the world. If they want to call me, they will; if they don't, fine, but we're still in touch at least twice daily. In fact, we're all on a group text message and, as time has gone on, we've become mates every bit as much as family. Mind you, they still grumble, as they always have, that I'm stricter than necessary.

To sum up, I think I'd say my actions have affected them in different ways. At times, I've disappointed them, which has led to anger and confusion. At other times, I've made them proud. They understand me, as their comments at the end of the book illustrate very well. They know I'm there for them and these days I know they're there for me too. Brooke, Jackson and Summer are my life and my number-one priority. It's as simple as that. I love them up to the sky and back.

Postscript

There is hardly any point in me denying that I love sex, but I also love working out a woman – finding out what makes her tick and then what makes her happy. I can think of nothing better than being in a strong relationship and caring for each other.

I love crashing out on the couch and watching a movie together way more than hitting the town. Being single, I miss that almost more than anything else right now. Like I miss the days when the kids were growing up and we did the family things – Marco Polo in the pool, walking down the beach collecting shells, throwing a tennis ball around, movies, even Monopoly. Gee, I love Monopoly.

They sure were better days than the week-on, week-off arrangements that had to be made after the marriage break-up. The kids hated that – it made them grumpy and insecure – so we changed first to a couple of weeks at each place and ended up with a month at Simone's and two weeks at mine. Over time, it worked itself out.

These days things are more relaxed about who goes where, but the principle is now that the kids spend equal time with both of us – at least until they too have kids and, hopefully, begin to feel the respect for Simone and me that we felt for our parents.

I admit I love a lot of what being single brings: the freedom to do what you want, with who you want, when you want. But for me, it's a no-brainer – the first preference is to have a great relationship. Second option, single. Bad relationship, no thanks.

I see mates who are in bad relationships, always on the phone fighting battles, justifying where and why, with no trust with each other about anything. I couldn't live like that. Believe me, I've tried. The other thing I know is that you have to accept people for the way they are. If you don't and you can't tolerate something, however small, it will become a slow torture until something gives.

The key to any relationship is what works for the both of you. Not what society dictates. Set the rules out and don't break them. Respect and honesty are the key, along with expressing yourself to each other.

I think I got it pretty right with Elizabeth and I think she would say the same. But that story comes later and, for a few happy years, it really did feel like a bit of magic.

Adventure of a Lifetime
(Aka The Art of Leg-Spin)

In the Beginning

THE FIRST THING I look for in young spinners – off-spin, left-arm orthodox, wrist-spin – is how much they spin the ball. Same as a fast bowler, I want to see them bowl fast; swing bowlers, let's see them swing it; seamers, hit that seam! If he or she is not trying to spin the ball then I give them another title: slow bowler.

Ashley Giles could spin one occasionally, but was more of a slow accurate bowler, and he played his role beautifully. I called him 'Ashley Hit-Me-Miles', because I liked to hit him miles. In the 2006 'Amazing Adelaide' match, I ran down first ball after the drinks break and donged him over mid-on. He said, 'You just don't rate me, do you?' I went, 'Nah!' (That's banter by the way, not sledging. They're two different things.) In fairness, 'Gilo' was a good cricketer – a man who made the most of his talents – but the point about spinning the ball is still valid.

Anyway, obvious as it sounds, the first thing I look for is spin. Then I look to see if spinners are trying to take wickets. It doesn't matter what form of the game – Test matches down to T20 – it's the same aim: to take wickets. I look at the fields they set and work out if they have a plan. Then it's the bowling action itself, and whether there are any technical flaws that are stopping them spinning the ball. I don't care so much about a textbook action, I'm looking for the position and angle of release, the drive of the hips and body, and the revolutions on the ball. If the ball doesn't spin, then they have to fix their action. Simple. After that, it's rhythm. You've got no chance without rhythm.

Let's move on to the grip. One of the biggest keys to spinning the ball is where you put it in your hand. Too far back in the hand and you can't get the leverage to release your fingers and wrist to spin the ball. I've heard coaches tell guys to grip the ball tight with their fingers spread wide. Wrong! In fact, in my view that's the worst advice you can give, because it immediately makes a bowler feel tense; so the trick is to grip it loose and relax. The fingers should be set at a width that feels comfortable. Younger kids, with their smaller hands, can go a little wider to get more purchase, but a loose grip and a wicket-taking mindset are the places to start from. That's basically it. Well, sort of.

The Magic

The art of leg-spin is creating something that is not really there. It is a magic trick, surrounded by mystery, aura and fear. What is coming and how will it get there? At what speed, trajectory and with what sound, because when correctly released, the ball fizzes like electricity on a wire! How much flight, swerve, dip and spin and which way? Where will it land and what will happen? There is no bowler in the history of the game that a decent batsman couldn't pick if he watched the hand, so a leg-spinner must distract and unsettle that batsman. Every leg-spinner gives the batsman a clue; some just disguise it better than others. Leg-spinners cannot create physical fear, in the way fast bowlers can, so they look to confuse and deceive. The intimidation factor in spin bowling comes from a batsman's ignorance and consequent fear of embarrassment.

Few batsmen, if any, truly know what I do. To maintain that mystery I look to develop an atmosphere of uncertainty and, if possible, go further and bring chaos. It all begins with being in control, with winning the psychological battle. When I say I create things that aren't there, I'm actually working with little things – subtleties like moving a fielder from one position to another and back again for no good reason other than to show the batsman I'm in charge of the pace of the game. As an example, I might move mid-wicket straighter but then decide he's too straight, so I move him squarer again. In the end he hasn't moved at all but I've held up the game and taken charge of the moment. Then, from the point at which I'm at the top of my mark, nothing can happen until I let go of the ball. The umpire can tell me to start 10 times if he wants but it doesn't start until I let go of the ball.

In summary, I'm looking to create an environment where I'm boss. I might be all over the batsman for any number of unrelated reasons, simply because I want to get into his head. Often I just stare at him for no reason other than to see if I can spark a reaction. Sometimes I'll hold up play by going to talk to my own captain or wicket-keeper about nothing. Nothing! But then, as I walk back to my mark, I'll suggest things to the batsman that he'll think are the result of that conversation. Then I'll follow up by tinkering with the field or switching to bowl round the wicket, or pretending to sneakily move a fielder so he doesn't see.

It never takes me much longer than an over or two to work a guy out. Does he like to play quick or slow? Is he fidgety or calm? Can I change that? I'll look for mannerisms – things like the way he walks to the middle, the way he takes guard, studies the field, grips his bat, calls for a single or two. Is he picking me from the hand, through the air, or off the pitch? Is he picking me at all?

I'm out to understand his vibe. What, for example, is his default position – attack or defence? Is he happier forward or back? To beat a batsman, I have to get under his skin and into his head. Every cricketer has an insecurity somewhere, the challenge is to find it and expose it. There are weak blokes who have the talent to bat but just fall at your feet, and strong guys who don't have the talent but fight you all the way. The art of leg-spin is not just bowling a leg-break; the art of leg-spin is to examine, deceive and outwit. That is the whole art. And within it is the magic.

The Set-Up

For me, the biggest thrill is the deception. Over a beer before Edgbaston in 1993, Allan Border asked me how I thought we could get Graham Gooch out. There was something in my subconscious that hadn't really dawned on me until I was asked the question. I said that now I thought about it, I'd noticed how Goochie just put his foot down the pitch rather than towards the ball. I reckoned I could get one around his pads if I went straight, straight, straight for a while and then suddenly bowled one really wide of leg-stump from around the wicket.

The Gatting ball is a rare thing because usually it takes time to nail a good player, especially if he's already settled when you first come on to bowl. You kind of have to stalk him and then set him up. If a guy is a good sweeper, your line has to be outside off-stump, spinning away, with six fielders on the off-side, and your length has to be fullish so he feels compelled to cover drive instead. By starving him of an easy ball to sweep, you challenge him to fetch it from dangerously wide of his go-to zone, and then, when you sense the frustration is eating away at him, you bowl faster and straighter, saying, 'There's the line you're looking for, mate, go for it.' I've hit the stumps and the pads more than a few times with a straight-forward plan like that.

For someone who likes to use his feet, you bowl quicker and flatter to keep him at home, keep him in the crease, and when you sense he's getting itchy, you bowl faster, faster, faster, faster, and then you slow one up and generally wider – away from his eye-line so he has to reach for it. Never in the same place you bowled your faster one, otherwise there's no deception. When you change your pace like that the ball must land in a slightly different spot from the previous ones, which makes it harder to detect.

For the players who drive well, use their feet quickly and cut effectively either side of point – Mark Waugh, say – you bowl a more leg-stump line, forcing him to work against the spin. You have to be accurate, otherwise you simply start again. I mean, you might go middle and leg, middle and leg, middle and leg. Then you think,

'Right, now it's time to bowl one higher and wider,' and you drop it halfway down the deck and he smashes you for four! Time to start again – just don't bowl another one there, you muppet.

Then there are basic, obvious things to look out for – like, when you drop one short the batsman knows the next one is likely to be fuller, and that's generally when they run at you. It's the same if you overpitch one; he knows you're going to bowl faster the next ball so he camps back a bit. You have to read those and react. Concentration is paramount. Miss a moment and you miss the trick.

Another thing to consider is the pitch. To get maximum spin, you have to bowl with different paces and trajectories on different pitches. Some days you might have to bowl a fraction quicker into the pitch, some days you have to bowl slower and higher. On fast pitches I use more over-spin, on slow pitches mainly more side-spin. It's a misconception that the slower the pitch, the faster you bowl; in fact, I often bowled slower on slow pitches to take the pace off the ball. I used to get frustrated by Adelaide, a batting paradise, until I learnt that I needed more over-spin and could attack the stumps more. I had kind of always gone with the idea that you get them driving by lobbing it up there around and outside off-stump at the Adelaide Oval, but it never worked real well so I pressed harder to suffocate them and hurry the defensive shots into mistakes.

The Sting

Let's get back to Goochie, a top-class player, and the best English batsman I bowled to. He was also hugely respected by Allan Border after his years in county cricket with Essex. We needed a good plan and I thought we had one. AB agreed. 'Let's go with it,' he said.

We didn't change the field at all because we didn't want to give anything away. We left the leg-side mainly open: a man at 45 degrees for the sweep shot, another back just behind square on the boundary and a mid-on. Sometimes I'd have a mid-wicket or short-leg too, but very rarely anymore. If you pack the leg-side when bowling round the wicket, you send out a negative signal. If a leg-spinner has more fielders on the off-side when bowling round the wicket, he is attacking.

I pretty much always bowled with that man saving a single behind square at 45 degrees because he was both an attacking catcher and a pressure builder when saving inside or under-edges. Then, of course, if I wanted to throw one out there to either bowl them round their legs or simply drag them outside leg-stump, I needed that fielder to keep them on strike. I always positioned him really fine. Most people would have him a lot wider, but I positioned him in my eye-line as I was running in, like my safety net. With the revs and bounce I got, I hated it if that fielder was beaten on his right-hand side. You should never get beaten on the right-hand side, never – not even from an under-edge, not if the fielder starts deep enough and knows what he's doing. It has to be a good fielder there and if it goes to his left there's a deep fielder for protection behind him too. Angles in the field are crucial and underrated.

Goochie had 40-odd, so he was seeing it well. We set the plan, denied him runs by bowling straight from round the wicket for a while and then slipped in the big wide one. Bingo! It spun a mile! If you watch the highlights of that dismissal, he just puts his foot straight down the pitch. Then you'll see me pointing at AB, like 'I told you!', and we gave each other a high five that it came off.

Most of the best plans are hatched out of hours, so to speak, not at those silly team meetings. A plan can come from anywhere at any time and the more you sit around and talk the game with good cricket minds, the more amazing things happen. In a formal environment they don't happen, which is why I never liked team meetings because all you did was talk around in circles. They were a waste of time, because it was the same plan all the time: build pressure and hit the top of off-stump, with the occasional bouncer. Yeah, we get that. Now let's go and chill.

Back to the sting.

Gooch wasn't the only one, not by any means. Here's another favourite.

At the Basin Reserve in Wellington, there was a great battle with Andrew Jones, who had this hugely competitive spirit. I dropped a top-spinner short, long-hop length, and he smacked it for four, swaggering round the crease afterwards like he was Viv Richards. I kind of smiled at the umpire, Steve Dunne, and quietly said, 'He thinks he can pick me now.' After that, I bowled three or four orthodox leg-breaks in a row and then whispered to Steve, 'Watch closely, I'll be shouting real loud.' I slipped Jones the flipper and as he went for the pull shot again, I could see the horror on his face. It hit him below the knee roll in front of all three. It was as good as the Alec Stewart one but didn't have the Ashes hype with it. Steve didn't smile much but I always thought his eyes were laughing when he gave that one out.

The Box of Tricks

The leg-break is key: you have to have a good, accurate leg-break. Then there is the top spinner, the wrong 'un, the flipper and the straight one. The straight one had a few different names – the slider and the zooter amongst them. The flipper was different because it comes from the front of the hand and is a faster delivery with back-spin on it, where a slider or zooter comes out of the side of the hand, like a leg-break, but goes straight on. And then I had what I called a back-spinner, which is the one I bowled by rolling my wrist so that it points to the sky before I flick the fingers up and out.

It's the same grip for every delivery, two fingers down, two fingers up. The ball sits in the space between the fingers and the palm of the hand and there should always be a gap between the palm and the ball; if there isn't, the ball is too deep in the hand. The thumb rests on the ball, sort of like a rudder, and the third finger does all the work.

For a leg-break, the back of the hand is at 45 degrees to the ground and facing in towards me. It is almost the side of the hand that is pointing to the batsman and the third finger flicks out and towards the target. For the top-spinner, you change your wrist position to come over the top, revealing more of the back of the hand to the batsman in a vertical position, and though you use the third finger to spin it up, it's actually the wrist that does most of the work. The wrong 'un is just the reverse to the leg-break, out of the back of the hand rather than the side. For the flipper you click your fingers. First, though, you put the ball in the front of the hand and squeeze it out between second finger and thumb, then click! It's bloody hard to control and tough on the fingers and wrists. (Years ago in LA, Bo Jackson asked me to show him all the variations. He loved the flipper: 'That's amazing. How do you do that, man?!')

The key to variation is not to change the pace of the mechanics. The temptation when trying to bowl a faster leg-break, say, is to use a faster arm; slower leg-break, slower arm. But there are ways you can do it by keeping your arm moving at the same pace. For example, by using a full rotation of the arc of the arm and releasing at a fractionally higher position at the top of that arc. The rotation is at the usual pace but the longer arc changes the pace of the ball. When I bowl a quicker one, I release it with a slightly lower arm – a little more round-arm in effect – so, even though it will travel faster, it's actually delivered by an arm travelling at roughly the same pace. The slower ball is the opposite and delivered with slightly higher arm.

The trick is to make sure you 'bowl' the variations, not just 'put' them there. My flipper was always the same pace. I would use the strength in my fingers to make the ball come out faster and flatter, which was fine until they started to show wear and tear. The flipper looked like a long-hop but skidded through real quick. When the flipper was on, it was some ball. Ask Alec Stewart, Andrew Jones and Richie Richardson.

Revolutions

The perception that the wind is the main reason for drift and/or dip is horseshit. It is all about angles and revolutions. Yes, if a right-arm leg-spinner bowls a stock ball on a breezy day and the wind is left to right, then, of course, it might drift in to the batsman. In that example, the angles matter most, both at the point of delivery and on the seam as it rotates. Get those right and there will be some natural movement of the ball.

LEFT: Mum and Dad's wedding day, 21 October 1967. It was Mum's 21st birthday and Dad reckons he couldn't think of a better gift!

BELOW: About 18 months old – go the smile.

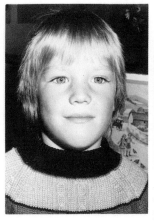

Aged four at kindergarten. I'm in the front row on the far right. Don't ever say I don't pay attention!

ABOVE: Half Moon Bay beach, which is directly opposite our home on Beach Road in Black Rock – a great place to grow up in the 1970s.

RIGHT: Ten years old, hooked on footy but starting to be seduced by World Series Cricket.

BELOW: Mentone Grammar first XI. I guess we've all got one of these photographs somewhere. The trophy, the blazers – it's kind of cute. Spot the mullet!

In 1988 the footy dream was alive and kicking, literally. Playing for St Kilda Under-19s switched my allegiance from the Hawks to the Saints forever more.

Our Cricket Academy group, with Justin Langer on the left, Damien Martyn partially obscured and Greg Blewett just behind me. The coaches were Peter Spence (left) and Jack Potter (right).

ABOVE: I like this picture. The shirt suggests it's from Academy days and the action suggests the boy has a future.

RIGHT: With Terry Jenner, the teacher. John Buchanan is in the background, where he should have been more often.

Test debut, December 1991. Ridiculous how young this kid looks!

My first ball in Ashes cricket . . . wow, not even in my wildest dreams! Mike Gatting says he answers a question about it most days – me too. My joy and . . .

. . . Gatt's pain.

Celebrating in the rooms at Old Trafford at the end of my first Ashes Test with AB and Tubby, the two best captains I played under.

'What a cool pic,' said Michael Jordan. Joke! Working with Nike was an incredible privilege.

The Gatting ball changed my life. I mean, how many boys from Black Rock suddenly hang out with Michael Hutchence?

On the town with the big boys – opening night at Crown casino in Melbourne in 1997 with Joe Montana, Sylvester Stallone, Sugar Ray Leonard, Shaquille O'Neal and Michael Johnson.

The Gabba, 1994, and the perfect flipper – Tubby and Heals seem to agree. Alec Stewart too!

MCG, 1994 – the hat-trick. Babs (David Boon) has already gone walkabout.

30 December 1997 vs South Africa – what colour is the couch, Daryll?!

Meeting Sir Donald Bradman with Sachin. You'd think we had called each other that morning and agreed what to wear!

January 1999. Every picture tells a story. John the Bookmaker lingered on, and on, in our lives. Here Junior and I are swamped by the press after the ACB had fined us heavily, almost five years after I met John in Sri Lanka.

Such a huge honour and really great fun to captain my country in the 1998/99 one-day series at home. This is the first final against England at the SCG, and me and my old mate are bringing down the Poms.

Moment of truth: World Cup semi-final 1999. The best cricket match I ever played in.

. . . And I was man of the match too. Even Chappelli looks happy – must have been good!

The World Cup final win, Lord's, 1999. Can you name everyone in the shot?

Facing the consequences of the diuretic pill. Such a contrast to four years earlier. This still breaks my heart.

Hampshire vs Kent, 2005. It's cold out there … and surely it's out out there too!

Boys of summer – Hampshire, 2006.

ABOVE LEFT: Marcus Trescothick was my 600th Test wicket at Old Trafford in 2005, but it meant less to me than the 'strength' wristband I'm wearing, given to me by Brooke at an emotional time in our lives.

ABOVE RIGHT: Caught on the boundary for 90 in the same match. Muppet!

Trent Bridge, 2005. 'Oh, Ricky, why didn't you let me open the bowling?!'

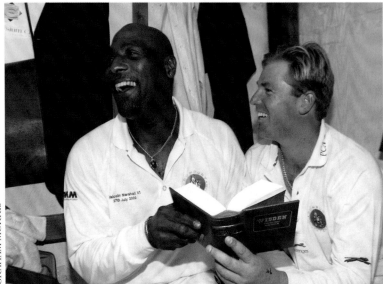

GRAHAM MORRIS

With Viv Richards, my favourite cricketer of all time and fellow member of the 'famous five' – the Wisden Cricketers of the Century.

SCOTT HORNBY/NEWSPIX

Arriving at the Quay restaurant in Sydney with Simone, 2002.

There are few words that can truly explain how much Richie Benaud meant to us all. Here, he's presenting me with the trophy for the 2005 BBC Overseas Sports Personality of the Year. No better man to receive it from.

Pre-Ashes 2006/07 – boot camp ... and respirator by the look of it!

This is the ball that bowled KP round his legs in the second innings at Adelaide, 2006 – a plan that worked and one of my favourite deliveries ever.

Ashley Giles kicks the ground in disgust and the scoreboard tells the story of England's demise. Amazing Adelaide was almost complete.

Number 700 from my perspective . . .

. . . and from their perspective! I was lucky to have a long and happy relationship with the Melbourne crowds.

But that's not how you get the drift, dip and late curve that plays with a batsman's mind. If he's half good, he can work out the wind. He's got to be very good to predict revolutions. The only way that you get curve and dip is from the amount of revs you put on the ball. There is a big difference between drift from the wind and curve from the revs on the ball. The curve happens later, for one thing. It doesn't matter where the wind is – sideways, up your backside or full in your face. If a leggie puts revs on the ball, the ball will dip in; if an off-spinner puts revs on the ball, it will drift away. The wind can exaggerate that but bowling against it won't stop it happening.

It isn't where the ball pitches but how it gets there that's most important. If there are no revs on the ball and it's just released out of your hand rolling over on its axis, you can pitch in one spot all day long but it won't do anything. However, if you spin the ball hard, with revs on it, and it curves and dips and lands in the same spot time after time, it becomes a threat. So, as I say, it's about how it gets there more than where it pitches – anyone half good can pitch it. The things that make the difference are the side-spin and the over-spin that create the swerve and dip; and the position on the crease from where the ball is released which then creates the angles that challenge the batsman.

Energy on the ball is a combination of everything working together through the combination of shoulder, arm, wrist and fingers and how quickly my body works into sync to drive the ball forward and especially my hips. This doesn't mean a fast arm but a fast, call it snap-like, release – the same as a batsman's hand speed at the point of his strike on the ball. Everything has to be right, not least the alignment of your feet and hips that allows you to bowl over your front leg. Good balance is essential. Any bowler off balance will get a soft, rolling release of the ball because only the arm is propelling it.

These mechanics really matter. At the moment of delivery, my feet were roughly shoulder width apart and, as my right arm gathered, so the left arm gathered too, acting as the sight for the target and the pulley for the action. This way I could look over my left shoulder to take aim. The actual delivery of the ball begins with the left arm, or front arm, pulling hard downwards, and the right arm working in tandem with it as the body weight is then transferred forward and over the front leg. It is then about how fast you can flick out the ball with your fingers and wrist, while using every muscle in your shoulders, back and right hip to drive directly at the target. If you can't drive your hips, you can't have bowled over your front leg. Alignment is crucial because everything has to work together and move straight at the target.

There have been front-on leg-spinners, of course – Abdul Qadir to some degree and Mushtaq Ahmed – but they didn't get the same curve or spin. The Gatting ball was the perfect leg-break because everything was aligned, including the stars!

Ideally, the seam rotates at 45 degrees – a little less for over-spin and a little more for greater side-spin. At 45 degrees, with max revs, the curve and the dip become as much a threat as the spin. Though the ball to Gatt spun a lot, it was the curve into him and the last split-second dip on the ball that confused him. Then it ripped. Goodnight, Gatt.

There are variations on this. I scrambled the seam occasionally and I rarely bowled the same ball from the same place on the crease. For example, I might repeat a delivery – a leg-break, say – 20 times consecutively, but from different angles on the crease, which creates the illusion that it's a different ball. Only if everything was in my favour – like, there were footmarks everywhere on a pitch that was ragging and bouncing – would I bowl leg-break after leg-break at the same spot and pretty much always from the same position on the crease. Just occasionally I'd switch to go wide, or even super close to the stumps, but in general I'd aim at consistency of release and target.

Stay with me here, because this is important regarding field positions and mindset. When I attacked with the ball, and by that I mean used more variations – which in turn meant the possibility of some bad balls – I would defend more with the field. When conditions were in my favour, I wouldn't worry about the variations but instead aim at leg-break after leg-break that gave nothing away to the batsman. I could then afford to attack more with the field placements. Understanding this strategy in detail makes a huge difference to the way you think – not just as a bowler, but as a cricketer in general.

For all that, wherever I bowled the ball from on the crease and wherever the seam was in the air, the one thing that could win me the moment – the game-breaker – was the amount of revolutions on that ball.

The Process

There are some givens. On a flat pitch, start at middle and off-stump with five fielders on the off-side. The easiest process for any young captain is: you've got nine fielders, so put four and four on each side and then you have one extra. Put him on the side to where the ball is spinning.

The more it turns, you're starting mainly on leg-stump but with plenty of sliders or toppies so the batsman doesn't get in the rhythm of kicking you away, unless you want him to. There is a valuable point there actually. The bowler should be dictating what shot is played. He should ask himself, what do I want the batsman to do? If I can get him playing my way, I'm winning.

Every pitch is different so you have to quickly work out what your stock ball is going to be and at what pace. This depends on the pace and bounce in the surface. The slower it is, the fuller you need to be, otherwise they'll play off the back foot too easily; the quicker and/or bouncier it is, the shorter you can be but with more over-spin. This gives them less time to adjust and why they nick off or get LBW. On slower pitches, you get them caught in the ring and off your own bowling as they drive too early or too hard or maybe shut the face of the bat too soon. And they chop on as well, trying to hit too square.

In general, I preferred less spin and more bounce, like the Gabba, because I felt bounce was the harder adjustment to make. I could bowl my leg-breaks, top-spinners and the odd slider, wearing guys down and bringing bat/pad and slip into play. I didn't like slower pitches so much, even though it was harder for batsmen to score. I didn't mind getting hit as long as that opened up the possibility of taking wickets.

It was interesting when the speed gun came into the game. The majority of the time, I bowled somewhere between 78 and 83 kilometres per hour and I bowled 'up' at all those speeds never down, which doesn't mean you can't bowl flat by the way, just that you have to release up and out; otherwise no drift. The flipper was different, often over 100 kilometres per hour and with lower trajectory, which is why it looked like a short ball.

I always want to bowl into the wind, because the ball holds up in the wind – I couldn't care less about being hit downwind – and I always liked to have the sun behind me. It's a lot harder for the batsman to pick up the hand, and therefore to read you, with the sun behind your arm than it is when the sun is behind him – try it.

The Teachers

Richie Benaud taught me something interesting that I've passed on to a lot of the young kids who tell me they struggle to take wickets regularly. 'Hey, Warney, I bowled 15 overs the other day and only got one wicket,' they say. I ask them if they think I was any good and they say, 'Yeah, you're the best!' Nice. Okay, how many balls do you reckon it took me to get a wicket? 'Oh I don't know, you probably got one every two or three overs.' No, I got one every nine to 10 overs – every 57.4 balls to be exact. Murali and all the other guys are around the same, nine to 10 overs to get a wicket. The message is that patience is very, very important to spinners.

Richie had given me a list of the strike rates of the top five spinners in Australia – surprisingly high – then he emphasised how important patience was. So I say to the kids, 'Look at how many deliveries it takes for a spinner to take a wicket. Patience, accuracy, perseverance and guts matter more than anything else, except spinning the ball. Spinning the ball is number one.'

I've talked a lot about Terry Jenner in previous chapters. He taught me the most about leg-spin. I was also lucky to have guys like Jimmy Higgs who backed me from an early age when he was a selector in Victoria and who was brilliant when he came and bowled in the nets. Bob Paulsen and Jack Potter were real good too.

TJ gave me a lot of tough love and he was the first person who'd challenge me on things. But he never tried to change my action, grip or approach to the crease. He let me be me and then showed me what I could do with my ability. He used to love to say, 'Don't say can't, Shane, let's just try.' He drummed in the importance of practice and accuracy, making me bowl each of the four main deliveries for hours, first at off-stump, then middle, then leg. He taught me the importance of an over-spinner too, convincing me that batsmen would mistake it for the wrong 'un. And he continually emphasised the three questions of what, when and why.

Not that I was a complete dummy. In fact, as I've often said, I love the strategy of the game and the tactics of a team or player in all sports. Even though I wasn't good enough for Aussie Rules at the top level, for example, I still read the play well and more often than not was in the right place at the right time. In golf, I generally take the right option, especially when I've hit it into trouble. In tennis, I understand the serve/volley game, I get the angles in both attack and defence and know how a change of pace in a rally can change the momentum. I might not play these things right but I know what's required. I'm sure that's why captaincy brought out the best in me – I was ahead of the game and could see things before they happened. Now I try and call it from the commentary box as if I'm still out there playing.

We all need a mentor. TJ taught me how important patience and a plan were – what to bowl, when to bowl it and why – and he gave me confidence. We had a strong bond, which had come instantly and effortlessly. He was a very good man, a true friend and a reliable offsider who knew a whole lot about the game. Ian Healy called him the spin doctor because wherever I was in the world, I'd call TJ and he'd chat for as long as need be. Sometimes I'd say, 'Ah mate, you wouldn't believe it, blah blah blah,' and I'd get all this stuff off my chest. He wouldn't say a word for half an hour and then I'd say, 'Thanks, mate, that feels better,' and hang up!

He came over to Lord's before the first Test in 2005. I wasn't happy with my bowling at all and had other stuff – marriage and family issues mainly – flying around in my head. We spent two days on the Nursery ground, six hours each day. The night before the game we didn't leave the nets till 6 pm, when I finally felt right. I had one of my best series ever and though we lost to England, I was proud to do myself justice under difficult circumstances. Thanks, TJ.

Spin Up!

It was TJ who came up with the phrase 'spin up'. Initially, when I got tired he noticed how my arm dropped too low to get any over-spin. I don't know how low but around 45 degrees at a guess, so in order to make the adjustment he got me to think high. At first it felt like I was bowling up by my ear, even past the perpendicular, which is no good. But I wasn't. In fact, looking at videos, it was close to where it should be. Then he added 'spin up' because if you fire it up and out you get the revs on it that will make it drop when it gets to the other end. If not, it's a full toss – believe me! So think high and spin up became a bit of a mantra, whether tired or not, and it helped to get my weight over my front leg and drive the right hip.

I reckon, more than anything, that this was what made me effective late in the day. However tired, I could find another gear and sometimes with the 'think high, spin up' focus, I bowled better than when fresh. I certainly got a lot of wickets towards the end of a day's play.

The Passion

I'm very passionate about spin bowling and in particular about leg-spin. I love to promote it and inspire others. I've worked with many of the best and we bounce off each other – Anil Kumble and Mushtaq Ahmed are great examples. I helped Mushy develop a flipper and then in the 1995 Sydney Test he took nine wickets in the match against us – oops. In the dressing-room our guys were saying, 'Mushy's got a flipper – he never had one before!'

Anil was a great competitor in all conditions and at his most dangerous on uneven surfaces. There's a lot of knowledge out there and most of the guys have come to seek me out over the years, just to chat and share the experiences we've been through and the challenges we face. I think they know about my passion and care for leg-spin and that maybe I've looked into the art of it deeper than most. It's my science and my gift, which is why I never treat it lightly. I still chew the fat with the brotherhood of spin and always will.

The world of spin isn't only about wrist-spin. I call off-spin Darth Vader because it's the dark side of spin. It's easy to bowl and easy to hit. Anyone can be an off-spinner but not necessarily a good one. That's harder. Off-spin is limited and predictable, so to step outside the box and make it effective takes some doing. The stand-outs in my time have been Tim May, who had a beautiful curve towards slip before that terrific off-break of his; Graeme Swann, who spun it hard at many different paces to suit all pitches and make life a nightmare for left-handers; and Murali, of course. Murali was something else. Eight hundred wickets is just incredible. One of the hardest bowlers to face in history. Genius. I'm going to talk about Murali later.

As a general rule, finger spinners need to find a way to beat the bat on both sides. Arm ball, drifter, high bounce or over-spin, doosra – whatever it may be, deception is their trick, almost as much as it is mine.

Leg-spin is bloody hard. It takes a big heart and a strong character; it needs a lot of love and good captaincy. I've seen so many guys messed about by shit captaincy. To me the best things in cricket are a fast bowler steaming in trying to knock the batsman's head off and him taking it on, and a leg-spinner challenging an aggressive stroke-maker, especially one who uses his feet. But if the captain doesn't get the fields right, well, the younger blokes have got no chance.

There are a lot of leggies out there right now – Mitchell Swepson and Adam Zampa in Oz, Mason Crane, Adil Rashid and Matt Parkinson in the UK, Imran Tahir in South Africa, Yasir Shah and Shadab Khan in Pakistan, Rashid Khan from Afghanistan is a wonderful talent, Samuel Badree for West Indies, and, as ever, a fair few in India, including Kuldeep Yadav, who is a very exciting prospect. The first question is: are they up for the fight? The second is: do they know enough about what they do? It's complicated and doesn't come easy. Then you wonder if their captains know anything about spin.

T20 cricket is great for wrist-spin; 50 overs too, because the batsmen don't have any option other than to chase the game, so you already know their mindset. Get the field right, land it right and a leggie will take wickets. Finding a way to take wickets in

Test cricket is another challenge altogether and can be a long and often disheartening journey. In my first Test, as I've mentioned, I took 1/150 and got smashed by Ravi Shastri. In Crane's first Test last summer in Australia, he took 1/193. That's a pounding but he bowled okay to be honest and showed a lot of courage just to keep going. I really rate Yasir Shah, he's got a great leg-break. I hope he recovers his best form but bad captaincy holds him back, along with his own lack of patience. The key for Yasir is to still have fun. That big smile tells us all we need to know about his attitude, which is so much of the battle. He's got plenty of courage too and never gives up.

Spinning the ball is supposed to be fun and people are always interested in how it's done. Everyone who likes cricket has a go at leg-spin at some time or another and they pretty much always find it difficult. You see guys landing the thing in the next-door net. That's because it is hard! I'm proud that I've done well and prouder still that I've inspired. A family came up to me recently and said their son had learnt how to bowl leggies by watching me on YouTube – highlights of matches, packages of great deliveries (even I watch those sometimes!), masterclasses with different TV channels, clinics etc. How good is that? He learnt off YouTube!

History Lesson

I've mentioned that TJ always said, 'Test cricket didn't start in 1991/92 when you arrived, mate, a bit happened before then.' However, because I grew up with Aussie Rules, I never got into the cricket history stuff. Not until World Series Cricket anyway.

I've had a look at the old leg-spinners on YouTube, though – Arthur Mailey, Clarrie Grimmett, Bill O'Reilly, and Richie, of course. Mailey didn't use his left arm much – it's probably why he wasn't very accurate. He whipped his right arm over aggressively, though surprisingly low – about 45 degrees at a guess. He drove his right hip more than most, which helped him out, and he's famous for 10/66 and all that – the day he got all 10 against Gloucestershire and the phrase then became the title of his autobiography.

I like the Grimmett story that he had a habit of clicking the fingers on his bowling hand real loud when he bowled a flipper and that, after a time, the batsman worked out when it was coming. So Grimmett started to click the fingers on his non-bowling hand when he bowled the leg-break too, and then the batsmen were all over the place! He was a New Zealander but he moved to Australia and ended up with 216 wickets in the days when not so many Tests were played. He was very accurate, they reckon, almost mean about giving runs away. They called him the 'miser' to Mailey's 'millionaire'. Apparently, he was the first to develop a slider. Ah ha, and I thought I was!

People reckon Bill O'Reilly was the toughest competitor and if Bradman says he's the best bowler he saw, that's good enough for me. They say he bowled it quick, nearer medium pace, and snarled his way through many a day. I love that. He and Grimmett bowled together for Australia for a while – the 'Fox' and the 'Tiger', as they were known. I just wish some of those guys had seen me in the mid-1990s. It would be nice if they'd known the leg-spin story was still being written.

I don't know enough about them, truth be told. I know a lot more about Richie, who was the first to bowl round the wicket into the rough and make it respectable, or accepted. It wasn't the done thing to bowl it out there in the old days, but at lunch on the last day of a Test at Old Trafford in 1961, England were cruising. Ray Lindwall was covering the tour for a news outlet and Richie asked what he thought about him going round the wicket and aiming into footmarks. Give it a go, said Ray, but you'd better be good at it, otherwise they'll be all over you: the press, he meant by that. Well, the great man knocked England over, took six in no time from round the wicket, and the vision on YouTube is great – Simmo takes an unbelievable catch. Richie was pretty cool, shirt unbuttoned and leaping about the place when wickets fell. There's been no-one better for the game than Richie, and in so many different ways.

The Rough

As I've mentioned, it was when I was 12th man against India in 1992 that Bob Simpson got me interested in bowling round the wicket. It was a game-changer for me.

It took a lot of practice and a lot of strength from round there – much harder to adapt than it looks – but I soon noticed how it helped my rhythm because if you don't complete your action you bowl rubbish. You have to have a strong action from that angle of delivery just to make sure you get the ball up there on the right line, and it takes a lot out of you.

I see too many spinners just 'putting' the ball into the rough, not 'bowling' it there. They expect the rough to do the work, but this means they don't get many revs on the ball so not much happens. Revs will bring irregular bounce, which is just as important as the spin. Mainly, this is because they're terrified of bowling a bad ball. However, the ball won't do much unless it's fizzed in there with energy and effort. I don't mean faster, I just mean a lot of revolutions at whatever pace is required for the surface you're playing on. As I keep saying, it's all about the revolutions!

To the right-handers I used to line up the pads and just try to bowl it outside their pads and spin it as hard as I could into that rough. Some of the deliveries I bowled to left-handers that stand out were Andrew Strauss at Edgbaston in 05, Shivnarine Chanderpaul in Sydney in 06 and Kevin Pietersen in Adelaide first ball later that year. These dismissals create that aura I was talking about earlier and create fear in the dressing-room.

Sometimes on dead pitches, I'd bowl a heap of big-spinning leg-breaks way out wide into the rough. Some spun and bounced, others skidded along the deck. They were all still missing leg-stump by miles but I did it to play with batsmen's minds. It was a nightmare for the keeper, especially as there was no chance of taking a wicket, but it built a picture of what might come and that was the plan. Remember, always have a plan!

People, Places

I backed myself against anyone but, in the cases of Sachin Tendulkar and Brian Lara, there was more of a game of cat and mouse to play in the search for the high ground. In general, I set out to tell the opponent *my* story and to make sure he felt a very small part of it.

I never rushed; in fact, my measured walk-in became a part of the overall impression of authority that I was trying to create. But Sachin and Brian weren't bothered by any of that – they had their own story to tell.

Sachin was the best judge of length I played against – he was unbelievable in India on the '98 tour – and very quick on his feet. He got down the pitch easily and could sweep well too, so the margins for error from my point of view were very small. Brian hit the gaps with uncanny accuracy, even when the ball pitched in the rough outside his off-stump, and because he played so late he could score off balls others did well to defend. He had a fantastic eye, a smart batting brain and really natural flair.

I know I've always said that Sachin was the best batsman during my time but, the longer I've thought about it, the harder it has become to separate them. They were the best two, for sure. Sachin was the better technician but Brian the more destructive shot-maker so, if I had to send someone out to bat for my life it would be Tendulkar; if I needed someone to chase 400 on the last day, it would be Lara.

Brian played the best two innings against us – 277 run out in Sydney in 1992/93 and 153 not out in Barbados in 1999, which won the game singlehandedly. He made 213 in Jamaica the game before, which wasn't so dusty either by the way. Sachin's unbeaten 155 in Chennai in 1998 is the next best. There was no bowling to either of them on those particular days.

I remember getting Sachin caught at slip fifth ball in the first innings in Chennai. In the second innings Mark Taylor brought me on as soon as Sachin came in and I quickly switched to bowl round the wicket and into the rough. He slogged the third ball into the stands at mid-wicket for six and just carried on from there, like a man possessed. After a few overs of this, Tub asked what I thought. 'I think we're fucked,' I replied.

There's no-one else close to them. Mark Waugh was probably the best of the Aussies – quick on his feet and he manipulated the field really well. Others who got me on occasions were Kevin Pietersen, brilliant on his day, and VVS Laxman – a fantastic player. Goochie was very good, but easier to control than KP or VVS. The one player I wished I had bowled at was Viv Richards. All the guys who played against him say he was different class, and in the days when Jason and I played in the backyard, Viv was always taking on Lillee, hooking him off his eyebrows.

I guess that, back then, I was subconsciously acting out the next phase of my life. I always loved the competition and the big stage. For me, it's all about the contest. Of course, some places turn you on more than others. The Gabba might not be the greatest ground in the world, but I had a lot of success there because I enjoyed the extra bounce in the pitch – 68 wickets in just 11 Tests! I'd always go for bounce over spin, but when you had both together, like at the Gabba, watch out.

My favourite place is the Melbourne Cricket Ground. It's a no-brainer. Ninety thousand people on Boxing Day – I mean, you can't get better than that. It's a happy time at Christmas and, being a Victorian, I get a fantastic reception each time I walk out there. The MCG is a coliseum and we are the gladiators. The noise when I took my 700th wicket, wow! It's a hard act to replace!

The MCG has been so much a part of my life. As I've mentioned, as a kid I saw the climax of the 1982/83 Ashes Test when AB and Thommo nearly pulled off the miracle. Later, I played footy there, which was awesome. I've seen the changes to the ground, the pitches move, the drop-ins arrive, two World Cup finals and so much more. The biggest crowds, the greatest showpiece – that's the 'G.

The Sydney Cricket Ground and the Adelaide Oval are different, Lord's too. The spectators sit a lot closer to you than at the 'G, so it's more intimate. These beautiful older grounds, theatres of cricket, make the game *feel* special. Then there are the personal favourites because of success – Old Trafford and Edgbaston were atmospheric and lively, Kensington Oval in Barbados as well. Both Colombo and Galle in Sri Lanka were great places to play. Cape Town is stunning and a special venue for me as I played my 100th Test match there – and I bowled a million overs in the game by the way, so it's got a place in my heart somewhere.

The Indian grounds have a sense of excitement about them; I suppose because you know the whole country is watching just about every ball. Eden Gardens is a great stadium – 110,000 manic people. But I didn't like playing there. Three for 364 in two Tests! No thanks.

And Finally . . .

Spin is hard and spin is fun. The great news is that leg-spin bowling is back in fashion, especially in the short form of the game. I like to think that I've played my part in that – helping to make it modern and sexy and worth the effort. I'm proud that whenever the PA system at a ground said, 'Coming on to bowl at the Members End is . . . Shane Warne,' the spectators would be excited enough to get back to their seats in expectation of something, *anything*, being about to happen. That's the magic.

To sum up, leg-spin is no half-hearted journey. You have to *love* to bowl leg-spin. I've been lucky to spin the ball further than most and to maintain consistency and accuracy. My personality has won a few battles and I've stayed strong when the chips have been down. I believed we could win every cricket match I played in and I have never, *ever* given up. If, after St Kilda sent me that letter saying thanks but no thanks, someone had said, 'No worries, Warney, give it a decade or so and you'll be voted one of the five greatest cricketers of the 20th century,' I'd have laughed at them. I suppose it's proof that anything is possible. As a mate of mine once pointed out about the challenges we all face, 'If you think you can or you think you can't, you're probably right.'

10

I'm Still Standing

Surgery

I'VE TALKED BRIEFLY ABOUT the mental demands of bowling so much over a relatively short period. The many thousands of balls and overs listed as examples in the previous chapter don't take into account the many thousands more bowled in practice. Believe me, they take it out of you too, particularly if you practise with intensity. I reckon I was at my best from 1993 to just before the 1998 tour of India, when my shoulder finally gave in so I needed surgery. It was five great years when I felt I was under total control of what I was doing and my body was injury-free. The 1993 Ashes tour to England and the home series in 1994/95 brought some of my happiest memories. A fantastic team came together to blow England away. The Gatting ball and a few others, 8/71 at the Gabba – my career-best figures – and the hat-trick in Melbourne are all personal moments to savour long into old age, but the quality of the cricket played by that team under AB is the memory that will never die.

For all the mental effort, only a very few people knew the physical toll on me. From being a skinny kid, I developed into a guy with powerful shoulders and a strong upper body. Leg-spin may not look much but it requires real strength to get the revs required to drift, dip and spin the ball properly; along with the ability to keep at it day and night.

I bowled really well at home against Pakistan and Sri Lanka in 1995/96 and then again in the World Cup. (The story of the semi-final, when we nicked past the West Indies in a thriller, is a whole lot happier than the one in the final, when Sri Lanka caught us off-guard and off-colour.) I was having a serious issue with my spinning finger around that time and though cortisone injections held the worst pain in check, the veins were starting to swell through the knuckle. There were other niggles too, the usual stuff – fractures, pulls, sprains – but I could kind of deal with those on an ongoing maintenance basis, especially under the guidance of Errol Alcott as he was the best physio on the planet.

In May 1996 I had surgery on the finger and immediately found myself surprisingly insecure. What I'd started to take for granted suddenly wasn't there. A period of rehab meant no bowling and then, when I did bowl, it felt completely different. In fact, I wondered if I'd ever be the same bowler again and various gremlins niggled away in the back of my mind. My aim was to recover that 'feel', which is not as easy as it might sound.

There's always a moment when you think, 'Enough of bowling with the attitude of "This is going to hurt",' so you protect it and not bowl flat out. Sometimes it's a game situation or a batsman that's getting on top and you say, 'I'm going to rip this and send a message to the opposition.' This particular moment of mine came in the 1996/97 home series against West Indies at the SCG when I bowled Shivnarine Chanderpaul with a beauty that spat back from way outside the left-hander's off-stump. We'd desperately needed a wicket and, as so often in my career, the situation of the game brought out the best in me. It pitched in the rough outside the line of Ian Healy's left pad, spun more than the Gatting ball, and probably would have hit leg had it not ricocheted off Shiv's pad and onto the middle stump. Gee, I enjoyed that ball. It was right on the stroke of lunch too – a killer for dressing-room morale on one side of the old pavilion and a huge boost for us blokes on the other side.

Given the finger op and the uncertain phases of recovery, it rates right up there with the best I've bowled. I was relieved as much as anything and those insecurities disappeared instantly. The feeling was different, but the feeling was back.

I've always said you need courage to bowl leg-spin – both mental and physical. My shoulder was the next problem and, annoyingly, it reached a point of real concern prior to the 1998 tour of India when Tendulkar vs Warne was being billed as the heavyweight fight of the decade. We hadn't played Test cricket against each other since my debut at Sydney in the season of 91/92, and, in the years since, both of us had had tremendous success and the extravagant publicity that came with it.

From the start of that 1998 series, Sachin, who had prepared well, played out of his skin. Increasingly, as the shoulder issues bit harder by the day, I didn't feel comfortable in mine. I was a whole lot better bowler than when Ravi Shastri hammered me at the SCG but the trouble was proving it. The competitive juices still ran fast and 'Hooter' – Errol Alcott – worked long hours with me to keep them going, but the truth was that the shoulder was on the brink. It needed a cleanout at best, a structural rethink more likely.

We had a pretty ordinary attack. McGrath was injured, Jason Gillespie too, and Paul Reiffel only played the first Test before breaking down. The bulk of the quick bowling came from Michael Kasprowicz. Paul Wilson and Adam Dale were in the squad but, no disrespect, were both a fraction short of Test class in those conditions; then we had the Waugh brothers, Greg Blewett and Gavin Robertson, who was the other spinner. Hey, this was Tendulkar and co! We were kind of clinging on every day. As the series went on, I struggled to get my arm high enough to release the ball from anywhere near the right position. The headaches were unbelievable, I struggled with sleep and was hardly able to train – in short, I was struggling and in pain. We lost the first two of a three-match series and though a good bounce back in the third Test helped save face, I knew my own career was soon to be on hold.

After Sharjah, where Sachin smacked us again and won every award on earth, the first thing I did on return to Australia was to go and see Greg Hoy, who'd done the operation on my finger. The MRI scan wasn't good. 'Listen, you might be lucky,' he told me. 'Another few months and, who knows, it might have been too late, but right now I reckon I can fix it with a SLAP lesion – a rebuild of your shoulder. Javelin throwers have it done but I have to say there's no guarantee. Your shoulder is hanging by a thread, mate. I don't know how you put up with the pain.'

I went under the knife straight away. I was then in a sling for six weeks, and wasn't allowed to move the shoulder. It had to repair naturally because it's a ball-and-socket joint that needs to move freely, but all the tendons were frayed and dysfunctional. I had a multi-directional shoulder that rolled all over the place, and the rubbing of tissue, tendons and joints had been causing the pain.

They shaved my bicep, shaved the tendons down and put four screws in my shoulder to hold it steady. After that it was rehab – twice a day, 10 separate exercises with therabands, which provide varying degrees of resistance to work the shoulder without impact or invasion. Quickly, I'd ramped up to five times a day, along with physio from a brilliant girl called Lyn Watson. For all this, I didn't play cricket for nearly six months.

While I think of it, I put Russell Crowe, who damaged his shoulder filming *Gladiator*, onto Greg. I was driving back from the airport one day and the car phone rang.

'G'day, Shane, it's Russell Crowe here.'

I said, 'Yeah, right,' and put down the phone.

The phone rang again. 'Shane, it's Russell Crowe again. Sorry to interrupt, but I got your number from a mate of mine who you know. I've got an issue with my shoulder . . .'

I said, 'Mate, don't be a dick!' and hung up.

Five minutes later, the phone rang again. 'Yes, who is this?!'

'Er hi, Shane, this is Lourene, Russell Crowe's fitness trainer. I know you probably get prank calls all the time, but this is very serious for Russell. His shoulder is in trouble. We're staying at the Park Hyatt in Melbourne under a code name of Mr Jones. Please call if you have a moment.'

I rang the Park Hyatt and reception answered. 'Can you put me through to Mr Jones, please?' 'Yes, sure.' It started to ring and

I quickly put the phone down. 'Shit, this might be true!' So I thought, 'Okay, I'll go and meet Russell Crowe, that's pretty cool.' I drove home, had a shower, put the kids to bed, rang Lourene back and said I was on my way.

Russell was great. We had a laugh about the phone calls, had a chat, and I told him my Greg Hoy story. Russell and I have hung out ever since and I also became good friends with Lourene, who is now a personal trainer and works with me when we're both in town.

I put Greg onto Pat Rafter too, as well as Daniel Kowalski, the swimmer, who had won Olympic medals. Greg is a fantastic surgeon and through him I made a bunch of mates, all with the shared ground of shoulder operations!

Back to my rehab. After the long hours of working on recovery you kind of think, 'Let's go.' It's also a mental test as the exercises are bloody boring. But your body has changed and so too the feel in the mechanics of the bowling action. The shoulder was so much tighter, which was predictable – there were screws in it! I'd done all the exercises, worked my upper body, and my chest and shoulders were massive. But it all felt stiff, solid even; it just didn't feel supple or loose. In fact, it felt like someone else's shoulder was attached to my arm. It took a long time. Not till midway through the World Cup in England in 1999 did it feel 100 per cent.

I played, but didn't bowl, in a pre-season friendly between the Vics and Tassie in early October, before a few games for St Kilda and then four Shield matches for Victoria. I was back in the Australian side at the SCG for the last Ashes Test of England's 1998/99 tour and got Mark Butcher with my fourth ball. Next thing I knew, I was pulling on the yellow shirt as captain of the Australian one-day side. More of that in a minute.

Revolution

My body wasn't the only thing in need of rehab through these strange and suddenly very different 'middle' years of my life as a cricketer. Our fee for the 1996 World Cup was around the 60K mark with another 40K if we won it.

Around that time, Pepsi had approached me to film a TV commercial for $US150,000 but the Australian Cricket Board refused to let me do it, because we were sponsored by Coca-Cola. The early days of ambush marketing in cricket! Though I could see the argument about a rival product, the board's general attitude to our commercial status opened my eyes to its inflexibility and, worse, its abuse of the players who were being paid peanuts in relation to the income generated for the game through their performances. Five of us – Steve Waugh, Greg Matthews, Tim May, Tony Dodemaide and me – set about forming a players association to fight for better returns, not just in international cricket – state cricket too.

Maysey approached James Erskine, who is now my manager but back then had just left International Management Group (IMG) to set up his own thing, with a mentor of mine and very dear friend who has now unfortunately passed away, David Coe. We were the best team in the world, made up of many of the best cricketers and personalities in the game. James said he wasn't interested in golf days and dinners – or chook raffles, as he called them – but instead suggested that the time was right to take on the board in a fight for better pay. The players were getting around 13 per cent of the pie, which was the lowest percentage of all the major sports in Australia – and James argued that 25 per cent should be the number. He said that Sports & Entertainment Ltd (SEL), his new company, would help us do it. Well, that got the boys buzzing!

Basically, we were split into three groups. There were those who were new to the scene – some of whom hadn't played for Australia yet, like Adam Gilchrist and Mike Hussey – whose dream was the baggy green, and though they saw the argument they didn't want to jeopardise their chances going forward and rock the boat. Then there were the sure-fire certainties with guaranteed places: blokes like Tugga, Junior, 'Pidge' (Glenn McGrath), Taylor, Slater and me. The third group were coming to the end of their time as players, and although they were fully in favour of action were reluctant to press too hard in case their next life after cricket was jeopardised by their part in a revolution.

Five of us – Tubs, Tugga, Maysey, Heals and me – met James in Canterbury before the end of the 1997 Ashes tour and came up with a plan for a collective bargaining agreement to take to the board that would be signed by 120 players back home. It took some doing. Each of us involved in that early planning got back to Australia and then visited the states to convince the players we had something good for all, not just an elite few. I went to Tassie, Tugga to Perth, Dodders to the Vics and so on. It was pretty exciting.

Then, at another specially convened meeting a couple of months later in Perth, Tubby told us of an offer privately made to him by Denis Rogers, the ACB Chairman. It dealt with some of our requests but fell short of the overall position we were looking for. The vote was 11–1 against the offer, with Tubby understandably feeling inclined to work with it given his conversations with Rogers. The main point of difference was Rogers' refusal to agree to James' proposal of a minimum $60 million a year deal for the players or, best of all, a guaranteed 20 per cent revenue share.

James is a smart guy. He set up a sideshow to distract the board, in the form of a bid for the TV rights at a price of $320 million that shook Kerry Packer more than a bit. The ACB Chief Executive, Malcolm Speed, almost shaking with fury by now, came out with a statement that he could get comfortably more for the rights from one of the major networks and it actually led to a really great deal for cricket with Channel Nine. At the time, Kerry was furious, thinking that (a) the players' threat of strike action was damaging his product and might even take it off air, and (b) the rights price just went up! I was also a very close friend of the Packers so was in a difficult position.

I had dinner with James Packer to explain there was more to this than just money. 'Yes, 13 per cent is bullshit,' I said, '20 per cent is fair – but it's only a part of the story.' He was amazed to hear we all still had to share rooms, fly economy, weren't offered a cent for our wives' travel or accommodation, were on pathetic expenses, and that much the same story existed in domestic cricket too. I said that we needed a say in the Sheffield Shield, the other formats, the amount of cricket played, the conditions and playing regulations. Actually, I think the key thing, and the message we wanted the Packers to understand, was that we wanted a partnership with the ACB, instead of being their bullied employees.

Once the news went public, we copped it from the fans, who said we were greedy, and from the board, who fought dirty. Every time we went to a meeting with board members, they seemed a step ahead, like there was a mole in there somewhere. We never found out who for sure, and, anyway, it's long gone now and things have worked out well.

At much the same time as I was with James Packer, James Erskine was telling Kerry to calm down, assuring him he had no interest in TV rights and that the players were not of a mind to strike, unless there was a complete refusal from the board to respond to any of our suggestions. As it turned out in the end, Kerry paid a higher price for the rights but accepted that the players deserved more. He had to. It wasn't such a different situation from his reasons for World Series Cricket 20 years earlier!

(By the way, Cricket Australia owe so much to the Packer family and to the Nine Network in general. The fact that the rights have now gone elsewhere tells us a great deal about how both television and the commercial side of cricket administration have changed, not necessarily for the better. The partnership between Nine and CA lasted 40 years and did the game proud. Fox and Seven have big shoes to fill; I'm looking forward to my part in the new age of television coverage with Fox Sports. I'm interested to see how some guys go commentating on six hours of slow Test cricket, as Big Bash is action-packed and very easy to commentate on.)

Anyway, after Speed's reaction to James' rights offer, we had all but won the fight. Speed could hardly say there was comfortably more out there than $320 million and then deny the players a decent chunk of it! We agreed a 20 per cent revenue share deal that increased to 25 per cent in the updated Memorandum of Understanding four years later. The principles of that Memorandum of Understanding existed in its mainly original format for 20 years, until slightly altered arrangements were negotiated under acrimonious circumstances in 2017.

I strongly believe in the value and power of the Australian Cricketers' Association. It is more than a voice, it's a true union that defends the rights of the players and works to improve them. In turn, Cricket Australia have to work more closely with the ACA to develop a partnership that will make sure they avoid the ridiculously bitter negotiations that gave the game such a bad name in 2017. The 'them and us' attitude is wrong and, whatever CA say, it does still exist all these years on. Fix it, guys. The ACA does great work on behalf of the current players, as well as those who have moved on and found life after a career in the game so difficult. I'm very proud of my role that I played all those years ago and my advice is simple – cricket should be a partnership with everyone in it together.

Sell the Ferrari, Son

From around the age of 10 my dream was to own a Ferrari, a midnight blue 355 Ferrari. So, with a few bucks coming in I drove down to Dutton's and asked if they had one.

'Warney,' he said, 'I've never seen a midnight blue 355 Ferrari – red, black, white, yellow, but no blue, mate, sorry. I'll keep a look out.'

'Okay,' I said, 'low kilometres, tan or white interior, and I'll write you a cheque the minute you find one.'

Two years later, in the middle of the players' dispute with the board, I get a phone call. 'Shane, I've found a midnight blue 355 Ferrari exactly the way you want it – 2000 kilometres on the clock, as good as brand new. The wife of the owner wanted yellow so he traded it in.' Oh, hmmm. Righto, I'll call the bank.

So there we are, fighting for better pay and preparing to strike, when I get a Ferrari delivered. It's now the days before the 1998 Boxing Day Test match and I'm telling everyone what I've given myself for Christmas. I'm pretty keen to show the boys so I drive it in to the 'G on Boxing Day morning with my foot to the floor. Next day, front page of the papers, 'Players Need More Money', with a pic of me climbing out of a midnight blue Ferrari. Oops! Warne came in for some stick.

Fair call, though in my defence, comfortably the main source of my income was sponsorship. I was probably making close to 1.5 million bucks a year, of which cricket was around 150K. So the

Ferrari didn't come from cricket money. Not that I said that in public . . .

A few months later, I was having a fun dinner at Crown Casino in Melbourne with Austin Robertson, John Cornell, Lloyd Williams – a very dear friend and mentor of mine who owned and built Crown casino – and both James and Kerry Packer. Kerry said, 'What's with the blue Ferrari, son? It's not doing you any favours. Be like the rest of the Aussies out there and get yourself a Holden. Everyone loves you because you're a champion who's still a knockabout kind of guy, but they'll soon think you're too big for your boots if you tear around town in a blue Ferrari. Buy a Holden, even a Ford.'

I said, 'Cool, I get it. Will do, Kerry.'

So I traded in the blue 355, bought a Holden VK Commodore . . . and a new silver 360 Ferrari.

Next summer, Kerry calls. 'Did you sell that Ferrari, son?'

'Yep, and bought a Commodore. It's awesome.'

'Good boy, well done.' I heard that eventually he found out the full story. And smiled. Great bloke, Kerry, he taught me so much and was such a loyal man. I miss him to this day.

Yellow

I always enjoyed captaincy. The game was in my blood in a way I hadn't realised until I'd grown up a little. I felt I had an instinct for it. I love the strategy and tactics; the detail, those little things that change the bigger picture. At times, I feel I can sense the overall pattern of a match even before most of it happens. That's probably why I like commentary so much and tournament poker.

When the selectors appointed me captain of the one-day team for the home tri-series with England and Sri Lanka in early 1999, I was pretty happy. Mark Taylor had retired after another convincing win in the Ashes series, Steve Waugh was taking over from him, and I'd been made vice-captain. But Steve got injured just before the one-day series began, so I became captain.

We played 12 games and won nine, including the last seven on the bounce to win the tournament. I captained aggressively and people said, 'Wow, Warney's good at this – imaginative and unorthodox.' I love the challenge of getting the best out of the players, encouraging everyone to think smart but in a relaxed and enjoyable environment. The guys responded with a lot of enthusiasm and the crowds got behind us. Fifty-over day/night cricket was the buzz back then and we had a lot of fun during the series. That's the idea, isn't it?!

The chapters about my time at Hampshire and then with the Rajasthan Royals in the IPL explain best how I see cricket captaincy and give examples of putting my principles into practice. They were two of the best and most rewarding periods of my career.

Dropped

West Indies 1999. We're 2–1 down after three Tests. Won the first easy, lost the next couple to Brian Lara; two incredible innings. I know he rates the first of them, the double hundred in Jamaica, as the best because of the pressure he was under. West Indies cricket was struggling, Brian was getting stabbed for his captaincy, the press and public were on the players' case, and then we go and win the first Test in Trinidad by a mile, bowling them out for 51 in the second dig. Whoa! That's heavy duty. Just about everyone wanted Brian's head and they were probably only a game away from getting it.

His response was to make that double century in Jamaica and then a wonderful 153 not out in the fourth-innings run chase in Barbados. I never thought anyone could bat better than he did at Sydney in 1992 when we saw him for the first time and he made 277. Given everything, though, I reckon his innings in Jamaica and Barbados in 1999 are the best two I've seen. It's a tight call with Sachin in India the previous year, but because of that pressure and the fact that he didn't have a great side around him, I'd probably give Brian the nod.

Anyway, we were 2–1 down. I was vice-captain and bowling pretty ordinary and Tugga opened the selection meeting between the two of us and Geoff Marsh, the coach, by saying, 'Warney, I don't think you should play this next Test.' (Remember the selectors on tour were the captain, vice-captain and coach.)

Silence.

'Er, right,' I said. 'Why?'

'I don't think you're bowling very well, mate.'

'Yes . . . fair call,' I admitted. 'My shoulder is taking longer than I thought but it's close now. The feel is slowly coming back and then the rhythm will come, mate. I'm not worried. The situation we're in is exactly when I perform my best. History proves that, so I'm looking forward to the match and I'm confident it'll work itself out.'

'No, mate, I'm not so sure. I really don't think it's right that you play. What do you think, Swampy?'

'I think Warney should play, mate,' said Geoff.

'Well, I'm captain and I don't agree,' said Steve.

Silence.

'Swampy' suggested we ask Allan Border, who was in Antigua with a tour group. So we found him and got him in that evening. All the boys were waiting for a team meeting to begin. There was a sideshow to this. Geoff was AB's vice-captain and when the selectors dropped him, AB refused to board the plane to Perth for the Test against India until he was reinstated. So Swampy figured AB's loyalty would win out.

Steve related our previous conversations to AB.

'Jesus Christ, I back Warney every time,' AB said. 'The situation is made for him. Anyway, we owe him. Think of what he's done for Australian cricket. We need to show faith.'

I thought, 'That should do it.'

Then Steve said, 'No, I appreciate your thoughts, AB, but Warney's not playing. I'm going with my gut here. Sorry, guys.'

Disappointed is not a strong enough word. When the crunch came Tugga didn't support me, and I felt so totally let down by someone who I had supported big time and was also a good friend.

At the team meeting, he said, 'This is the hardest thing I've had to do as a captain but Warney's not playing – plus these changes too. It's Blewett for Elliott, Dale for Gillespie and Miller for Warne.' There was complete silence.

(Diversion. Just before the tour of the West Indies, I signed a deal with Nicorette to give up smoking for the first time in my life.

They said, 'Listen, 85 per cent of people take at least three attempts to pack it in, so if you have a cigarette let us know because there are steps in place to help you.'

At the time I would still have the occasional one, the plan being to slowly stop with the help of Nicorette. That night I got dropped, I went out with Brendon Julian and Damien Martyn. Geez, I had the shits and felt embarrassed. I got plastered, we all did, and Marto lit up a fag. I said, 'Give me one of those things, mate.' And at the very second I lit up, a flash went off and some bloke shouted, 'I'm going to sell this!'

I thought nothing of it – whatever, mate, just fuck off! – continued to get hammered, smoked a few more, and the next morning I woke up thinking – not for the first time in my life – 'You idiot!' I rang Jase, who was my manager in those days, and said, 'You better call Nicorette.'

They got back to me straight away. 'No worries,' they said. 'We told you it would take at least three attempts. We knew this would happen, we just didn't know when.' So they put out some great PR stuff and made it clear they were backing me. *Phew*.)

Anyway, I smoked in the toilet through most of the match, so no-one could see me. Errol Alcott and a few of the guys joined me in the dunny too. I conducted myself badly, to be honest. I wasn't that supportive of the team, which I regret.

Looking back, this was probably a combination of the shoulder issue still eating away at me and the pure anger bubbling inside at Steve's lack of trust. During the first three Tests, at various times some of the bowlers came to me, grumbling about Tugga's captaincy and field placements and stuff. I said I was backing him to the hilt and if they had a problem with the captain they should go see him direct. Perhaps because of this, I was deeply disappointed that he didn't back me in return.

I understand he had a job to do. He wanted to win the game and, yes, they went on to win it and draw the series, but who's to say they wouldn't have won it with me in the team? Steve will always say the result justifies the decision, but I don't think it's as simple as that. I lost a bit of respect for him after that. I believe he should have backed me – as I always believe the art of captaincy is to support your players and back them every time. This gains the respect from the players and makes them play for you. He didn't, it's history, but I never found it easy with him after that.

We won in Antigua by 176 runs. Brian got yet another hundred out of West Indies' first innings 222 but it wasn't enough to save them this time. What a performance by him all tour. The wickets were shared around in both West Indies innings – Colin Miller got three in the match, Stuart MacGill five. It was a great series that finished 2–2 and kept Brian in the job.

I'll say one thing for being dropped. It made me realise how much I loved the game and how much I missed not being out there on the park with the guys. It gave me focus, but a part of me wanted to throw the towel in.

Magilla

Stuart MacGill and I always got along well. His folks and my folks catch up all the time. They have mutual friends and enjoy hanging out together much as they did when we were playing together for Australia.

He had a great attitude, and was more a snarling fast bowler than thoughtful spinner. He was kind of furious, come to think of it. Off the field he was great company but he had a rage and you needed to dodge it. Just occasionally he could be like a light switch – one minute fantastic, the next a bit ugly. When the switch flipped, some of the guys – Andy Bichel and Matthew Hayden in particular – used to tell him to pull his head in or risk getting it knocked off.

He could really rip those side-spinning leggies of his, and in an aggressive sort of way. When 'Magilla' was on top he was pretty hard to peg back. Sure, he bowled bad balls – two, sometimes three an over – but the good ones were ridiculous when he was on. He was a wicket-taker, simple as that. Two hundred and eight wickets in 44 Tests with 12 five-wicket hauls speaks for itself. He took 12 against England in my comeback match at the SCG in the

1999 New Year Test. Brilliant performance. Then he got on it with Ian Botham that night and wonders to this day how he survived. He's no slouch himself by the way and these days is right into wine – a special subject for him.

Other than when I wasn't around, he mainly got picked when the pitch was a big turner and we decided to play two spinners, so most of his career he played in conditions that suited – lucky bastard! The argument that his record ended up better than it would have if he'd played on the flat decks, or the green seamers, when conditions didn't suit him, might have something to it, but it's pretty unfair on him. You can only do what you're asked to do and he did that very well.

Steve stuck with him for the Antigua match because he had a decent run while I was out injured but, in truth, he didn't bowl much better than me in the defeats in Jamaica and Barbados. I never thought two leg-spinners was a good idea. I preferred someone who spun it the other way, so an off-spinner like Maysey or 'Funky' Miller was always my choice during those years. Two leg-spinners will almost certainly want the same end and, anyway, batsmen get used to the ball turning one way and, I believe, it negates both of them.

Magilla doesn't have a problem with that. He always said that he played as much as he did because of me. He says, 'Warney opened the door to leg-spin and the rest of us just tried to walk in.'

World Cup 1999

Soon enough we were in England for the 1999 World Cup. We lost to New Zealand and Pakistan almost immediately and the pundits wrote us off. Trevor Hohns, the chairman of selectors, rang me to say that if Steve doesn't get a score or we don't make the next stage of the tournament, we're leaving him out of the side and making you captain. That was fine, but right there and then our full attention needed to be directed towards getting back on track in a tournament we were fast disappearing from. In effect, we had to win six games in a row to make the final and one more to win the World Cup at

Lord's. There was no room for another mistake: one more loss and we were gone.

Next up was South Africa at Headingley. This was the game when Herschelle Gibbs famously dropped Steve – and, by the way, it's a load of crap that he said to Herschelle, 'You've just dropped the World Cup.' It's totally made up.

Sorry, let's go back a step. At the end of the team meeting the night before, Swampy asked if anyone had anything else to offer. I said, 'One thing. If Herschelle Gibbs catches you, stand your ground, because he never holds the ball long enough before he throws it in the air in celebration.' And everyone said, 'Yeah right, whatever.' I said, 'No seriously, remember I said that because he'll catch someone tomorrow and throw it up too quick. I reckon the umpires are watching for it, but, if not, we should point it out.' And guess what. Some of the guys have told that story in their own books, saying they couldn't believe I came up with it. Maybe it saved Steve's one-day career. It certainly saved our World Cup.

To Steve's credit, he made a fantastic hundred – after Herschelle had missed him on 56. The win gave us confidence and we marched through the remainder of the Super Six group and the quarter-final. All of which meant we played South Africa again in the semi at Edgbaston. What a game! Best one-day match ever.

We got knocked over for 213, Shaun Pollock nipping the ball around in typical fashion. Steve hung on in there, putting on a crucial 90 with Michael Bevan. I've watched this game twice through on video, from first to last. It's a great plot line and a lesson to any cricketer that each and every ball is priceless.

We were slow out of the blocks, South Africa 0/43, and when Steve threw me the ball, obviously the situation was dire. A hint of irony in that – as he needed me!

I thought, 'Stuff the shoulder, stuff everything, let's give them a rip and get the boys back into the game – and make them believe we can win this.'

It went like this: I bowled Herschelle Gibbs with a Gatting ball; then I ripped one through Gary Kirsten before knocking over

Hansie Cronje. Eight overs, 3/12, that's as good as I can do. We were back in the game and I could sense I was dragging the boys with me, to believe that a place in the World Cup final was still on.

I came back in the 43rd over, when Kallis was threatening to win the game. I was in the groove immediately and remember thinking that this was the most tense I'd known a cricket match – both sides on edge, each run precious, each wicket gold. After Jonty's dismissal, Shaun Pollock began by prodding around nervously, which, for a short while, played into our hands. Then, out of nowhere, at the start of my last over, he smashed me for six and four off consecutive balls, followed by a single.

'Make Jacques wait,' I thought. 'Draw it out. Slow down, mate, slow down. Dot ball. Slow down, Shane, mate, slow down. Make him wait again.'

I let it go higher, slower, a touch wider, and he drove hard, sliced to Steve at cover. *Out!* Warne 4/29. Not a bad effort, that.

With 39 runs to win and four wickets in hand, Lance Klusener walked to the wicket. Player of the tournament. We managed to get Pollock, Boucher and Elworthy out, but in what seemed like a flash Klusener had 31 from 16 balls, with four fours and a six. Shiiit! The last two of those boundaries came off Damien Fleming in the final over of the match, which had started with nine still required, and now ... one run needed off four balls. There was only one winner, surely.

Klusener swung hard at the third ball of the over, which dribbled to Darren Lehmann at mid-on. Allan Donald just ran, kind of crazy. 'Boof' threw and missed. It would have been out if he'd hit. Chance gone now. Or had it? Had Donald learned his lesson? Pressure is the weirdest thing; smart men lose the plot. The player of the tournament was on strike, unbeaten on 31, and now, with three balls remaining, required a single, solitary run for a place in the World Cup final. A place where South Africa had never been before. And, almost certainly, that was the problem.

Once you've reached a certain level, the hardest thing is getting over the line. It's what separates the great from the very good – think Tiger Woods, Roger Federer and Rafa Nadal. The South Africans were good, but against us, well, we felt they just wanted it *too* badly. Add in the fact that after years of isolation because of apartheid, they were desperate to win the World Cup and you begin to understand what Klusener and Donald were going through mentally. The whole of South Africa was watching: they could not *not* win. One run from three balls – no way you don't get that. Except they didn't. They *did* not win. I think Klusener – or 'Zulu' as they called him, Natal's Zulu warrior – would have got four or six to win in one hit. But one run, nine down, I reckon he was thinking, 'Don't blow this, not now.' Four or six to win would have meant less pressure – after all, fours and sixes were his game. But one – just a single, damn it – was suddenly, weirdly, very difficult.

I don't remember Klusener and Donald talking, even after that mix-up. It was like fear had set in. The one thing we knew was that a tie worked nicely for us, very nicely. We'd go through to the final courtesy of our win at Headingley in the Super Six stage of the tournament against them.

We had a kind of ring field saving one, with a few guys dotted here and there for the ball off the pad, or dropped down soft. We couldn't cover for the big hit. Zulu was a power leg-side hitter but the two boundaries he pummelled at the start of the over were through the off-side, so who knew where the ball would go if he connected? So we crowded him and I clearly remember how nervous I was and how I was thinking, 'Wow, this is awesome. C'mon, Flemo.'

The sense of chaos settled and Flem ran in to bowl a great ball, very full, pretty much a yorker and wide of off-stump. Credit to Flem here. He'd bowled the final over of the '96 semi-final at Chandigarh against West Indies too. You need big kahunas to do that job – twice! He had them.

Klusener went hard at it but it was so well executed by Flem that he couldn't get under it. The ball dribbled to Junior at mid-off, who, seeing that Klusener had charged down the pitch for the single, backhanded it at the stumps at the non-striker's end. He missed. By now Donald realised that Klusener was committed to the run and set off himself, but sensing it was hopeless, turned back and dropped his bat. It was mayhem. Both batsmen were alongside

Flem, stranded. Our guys were screaming and shouting at Flem but he had it covered. Cool as you like, he picked the ball up and rolled it underarm down the pitch to Gilly who did the rest. We went nuts. The crowd went from confused to ecstatic to suicidal, depending on who they were barracking for.

The freeze-frame of that moment is a great picture. At least for Australians, it is. In a way I felt for the South Africans as they were the best team in the tournament.

In the final, we just blew Pakistan away. I never understood why Wasim chose to bat when he won the toss, other than the fact that they won a lot of games defending with that brilliant bowling attack of theirs. But it was a damp, misty morning at Lord's – a nice bowling morning. We knocked them over cheaply and made the 133 we needed to win by mid-afternoon. As I mentioned in an earlier chapter, the party began right there and never really stopped. I was man of the match in both the semi-final and the final. The shoulder and finger were fine. And I felt back on top of the world.

When September Came

In late August 1999, we went to Sri Lanka for a triangular one-day tournament with India. Continuing our World Cup form, we were unbeaten in five matches up to the final and then got bowled out for 202 by Sri Lanka in the one that mattered most, and lost it easy.

Next up, in early September, was the first Test in Kandy, and not just any old first Test – the first since I'd been dropped in Antigua. Funky kept his spot, while Magilla was left out. I took 5/52 in the first innings but we batted badly both times round and went under. There was a Sri Lankan bogey on us for a time back then – in more ways than one.

In the first innings, Steve Waugh and Jason Gillespie had this massive collision running for a catch in the outer. It was really nasty and no one knew the extent of the injuries.

This is where it got really interesting. We were one down in a three-match series and at the selection meeting for the second Test, Steve, who was up and about now, said he should play.

'I'm not sure you're right,' I told him. 'You've just had this dangerous collision – take it easy, mate.'

'No way,' he said, 'I'll field in a helmet.'

I said, 'You can't field in a helmet.' Geoff Marsh said the same.

I admit there was an element of bitterness in my attitude to Steve after what happened in Antigua. Equally, it's my honest belief that you can't field a whole Test match in a helmet, even in the gully. As the conversation went on I got more and more facetious about it. I'd even say I was being a dickhead and looking for a bit of revenge. He hadn't backed me and now I wasn't going to back him.

I have to emphasise that my attitude had *nothing* to do with me wanting to be captain. It was all about him not playing. Someone else could have captained, I wouldn't have given a shit. Steve Waugh was the most selfish player I ever played with and was only worried about averaging 50. It was about a lack of loyalty. Pretty childish, I know, but that's the way it was.

It wasn't that he dropped me. I have no issue about being dropped if I'm not performing; if you don't perform, out you go. But there was more to it than my performances – I think it was jealousy. He started to niggle away, telling me to look at my diet and spend more time on deciding what sort of person I wanted to be in my life, how to conduct myself – that sort of stuff. I said, 'Mate – worry about yourself.'

Anyway, the meeting got pretty tense and eventually Steve said, 'Fine, I won't field in a helmet but I *am* playing.'

Geoff said, 'Okay, I'm good with that,' so I lost the vote 2–1.

Steven and I got on with playing, no problem. I've always said you don't have to have your best mates with you on the field, but that when you cross the white line to represent Australia, you play as if every one of those 10 guys is your best friend and – here is the key – you support them to the hilt. It's how a team has to work, otherwise the negative energy seeps in and breaks that unwritten bond.

But that moment was really it for me. Our friendship had been on the edge for a while. After the West Indies and Sri Lanka it was pretty much done.

11

Mixed Emotions

A Famous Five

TO CELEBRATE THE TURN of the 21st century, *Wisden* picked the five cricketers of the 20th century. I knew nothing about it until one day in early 2000 I got a call saying I was voted number four. The five were Sir Jack Hobbs, Sir Donald Bradman, Sir Garfield Sobers, Sir Viv Richards and Shane Warne. Spot the odd one out! I don't suppose a knighthood is coming my way anytime soon, but I can hope! But that's fine – just to be recognised and talked about alongside the greats in the history of the game was mind-blowing. (Many years later, the Mayor of Melbourne appointed me 'King of Moomba' – see Chapter 18. So, you know, I had my moment too!)

The *Wisden* people asked 100 former players, expert observers, writers and commentators from all over the world to vote. Each of them chose a top five and the most polled got the nod. What an honour. I was very surprised – I couldn't believe it, to be honest – and felt a huge surge of pride in myself, and of gratitude to all the people who had helped me along the way.

It also made me think back to all the wonderful cricketers over so many years and across so many countries and continents – from

Victor Trumper to Greg Chappell and Allan Border in Australia, for
example; from Wally Hammond and Len Hutton to Ian Botham in
England; from Vinoo Mankad to Virat Kohli in India. I was the only
current player, which made it all the more amazing. Viv Richards
started in 1974 and finished at international level in 1991, just before
I started. Viv Richards and Shane Warne, the only youngsters in a
short list of names that covered 100 years of Test match cricket! The
more I thought about it and the more often I said those words to
myself, the prouder I became.

I began to wonder who I would have chosen. Bradman, of course;
and my favourite player of all, Viv Richards.

I didn't really know about Jack Hobbs but I then read about him
and saw that he made 197 first-class hundreds – 100 of them after the
age of 40! I'd have had Dennis Lillee in my five, and in fact, the next
day, when I saw the full published list of all the players who received
votes, I saw that Dennis was sixth. Others in contention for me would
have been Tendulkar, Lara and Wasim Akram, who combined serious
pace with the most skill of any bowler I came up against. Any cricket
match was alive when Wasim was on the field. He was a ferocious
competitor and one of only a very few cricketers able to break out
and change a game with both the new ball and old, and with the bat.
Great bloke too. I saw Malcolm Marshall but didn't play against him.
No doubt he was a great bowler. Most good judges have him up
there with Lillee. Sir Richard Hadlee too – he pretty much carried
the New Zealand attack on his own.

In the end I think I'd choose Wasim to make up the numbers. So
my five, if I'd been asked to vote, would have been Bradman, Sobers,
Lillee, Viv Richards and Wasim Akram.

I asked about the criteria for selection. Broad appeal and
match-winning ability, they said, which I suppose meant more than
just the statistics. And as I always say to young players, people won't
remember your stats – it's all about the way you play the game. *Wisden*
says that the 27 votes for me came from a wide selection of the
voters and across the generations. One comment made me particularly proud. An English journalist called Crawford White, the former
cricket correspondent of the *Daily Express*, who had apparently been

around long enough to have watched both Bill O'Reilly and me, said that 'O'Reilly didn't rip the ball through like Warne does … And I don't think he caught the imagination quite as much as this lad.' Given everything I'd heard about O'Reilly, that was very flattering. Elsewhere, I read stuff like 'Warne brought leg-spin back after it seemed to have died' and 'Warne brought a new audience to the game every bit as much because of his ear stud, hairstyles, modern clothes and rock 'n' roll attitude as because of his bowling.' I liked that too.

There was no event to mark *Wisden*'s announcement of the Five Cricketers of the Century, just 10 posters that we each signed. Obviously not Jack Hobbs but they managed to get Bradman to sign before he died in 2001 – so that's a treasured possession.

For what it's worth, the top 15, down to Bill O'Reilly, with the amount of votes they received beside their names, were: Bradman (100), Sobers (90), Hobbs (30), Warne (27), Viv Richards (25), Lillee and Worrell (19), Hammond (18), Compton (14), Hadlee and Imran Khan (13), Gavaskar (12), S. F. Barnes and Hutton (11), O'Reilly (10). The highest-placed current player after that was Sachin, who was 17th.

It's pretty cool for us both to be up with those guys!

In my thinking, the best of the best have to be so good that no-one argues their status; so different that they challenge the way the game is played, its tactics or its laws; so skilful that they almost single-handedly win matches for their country; so confident that they drag others with them; and so exciting to watch that their X-factor brings in the crowds.

Bradman had all of those attributes and he received 100 votes out of 100. Think about it. He finished up with a record nearly twice as good as anyone else; Bodyline 'restricted' him to an average of 56.5 over the four matches out of five that he played in the series, a phenomenal performance by anyone else (the next best Aussie was Stan McCabe with 42.7); he won countless matches for the teams he played in; and when you watch the old black-and-white film the crowds are packed in to watch him. Think of the shock around the ground when he got out, particularly in his last innings, and the disappointment that came with it. And then remember that more than 60 years later he was still the most sought-after personality in the game and the cricketer whose signature was most wanted.

I met Bradman in 1998. Sachin and I were asked to go and see him on his 90th birthday. We were told we were his two favourite current players, an incredible compliment, so we went to his home in Adelaide and talked for three hours. His son John was there too.

Sachin asked him about preparation and he said that when he moved to Adelaide he worked as a stockbroker first thing in the morning and then walked down to the ground to play Sheffield Shield cricket! Otherwise he had nets but no other specific methods of preparation. No sports science in those days, no video tape or digital replays, just blood and sweat.

I asked him about the modern game and, surprisingly, he thought the game in general hadn't changed a great deal – except for the standard of fielding, ground fielding that is, which he thought was fantastic, as against slips catching, which he said was about the same or a little lower than it was. He would have liked to have played one-day cricket – right up his street, he said. He talked about O'Reilly being the best bowler he had seen and Harold Larwood the fastest, but he didn't talk about Bodyline at all. He said O'Reilly spun it hard and was very aggressive and that there were similarities between us. He liked watching me, he said, and enjoyed seeing batsmen intimidated by a spinner. He told Sachin he reminded him of himself as a young man, that they batted in a similar way. Nice things to say.

We were nervous, just two kids really. We had dressed in very similar suits, shirts and ties, and a nice picture was taken of the three of us, at Don Bradman's house, a normal suburban home in Adelaide. I'll never forget it.

I've heard so many stories about Garry Sobers – how good his eye was; how hard he hit the ball; how late he swung it in at pace; how he could bowl chinamen and left-arm orthodox; how his outrageous fielding close to the bat shocked everyone. He sounds like Superman. Ian Chappell told me a story about the last ball of a day in a Shield game when Sobers was playing for South Australia and fielding at bat-pad to either Terry Jenner or Ashley Mallett, I don't remember. Sobers pre-empted the batsman's defensive shot and, diving forward, caught the ball before it hit the ground. 'Chaps' said everyone just stood there in disbelief.

Sir Garry got 90 votes out of 100, by the way.

Viv was my first hero and the greatest cricketer in my eyes. He had everything I liked – the swagger, the intimidation factor, the aggression – and he delivered when his team most needed him. We used to go and see him at the 'G. Some of his shot-making was just insane, outrageous! He was pulled in as a mentor for the Melbourne Stars and I loved spending time with him. One day, after a long dressing-room debate about team spirit and the need to work harder for each other in general, we asked him if the West Indies team of the 1980s, arguably the greatest team ever, got along okay or if they ever bitched and fought.

He said, 'Man, we never got along that well. Yes, there were friendships when we walked on the field and we were all together in the heat of battle but, off the field, a lot of the times this guy didn't like that guy and that guy didn't like this guy and so on. I had a couple of the fellas I didn't appreciate so much – not my cup of tea, that sort of thing. But it never affected our cricket. We played hard and to win. We took no prisoners and, in that, we were always together.'

It's an interesting subject and comes back to where I finished the last chapter. The Australian team I started in got along fine, but the new guys who came in during the late 1990s, well, they were different and I didn't get along with all of them. That's not to say that when we were out on the field, we were anything but in it together. We never spoke publicly about differences – Viv said that too – and anytime any of us were asked about a team-mate in a press conference we always said good things. At least, that was the principle with which we operated in our team environment, that every message put out there was to be positive. Once you crossed the white line, you'd die for your team-mates.

The great teams in history are considered to be the Invincibles under Bradman in 1948, West Indies under Clive Lloyd and Viv Richards, and Australia from the mid-1990s to early 2000s, first under Mark Taylor and then Steve Waugh. Perhaps the friction amongst the various personalities and very strong characters in the best teams led to a greater intensity in the way those teams played and prepared as well as trained.

Two More Men at the Turn of the Century

I've already explained why Tendulkar and Lara were in a class of their own. Wasim Akram too. I should also mention Jacques Kallis, whose record is absolutely outstanding. Over 13,000 Test runs, which is the same as Ricky Ponting, as well as 292 wickets at 32.6; 200 catches. I remember Jacques' near-perfect innings to save the 1997 Boxing Day Test with an unbeaten hundred – it was his first of many. Occasionally he would throw off the shackles – not often enough in my view – and parade his wonderful array of strokes, but in general I'd say it was the excellence of his technique that shone through in long innings played to set up South Africa's bowlers. He was just a magnificent all-round cricketer with the biggest heart and a strong mind; surely one of the greatest of all time and, among modern players, easily the stand-out all-rounder.

South Africans claim he was better than Sobers. I think that's because the figures stand up. Comparing is almost impossible but from what I've heard from the guys who saw both, Sir Garry had everyone covered for talent, flair and game-changing genius.

I want to talk about Muttiah Muralitharan too. The things Murali could do with the ball were unbelievable. Once you combine a big spinning off-break with a hard spun doosra and you do so accurately and with lots of revs on the ball over a consistent period of time, well, you've got the game in your hands. Murali put batsmen under so much pressure through accuracy, patience, perseverance and the likelihood that eventually he'd make something happen.

Unfortunately, there is divided opinion over his action. The law changed to a 15-degree elbow-flex allowance because of Murali. Once they started testing him, they tested others too and found that more bowlers had a significant degree of flex than was imagined. The biggest problem for Murali, or for his action, was the doosra. It's hard to bowl it with a straight arm and virtually impossible if you're really spinning it and getting it out there at a good pace. I think Murali was measured at 14 degrees, so you could argue that the laws changed for no other reason than to allow him to bowl. That's fine. I have no problem with cricket evolving, but I do feel for guys like Ian Meckiff who got called for throwing and were drummed out of the game. They would have been able to play today.

My view is that if a bowler's action is suspect and analysis confirms that it's a 'throw', the bowler shouldn't be allowed to play the game. But now that the law has changed, young kids, especially in the subcontinent, will grow up bowling with a 15-degree flex and think it's normal. My concern is that youngsters will, understandably, want to emulate their hero, but will pay for it in the long term. And I worry that the game changes to the point at which the past becomes irrelevant and every spinner has to be pulled up and analysed.

In summary, I respect Murali and his achievements. What he did with the ball was insane and very special. We're good mates and when that terrible tsunami hit Sri Lanka in 2004, I went over to help his initiatives, taking stuff for children – simple things like colouring books, toys and cricket equipment. It was a pleasure to be able to help in a small way.

The Warne/Muralitharan Trophy for the Test series between Australia and Sri Lanka is something we both have great pride in.

At first it seemed surprising that neither Jacques nor Murali received a vote from the *Wisden* judges – not one – especially as there were 11 South Africans and three Sri Lankans on the panel. Probably it was because so much of their careers ran into the 21st century. The bottom line is that they were both very great cricketers.

The Other Side of the Coin

For all the happiness at being chosen in that great list, the turn of the 21st century was a period of sadness and frustration in my life too. Some of the blame lies with me, some with Lady Luck and some with a few others!

In the 'Changes' chapter I addressed the mess I got into over texts and messages swapped with a girl I met in a nightclub. The biggest shock came when Cricket Australia sacked me from the vice-captaincy. After the disruption to our family life, this was another blow that hurt badly. I'll always argue that those texts and messages had nothing to do with cricket.

From what I heard CA were fearful of what might happen next.

The previous summer, I'd been wrongly accused of sledging one of our own players, Scott Muller, during Channel Nine's coverage of the Hobart Test against Pakistan. An effects microphone had picked up someone saying about Scott, 'He can't bowl and he can't throw,' and for some reason fingers pointed at me.

A cameraman at Channel Nine, Joe Previtera, admitted to having said it, but that didn't end the story. It even came up in Federal Parliament, where a Labor MP, Mark Latham, called the camera guy 'Joe the Patsy'. It was ridiculous. It was proven that it wasn't me, because the TV footage had me standing halfway down the pitch with my arms folded, not saying anything. And an independent ABC Radio stump mike, which would have picked up anything, didn't pick up a thing – apart from something in Urdu, the Pakistani language.

Unfortunately, Scott didn't believe the evidence, and spoke out in the media. I was disappointed that he didn't believe me – that he believed the hype.

Then in March, in New Zealand, I lost my cool with a couple of teenagers who were taking photographs of me smoking. At this time in my life, it seemed like everything was my fault! You could say much of it was, but I'd argue I was an easy target.

Anyway, Malcolm Speed, the CEO of Cricket Australia, rang me and delivered the news.

Gilly

Adam Gilchrist was made vice-captain in my place, and he took over the following season in Australia, after only 12 months of playing Test cricket. I guess he was the clean image they were looking for. I thought Ricky Ponting was the next cab off the rank, but he had one or two off-field black marks against his name too, so Gilly got the job. He hadn't been in the side long and was still establishing his place at the table after 'Heals' had surprisingly been dropped at the start of the previous summer.

In general, over the years the Australian selectors have been quick to move if a player who has been around a while is on the downward spiral and a replacement is ready to go. I think it's been one of the strengths of our cricket and why Australian teams have a good blend of experience and youth. There was a period after Pidge, the Waugh brothers, Marto, Gilly, Haydos, Lang and me all retired that it didn't happen quite so much, but it looks like they're back on track with Trevor Hohns as the chairman again. A very good side was shaping up until the Cape Town ball-tampering controversy. Usually, as one door closes, another opens. How Australian cricket reacts now is the true test of the system.

Gilly quickly became an important part of the team. His batting was so dynamic and although he wasn't the best keeper going around – Darren Berry, Phil Emery and Wade Seccombe were better glovemen – his package in both Test and one-day cricket gave us a new dimension in our cricket, along with Brett Lee's pace. I think we could have played two spinners a lot more than we did actually. He gave us such flexibility and I never understood why we didn't use it better. It's no secret that his keeping wasn't in the same class as his batting, where 5/200 could become 5/350 before anyone could blink. It just happened so quickly and, of course, it completely demoralised teams who thought they were getting back in the game against us. He was good for us tailenders too, because being thrashed by Gilly at one end meant the bowlers tried too hard against us at the other end, and we cashed in. Without Adam Gilchrist, we wouldn't have made anywhere near the runs we did.

For all his brilliance as a cricketer, he sure pissed me off a couple of times. In the build-up to the start of the summer in Australia against Pakistan/India, he asked if he could see me in my room. He looked a bit sheepish when he came in and I thought, 'What's this about?' He said something like, 'Mate, I know I've only been in the side for a year or so and just taken over from you as vice-captain, but if you ever need some advice or support over anything, let me know. I'm here to help any of the guys, and that includes you.'

Was he serious? After laughing, I said, 'Sure, Gilly, thanks. You do your thing, mate, and I'll do mine.' Worry about catching them behind the stumps, I thought. In the end, it was just kind of cheeky of him, I suppose. My guess is that as the new vice-captain he'd probably been encouraged to have a chat with the guys who'd been around a while.

The second time was when he publicly nailed Mum and me in the diuretic incident prior to the 2003 World Cup, blaming her for misleading me. He rang to apologise, which to his credit took balls. But the fact is there was no need for him to comment, and our family felt very let down. I've already explained how a team can work perfectly well without everyone being best buddies, but that, in public, you have to support each other. He broke that code and, in my view, it was wrong to go public and nail my mum.

For all that, I never lost respect for him as a cricketer. The impact he had on our team and on the game, not just in Australia but all around the world, was exceptional. After Gilly, everyone wanted a keeper who could counterattack with the bat from number seven. There were some good imitations, but the truth was that no-one quite had his talent! In the modern game, people want a batsman/keeper and not a keeper/batsman anymore.

Surgery Again

26 October 2000. Victoria were playing New South Wales at Punt Road Oval. Mark Waugh slogged at Colin Miller but toe-ended the ball, which went straight up in the air. 'Chuck' Berry was keeping and I was at slip. I shouted for it. It was a ball that barely lobbed five metres high, but was spinning away from me and I misjudged it. It hit the top of my fingers, bounced out, and I only just caught it second time around, before throwing it to the umpire in disgust with myself. Dumb-arse, I thought, and then I looked down to see my spinning finger at an angle. There was no pain, not even throbbing – it was just fucked. I went off, thinking it must be dislocated or something. I figured the physio would just click it straight back in. If only it had been that simple.

The X-rays revealed a lot of damage and within three days I was back at the hospital with Greg Hoy. He put two screws in a fractured dislocation of my right ring finger, the same one that had been fixed up in 1996. It was immobilised for three weeks and I thought I'd be out for four to six months.

I remember screaming inside myself. What was going on during this unpredictably weird year of my life?! I'd gone from the highest imaginable honour to that bloody hospital again, and somewhere in the middle I'd lost the vice-captaincy of Australia. The answer, of course, was a roller-coaster that asked me a lot of questions about myself. I didn't know it at the time but I had to find some answers. They don't always come along immediately, and there were some rough times still to come.

The finger healed well, faster than even Greg predicted, and I was able to bowl a few gentle overs for St Kilda in two matches just before Christmas. Then I played for the Vics on 2 January and in the Carlton one-day series against West Indies and Zimbabwe that began on 11 January. Six weeks from woe to go and only another three and a bit before being back in Australian colours. Awesome! Up to a point.

What wasn't so awesome was that I'd let the injuries drag me down, both mentally and physically. I'd lost interest in training and put on weight. I'd only played 17 of Australia's 30 Tests between 1998 and 2001. It showed in everything I was doing.

Yes, it was great to have come back so quickly, but there was a price to pay. Among some good spells, my bowling was only average. Remember, in India in 1998 I'd had the shoulder issues. Now I had the finger problem – shaved tendons in '96, two screws in late 2000 – and, guess what, I'd lost the 'feel' again. But India was the great challenge, the one I couldn't resist and wanted to put right after '98.

Kolkata 2001

I love India's passion for cricket. Over the years I've come to understand the people and their culture. In fact, my time as captain of the Rajasthan Royals taught me some of the things that make India tick. It can be a frustrating country, often annoying, with the stampede that follows cricketers – autographs, photos, people closing in around you on the streets, people looking for interaction in hotel lobbies. But I've learnt to control my responses and appreciate that their admiration for cricketers and what they achieve is very flattering. These days, I can feel the love!

I've made good friends in Jaipur, Delhi and Mumbai. It's a fast-changing country, mostly for the better, and the changes are easy to see whenever I go back. It is more comfortable for visitors than when I first went and, though occasionally I still think, 'Get me out of the chaos!', most of the time I can see the beauty of India in the smiling faces and positive outlook of the people that make it so rewarding. Their passion for cricket is unmatched and particularly for the heroes – Tendulkar, Ganguly, Dravid, Laxman, Kumble, in my time; Kohli and others today – who are worshipped almost as if they're gods.

Indians are thoughtful and kind by nature. However, in the time I've been playing there, they've thrown off the submissive side that other nations took advantage of and become so much more confident in themselves. They are punchier now, more likely to look you in the eye and take you on. Maybe that began to come out in their cricket on our 2001 tour. It was as if they were saying, 'We won't be pushed around anymore.' In fact, Sourav Ganguly, the captain, operated like a dictator and this rubbed off on the players, the media and the fans, who were more aggressive than we'd seen previously.

Of course, our 2001 tour will always be remembered for one thing – India's great win in the second Test, only the third time in history a team has lost after enforcing the follow-on. It was some match, one I'll always believe we should have won.

Glenn McGrath used to say we'd win every Test match we played because we're the better team. Not many cricketers think like that, mainly because it's human nature to have insecurities about performance. The more you play and win, however, the more confident you become. We went to West Indies in '95 thinking we'd beat them at last. And we did. We went to India in '98 convinced we could win over there. Wrong!

I wasn't so sure in 2001, in fact the tour made me nervous for some reason. India was referred to as the 'final frontier' because it had been 31 years since Bill Lawry's side last won a series for Australia over there. They had a lot of very good players and an increasingly feisty new captain in Ganguly.

Well, first Test we hammered them: 10-wicket margin, no problem. Pidge must be right! I bowled fine, picking up 4/40 in the first innings and getting a bit of feel back in my finger. Why had I been nervous? I guess it was an indication of how much an injury to a crucial part of the mechanics of a bowler's action can lead to the insecurities I mentioned.

We were very confident heading into the second Test in Kolkata. We won the toss, batted first and made 445. Then we blew them away for 171 – Pidge at his best with 4/18. He really was right! There was no way back from that. No way. Except there was.

My view is that Steve Waugh had become obsessed with our record winning run of 16 consecutive Tests, and forgot that patience goes a long way in winning cricket matches. Instead of applying common sense to the decision of whether to enforce the follow-on, he went with arrogance.

After we took the seventh first-innings wicket, we all came in to the huddle and Steve asked us how we were. Kasper, playing in his third or fourth Test, said, 'Yeah, I'm ready to go, let's do it.' But then any young player would say that in front of the captain. Jason 'Dizzy' Gillespie was like, 'Yeah, I'm not bad – a bit weary but ready to go.' Then we got another wicket and went back in the huddle again. Steve asked McGrath how he was feeling. 'Tired, but always ready to bowl if needed' came the reply. After the ninth wicket, Steve asked me. 'I'm pretty knackered, actually. I've bowled 30 overs and I'm tired too. It's like 40 degrees. Let's rest up and bat again.'

There was some mumbling. I can't remember exactly what was said, but I pushed hard for us to put our feet up and the general view swung back towards 'Yeah, on balance, let's bat again then.' I got the last wicket. VVS Laxman, trying to sweep, hit it straight up in the air – out! A lead of 274. Time to chill. There was so much time left in the game, we were all but certainties to crush the Indians' spirit in the third innings of the match and then bowl them out in the fourth.

As I say, it was common sense. But Steve failed to see it and decided to bowl again.

We started well enough; three out for 115, including Tendulkar. Then Ganguly played fluently before he edged McGrath to Gilchrist. At this point – 4/215 and Australia 59 in front – Dravid joined Laxman, who'd come in at number three in the second innings after batting with more freedom and confidence than the others in the first dig.

Two days and two nights passed with no change to the wickets column. Laxman and Dravid were ever-present as the score spiralled out of control.

There have been plenty of good innings against us but that one by Laxman was right up there with anything by Tendulkar or Lara at their best – in the top three or four I've seen. He handled the short ball comfortably and played his strokes late and with no fear.

As an example, when I bowled around the wicket into the foot-marks he'd whip it through mid-wicket. I'd think, 'He can't keep doing that,' and I'd land it there again, exactly the same ball, and he'd run around it and smash it inside-out over cover. He played brilliantly against the spin and equally brilliantly with it – just good shot after good shot. I tried everything: over the wicket and round the wicket; slow and high; fast and flat; sliders, flippers and wrong 'uns. On the day, or days, I wasn't good enough.

In the slips, Gilly and me went through our favourite movies and TV programs, best songs and, of course, picked cricket teams – best ever, best to watch ever, ugliest, most dangerous etc. Imagine me staggering off to slip and saying, 'Right, I've got *Gilligan's Island*, David Bowie's "Heroes" and all the James Bond movies. What have you got?!'

We were out there for 178 overs, spread over 12½ hours and three days, in 40-degree heat. When India finally declared on the last morning at 7/657, we were all but on our hands and knees and begging for mercy. VVS made 281 and Rahul, who I otherwise had a good record against over the years, 180. Their partnership of 376 was outstanding.

Ganguly set us 383. No chance. We had to bat out 75 overs – not easy, not impossible. I remember being painfully tired. Coming off shoulder and finger injuries, being unfit, and losing the vice-captaincy and all the stuff that came with it, I was physically and mentally exhausted. Sitting there watching us bat, I began falling asleep. I'd bowled 54 overs in the game – not massive but it always feels more when you're on the end of a pounding. Out of nowhere came a loud roar: shit, someone out. Then another. Next minute I had the pads on. I was still half nodding off and going, 'Geez, I need to switch on here,' so I got up, walked around a bit, splashed my face and, boom, I was in.

Sachin was bowling these massive wrong 'uns that not many people were picking; fizzing it and turning it miles. I saw the seventh ball I faced better than the previous six, picked it as the wrong 'un and went to pull it through mid-wicket. Oh my God, embarrassing, missed it by miles, and as the ball smashed into my pads, they all appealed like wild dogs – ooooh no . . . ohhh yes! Out, got 'im! The crowd went nuts. Warne, LBW Tendulkar.

'Christ,' I thought, 'we're gone here, gone.' And we were. We lost the Test easy. Harbhajan got six, Sachin three. Some of the LBWs were a bit dodgy, but that's the way the game goes when you boss it. I should know! We were a mess. Completely outplayed. Harbhajan had 13 in the match, including a first innings hat-trick. Not bad for a 20-year-old starting out! India were awesome.

Hindsight is a great thing because it gives you a new perspective. Kolkata was good for cricket. VVS played an innings that brought a lot of joy to a lot of people. Rahul too. The world took notice and the fact that the follow-on cost a dominant Australian team so dearly attracted a lot of interest and analysis. Our long unbeaten run was finally over and a great performance had ended it. Fair enough. Very few sides have enforced the follow-on since: once bitten, twice shy. In my view it still has a place, but without rest days and with the scheduling of back-to-back Tests making most series so draining, it's understandable that captains have become increasingly reluctant. Michael Vaughan enforced it at Trent Bridge in 2005. It nearly cost him too! I've never been a great fan because I like to be bowling in the fourth innings, but I see both arguments.

The day after Kolkata something very disappointing happened. John Buchanan, the Australian coach, came out in the press with a statement saying I wasn't fit enough to play international cricket. I heard about it and thought, 'Muppet!' Yes, agreed, I was out of condition, but if Steve hadn't enforced the follow-on, we would have all come out fresh and probably knocked them over in 50 to 60 overs. Steve made the wrong decision and the coach made me the scapegoat? Please.

I don't know if Buchanan was looking to fire me up or something, but it showed how little he knew me. If he'd come to me in private, we would have thrashed it out. I didn't necessarily disagree with the issue of my weight, but why try and humiliate me? I didn't understand.

Needless to say, his comments had the reverse effect. I was furious and immediately went to see the captain to tell him to pass on to the coach that he was not, under any circumstance, to speak to me again unless he discovered the balls to make his point straight to my face, which I wanted to do, but I wanted to see what the captain would do!

'Buck can't know me very well,' I said, 'because if he wanted to pump me up for the next Test, he'd have gone about this very differently.' I added that if he had a problem with any player, he'd do well to talk to them direct, not via the media. Steve agreed and said he'd speak to him.

If Buchanan had come to me in private, made his point, and offered solutions for working through it together, I might have even listened.

The third Test, at Chennai, was the decider and it lived up to its billing. Harbhajan took 14 this time and he was at the crease when India got over the line by two wickets in a thriller. The old cliché ran true: cricket was the winner. I had a disappointing match. For the first time I could remember, the fight, never mind the magic, was missing from deep in my heart. I was tired and felt let down by the management of the team. Instantly, I blamed Buchanan. But as the days passed, I thought, 'Mate, you have to get yourself sorted.' In the end, there was no-one else to blame.

My record in India is not as good as it should be. There are a couple of reasons. From 1993 to '98, when I was at my best, we didn't tour there. In 1998 we had a pretty ordinary bowling attack and, with my shoulder about to fall off, I wasn't able to carry the workload.

In 2001, as I've mentioned, I'd just come off a finger operation and was struggling for the feel that is the difference between average and good. My fitness levels were poor, my state of mind a bit low. In short, I twice agreed to tour India when a long way below my best. I'm proud that I didn't shirk the challenge and gave it all I had, as you can't pick and choose what tours you want to go on. But, if I had my time again ... well, I don't know, but maybe I wouldn't have gone, especially in 2001. The trouble is, that's not my style. To opt out is not me.

For the 2004 tour I was back, fit again – super-fit, actually – and bowling well. 'Bring on these Indians,' I thought, 'bring them on.' The first Test, I got Laxman out both innings. It was hardly revenge but certainly satisfying. I took 14 wickets in the first three Tests and we had the series sewn up by the time we got to Mumbai for the last one.

None of us will ever forget our first view of that wicket. It was a minefield! The day before the game, I was in the nets having a long hit because I figured every run would be crucial in the conditions. I had a brand new pair of gloves with extra chunky, newly designed protection around the thumb that was unusually uncomfortable. I thought of borrowing someone else's gloves but, instead, just pulled out the hard rubber cup-like protection that slots over the thumb. Unbelievably, a 16-year-old net bowler, a spinner for goodness sake, hit me on the thumb and broke it. Nooo! Not again!

I was like, 'You have got to be kidding! I only need to turn my arm over on this pitch and we'll walk it in. I'll get six, seven, 10 even, wickets in the Test match.' We'd already won the series and I was thinking that 20-plus wickets in a series in India would shut up the critics. Instead, I was on a flight home. Michael Clarke took 6/9 with his left-arm orthodox on the worst wicket you've ever seen in your entire life. We were bowled out for 90-odd in the last innings and lost by a whisker. I like to think we would have got over the line if I'd been there.

In general, the Indians are terrific players of spin, because they're brought up on dry pitches and have played against good spinners since they first picked up a bat. They see the ball early and play it late, using their wrists to skilfully manoeuvre the ball and keep scoring, which is the secret. Dravid, Tendulkar, Ganguly and Laxman – batting in India – make up the best middle-order I've bowled to. Sachin, of course, was amazing anywhere, but I wouldn't say the others were quite so exceptional outside India, though still pretty good. Throw in Sehwag and it's a good side. I love the fact they are such heroes, who bring hope to people's struggles and joy to their lives. It's almost like India loves the cricketers more than the cricket match itself.

As the team has been shedding its old submissive ways, so too has the Board of Control for Cricket in India. The IPL has played its part in making the BCCI confident, outspoken and, for that matter, often confrontational. I'd even say there was an arrogance that has helped change the way India thinks about itself and its place in the global game. That's fine but with it comes a bit of responsibility. Go for it, guys, help lead our great game into the future while keeping your eye on the things from the past that really still do matter – like Test cricket.

One More Thing

I don't like curry. Jason Gillespie wasn't so keen either. In fact, back in the day me and Dizzy only ate omelettes, fries or garlic naan, and drank milkshakes. Now when I'm in India I live off chicken, either tandoori or tikka. In 1998 I called room service and ordered a toasted cheese sandwich. It arrived with ham, cheese, tomato and onions. I sent it back. Then it arrived without the tomatoes, but with the onions and ham. I sent it back. Then it came without tomatoes and onions, but with ham. I asked, 'What part of a toasted cheese sandwich comes with any of tomatoes, onions or ham?' The waiter didn't get it really, so I said, 'I tell you what, mate, I'll have a plate of French fries.' In 2001, I took my own toaster and processed cheese and got the waiters to bring up white bread and butter.

Love India!

12

No Surrender

King of Pain

TEARS WERE STREAMING DOWN my face. Errol Alcott moved my arm, rotating it as if he was separating it from my shoulder. Describing the pain is almost impossible, other than to say that none of the other injuries that led to surgery had come close to this. We had five weeks till the deadline for the 2003 World Cup in South Africa. Five weeks, that's all.

I'd started the summer of 2002/03 in great shape. I had confidence and a better sense of how to move forward in the coming years, both in my home life and with cricket. It was an Ashes summer too, so the juices were flowing.

The Ashes proved to be an anti-climax. We wrapped up the series in Perth after just 11 days of play across three Tests. Nasser Hussain sent us in to bat at the Gabba and never looked forward. We blitzed the Poms, with the gulf in class between the sides never more obvious than over this pretty shocking three or four-year period for English cricket. Only Michael Vaughan could hold his head high as the margins of victory told the story: Gabba – 384 runs;

Adelaide Oval – an innings and 51; WACA – an innings and 48. We were good, very good.

After the Perth Test, the schedule reverted to the old format of the one-day triangular tournament – or VB Series in this case – that began midway through the Ashes series. It was an exciting build-up to Christmas and kept cricket in the headlines. On 15 December, we played England at the MCG and I bowled an uneventful straight ball that Craig White drove back just to the leg-side of the stumps behind me. Throwing myself hard right to stop the thing, I landed badly and dislocated my right shoulder.

A dislocation hurts like hell anyway, but a dislocation with four screws already bolted in to keep the joint tight and stable is another thing altogether. I was in absolute, utter bloody agony.

They carried me off and when I got to the dressing-room there were that many people in there – doctors, physios, staff and all sorts wanting to know what had happened. (I've just looked at the dive again on YouTube, it's *so* innocuous. Maybe that's why I was immediately so grumpy, or maybe I sensed danger, like long-term damage.)

It was Groundhog Day at the hospital with Greg Hoy. He did what he had to do – where would I be without that guy?! – operated, strapped me up, put me in a sling and said, 'Hold tight, you'll be fine.' I'd resigned myself to missing the World Cup, however Greg wasn't so sure.

'Usually,' he said, 'this would be two to three months at best, but you've beaten the odds before and I think this can heal quicker than that. It's certainly a possibility, anyway. Commit your mind to making it and you just might.'

Errol Alcott was even more convinced. 'No way you're missing the World Cup,' he said. 'I'll get you back, fit, strong, ready. It'll hurt, mate – pain-barrier stuff – but I'm going to push you all the way through this and on to South Africa. You're going to be right.'

Great fella, Hooter, and a genius physio. I was up for it. He gave me 48 hours for the inflammation to settle and away we went, hardcore physio work, day upon day. That's when the tears were streaming down my face.

I was back with the team for both the Melbourne and Sydney Tests, working with Hooter in the changing-rooms and then in the gym with all the theraband stuff. The aim was to create mobility and strength in the shoulder, while also working on chest, lats and the muscles that support it. It was full on 24/7 rehab but less mentally draining than some I'd been through, because the goal was so close, like I could touch it.

I remember the evening at the SCG when we stopped work on the table to go out onto the balcony for the last over of the day. It got to the last ball with Steve Waugh facing Richard Dawson and needing four for a hundred. The excitement as Dawson paused at the end of his mark was incredible. The place went off, we stood and applauded, and then went back to the table for more shoulder manipulation. And pain.

I said Groundhog Day for a reason. In 1996 it was the finger and finding that feel again. In '98 it was the first shoulder op. Then in 2001 the finger again. Now, in 2002 a shoulder dislocation tested me once more. It's a difficult test in a way people might not understand. 'Feel' in the fingers is one thing – for a start, the ball feels like it's in someone else's hand – but the shoulder is another: different but kind of similar too. At first, the shoulder also feels as if it's not mine. It's tight and refuses to rotate in the way it has done all my life. In fact, it hardly relates to my upper body at all, which is pretty scary. 'Will I be the bowler I was?' I was asking myself once again.

Then there's the pain threshold. How long will this take and how much do I have to go through? Is it worth it? If I'm not the bowler I was, do I want to play? I need patience and time. But I don't have either.

You can throw confidence into this mix as well. Standing on my mark and looking down the pitch at the batsman, in most cases over the years I've been able to sense his uncertainty, maybe even his fear. This gave me an immediate advantage, a headstart if you like, in the race to win the ground we were competing on. He knew I had a box of tricks and I knew that he knew and would therefore be distracted by unravelling it. But right now, on the back of another op, I didn't know if these advantages would still exist. In fact, I figured most batsmen would think, 'You're not what you were, matey, I can take you down.' This is how damaging an injury can be and how the mind plays tricks. In summary, I was worried that my psychological advantage was threatened.

The longer I thought about these things that confronted me – and over that five-week period of rehab, training and net practice I didn't think about much else – the clearer the answers became. I did want to play on; in fact, I became almost manic about it. I realised I had to stay brave and mentally strong – and I figured I had to trust myself. Yes, I'd lost some feel and confidence but no-one else need ever know. Come the first competitive ball I bowled, I'd be in the batsman's face, big time, reminding him who was the boss.

I really had to work at it in the nets but it was a hard juggling act because I could only bowl for so long before the shoulder, and the finger by the way, got too sore. The flipper suffered and the wrong 'un too. I could deal with the pain but coping with the fear of pushing it too hard and the shoulder or finger going again was harder. Therefore I couldn't get the miles under my belt to find the rhythm and groove that is the key to performance. I'd bowl one good ball, but then four shit ones. I persevered, though, searching for consistency and in the hope of a few miracle balls that would send out messages, both to opponents and to my own brain.

I first bowled a ball on 3 January, just 19 days after the dive and dislocation. That day, I bowled seven painful overs in the SCG nets. A month later, I was on the plane to South Africa, ready for the World Cup. I'm very proud of that and have Greg and Hooter to thank, along with my parents and grandparents for giving me some sort of willpower and determination that helped me beat the odds time and time again. By the time we landed in South Africa, I was super-fit, fresh and bowling just fine. I kept my secrets to myself. As far as anyone out there knew, I was the Shane Warne of old.

The Diuretic

The day before our defence of the World Cup began at the Wanderers in Johannesburg, I got a phone call from a guy who said he was from ASADA – Australian Sports Anti-Drug Authority – telling me that I'd tested positive to my 'A' sample. Yeah, whatever, mate, are you stitching me up? I've never done drugs in my life, so piss off.

He rang back, repeating that I had tested positive and that the 'B' sample test would follow in a week or so. He warned of a hearing, if that test was positive too.

I'd guess I had around 15 random tests during my career which all came back the same by the way and never been positive. I hate drugs. I'll happily admit to a couple of joints in my life, both years back, one at a mate's wedding and one while surfing down at Sandy Point when I was 16. I told the ASADA guy that I'd thrown people out of parties for doing drugs; that I just didn't do them under any circumstance; that I'd seen what they had done to some of my friends growing up; that I was an anti-drug person and that he was bullshitting me. Then I hung the phone up.

My heart was racing. What could this be about? I called Hooter and said, 'Mate, some bloke saying he was from ASADA just accused me of taking drugs.'

'What are you talking about?' said Hooter.

'I don't know what they're on about, if it's a prank or whatever,' I told him.

'Give me 10 minutes,' said Hooter.

When he called back, he told me he'd been instructed to search my room and my possessions. He arrived and we went through everything. What the fuck could I have possibly taken? Nurofen Plus, Panadol and Voltaren were all there, but there was no problem with any of them.

'Have you taken anything else?' asked Hooter. 'Has anyone given you any other tablet?'

At first I said nah, but then, suddenly, it came to me. Mum had given me what she called a fluid pill. It was something she took to help with water retention. She gave me one because she said I had a few extra chins.

'Sure, what does it do?' I asked.

She said, 'It gets rid of water in your body.'

So I took it and pissed a lot of water and that was that – I didn't think another thing of it.

I rang Mum, with Hooter listening in. We were all in a panic. She said it was a Moduretic, which Hooter quickly looked up on Google.

'It's a form of diuretic,' he told us, 'used to mask other stuff, such as steroids.'

I said, 'What the hell, it just made me piss.'

'Yeah,' he said, 'it does that too but it's a masking agent.'

'Well, I'm not trying to mask stuff,' I told him.

He said, 'No, I know, but that's why it is on the banned list.'

The 'B' sample came back a few days later, positive. It meant a hearing, back home in Australia in front of the anti-doping policy committee. From this point, everything went mental. Cricket Australia informed the world that I was being sent home from the World Cup and that there would be a hearing. I was shattered.

'This is unbelievable,' I kept saying to myself. 'I cannot be sent home for taking one of these tablets – this is horseshit.' I was ropeable, just so, so angry that (a) I was in this mess, and (b) I might be thought of as a cheat.

Ricky Ponting wanted me to speak to the team, so at six o'clock that evening, distraught and emotional, I explained to the guys how frustrated I was by what had happened and how terrible I felt letting everyone down. They were fine with me, and supportive. I said that I'd never done drugs and I felt sure they would know I was telling them the truth. I explained how stupid I'd been not to check before I took it. Then I apologised and left it at that. You could have heard a pin drop.

Ricky broke the silence and told everyone to go and get some food and come back at 9 pm to talk about the game we had to win the next day. The next morning I did a press conference explaining what had happened and admitting my mistake. I did all I could to protect Mum by being open about her getting the diuretic from a pharmacy (not from the black market!) and me taking the tablet innocently.

A few days later, Adam Gilchrist wrote in a newspaper that he thought my mum and I had deceived people. Thanks, Gilly, that was a help. Even to this day, people out there think I was blaming Mum, which is rubbish, total rubbish. I was obliged to say where the pill had come from, which I did – but at no stage did I ever blame my mum.

I was deeply upset that people immediately associated me with drugs – like I'd done cocaine – because it was so far from the truth. As kids, we were into sport, sport and more sport, and never came across drugs. Only in my late teens did I see the damage that drugs could do. Around me, some guys I knew got into a real mess; one of them, a close mate of mine, needed financial help to escape the vicious circle, which I gave him.

Back then, I could see how the threat of drug addiction might affect me. I have an element, a gene perhaps, of an addictive personality that needs monitoring. For example, if I diet, I don't eat. Bang. If I commit to training in the gym, I go twice, maybe three times a day. If I go out on the piss, I get hammered. If I play golf, I play every day of the week. If I'm at the roulette table, I go with everything I've got at the time.

All those examples reflect the way I don't do things by halves but, equally, they are conscious decisions and very rarely get out of hand. So I know if I ever tried the drug thing and I liked it or had fun with it, I wouldn't be able to stop. That's why I've never been tempted. And anyway, I've never felt like I needed that sort of buzz. I'm happy with 10 vodka/Red Bulls and a few shots to get my buzz on the occasions I have a big night out. Otherwise, bowling under pressure works just fine for me. I loved that more than anything and would never have jeopardised it.

Anyway, we finished the presser, hopped on a flight with the Cricket Australia guy, Michael Brown, and I was about to chill when he said, 'Geez, at least we've got 24 hours to sort things out, mate, to be ready for the next hurdle when we land in Oz.'

I said, 'Mate, without trying to be funny, I'm pretty pissed off right now because I'm being portrayed as a drug cheat, so I'm not much up for a chat. But I'm innocent and my conscience is clear. I sleep well on planes, so I'm planning to crash out.'

'Oh, okay,' he said, 'have a good nap and we can chat after.'

I said, 'There will be no after. Once I'm out, I'm like a 12-month-old baby in the back seat of a car – I'm out.'

'Yeah, right, mate, talk later.'

Michael had to wake me up in Perth when we changed planes and then again in Melbourne when we arrived. Not a word passed our lips. He still tells the story and points out that I can't have been all that worried about being found guilty. So I slept.

When we landed at Melbourne airport, it was pandemonium, and then every bit as bad back at home, where journos and paps were camping outside the house. I met with Cricket Australia first and then tried to explain things to the journos. There was a lot to get through. Back in Johannesburg, Andrew Symonds, who'd replaced me in the team, made a great hundred and we beat Pakistan in our opening game. I heard later that the guys packed down together and resolved to keep their focus on winning the trophy, and not be distracted by what was going on with me. Good decision. They stayed unbeaten throughout the tournament, smashing India in the final, with Ricky making a brilliant hundred. A great effort that made a lot of people, particularly me I have to say, feel very proud.

For the hearing at the CA offices in Melbourne, I needed legal representation and that was when I had a phone call from Kerry Packer, who I'd first met in 1993 with our mutual great mate, Lloyd Williams. He became one of my closest friends and a valuable mentor during the years that fame first came my way. He still is.

'Tell me the truth, son,' said Kerry. So I told him exactly what happened. He was relieved there were no drugs involved and said, 'If I find out anything different . . .'

'Kerry,' I said, 'there is no reason I'd lie to you and on my children's lives, I'm telling you the truth.'

'Great, I figured it was bullshit,' he replied, and then said about the nicest thing anyone has ever said to me. 'I love what you have achieved, you're one of our greatest sportsmen, and you need to be represented properly at this hearing. I'll provide you with my legal team down in Melbourne. I'm not asking you, I'm telling you. These people will get you the best possible result. Mates stick together, son. Good luck with it.'

I was blown away. Kerry fixed the best representation out there and saved me a lot of money. Going forward I felt that, even under the pressure of the hearing, the chance would be there to make my side of the story clear. Kerry's team were quick to find loopholes in the case against me and seemed hugely confident of getting me off.

The hearing was chaired by the Queensland appeal court judge, Justice Glenn Williams. In the room were Andrew Thwaites, the CA lawyer; Peter Taylor, the off-spinner whose place I'd taken in the team in the early '90s, representing CA; the sports doctor, Susan White, other ASADA reps and my, or Kerry's, legals. It was a room of dark suits and ties and serious faces.

Thwaites grilled my mum in an unforgivable way. Obviously, there was a necessary line of questioning but there was no need for it to be an aggressive one, so full of suggestion and accusation. She was lost in the whole process and the more she stumbled or asked for questions to be repeated, the more he went after her in that bullying way. Sitting there watching and listening to this, I became more and more angry, wanting to literally take matters into my own hands. Thinking about it now makes me madder still. One day the karma bus will get him.

Kerry's lawyers were quite taken aback by the way Mum was treated and began to think that the whole motivation of the hearing was to hang me, not to establish the truth. ASADA didn't seem interested in the real facts at all, only that an example was to be made of a high-profile player.

When the scientific documentation came up, every test I'd taken over the years showed the same pattern. Nothing. Until the one taken three weeks before the 2003 World Cup, which had the anomaly. Thankfully, the small amount of the diuretic found in my system showed up as too weak to mask anything, least of all steroids. Ironically, the very same Moduretic is now off the banned list for exactly that reason – it does nothing except help with fluid-retention issues. I could have 10 of those tablets now if I wanted and they wouldn't show up in any cricket drug testing.

My legal team warned that if found guilty I could receive a two-year ban but that, on the positive side, the drug had no performance-enhancing property, so I should get off, no problem.

But Justice Williams saw it differently. As he said to reporters outside the CA offices in Melbourne, 'The committee found the charge proved and imposed on player Shane Keith Warne [a ban] for the period of 12 months dated from February 10th 2003.'

I was furious and responded immediately. 'I am absolutely devastated and very upset. I will appeal. I feel I am the victim of anti-doping hysteria. I also want to repeat that I have never taken any performance-enhancing drugs and never will.'

It was a weird decision and sentence. What was the reasoning? Did they think there was more to it? So now I'd had two serious shoulder injuries, two ring-finger ops, been dropped from the Test team, sacked from the one-day captaincy, rubbed out of the game for a year. What the hell would be next?!

I was all over the place and felt this terrible sense of injustice. Simone was terrific and stood by me throughout, but there was no escaping the fact that I was at one of my lowest points. I was stuffing things up for myself and for everybody around me that I cared about. So then I got angry again, this time with myself. Why hadn't I checked out the ICC book of rules? I might not have taken anything performance-enhancing, but I should bloody well have checked out whether or not that tablet was legal. Stupid, but innocent.

I had the right to appeal and my first reaction was to do so. But I changed my mind. The lawyers explained that if we lost, I'd get the full two years. They said I'd been nailed for the mistake of not checking out the tablet and then of failing the drug test. They made the point that my profile allowed both ASADA and Cricket Australia to make an example of me. What with Dick Pound, the President of the World Anti-Doping Agency, weighing in, saying it was a disgrace for Australian sport and that he couldn't see the reason not to ban me for the full two years, my lawyers figured that, in the end, I was better off taking the hit for a year than taking them on.

My last words on the subject were: 'Although I find this penalty very harsh and I am extremely disappointed that this has happened, I have decided that I no longer want to put my family under even more stress. Enough is enough.'

Remission

Simone and I took the kids to Spain. We were being hounded at home in Australia and it was affecting our life with the kids, young as they were. We had a good time together in Spain; in fact, most of that year was good because, for once, family took precedence over cricket.

When we got back to Australia after our holiday, there were two things I wanted to do – learn how to drive properly and get my golf handicap down as low as possible. I enrolled in all the advanced driving courses with BMW. I wanted a CAMS (Confederation of Australian Motor Sport) licence that would allow me to race on the track and enter pretty much anything, even the Bathurst 1000.

I wanted to get my golf handicap down to single figures as well, so I played with Lloyd Williams at his club, the Capital, 27 days in a row. It was just Lloyd and me, 6 or 7 am hit-off, done by 10-ish, breakfast and away. I got it down to 6.7, the best it has been.

It was the first year I'd played in the Dunhill Links Championship in Scotland, the best pro-am golf event on the planet and the most fun week of the year, every year. It's a four-day event where you live and breathe the life of a professional golfer. What a privilege it is to be asked to play and, that year, for obvious reasons I particularly appreciated the invitation from Johann Rupert, the great South African who sponsors the tournament and puts his unique stamp on it time after time. Johann has been a tremendous friend and supporter of mine ever since. At the time I was black-banned everywhere, so this was a gesture I'll never forget.

I didn't touch a cricket ball for six months. The ban meant I couldn't train at any facility in Australia or the government would withdraw their funding for it. So I couldn't practise at the MCG, at any club or at any indoor nets – nowhere. A mate of mine owned an indoor cricket centre in 'Woop Woop' – in other words, miles out of town – and he agreed to open it up for me at six in the mornings. I drove in the dark and would bowl for an hour at a handkerchief before he ushered me away, locked up the building, and came back at eight to open it up formally for the day's business. On a couple of occasions I bowled at the actor Glenn Robbins, a great mate of mine, but then someone found out what was going on and we had to bin the whole exercise.

I thought, 'Right, I'm not allowed to bowl but no-one can stop me from getting fit.' I hired Russell Crowe's fitness trainer, Lourene – who I mentioned earlier – for a six-week period, which became eight weeks while I became the fittest I've been in my life. I trained my arse off, didn't drink, fed off protein shakes and went for it. I did yoga too, stretched and worked on core strength. I'd never felt better.

I've kind of done that most of my life, lurched in and out of fitness. Most of the time I just can't be bothered but then, when the bug gets me, I just tear myself apart and start again. I can drop from 90 to 80 kilos in next to no time.

Basically, it's cereal – Special K – plus fruit and water for the first 10 days, then protein shakes. I love fruit – watermelon, grapes, apples, bananas – and within a couple of weeks I've stripped 4–5 kilos. After that I'll eat in moderation, maybe some bacon with the morning protein shake and then pasta for lunch, but I never eat in the evening. Oh, and I cut out all the junk. No fries, no chips, no pizza, no lollies. The cigarettes stay.

Anyway, the day the ban ended, Victoria were training at Junction Oval so I went up to roll my arm over. The guys saw me and were saying, 'Wow, you're looking good, Warney.' And I was like, 'Yeah, I should get rubbed out more often!'

A few days later I played for the Vics' second XI against Queensland and got the shock of my life. Gym fitness is one thing, cricket fitness is another. A year out of the game and then a day in the field – geez, that hurt; just everywhere. Shoulder, legs, groins, back, hips, lats, wrists, fingers ... holy malloly! So I had to get some miles in very, very quickly.

I played one Shield game and two one-dayers before the selectors picked me to tour Sri Lanka 10 days later. As we got there, I said, 'Whoever wants to bat, I'm bowling. And if you want to have another bat after the session, I'll bowl again.' I didn't play in the five-match one-day series that kicked off the tour, but when Ricky said I was in for the first Test, I felt a huge amount of pride. I knew I was ready, and hungrier than I'd been since those Terry Jenner days. Stuart MacGill had done well in my absence and picking the two of us together was a great thing for the art we loved most. The art of leg-spin.

The date was 8 March 2004, barely more than a year since the humiliation of the positive tests, removal from the World Cup, the hearing back at home and the ban.

It was, how should I say, tricky to integrate back into the side. Maybe the word is awkward. The guys had lived in each other's pockets for the best part of 12 months, and won a World Cup, remember, without me around. Then, suddenly, I was back, like I was someone new, and we both had to get the feel for each other again. I'd played for 13 seasons and over 100 Tests before the ban, so I was actually more senior than any of them, but it didn't feel like that. For a few days, to be honest it was pretty weird, but to everyone's credit the guys were great and that welcome back was something I won't forget. I even joined in the sprinting sessions. That caught 'em off guard!

In hindsight, this was probably the most focused I had been in my whole career. It was, like, you blokes in your dark suits and ties that judged me at the hearing but don't know me, you're not going to stop me doing the thing I love most. You want to try and rub me out? Well, I ain't going anywhere.

It had taken a while for me to get to that point. At the start of the ban I was sulky and weighed down by the questions that nagged away: why me, why this? But time was the healer. I eased off a bit, had a great time with the family, loved playing golf with Lloyd, driving the race cars and looking at life from a different perspective. I guess that's a problem with professional sport, the bubble you live in and the danger of a siege mentality. My mindset was so much better from having allowed it to relax. Test cricket and the lifestyle that came with it had a high tariff in many ways and the downtime taught me a bit about myself.

From the moment I started training hard, late in 2003, and then bowling again in early February 2004, I felt comfortable with where I was at. I had unfinished business on the cricket field, strongly believing I still had a contribution to make to Australian cricket. To be honest, I'd missed the game terribly and resolved to show people what they'd been missing too. When I walked out onto the field in Galle, I felt 10 foot tall and there was no way I was going to let anybody down. Least of all myself.

I took 10 wickets in that Test match – which included my 500th – 10 more in the second and six in the third. It was the best tour I ever had. The Sri Lankans were super players of spin – Jayawardene, Sangakkara, Atapattu, Tillakaratne, Jayasuriya, Dilshan – and they prepared big turning wickets in the belief that Murali would outbowl us. We were behind on every first innings but we still won 3–0. I flew Mum and Dad over for that first Test and was able to share the occasion and result with them. I thought back to 1992 and the Test match in Sri Lanka that changed my life, and reflected on the fact that, once again, this country had been good to me. I was back, the memories of a nightmare year pretty much erased, and the fun of cricket stretching out in front of me.

Footnote

Nine months later, the tsunami hit Sri Lanka and tore the island and its people apart. I rang Murali and said, 'I want to come over and help.' He was excited and asked how quickly I could get there. Within a week or so was the answer. I rang TNT, the courier-service people, and I said, 'Right, I've got Gray-Nicolls and County willing to fly out cricket kit. And I've got toys, colouring books, pens, pencils, and lots of other stuff too.' They said, 'Sure, let's do it.'

It was flown to Galle, where I met Murali, and we handed it out to children who had been through hell. There was a guy there called Kasheel, who'd been teaching the kids how to use computers and to speak English, but their village had been destroyed by the waves. The joy and gratitude on his face when we arrived was unbelievable. Then there was the truly horrific scene of a train in Galle that had been hit by the tsunami and was lying wrecked by the side of the track. Many people had died, including the parents of a family of four. When the two children came forward for their gifts and smiled to say thank you, I just teared up. Their courage and hope, after such heartache, was one of the more incredible things I've experienced in my life. Sri Lanka is a beautiful country, made even more beautiful by its people. They have a special place in my heart.

13

Fields of Blue and Gold

Hampshire . . . or Lancashire?

THERE WAS ALWAYS SOMETHING about county cricket that I liked. When I played the leagues in Bristol in 1989 and Lancashire in 1991, I used to go and watch with a few mates and think, 'Yeah, I'd like a go at this.' The standard was better than first grade in Melbourne but not as good as the Sheffield Shield at that time. I liked the traditional aspects of it, the pretty grounds full of people happy to spend a day enjoying the game.

After the '93 Ashes tour and the Gatting ball, a lot of counties hit me up to see if I was interested in playing county cricket. Sussex offered £75,000 – a lot in those days – but Kerry Packer talked me out of it, saying it was more important I stayed fresh for Australia – and he did this as a friend, not for ratings! That was really the start of my great friendship with Kerry.

I didn't think much of it for the next few years because we played so much international cricket, and then injuries hit me – surgery, rehab, training. A lot of mental energy was used up, so I didn't want to waste any of it on the county circuit, but save everything for Victoria and Australia.

At the start of the 1999 World Cup in England, we had a function at Buckingham Palace and the Hampshire chairman was there – a big bloke with a beard, Brian Ford.

He said, 'I hear you want to play county cricket.'

'Really?'

'Well, that's what I heard,' he said.

'Righto,' I told him. 'Yep, I spoke to Sussex a few years back but it didn't work out. I'm up for another look at it.'

And he came straight out with 'Come and play for Hampshire then.'

'Er, okay, mate, best if you speak to my agent.'

Brian later said it was a nightmare because I had two agents and they saw the world very differently.

Anyway, I didn't hear from Hampshire for a few weeks. Meantime, we were playing West Indies at Old Trafford and I was approached by the Lancashire chairman, Jack Simmons, to play for the Red Rose county. Jack was a good bloke, a much liked character in Australia where he'd once captained Tasmania to some success, and he didn't have much selling to do given my success story at Old Trafford! We basically did a deal there and then: £100,000 plus all expenses.

I said, 'Look, mate, it sounds good, but I won't fully commit for a month, maybe two, and certainly not until the end of the World Cup when my head is clearer. At this stage, your offer is great, I'd love to play at a big Test ground, I've got some great memories at Old Trafford, I've got mates in the leagues, and I like the way Lancashire play their cricket.'

I never fully committed but, in principle, I was definitely going to play for Lancashire. Then, on the morning of the final at Lord's against Pakistan, we'd just finished our warm-ups when Robin Smith, who was doing some radio work that day, came over and spoke to me. 'Do you want to come and play for Hampshire?' he asked.

Judge and Jack

The first thing to say here is that I've never come across a better bloke in cricket than Robin Smith. I first met the 'Judge', as the world knows him, in the 1990/91 season in Adelaide when I was bowling to the Poms in the nets and kept knocking over John Morris, a bloke who didn't last long in Test cricket, but who is a good and funny man. In the end they moved me out of that net because it was getting embarrassing, so I went next door and bowled to the Judge.

Anyway, our Academy team – guys like Blewett, Martyn, Langer and Cottrell – played two games against England and I got the Judge out for 30-odd in the second of them. Afterwards, Allan Lamb came up to me and said, 'We hear you're the guy to show us round town tonight.' So off we went – Lamby, Judgey, me and a few others in tow. We had a great night and we've stayed good mates ever since.

I reckon England binned Robin too early, but perhaps the reputation for having a good time became a kind of noose around his neck. He was a helluva player, a magnificent striker of the ball with a huge heart. He had the respect of the Australian dressing-room, which wasn't given out easily. People said I finished his career, because of the way I got him out a few times. That's bullshit. Robin's record against spin is better than most people think – particularly against India and Sri Lanka. In the early days he used to smack it out of the park, but as he got older he attacked spin less. Age definitely changes the way batsmen think and most go into a shell – reactions slow up and the carefree instincts of the early years are affected by knowing too much. Fine player, though, the Judge, and a great bloke. He had the fiercest cut shot I've ever seen, and I've never heard a bad word said about him.

So there were the two of us, as the drizzle began at Lord's and delayed the start of the final. 'Hampshire are a small county with a very talented cricket side,' he said, 'but we lack leadership. We like to party a bit too much, and we don't take our cricket too seriously, which may or may not be a good thing. We should be better than we are and I think you're the man to help us, and impart your knowledge along with your winning mindset to the group.'

It was a pretty smart approach by Judgey. I like a party too and the idea of trying to bring success to a club that hadn't had any of late was very appealing.

'Leave it with me, Judge,' I said, and, heading back to the dressing-room, I was thinking that I sort of liked the Hampshire idea but I'd partly given my word to Lancashire. Hmmm ...

That afternoon, Australia won the World Cup. We outplayed Pakistan in every department of the game, which was a fantastic end to a campaign that didn't start so well. The celebrations in the rooms summed up why we play in the first place and they went long and hard from mid-afternoon to around 10 pm, when the officials moved us on. But not until we'd sung our team song out in the middle on the hallowed turf of Lord's.

When we got back to the Royal Garden Hotel, a little guy came over from the far corner of the lobby in a hat, suit and cufflinks that each had the initials MPC on them.

He said, 'Excuse me, can I have five minutes of your time?'

'No, mate,' I told him. 'We've just won the World Cup and I'm hanging with the team.'

He said, 'Well, if you do find five minutes, I'll be waiting here.'

I went up to my room, had a shower, got changed, made a couple of calls and headed down to the bar to meet the guys. The little bloke was still there.

'Whenever you have five minutes,' he told me again. 'I'll wait here all night if need be.'

I had a couple with the guys in the bar and came out for a smoke. He was *still* there. I said, 'I tell you what, I'll finish my smoke and then give you five minutes.'

I did and then he gave me this spiel – he said he was Michael Cohen and asked me who managed me in England. I said I had a real good bloke in Oz, Austin Robertson, but, no, I didn't have anyone in England. He said there was a lot he could do for me in the UK, so I suggested he ring Ocker and headed back to the bar.

I rang Ock myself the next day and he said Michael Cohen had already called him. 'He's tenacious, you gotta give him that,' said Ock, 'and he sure knows the English market better than us.'

'Good point, Ock,' I said. 'Tell him we want to play county cricket next year. See if he can package up the best deal on the planet, with other gigs surrounding the cricket to make the most of my time there. No commission, first year for free. That way we find out if he's serious.'

Three months later we were playing a short Test series in Sri Lanka, and MPC – that's Michael, the little bloke! – called with an offer of £150,000 from Hampshire, plus car, house and flights. Then there was a radio deal: me and Jamie Theakston, very much the young radio and TV guy of the moment, hosting our own Sunday show – six shows at £5000 a pop; an agreement with *The Times* for 10 columns at 12K each, and a £200,000 book deal to tell my story so far with Hodder & Stoughton. £500,000 in one phone call!

I rang Ocker and said, 'You'd better pull your socks up, mate, this Michael Cohen is pretty damn good!' I said he could split his commission with Michael if he liked, but it was up to him. The next thing I did was to ring Lancashire and tell them I was signing with Hampshire. I explained my decision – it was partly the financial offer, partly me being a mate of Robin Smith, and partly the chance to turn a smaller club around. Apologies, Lancs, it's the way it had to be.

Nearly 20 years on and MPC still manages me in the UK. He's a really good guy, he's done an excellent job, and I've become firm friends with him and his family.

Australia played a one-day game against South Africa at the Wanderers in Johannesburg on 16 April 2000. Three days later, I made my debut for Hampshire. I drove to Chelmsford in Essex with the Judge the evening before the match, having crammed in some media stuff, met with sponsors and committee men, moved into a new house and opened a bank account, all in less than 48 hours. Judge had plenty of cold beers in an esky on the back seat so we got stuck in. I thought, 'Right, I get the party thing.'

I hadn't met many of the Hampshire guys and I remember walking into the dressing-room for the first time the next morning and thinking that some of these blokes looked past their sell-by date. I was 30, turning 31 later that year, and you know how some people look older than they are and others look younger – well, I sat next to Judge, pointed to Peter Hartley and, assuming he was the manager, asked him to introduce us.

Judge just laughed. 'He's our opening bowler!'

I said, '*Whaat?* He can't be our opening bowler, he's got to be 50.'

'Turned 40 yesterday,' replied Robin.

'What pace does he bowl?' I asked.

'Mid-80s.'

'Come on, mate, there's no way he'll bowl mid-80s,' I said, and at that moment Peter – or 'Jack', as the boys called him – sucked deep on a gasper and came over to shake my hand. An hour and a half later, I was standing at slip and Jack bounded in, let go of one that flew with a beautiful outswing shape and slapped into the keeper's gloves nice and hard. Jesus! Tidy, that!

We won by five wickets and Jack could bowl. He played the game hard and fair and we became good mates and driving buddies, both of us smoking like a chimney.

Captaincy

It wasn't long, though, before the alarm bells started ringing. In the nets, the boys were really casual and would just get out, like it didn't matter. Then they'd get their phone out and mess about on it for ages – girlfriends, business ideas, music, games.

I was like, 'What the hell is going on here – are we serious or what?'

Judge wasn't worried. He just kept saying, 'They're out now, it doesn't matter.'

But it did matter. There was no focus and certainly not on winning. As you've heard, I love Judge to bits but I didn't agree and I snapped one day when he offered an opposing batsman, who was going well against us, the chance to change his gloves and have a drink. *Offered him!* Oh my God, this is not my cricket, not at all.

I hate going soft and I hate losing even more. The guys would come out of the shower, ramp up the product in their hair and say, 'Where are we going for a beer?' I didn't say much to start with, but by halfway through the season it was getting to me and I snapped a few more times.

I talked a lot about it to John Stephenson – good cricketer was 'Stan', I enjoyed playing with him – because he and I always shared an 'oily' (cigarette) and a beer or two next to each other in the change-rooms, long after the others had gone. He was in my camp but had found it hard to change the culture in the two years he was captain. Look, it was fun because they were such a great group of guys, but they weren't taking their lives as professional cricketers seriously enough and I began to see the extent of the challenge ahead if I was to honestly consider coming back.

At the end of the year the new chairman, Rod Bransgrove, asked me to write down everything that I thought needed to change at the club. I wasn't sure it was my place to do so, but he insisted, saying we all want you back: the members who loved the way you just kept bowling and smiling, signing autographs every day for the kids; the players, and most of all me, he said, and we won't get you back unless it's on your terms. True.

'Okay, here goes,' I told him. 'Get rid of all the deadwood, the guys who've been at the club for four or five years and only played a handful of games. The talent is here – blokes like Derek Kenway and Jason Laney – but the culture has to change. There's a time and a place to drink and that's when you celebrate a victory. Sure, have a few during the game, but if you do then you better turn up and perform.

'Sport is performance based – you perform, you keep your spot. There have to be stricter dressing-room rules and everybody should sit out on the balcony, watching where blokes field, who's the left-arm thrower, right-arm thrower, who's looking tired and easy to attack, who's alive and dangerous. Study the game, guys! What about the pitch, the boundaries, the angles, the tactics? Where does gully field, how fine is backward point, and why?

'These guys need to start looking closely at cricket, getting inside cricket, and they have to start to openly support their mates when they're out in the fight. I don't want blokes on the phone in the dressing-room talking to a stockbroker, I want blokes who are committed to bringing success to the club, strong characters, good people with a work ethic. Trust and belief have to replace jealousy and laziness. Cricket is bloody hard, and sponsored cars, free every-thing, long-term contracts shouldn't come easy.' But, back then, they did.

Rod listened and didn't argue. Then I wrote it down for him too.

2001 was an Ashes year so I didn't play county cricket. 2001/02 was a tough time for many reasons, so I needed some time away from the game in the Australian winter. 2003 I was rubbed out because of the diuretic. But, and this is what I loved, Hampshire never gave up on me, and in 2004 I signed a four-year deal to be captain. It was for less money because the club were under severe pressure financially, but that was no problem – I wanted to do this. So, that summer I got there early to spend time with the guys, talking about my philosophies on the game and what it takes to win. John Crawley had joined the club from Lancashire and played really well. We had some good players, and some not so good, but we began to move as one in the right direction.

My message was simple enough. 'We're playing to win,' I told them, 'and if that means losing occasionally, then so be it. I want you guys to learn how to win, and how to bat, bowl and field under pressure.'

Hampshire had won just four games in the previous two seasons. It was a pretty poor effort, given the talent was there to compete and get promotion to the first division.

'I guarantee you we'll win more than four games this year alone. We might lose a few too, but we'll win more than we lose. This cricket journey is not about averages – I don't give a rat's arse about averages. I care about how you play the game, and that you love playing it.

'Yes, it's cool when you make a big hundred in a run chase, but it's also cool if you make 40 when we desperately need it. It's great if you take five-fer, but also pretty awesome if you keep it tight when we're under the cosh. I care about how you treat your team-mates and how you look to improve yourself. Cricket is what we've chosen to do, so let's do it properly.'

I also wanted the other counties to hate us; to be so intimidated that they dreaded playing us. Equally, I wanted the team to be respected as well, so I made sure we thanked the ladies who made the lunches, cleaned the change-rooms etc. Manners are free.

In 2004, we nearly won the second division title, but had to settle for second behind Nottinghamshire, which at least meant promotion.

The bowlers ticked over fine, although the truth was that we were one gun batsman short of being really good.

KP

We were on the bus to Notts and all the boys were saying, 'Warney, please, get the big-head out.'

'Who's the big-head?' I asked them.

Kevin Pietersen, they said, a cocky, strutting South African, the most arrogant prick you've ever seen.

I'd never heard of Kevin Pietersen, never mind seen him play. But I figured that this guy must be good because no-one likes him.

Next day, I knocked over Russell Warren and in he came. I thought this *will* be interesting. I was standing at the top of my mark and everyone went quiet. Were these blokes scared of this bloke or what? Weird.

Anyway, I was about to bowl when he pulled away. I thought, 'Fair enough, he must be having another look at the field.'

I went back to the top of my mark, made him wait a bit, then came in to bowl and he pulled away again. So I said to him, 'Mate, I haven't heard one thing about you that's any good. Everyone on this field hates you. Even the non-striker told me he thinks you're a prick, so I don't know what's wrong with you, but you must be a fuckwit. I was going to give you the benefit of the doubt, but now I'm not sure, so if we could get on with the game, we'll find out if you're any good and, either way, you're still a fuckwit.'

Two balls later, bat-pad, leg-side – bang, bang – catch, out. I said, 'Now fuck off.'

All the boys were screaming, 'Yes, that's it, fuck off. Give it to him, Warney!'

I thought, 'They really don't like this bloke.'

That was my first impression of Kevin Pietersen – not good.

✧

At the end of 2004, I got a call from Ian Botham, who was managing KP at the time (go figure!). He said, 'KP would like to talk to you about playing for Hampshire. I've told him if you want to learn how to play the game properly and to take that talent of yours into Test cricket, there is no-one out there who knows more about it than Warney. So the question is, are you interested and, if so, can I pass your number on to him?'

'Yeah, sure,' I said.

So KP rang me and said he loved what we were doing and that we were an exciting team. He said he wanted to leave Notts and come to us because Beefy reckoned this was where he'd learn fastest, alongside me and under my captaincy.

I said, 'I'm very flattered, mate, but we've started something here which is pretty good, and we're all in it together. What I hear about you is that you're not a team man. Now, I don't give a fuck what other people say. I want to make up my own mind, so I'm happy to meet you, with a couple of Hampshire officials. In the end, they'll make the call.'

KP turned up in a singlet and shorts, while me, Rod Bransgrove and Tim Tremlett, the Hampshire director of cricket, were in pants and a jacket. He swore like a trooper and bagged the guys at Notts. Basically, he'd fallen out with everyone there and was desperate for a change.

KP was getting heaps of runs everywhere and I liked his individual style – the stance, the intent and the desire to succeed. There was something about him, for sure.

I said, 'Look, with me, you start with a clean slate. I'll only treat you based on how you conduct yourself in the group. We all play for each other here and I think you'll fit in beautifully. In fact, you're just the cricketer we need to take us to the next level. We'd love to have you.'

Well, that stopped everyone in their tracks. We did the deal soon after and Kev was with us for the 2005 season.

He lived with me for a time, like Michael Clarke had done when he played the 2004 season. A few good Aussies started to come to Hampshire – apart from 'Pup', there was Shane Watson, Simon Katich and Stuart Clark back then.

Pup stood next to me at slip and wanted to learn about the game. I said, 'Ask me about everything, every move I make,' and he was like a sponge. We hung out all the time, became great mates and talked cricket like you couldn't believe. The next year the same sort of thing happened with Pietersen – me passing on everything I'd learnt.

I liked the way the two of them played the game and I was happy to have them under my wing. It was great to watch them succeed the way they did.

The sad thing was that KP didn't stay longer. Once he was in the England side, he was spending all his time in London and, of course, playing less and less. Sometimes he would helicopter in and out for a game, which was crazy really. I think we played our part in his progress, refining him, teaching him, and the club were very support-ive, even though we saw so little of him. I know KP really appreciated everything that Hampshire did for him.

KP was a sensational player, similar to Adam Gilchrist in the way the ball came off the bat, the sound it made and the fact that the game could change in an hour when they were at the wicket. Guys like Sachin Tendulkar, Ricky Ponting, Jacques Kallis and Kumar Sangakkara were great players but orthodox, dependable. Then there was Brian Lara, Gilly, KP – the ones with X-factor, the matchwinners who play some shit shots, make a few noughts, and then win a game out of nowhere. KP was so destructive. Some of the shots he played off McGrath and me, I've never seen anyone play those sorts of shots. What about when he smashed McGrath over mid-off and into the pavilion at Lord's!

As I've mentioned, I think in my time the best two were Lara and Tendulkar; after them, daylight. Then there were Gooch, Ponting, Kallis, Pietersen, Sangakkara – they're all in the next best. Dravid and Laxman weren't bad, by the way. But of all of them, KP was the most different, and I like different.

I don't have a bad word to say about him in the dressing-room because I understood him and he understood me. The trick with KP was to make him feel important and part of the decision making process and ask for his opinion. So, for example, we'd walk out to look at the wicket on day one and I'd say, 'KP, what do you think? Shall we bat, shall we bowl?' Then we'd talk it through.

Some of the time, I already knew what I was going to do; other times he had good ideas. I wanted him to feel involved. It was an ego thing to some degree and if KP felt important and wanted, he delivered to the team and with the bat. 'What do you think the team should be, mate?' 'Who should be 12th man?' 'What do you think about the batting order?' 'Who do you like following you at five?' 'What do you reckon?'

Any team leader, whether they like KP or not, should still pay him that respect. Being a captain or a leader is about understanding the person, and in KP's case he is so important to the team, he deserves the respect. Make him feel important and you'll never have to pull him up. That was England's mistake. Instead of pumping him up, they began to diminish him. It's the tall poppy thing and no good with Kev. In the end, he's a bit insecure and wants to be loved. (I can think of a few who are like that!) He's a decent fella underneath all the bullshit, but England, being England, couldn't see that because he didn't conform. The English hierarchy and the Pietersen bling – car crash!

Listen, he played his part in the relationship falling apart two years before it needed to. You can't do some of the things that KP did. He thought he was irreplaceable, but no-one is. So, for me, 'Textgate' in that South Africa series in 2012, and all those kinds of things that went on, were a sign of England not showing him enough love and KP reacting like the wronged party in a broken marriage. Not that it's an excuse for what he did – texting a couple of the South African players with his uncomplimentary views on the England management team – because he was out of order, but it's a reason, and I believe England brought some of it upon themselves. We know some of the other senior guys didn't like him and an atmosphere was created that couldn't possibly work in a dressing-room.

As for us at Hampshire, we had no problem; and I never had any issue with him as a captain either. Over the years, I think KP has been a bit misunderstood because he is different, but my view is that that difference is worth the effort. I can see he hasn't always helped himself but, when a guy has got a talent like he has, you have to work with it. You just have to.

Hampshire vs Nottinghamshire 2005

We were promoted with Notts in 2004, and both sides started the 2005 season well. We met at Trent Bridge in the sixth championship game and were up near the top of the table. Our guys had good energy going and other teams had become kind of wary of our attitude and confidence. KP was so pumped for this game, like, 'I'm going to smack these blokes from Trent Bridge to Timbuktu – blah blah blah.' The tension between him and them, and therefore us and them, was pretty obvious even in the warm-ups.

John Crawley used to make a heap of runs against Notts – he got a triple hundred in 2004 and was to get another in the game at our home ground, the Rose Bowl, later in 2005 – so they were nervous of him alone. Mind you, Notts were getting it together under Stephen Fleming's smart captaincy. This definitely felt like the match-up of the season so far.

I said to the guys, 'This is a great test of everything that we now stand for. It's a flat pitch at Trent Bridge, we have to play attacking cricket and be prepared to take risks to win.'

Everyone was so up for it. Then it rained, and rained. We didn't start till after lunch on the second day and were bowled for 277 the next morning. Kev was LBW second ball for nought: the Notts boys went off on one. They were 5/225 at the close. Three days gone, the match going nowhere.

I thought, 'This is no good. If we're to be anything as a team, it has to be now.'

Remember I'd told the guys we were going to try and win every game, and if we lose so be it. This was a great test. There had to be some manipulation for this match to work, and a gamble.

I'm very good friends with Flem, so I was thinking we might be able to fix up something when we had dinner that night at an Italian joint he'd booked. First, though, I talked to our guys, saying, 'Righty-ho, full day's play tomorrow plus the extra overs we have to make up. Maybe 104 overs in the day. Let's say we smash a quick 250 and set them a target. How many, in how long?'

They ummed and ahed and ended up suggesting 330 in 80 overs – cautious. Not gamblers, these blokes. I got them down, reluctantly, to 300 in 75. At least, that's what they thought it was going to be!

In the restaurant I asked Flem what he was thinking. He said, 'Well, let's get a game in – neither of us want a boring draw.'

I said, 'Exactly what are you thinking?'

'You tell me,' he said.

I said, 'Well, what do you have in mind?'

It was like we were dipping our toes in the water. I knew what I had in mind, but I didn't want to look like I was asking for too much. Let's think about it overnight, we decided, and have a chat tomorrow morning at the ground.

The following morning I said, 'Flem, let's not haggle – here's a plan. You lob it up for 25 overs, we then score real quick, and we'll set you 275 off 65 overs.'

Flem said, 'Sorry, are you serious? That sounds more than fair!'

'Serious. Now I want a dart, so you happy?'

'Yeah, let's do it,' he said.

I told the boys and they were like, 'That's a bit light, skipper!'

I said, 'I know, but he wouldn't budge. It's better than a dead day, guys. I tried for 300 but I just couldn't get there – sorry.' Let's just call that a necessary white lie!

Notts spent the first part of the fourth morning bowling some filth, while we pasted 4/220 in 28.3 overs. The chase was on: 275 in 65 on a flat deck.

I'm telling this story in detail because I believe it sealed the deal for a newly committed and talented Hampshire team. From this match on, I felt the guys bought in to everything I'd been trying to apply to the team. They began to approach matches in all competitions with exactly the right attitude, preparation and level of genuine confidence in themselves.

It wasn't that nobody could beat us, more that we just didn't think they would, and that belief carried us through the season and almost – bloody well almost – to the championship title. It was chalk and cheese from the dressing-room in 2000.

Anyway, back to the match, which was going pear-shaped. Stephen Fleming got a hundred and they were 3/227 with only 48 to win, seven wickets in hand and 12 overs to get them. I was thinking, 'I've fucked this up,' and out of the corner of my eye I could sort of see Flem going, 'Ha, ha ha.' At this point, Shaun Udal – 'Shaggy' – had him caught at deep mid-off for 105. Four down, 48 to win.

Now I needed a three or four-over burst from Chris Tremlett – nasty, short, fast – that would send a message to the new batsmen and the dressing-room that we weren't giving up.

I turned to Chris – 'Goober', we called him – who was walking in from deep backward square-leg looking uninspired, like the responsibility was too frightening. I gave him a terrible spray. It was harsh and unfair really, but with a few cold, hard facts in there too.

I said, 'Goob, what the hell have you ever done for Hampshire? You're six foot 35 and built like a brick shithouse. In the nets, no-one gets close to you – in fact, they shit themselves – but out here you're a pussycat. I don't want you to be someone you're not. You don't have to sledge or anything like that – just bowl hard, fast and hit them in the head.'

Goober said okay.

Right: three slips, gully, leg-gully, bat-pad, third-man for the upper-cut, cover, long-leg. I remember it like it was yesterday. Give it to 'em, Goober! He bowled like the wind and real nasty, took a hat-trick – Mark Ealham, Graeme Swann and Greg Smith – and ended up with five. At the other end, I knocked over Chris Read and later Ryan Sidebottom, the last wicket, with a nice little slider that hit off peg to win the match by 14.

We went nuts! I'd never seen anything like it from the guys. It was one of the great wins of my life in cricket.

✧

I played 11 championship games that year either side of the Ashes, which ran later than usual, into the second week of September. We missed out on the title by 2.5 points. I got back to play two games and we won them both – first against Glamorgan, then the return Notts match in which 'Creepy' Crawley made his second triple hundred against them. We beat 'em twice but finished behind them in the table by a whisker. Jeeeesus!

At the time I was angry about the penultimate Notts game at Canterbury, the one before they came across to the Rose Bowl. Kent were third, 19 points behind Notts and about 16 behind us. Desperate to win, their captain, David Fulton, agreed to chase 420 in 80 overs in the last innings and Kent were rolled over pretty easily.

It was a ridiculous agreement but, of course, Flem had Fulton over a barrel. I've often wondered what I would have done, because what happened at the time didn't seem right, or fair, to me. Maybe we would also have agreed to chase almost anything for a win, however small the chance, but I think I would have negotiated a lower chase or, if that fell on deaf ears, decided to take my chances with the final round of matches. I'll always be proud of that English summer – the Ashes, of course, but the achievements with Hampshire too.

We won the Cheltenham and Gloucester Trophy, though the Aussie management wouldn't let me play in the final at Lord's for fear of injury midway through the Test series. Shaggy captained the team and we played great. I went on to play two more successful years and I like to think that from where the club was when I took over in 2004 to my final season in 2007, things changed for the better. And in that time we won more first-class games than any other county.

Reflections

KP, Googa, Dimma, Shaggy and another team-mate, Michael Carberry, all said publicly that I was the best captain they ever played under! But not all players will love your style. A guy like James Bruce could really bowl, but he'd rub me up the wrong way. He was a posh kid from Eton school who did a nice turn in sarcasm, and I found myself nailing him more often than maybe I should have. Anything I ever said to Brucey was to get the best out of him, but he just saw me as having a go at him. Not true. I was looking to fire him up more – he was too passive for a quick bowler – and to add a bit of discipline to his cricket by pushing him to stick to plans instead of veering off in his own direction. I'm sure if you asked him – and maybe one or two others – he'd say I was too hard on him. Hmm . . . thinking back now, I probably should have put my arm around Brucey a bit more.

In general, though, I challenged the players like that because average isn't good enough. Bring more to the table, mate. Be a gun fielder as well: practise, hit the stumps more than the others; catch everywhere not just where you're comfortable; be the best point fieldsman, gully, slip, bat-pad, anywhere you like, but *improve*. Be the best cricketer you can be. Otherwise, why play?

So, yes, I would give them a kick up the backside and if they didn't like it, well, leave, mate, go somewhere else. I'm not into mollycoddling people. I didn't want anyone at the club who was just playing for a contract – I wanted people to push themselves and become the best player they could be.

Honestly, I think I earnt the respect of the players and of the supporters too. They came to see that I absolutely loved Hampshire cricket. No doubt, there is something special about that club. I have only ever been a one-club player – St Kilda, where I'm a life member, Victoria, the Rajasthan Royals, Melbourne Stars and Hampshire. That's the lot.

I have to say that I've never felt more liked and valued than I did during those eight years involved with Hampshire, and especially the last four as captain. I sensed people were grateful for the time and effort I put in. I'm very thankful to them too. The county was my second home for a long while and I loved every second. I loved living at Ocean Village in the house I bought from Matt Le Tissier – the brilliant Southampton and England footballer – and loved life on the road with the other players too.

Throughout that four-year period of my captaincy, the standard of the first division of county cricket was high. In fact, I'd say that the top four teams – Notts, Sussex, Lancashire and us – would have gone well in the Sheffield Shield at that time. Victoria vs New South Wales matches are the toughest first-class cricket I have played, but 2004 and 2005 in England was pretty good. I'm proud to have played my part in that.

Thanks . . .

. . . Go to that sensational man Wilfrid Weld, President and then Patron of Hampshire, who so sadly passed away a couple of years ago; to Tim Tremlett, 'Trooper', a former player who became director of cricket and the best of blokes with a sneaky good sense of humour; and to Rod Bransgrove, the chairman, for his vision, support and friendship. If you go down to the Ageas Bowl now – as the Rose Bowl is known these days – you'll find the most beautiful place for cricket with the best facilities anywhere. It's Rod's baby and just amazing. Geez, the more I think about it the more fun I remember it being. Perhaps, best of all, the brand of cricket we played brought a lot of pleasure to a lot of people. There is not much more rewarding than that.

When Wilfrid stood down as President in 2002, he was succeeded by Colin Ingleby-Mackenzie, the captain when the club won the championship for the first time in 1961. A great bloke, very funny, but a loose cannon on his day. At the AGM when I took over as captain, he stood up to make the big welcome speech and in that slightly mad, incredibly enthusiastic voice of his said, 'Well, we are very, very lucky to have one of the great men and one of the greatest cricketers of all time as our new captain. What's more he's been voted one of *Wisden*'s Five Greatest Cricketers of the Century so nothing is beyond him. For goodness sake, we've seen him give us Poms a monumental thrashing for years, but the great thing now is that we can call him one of us, a Hampshire player through and through, and a terrific captain – just the best! It's going to be an exciting ride for us all.'

Then he paused, and said, 'And for all the women out there, lock up your daughters because Warne's in town!'

He did, honestly. And there were 500 people there who knew I was married. Worse, Simone was sitting next to me. 'Did he really just say that? Is this bloke for real?!' she asked.

I said, 'Yes, oh yes, great bloke Ingleby, just taking the mickey.'

Everyone's gone, 'Oh, no!' You could feel the room cringing, but he got away with it. He would – he was Ingleby.

I invited him into the dressing-room all the time. 'Come on, tell us a few stories, Pres,' I'd say, and, sure enough, the President could tell a story! 'Play started at 11.30 in those days and as we headed to the bar after stumps had been pulled for the day, I used to tell the lads it was crucial to be in by 11 o'clock, to be sure you get a good half hour's sleep before the start of play the next morning!'

He had us in stitches every time. I know the stories are old hat now, but we didn't know them and loved hearing them and feeling his huge optimism rubbing off on us. What a special guy.

I mention Ingleby because the two of us have had stands named after us at the Ageas Bowl. It's such a great honour. I'm very, very proud of that. He was a legend of the club and to be alongside him is really something. I think it shows we did some good things in those years, some of the happiest of my cricket life.

The Future, Briefly

I can't pretend I've made a detailed study on another way forward for first-class cricket in England, but I've always had strong views, and after playing for Hampshire I feel qualified to put them forward. A lot of people think the two-division format works well and that the new T20 league will shore up the other comps that struggle to make ends meet. I know many counties wouldn't exist without the money they get each year from the ECB, which, in the end, is money from television rights.

I always felt there were too many teams, too many players and too many games, which dilutes the standard. There are plenty of talented players in England but a whole bunch of them just cruise, earning a living without pulling a finger out. It's a nice life and difficult to leave behind once it's over. That's why a lot of guys struggle in their next life. The system has allowed them to drift and the price is higher than people understand. If they were told at the start that they weren't good enough, they'd go off and find another way to make a living, instead of wasting five, maybe 10, of the best years of their lives.

County cricket should be a representation of international cricket, and to make the competition tougher they need to get rid of the deadwood. Twelve county teams playing each other once in four-day cricket seems about right to me; maybe with a final, as in the Sheffield Shield, to give the county season a climax. Though a part of me thinks that the team which has worked hardest to win the league should keep the trophy. I leave that choice to the marketeers!

Then a 50-over knockout, replicating global tournaments, and one big, all singing and dancing T20 super league – definitely not The Hundred that has been proposed. Cricket does not need another format. It's arguably overkill to have three different types of the game as it is.

Each club would employ a maximum of 25 players and run a second XI that competes on a similar basis. This means a few counties would have to merge, providing greater strength anyway. I know I'm a bit one-eyed about the standard of first-class cricket in Australia, but not many people would deny that the Sheffield Shield has been the strongest first-class competition for 100 years, and that nowadays the Big Bash is pushing the IPL to be the best T20 comp in the world. England could do worse than follow those models.

I think loyalty to the club that raised you is really important. At the moment people are swapping counties like kids used to swap football cards. If you're any good, you want to be in first division so you're not going to stay with a club that struggles in the second division. If there was one division, the loyalty would be easier to demand. I also believe that international players have to play first-class cricket for their counties more than they do. And, by the way, that doesn't just apply to county cricket – it's a global thing. There's not enough respect for the roots that made you what you are in the first place.

People say there's so much more cricket these days. That's rubbish. I'd argue there's less. For instance, take an Ashes series. We used to arrive in early May and leave in September. Before a series there were at least three three-day county games and then between Test matches plenty more. In 1993 I bet I bowled more balls than just about anybody out there.

The challenge for the guys these days is the different forms of cricket, which are hard to adjust to and hard on your body. Twenty20 cricket alone is a massive physical challenge – four pressure overs, sometimes in one-over spells, and throwing yourself about in the field. I've heard people say, 'It's only four overs,' but, believe me, those 24 balls take it out of you. So T20 needs its own window, like the IPL. Obviously that has to happen when it's most commercially viable, because the current T20 Blast – never mind the new super league or whatever they end up calling it – is a key element of county income outside of the ECB handout, and what all the boards need to remember about 20/20 is that less is more.

There would be no problem finding that window if there were only 12 fully professional county teams. Fewer players means a stronger tournament. End of story.

14

Ashes to Ashes

I DIDN'T GROW UP salivating about the Ashes. As I've mentioned, the first Ashes experience that made an impression on me was when my brother Jason and I saw AB and Thommo's last-wicket stand at the MCG in 1982/83. I was in my early teens by then. Ian Botham was a huge figure at the time, a Pom we loved to hate. He played the game a bit more like an Aussie – attacking and in your face. If anyone was taking that final wicket, it was a relief that it was a bloke who played like one of us. Having said that, we went home with a kind of hangdog expression. Losing hurt, even then.

The Ashes really got a grip of me in 1989 in England, when AB's team won 4–0 against the odds. I was watching plenty of county cricket and kept an eye out for the blokes who could play – Gooch, Gatting, Gower, Lamb and Robin Smith, already a favourite of mine, were the best. England had won the previous two series, home and away, so this was a turn-up and great for a young Aussie playing the Bristol league. It meant the Poms couldn't gang up on me in the pub! Did I think I'd be a part of it one day? No way. I still had footy ringing round my head, but I suppose just through being in England as a club pro, my ambitions were changing.

By the time I came back to play in the Lancashire League in 1991, I'd already made my debut in first-class cricket and was all over it. In fact, I was so driven to succeed that I could already see how far I had to go and that I wouldn't get there without a real lifestyle commitment to the game. It was another seven or eight months before Terry Jenner explained exactly what that meant.

By the English summer of 1993, when I was picked for my first tour of England, I couldn't get going fast enough. The Ashes had its grip on me and that flight to the UK, sitting next to Merv and listening to his stories, had me pulling on the leash! It was a great series for me, not least because of that moment that changed my life; and it was an even greater series for the Australian team as we gathered more experience and belief in the quest to beat West Indies and be acknowledged as the best cricket team in the world.

I strongly believe there is a kind of magic in the Gatting ball, something that leaves the audience at first shocked, and then amazed. This applies to the person who made it happen too – I was pretty overwhelmed myself. I think that when a sportsman does something out of the ordinary – something so spectacular that those watching couldn't imagine doing themselves, especially on that kind of stage – the audience is taken to another place. Peter Such got 6/67 in our first innings, a good effort against a good side, and I took eight in the match, but that one single delivery to Gatt is the piece of cricket that everyone remembers. I was there, they say, or I saw it live. It must have been a big audience then!

In the series back at home in 1994/95, I bowled about as well as I can, with a career-best 8/71 at the Gabba and the hat-trick at the MCG. I still love listening to Greigy's call when Devon Malcolm prods forward and Babsie takes off to his right. 'Oh, he's got 'im, has 'ee caught him, yes he has, he's caught it at short-leg, he's gone, he's got 'im, it's a hat-trick, that's the hat-trick for Shane Warne, a great moment in his career, what a catch by David Boon . . .!' Love it!

I remember how clammy my hands were before that ball, how everything went by in a flash and suddenly I was running at Babs. I was relieved. I mean, I'll never get a better chance – no disrespect,

Dev! – so I was relieved to get it. I caught a few in my time at slip but when I dropped Damien Fleming's hat-trick ball against India in 1999, I felt sick. Flem says he's spent every day since thinking about it. I say no-one deserves two hat-tricks. He'd got one on debut, and only two other blokes have ever done that. So don't be greedy, Flem.

The more you play Ashes cricket, the more you feel the history. At first, it's a bit of a blur, with the event seeming even bigger than the game itself, especially in the first match of a series. After a while, you begin to understand the legacy left by the past players and matches and where the heated rivalry comes from. It's a part of national identity. This was shown really well in the documentary Cricket Australia released on Channel Nine last year called *Forged in Fire*. Former players from both countries talked passionately about the reasons it means so much to them, like it's a human drama as well as a sporting one. That old thing of the toffee-nosed English and the convict Aussies will never go away. It's something we play on but actually I think we truly respect each other. We like their humour, they like our never-say-die attitude to life.

The Ashes is bigger than ever now, and getting bigger still. Social media, extensive TV coverage and the desperation of the two cricket boards to milk it dry have seen to that. Most players would agree that an Ashes series can define their career. Think Andrew Flintoff, for example, in 2005 and 2009. His performances over those two English summers turned him into a superstar, even though his overall Test record never reached that Ashes level.

If I was honest, I'd say that beating the Poms lost a bit of its gloss after the eight consecutive huge series margins between 1989 and 2002/03. The result had become predictable: we knew we'd win, they knew we'd win. It wasn't as if we weren't proud of what we achieved but, other than the odd game here and there, England just froze against us and everyone realised what was coming. This really came home when Channel Nine decided not to bid for the rights to the coverage of the tour to England in 2005. SBS got it and, had the series followed the pattern of the previous 15 years, it would have been pretty much hidden from view in Oz. But it didn't and it wasn't. England won, with the better team over the five matches. The tension at Edgbaston, Old Trafford, Trent Bridge and the Oval was incredible.

I figured England would be good. After my first summer back with Hampshire in 2004, I sensed a much more competitive game and a much more professional attitude towards it. Michael Vaughan was a smart and steely captain, happy to mix it with anyone. The bowlers had pace and aggression. I wasn't so sure about the middle-order batting but the top three could play – Marcus Trescothick, Andrew Strauss, Vaughan – and score quickly when need be. Then when KP came to Hampshire for the 2005 season and I saw him up close, I said publicly that I thought England should pick him straight away and, to their credit, they did just that.

I watched them in South Africa, a few months before we played them, and was impressed by their willingness to go all out for a win. Before Vaughan became captain, the England sides that I played against erred on the side of safety, first trying not to lose, even from a position of strength. Mark Taylor was a master of the declaration because he understood that the risk of losing created the chance to win. I loved that. Vaughan understood it too.

Of course, we'd won a lot of Test matches over a long period. England hadn't. That breeds confidence and self-belief, or some might call it cockiness. The Judge told me that England won only 14 of the 62 Tests he played in. A reason might be the 69 players chosen alongside him over the eight years he was in the team. To put that in perspective, I played with 58 different guys over 145 Tests and was on the winning side 92 times.

Selectors have a lot to answer for if they're indecisive and/or inconsistent. But when they get it right, they show how crucial a role they play. Sportsmen need to feel safe to feel free. Caution can easily override instinct and if your place in the side is uncertain, you'll never relax and be the performer you are deep down. The Aussie selectors got it right for the Ashes last summer for example, and a good side was shaping up until the ball-tampering day in Cape Town in March when the whole thing went pear-shaped. Trevor Hohns must have been spitting. He'd come back to the job in difficult circumstances

16 months earlier after the humiliating defeat by South Africa in Hobart and made a lot of smart decisions. Then a moment of madness set everything back again.

Back to England in 2005. For the first time that I'd known, they definitely thought they could beat us. It was Vaughan who got that change of attitude across to his players, convincing them that they had nothing to fear. The selectors supported his approach by making a couple of brave choices in KP and Ian Bell, which meant dumping Graham Thorpe who was carrying a lot of baggage, especially against Australia. Thorpey made his debut in 1993 and was a good player, but 12 years later still hadn't played in a winning series against us. Bell was a gamble, one for the future. Pietersen was a no-brainer.

The hype before Lord's was something else. The papers were full of it and tickets were going nuts on the black market. It felt different, like the real deal. I remember thinking that Kerry might have made one of his few mistakes in not getting those television rights. The day before the game, the Nursery ground was heaving with spectators, more like Kolkata than London. The nets had a million cameras everywhere and media people were requesting interview after interview and filing report after report. There were features all over the television channels and radio networks and more selfies and autographs than seemed possible, day after day.

To be honest, I wasn't in great form with the ball. With the bat, yes; in fact, I made two hundreds for Hampshire that year, the second of them at Southgate against Middlesex in the last county game before joining the Aussie boys for the Test series. Truth be told, though, I should have bowled Middlesex out on a pitch that turned miles, but I didn't. I bowled crap. The ball felt kind of stuck in my hand, like I couldn't release it with much more than a push of my wrist, arm and upper body.

It was the old story – no feel and no rhythm means no form. I called TJ, who joined us for the voluntary top-up net session we always had the day before a Test match, and he and I stayed till 5 pm that evening. For me to bowl for almost five hours the day before a game was, to say the least, unusual, but I wasn't walking away from those nets till I was right.

Gilly stayed for a while, taking a lot of balls. It was a valuable time for us both. TJ got my arm a little higher and had me spinning the ball 'up' rather than firing it into the pitch. When a pitch really spins, like Southgate did, the temptation is to bowl it hard into the surface and especially into the rough. This means you lose shape out of the hand and tempo in the action. Nothing is in sync, like a batsman trying to hit the ball too hard. In county cricket I was bowling a lot of overs, often blocking up an end, rather than looking to take wickets. Maybe that's why I lost rhythm. Anyway, by the time we finished I was happy, really fizzing them again – got the slider humming, actually, which it hadn't for a while – without any sense of effort. From nowhere when I got up in the morning, to the close of business on the eve of the 2005 Ashes, I knew I was ready to go. What a turnaround. I was excited. My mind was clear and my body had recovered its relationship with leg-spin.

If You Fail to Prepare, You Prepare to Fail

I was huge on my preparation. I didn't like all the silly team meetings, they were just a waste of time because generally, as I've mentioned, no matter what team you were playing for, everybody would talk about the same stuff. Occasionally, there would be an obvious weakness to exploit, like someone who couldn't play the short ball – Graeme Hick in 1993, when Merv just went for him in a hardcore kind of way; Jonathan Trott in 2013/14, when I told Michael Clarke that the quicks should just pepper him, nothing else – or a guy who was clearly weak against spin, like Daryll Cullinan. Otherwise, it was all pretty repetitive and not worth the time spent on it. *Yawn*.

(Actually, on the subject of the fast bowlers, in the Caribbean in the mid-1990s Mark Taylor told us we were going to bounce the shit out of their tail, come what may. It's time for the bullies to be bullied, he said, which got the bowlers looking sideways at each other! We took a few hits along the way, but overall it worked well and we won in the Caribbean for the first time since 1973. Give as good as you get!)

The ideal preparation is both physical and mental. If you have things on your mind, you have to get rid of them, otherwise no way can you feel fresh and relaxed. These might include anything from a lingering business issue, to a family thing, to comp tickets that need sorting for mates or a tough cricket decision on the morning of the match. For me that summer, it was the stress I'd caused the children that made the build-up to the series so difficult and mentally consuming. I'm lucky that I sleep well, whatever my state of mind, but it was harder during that series than ever before.

The day spent with TJ probably saved me. It occupied my mind with a series of other issues, each of which could be resolved with some hard yards in the nets. In summary, whatever it takes to close the door on the things that are nagging at you, do it; otherwise your concentration will suffer. In general, once I was across the white line, out there in my space, I was fine. In 2005, I left it late.

Then there's the physical side. On the days before a Test match I would never, ever leave the nets until I was happy with my bowling. The hours didn't matter, the ball I was bowling did. Some days it would only take half an hour to be sure that I had the rhythm and feel, other days five hours. After that I'd have a massage; treatment to loosen up my shoulder, forearm, wrist and fingers. My forearm used to get really stiff, so Errol Alcott used to massage the thing until it hurt really bad and I couldn't take any more. Then he'd move on to the back of my shoulders and my neck, everywhere in that area, so that it was all as loose as it could possibly be. Thinking back, we could go through this process almost every day.

I stopped batting in the nets after 2000 when I lost confidence on a bad surface. I went to throw-downs only, which worked fine for the two things that mattered most to me – watching the ball and timing the ball. We all spent a lot of time with short, sharp catching sessions – not more than 20 minutes but very active and full of purpose and energy, which we'd learnt from Simmo – and ground fielding, where we rehearsed attacking the ball hard and throwing down the stumps. That was about it.

The guys used to play a lot of that stupid touch rugby or other games that I hated. I just had no interest at all and kept asking how much longer this rubbish was going on for. Honestly, on the morning of the match even an Aussie Rules ball didn't do much for me. I just didn't get that stuff and I still don't when I see sides warming up with a game of football on the morning of a Test match.

The days before the game are a slightly different story. I was always up for throwing an Aussie Rules footy around, but not much more. The other thing I hated was the stretching but, if I had my time again, it's the one part of my preparation that I'd look to improve. My upper body was okay, hips not bad, but I've got the worst hamstrings you can possibly imagine. It probably goes back to when I was a kid and broke both my legs. Whatever, all I know is that I wasn't the most supple person on the planet and should have stretched a whole lot more.

When you bowl 35 overs in a day, the next day hurts. To get out of bed then, geez, everything hurts – everything. Add in a late night, 10 vodka/Red Bulls and 50 fags: well, I'd have to say I was a legend to have turned my arm over the following morning! Apparently, Garry Sobers was a genius of the 'next day' after a big night out. Ian Botham wasn't bad either. I get it. Sometimes you need that escape, for whatever reason, and then, wow, you'd better perform, so you do.

It's X-rated, though. I mean, if you said to Justin Langer or one of those guys, 'Come out with me till three or four in the morning drinking and smoking,' they wouldn't be able to turn up the next day, let alone play. But it worked for me because I was being myself – not every night, but often enough to escape and chill. For some guys a few beers in the changing-room is enough to relax. I'd have the odd ice-cold one after a hard bowling day, but just a soda or a lemon, lime, bitters if we'd been batting.

People think I'm this bloke out on the piss every night, but I go three, four days or much longer without a drink. I don't need to drink but I do need some fun. If you remember, I said that when I started, all I drank was beer. Having learnt how to drink 10 pints in my Bristol days, I'd have 12 or 15 cans after training, out the back of Mum and Dad's house back in Oz. Then TJ got into me and changed the way I thought. Why ruin it all for beer? Good question, so I didn't. When we won a Test match, I'd be the first one to party and the last one to leave. Thank God I came to realise there was a time and a place.

Let's get back to the morning of a match for a minute. With the Rajasthan Royals in the IPL, I came up with a theory that warm-ups were not warm-ups at all. Throughout most of my career, the routine was to get to the ground, run around together, have a net, drift back to the rooms, listen to the result of the toss and then we'd cool down for half an hour. To me, that's crazy. A warm-up is to warm up! So, with the Royals, I changed that. We'd get to the ground 15 minutes before the toss: if we were batting first, the batsmen had some throw-downs; if we were bowling, the bowlers had a few looseners. Everyone went through some short, sharp and simple fielding drills.

My theory was that your preparation should have been completed the day before a match, so that you didn't have anything to do on the day itself, other than loosen the body and mind. Don't use up the energy and focus that you'll need later, I would say. No worries if you're the sort of person who needs to feel bat on ball, take a few catches, calm your nerves, get a feel for the ground, meditate at the pitch. That's all fine, but it doesn't have to take an hour, or two hours, or whatever some teams take. You don't need a lot of time, you really don't, you just need to be ready. Then it was a quick reminder of how we wanted to play, the things we did best and an emphasis on the fact that if we stuck with our game plan we'd win through. 'Let's give it to them early,' I'd tell them, 'take wickets in the first six overs; hold nothing back. Just go for it, guys.' No stupid huddle thing – or the cuddle, I call it – just get out there and get stuck in. I really enjoyed that.

There's no reason this method can't be applied to Test cricket. It makes sense, common sense. Most warm-ups are for show, justifying the jobs of the too many people who hang around the team these days – the fitness guy, the masseuse, the analyst, the therapist, the bowling coach, batting coach, team coach, manager. There are more, actually, but I'm tired just thinking about them. I think Gavin Dovey, the Aussie manager in South Africa, had 12 blokes on his support staff. That is too many!

A Test match day is made up of three sessions of play, every one as important as the last. Why add a fourth?! Save energy and give it to 'em after tea. That final session, even the final half hour, can make or break a day. Don't be knackered for it, which so many current players are. The number of runs scored between lunch and tea on an average Test match day is ridiculous. And guess why? Bowlers and fielders lose concentration because they're tired!

Finally on this subject, outside of stretching and loosening the muscles and joints, the hour before play should be based entirely on traditional cricket-specific skills. All this reinventing the wheel of how to pick up, throw and hit the stumps with balls flying everywhere drives me crazy. Just hit the ball at me, let me pick it up properly and throw it at the stumps, because that's how it happens in a match. Simulate that match skill with proper nicks, proper ground fielding, high balls and low balls, just as they come in a match.

It is *not* a fitness session. If it's a fitness session you want, do one on another day – but don't combine the two. Cricket is about doing the basics better than the next bloke, so simulate the basics, focus on match awareness, and understand the angles. Establish some facts that might provide you with an advantage: where is the sun; where are the good and bad backdrops for picking up the ball; is the pitch on a higher level than the area on which you'll be catching that ball; is one boundary particularly short, or another ridiculously long?

It's simple – practise the challenges you're most likely to face. The focus on tactics is no different – yes, keep an open mind and stay flexible, but keep it simple. In the field, if you concentrate on bowling dots, stopping the ball when it comes your way, catching it in the air, and therefore building pressure, you'll be hard to play against. Again, with the bat, if you rotate the strike, punish the bad ball and don't lose wickets in clumps, you'll go okay. If you do these things better than the opposition, you'll win.

London, Birmingham, Manchester

At least, that's the theory. One of the things I like most about cricket is that you never really know what will happen after you've walked through that little gate. For example, I was an odds-on favourite to bowl Middlesex out at Southgate, but couldn't do it. Some days you knock 'em over and others they slog you into the stands; some days you catch a ripper and others you drop a soda; some days you feel like Bradman, others like Benny Hill. That's the game.

Ricky won the toss on that first morning of the 2005 Ashes and batted. The noise when England walked out was more AFL grand final than Ashes first morning at ever so polite Lord's. Matthew Hoggard knocked over Matthew Hayden and Steve Harmison hit Ricky in the head. Suddenly, it was more heavyweight title fight than AFL. We were bowled out in 40 overs for 190 and then bowled England out in 48 for 155. 'Christ,' I said to Pup, 'this series won't take long!'

Pup had other ideas and played well for 91 in the second dig. England had to make 420 to win and made 180. Pidge took nine wickets in the match. In the first over after tea on the first day, he got rid of Trescothick and Strauss with good balls. Not long after, he hit the stumps three times – Vaughan, Bell, Flintoff. Nice job. Pidge loves Lord's. I took six wickets and like it too. I'd have a lot more wickets there if Pidge hadn't been around. What a place to play cricket it is. (Oh, and KP played great. Those English selectors never miss a beat, eh!)

I don't think Pidge is so keen on Edgbaston. Before the second Test, during the morning 'warm-up' – ha, ha – a game of touch rugby ('When will this be over?!'), he trod on a cricket ball and did a ligament. In came Kasprowicz for McGrath and up went the coin. Ricky won again and batted, of course. Errrr, no. Ricky won the toss, and bowled. At lunch England were 1/130 and I was already hard into it; or maybe I should say the Poms were hard into me. Ricky's decision was a shocker, presumably thinking that one good morning with the ball would finish England off. He didn't rate the English batting and it cost him, and us.

Here is the truth. Forget anything else you've heard or read. Ricky relied on John Buchanan's stats, which indicated that the bowl-first, bat-last tactic at Edgbaston won more games than it lost. He looked back at the filthy weather of the previous few days, not forward, and made an assumption about the pitch having moisture in it. Wrong!

It was a belter, an absolute road, which was to spin later in the game. He ignored McGrath's injury because arrogance refused to let him believe England could play. The entire series was defined right there, at Edgbaston, when Ricky was blind to the cricketing facts in front of him. England were thrown a huge bone and fed from it for the rest of the series. I rate it as the worst decision made by a captain I played under, just topping the charts ahead of Steve Waugh when he made India follow-on, because it was based on arrogance about the opposition and our own supposed invincibility, not the cricketing facts.

England scored 407 in 79.2 overs at more than five an over, the fastest run rate in a single day by an England team since the Second World War! They should have made more, actually, but got over-excited, which is why we took 10 wickets. There you go, that's the reason I like cricket. You just never know.

Both sides batted at breakneck speed, but with the opposite effect to Lord's – i.e. England better than Australia this time. Two days later, when Saturday's play finished – the third day, that is – England had claimed the extra half an hour to try and win the game, but not managed to do so. I was still there, slogging sixes off 'Gilo', but then watched in horror as Pup was cleaned up by Harmison's slower yorker off the last ball – as it turned out – of the day. Eight down at the close of play and still needing 107. Nothing is impossible, I said to myself.

Next morning, with the crowd on the razzle long before play even began, Brett Lee – 'Binga' – and me decided to just enjoy ourselves in the distant hope of chasing down the remaining runs to go 2–0 up. This approach took the pressure off a bit and England began to get edgy. Binga took a few blows, while I cut, swept, slogged and slashed. He survived, I scored. Suddenly we'd put on 45. Then I went back to Freddie, right back to a full ball around leg-stump, and trod on my stumps. I'd never done that before in my life and never did again. Nine down now, and we still needed 62.

The England bowlers were swinging the ball at pace, but not so accurately as the day before. Bing and Kasper continued to play freely, pretty much like it didn't matter, because no-one thought it did. England tightened up as the expectation gnawed away at them. We all know what it's like – LBWs turned down, a catch dropped, a mistake in the field. They all build up. As we crept closer to the target, the pressure levelled out. With only four needed, Binga smashed a square drive off Harmison out to deep cover. A couple of yards either way and it would have been over. Next ball, it was.

We've all seen the Kasprowicz wicket a thousand times. Short ball from 'Harmy', Kasper half-ducks, half-fends, and Geraint Jones dives down the leg-side to take an important catch – the most important catch of his life, the catch that woke up a whole nation! These days, DRS would have overturned it because the glove the ball hit was just off the handle. No worries. England deserved the win. Freddie had a great match. I had a good one too. But what mattered was the cricket. It's been called the greatest Test match ever, and it's hard to argue with that.

The picture of Freddie consoling Binga is right up there with any sporting photo I've seen. It summed it all up better than words in press conferences; in fact, it summed up the series every bit as much as the Edgbaston Test. Both sides played tough and fair and appreciated each other's performances. That sportsmanship and the level of skill in the cricket captured the imagination of cricket lovers from Manchester to Melbourne.

And, talking of Manchester, on we all went to Old Trafford, that place in Manchester where it rains a lot and Mike Gatting missed a good ball. And, this time around, Shane Warne missed another chance to make a Test match hundred.

Edgbaston 2005 was the ultimate sporting drama, marginally ahead of Headingley 1981, Adelaide 1993, Barbados 1999 and Kolkata 2001. Why do we always lose these thrillers? I guess it's because when we win, we clean up, and when we get pushed hard, we stay with it till the end – until the ship goes down, so to speak. Old Trafford 2005 wasn't so bad a game either. The clue is that it went to the last ball and, by then, everyone's nails were chewed off and down their throats.

England were due to win a toss and made it count. McGrath bowled Vaughan with a no-ball and Gilly dropped him the very next ball. Vaughany made a brilliant hundred after the let-offs and others weighed in. Trescothick was my 600th Test wicket. The moment was an anti-climax as it kind of came off the back of Tres's bat and gently looped up to Gilly, but the achievement, at that time in my life, was something I shall always treasure.

A lot was made of me kissing the white wristband Brooke had given me. 'Be strong, Daddy,' she said, when a tabloid newspaper printed more accusations against me by a woman just a day or two after the family arrived from Australia in the build-up to the Lord's Test. By then, my marriage to Simone was all but over, not that we had told the kids. Therefore the shock of this story was exaggerated. Simone took them back home immediately, like a couple of days later, which made the tour painful for me off the field.

It's one of the reasons I'm especially proud of my performances over all the five Tests. And I was even more proud of Brooke, who was seven, going on eight, and old enough to understand that things weren't good for her mum and me. Once the family was back in Oz, I spoke to the kids pretty much every day on the phone, and when I raised my arms to thank the crowd for their applause, I kissed the wristband as an open message of thanks and love to Brooke. Printed on it was the word 'Strength' – pretty good from a seven-year-old.

Not even that wristband could get me a hundred in a Test match, though. I holed out to deep square-leg hooking at Simon Jones. Four years earlier, I was one short when I slog/swept Dan Vettori to deep mid-wicket in Perth; this time, at Old Trafford, I still had to get 10 more. You'd think I'd have taken it a bit easy in the 90s, but that's not how I roll. Once adrenaline kicks in, the native instinct to attack takes over. (I twice made 86s, out hooking Wasim Akram at the Gabba, and LBW to Kumble in Adelaide playing all round a straight ball in an attempt to steal the strike!)

It's well known that we drew the game, nine down, thanks to a special innings by Punter. Those lucky enough to have tickets spent the day on the edge of their seats after 10,000 more had lined the streets outside the ground begging for a way to get in.

Briefly, Punter had looked like he might win it on his own, but more than 400 in the last innings of a Test match is exactly that, more than 400, and usually well out of reach. I hung on for an hour and 40 minutes with him, and hope remained while Ricky remained.

He was eventually caught down the leg-side by Geraint Jones off a Harmison short ball – echoes of Edgbaston once more – after batting for nearly seven hours. Binga was good again, batting really bravely for 45 minutes till the end, and, incredibly, so was the Pigeon, who survived an unlikely nine balls in the final 17 minutes of the match. Our dressing-room was a relieved place, though the smiles and handshakes on the balcony prompted Vaughan to get his guys together and say, 'Look, the mighty Aussies are celebrating a draw with England. We've got them now.' Not a bad team talk that.

Those balcony smiles of ours hid an increasingly moody attitude. We weren't playing as well as we should or could, and it was niggling away at us. You could say the boot was on the other foot and the challenge was to drag ourselves back into the series with better cricket.

On the bus on the way back to the hotel after the game, John Buchanan called a team meeting. I was like, 'Oh no, what's he going to say now?'

We collected in the team room and he started with an obvious line, something like, 'We didn't play very well again this game.'

Yep, true, Buck.

Then he said, 'But why didn't we play well?'

Maybe you tell us, Buck. So he did. It was along the lines of 'I don't think you blokes care enough and, playing like you are, I don't think you're worthy of wearing the baggy green cap.'

I could sense the rage bubbling in the room and could feel it burning inside me, but I waited for the captain, anyone, to say something. Everyone sat there quietly, heads down, no-one willing to get involved.

I thought, 'To hell with this,' stood up and said, 'Buck, don't you ever tell me I don't care enough and that I'm not worthy of wearing the baggy green cap. I've busted my balls for a long time, so has everyone else in this room, so how about we just play and you keep your thoughts to yourself.'

McGrath said, 'I'm with Warney.' Magilla said, 'I'm with Warney too.' Ricky was like, 'Hey, hey, alright, calm down, you blokes.' I said, 'Fuck this meeting, I'm not taking this shit from him,' and started to walk out.

There is no-one who can say I'm not worthy of the baggy green – no-one. John Buchanan would have no idea how much blood and sweat I've put in, never mind the tears, especially on that tour. That's not just me either, it's all the guys. We've all busted our guts and given it everything. Punter said, 'Hey, let's calm down.' But I had mentally gone. 'This meeting is over, Punt,' I said, and was out of there. Buck never really understood when to make a point and when not. It was like he couldn't judge the moment. He thought he knew us but he didn't. And that was proved time and time again with these ridiculous meetings.

Coaches

Here is the thing with coaches. They're an integral part of the game in first-class cricket, second XI cricket, age groups, development programs, all those areas. Basically, at every level of the game beneath international cricket, because by the time you play for your country, you should know the mechanics of what you're doing and you should know yourself. Having said that, I know how valuable it is to have someone to talk to, like Terry Jenner. So, as far as I'm concerned, the role is less coaching than mentoring and guiding – a job the manager should be able to do.

The power of the mind and the intricacies of tactics are things you find out about along the way. Simmo was the best, then Greg Shipperd. I rate Trevor Bayliss and Darren Berry too. They all know every aspect and detail of cricket and had relevant things to offer. I had the impression that was the case with Duncan Fletcher for England, who the England boys said was very good too. Whoever it is should be in the background and allowing the captain to run the team.

Say, for example, if Kevin Pietersen gets out three or four times in a row for low scores, it might not be anything to do with technique but, instead, will be about concentration or a thought process. KP loved to smack people out of the ground. There is a time and a place for that approach and only a person with an understanding of the game and KP could have taken him aside and talked in detail to him about shot selection. Simmo would have been able to; maybe Fletcher did, but Buchanan couldn't.

In 2001 Buck came up with this theory based on a book called *The Art of War* by a Chinese military leader from way back, Sun Tzu. *The Art of War*, I mean, please. We all had two pages of A4 with Sun Tzu's teachings on them put under our hotel-room doors. At a meeting Buchanan said, 'Right, who has read these?' Mark Waugh, Andrew Symonds and me said we'd thrown them in the bin. Next day, one of the British papers printed a front-page picture of Steve Waugh dressed like a Chinese general, sword and all, and with the rest of us in smaller pictures as old-style Chinese soldiers all around him, like in a picture frame. We were 2–0 up in the series and a laughing stock.

Next day, Darren Gough was bowling to Junior, who easily drove him through mid-on and mid-off for a few boundaries. Exasperated, Goughie stopped in his follow-through after the last of them and began a long spiel to Athers at slip in mock Chinese. During the spiel he reset his field with a couple of blokes out deep on the leg-side. Then he charged in and, with a quick bouncer, smashed Junior full on the helmet. Junior hit the deck, hard. Goughie followed through and, standing near Junior now, said, 'Hey, Athers, I fookin' told you he wouldn't oonderstand Chinese!'

Sun Tzu!

On reflection, to have or not to have a coach is about that coach being the right person. Then a kick up the arse from that person will mean every bit as much as an arm round the shoulder. John Buchanan kicking us up the arse was a disaster, partly because he coached by a book, rather than a feel, and let analytics overtake common sense. The job, whatever you call it, is about knowing the people you're working with. Time after time, it was clear that he didn't know me or a number of others in the team. This created disharmony and led to problems and, at times, conflict.

Buck also finished up on the wrong side of other teams he worked with, so it isn't just me who's had a problem with him. He was once asked, 'Do you think the Australian cricket team has made you or have you made the team?' 'No comment,' he said. No comment! Is he kidding, or what? Enough said.

In writing my own book, I've altered my position on a few things and, having thought more deeply about the role of a coach, I would no longer say that the only thing a coach is good for in cricket is to drive the players to and from the ground. A good coach has a role if he is the right bloke. Simple. It doesn't work if it's the wrong bloke. Anyway, I think it's the title I don't like – manager will do nicely.

Trent Bridge

Only once in my career did I get on the piss during a Test match and let it affect my cricket the next day. That once was Trent Bridge, 2005.

England won the toss again and made plenty first up. Freddie got a hundred. We were bowled out cheaply; me, first ball. I couldn't see the bloody thing because I'd been up till five or six in the morning and spent most of the day nodding off in the changing-room. When Simon Jones bowled a normal length ball, I just spooned it up in the air like I was a clubby. Embarrassing. It was the one time in the series when the pressure of everything that summer had got to me a bit and I desperately needed to let my hair down. Not good. I just sort of sat there thinking, 'Please make us follow on, Vaughany, I need some sleep. And if you do, and we bat better second time round, I promise to all Australia I will win us the game.'

He did, he put us back in! The first two things I thought were *phew* and Kolkata.

The guys really battled in the second innings, with just about everyone chipping in with useful scores, but never quite putting England away. I was going well with Simon Katich when he got a shocking LBW. There's no way it was out. It pitched way outside leg and hit him high anyway, but at the time it was one of those that looked kind of okay, even though replays showed differently.

He came to me at the non-strikers end and said, 'Was that out?'

'I don't know,' I answered. 'Maybe not.'

'Was that fucking out?' he asked, by now steaming. I thought he might hit me, never mind a Pom or an ump.

'Er, no, don't think so, mate. It pitched outside leg and was too high.'

Then he turned to the umpires and went 'Fuck you' before storming off, yelling at everyone like the angriest man in the world. Not that I blamed him. He'd worked his nuts off for 59 runs over four hours and 20 minutes. Another half an hour or so of the two of us might have swung it our way.

It's worth saying here that the whole changing-room was already steaming after Punter's run out by the sub fielder, Gary Pratt. An English journo, Martin Johnson, wrote that there were two Pratts involved – meaning Pratt and Ponting – but it was probably more Marto's bad call and Punter's slow response than anything. So maybe there were three Pratts!

England had taken advantage of the sub-fielder rule all tour by having county specialists available and getting them on where possible in place of tired bowlers. When Punter reached the pavilion steps and looked up to see Fletcher looking down smugly, he gave the England coach a gob full. Actually, in this instance Pratt was on for Simon Jones, who was genuinely injured and didn't bowl all innings. Anyway, Binga came in, hit a couple of massive sixes and played great again. I made 45 before Ashley-hit-me-miles had me stumped by Jones – that's a death and a half! We were bowled out for 387, leaving England 129 to win.

I said to Punter, 'Let me open the bowling.' I was desperate to get at them with that new nut. But he didn't. Unfortunately.

Trescothick was hammering the new ball and I was just watching the scoreboard roll over like a pokey machine. 120 to win, 110 to win, 100 to win, less than 100 – I was like, I need to bowl, mate. At 0/32, Punter called me up and first ball I got a wicket, Trescothick bat-pad; then Strauss caught down the leg-side, before Vaughan tried to whip one through leg-side and was caught slip.

I had three for nothing and there was an England panic on. Flintoff and Pietersen reined it in a bit. Then Binga knocked over KP caught behind, as well as Ian Bell, before he found a ripper delivery for Flintoff. England were now on 111, 'Nelson', their famously unlucky number. Six down and sweating. Pommie fingernails were on the floor of the stands and on the carpet of lounge-rooms all over the country.

Giles came in to join Geraint Jones. A nick here, a nudge there. *Geez.* Everything so tight. I could just see Jones' eyes – they were so wide. I said, 'This guy is nervous. I'm going to lob one up here and he's never going to resist.' So I bowled really slow to him and he ran down the line of leg-stump to hit straight or mid-off, and got it wrong. Kasper took the catch back towards the fence and we mobbed him like grand final winners.

7/116, Giles and Hoggard in. The tension was extreme. I was ripping them and Binga was reversing it at serious pace. But they only needed 13. 'Ohhhh,' I was thinking, 'I'd give anything for another 20 runs here,' but with 13 you have to go for broke. Patience, plans, all that stuff is nowhere. Every ball has to be a wicket ball, so you bowl a mixture of everything you've got.

Gilo played well; Hoggy too. Straining, we offered a couple of low full tosses which cost us two twos, I think, and a boundary. At that stage every run was like, 'Oh shit.' A few more runs up our sleeve and I truly believe we would have won. Unfortunately I came on too late. Enough said. England avoided their Kolkata moment, just.

Vaughan led them round the outer as the crowd sang songs about the Ashes coming home. It was a bit early for that. But then 18 years is a long time.

The Oval

My last Test in England; Pidge too. We took a bow at the end and felt honoured to be so appreciated by the English fans. We'd done some damage over the years but, I think, were recognised for being pretty good at what we did and providing more than decent entertainment. There was no sadness. In actual fact I had a smile when the crowd started singing to me, 'We wish you were English'. We weren't retiring, though that was soon to come – we'd just accepted that another Ashes four years down the road was out of reach.

The sadness came with Richie Benaud's last broadcast in England. He'd moved from the BBC to Channel 4 in 1999 and for seven years gave the Poms all the old magic on a new network, just as he was still doing on Nine in Australia. He was in the middle of his goodbye speech during a commentary stint when KP lost his off-stump to

Pidge and, apparently, the great man never missed a beat. Well, of course he didn't.

The ground announcer came on the PA system, thanking him for 40 years of cricket broadcasting in the UK and wishing him well. We all turned to the commentary box, doffed our headgear and applauded. I loved him, always had. After the match ended, during the wait for the presentations, he walked the whole way across the ground with Greigy, to be interviewed by Mark Nicholas, as Channel 4 said goodbye to cricket broadcasting themselves, having lost the television rights to Sky. The response to Richie was incredible. The whole ground stood and the applause got louder and louder before it turned to cheers. I don't suppose any Australian has been as popular in England.

To retain the Ashes, we needed to win the match and draw the series 2–2, but it didn't happen. Having said that, England's second innings had a hint of Adelaide 2006/07 about it, as batsmen caught between the defensive instincts that were needed for the draw to secure the series and the attacking ones that related to their 'natural' game collided. When they were 7/199 in the middle of the afternoon and only 205 ahead, there was time for three quick wickets and a doable run chase. But it wasn't to be.

In the morning Gilly had missed KP off my bowling before he'd scored – one he would take more often than not. It ricocheted off his glove towards Haydos, but he couldn't hang on either. On 10, KP narrowly avoided being run out and on 15 I dropped a straightforward chance at slip. After that, it was one-way traffic.

Apparently, at lunch he asked Vaughan how he should approach the rest of the day and the answer was 'Smash 'em'. Which is exactly what he did. Sure, he lived by the sword and risked dying by it but, in doing so, he made 158 off 187 balls with 15 fours and seven sixes! I went over to congratulate him as he walked off. Before the series began, I was sure he could transform England's cricket from predictable to potentially electrifying. I was proved right. He is a once-in-a-generation player. You just have to accept that mixed into the magic will be some madness.

Understandably, people remember that innings as the highlight of the day, and one of the highlights of the series, but people don't make much mention of Ashley-hit-me-miles, who hung on for a pretty gutsy 50 that stopped us getting through to the tail. I think I'll rename him. 'Ashley-block-for-hours', well done, mate.

A great last day's play – a very good Test match overall, actually – did justice to a memorable series and the draw gave England back the Ashes. Fair enough. Over five Tests, Vaughan's guys played better than we did. It happens. I can't say I was pleased for them, because that is bullshit. If anyone on a losing side says they're happy for the winners, they'll never be a winner themselves. Losing should hurt. I took 40 wickets in the series – 12 in that last-ditch effort at the Oval – at 19.92 each, and I made 249 runs in nine knocks. Pleased as I was with those performances, I still hurt as bad as ever. What I can say is that it was a good thing for English cricket to win the Ashes again and the huge viewing figures proved that the country still had the sport in its blood.

It was a good result for world cricket as well, because a strong England lifts the game in general. Best of all, it was a reminder that in Test cricket, the best team wins. There is a beauty there that is worth persevering with at a time when the game is changing shape and direction so fast. Test cricket will always be the most beautiful game, in many different ways.

As for us, well, we had blood on our minds alright. No way would we let this happen again, and definitely not in our own land. The return of the Ashes was barely more than 14 months away.

Fifteen Months, That's All It Took

I reckon the 2006/07 series is the most determined I've ever seen any Australian cricket team I played in. We were so motivated, determined, switched on. We trained hard, a precise and steely sort of training – extra nets, no slogging, just all proper batting, extra catches. No mucking around. Look, we had some fun – you always should, it's a game after all – but in general I'd say we were super focused about what we wanted to achieve and therefore our practice was even more intense than usual.

Honestly, I believe we could have turned up two days before the first Test and been the most motivated team of sportsmen on the planet. Add in the preparation, concentration and commitment, and I'd argue no-one could have beaten us over that series. England had stolen back the little urn that means so much to both countries. We saw Michael Vaughan and his team paraded around London on a red bus, turn up at Trafalgar Square to be greeted by tens of thousands of fans and then head off to the Prime Minister's place. Watching that sort of stuff sure brings it home. Our quest to get back the little urn that guys like Bradman and O'Reilly, Miller and Harvey, Benaud, Davidson, Lawry and Simpson, the Chappells, Marsh, Lillee, Border and Taylor had fought for, left no stone unturned. That's what the Ashes means. It's national identity, and pride.

Boot Camp

Three months before the first Test, we had this boot camp. I've been on record so often about this – it is just a fact that John Buchanan and I didn't, probably still don't, see eye to eye. And that isn't just about the boot camp, by the way! I'm going to try to pull my head in as I talk briefly about this, because the temptation is to lose the plot again.

Put simply, it was a waste of time and, worse, led to injuries – as proved by Stuart MacGill, Michael Kasprowicz and, to a lesser degree, me. Going away to the Queensland bush, pushing cars eight or 10 k's along tracks, carrying jerry cans of water up hills, getting woken by explosions after dark, and reporting somewhere in the jungle to sing the team song. I just can't see how in any way it benefits playing cricket or team spirit. And what got to me most is how it panders to that whole worship of the baggy green crap.

I got off on the wrong foot with the idea of this boot camp and never got anywhere near the right foot. First up at the briefing, Buchanan, along with Steve Bernard, the team manager, and Reg Dickason, the security guy who works for England these days – both good blokes – told us there would be no this, no that; you can't do this, you can't do that; here's your backpack and sleeping bag; here's your clothes; no drinking, no smoking etc.

Oh, right. 'Sorry?' I said. 'No smoking? I think we have an issue, boys, because if I can't smoke, then I don't think I can go.'

They said, 'You have to go.'

I said, 'No, I don't.' And I told Reg, 'Even if you go with your best shot and talk me into it, I'll be smoking, so let's save time. Are there smoking sections wherever we go on this trip?'

'No!' he said. 'No drinking, no smoking, Warney!'

So I said, 'That's fine. You all go off and play your games, but I'm out of here.'

I guess I had to be that guy, the one who behaved like a dick, but I couldn't go three days without a smoke.

They said, 'We'll talk to you after, Warney.'

Okay, fine. So they got me on my own and said, 'This an army thing – there are rules.'

I replied that I totally respected that, but since I was a smoker, I wouldn't be able to come along. 'Three days without cigarettes will make me very grumpy,' I said, 'and probably very unpleasant. So you choose.'

There was an awkward silence. 'Okay,' they said. 'You can smoke away from the group and discreetly.'

'Cool, we're all good,' I thought, 'I'm a team man' – so shall we say we compromised.

The Gilchrists, Haydens and Langers loved the experience. The others had mixed views, but myself and Magilla hated it.

(The one thing on that whole trip that made some sense was when we each had to write about each other's strengths and weaknesses. We could have done it back in town, of course, but it was good because you learnt something about yourself. The verdict on me was that I'd never, ever give up on the cricket field, but that I was too quick to be judgemental about others and never prepared to change my mind once I'd formed an opinion. 'Okay,' I said, 'I'll try to change.')

After the explosion that shocked the life out of us in the middle of the night, we were instructed to pull on some clothes, do up our boot laces in the dark and follow the army into the bush, where we sang 'Underneath the Southern Cross' and listened to Buck talk about how great was Australia and what the baggy green should mean to all Australians. I've said it before and I'll say it again, you don't need to worship, or even wear, the Australian baggy green cap to love what it stands for. Oh, and I don't need someone to tell me how much I love playing for Australia.

My messages to the coach were simple. I'll bust my gut for my country on the cricket field, but I won't wear the cap because I find it uncomfortable – I'll wear my sunhat, thank you.

Amazing Adelaide

At the Adelaide Oval in the second Test, both teams made more than 500 in their first innings. At the close of play on the fourth evening, England were 1/59, a lead of 97. The game appeared dead, but no, far from it.

Meantime, let's rewind to the first Test at the Gabba in Brisbane, where we just blew England away. Ricky made a hundred in both innings and we smashed them, playing some of the best cricket I've been part of. So, going into the second Test was strangely like Birmingham 16 months earlier, after we'd hammered them at Lord's. This time, though, we kept our foot on the floor and Pidge kept his foot miles away from any practice balls lying loose on the outfield. The second Test match in a five-match series is always pivotal – the team that is down can get back into the series, level it up and, effectively, set up a three-match series with the momentum on their side. But the team that is 2–0 down with three to play is sort of gone.

In Adelaide, you know the toss is massive. The wicket is, or was, very flat, so if you lose the toss, it's a psychological thing, like, 'Oh shit, we're chasing leather today.' Well, we lost the toss and England played bloody well. Paul Collingwood got 200 – I still can't believe it, Colly, mate – and KP 150. It was one of the few times I bowled purely to dry up an end. Like at Edgbaston, actually. We chased leather all day, and this time all the next day too.

By the time England passed 500, Freddie, who was captain, was slogging us everywhere. I walked past him and said, 'Mate, any chance of you declaring? We're on our knees out here and begging for mercy!' He waited till 551!

So we went in to bat and did alright in conditions that were still perfect for batting – Ricky made another brilliant hundred – until

Hoggard found some reverse. I remember walking out to bat with Michael Clarke at 6/384, still 167 behind. While he went on to an excellent hundred, I managed 40-odd before the partnership was ruined by a ball that tailed in late and hit me so high it hurt where it hurts most. Yup, hit in the nuts and given out LBW. The other guys down the order played really well too and we made it to 513. England were 1/59 at stumps, and looking pretty comfortable. Having said that, as we walked off the field I kept thinking, 'Day five in Adelaide, anything can happen – reverse swing, spin, low bounce etc.'

That evening, I spoke to McGrath about his wife, Jane, who had had a relapse after a promising period in her recovery from breast cancer. It's such a sad story – she was such a great woman. We talked a bit about the game too. Pidge was with me. It's winnable, we thought.

Later that night, I was sitting in my room with Michael Clarke, having a pizza and watching *American Pie* (Pup was having a salad!). During the film, I said to Pup that England would probably come out trying not to lose, blocking the shit out of it to eat up time and secure a draw. My view was that even if we didn't take wickets in the first 15 to 20 overs, they wouldn't have moved too far ahead and there would be plenty of time for us to chase down anything under 200. I didn't say we were going to win, I just thought that given England's likely mindset there was still a good chance of a result and, with the time left, that result would be us winning. So there we were, watching *American Pie*, and the 'Sherminator' came on.

Pup said, 'Don't you think he looks like Ian Bell?'

'He does too!' I said. So we had a bit of a laugh and that was that.

I woke up the next day and went to the ground. There wasn't much happening, no great excitement, just the usual routine. In the dressing-rooms, Punter started talking and asked what we all thought. Most people agreed it would be hard to bowl anyone out, because conditions were still good.

I was listening while having a dart out the window of the rooms and I turned back in to say to Punter and the guys all the stuff I'd said to Pup the night before. Mike Hussey was like, 'Yeah, good thinking, Warney.' And then I added that it was a mindset thing and ours was better than theirs, so if we rotated quicks from one end and I got it to rip from the other, the Poms might well panic if we got a couple of early wickets. We agreed that unless KP got in, they couldn't hurt us on the scoreboard and we could make up runs late in the day given that Adelaide is a hard ground to defend. Punter said, 'Okay, let's go hard with the mindset of winning the game, not letting it peter out.'

So we headed onto the field to prepare for the day and there was a very obvious change of mood from how we'd felt in our cars on the way to the ground. Everyone was more buoyant. Suddenly there was a plan and some focus on what we were trying to achieve, rather than just the sense of letting things unfold as we went through the motions. It was like, 'Let's get desperate in the field, not let anything through, take early wickets, suffocate them and see how they cope.'

I don't care how good a side you are – and we were among the best – it's human nature to take something for granted. We had a positive group of guys but, that morning before play, it wasn't easy to see a way to win. It just needed a plan, and some belief to have a go. That day, it was me who came up with it. I guess it's the way I played my cricket. I know I hardly ever bowled without thinking of a way to help us win.

If at one end you had Glenn McGrath – one of the best fast bowlers of all time – alternating with Brett Lee's pace and ability with reverse swing, as well as Stuart Clark's subtleties, and at the other you had me ripping them, there was a decent chance of knocking anyone over. We also had a great fielding side and the conviction that most half chances would be accepted. Above all, we had a very positive attitude to just about any situation a cricket team might find itself in. That was a hard thing to play against.

When play began, it immediately became clear that England were looking to bat time out of the game. I remember the first wicket like it was yesterday – Andrew Strauss, caught bat-pad, which he might not have hit (well, he claims he didn't). But these were the days before DRS, so Straussy was gone. Then the Sherminator came in, and this triggered the point when the game truly started to change face.

I walked past Ian Bell and, just loud enough for most of the guys to hear, said, 'What are you looking at, Sherminator?'

'I've been called worse,' he replied.

'No you haven't,' I said.

The guys around the bat laughed. A few balls later, Bell, who was obviously flustered, got into a mess after a bad call and was run out by Pup's slick pick-up and throw to me in my follow-though. I was three or four metres from the stumps and hit direct. From that moment on, we were humming.

Next up was KP. We knew he'd look to be aggressive after the first innings hundred, so I fancied him to take a risk or two early. I said to the guys, 'I'm going to bowl him round his legs,' and bingo, first ball! It curled, and then it ripped alright, from outside leg-stump to hit off! Loved that delivery! We were more than just humming now, we were sensing something very special.

The Pommie panic was definitely on. We were in their heads, a nice place to be. The score was 4/73 – only 111 ahead. Almost immediately after the KP ball, Binga ripped out Flintoff. 5/77! Oh my God, now every ball had a danger sign attached to it. It was just a matter of time. Collingwood hung on a bit but the rest fell apart. I bowled all day at one end, 27 overs, 11 maidens, and took 4/29; McGrath and Lee got two each. Stuey Clark had got Cook the night before, when I'd bowled five overs, 0/20. How the great game spins!

The atmosphere was electric, like the crowd fed off our energy and from the expectation that a wicket was going to fall every time we ran in to bowl. England lost 9/70 in 54 fear-ridden overs. It was something else really – as if nothing, and nobody, could stop us from what we wanted that day.

We needed 168 off 36 overs and cruised home with three of them to spare. Lang set the tone by running down at Hoggard and slogging him over mid-wicket. Ricky and 'Huss' played one-day cricket, running hard and smashing the odd loose ball. As we approached the finishing line, I was thinking how we'd just stolen an Ashes Test match; and how it's worth remembering that, in sport, pretty much anything is possible. All that matters is to think clearly and to never, ever give up.

I've looked up all the details on Cricinfo. There's a kind of bullet-point summary of each day's play. The bulletins and verdicts from the match preview right through to the final-day report make for good reading. In chronological order, they go: 'It's Edgbaston all over again'; 'Collingwood and Pietersen make it England's day'; 'England revival in full flow'; 'Australia must sense warning signs'; 'Heading for a draw but certainly no bore' – which comes at the end of the fourth day; 'Warne and Hussey sink England' – after the fifth. Ian Chappell sums it up with: 'The difference was in the mind.' Among other quotes are 'Ponting and Warne hail greatest win.' There is also 'Warne hits back'. Apparently, after England's first innings when KP got into me and my figures read 53 overs, nine maidens, 1/167, there was a headline 'Pietersen outwits the master'. Not for long, he didn't.

The celebrations were fantastic, everyone on a high, and we went late into the night. Channel Nine released a video of the match called *Amazing Adelaide* within weeks. The whole country talked about it as if every one of them had watched. Perhaps they had. There was no way back for England. If you lose after making 550, you're shot, I don't care who you are. In the rooms it was all about the moment of victory and then the thought that we'd hammer them in the three remaining matches. Which we did. Five–nil was proper revenge. There was no bus trip round Trafalgar Square after that.

What a summer that was. At the MCG I had my 700 moment; at the Sydney Cricket Ground we had our final bow as me and the Pigeon retired from Test cricket together with 1271 wickets between us. Lang bowed out too and the crowd shared our final hours in the Test match limelight with wonderful enthusiasm.

It definitely felt right to finish up after a series against England. Ashes cricket certainly defines you and it brought out the best in me, time after time. Beating the Poms in 2006/07 was made all the sweeter by having lost in 2005 – it felt like the old rivalry was alive once more.

What I could never have imagined – and neither could anyone else – was that an even greater challenge was around the corner. In India a cricket storm was brewing. Lights, camera, action . . .

15

Start Me Up

The Story of the Rajasthan Royals in the First Indian Premier League

HAVING RETIRED FROM TEST cricket in January 2007 – aged 37, I should add! – it soon became obvious to me that I'd lost motivation to play any cricket at all. My shoulder was sore, my body tired – the kind of sore and tired that makes it hard to get out of bed in the morning, never mind bowl 20 overs off the reel. It was, like, Test cricket is the pinnacle; after that, there's no other mountain worth the climb.

However, I was determined to honour my contract with Hampshire. The club had been good to me, and I wasn't about to let them down. Halfway through the English season I was in Southampton when Tony Greig called to tell me about the new Indian Cricket League.

'We want you as a marquee player,' he said. 'It will be a privately owned Twenty20 tournament, televised by Ten Sports (the Indian network now owned by Sony) and the owners will pay you serious money.'

I told Greigy I was finding Hampshire hard work and that my heart wouldn't be in it. But he was like a dog with a bone – typical Greigy, I always loved his enthusiasm – and wouldn't let go.

A few weeks later, Stephen Fleming, a good mate, rang to say he'd just had a very interesting meeting with a guy called Lalit Modi from the BCCI. I said, 'Oh yeah, what about?'

Flem said they were doing a rival Twenty20 called the Indian Premier League that was going to be owned by the BCCI and probably aired on Star TV. He said Lalit was pretty keen on getting me as one of the marquee players. I told Flem that I really didn't have that much interest in playing any more, but he was no less insistent than Greigy. Just don't sign with the ICL, he advised, let me get you some more info about the IPL.

A few days later, a guy I went to school with called Ravi Krishnan, who'd been running the commercial side of IMG in India, called to say that the Jaipur IPL team had recruited him as their vice-chairman and that he'd recommended me to the main owner of the franchise, Manoj Badale, as captain/coach.

Ravi knew his cricket. He'd played first grade for St Kilda and followed the game at the top level closely. He explained that the IPL would consist of eight franchises, each of which would buy their players at auction – internationals included. Ravi said he was selling me to Manoj as the one man who could make his team into something special.

It sounded interesting but I just couldn't convince myself I wanted to play cricket anywhere, least of all Twenty20, which I really hadn't played at all. I was still wondering if it was a hit and giggle form of the game, though I admit that the tactical side of something so new caught my attention. Yes, I was intrigued.

Manoj called to introduce himself. He sounded more English than Indian which, after many years living and working in London and holidaying on the Devon coast, he almost is.

'Ravi is convinced you're my man to lead the franchise,' he said, 'so tell me why you would make a good captain/coach and how you would run your own team.'

'Well,' I replied, 'firstly, I didn't say I would, Ravi did. I'm intrigued by T20, but the truth is I'm not sure I want to play any more cricket for anyone. I need a better understanding of the tournament so I can make an informed decision on whether or not

I'm willing to put my name into the auction and pull on those boots again.'

He went through his ambitions, chapter and verse, especially the idea of a Jaipur franchise surprising the rest of India with its signings, commitment and, best of all, smart thinking and desire to win – all of which whet my appetite nicely. Then he said, 'Okay, let's say you have put your name in the auction. Explain your cricket philosophies to me.'

This was a persuasive guy, and I liked his style! So I told him.

'I think there are too many coaches trying to reinvent the wheel. Cricket is a simple game, dependent on doing the basics well and keeping alive to the opportunities that present themselves. Leadership is the key, both in backing players – publicly and privately – and creating an environment where everyone is treated equally and encouraged to express themselves. Ideally, the players buy into an aggressive style of play and learn the value of taking risks in order to win. That's not as easy as it sounds, by the way – most cricketers worry about their place in the team.

'Lastly, it's really important to enjoy playing, to have fun out there. The captain should be accountable for performance, no-one else. Yes, he needs a strong team of support around him, good characters who understand the game, but in the end, he is accountable.'

'Great, I love it,' said Manoj. 'I would like to advance this chat and talk about you being a part of the franchise.'

I was thinking that this was all a bit weird because I hadn't really said to him that I much wanted to play yet. Anyway, time flew by and towards the end of January 2008, it was announced more formally that the IPL was going to launch in April and that the auction for it would take place in February.

Ravi called me again, saying, 'You've got to make a decision. Every player has to put his name in the auction within the next week or two.'

I said, 'Mate, I just don't know.'

It was then that Manoj rang, this time with his killer line. 'How are you feeling about this? We need an answer and, for what it's worth, my view is that it gives you the chance to show you were the best captain that Australia never had. That's an opportunity you shouldn't miss.

'Come on, let's do it, come and run the franchise exactly as you believe a cricket team should be run. It's a great chance to do the one thing in cricket you haven't done yet: win a title in a big new event that is going to change cricket. Let your leadership make a real mark on the game.'

Well, by now I was interested! You have to say his approach was pretty smart. Then he said, 'We will make you captain/coach with the final say in all cricket matters, including, of course, selection. You will run the cricket aspect of the business and we will ensure that you won't be distracted by anything outside of that. Everything cricket, you're in charge.'

I asked what would happen if other teams wanted me?

'I'm assuming things go to plan: that the others won't be alert to the detail of how the auction works, that we are well prepared, and that we get you!'

I liked it. Okay, I was in. What about guarantees? My price was $US450,000 and the understanding with Manoj was watertight. He was right about the auction, I was the first name out. Everyone seemed to be thinking, 'Do we bid? Don't we bid?' So . . . no bids. Going once, going twice – Shane Warne sold to the Rajasthan Royals.

I don't know exactly how it happened but I was pleased that it did. The big guns, the high-profile Indian owners, were waiting to see where to spend their money. No-one dared dive in and that worked in our favour.

On a more limited budget than other teams, the auction went okay. We had three Pakistanis, a South African, a Pom and two Aussies as our overseas players, alongside some very young, enthusiastic Indians and the more experienced Munaf Patel. So a lot of different cultures and nationalities.

We had a couple of months before the start of the tournament, and I spent a lot of time chatting to Manoj and others about the philosophy of cricket – T20 cricket mainly in this case. My main observation was that cricket matches are won by bowlers. A single T20 batsman will win you one-offs, but given it was going to be hard to bowl a side out in 20 overs, the role of the bowlers was not to contain but to take wickets – early wickets to change tempo and then later wickets to peg back acceleration.

'Interesting, interesting,' Manoj kept saying.

Then he elaborated on some of the reasons he picked certain players. In the case of batsmen he noted the ration of boundaries as against dot balls. If someone was striking at 100 runs per 100 balls but hitting a lot of boundaries, it meant he was wasting a lot of dot balls. So Manoj's ideal team had batsmen with good strike rates and the least amount of dot balls. Graeme Smith was a key choice there.

With bowlers, he went for early strikes, the ones who knocked blokes over for nought or for single figures. He wanted fast strike rates every bit as much as economy. He was influenced in his thinking by the book *Moneyball*, the story of the analyst at the Oakland Athletics baseball team who used algorithms to determine a player's value. It was an alternative approach and fascinating – in fact, working with Manoj was terrific.

When I arrived in India, all the IPL captains were flown around the country for launch events and Spirit of Cricket stuff that the MCC had introduced in a partnership with Lalit. The others were Tendulkar, Ganguly, Laxman, Dravid, Sehwag, Dhoni and Yuvraj. All Indians and little ol' me. Luckily, I sort of knew them well enough, but it was a very different dynamic. Every conversation was about India, the country's fast-changing philosophies and the complex social issues faced every day that affected the BCCI, and more specifically the players' contracts and money etc.

I just sat there, listening to their vibe. It occurred to me that over all the years of playing against each other, we'd never really known each other at all. There was mutual admiration and respect, but not real friendship. Having said that, after a few two-hour plane rides and a lot of cricket talk too, you sure learn a lot about each other!

At the start of the first Rajasthan Royals 10-day training camp in preparation for the first game, Manoj said we had to prune 50 players down to a final squad of 16. That included six overseas players – and only four could play at any one time. I went with Smith, Shane

Watson, Kamran Akmal, Sohail Tanvir, Dimi Mascarenhas and me. This meant leaving out Younis Khan – a great bloke, by the way – and bringing in Darren Lehmann for just two games while we waited for Smith to arrive from South Africa.

Then it got interesting because the Royals philosophy was to give young kids a go. The biggest name Indian player we'd signed was Mohammad Kaif – hardly Sachin Tendulkar or MS Dhoni. What people didn't understand was: why pay a massive $US650,000 for Mohammad Kaif? It was the auction process. If you missed out on two or three batsmen you wanted, you might get left with one you didn't want so much, but have to buy him because there was a gap in your team to fill. You could be lucky or unlucky, pay under or over, depending on timing, demand and the vacancy that needed filling. It was what made the auction so exciting.

It was Mohammad Kaif who, unknowingly, brought our attention to something that needed fixing straight away. When we checked into the hotel as the Rajasthan Royals group, everyone got their room key and disappeared. Minutes later, while I was chatting with the owners in reception, I noticed Kaif go to the front desk and say, 'I am Kaif.'

'Yes,' said the receptionist. 'How can we help?'

'I am Kaif.'

I went over. 'Everything alright, mate?' I asked.

'Yes, I am Kaif.'

'I think they know who you are, mate, what do you mean? What are you looking for?'

'I have got a little room like everyone else.'

I said, 'Right, okay. Do you want to upgrade yourself or something?'

'Yes, I'm Kaif.' I knew exactly what he wanted: 'I am a senior, an Indian international player, so I get a bigger room.'

'Without trying to be funny, mate,' I said, 'everyone gets the same room. I'm the only one with a big room because I have to meet with people.'

'Oh.'

And off he walked.

We realised that the senior Indians expected preferential treatment and the youngsters were treated like, you know, pick up my bag! So I figured I had to gain the respect of the whole squad of 50 by quickly laying down exactly the same ground rules for everyone.

At the first team meeting, I said we'd all start with a clean slate. 'If you step out of line, there will be consequences. We're all in this together, no-one is bigger than the team, and there's a rude shock awaiting anyone if they think they are. However, if you want to play and learn, then, great, we're on the same page. After all, we have the same ambition, to win the IPL.'

Alongside me to work with the players were Darren Berry, the former Victorian keeper who'd gone into coaching back home, and Jeremy Snape, a good county off-spinner who'd played a few one-dayers for England and had studied the psychological side of sports science. Berry was my pick, Snape wasn't.

From the start, I'd told Manoj, 'I don't need any shrink – I just don't believe in them.' 'Chuck' was very good at planning, analysis of the opposition, tactical stuff. His man-management skills needed work but he was the perfect background assistant. When Manoj first rang me for my thoughts on cricket, I said that modern cricket teams had too many people hanging around the dressing-rooms, getting in the way, but he insisted on Snape and was proved right. 'Snapey' is good with people and a very good bloke himself. His energy and insight were terrific for us and he and Chuck complemented each other well. Their impact can't be overestimated. They were very much a part of the magic we created.

After the first day with all 50 of the players together – doing sponsorship stuff, having various meetings and a gentle loosener – the three of us shared our first impressions of the interaction we had picked up on. Mohammad Kaif thinks he's Don Bradman, we agreed, but he ain't that good. Do we chop him off at the knees or do we put an arm around him, pump him up and say how important he is to us? We went with the carrot, not the stick, and decided to include him in a lot of what we did in preparation.

Kaify was a decent player, not a gun but full of purpose and ambition, and we needed him on board. As an Indian 'name' the other guys looked up to him and we figured we could use that to our advantage. We called him over to say, 'We want you to help us – who's this guy, who's that guy, what do you think of him, what's he thinking about us etc?'

He helped us understand the way the Indian players thought and became a useful middle man. We had a couple of other young Indian coaches who looked after the kids, Monty and Zubin, both very good. Zubin was left-field with a lot of original thinking, and he was still going strong with the Royals during the 2018 IPL. Monty was just a really nice guy who would throw 1000 balls, or whatever was needed.

We quickly realised that net practices weren't teaching us enough. We needed match simulation to see how the guys thought and reacted under a bit of pressure. We picked two sides of those who looked the best first up and two more sides for the next level down. Then we manufactured game situations and manipulated head-to-heads that set them more intense challenges than a net can provide.

Here's a good example. There was a 19-year-old left-arm spinner called Ravindra Jadeja, who'd come to us with a reputation of being able to bat a bit too. We brought him to the wicket against a 17-year-old off-spinner and made a bit of a scene about bringing the field up and demanding that he keep the scoring rate moving as if it was a run chase, but retain his wicket because he was the last of the recognised batsmen.

Well, first ball, he hit the off-spinner into the changing-rooms.

The poor kid said, 'Please, sir, can I put the fielders back?'

'Nope,' I said, 'we'll leave them up.'

So Jadeja hit him straight, and very long, for six again. Then we put mid-on and mid-off on the fence. He rocked back and cut past point for four. Next ball, cool as you like, he took the easy single down the ground. I thought, 'Yes, the boy can play,' and told him to come out now.

He begged me to let him bat on. 'Please, sir, please.'

I said, 'No, mate, you're fine,' and thought, 'Let's hope he can bowl and field that good too.' He could. I sensed that his air of confidence would rub off onto others, so I nicknamed him 'Rockstar.'

He loved that. Within a year or so, Jadeja was playing one-dayers for India and every time we see each other now he still calls me 'sir' and talks about those days. I tell him I should be on 10 per cent of everything he earns!

So then another young kid came in – for the purposes of the story, let's call him Asif – and within three balls of spin and three of pace, I thought, 'Yep, okay, mate, not bad but no Jadeja.'

'Sir,' he said, 'a bit more, please.'

I said, 'No, no, it's okay, thanks.'

We went through this routine with all the guys and often fired up Tanvir and Munaf to bowl bouncers, yorkers, the lot. We were looking at character as much as skill. Then at the end of each day, Chuck, Snapey, me and Kaif sat back with pen, paper and a bunch of notes and went through everyone.

A couple of guys stood out. One was the young Swapnil Asnodkar, who was tiny – five feet one, at a guess. He had a good technique but just wanted to hit the ball, which he did more often than not. He was a natural to open with Smith.

The other was Jadeja, of course. The more we saw of him – the way he moved in the field, the athleticism, the swagger – the more we thought, 'We've got something here.' It was even obvious in the way he walked out to bat.

I said, 'This guy can do it for us in the top four or five.'

They said, 'He bats nine and bowls a bit of spin.'

'No,' I said, 'he can come in after the first six-over power play and chase down the spinners.'

After 10 days of this assessment process, we had a group of 16 guys we were happy with. I rang Manoj and read out the names.

'Great,' he said. 'A few surprises. Tell me why him and not him?'

So I explained it all and he was happy. Or nearly.

'Just one dilemma, Warney.'

'Oh, what's that?'

'Why no Asif? The kid can really play. I've done the stats on him.'

'Yeah, he's not bad . . . but he's not that good either.'

'He has to be there, Warney, at least as a squad player. I'm convinced.'

'Why does he *have* to be there?'

'Because I kind of backed him from the start and, anyway, I think his figures match up.'

'Manoj, you asked me to pick the best squad I possibly could, and with the help of Darren Berry, Jeremy Snape, Mohammad Kaif and Munaf Patel, that's what I've done. We've worked pretty hard, spending a lot of time with these guys personally. We've gone into great detail about the cricket we're looking to play and about the roles they'll each have. We've analysed potential match situations and made plans for specific periods, overs and balls. We've gone though options, pressure, choices under pressure, hype, karma, match awareness, anticipation, expectation.

'For 20 years I've been learning about the game at the top level and I've tried to impart as much of that knowledge as I possibly can to these guys over an intense period in all of our lives. We've sifted the best 16 cricketers from 50 you gave us. And now you want me to change one of them? No, absolutely not. We've chosen the very best. Making a change will betray their trust, set us back and compromise our chances. You gave me complete control over the cricket and that is my decision. So, no.'

'Warney, you're not hearing me.'

'Really? Right, well that's fine then, mate. If he has to be in the 16, he takes my spot because I ain't in it.'

'Don't be stupid.'

'Manoj, over 10 very full-on days I've earned the respect of these guys. One of the reasons for that is I've treated everyone fairly. If I put Asif in that group, they'll know he's not good enough and that he's there because of some hidden favouritism. At that point, I'll lose them. So if you want Asif in the squad, that's fine, but I'll give you your money back – I don't want to be part of it.'

'Are you serious?' asked Manoj.

'I'm deadly serious,' I said.

'Let me sleep on it.'

I was serious, but I was bluffing a bit too. For one thing, I didn't want to hand back 450 grand; for another, I was enjoying the job and looking forward to the tournament. I told Snapey and Chuck about the conversation with Manoj.

They said, 'Geez, did you really say that?'

I said, 'I did, guys.'

And they said, 'Good on you. The players will respect you even more for that.'

Next morning, Manoj called.

'Can we compromise?'

'Depends what the compromise is, Manoj, because I ain't compromising on the squad of 16.'

'Okay, that's fine, but can he be part of the squad at home in the dugout with a Rajasthan Royals shirt on? It will be a great learning curve for him.'

I didn't like the sound of that. 'No, the area is too small for all of us as it is, and, anyway, I don't want him just sitting there, because again it looks like we're doing him a favour. So no.'

'Okay,' said Manoj. 'I asked you to do a job and you must do it. I hope you're right and if so, I'll be the first to say so.'

'Great, thanks,' I said. 'Are we done?'

'Yep, I guess so. Good luck with the guys.'

Then I went and saw the players and read out the 16 names. There were people crying, which was the moment it dawned on me just how big this was. I'd picked a kid called Dinesh Salunkhe, who was runner-up in *Cricket Star*, the Indian talent show, which Manoj and Charles Mindenhall, his business partner, had launched in 2006. He was a leg-spinner who hadn't played any first-class cricket, and I was his idol. He came up crying with joy and hugged me. He wasn't the only one. Others were crying because they'd missed out. I realised that this meant the absolute world to them. These were kids who sat in their rooms watching cricket all day long on TV. To be named in the squad, get their gear and later walk out at the opening ceremony representing the Rajasthan Royals was beyond a dream.

It occurred to me that we were all starting from scratch. We were now the first piece of history in the story of this new club, which was kind of awesome in its way. In fact, the start of the IPL was a pretty special time in all of our lives.

Those 10 days, getting to know all those players, putting my arm around them, teaching them, I'll never forget it. We had no big Indian superstars but we had a great dynamic. I think when you look back at teams you played in, there was often something you can't quite put your finger on that makes it tick. A vibe, specific to that collection of people. I knew that our internationals – Smith, Watson, Tanvir and me, mainly – had to play incredibly well for us to challenge, but I also knew we'd created an atmosphere that made anything possible if a bit of luck went our way.

It Couldn't Have Gone Much Worse

So we get to the first game, Delhi Daredevils in Delhi. We had Yusuf Pathan at the top of the order with a guy called Taruwar Kohli, who played unbelievable inside-out shots over cover, just crunched them for six. We knew McGrath was opening the bowling for Delhi, and that he'd land it on a good length around off-stump. So I told Kohli not to be shy with that over extra-cover shot of his. 'Mate,' I said, 'you're playing because you can run at him first ball and take him down. Set the tone and let everyone know the Royals are here.'

We also knew Delhi would bomb Yusuf with short balls – Pidge would tell them to – so in training we had the quick bowlers crank it up against him and worked with him to stand tall and drop the short balls down at his feet so he could rotate the strike with singles. After that, I told Yusuf to smoke 'em against the other teams.

After the toss, I had a smoke and then sat down to watch. What? Whaaat? I saw that Yusuf was on strike! No, guys, Kohli is out there to take down the Pigeon from the off! I sent a message out and they switched last minute. And Kohli did hit the last ball of Pidge's first over for six, but fell to the third ball of his next over. It was a bad omen.

One thing led to another and we got hammered by nine wickets with five overs to spare. I did the press, came back, and Shane Watson was crying in the corner.

'I am so much better than this,' he said.

'Well, bloody well show me then!' I fired back.

With the exception of that brief exchange, the general silence in the room was deafening.

I said, 'Boys, are we okay? Listen, we lost a game of cricket, it's not the end of the world. We are better than we were today, much better, and we'll prove it. The bus leaves in 20 minutes, be on it.' And that was that. Played one, lost one.

I had a drink with Manoj back at the hotel and he asked how I was going. Like, was I still happy with the squad and, if so, were the problems of the game mental, skill-based or just nerves? Those sort of questions.

I said, 'Yeah, yeah, I'm happy and whatever problems you saw tonight will be fixed up by the next game.'

'Tonight didn't go so well,' he said.

I said, 'Too right . . . in fact, it couldn't have gone much worse!'

'Yes, it's a big game in a few days when we take on Kings XI at home.'

'Yep,' I said, 'and we'll be right.'

It was a tense conversation but I knew he was 100 per cent supportive. So now the next two days were like, 'Jesus, we have got to win this game!' I spent the first 24 hours speaking privately to every one of our Indians who were going to play in the Kings XI game, reiterating their roles and reminding them of all the things we'd worked on in preparation and where our strengths lay. Then for the next 24 hours after that, I talked to our international stars. It was a simple message: *'Lift, guys, lift!'* Oh, and I bowled my own arse off in the nets, to find a rhythm and groove that weren't quite there against Delhi.

It Couldn't Have Gone Much Better

We beat them, and beat them well. I got 3/19 – Hopes, Sangakkara and Yuvraj – and had a straightforward catch dropped. Watto got 70-odd not out and the man of the match award.

My favourite story of that game, though, was Dinesh Salunkhe, the *Cricket Star* kid. I kept him in the side because I fancied him against Mahela Jayawardena, who often went inside-out over cover against the spinners. I liked Salunkhe's shape and pace for Mahela, but even I couldn't have predicted one of Sri Lanka's greatest-ever batsmen coming down second ball, getting beaten in the flight and stumped.

The crowd, who had all watched the *Cricket Star* program and knew about this young kid, went bananas. And I mean bananas – screaming and yelling. Salunkhe went berserk, our whole team went berserk. It was one of those moments when you think, 'Oh, how nice is that! That's just worked beautifully.' And, of course, from there we were hard to stop and won the game by six wickets.

This time I came back from the presser to the dressing-room and the music was going, arms around each other and they're all dancing. Even Watto's got a big grin on his face. I'm thinking, 'Wow, how good is this,' and said, 'Boys, we all good?'

'Yes, yes,' they answered this time, and they were cuddling, hugging and singing songs.

I said to Manoj and to Fraser Castellino, the CEO, 'Right, now these guys have to understand what happens when you win.'

'What do you mean?' asked Manoj.

I said, 'Let's throw a party.'

He said, 'What?! Some of them are 17.'

'Throw a party,' I said. 'Find me some dancing girls – the cheerleaders at the ground would be perfect – get a DJ in that big reception room at the hotel, set it up as a nightclub, get some alcohol, get some of the girls on the dancefloor, and I'll tell the guys we have an important meeting back at the hotel that they have to attend.'

'Okay,' said Manoj, 'let's do it!'

As the bus pulled up at the hotel, I said, 'Boys, congratulations today, a fantastic performance. Now I'm going to show you what happens when we win. You guys all love dancing. Well . . . let's dance. Everyone down in the lobby in 15 minutes in the best gear you've got.'

'Yes, sir, yes, yes.'

'Best gear, down in the lobby,' I repeated. 'Don't be late.'

I had a fast shower, put on the glad rags, and made sure I was down there first. Manoj was already there, however, now keen to party. So they all came down to the lobby.

I said, 'Boys, let's go!'

We opened up the doors to the ballroom, the DJ was rocking the joint, there were a dozen girls dancing, and you could hear all the Indians laughing and cheering, just loving it. Within a few minutes their collars were up and they were dancing for all they were worth! It was a great sight. At that stage, the internationals were at the bar, quietly having a beer and reflecting on how much better it was to win than lose.

The vibe that night was something else, unforgettable. When we won our third game, the Indian players said, 'Sir, is there a party?'

'Yep, every time we win there's a party, guys.'

So on we marched, partying a lot, because we only lost one more game en route to qualifying for the semis – away to the Mumbai Indians. We then lost the final group game in the return Kings XI match, deciding to rest key players having qualified. Other than those two matches, the Royals were unbeaten from the woe of the Delhi debacle to the go of the play-offs. Not bad.

Guess what, we got Delhi again in the semi-final. I said to the guys, 'This is one of the things we look forward to – the chance to play a team that hurt you. This is revenge time. Let's go teach them a lesson.'

We smashed them with the bat and made 192. Watto played like the cricketer he always promised to be and Yusuf slammed them at the end. What a ball striker that boy was!

Out came cocky Gautam Gambhir and the incredibly dangerous Virender Sehwag, India's opening pair, to open for Delhi. Watto now bossed the game with the ball, finding surprising bounce in the Wankhede pitch. Sehwag lasted only four balls before holing out at deep point. I stood at the non-striker's end and looked Gambhir straight in the eye.

'Absolutely no-one at this venue, including the Rajasthan changing-room, has spoken a word about you,' I said. 'It's Sehwag we were worried about, mate, not you, so you might as well get out, because it doesn't really matter what you do out here – no-one cares.'

He looked at me like he wanted to kill me, eyes spinning, completely losing the plot. Soon enough, he shelled one to point, where young Kohli, on as a sub, took a blinder. So that sledge worked pretty well. Immediately after that, Shikhar Dhawan pulled into the hands of square-leg. Three for spit to Watto, all plans that worked perfectly. The guys were ecstatic.

We knocked them over for 87, just blew them away with an amazing performance. Payback for the first game was complete. One of the things that stands out from that semi-final was how much tougher we'd become. An illustration of this came near the end when the match was long over as a contest.

In the practice sessions prior to the tournament, I'd told our fast bowlers that when the tail comes in, we bounce the crap out of them, trying to hurt them mentally and physically. Part of this was to set a tone of no free runs, whatever the situation of a match – no easy slogs off yorkers that become half-volleys and stuff. We had mid-off and mid-on up, and everyone square of the wicket back. The other part of it was to show a bit of muscle, and decent bouncers were as good a way as any.

In that semi, Delhi were nine down and gone, still needing another 100, when McGrath came in.

Munaf Patel was on and said to me, 'Captain, still short?'

I said, 'Munaf, if I tell you to do something different, then we do something different.'

So . . . okay. Munaf bowled four bouncers in a row to Pigeon. The last one broke his thumb.

He was absolutely spewing, threw his bat, saying, 'What the fuck – is this a joke? What are you doing?'

To this day, his thumb is still a mess. The point was that everyone round India was watching that game, so it set the tone for the business we were in. It wasn't personal against Pidge, because if it had been, I would've said pitch it up to him. As it was, people could see that if I was after one of my best mates, I'd sure be after them too.

That was the semi-final. Very satisfying. But people remember winners and there was still a game to go. A very big game.

The Three-Second Chill

T20 was relatively new. We were always on the lookout for ways to play the game differently and stay ahead of the other teams. And not only was T20 new, it was very fast, so much so that much of it passed by in a blur. We began to understand each ball as an event of its own and therefore the need to give it some serious attention. In essence, we talked about 120 separate contests – in other words, one per ball.

T20 batsmen have to be hustlers, constantly running hard and hitting hard, and because bowlers look to upset their rhythm by rushing them even more, we wanted our guys to stand back and take a breath. Equally, because the bowlers were looking for the best yorker, say, or the best slower ball or bouncer that they'd ever bowled, the pressure on them was intense, and we figured they needed to take a breath too. So we came up with the three-second chill.

I'd used it for a while in my own bowling, just steadying myself at the top of my mark, taking in some deep breaths, looking round the field. It became a sort of psychological tool, to make the batsman wait for me, rather than me wait for him. The generally frantic nature of a T20 innings affects everyone. The guys who take stock, the ones who stop, think and reboot, have the best chance of coping.

An amusing insight into the benefit, or otherwise, of the three-second chill involved a batsman, Tyron Henderson, the South African who had a good T20 season at Middlesex in 2008. Manoj had seen him smash it in the English T20, loved his stats and signed him. Before the start of the second IPL season in 2009, Tyron came out to bat in a practice game for us and, first ball, went for an almighty six – he swung so hard, he threw himself off his feet, missed it, of course, and lost his middle stump.

Snapey asked him later what was going through his head.

'Oh, mate,' he answered, 'I get so nervous, I just swing at the first ball.'

Snapey said, 'Well, I tell you what you should do, Tyron. Take centre, face up, step away from the stumps, and swing as hard as you like for a few seconds before the first ball is bowled. Then, instead of playing a shit shot, face up to your first ball and play it properly.'

Tyron played two games for us, made five runs and got hammered when he bowled. A Manoj beauty at $600,000 a year. But he'd won the English Twenty20 with Middlesex, finishing with a strike-rate of 180.12 and 21 wickets at 7.42 runs per over, which is probably why Manoj saw him as a good buy. Go 'Moneyball'!

To be honest, we both got a few right and a few wrong. The core of our team was made up of good people who we trusted under pressure. We didn't overspend; in fact, our $US5 million was nothing compared to some of the big guns.

Shane Watson was a masterstroke and he was eventually chosen as the player of the tournament – 472 runs and 17 wickets. I knew him as a youngster and could see all this talent and desire. When he was starting out, he sometimes stayed with me in Melbourne and we talked a lot. You kind of had to force self-belief on him, but then, cruelly, those injuries that came early in his career damaged much of the confidence he was busy building. I just tried to bring that confidence back.

I felt for him, being on the fringe and not quite nailing it. He was always a very determined guy, and very competitive, but he had a soft side. When I think back to that first game and him in tears in the corner of the changing-room, well, what a comeback he made from that.

A couple of days after the Delhi game I asked him what he wanted from his career and he just kept answering, 'I want it. I desperately want success.' He was almost in pain with his frustrations.

'Okay,' I said, 'you can bat at three and open the bowling. You've got it all – strength and power, touch and timing, pace, control and variations. Plus, you've got guts and determination.

'And Watto,' I added, 'there's no need to be nervous. We're all nervous but you have nothing to prove to anyone. We all know you can play, so show us how good you are.'

And did he! I think he really enjoyed the responsibility, and the support and backing from a captain. In turn, I was so proud of him. From there, he kicked on to be the cricketer we all knew he could be.

Graeme Smith was a top man to have in a team – committed, honest and tough. We wanted him to play cricket shots for the first six overs and then expand a bit if we'd made a decent start. He's such a reliable guy and a good judge of the pitch and the likely par scores. Chuck had given everyone a nickname that applied to their role, and Smithy was 'The Rock'.

Alongside him at the top of the order – after we'd moved Yusuf down a bit to smash the spinners with Jadeja – was Swapnil, the kid from Goa. We called him the 'Goa Cannon' because we wanted him to go off like a cannon. He was five foot high and a very funny sight in the middle between overs when discussing stuff with Smithy, who is six foot five and built like a block of flats. (I'm being very kind to you here, Smithers, boy!)

The quick bowlers were just as fantastic. I had a lot of time for Munaf Patel, who had a huge heart and a great sense of humour. I was sitting at the back of the bus with him one day, early on, and asked how old he was. 'Skipper, do you want real age or IPL age as others would ask?'

I said, 'I just want to know how old you are.'

'I am 24 but if my real age was 34, I would still tell you my IPL age was 24, because this is a good gig and I very much wanted to play. If I am 34, no-one picks me. If I am 28, people think I have a few good years left . . . I'm going to stay in my 20s for a long time to come!'

Good thinking, Munaf. He was a true leader of the attack, taking some of the younger guys under his wing. He's such a nice guy. People criticised him for too many bad balls, but he was always searching for wickets, which we liked.

Tanvir was a gem. He had that awkward, ungainly action and real pace when he got it right. Smithy and I hung on in the slips as he constantly surprised people with zip and bounce. We caught plenty. It was hard to pick his action when you first got out there and I was frequently tempted to bowl him more than two at the start. The thing was he was bloody good at the death too. A great signing.

The most underrated bowler we had was Sid Trivedi, just medium pace but with an excellent slower ball and a good bouncer. He played for Gujarat in the Ranji Trophy and was one of the team's most successful 'Moneyball' signings. Sid, or Siddarth really, loved a dart and a beer, but he didn't like to be seen having either, so he always came to my room.

'Skip, can I have a cigarette with you?'

I loved that and we talked a lot of cricket together; also with Munaf, who liked the odd dart too. Two great guys, and pretty smart.

Yusuf Pathan linked everything together for us, as a pretty smart off-spinner and a devastating batsman. His innings in the final was a belter, but we'll come to that in a moment. He needed to be released as a cricketer, like given permission to be himself. In fact, this was something that the IPL, and T20 in general, has done for a lot of players: freed them up to show off their talents. We liked him because you knew he was in it for everyone else every bit as much as for himself.

Before our third game, the Deccan Chargers in Hyderabad, I told Chuck and Snapey that Adam Gilchrist was a bad starter against spin and I was going to open the bowling with Yusuf.

They said, 'You're nuts – Gilly will smash him.'

So I opened with Munaf and Watto. He smashed them. Third over, I brought on Yusuf and straight away Gilly walked past one to be stumped. Soon after, Yusuf got Shahid Afridi too. Not that that stopped them making 5/214, of which Andrew Symonds thrashed 117 in 53 balls. We chased them down, though. We needed 14 off the last four balls. Warne hit Simmo for 4, 6, 6, and the Royals won with a ball to spare. Nice job, King!

I don't tell that story to show off – I tell it for a reason. Working backwards, the win was crucial for our momentum. Having lost the first game and won the second, victory in the third cemented our progress. For us to take it so deep with the bat and then pull it off from such an unlikely position proved that anything was possible if you wanted it enough.

Next, I'd switched the batting around to prove we could be flexible depending on the needs of the moment. And, at the start of the match, I'd done the same with the bowling, bringing Yusuf on so early. By always moving the bar, I was creating a sense of possibility in the minds of the players. I didn't want them to feel limited or restricted. I wanted a cricket field to be their playground.

The bottom line was that from performances like this, the guys started to believe.

I've talked a lot about Jadeja. We loved him from the minute we saw his approach and enthusiasm. There was bit of the 'boy wonder' in him so we gave him a longer leash than most, but his lack of discipline was a problem because it sometimes led the younger guys down the wrong path.

We let a few things go but I can't stand anyone who is late for anything and Ravi Jadeja was always late. First time, there was a bit of confusion with bags and stuff, so I let it slide. Second time, no good – the bus left at 9 am for training and he wasn't on it, so he had to make his own way to the ground and, of course, was late again. On the way back after training, I stopped the bus halfway to the hotel and said, 'Guys, we had someone late again this morning. Ravi, mate, get off here and walk home.' One of his mates made a fuss, so I told him to get off too and they could walk back to the hotel together. No-one was late after that.

There are many elements to captaincy. As I've explained before, the detail of strategy and tactics interests me most; then the study of people – how to get the best from your own guys and make life most difficult for your opponents – followed by the philosophies that set out the way I want to play the game. Strong characters and lively personalities are the central part of any group of cricketers who are successful together. As I've mentioned, you don't have to be best mates to make up the best team, but you do have to stick together, otherwise the opposition have something to go on.

Both at the Royals and at Hampshire, a lot of the guys were basically soft. I think Australian cricketers were harder than any in the era I played, with the exception of the first West Indian team I came up against and most of the South African sides. So at Hampshire and the Royals I tried to toughen the guys up. Hard but fair was my way of doing it.

The IPL made a lot of the Spirit of Cricket. Okay, I get that. And the tournament had a Fair Play Award, which I didn't think was so fine. I told our guys, 'I want to be at the bottom of the Fair Play table and the top of the Indian Premier League when it comes to qualification for the finals.'

I wanted the other teams to hate us so that when they came up against us they were thinking, 'God, I want to beat these blokes so bad,' and they'd lose focus on what they did best. The tougher we became and the more matches we won, the more unpleasant we were to play against.

I was reprimanded a few times, sometimes fairly sometimes not. In one game midway through the tournament, I pushed it too hard and was reported by the umpires to the IPL playing committee, which, back then, basically meant Lalit Modi. The IPL was Modi's genius – he made it what it was, no-one else, whatever you hear – and he made it a whole lot more than just a tournament of cricket matches too. Those first IPLs were incredible events, the best of everything and great parties night after night. It's still a great tournament but doesn't have quite the razzle and dazzle of the first couple of years. I was blown away by it and Lalit Modi couldn't do much wrong in my eyes, so this was going to be an interesting meeting.

Manoj came with me to the Rambagh Palace hotel and we were directed to a huge private suite, a room as big as the Oval, where Modi was having a foot massage – two people, one on each foot. We suggested to him that we come back later.

'No,' he said, 'let's have a chat.' He didn't waste much time. 'You've been a naughty boy, haven't you? Please don't be a naughty boy again.'

I said, 'Ummm . . . sorry about that, Lalit.'

'Put your hand out,' he said. So I put my hand out and he smacked it. Then he said, 'Right, what do you want to drink?' We all laughed and that was that. Then we spent an hour talking about the tournament, about cricket in general, and then about his thoughts for the future of the game, which weren't bad actually. Lalit has been a loss to cricket ever since he fell out with the BCCI and became sort of exiled in the UK.

Back to the cricket and the journey to the final. One of the things I thought we needed in such a short cricket match was a series of set plays we could turn to under pressure: things like the first and sixth ball of overs, when the bowlers would go full and wide, short and wide, straight bouncer, slower bouncer, leg-stump yorker, or wide yorker.

These options depended on the batsmen and the pitches, of course, and I would always ask the bowler for his preference. So, if the answer was short and straight, I'd say short, or whatever, to the guys and the fielders would revert to the positioning we'd planned before the game. Often the batsmen heard the instruction but that was no big deal – they could see it from the field setting anyway. With any of the short plans, for example, we had mid-on and mid-off up and everyone square to the wicket or behind it back. Obviously, the success of this depended on execution by the bowler and reaction from the batsmen. The point was that with so little time we had to focus everyone's brain quickly and this discipline really helped.

Then there were things like the first six overs, the power-play overs, when I said to the bowlers, 'I don't care how many runs we go for, I want four wickets. We'll keep two slips in if you want to go normal "corridor" bowling – Test-match bowling – and try to nick them off, or if you want to bowl yorkers at the stumps, slower balls, whatever, but let's work that into our plan for four wickets.'

Here's why. If we take three to four wickets in the first six overs, all they can do is bat out the time, in an attempt to post some sort of score. In other words, the more wickets we take early, the harder it is for them to take risks because they might be bowled out.

Most bowlers wanted a ring field with one slip and then when someone played a cover drive, the slip would move to cover to block the gap. I'd say, 'No, no, I'm keeping the slips in. I don't care if you get hit for boundaries, go for wickets.'

A couple of times early we got tested, *smack*, *smack*, and the bowlers would panic and I'd say, 'No, mate, wickets!'

Smithy and I took a lot of catches at first and second slip. We definitely weren't there just for the sake of it. Sometimes, I'd go to gully or short point – wherever – but there was always an extra catcher in those first six overs.

After that, I wanted spin. The pitch in Jaipur was very dry and didn't bounce much, but it did turn. We had big boundaries and I had the rope back as far as it would go. Ideally, we had four spinners – just hit 'em with spin was my theory at home – which had the added bonus of allowing us to sneak up on batting sides by bowling a high percentage of our overs in super-quick time.

Obviously, away from home, we used the different options in our attack for different surfaces. But in Jaipur, over the four years I played, spin was king.

The Royals Win the Cup!

Never in my life have I experienced anything like it. On the day of the final, we came out of our hotel and the Mumbai streets were lined with Rajasthan Royal blue, walls and signs were painted with 'We love the Royals' and the overwhelming feeling was that the people had fallen in love with the underdog. Our opponents were the Chennai Super Kings, which meant MS Dhoni, Suresh Raina, Albie Morkel, Chamara Kapugedara, Makhaya Ntini and Murali – all the heavies.

I could sense this mix of nerves and excitement amongst our guys, so we decided to arrive at the stadium earlier than normal to settle down, mill around and take it all in. Just as everyone relaxed, we were told there was an official ceremony before the match. It was the Cirque du Soleil and it went on forever, which kind of made people edgy again.

We won the toss and bowled first, as much as anything to take the pressure off the batsmen. It went well. The bowlers were good, Yusuf particularly so, with three big wickets. We had control until Dhoni slogged a few near the end to take the Super Kings to what we felt was no more than a par score – 5/163. Having said that, in a final, runs on the board are gold.

After a good start we got bogged down in the middle. To make things worse Murali came on and asked some questions. In the 11th over a big moment went our way. In an attempt to up the ante, Yusuf skied Murali out to mid-on but Raina, running in, spilt the chance.

An over later I got a signal from Yusuf. Now, as I've said, this boy can smoke 'em, and in an earlier game he'd given Murali a pasting. We sent the 12th man out with a drink to see what Yusuf wanted.

A truly memorable message came back: 'Skipper, I want to smash Murali, but we just lost a couple of wickets and I was dropped. What shall I do, smash him or block him?!'

'Smash him,' I said.

At the start of the 13th over, we were 3/87, still needing 77 from 48 balls. Yusuf hit the last two balls of that over, bowled by Murali, into the crowd. Two overs later, Kaify hit Murali's first ball for six; Yusuf hit his fourth ball for six. We were edging ahead of the rate, out of the danger zone a bit, thanks to this guy who, outside of India, no-one had heard of before the IPL began. Yusuf had no fear, which makes anyone a threat.

Anyway, that was by no means the end of it. Kaify got out and, in another twist, Yusuf was run out by Raina's direct hit from backward point. Whoa, we were twitching now!

I came in at number eight with 17 balls remaining and 25 needed. Immediately I arrived, Jadeja holed out in the deep. Suddenly, Chennai were the hunters. One boundary and three singles later, 18 runs were needed and I was at the wicket with Tanvir. Makhaya Ntini had the ball in his hand and two overs, just 12 balls, of the very first IPL remained.

Ntini bowled five pretty good deliveries – only a two and four singles from them – yorkers mainly. Then I was on strike with seven balls to go, 12 runs to win.

'Hmmm,' I thought, 'they've got a guy called Balaji – we used to call him the "Bellagio Hotel". He bowls pretty good slower balls, he's good at the death. It'll be tough to get 10 or 11 off the last over, so we need a boundary. *Now*.'

Ntini was at the end of his run. *I had to find a boundary here.* I bet on another yorker and as he reached the crease, I shimmied outside leg-stump to free up my arms and try to hit something through, or over, cover. I won the bet with myself, but he missed the perfect length by a fraction – thank God – and I smashed it straight over cover for four. I remember that shot so well. I probably always will. I hit it flat and hard and the relief was, well, relief.

Okay, so the pressure had eased a bit. Eight off six now – we should get those. We started with a couple of singles and a dot.

Not good. Three-second chill. Six needed off three now. Then the Bellagio Hotel slipped us a wide that went for a bye – so a lucky two added! The pressure was everywhere – four off three now. I got a single, and Tanvir scrambled a couple behind square.

The scores were level, there was one ball left. MS rearranged the field amidst ridiculous tension. Balaji dropped short and Tanvir pulled it wide of mid-on. It beat the fielders and raced away.

'Oh my God, we've won the first IPL!'

The team that Delhi smashed all those weeks ago had won the whole bloody tournament! I was ecstatic. This was right up there with anything I'd done in the game before.

Suddenly, we were swamped. Everyone was charging out to the middle, it was just total chaos out there – guys, young and old, crying everywhere you looked. It was the young kids I cared most about, and this meant so much to them.

I'll never, ever forget that moment. It's a memory that lives on, almost like it's still happening; a memory I can call up and see right there in front of my eyes: it's the moment the Royals won the cup. Imagine the euphoria, imagine those Indian faces and the amazing unbridled joy.

At the presentation ceremony, everyone was on the podium dancing and cheering and chucking champagne around. Manoj and I were hugging. Then, on our way across the ground to the press, I stopped in the crease of the pitch we'd just played on and said to him, 'Stand here for a sec, mate, right here. This is where I smashed Ntini for four and won us the tournament. Hahahaha.'

Half an hour earlier, right there, I'd been wondering how the hell I was going to find a boundary off Ntini. Now the cup was ours! Manoj liked that.

We had one of the great nights, a party to match any Ashes victory and anything else. It's a night like that you play for. From the moment Manoj and Ravi talked me into the IPL, to the party after the final that went deep into the next morning, this was one of the best experiences of my life. We all felt the same. It wasn't just me – Smithy had done pretty well for South Africa but he was on a high too; Watto was on a cloud; the Indians, well, they were off the planet.

The thing was, no-one knew what to expect. We all came at it cold. What was franchise cricket? How would player auctions work? Could such a long tournament maintain interest? From our point of view, could a low-budget team mix it with the heavies? The answer was emphatic. Yes. We won 13 of 16 matches and we won the one that mattered most. The last one. Wonderful.

Manoj Badale

Manoj is a super-clever guy. He's my sort of age and, once we'd worked out that initial deal for me to become a Royal, we hit it off together in almost every way. He does sarcasm well – it's his way of testing you out – so you have to keep on your toes, which is no bad thing. Getting to know him was one of the best aspects of the whole journey and earlier this year we teamed up again to relaunch the Royals in the 2018 IPL.

He loves cricket, and understands it, but having put me in charge he basically left me to it. We had the occasional disagreement, but always for a good reason – not because he was interfering for the sake of it. He has a good handle on things and is right into stats as a measure of performance. His research and my feel for the game clashed occasionally but, overall, worked well together. He kind of challenged me with the statistical stuff, which was interesting, and gave me another perspective on the game. Like Snapey, he introduced me to alternative ways of thinking.

He's been up against it a bit the last few years. The Royals were targeted by the BCCI because Lalit's brother-in-law was in the original ownership group. Then, when Rahul Dravid was building a great Royals team, three players were accused of spot-fixing. As if that wasn't enough, the team was suspended from the IPL when Raj Kundra, husband of the Bollywood actress Shilpa Shetty, and a new 10-per-cent shareholder of the business, was alleged to have placed bets on matches, which you can't do as an owner. Manoj rode all that and looks stronger than ever to me. We made the play-offs earlier this year and the Royals story is back on track.

In 2009 the tournament was moved to South Africa at the last minute because of the elections in India. It was a lot harder for our young Indian players, most of whom hadn't left home before. In India there would be 20 or 30 people waiting for them in the hotel lobby every day – family, friends, fans – but in South Africa they got lonely in their rooms.

We played well, though, and to be honest it was a joke that we didn't make the finals. We had Kolkata Knight Riders 6/45 chasing only 102 to win and I had Laxmi Shukla plumb LBW – like French cricket plum. Not out! Yeah, right. He slogged 40 and we missed out on qualification for the semis by one point.

Over the four years I played we were always there or thereabouts, but I began to run out of gas. At 40 years old, the body hurts and my bowling suffered. Add in the fact that with each year, I had less and less to pass on to the players, so it got harder to motivate myself. Every little thing that happened seemed less important and more draining, however important it may have been. That tells you a lot. At the end of the 2011 season, 20 years after making my debut for Australia, I called it a day.

The IPL is still a great tournament but that period when Lalit ran it was spectacular. The pizazz, the razzamatazz, the entertainment – the story off the field as well as on it – was just incredible. Lalit linked the cricket to the fashion industry and games were followed by shows where the best designers had the best girls modelling their gear. The players of both teams sat either side of the runway with a drink, or whatever, and 300 guests would stare, starstruck, not at the models, but at us! Then there'd be a huge party. Vijay Mallya, the Royal Challengers Bangalore owner, had flown the Dallas Cowboys cheerleaders over for the tournament, so the games against them had added spectacle and glamour. The downside was the collection of security guards that followed their every move!

I'll never forget those years, which remain among the most fulfilling and satisfying of my life. I made lifelong friends, won the IPL with a great bunch of guys, inspired a few kids to great things and ended up understanding India a whole lot better than when I started. What a fabulous country it is. Thanks, Manoj.

How the Stars Didn't Win the Cup

In the English summer of 2011, I based myself in England and that autumn I became engaged to Elizabeth Hurley. We lived between our London homes, the Gloucestershire countryside and New York, where she was filming *Gossip Girl*.

One morning I got a phone call from Eddie McGuire, the Australian television and media star and President of Collingwood Football Club, who told me that Cricket Australia were starting their own T20 extravaganza, the Big Bash. He said he was running the Melbourne Stars and wanted me to captain the team. I had no interest in playing anymore.

'Ed,' I said, 'mate, I've had enough. I'm 42, the body's had it and I just don't have the motivation to start it up again.'

'That's fine,' he said, 'just play one game – the first game – at the MCG. You'll put 50,000 bums on seats.'

Typical Ed, one of the most persuasive blokes going around.

'Leave it with me,' I said.

I hadn't had a bowl for six months, but on the tennis court, turning over my arm with Elizabeth catching them and throwing them back, it came out alright. Better still, my body felt surprisingly okay. I was very fit then too, having trained hard, improved my diet under Elizabeth's guidance and lost a bunch of weight. I thought, 'Hmmm, maybe,' and spoke to James Erskine, my manager. He reckoned there was a good deal out there if I was up to it.

I said, 'It's not about the money, James. I'm not going to come out and embarrass myself, and not be able to run in the field or bowl with energy and strength.' He asked how much I wanted to play, to be part of something new in Australian cricket. The answer was: I kind of did. He said he'd see what he could put together with Cricket Australia, who wanted me from a PR angle, Fox Sports, who were televising it, and the Stars, who needed a big-name signing from the get-go.

James came back a week later saying that Foxtel wanted to mike me up, so I could talk the audience through each delivery of an over as I bowled it. It was a step up from the other miked-up stuff players had done before, which was just conversational.

I thought, 'Ohhhh, that's a bit of pressure for an old man, to say I'm going to bowl a slower leg-break wide of off-stump but then I go and bowl a long hop that's crashed through point; in fact, I can see the flipper disappearing into the stands already!' Hmmm . . .

So there was this uncertainty, but, at the same time, it sort of intrigued me too. I liked the idea of talking to the viewer, but wanted to be sure I wouldn't look like a dick. I wanted to help Cricket Australia launch a Twenty20 comp because I'd been so involved in the success of India's equivalent, but I didn't want to be seen to be doing it for money; and I liked Eddie, who is a pretty damn good salesman and loves Melbourne like I do, but I didn't want to fall under his spell if I wasn't truly into it.

Then Elizabeth made a great point. She said, 'You know what, if you're going to do it, do the whole year. Don't just play one game, that's silly – it's like they're wheeling you out, which is the issue creating the doubt in your mind. Do it properly or not at all.'

I said, 'That's spot on. Fuck it, let's do it.'

'Yeah, go for it,' she said.

So I rang Eddie, who was sitting on one of those little plastic chairs, watching his son play a school cricket match, and he said, '*Whaaat?!* You're going to play the whole year? *Yesss!*' And in his excitement, he fell off his chair. 'Shit, Warney, shit . . .'

He was so excited he just lost it, which made me and Elizabeth feel great. James did me a very good deal with Foxtel, Cricket Australia and the Melbourne Stars, a deal that included a small percentage of the Stars, in case CA ever changed the business set-up of the Big Bash to a franchised model.

Soon after the deal, I was playing in the New Zealand Open golf pro-am and got chatting to Viv Richards. I rang Eddie about signing Viv as our batting mentor.

'Ohhh, yesss!' Ed loved that. He said, 'Do it, mate, and then tell me how I can get Garry Sobers too. We've got two of the cricketers of the century, and two are no longer with us, so let's get the other one who is!'

Farewell to the MCG – or so I thought . . .

FAIRFAX SYNDICATION/VINCE CALIGIURI

CAMERON SPENCER/GETTY IMAGES

And goodbye, Sydney, from me and my mate, the Pigeon.

IPL ecstasy . . .

And IPL glory. This picture reminds me of a wonderful time and an amazing success story.

Warne: The Musical. Eddie Perfect did a close to perfect job.

Joe Hachem – great player and great mate.

World Series of Poker Main Event. Contemplating the next move – do I shove, check or call?

Elizabeth days – Flemington races and the opening of Club 23 at Crown. It was wonderful to have her by my side.

Aaron Hamill, my best mate.

Fun at the tables with James Packer – both James and Kerry have been important figures in my life.

The Great White Shark and the King of Moomba. Greg Norman was the face of Australian golf for a couple of decades – we all loved him. Melbourne's sandbelt has a truly wonderful collection of courses, of which Kingston Heath, Metropolitan and The Capital are my favourites.

Eighteenth tee, first round of the 2014 Alfred Dunhill Links Championship at The Old Course, St Andrews. It is right here that you walk with the ghosts of the game.

Channel Nine commentary team, November 2014. This a special picture because it was the last time we saw Richie. His passing is still felt all over the land. Greigy had gone too, of course, and televised cricket in Australia will never quite have the same magic again.

But others do a good job too. These days Sky set the standards. Here I am on air at Lord's with Andrew Strauss, Ian Ward and the Sky cart.

Miked up and just as predicted. Dismissing Brendon McCullum for Melbourne Stars, December 2011, having talked it through with the Fox Sports viewers.

Cricket All-Stars in New York. 'Sachin, I think this was a good idea, mate!'

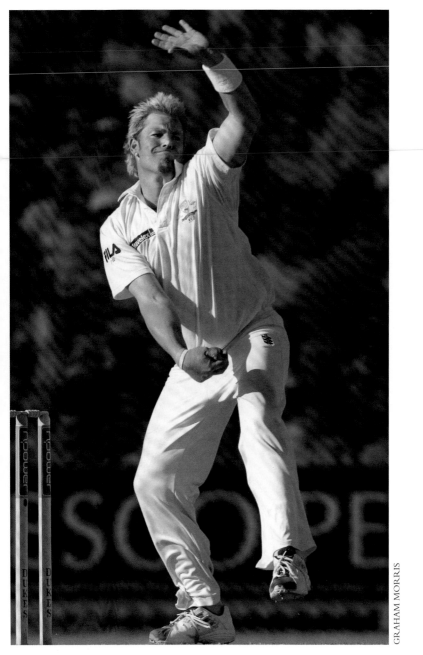

Everything nicely lined up here and ready to pull the trigger.

A lot goes into winning a Test match and the celebrations are well deserved once it's over.

Pup's World Cup, at home, in 2015. The MCG roar when Mitchell Starc bowled Brendon McCullum in the first over of the final is the loudest I've heard on a cricket ground.

WILLIAM WEST/AFP/GETTY IMAGES

With Brian Lara in Melbourne in 2005. He was playing for an ICC International XI in a one-off series against the Aussies – a worthwhile experiment that didn't really come off.

With Murali. 1508 Test-match wickets between us, so lots to talk about.

Suited with 'Beefy' Botham for the 2013 golf Ashes. Come on, Aussie, come on! We lost.

SCOTT BARBOUR/GETTY IMAGES

ABOVE LEFT: Boxing Day, 2010. No worries, Hugh can play . . . err . . . a bit!

ABOVE RIGHT: With Ed Sheeran, as well as my other great mates Dimi Mascarenhas, as good a human being as there is out there, and Ross and Stephanie Desmond, who aren't too dusty either.

A favourite picture of mine – the kids and a couple of their mates with Chris Martin and a couple of his. Yes, Coldplay came for a BBQ before the concert in Melbourne in 2017.

Wannabe rock star: this confirmed it was never going to happen! Having said that, what a night!

Guess what – me and Becks were discussing haircuts and face creams.

The King and Queen of Moomba.

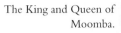

Spiders excluded, I enjoyed almost all of *I'm a Celebrity* – no, really, I did!

The first-ever hole-in-one to the back right pin position on the 16th hole at Augusta National. A ridiculously exciting moment and a picture that will take pride of place forever.

With Mum and Dad at a Foundation event in 2015.

Jason and Dad help me celebrate.

The family album. Geez,
they've grown up quick.

It's all about the balls . . .

I said, 'Mate, calm down, Viv is plenty good enough.'

And he was. He was brilliant on the approach to batting. The room just sat there open-mouthed when Viv spoke. He said things like: 'The better I thought the bowler was, the more I'd look to impose myself and win the early skirmishes. To me, this was war; not just a game, war. Me against him and there could only be one winner. I loved the battle. Loved it!'

We had Ian Chappell too, as Chairman of Selectors, because David Evans, who is the ultimate Chappelli fan, was on the board with Eddie. I played with 'Godfrey', as we called him, at St Kilda Cricket Club in the 1980s. He became a hugely successful businessman and has built a fantastic new golf course, Cathedral Lodge, with Greg Norman. So Godfrey wanted Ian, the best cricket brain going around, and I said he's the perfect Chairman of Selectors. Eddie just said yes to everything.

The build-up to the first game was great, such a buzz everywhere round town. Oh, wait, my first net session, how's this . . . I came in to bowl and, first ball, a young kid I'd never seen before reverse-swept me and I went, fucking hell, what?! It was partly the audacity of the shot, the lack of fear in it, but more the power. He hit it so hard. Next ball, he ramped me. I thought, 'Hello, times are changing.'

After that, everyone was just hitting the ball – attack, attack, attack – and I quickly realised that the pressure on bowlers was massively more intense that it had been even just a year earlier. I was now into my 40s and thinking, 'Hmmm, maybe I've gone a road too far with this T20 thing.'

I mean, in that last IPL – nine months earlier – if you had mid-off and mid-on back, they'd try and hit it in the gap, not over their heads. But here, in Australia, they were just trying to hit it as hard and far as they possibly could and didn't seem to care about the consequences at all. It was like the loss of a wicket was irrelevant. This new mentality was even more apparent in our first game, against Sydney Thunder, when David Warner, who'd just made his debut in Test cricket, made an unbelievable hundred. He smashed all of us everywhere, and I mean *smashed*. We lost. I said, 'Don't worry, guys, I lost my first IPL game too.'

Eddie wanted me to captain the Stars, but Cameron White was captain of the Australian Twenty20 team and he didn't want to be compromised. Fair enough. It wasn't what I'd agreed with Ed when we did the deal but I was cool and saw Whitey's point of view.

So, second game we went to Brisbane, and having talked the TV viewers through being hit 10 rows back by Warner, I thought, 'Righty ho, I'm pissed off with the first game, let's get it right this time.'

I bowled a really good over to Brendon McCullum, beat the bat once and beat him in the flight off the last ball as he tried to hit me down the ground, but it dropped to safety. Next over, Brendon Julian, an ex-team-mate now Fox commentator, was in my ear.

He said, 'Right, Warney, what you thinking here, mate?'

'Well,' I said, 'the last ball of the last over, he tried to hit me down the ground for six, so I think he's going to try and sweep this one hard and square, so I'm going to go for a faster slider, very straight, looking to get him bowled or LBW.'

'Great, good luck,' said BJ, like, *Yeah, right, no chance.*

'I think I might need it, Beej,' I replied.

Here we go. I bowled a fast, straight ball, the flat slider, that he tried to sweep. It bowled him.

'How good was that?!' said BJ.

That delivery was the lead news story in Australia that night. It really helped the Big Bash, especially so early in the tournament, because people who wouldn't normally watch tuned in out of curiosity. We won the game and got on a good run, but lost the semi-final with a disappointingly lacklustre effort in Perth against the Scorchers.

I signed for a second year, as captain. Cameron White was having a rough time and was happy to get out of the firing line. We lost in the semi-final again, to the Scorchers in Perth. Again!

Whitey and Brad Hodge were hammering them and we were 1/159 off 15.2 overs – Hodge 50 off 30, White 88 off 52; 10 sixes between them – when the rain came. The first ball after we came back on, Whitey got out and the momentum was lost. We reached 2/183 off our 18 overs, so we were very much in the game – favourites, in fact, but not out of sight as we had promised to be. Then the rain hit us again, in Perth of all places! The target was reduced to 139 off 13.

I still seethe about the end of this match. I concede that I made a mistake bowling young Alex Keath instead of myself. The thing was, it was so wet out there, I couldn't grip the ball. Brad Hogg had gone for 44 off three overs when the Scorchers bowled early, and it wasn't even so wet then. Keath went for 27 in his one over – Shaun Marsh just manhandled him. Not that that meant the end of things, but it did make defending the score more difficult. When I talk about what happened next I lose the plot a bit.

Rain reduced the game from 20 overs to 18, after our pretty awesome batting effort had made us strong favourites. Then more rain came and the match got reduced twice, finally settling at the 13-over chase – so definitely a wipe-out of our odds and now advantage to the Scorchers.

I could spend ages on the 10 runs needed from James Faulkner's final over, and on Jackson Bird's drop of Mike Hussey from the first ball of the over alone. But the match, the BBL final, and a Champions League place all came down to the last ball of the match.

Adam Voges on strike, three to win, and two to force a one-over shootout. Faulkner, who was captain by the way because me and Cam White were serving time for slow over-rates earlier in the tournament, stood at the top of his mark with me and Cam setting the field.

Then we went to our own fielding positions to see James bowl a brilliant wide yorker that 'Vogie' missed and, though Huss ran through for the bye, we assumed we'd won. Until we saw standing umpire Mick Martell signalling a no-ball. Now you'll understand why I lost the plot.

Cam, who should have been one of the four inside the circle, was outside it! Only three inside the circle! As it turned out Jimmy Faulkner had overstepped the front-line too, so it was a kind of double no-ball. Jeeeeesus!

Huss smashed the extra ball over mid-on, and the Scorchers had a home final at the WACA to shout about.

The whole thing was nuts, just ridiculous, but we only had ourselves to blame.

We'd lost the semi in the first year at the WACA, and lost it there in the second year too. It was hard to take. But we had a fantastic time and I'm glad I went for it with the Stars. I'll always thank Eddie for calling me up and trusting me in my old age. After that game, I packed it in for good – 44 years old and proud of a 'second' playing career that went way beyond even my sometimes extravagant imagination!

16

Photograph

Elizabeth

I FIRST MET ELIZABETH at Goodwood in England. I don't often go to the races, aside from the huge spring carnival in Melbourne that I take Jackson to most years nowadays. If I'm going to have a punt, it will more likely be on the roulette and blackjack tables or in a poker school. I've only been to the horses once or twice in the UK, so I think we can call it fate that one Elizabeth Hurley was in the same private box as me at Goodwood in the English summer of 2010.

We just clicked straight away – lots of laughs, just a natural chemistry, I guess. She was still married, although in the process of breaking up with her husband, Arun Nayar. I was giving it another go with Simone, so it wasn't anything more than one of those first-up things most people have when they meet and like each other.

We swapped numbers, kept in touch and met in a bar in London a few weeks later. There was more than just a connection this time, there was a sense of excitement. You meet a lot of people in your life, anywhere from the racecourse to the supermarket really, but only very occasionally do you immediately feel on the same wavelength with someone completely new.

It's pretty hard to say what brought it on – don't the French say a certain *Je ne sais quoi* – but pretty quickly we both knew there was something special going on, something real. We had a drink, then dinner, and that was that. Nothing else happened – we were both in a situation that needed resolving first.

I went back to Australia, but we kept texting and even tweeted, which of course was public and aroused suspicion. I went with something like, 'Looking forward to dinner next time, hope you'll be cooking at home though'; she replied with 'Yes, sure will, can't wait to see you!' type thing. Pretty lightweight. Suddenly, *Woman's Day* came out with a front-page picture of the two of us at Goodwood and the headline 'In Your Dreams, Warney'. The article with it included the tweet. It was funny in a way – if only they knew. We just giggled and moved on.

Simone and I went to Topolino's in St Kilda and I said to her, 'Listen, I think . . .'

'I know,' she said. 'We knew on the first night we got back together, didn't we?'

'I guess we did,' I replied.

We agreed it was over, for good this time. 'So what are we going to do?' I asked. 'How do we tell the kids again?'

She said, 'Oh my God, we can't tell the kids again. Not right now, anyway. The summer is starting soon, and you'll be all over the place commentating. Let's get through Christmas and the school holidays and tell the kids before they go back to school.'

Good plan, I said. Which was exactly what we did.

Later in the year, I was back in the UK to film some interviews for my new TV show, *Warnie* – more about that in the next chapter – and a couple of days later I met Elizabeth at a function that she'd invited me to. About 20 of us sat at a long table but, by now, we were struggling to hold back. As both of us were now single, we left early, kissing in public, and she came back to the Bentley hotel where I was staying.

As we entered the room at about 1 am, the fire alarm went off. We both thought, 'This is a bit weird,' so we looked out the window onto the street and didn't see a thing going on. We figured someone had lit a cigarette in their room or something and then, wow, the next thing we knew there was banging on the door and shouts of 'Evacuate, evacuate!' The sirens were going nuts, people were running all over the joint and we ended up outside on the street. We waited a while but not much was happening, so we disappeared up a side street and started kissing again. Anyway, Elizabeth left soon after this drama and that was sort of it.

During the next few days, I was busy recording interviews for the show and the best part of a week passed before I flew home.

I will never, ever forget landing in Melbourne. There were a thousand messages, some of which were from Elizabeth – call me, call me. The front page of the *News of the World* had a double-page spread on us leaving the party, hugging, kissing, standing outside the hotel in the middle of the night, up the side alley, the lot. We reckon that someone who saw us at the party tipped off the press and then the hotel, and someone there set up the fire-alarm thing. Pretty easy to fix with a wad of cash!

Now, remember, Simone and I hadn't told the kids we'd split up and although Elizabeth and her husband had agreed to separate, she was still technically married. The press put two and two together and made five: 'Cheating Warne, again', 'Hurley cheats on husband' type stuff, which wasn't true, but they could be excused for thinking it was. The moral of the story is: deal with things instantly, no matter how hard it is to do.

The kids were 13, 11 and eight, so they knew enough about what was going on in the world. Most importantly, they thought their dad and mum were together. They were angry, which was fair enough. We should have told them straight away. In trying to protect them, we let them down. Simone and I sat down with them and ran through everything, this time coming completely clean, and in my case, that included Elizabeth. Summer, the youngest, and I had watched the *Austin Powers* film together, which made us cry with laughter, so, she had 'met' Elizabeth in that movie.

'Is that really her, Dad?' she asked.

'It is, Summer, it is.'

Brooke wanted detail. Is this serious and, if so, what happens next?

I said, 'Yes, I think so, but we live on opposite sides of the world and we can't be sure how it'll pan out. We really like each other and feel we can be very happy together.'

Jackson kind of shrugged his shoulders, as if the world was passing him by in its usual confusing way. Hidden deep down was his belief that I'd hurt his mum again. All three of them thought that. Their blame fell on me. I could sense it and understand it.

Of the many things I've learnt about my children, their resilience and loyalty stand out. When I introduced them to Elizabeth, it was the first time they'd met any girl I had been with since either of the break-ups with Simone. The reason was simple. I didn't want the kids exposed to anyone unless my relationship with that person was serious. Contrary to the rubbish often reported in the media, EH was the first serious relationship I had with anyone outside of Simone. Their attitude to meeting her was fantastic – open, warm, welcoming and natural. Thanks, guys, I'll never forget that.

Elizabeth had flown to Australia at exactly the time I was moving into a new house that had taken 18 months to renovate. The day the beds arrived, the press were there and wrote the story that the biggest new bed was for her. It was a circus, so much so that the next-door neighbours set up a cordial stand, selling drinks for a dollar to the press and other sticky beaks out the front. We had 50 to 60 people camped there, for goodness sake, so the market for cordial was real good!

That evening, a strip club, or escort agency – looking to drum up business, I suppose – sent one of their pink stretch Cadillacs and took photos of girls hanging out of it with the new house as the backdrop to the shots. Callaway sent us Mr and Mrs golf clubs. Helicopters hovered overhead with cameras poking out of them, waiting for us to move a muscle. It was just a joke – absurd – and it stretched our sense of humour at a pretty intense period of our brief lives together. And, remember, most importantly this was meant to be a trip for EH to meet my children.

I wanted to show Elizabeth a bit of Melbourne but we were housebound. When we did break out, cars would follow us, cutting off other drivers and running red lights. The chaos was so extreme it moved from dangerous – certainly dangerous on the road – to funny. Elizabeth enjoyed Melbourne otherwise and even agreed to Eddie McGuire's idea that she toss the coin at the start of the Stars' campaign in the first Big Bash.

Things just grew from there. My three children went to England, Elizabeth came a few more times to Australia, and we went on holidays together as a family to Sri Lanka and the Caribbean. Though my kids were different from her son, Damian, they got along pretty well. Mine mainly sporty; Damian, more arty. Damian and Summer were the most alike, singing and dancing together and putting on shows for us. They had a terrific bond and still keep in touch to this day! Brooke and Elizabeth got along well together and Jackson bought into all the times we had as one big family.

That was how we rolled. Elizabeth signed to do *Gossip Girl* in New York so we spent six months there, on and off. I was also between Australia, seeing the kids, and England for TV work, as well as other sponsor commitments globally. To be honest, it was pretty draining but we kind of rode through it, in our determination to make the relationship work.

In the European summer of 2011, James Packer invited us to his boat in Spain and – wait for this – sent his private plane to New York to pick us up. Well, what are mates for! We arrived, and the boat, the *Arctic P*, was exactly as I remembered it from previous visits – just out of this world. To be on that boat – ship, really – is just the greatest experience and Elizabeth loved it.

We had a few drinks on deck, and a few more, cranked up the music and, as we started to dance the night away, I began to think of proposing right there and then. After 18 months together and completely on impulse in the middle of a dance, I grabbed Elizabeth, dropped to one knee and said, 'I'm not sure about you, but I've never got along with any woman as well as I get along with you. I'm madly in love with you. Our kids get along great. How would you like to spend the rest of your life with me?'

Without hesitation, she replied, 'Of course I would, silly, I'm madly in love with you too. I feel exactly the same. I've never got on better with anyone than I do with you either.'

So I shouted, 'Yessss!'

'Pack' was on deck too. He turned around and said, 'You haven't, have you? You just haven't . . . have you?'

'Errrr, yep,' I said, 'and, guess what, you're the first to know, James!'

'Your secret is safe with me,' he said, and on we partied.

I didn't have a ring, nothing, but the moment was right. The Warne impulse was in action. So we danced and sang and drank and blew the speakers before we crashed too. On our way to bed, Pack said, 'Superstar, when you wake up, you are going to be somewhere special.'

No kidding – we had breakfast off the coast of Morocco. There was no-one in sight, no-one for miles, and Pack and I just hammered the jetskis off the African coastline, laughing and racing and having a ball.

After a while, we stopped for a dart – yep, I kept them dry under my wetsuit somehow – and, bobbing on the ocean, he said, 'How about last night? How cool was that!'

I said, 'Mate, it was sensational. I've never been so happy in my life. Thank you so much, buddy. I've found the girl for me. And, while I've got you, mate, thanks for everything you've done for me and, best of all, thanks for being such a great mate over a long period of time. I owe you so much.'

'Mates never owe or judge, Warney,' he said, 'they just look out for each other.'

Amen to that. We stayed on board for a couple more days and the sense of euphoria never left that boat.

Back in England a week later, I was working for Sky on a Test in Birmingham. I came off air and my phone rang. It was EH.

She said, 'Have you seen this article in Australia saying we're engaged?'

'What the hell?' I said. 'I haven't said a word.'

Elizabeth told me that she hadn't either, as we'd agreed we wanted to sit down face-to-face with our kids and tell them the great news. The only other person who knew was Pack. I said I'd call him.

'Maaaate, as if I would tell anyone,' said James when I rang. 'I haven't told a soul.'

'Well, there was only three of us there, Pack. Elizabeth hasn't told anyone, I haven't told anyone, and you're saying you haven't told anyone, so it must be the crew on your boat.'

'Maybe, mate, I don't know. The journos find these things out – they just do.'

I was pretty stressed. This could not be happening. I hadn't told the kids, so this was bad. That night, which was early morning Australian time, I called them. They weren't happy. Brooke came on the line on behalf of all three of them.

'Dad, what the hell is going on? You haven't mentioned anything to us. Is it true?'

I was put in a situation that I shouldn't have been and didn't want to lie to my children.

'Yes it is,' I admitted. 'I wanted to tell you when I got back in a couple of weeks but unfortunately the press have got it.'

'Dad, this is ridiculous. Look, we're happy for you, but . . . geez, why didn't you think to ask us or at least tell us straight away? You can't just go off and get engaged and not tell us what's going on.'

The longer they talked about it, the angrier they became. I'd let them down, though through no fault of my own this time. I was pretty angry too and once again it caused grief for our families.

(About six months later, Elizabeth, Tiger Woods and I were opening Club 23 at Crown in Melbourne. James was there too. Up he came and said, 'Okay, it was me. I'm sorry – hit me, do whatever you want. I told them you guys were engaged. I'm really sorry.')

For a while, the stories about me and Elizabeth kept coming, which made for a rockier start to the engagement than we'd hoped for. Looking back, I don't know why we thought we could get away without too much media coverage – maybe we were lost in ourselves. It was kind of nice that we thought that way too.

Anyway, things settled and I can honestly say that the time I had with Elizabeth were the happiest years of my life. I was more in love with her than I'd ever realised I could be. The more I thought about it, the more I understood that my relationship with Simone was based on a wonderful and close friendship between two newly married 24 year olds. With Elizabeth it was what I had been searching for.

There was the initial physical attraction, how she looked, acted, spoke; then the things you talked about, related to and liked to do together. But the substance, that chemistry, comes over time and is part of how much you grow to respect each other. The more I got to know Elizabeth, the happier I was in general. We lived between Melbourne, London and her house in the Cotswolds before buying a bigger house near Ledbury in Herefordshire. I loved the country lifestyle and, contrary to what people may think and say, I was pleased to be out of town and enjoying the country lifestyle.

We bought a house together because we wanted to start the journey of shared experiences. It was an investment in the relationship. We did the house up the way we liked as a couple, making sure each of the kids had their own room and that there was space for them to be there at the same time without falling over each other. We created a big, beautiful family home. If only we could have been in it more.

Elizabeth was meeting a whole new set of people, mainly sports-driven of course, and travelled back and forth from Australia establishing new friends and loving the outdoor life. In turn, I hung out with a different crew too, some high-flyers among them. Because Elizabeth was in fashion, eyes were trained on us. It was funny to be critiqued for my clothes, having been brought up in a town where no-one gave a damn about what you wore. We featured in magazines and newspapers and, as social media took off, everyone had a view.

The change in my appearance had nothing to do with Elizabeth at all. I'd watched the first pilot of my interview show and been taken aback at how overweight I looked. TV is a shocker, of course, puts on three or four kilos, they say. I didn't look good and decided to sort it for myself. I went on a monster fitness regime, ate better and trained hard. This was almost exactly the time EH and I were getting it together properly and, well, there's no rubbish in her fridge, no chance – nothing processed, no junk whatsoever. It made me rethink the way I lived and, put simply, made me want to wake up in the morning feeling great and excited about the day. Training became a routine. I lost 12 kilos in no time, and felt fantastic.

It shits me that people think I've had plastic surgery – or any work, for that matter. I've never gone under the knife. Yes, Advanced Hair

Studios have been looking after my hair since I first signed with them in 2004, years before I met Elizabeth. And yes, my teeth are whitened – big deal. I'm a smoker and they'd be a revolting yellow if I didn't. And, for the record, I get them done regularly. Who cares? People made out that I'd become some kind of skinny, wacko freak. Nah, I just wanted to feel healthy and look good. So that's vain of me? Yes, fine, I'll take that. I'll also say that Elizabeth's encouragement inspired me to look better. Eating healthier food was cool and helped me to feel better too. Blaming EH for the change in the way I looked was ridiculous.

The relationship wasn't always plain sailing. During the 2010/11 Perth Test match, I thought I lost her. I'd done a couple of silly things, like texting a few girls from my past, and one of them made it public. It was the girl from a shop across the road in Melbourne, actually, who I'd been in to see. A picture appeared of us in the paper a couple of days later. Obviously, I shouldn't have gone to see her but as it was early days I didn't realise how serious Elizabeth's and my relationship had become, and certainly not how committed to it she was.

I knew I was serious about her but I didn't immediately get the same vibe back and I misjudged that. It was a stupid thing to have done and I flew to LA to meet her at the first opportunity. We talked things through, got to grips with each other's understanding of the relationship – the trust issue was huge, given my history; that, and nights out with the boys, poker, too much golf – but we never really looked back after that trip cleared the air and gave us a path forward.

So, how come that around Christmas in 2013, we broke up?

There was no single, clear reason. Elizabeth never did the wrong thing by me; I never did the wrong thing by her. She signed a seven-year deal to play the Queen of England in the TV series *The Royals*: a dream role. I was genuinely happy for her. The problem, as it turned out, was filming for five or six days a week, eight to nine months a year, which left little time for us to be alone together, as well as spend quality time with our children.

I was back and forth from Australia and she'd lost her flexibility to travel pretty much anywhere. The immediacy to our lives was lost and the friendship between our kids – that we'd worked so hard on – was compromised. We were living on a whiteboard timetable and the long periods apart were just becoming too difficult. I mean, we can all do three, four, five weeks every now and again, six weeks if we have to, but not three months.

Of course, the more you're apart, the more you ask questions. I got jumpy about the time Elizabeth still spent with Hugh Grant, for example. He is her best friend but they saw each more when I wasn't around so, well, you know. Hugh was also her go-to for advice on pretty much everything, and on acting roles in particular. So they were always bouncing ideas around. My world, cricket, was nowhere near her world. Add in the distance, and the children, and you get issues that are harder to resolve than perhaps they sound.

We still love each other in many ways – we're not *in* love, like we were – but I still care for her deeply. She showed me what a relationship should mean and she guided me in other areas that went on to make a huge difference to my life. I think we were good for each other and I know that I miss the love we had.

Three things I would pick that lead the way about Elizabeth – a silly and really enjoyable sense of humour; great affection; and a supportive thoughtfulness that is harder to describe but was incredibly important to the way we were able to spend our time together. Did we buy the Ledbury house too early? Yes. But we were planning a whole new life, so I'd call it bad timing, not bad thinking. It ended up costing a lot of money, which was annoying but not worse than that. It's the same with the ring, though I think it's time I had that back! I'll always care about her and would be there if she needed me. We had something very special. I regret none of it and now have a special friend forever. Who knows what the future holds? Maybe the romance and relationship will one day come alive again.

Regrets? Come to Think of It, I Have Had a Few

I've often wondered about the point of regret: if something is done, just move on. My mantras are 'Always get too far ahead of yourself' and 'Always shoot the messenger'. But while working on this book, I've seen light through new windows. There are choices I've made and actions I've taken that have both embarrassed and let down other people – my children, in particular. Those things I regret.

Most of them have concerned women. I'm not always guilty as charged, but more often than not I've been to blame for stories that have become public and caused a lot of pain. I often feel misrepresented, especially when events get out of hand and the accusation against me becomes national news. After all, I haven't committed crimes, nothing I've done is illegal, and, in my view, it's not anyone else's business either. Why do these girls want to tell the world about a night with me?! Because I'm Shane Warne, that's why, and that means public property. When these stories have broken, it's like I've been unfaithful to the whole of Australia. This attitude continued long after I was divorced and leading a single life. On the basis of these judgements, I've been guilty of some howlers.

Here's one the tabloids particularly liked. Is it really that shocking?

Rewind, Early May 2006

Me and my best mate, Aaron Hamill, the footy player, caught up for lunch in Chapel Street, Melbourne on the day I was leaving for the county season in England. Walking back to the car, we stopped outside a Playboy shop that sold all the gear, underwear included. There were two gorgeous girls inside, so in we went to have look around. We had a giggle but with the flight looming that evening we had to move on. I bought a three-pack of the Playboy undies, the ones with the big bunny-ear logo on the crotch.

A few days later, I was in the middle of a home match for Hampshire against Middlesex and there hadn't been a lot of washing done. My suitcase still hadn't been unpacked and lying on the top of a pile of new shirts, pants, ties etc were the Playboy undies. Needing some fresh jocks, I grabbed a pair, thinking this would give the boys a laugh. I wore them to the ground, changed into training kit, then playing whites, and at the end of the day climbed back into the clothes I had on in the morning. The boys loved the jocks.

That evening, the physio, Paddy Farhart – 'Jaws', we call him, he's a great man – and I headed out to La Lupa for a pizza. About nine o'clock, a text pinged through: 'You should be here with me'. It was a girl, Coralie, I'd known for a while – 10 years to be precise – with a group of London mates. Immediately following on from the text, she sent a picture of her kissing a girlfriend. They were in London, I was in Southampton. I texted back, saying I'd be there in an hour.

I apologised to my dinner mate – 'Sorry, Jaws, I've gotta go to London Town, see you in the morning' – grabbed a bottle of vodka, two bottles of champagne and hit the road.

'No worries, Jaws,' as he called me too (it was like the old days at home when we all called each other Harry!). An hour and a half later I rang the doorbell and Coralie opened up.

She was flying, her friend too. 'How are you, babe?' she asked.

'I'm great but I need a drink to catch you guys up.'

'This is Emma,' she said, turning up the music and lighting a cigarette. Next minute, they got up and started dancing with each other, very provocatively, very sexual, kissing each other.

I said, 'Don't mind me, just keep going – I'm quite happy just sitting here.'

I sat there having a smoke and a drink as they started to take off their clothes. At the bras and knickers point, they got out a massive inflatable sex toy – kind of drunken, silly stuff. At this stage you have to understand my mindset. I'd known this girl for 10 years, never done anything with her, just known her as a friend. She was with a friend, they were both pissed and, if I'm honest, it was a fun kind of vibe.

Soon enough, though, I was joining in. There was a lot of laughter, another drink, and one thing led to another. I started kissing them both, clothes off, and then, from nowhere, they pulled a bed out of the wall! Well, we just went for it.

Around 2.30 am – two drinks and two girls later – I was back in the car to Southampton. I was fine to drive and, on the journey back, started thinking about the next day's play against Middlesex and how badly we needed to win it. Because I figured I'd miss the alarm, instead of going home I went straight to the ground, parked in my spot, put the seat back and crashed.

It felt like five minutes later that Paddy banged on the window. 'G'day, Jaws, how was your night?' I asked.

'All good, Jaws – more to the point, how was yours?'

'Late!' I said.

(I should explain this Jaws thing. Paddy is an Aussie and when he came to Hampshire I said we'd signed the biggest fish in physio, so he said the club already owned the biggest fish in cricket. You had to be there!)

So I hit the shower, had a shave and started telling Jaws the story of the night. Then I had a dart, a chat with the team about the day, and five hours later we were back on the piss. We'd won inside three days, and I knocked seven over, my best return for Hampshire: 7/99.

Sometime that evening I had a call from a number I didn't know. I left it. No message. Then it rang again. And again. Do I? Don't I? I do.

The voice at the other end sounded kind of nervous: 'Errr, hello, this is Andy Coulson – I'm the editor of the *News of the World*.' This is the bloke who ended up as the Prime Minister's offsider. 'We have pictures of you with a girl called Coralie and a friend of hers.'

'Mate, plenty of people pretend they're me. Fuck off,' I said and I hung up.

He rang back again.

'We're going to print the story, the pictures are good quality – it's you, for sure. Is there anything you'd like to say?'

'Mate, I've got nothing to say – now piss off.'

'How the hell?' I thought. There were just the three of us. I didn't see any camera, didn't hear any motor or clicks. Jeeesus. I called Coralie.

'Oh my God,' she said, 'you wouldn't believe it, my friend has sold the story. She got pictures – she had a hidden camera.'

I said, 'Tell her to effing well stop.'

'It's too late,' she said. 'She's already sold the story to the *News of the World*.'

Coralie has always maintained that Emma set us both up. She did a good job. The pictures came out with me in the Playboy undies, so a lot of people assumed that 'Warne the Playboy' poses around in Playboy jocks. My mistake, if that's what it is, has been to grow into a larger-than-life character, this guy who has 50 beers at the bar, bets a wad at the tables, celebrates like a mad dog, and all those sorts of things.

Honestly, that's really not me, not deep down. I'm a pretty simple sort of guy, who has worked hard to reach the top of his profession. That's not 'work' like nine-to-five but, as I've tried to explain, bowling makes huge demands on body and mind and means you live with a lot of expectation of your performance and behaviour.

I like to go out and have some fun occasionally. I like my golf and poker. I love my kids and folks and have had two fantastic women in my life. That's sort of it. Of course, not many see the real me. My inner circle, family and close friends, see a very different person from the one that's been portrayed to the public. It's like two different people are out there.

Anyway, the evidence in the *News of the World* was pretty concrete. Warne guilty. 'But of what?' I would plead in a court-room. Not that my plea would matter. 'Guilty' is the end of the story in the media.

I've always struggled to deal with these tabloid stories. What sort of person hides a camera and then sells the pictures? As I've said, I'm not a criminal – a murderer or drug-runner. Yes, I'm into women, which has cost me massively, time after time. To me, only a pretty sad mind goes undercover to make a few bucks out of a friend and a guy she's never met before. Either that or Coralie was lying and she set the whole thing up. Then it's even worse. Either way, in general, I just don't get it, never have. I know, it's naive of me, but my inclination is to give people the benefit of the doubt.

The Snape Sessions

When Elizabeth and I decided to pull the trigger and start dating seriously, we knew the outside interest in our relationship would be challenging. Our feelings for each other were very strong and

I know that, in my case, I'd found what I was looking for. But, as I said, it wasn't always easy. My history was everywhere and therefore hard to avoid. For example, I thought I'd lose Elizabeth because of that innocent picture in the paper of me and an ex-girlfriend. Thankfully, that wasn't the case, and, as I've mentioned, after a fraught period, Elizabeth and I sorted it out. From that incident, we came to understand each other better and our bond was stronger than ever.

I'd had a scare, though, and became more determined than ever not to stuff things up. During the IPL, I had come to enjoy working with Jeremy Snape, the sports psychologist Manoj had hired, and, I have to say, I learnt some good stuff from him. Although I've never been one for shrinks, I trusted Snapey, both as a friend and an advisor. He didn't do the psychobabble thing, he just talked good sense and understood what made me tick.

So, in January 2011, I called him in the UK and said, 'Snapper, have you got three days to spare this week? Because if so I'm booking myself a ticket to London and taking you up on the offer of some time on your couch.'

He said, 'Lock it in, mate, no distractions, just us. Let's do it.'

I booked a hotel in central London and we shut the door to the outside world. It was an intense and sometimes brutal experience. Here's Snapper's recollection of a period that reshaped my life.

> It was an interesting call to get out of the blue. I had a lot on but sensed Warney was serious about needing someone to bounce things off and help if they could. I postponed some commitments and met him in London just a couple of days later. The first thing was to encourage him to stop and think, so I mocked up some TV 'newsflash' footage of a plane crash in which he was killed – the imagery was quite shocking – and then I asked him to write his own obituary. In other words, how would he like to be remembered?
>
> I'd run similar discussions and practical examples with some corporate CEOs that had worked well, and I hoped it would make him recalibrate the way he went about aspects of his life. Warney

never has time to stop and think, so I asked him to consider the way people would remember him, the images in their mind, the phrases they'd use and the impact he'd made on them, both positive and negative. He didn't like some of the answers he gave and that was the start of the turnaround.

Warney's children are a big motivation in his life and his number one priority, so I asked him to imagine their memories of him. They were at a critical age in their development (this was 2011, don't forget), so they still needed his guidance and support. The outcome was that if he'd died at that time, he wouldn't be remembered by them in the way he wanted. This gave us a chance to plan a rewrite of the second part of his story, the post-cricket story – his legacy to those he loved.

As another reference point, I asked my graphic designer to create an image of Warney aged 70 and used it alongside some images of a family at a beautiful beach house. It was meant to show him the life he'd love, surrounded by his kids and grandkids. This was an ending he could create and he was quickly excited by the fact that its potential was in his own hands. The challenge was that he would need to be driven by different motivations from those that fuelled the success of his earlier career. This called for renewed focus on relationships, trust, stability and helping others, as opposed to the drive and relentless urge to prove people wrong that had motivated him previously.

He started to construct a set of goals and plans about his key relationships, his health, his career – his long-term success and happiness. Thinking about your life aged 70 gives you a different perspective, away from the hustle and bustle of next week's or next month's commitments. Most of us focus on the day-to-day stuff, but he was able to make bolder choices in the search for this new dream that he believed strongly could become reality.

He started to prioritise his fitness, sleep, diet, his Foundation too, and to spend more quality time with his family and close friends. It was like he'd realised that he could be in control of his life again, rather than being thrown from commercial commitment to official function to airport to hotel and to cricket ground every minute of every day of every year. He started to create better long-term choices that gave him a routine, within an environment that allowed greater happiness.

Generally in these situations, the new choices we make lead us to better perspectives and from them we can grow again. For example, when we decide to drink less, we find we eat better, sleep better and then our relationships are less tense etc, because we are well rested and thinking more fairly and more clearly.

From my side – Warney is one of the most creative, ambitious and single-minded people I know. At the exact moment when he called me, I could sense that his greatest strengths were pointing in the wrong direction, so we set about getting them lined up straight again. It was like a weight lifting off his shoulders and the way he changed his life in the months ahead was a joy to see. Suddenly, he was channelling those strengths and able to create the life he wanted, rather than risk ruining the one he had. It's an enormous credit to him that he did change – not just physically either, though that turnaround was amazing, but mentally too – and went on to have a happy time with Elizabeth and to make his children proud.

Wow, great job, Snapper. The bottom line was that when I was 18 years of age and told I wasn't good enough to play Aussie Rules football at the highest level, I was heartbroken. I'd used that as my motivation to be good enough in whatever field came next, which happened to be cricket. Snapey explained that the motivations we had as a youngster aren't always useful when we get older, and that it's better to think about what we want to achieve in our time left.

This was a different perspective and I thought about the kind of father, brother, son and friend I wanted to be. We came up with plans for fitness, business ambitions and my relationship – all of which became routine. I'll always be very thankful for Snapey's time and effort in helping me find some peace of mind and improvement as a person.

Thinking about this now, aged 49, I know that I've had enough drama. I don't actually like drama, not off the field anyway. People think I manipulate it for self-promotion in my private life. They're wrong, I hate it. A moment ago, I mentioned those mantras of mine. Well, the bit about always getting ahead of yourself kind of explains that I act on impulse and let the thinking happen later, if at all. For most of my life I didn't really consider consequences, but as a father of three grown-up children – 21, 19 and 17 – I sure have to now, otherwise their maturity will go past mine.

I probably share too much that I see as funny about myself, with people I consider mates. They then sort of live their life through me, but that means they talk and so the stories become embellished, which is *not* a good thing. What I'm actually doing is sharing my experiences with a sense of humour about the situations I find myself in. These get distorted and, understandably, people close to me then wonder why I open myself up in such a public way. So I'm going to keep things to myself a lot more and live less of my life on the edge. I'm going to try to show the real me.

The truth is that I want to share a life with a wonderful woman, not be a lonely old bastard turning up on news bulletins here and there. The more I think back to my time with Elizabeth, the more I reflect on how rewarding a good relationship can be – the best thing you can have in your life really.

People don't want to read about the crap Shane Warne gets up to. Whether most of it is true or not, the one sure thing is that I've put myself in a situation where I've given it the chance to be true. That is just plain stupid. So, not anymore. I don't want to be reading about Shane Warne in the wrong part of the paper. Honestly, who does?

17

The Great Gigs at Nine, Sky and Star (Meantime ... Get Me Outta Here!)

Nine

My journey with Channel Nine began soon after the Ashes tour of 1993. It was Kerry Packer's idea to sign me as a personality for the network and I'm forever grateful to him. Earlier this year, Nine's 40-year hold on the cricket rights was broken by Cricket Australia's new deal with Fox and Channel Seven. I'd never have left Nine but cricket is in my blood and I love commentating so much that there was no option. Fox were very enthusiastic about continuing where we'd left off after my brief appearances as a player in the early days of the Big Bash.

Kerry would understand, I'm sure of that. Throughout the years when Nine had the rights, he liked to have a couple of key Australian players in his stable and, back in 1993, he said they'd be looking to have me on air as often as possible. I got a thousand bucks a week and my mobile-phone bill paid. It was like a retainer fee. I was very flattered. For about 24 hours, that is.

I signed the contract one Friday evening and on the Sunday night had a phone call from a producer saying that their sports presenter Dermott Brereton was crook and they'd like me to read the sports news on the *Ernie and Denise* show – that's Aussie showbiz legends Ernie Sigley and Denise Drysdale.

I said, 'Errr, okay, yeah sure, no worries.'

They said, 'We need you here tomorrow morning at 5 am.'

I was like, 'Oh, 5 am, right.'

So I got in there and we did wardrobe, make-up and all that sort of stuff. Then this guy, the producer, I guess, or maybe the floor manager, said, 'We need to teach you a bit of autocue.'

'What's autocue?' Remember, I'm just a kid out of Bayside, 23 years old and with no idea about television production.

He took a deep breath and said, 'Well, it's, um . . . hmmm, tell you what, let's get into the studio and give it a go.'

So I sat behind a desk, three cameras pointing at me, and the one in the middle with a monitor above the lens. On the monitor my script was slowly rolling over.

'Read at your own pace,' he said, 'but try not to look like you're reading.'

'Errrr, okay, but I *will* be reading,' I thought.

Away I went. 'Over the weekend, we've had some fantastic tennis, a surprise winner at the golf in . . .' But I was reading it. Obviously I was.

He said, 'No, no, stop for a sec. We have to make it look like you're *not* reading it. Look at the words, turn your head occasionally, read, pause, read, up the pace, slow the pace, read.'

Okay, so I tried that, but just kept stuffing it up. It's harder than it looks. It took an hour before I got the hang of it. Or thought I did . . .

So, Ernie and Denise were live and doing their thing – it was a chat show, with a bit of music. I was sitting in the chair next to them and, on a cue, Ernie said, 'We've got a special guest this morning. He's just signed with us at Channel Nine, and he's a fantastic cricketer as we saw during the recent Ashes over in the UK. Yes, it's a wonderful time to be introducing Shane Warne to bring us the weekend's sporting news.'

'G'day, Ernie. G'day, Denise.'

'You've got the sport for us, Shane. What's been happening?'

'Well, yeah, thanks very much, guys. It was another big weekend in tennis. Mary Price had a great win at . . .'

'Do you mean Mary Pierce, the French player?'

'Errrr, yes, Pierce, ummm . . .' Pause. 'Ah, Mary Price, no Pierce, sorry!' *Gulp.* Two lines in, the panic was on and I was dying.

It's true, I just stuffed the whole thing up. In fact, all the way through my segment, it never got any better. Hence I never did it again. But it was an experience – my first-ever experience of live TV – and, looking back now, quite funny.

Cricket commentary was a different thing. Kerry detailed a super guy called John Murphy to guide me, and we watched tapes of old matches and listened to Richie, Bill, Tony and Chappelli. Not that I didn't already know the sound of them. When Jason and I played in the backyard, the volume was up loud enough on the TV: 'Here we go!' roared Greigy; 'Got him,' screamed Bill, 'yes, he has!'; 'Quite brilliant,' said Richie. They'd all go off in their different ways and, from there, you just knew it was summer.

I did my first-ever commentary for Channel Nine in 1996, when I was recovering after the first finger op. It was pretty daunting. The Test was in Adelaide and I just sort of rocked up and was told I was on with Tony. I had an earpiece but didn't know where to plug it in or have any idea about any of the technology. I didn't have the courage to ask, so I'd just sat in the chair being interviewed by Greigy, more than commentating myself. It was fun. I'd already thought way back then that commentary could be a good way of staying involved in the game and giving the viewers a new insight.

Kerry had a few things he pushed real hard: (a) take the viewers into the middle because they'll never get the opportunity to experience what it's like out there; (b) don't tell us what we can see – we're not dummies; tell us why it's happening; (c) don't alienate people by assuming they know the game like you do; like, don't say mid-off and not explain it because the wife might be sitting there with the husband – or vice versa! – and have no idea where mid-off is; (d) relate to children in any way you can; (e) have fun, because if you don't, neither will the viewer.

I sometimes talk a bit too much in my commentary, but I like to think my skill is to read the play and give the viewer the options – the captain's perspective really. I like to educate, especially when it comes to wrist-spin, and I like to entertain.

I spent a lot of time with Kerry and Lloyd Williams. After my dad, they're the two men who've helped me the most in my life. Lloyd has so many strings to his bow and, being a brilliant entrepreneur, is a good man to have looking out for me – backing me in ventures, supporting me through personal issues and public crises, and guiding me through the best and worst of my own daftest ideas. Kerry was great on getting my house in order from day one of playing for Australia – the right tax people and financial advisors, the people to trust, in all the walks of life that suddenly hit you when a bit of fame and money comes your way. 'Surround yourself with good people, son,' he used to say.

They both loved the fact I had a punt. Neither of them were allowed to gamble at Crown, their own casino, so they used to stand behind me at the blackjack table watching every move. Kerry, typically, called the shots and one night we had a big argument about a 12 versus a two.

I said, 'Depending on where you're sitting at the table and what cards have fallen there previously, you get a sort of a feel that sometimes you take a card and sometimes you don't. It's instinctive.'

He said, 'That's wrong, son. Whatever you do – taking a card or not taking a card – you keep doing it for the whole night. You never let instinct overtake common sense. Stick to the book,' he kept saying, 'and you won't upset the cards.'

I spent many a day with Kerry in Sydney, at his main house in Bellevue Hill, and also with James out at their amazing Ellerston estate, where I once took Elizabeth and the kids for a memorable New Year's Eve – beautiful for us, go-karting for the kids! They were special times. I was so lucky to be thought of as a friend by the Packer family.

I got to know James and his best mate, David Gyngell, really well. They were like brothers. We were the same sort of age and the three of us hung out together a lot. James is a very clever guy, but living in Kerry's shadow wasn't easy for him. He stepped up when Kerry so sadly passed away at the end of 2005. Of course, there was only one Kerry Packer. He had this massive personality, dominating everyone and everything around him. He could be scary – brutal even, if you were on the wrong side of him – but to those he liked he was warm, generous and surprisingly charming.

If I was picking out one thing that touched me the most, it would be his super loyalty and an unwavering level of support through thick and thin. That, and his brilliant sense of humour. After his memorial service in Sydney, I stood on the steps of the Opera House with Ian Wooldridge, the great British sportswriter, who loved Kerry every bit as much as any Australian. I lit a cigarette and said, 'Bloody marvellous service.' He lit one too and added, 'For a bloody marvellous man.'

James had a lot to live up to and, sensibly, focused on hotels, casinos and the other stuff that interested him. TV wasn't his thing in the way it had been Kerry's. When he finally took over the empire, he made an amazing job of it, but in different ways to his old man. It can't have been easy but he has become hugely successful in his own right and, I'm sure, would have made his dad very proud.

Gyng is a great TV guy, really smart. He took over the Nine Network very young – still in his 30s, as I remember – and clashed a bit with an ageing Kerry at that time. When he came back after Sam Chisholm's second run at being CEO, he did a great job getting the business back on track and saving the cricket from going elsewhere. Gyng has a positive energy that flows through everyone around him. If he'd been at the helm in 2018, no way would Nine have lost the cricket rights.

Gyng was right behind *Warnie*, my show on Nine that didn't turn out the way I hoped. My idea was for a half-hour interview show across a desk – 22 minutes of TV, eight minutes of ads. The producers turned it into an hour-long prime-time Thursday night show with a whole lot of other off-beat stuff going on – like, say, a pre-recorded segment of Merv Hughes with the Barmy Army. The show wasn't much good, but people did seem to like my interviews. I'm no journo, or current-affairs guy, nor am I a full-time interviewer. I'm a sportsman with interests outside cricket – music and cars among them – and my idea was to chat to a few big names that I knew well and try to bring out their relaxed, social side.

I accept that me doing the product-placement reads just didn't work, but, as I say, the interviews were fine: Sting, Chris Martin, Dannii Minogue, Susan Boyle, Jeremy Clarkson and James Packer – all of them happy to chat in a more relaxed style than usual. The problem was that they were cut so short the show never did them justice. I mean, I did an hour and 20 with Pack, his first interview in 20 years, and the show had nine minutes of it! Ah well, an experience that ended up being a disappointment, though all those people I interviewed said they enjoyed our chat.

After Gyng retired in 2015, Nine saw cricket as business and took all the emotion out of their thinking when it came to negotiating the new deal. It's too early to judge, but I think Cricket Australia might one day see their decision to ignore Nine's bid as a mistake. Nine gave cricket a home for 40 hugely successful years and provided the money that allowed a beautiful and traditional game to move into the modern age. Now the same game settles into a new home, hoping that the viewers move in with them too. Good luck to Fox and to Channel Seven – they're big shoes to fill.

The Sky and Star

Nine didn't have the rights to the Ashes in England in 2009, which was when I was first asked to work for Sky. It was interesting walking into that commentary box, which, of course, was based on English ideas and thinking, not Australian. I knew Ian Botham very well, David Lloyd and Ian Ward a bit and, of course, Nasser Hussain and Michael Atherton as opponents that we hammered more often than not. I hadn't come across David Gower or Michael Holding much.

The English philosophies are different from ours, for sure. I was fascinated to hear how these guys felt about cricket on and off the field, as I had been when travelling around India with the other IPL captains. In general, I'd say Australians see the game aggressively, whereas the English still have a love affair with village greens and country houses – though not in the leagues up north, to be fair, where cricket's relationship with working-class communities can still be found. Australians don't really do that social cricket thing at all; it's full-on play to win from early schooldays and never wavers much from that. The pathway from school to the top is complicated in England, but in Oz it's simple – school; grade, or club, cricket; Sheffield Shield and the national team.

Anyway, back to the commentary box. Sky doesn't break for an ad every over, so there's much more on-air discussion and debate between the commentators. This gives a better opportunity to explain the nuances and listen to everyone's take on situations we might not necessarily agree about. The production values are good and there's a lot of air time to fill, so the guys can go to town on content.

Everyone always thought of Channel Nine as the best, but the money available from satellite television changed that. I think Sky's coverage is hard to beat right now and, given the new billion-pound deal that runs until 2024, and the likely spending power on production that comes with it, it might hold its position at the top for a long time yet. I've had nine happy summers with Sky. It's a great company to work for, and though I'm now out of contract, it'll be interesting to see how things pan out going forward.

I signed with Star Sports in India for the England tour of 2012/13. Kevin Pietersen and Alastair Cook both got great hundreds. Graeme Swann and Monty Panesar bowled out of their skin and England won over there, a great achievement. There were good days and bad – I was in Mumbai for Sachin's 200th Test, watched the Australian team getting hammered first-hand on two different tours, and saw the silly Homework-gate saga embarrass Australian cricket in general.

Star's production is both amazing and chaotic at the same time; pretty much like India, come to think of it. Everything is fixed only at the last minute and then works surprisingly well. It's great fun being with guys like Ravi Shastri, Laxman Sivaramakrishnan, Sanjay Manjrekar and Sunny Gavaskar. Again, the different philosophy thing stands out, but also, just in general conversation, it's interesting to hear how these guys think about everything from commentary to playing against Australia back in the day. What we all said about each other at team meetings gets us laughing the loudest and is proof that you don't always see yourself as others do.

I think Ravi is a great commentator and I love the way he says, 'Bowled him!' *Love it.* I sort of say it to myself quite a lot, and then on air, when I'm the lead commentator, I'm still trying to incorporate Ravi's gruff, rasping tone into my way of calling an exciting moment.

I've always loved the Indians and their passion for the game. Everyone from exec producers to cameramen and runners, they're all so lovely and generous. They say things like, 'Oh, I remember the first time you came over, sir, you are my favourite cricketer.' Come to think of it, maybe they say that to everyone! I don't do much for Star – 20 days max a year in total – but it's really fun. I like the innovation and the optimism. Oh, and the dugout for the players, with the TV interaction, was an outstanding idea. Good job, guys.

I'm a Celebrity, Get Me Out of Here

I'd been asked a few times to do the British version of the show, but didn't fancy it. I was asked onto the British *Big Brother* too. In Australia they tried to get me to do *Dancing with the Stars*. All noes. With due respect, I thought these shows were for wannabes and washed-ups.

The Australian *I'm a Celebrity* rang the first year – 2014 – but I scared them off with a figure of two million bucks or nothing. They said, 'That's our budget for everyone,' so there was no deal. I watched that first series and quite liked it, and I got tempted by the chance to portray myself in an environment outside cricket. Then the reality of six weeks in the jungle with no contact with the outside world kicked in. No chats to the kids – no way! So I binned the thought.

However, the following year, Brendan Fevola, the AFL footballer, was over at my place one night and said he was doing the show. He asked if he could represent the Shane Warne Foundation while he was on. That really got me thinking. There'd be a guy in there who I know; I'd have the chance to show Australia there's more to me than people think; and two million is serious money, so my charity could benefit massively. The question was: could we get them to pay that figure?

I called James Erskine, my manager, who said he knew the main guy at Channel 10 and would speak to him again, which he did. Bingo! Next day, James rang to say we've got the $2 million! Oh shit! When you throw a big number out there, you're not really expecting to get it; but now . . .

So I asked the kids. 'Oh Dad, you've got to do it,' they said. 'You'd be awesome. It's a great show – we love it and everyone will see the real you.'

'Right, the kids are the deal-breaker,' I thought, so I rang James back. 'I'm in,' I said.

When the Big Bash launched in mid-December, Channel 10 were relentlessly promoting *I'm a Celebrity* every night, saying they had a pop star, an AFL Hall of Famer, an actress, a cricketer – and everyone thought it'd be Andrew Symonds, until someone on TV, maybe one of the Big Bash commentators, said out of nowhere, 'I'll bet it's Shane Warne.'

Ricky Ponting sent a text, 'Is it you,' and I replied that no way had I signed to do the show. It was my way of not lying. I hadn't signed – I had only agreed. I didn't sign till I was off the radar, on the edge of the Kruger National Park in South Africa.

I stayed in a hotel for a night – I was sort of held back for the first 24 hours of the show – and was then moved in a private plane to the bush. I was asking all the producers who's in – 'Come on, tell me' – but everyone was sworn to secrecy. They put me in a box, left me at the camp and disappeared.

After an hour the other contestants came back to camp, having heard a rumour that Warney was the last man in. They kind of circled the box and took a while to open it. When they did, out popped Warney, me thinking, '*What the hell am I doing here?!*' And they were probably thinking much the same!

And Brendan Fevola was, like, 'You bastard, what the hell *are* you doing here?!'

James negotiated me leeway on three things. One was smoking. I could smoke but had to follow the process of being about a hundred yards from the camp with a security guard accompanying me. After a few days, some of the others smelt the cigarettes on me and there wasn't much the producers could do when the smokers among them insisted on coming along for a dart as well.

The next was my hair. It has to be redone by Advanced Hair every three weeks, so the company flew out to the bush midway through the filming of the program. It was a simple enough strand-by-strand process to the crown of my head and took no more than 45 minutes. So, at 5 am on the third Saturday morning, before anyone else woke up, a couple of the production people from the show came and grabbed me. First they blindfolded me, then led me to a car and drove me to a house where the hairdresser fixed me up. I was back by 6.30 am and, at exactly the time everyone else was getting up, I wandered into camp as if I'd just been to the dunny. It was quite a cool experience, and certainly kept the Advanced Hair people sweet.

My 'bed' buddy was Havana Brown, a big name DJ in the States – she's such a cool girl and we've become really good friends. Fevola was a long-time mate anyway, and I really enjoyed Anthony Callea, the singer. There were a couple of people I didn't like – Laurina Fleure, a kind of reality-show specialist and just loopy to the point of being a pain in the arse. In fact, as the days passed we realised she was not to be trusted.

Then there was Val Lehman, who played Bea Smith in *Prisoner*, which was a massive show that I loved. I was a bit of a fan boy with her until I got to see how she behaved in the camp. She was bitter, basically, and in that small space it came over too strong. She's not a bad person but it was hard out there, and much as we tried to make her life easier, her stubbornness drove everyone crazy in the end. I felt for her in a way – and in another way I didn't feel for her at all.

The show ran for 24 hours continuously from Monday to Thursday. Then Friday and Saturday were days off and Sunday was the big one, the ratings winner. Everything was exactly as you saw it on TV. The camp, accommodation, the challenges, all the general restrictions such as alcohol, and the food – strictly rationed beans and rice for the first two weeks only. The reason for food rationing was to make us so seriously hungry that we became agitated, moody and edgy, which adds to the show. In short, when you're hungry it doesn't take long to piss each other off.

I was the camp captain for the first three weeks and then lost a split vote to continue in the job to the ex-rugby league star and media personality Paul Harragon. Paul immediately had me on dunny duty – yep, cleaning them. So that's number one and number two and the job required emptying the buckets after both and cleaning them out. Any time someone walked towards the dunnies, you just thought, 'No, please, not a dump.'

Some of the challenges were pretty shocking too. First up for me was the field of maize. It doesn't sound much but just hang on a minute. I chose Fev as a partner. 'Sorry, mate, I don't know the rest of these guys yet, but I know you, so you gotta come with me.'

We walked for 45 minutes through the hills and were shown these two perspex coffin-like boxes that were upright in the middle of the maize field. The challenge was simple – there were 12 camp members and the longer we lasted in the boxes, the more of them got to eat that day. Each minute was equal to one person's tucker. Last for 12 minutes and everyone eats.

They began by pouring in corn right up to our necks. We were fixed in real tight and it was hard to breathe. Fev didn't seem to give a shit – he was up for everything, tough bastard. Whenever we went for a challenge, the added pressure was not to let the others down. To ease this, we had a pact: if there's something you can't do or are just too scared to do, don't feel you have to do it. We expected everyone to try but not to suffer. Fev had no trouble with that; in fact, he was ridiculously gung-ho about everything. Nearly . . .

It was 30 degrees without a cloud in the African sky. We were squeezed in super-tight, no movement at all, with the wall of a perspex box centimetres from our face. There was corn up to our necks and we were choking from the dust. The only concessions were goggles to protect our eyes and a small, thin cap-like thing on our head so that what was to come didn't get stuck in our hair. Then they said, 'Right, let's make this more interesting.'

First, they tipped in bull ants, which nibble and bite at your ear and then disappear inside it, just like they do to the nose. Then cockroaches. There were 12 insects in total and they kept coming fast. Which had nothing on the snakes. *Yep, snakes too. Oh my God!*

'Fev, are you okay?' I asked.

'Jeeeesus!'

Snakes changed the game. Fev wasn't quite up for everything after all.

The snakes attached themselves to our necks, sliding around as we squirmed and began to panic. Twelve minutes took a long time. Longer than 12 minutes, for sure. But we made it.

Now get us out! This took some time. They had to suck out all the corn and then, once we were out, they had to apply tweezers to remove the bugs from parts of the body I didn't know I had. Look, in general I'm alright with snakes, so it was doable. Spiders are my killer. I've got a phobia – I'm past scared of spiders.

We returned to the group, told them our story and that 12 meals, if you call them that, were on the way. Then, stinking, I headed for the shower. Shower on, cameras on, clothes off, just go for it. Some of the contestants wouldn't shower with the cameras on them. I was past caring and within 20 minutes was crashed out in bed – if you call it that.

I could go on forever. Of all the challenges, the ones with insects and reptiles were the worst, especially when they were food. Errr . . . except for the century egg. That was bad.

They'd taken the shell off this 100-year-old egg. It was raw and was black in colour. You only won the challenge if you ate it without throwing up, so I wasn't favourite.

I thought, 'If I put it all in my mouth at once, should I chew or swallow?'

The trouble was that as soon as I picked it up and lifted it to my mouth, the stench overrode any plan. *Ohhhhh my God, it stunk!*

So I said, 'Right, ready, yep; go, mate, go.' And in it went. I physically couldn't swallow the thing, so I chewed. It was so bad. I gagged internally, up into my throat, but swallowed it back. The process took ages but, bit by bit, runny little globules of century egg slithered down my throat. I don't know how long it took – five, six, seven minutes? – but I didn't throw up. Good effort.

We ate rats, fish offal, cockroaches, frogs, and we drank cow's blood and antelope blood. I completed challenges where, with hands tied behind my back, I put my head into boxes of rats, snakes and lizards, amongst other things, to get a key out with my mouth that would open the door to a reward for the team.

I was the guinea pig, the go-to for challenges. I know why. Either the public voted to see how I'd cope or the network thought I'd better earn that money.

I snapped just once, after another vote for me to do something disgusting. (This was the day after an anaconda, which was in a box we had to extract a key from, bit my forehead and the medics came rushing in with a serum, which wasn't needed, thank God.) I'd had a gutful, simple as that. I think they bleeped out most of a few paragraphs of swearing about the whole bloody thing. It sounded like I was at breaking point, but it turned out I wasn't – I just had a few things to get out of my system.

That hissy fit of mine became the inspiration for a trick the producers wanted to play on Brendan Fevola. The idea was that I was truly over it and planned to leave – the call if anyone wanted out was, of course, 'I'm a celebrity, get me out of here!' – and that Fev was detailed to talk me into staying. He got into a real state about it, confiding in the others that he thought I was serious this time.

Initially, the others were in the dark too but the more emotional Fev became, the more most of them worked out what was going on. His heart sank when, after a couple of days of pleading with me to stay, I told him that nothing – nothing on earth – could change my mind, not even him. Then I went off to pack my bags.

'Don't go, mate, you can't give in now. You can't.'

'I can, mate, that's it, I'm out. Thanks very much, everyone, I'm going. I'm a celebrity, get me out of here.' And I walked over the bridge and disappeared.

Fev was, like, 'I couldn't convince him to stay – oh my God, we're going to miss him in here.'

Ten minutes later I walked back into camp, gave Fev a huge hug and said, 'I love you, mate, I'm not going anywhere.'

Everyone started laughing and we all got a beer, because the challenge had worked so well. Then we sat round the camp with Callea singing. It was a good vibe and much needed for morale at that stage of our stay.

After 40 days living this weird existence, and with only five contestants remaining, they told us about a challenge that had chocolate and ice-cream as the reward. The challenge was to hold a spider in your hand for 30 seconds: 'A South African baboon spider, a highly venomous species of tarantula.' This thing eats birds, for Christ's sake.

I repeat, I have a phobia about spiders. For people out there who don't know what a phobia is, it's as good as thinking you're going to die. If you have a phobia, you just can't get in the vicinity of what you have to do, because you have no control over your body or mind. It is truly frightening.

In the build-up to the challenge, my body started to shake as sweat gathered around my head, chest, arms and legs – everywhere. The spider was brought onto the set. It was hairy, and as big as a hand. From 20 metres away I watched the other four have this thing placed in their palm for 30 seconds. The spider stayed dead still. It was over in a flash, but me, well, I just couldn't imagine dealing with it.

My turn came. My hand was covered in sweat, my clothes drenched. The bushranger guy didn't want to put the spider on my hand while it was shaking.

I said, 'For fuck's sake, mate, I'm shitting myself. This is as good as I can do.'

Fev put his arm around me and said, 'Think of your kids. Do it for them, mate – it'll be over before you know.'

He rubbed my back and shoulders and tried to calm me. This is all on YouTube, not that I can watch it.

I started bawling my eyes out. The spider was on my hand now and everyone was urging me on. I knew I had to complete just 30 seconds, but I was overwhelmed with fear, panic, tears and even prayers. My mind felt separated, my body detached. These moments will live with me forever.

My hand steadied a little, the spider was placed in my palm. The 30 seconds passed. I went into shock and curled up, burying my head in my chest and crying like I can't explain. I was taken to the medics, and the psychologist got involved too. I was scared – really scared – even though I knew it was over and I was going to be fine soon enough.

The next day I was voted out. The story ended at the one place I would have known it would end if anyone had told me about the spider. Anthony Callea went the day after me, then Laurina Fleure, and finally Paul Harragon. Brendan Fevola won it. He deserved it too – he was different class. Respect, mate.

I regret none of it; in fact, I'd say I mainly enjoyed it. No phone, so no contact with the outside world, was a bit of a relief. All I missed was the daily chat with the kids. Actually, that reminds me. Halfway through, we all received messages from family or friends. Summer said, 'Dad, you're killing it, smashing it, we are so proud of you.' Jackson said, 'Hey Dad, you're awesome, you rock, we're all watching and we're really proud.' And the next message read out was to the person sitting next to me.

I said, 'What? Where's Brooke's message?'

The producers said they'd tried her for a week, but she was always out partying. Well, she is her father's daughter!

I've often been asked if there was a moment when I'd have given a million bucks back and walked out of there. The answer is yes, just the one I mentioned when I flipped. I'd done a bunch of challenges in a row and remember sitting there in the evening, thinking, 'You know what, I've had enough. I can't keep doing this, not for another three or four weeks.' But I did.

The food challenges were shockers and sapped my morale. And, of course, I lived in fear of spiders, though I was surprised at how quickly I came out of the shock. '*You're weak as piss, Warne,*' I said to myself, '*get on with it!*'

A bonus was losing 13 kilos. I don't like rice and beans and didn't like any of the reward meals either. I mean, crocodile and wild boar . . . please! There was no pizza or pasta, no bread, no cheese. I fell asleep all the time because I had no energy. I went from 91 to 78 kilograms and the minute I was out of there, I necked a whole bottle of champagne and the biggest bowl of spaghetti bolognese you've ever seen.

To sum it up, if I had my time in the jungle again, I wouldn't do anything different. I enjoyed it and learnt a lot. The public got to see the real me, the kids were super proud and I got to make some unbelievable friendships that will stay with me forever. So thanks to the Ten Network and all the guys in that camp. It was a blast.

18

Reasons to Believe

The Shane Warne Foundation

DURING MY BAN FROM cricket in 2003, I went on a 'Trip of a Lifetime' with Challenge, the charity set up in 1983 by David Rogers for children and families who are living with cancer. We took 10 kids who were in remission to the US and, among other great experiences, had a ball at Disneyland, saw a Celine Dion concert in Vegas and visited the New York City Fire Department not long after the 9/11 attacks. This last part of the trip was intense and incredibly moving.

In fact, the whole journey was really something – a month across America on a kind of magic carpet ride! One of the kids, Chris Hirth, used to knock on my door and say, 'C'mon, Warne, tell us one of your cricket stories,' and the kids would gather round and listen to tales about World Cups, the Ashes and tours to India and South Africa. Chris and I became quite close over those weeks and stayed in touch. There's no doubt that his predicament inspired me to try to do more.

I'd wanted to start a charity venture of my own for a while, but couldn't come up with an idea that stood out from other success-ful charities out there. It was the 'Trip of a Lifetime' that did it for me. That trip truly touched my heart and made me aware of how important it was to raise money that could then focus on children and their families whose lives had fallen through cracks and become particularly difficult. More than a decade of non-stop professional cricket had meant there wasn't the time to commit to anything more than visits to children's hospitals whenever there was the chance to do so. That year out of the game convinced me to think big.

I began by putting in $50,000 of my own money to start the Shane Warne Foundation. I then got on the phone to friends who I knew would want to help me in setting it up. Kerry, Lloyd and David Coe – the businessman who was Chairman of SEL, my management company, and one of the most fun guys going around – all gave me 50K straight away. So did 'Crazy John' Ilhan, who I didn't know so well back then – his daughter, Yasmin, was and still is Brooke's best friend – but who became a great mate and reliable support. (Incredibly sadly, both John and David have since passed away and they're missed more than words can say.) So that was $250,000, which meant I could hire a CEO, rent an office and start planning some events. Err, not quite.

It took most of 2003 and the early part of 2004 to sort out the legal aspects of founding a charity and then to register with the Australian Tax Office. The admin was complicated and left me respecting successful charities more than ever. Having explained my goals to Annie Peacock, Ray Martin, Garry Lyon and Rob Sitch, they all agreed to come onto the board straight away.

Over the years, as schedules and lives changed so too did the board, and guys like David Evans, Glenn Robbins, Andrew Bassat and Eddie McGuire became involved. I only asked people I trusted and believed would make a difference. These were outstanding Australians, from many different walks of life. They were credible, intelligent, and in it for the right reason, to do something worthwhile for both seriously ill and underprivileged children.

We also had three ambassadors – Russell Crowe, Elizabeth and, later, Greg Norman – who gave us fantastic profile and networking opportunities. I was Chairman and in it very deep. The main reason I was so hurt by the accusations against the Foundation in 2015 is that we had such highly respected people involved. No way were these guys using our events for their own ends or creaming money off the top of our fundraising. I mean, why would they? They were successful in their own right! Please. No way.

Brad Grapsas had come on as CEO. He was the Oakley guy who looked after all the sportsmen and women who wore the Oakley gear. I'd known him for 15 years, since Academy days. We paid him $50,000 a year, hardly a rich man's wage, because we were super conscious of our spend and the need to hand over a high percentage of earnings to the causes we supported.

I remember the board's first fundraising meeting when everyone said, 'We've had enough of black-tie dinners. We'll pay a grand not to go to another!'

So our mantra was to come up with new and fun events. We did poker nights, footy finals lunches, golf days, and the big one, the Boxing Day Breakfast, which became a regular and very popular event. In addition, we did one-off private experiences. For example, James Packer gave us Ellerston for the day and punters would pay 10 or 15 grand to go up by private plane, play the course and have lunch or dinner with us.

We had a couple of funny nights with Russell Crowe, who would invite 10 of his friends for dinner and then charge them 10 grand each to listen to me and a 'name' mate talk about the game and tell stories.

One that stood out was when Stephen Fleming came over especially from New Zealand and Russell said, 'Righty-ho, there's no such thing as a free meal. These blokes have paid $10,000 each, your Q&A stuff was okay, but now you have to perform the Australian team song!'

Flem said, 'For Christ's sake, no way! How many times do I have to hear that effing song? I'm outta here.'

And, sure enough, out he walked! So the rest of us got arm in arm and sang it, loud as we could. Then Flem came back in and said, 'Right, you blokes, I've got something for you,' and proceeded to give us the full-blown haka, as good as an All Black. It was just awesome.

I learnt fast that in the event world, even charity events, costs are high. Crown were fantastic and would give us a small room for next to nothing, but the ballroom, for example, cost massive money when employing a huge number of staff, setting up high-quality audiovisual equipment and providing the standard of food and wine that people expected for a $10,000 table of 10.

The poker nights there with the former world number one Joe Hachem were great, but if the auction didn't go well at any of our events, it was hard to make the kind of money that we hoped for. There was a time when a signed cricket bat would get a good price, but nowadays you put a bat in a raffle and hope someone doesn't mind winning it.

These days, it's all about money-can't-buy experiences, as well as access to big-name celebrities. For example, the footy guys – Sam Newman, Garry Lyon, Dermott Brereton, Nick Riewoldt, Billy Brownless, Aaron Hamill, Campbell Brown – would turn it on at footy finals lunches, with TV personalities Mick Molloy and Luke Darcy interviewing them and turning the whole thing into a fun and terrific event.

My mates were unbelievable. Dermott did *Celebrity Apprentice* and chose the Shane Warne Foundation as his charity of choice; then he won *Celebrity Singing Bee* and chose us again. In total, Dermott gave the Foundation over $250,000. Pretty amazing guy is my man Dermott Brereton. So too Campbell Brown, who attempted to swim the English Channel for us. The Browndog would still be out there if he'd had his way, battling on. They had to drag him out of the water, almost kicking and screaming – and all that for the Foundation.

I found myself putting a lot of my own money into the pot each year just to keep the ball rolling by buying tables at events, auction items etc.

On those occasions, you just had to laugh. Here's an example: a jewellery company very kindly donated some special cufflinks – a cricket ball with diamonds all around it and the logo 'SW23'. The auctioneer started the bidding at $10,000, but no-one offered, so I put my hand up.

'Anyone else?' he asked. 'Anyone else?! Okay, going once . . . come on, you can't leave Shane with it. Anyone else? Going twice . . . I say again, going twice . . . no, we're all done then. Sold to you, Shane!'

So I paid 10 grand for some cufflinks with my initials and shirt number on. Mind you, they're pretty cool! Ha ha ha!

The rewards were worth it, though, like getting to know Chris Hirth a bit and driving out to the country to see him for an afternoon here and there. It was desperately sad when he died, but the family felt he'd got all he could from the last years of his short life.

Obviously, financial generosity is essential but it was the time everyone gave to us that was so valuable too. Eddie McGuire, one of the busiest guys going around, came with me to Monash Hospital to sing the Collingwood team song to the children in there who were huge fans of the club. We also used our influence to persuade Foxtel to install set-top boxes into the wards and, well, there was so, so much more.

I could go on about the various aspects of the Foundation's lifespan that made me so proud. It is just a fact that we did some very good things for people less fortunate than us. We donated a substantial amount of money until the GFC hammered us, and after 08/09 it got really tough.

We had a bit of money in the bank that kept the Foundation going, and slowly but surely we recovered some of the lost ground. We were able to do more great things right up to the time in 2016 when we were left with little option but to close down.

In the end, from 2004, when we launched properly, to 2016, when we were winding down, we gave away $4.1 million to children and families, which is a very significant amount of money. The last donation was one of the most satisfying – $436,000 in total to a 14-year-old boy called Will Murray, who'd become a paraplegic after a fall from a pier. Will was an unbelievably talented sportsman, possibly reduced to life in a wheelchair. The family house had to be altered and upgraded, a special-needs car was required – all the stuff we read about but pray doesn't happen to our own. It was just horrific. You marvel at how a family copes. Will Murray could have been anything in sport. Life can be so unfair.

Deciding how we directed the money that we raised was an ongoing challenge. We wanted to help as many children as we could, but which children? Cancer, leukaemia and all that goes with them are horrible, but then so is autism. Our initial aim was to help the families who couldn't find a way through the mire themselves. Even that got complicated, though. I mean, how do you prioritise one worthy family over another? So we hired a company based in Sydney called Australian Philanthropic Services, who advised us on the families they most thought our Foundation would relate to, and then did due diligence to ensure they were above board.

This was an expensive but necessary cost and gave us further credibility. Most applications came through the usual channels, others via the NCF, the Necessitous Circumstances Fund, which provided for one-off cases such as accidents that led to sudden, unexpected needs.

You can imagine how many applications were coming in and how tough it was to sit down as a board and make choices about people's stories, each of which was as tear-jerking as the last. The practical applications you could cope with – a library full of books for kids, for example; that was a tick straight away – but the emotional ones . . . Oh wow, I shudder looking back now. Deciding was just so hard. Annie Peacock was the best at this. She had the clearest mind when it came to what fitted our criteria and what didn't, and she knew the charity world inside out. Annie is a very special lady and a very dear friend. She was the heartbeat of the Foundation.

In a way which is hard to explain, this role in our lives became a privilege. All of us on the board were shocked by the traumatic experiences good, honest people went through, and being able to do just a little bit to help them opened our eyes to the possibilities out there; and to the dangers out there, for that matter. It was incredibly rewarding when the money we gave or the time we put in had an effect. I only wish we'd had more of both.

Take Maxi, as an example, a little boy who was so seriously ill with an undiagnosed genetic neurologic metabolic condition. We weren't able to achieve everything for him we would have liked, but we did help improve his situation. No-one in Australia could diagnose the problem but we used our influence to push very hard for him to be accepted into a specialised program at a hospital in America.

When we eventually won that battle, he became the first non-American citizen accepted into the program – in 2014 – and diagnosis was reached that gave real hope. We were a very, very small part of the journey Maxi took with his fantastic mum, but we made a difference. At the Footy Finals Lunch, we played a three-minute video and big, strong AFL players were reduced to tears. Many of us have these sorts of stories to tell and the very least we can do is look to improve the lives of these very brave children.

I'll never forget when Chris Martin came with me to meet Aiden Buchanan, a young boy I'd got to know who lost members of his family in the tragic Black Saturday bushfires in 2009 that claimed 173 lives. Chris had read of the traumatic experiences everyone had been through up there at Kinglake – about 50 kilometres north of Melbourne. When we went to Aiden's school, the response to Chris coming along was just incredible. There's no price you can put on that sort of genuine interest in, and concern for, people who have suffered such devastating loss.

◇

In November 2015, a story appeared in the Melbourne *Age* taking potshots at the Foundation. I had no idea why this journalist suddenly went after us after all the good we had done. Consumer Affairs Victoria conducted a thorough investigation that lasted 11 months and, apart from the late lodging of the 2015 annual accounts, cleared us of any wrongdoing. My statement at the time reads true now:

> As expected CAV and the Commonwealth charity regulators have cleared The Shane Warne Foundation of any wrongdoing besides one late lodging of annual accounts by the due date in 2015.
>
> The foundation, myself, management, ambassadors and the board have always maintained that nothing inappropriate had occurred and now it's official after these thorough investigations. It's disappointing one particular media publication continued to run inaccurate and baseless articles that misled the public. Thank you to everyone for their unwavering support, it has meant a lot to all of us.

We also released a statement announcing our next step:

> The foundation announced its intention to wind up in January
> 2016. Since that time, it has spent significant resources responding
> to inquiries from the Victorian and Commonwealth charity
> regulators. Now that those inquiries are complete, with no
> finding of any wrongdoing relating to its fundraising activities,
> the foundation will take all steps necessary to wind up its
> operations as soon as possible and make a final distribution to its
> beneficiaries.

After 13 years of time and effort given to something we were so proud of, the criticism and accusations really hurt. It made no sense either. As a board we felt we were the target of a witch-hunt, and the public questioning of our integrity meant we began to doubt our willingness to carry on. The story spread like wildfire and definitely affected us.

For all that, the final straw in the decision about whether to wind up the Foundation or not was the Christmas Eve raid by the charity regulators – 4.30 pm on Christmas Eve, for goodness sake! – at the offices of the accountants who acted for the Foundation. It was such a stitch-up and very unpleasant apparently. The accountants handed everything over, and, as I've mentioned, it was found to be all in order.

I tell you what really got to me. Channel Seven put two children in wheelchairs in front of their cameras and said the Shane Warne Foundation wouldn't help them. That is just the lowest act. Unfortunately, it isn't as if any one organisation can help everybody. And what about all the children we did help? I felt sorry for those children but what Channel Seven did was unforgivable and misleading.

I would have gone on television – Seven, if need be – to defend myself and the Foundation, but I'd just arrived in the African jungle for *I'm a Celebrity*. Given that I wasn't allowed to have any contact with the outside world, well, it was pretty obvious there was nothing I could do. Six weeks later, when I came out of the jungle, the moment had gone and the damage was done. There was even an implication that I went to the jungle to avoid the exposure. Oh my God! How unfair was that? Disgraceful, in my view.

The same journalist at *The Age* said I paid my brother 200K to be CEO. True. I paid him 70K per annum, like the other CEOs after Brad Grapsas. Therefore, if he worked for the Foundation for three years, he would have earned 210K, so where's the problem? Jason got the job because he's a good operator, he knew me and the demands on me well, and had done plenty of work for the Foundation for nothing in previous years. I trusted him, he had experience in the business of sport from his years with IMG/TWI and he knew the Melbourne powerbrokers inside out. Good reasons to employ him, in my view.

Then there was the issue with the raffle. Helen Nolan, my former PA, bought a ticket in one of our raffles one year – as did many of my friends and all my family – and then won a Mercedes. Some people said that was a fix too, even though Mick Molloy did the draw live on the Triple M breakfast radio show in front of the cameras!

I'll always be sad – and angry too – about the way the life of the Foundation ended. Making a difference to children has been, and remains, a special part of my life. It's the smiles that do it for me – Chris and Maxi are the examples I've written about here, but there were many, many more.

I should also say that I'm relieved too. The witch-hunt was unkind, unfounded and very depressing. It left me feeling responsible for the reputation of mates like Eddie, Pack, Lloyd and others, which had begun to wear me down. They'd backed me, and, by doing so, had given a massive amount to children who needed their support. The Foundation improved lives and helped to save lives too. We're all proud of what we achieved.

Lloyd Williams

My father has always been my hero and mentor – sound with his advice, both financial and personal, and very worldly. But, as I've mentioned, the trouble is I probably don't listen to him enough.

I believe it's important for sportsmen to have good people around them. I've been lucky that very successful business guys have looked out for me and always had my back and I've been able to tap into their experience when need be. One of these – the main man for me – is Lloyd Williams, the smartest man I've ever met. He's a father-like figure, a sounding board and an essential filter – separating sanity from occasional insanity and making sure that however hard I try, I don't, actually, get too far ahead of myself! Without his unwavering support, I wouldn't have achieved many of the things I have. His friendship means more than I can say here.

Most of our time together has been spent at the Capital Golf Club, which Lloyd built at much the same time as Crown casino in the 1990s. It's a private club with no membership, but he gave honorary guest status to a few good friends of his, and our times together on that fabulous golf course have been terrific. I've played there with Fred Couples, John Daly and Brad Faxon; I hit balls on the range with Tiger Woods. Pretty cool.

Going back a while, and over the best steak sandwich on earth, Lloyd sat in the clubhouse lounge and told me about a guy called Robert Earl, who started, owned and ran all the Fashion Cafes, Planet Hollywoods and then the All Star Cafes. Lloyd thought they were great businesses and when he put an All Star Cafe into Crown, he gave me some of the equity. It was fun. And very generous. In 1997, global superstars turned up for Crown's opening night – Wayne Gretzky, Shaquille O'Neal, Monica Seles, Michael Johnson – and they all had a piece of the All Star Cafe business. Sylvester Stallone and Hollywood people also turned up. It was a great occasion for Lloyd, for Melbourne and a great night for the paparazzi. What Lloyd has done for Melbourne is nothing short of inspirational and has really put Melbourne on the map.

Anyway, next day we played golf with 'Rocky' (who is five feet six, by the way!). He arrived at 2 pm for a midday start. Usually that would have been fine, if rude. But it was my wedding anniversary and Simone and I were booked to go out. Having turned up late, Mr Stallone wanted lunch, then practice balls, then he took 10 shots on the first hole and 12 on the second. You get the picture.

It was pretty much dark when we were done. Then he wanted a drink and a chat. I made it back to Crown, where we were staying, at 9.30 pm. Simone wasn't happy. I don't blame her. I knocked on the door – *knock, knock, knock.*

'What time did you start cracking the shits?'

'Two hours ago.'

'You letting me in?'

'Nah.'

Thanks Rocky, great job.

Lloyd loves cricket. He would be in Melbourne, Kerry in Sydney, and they'd have the speaker-phone on, chatting away for seven hours while watching the game.

One summer Lloyd said, 'Right, Warney, enough of this just trying to smash every ball. I want you to get a couple of hundreds this year.'

'Okay,' I said, 'I'll get you one this summer.'

I made two 86s and got myself out both times. I called Lloyd to apologise.

He said, 'No worries, Shane, awesome batting – the hundred will come.'

For once, Lloyd was wrong.

Shane Warne: the Musical

Not many people have had a musical written about them. Early in 2008 I was approached to be a part of it, but I didn't think it was right that someone could just churn out a show about a person they didn't know from Adam, so I took legal advice. It turned out that they could, but I didn't want to be part of something about my life story that I couldn't control.

Having said that, I liked Eddie Perfect, who was behind the whole thing and I didn't want to bag it in case it turned out okay. I mean, Eddie was a big fan of mine, so maybe he'd do a good job . . .

James Erskine made the point, 'If it's done well, it could be very good for you.' He also thought we should go and see the first night, so we knew what we were talking about if the press came onto us.

He fixed up a secret last-minute arrival, and on 10 December 2008 we snuck in through the curtains at the back of the stalls at the Athenaeum Theatre in Melbourne and took our seats in the back row.

It didn't take long. 'Oh my God,' we whispered, 'this is pretty good!'

'How the hell does he know some of this stuff?' I said. 'It's, like, spot on!'

Eddie had me in my late teens, slumped in a beanbag with 12 cans of beer alongside me, watching footy on the telly while Mum did the vacuuming. I thought, 'That's exactly how it was. How did he know this stuff, because there's no way Mum or Dad would have talked to him!' Nor Jason or anyone else I could think of. Obviously, I missed someone!

He'd done his homework alright. He even had me and Simone in the supermarket, her looking at stuff on shelves and me strolling down the aisle texting some girl. Far out. The John the Bookmaker stuff was very funny and when he brought in Elizabeth for the 2013 revised show, he got most of that right too.

Overall, he'd done the show in a fun, respectful and sympathetic way. He captured that larrikin thing in me and I heard that blokes would go to their seats carrying armfuls of beer for their mates, as if they were living the moment live at the cricket. That's pretty cool.

Eddie is a super-talented guy. He wrote the show, produced it and performed it. Kudos to him. Then, at the end of the first night, he came out on stage after the curtain call and said that the man who this is all about is in the house. I was like, 'Oh no!'

'Please come up on stage, Shane!'

Ohhhhh . . . no option here. Up I went and we had a hug. I thanked him and said what a good job he'd done. I then thanked everyone for coming and said, 'Tell your mates about it!'

Eddie and I became good friends, almost a partnership during that time, because he had collections for my Foundation at every show and we stayed in close touch. In just about every way, he did a very, very good job, and, as I say, not many people are lucky enough to have a musical written about them. Thanks, Eddie.

Melbourne Days

I grew up in a city that is now voted the most liveable in the world and has been so for the past seven years. I love it, with only the occasional reservation, like when we got home from England in 1997 and I moved house to Beach Road, which made the news. One morning I woke up late, threw on a pair of undies and went out the front door to get the paper, which we all used to have delivered back then.

A bus tour pulled up and a bunch of tourists scrambled for position to take photos. *Are you serious?* Then they got out and wanted selfies, or the equivalent of the day. I was like, 'Really?' So I was out there in nothing but my undies, paper under my arm, with 10 people I'd never met, and would never meet again, clicking away.

I hang out a lot with Sam Newman, the ex-footy player and gold-level television star, who is a great mate (and contrary to what people may think – shy!), Dimi Mascarenhas, who played at Hampshire with me, and guys like Brendon Goddard, another AFL footballer.

Sam was a 300-game Hall of Famer for Geelong and is a super-bright guy, very funny and very, very competitive. We have serious ding-dongs on the golf course; heated matches for a bit more than just 10 bucks! 'Dimmer' moved to Melbourne a while back but free-lances as a coach both internationally and in the IPL. He's another golfer and a true companion. Goddard is a scratch marker; he and Tim Henman are the two best sportsmen from another sporting field that I've seen play golf – not necessarily better ball strikers than Ricky Ponting, but more effective all-round players.

I also spend a bit of time with Eddie McGuire, mainly in town over a few drinks or dinner, or at Crown. Ed's a good guy – always on the go, full of enthusiasm and energy. I see a lot of Johnny Williams and Nick Williams as well, Lloyd's sons. Johnny and I once played a one hour, 45 minute golf match against each other in carts and for a lot of cash. No talking – just hit it, find it, hit it again, and then pay up!

Aaron Hamill, who as I've mentioned is another former footy player, is my best mate. We've been alongside each other for a long while. I was on the bridal party at his wedding earlier this year and I reckon we'll be mates till one of us falls off the perch.

Outside of golf, I've got the poker bug. Every year I go to Las Vegas and play in the world championships, or the World Series of Poker Main Event, as it's known. We have a weekly poker night at my place with Joe Hachem, his brother and a few other mates. There's usually about 10 of us, with a glass of wine, a cigar and some deep pockets!

I've just sold the Brighton house, in Middle Crescent, that I've always loved the most; the offer was too good to refuse. It's a shame, because it was done up pretty nice and I could never have wanted more in a home. I'm buying up the road and that will be good too, with a bit of time and TLC. I'm happy in Brighton, just 20 minutes from the centre of the city I love more than any other, and will probably never go elsewhere.

Above all, Melbourne remains the sporting capital of the world. Whether it be the Boxing Day Test, the AFL grand final, the spring carnival, the Open tennis, the Grand Prix, the Masters golf, the soccer, the rugby, the swimming, the athletics, Melbourne has it all and full houses turn up year upon year to prove that there's no place like home to celebrate sport – a central theme of Australian life.

Saints So Near, Saints So Far

There were 100,021 people at the Melbourne Cricket Ground for the 2017 AFL grand final. That's about right – it's a six-figure match year upon year. Richmond won it after years of infighting and upheaval. It's a great club and no-one with a heart for the game would begrudge their players or supporters. They hadn't won the flag since the famous smashing of Collingwood in the 1980 grand final, so you can imagine the party.

As I've said, up until the age of 16, I was a fanatical Hawthorn supporter. My cousin gave me his Peter Knights footy jumper with the number 24 on the back and the only sportsman on the planet

I wanted to be was Peter Knights. Then, when I went to Mentone Grammar, I got scouted by the St Kilda Football Club. I've been a Saint through and through ever since. I never abandoned Peter Knights but Trevor Barker took over as top dog in my eyes – my number-one player who wore the number 1 on his back. St Kilda won the premiership for the first time in 1966, when the great Barry Breen kicked a point in the dying seconds, but never in my lifetime. It'll happen, though – I know it will.

Footy is a religion in Melbourne and a passion for those who have followed a club, any club, for any part of their lives. In my case that means the Saints – as it does for Hamill, one of our greatest-ever players. These guys are super-fit, super-flexible and super-strong, like no other athletes in the world.

The game is hard and the game is fast, a hybrid of many ball sports. Outsiders have called it Aussie No Rules on the basis of the speed and freedom of movement and the extreme physical contact – these guys just hammer each other. The demands, both physical and mental, mean the players have mainly short careers and finish up bruised and battered in more ways than one. There is no padding or protection of any sort and for two hours once or twice a week through the long winter season, they take a pounding.

When they're done, nothing can replace the adrenaline, the rush that comes with the sound of the siren to start a match, which they've known since they first picked up a ball. In return, they are local heroes – as big as Elvis in Memphis. Well, you know what I mean. The point is that they're big, like the soccer players in Manchester and Sachin Tendulkar in Mumbai. Anyway, I love it. Footy is my favourite game by a mile.

I was in nappies when we lost the grand final to Hawthorn in 1971 and in a seat at the 'G when Adelaide beat us up, 125 to 94, in 1997. Not good. Darren Jarman kicked five goals in the last quarter – an incredible achievement under pressure. He wasn't Elvis to us, more Darth Vader.

There have been two premiership chances on the big day since. We lost in 2009 to Geelong, which hurt; but nothing like the following year when we were losing by one point with less than two minutes to go and Stephen Milne, a good mate, was chasing the ball in the forward line with an open goal in front of him. I was watching on the TV in London, shouting at the screen, when the last bounce of the ball went sideways – like, at right angles – and the ball went through for a point, instead of a goal. I can see it now. Jeeeeeesus! You know the gods don't fancy you when that happens. Had the ball sat up for him . . .

So there was a replay the next weekend (after 2010, they changed from a replay to extra-time). The guys couldn't get over the shock of having the premiership flag in front of their eyes and having it stolen by a very cruel bounce. I was in Scotland at the Dunhill Links golf and got up in the middle of the night to watch the game. It was an anti-climax. Collingwood fed off their own excitement at getting a second chance and outplayed us. Everything that could go wrong for the Saints went wrong, and I really felt for the players. It just wasn't meant to be.

23

When I went to St Kilda in 1986, they threw me a jumper and it was number 23. Complete coincidence, and nothing to do with Michael Jordan. That was years before I signed with Nike. I was number 23 for the Under 19s, then went to the reserves but was given the number 59 jumper. By the time I finished football in 1988, I was 23 again. In casinos I started to bet on my footy number – 23. It still had nothing to do with Jordan. I loved Dermott Brereton, who happened to be number 23 for Hawthorn, but, as I say, my favourite players were Peter Knights and Trevor Barker, numbers 24 and 1 respectively for Hawthorn and St Kilda.

There were no numbers in cricket when I started, but when they came into the one-day game with coloured clothing, they were 1–11. I said, 'No, no, I want my footy number, 23.' The board agreed and gave me the number. So I was the only player in the world who didn't have a number between one and 11. After that, everyone started wearing their own numbers in one-day cricket.

(Chris Gayle had 333, his highest Test-match score. So I guess he likes Test cricket more than he admits.) When I retired, my best buddy in the team, Michael Clarke, took over the number. It worked alright for him too.

The King of Moomba

Moomba is a free community festival that happens every year over the Labour Day weekend. Basically it's a huge party that celebrates all that is good about Melbourne, and it crowns two local people as monarchs for their contribution to the city. In 2015 I was crowned King of Moomba, alongside Pallavi Sharda, who was crowned Queen.

Pallavi was born in Perth but came to Melbourne with her Delhi-born folks when she was a toddler. Her big break was moving to Mumbai to act and dance in Bollywood. She co-hosts the IPL TV coverage and was in the brilliant film *Lion* with Nicole Kidman. She still calls Melbourne home, though.

It was a kind of unreal experience for us both as the Moomba Parade took us through the city on a float with 80,000 people cheering and partying. It's a really eccentric thing but it truly displays Melbourne's amazing spirit and sense of fun. There are huge programs of activities and shows for music, the arts and sport.

There's a lot of humour to it too. I love the Birdman Rally, on the banks of the Yarra, when crazy people turn themselves into flying machines – made of cardboard or plastic or whatever – to sprint along the bank and take off into the water. The one who goes furthest wins. Simple. Except that most never really take off and just nosedive and fall in. Ridiculous, mad Melbourne, but it raises great money for charity.

Moomba has been around for over 60 years. A couple of Pommies have been crowned King, actually – actors Robert Morley and Alfred Marks after their performances in Melbourne – along with local favourites like Lou Richards, Johnny Farnham, Bert Newton, Graham Kennedy, Denise Drysdale and Lucy Durack.

Pallavi and I did a few press events that were basically about selling Melbourne's attractions, which was hardly difficult. It was an honour and pretty special to represent the city that, in my view, just cannot be beaten on any level.

19

New York, New York

The New York Stock Exchange welcomes cricket icons, Sachin Tendulkar and Shane Warne, to ring the NYSE opening bell to highlight the inaugural 'Cricket All-Stars' three game series in New York City, Houston and Los Angeles. This historic tour marks the first time Tendulkar and Warne play on US soil.

Cirencester CC, 9 June 2013

ELIZABETH AND I PUT on an exhibition game at Cirencester in Gloucestershire to raise money for our respective charities – the Shane Warne Foundation and The Hop Skip and Jump Foundation. The game was billed as England vs Australia, my team against Michael Vaughan's, and we had a lot of great names out there – not least Merv Hughes and Allan Lamb, two of the best and funniest guys in any era of cricket.

A huge crowd turned up on a sunny day and more than just a few of them asked why us old blokes didn't do this more often. Elizabeth asked the same thing, suggesting it might have a business angle to it. They got me thinking. We talked about a world tour, a Harlem Globetrotters kind of thing, and on the set of *The Royals* in New York, we sat killing time in the trailer and began to map out some ideas.

The recruitment of household names mattered most, then venues and pitches: no point in good players struggling on substandard surfaces. We wanted the fans to see their heroes play live and somewhere near their best. You need a good pitch for that.

We mapped out the concept in detail and with each cricketing thought of mine came another with a different angle from Elizabeth. It was fun and the foundation of something really good began to emerge. Instinctively, we thought it right to start in America, where so many ex-pats are starved of cricket. We were excited by the potential of social media in promoting to them and to the young Americans they might bring along with them, who might see T20 as a trendier and more exciting hybrid-type thing of baseball. Then we put our not very financial minds to the cost and realised we needed a serious and committed backer.

Then, just as we thought we had something to take to a few big hitters, Elizabeth and I split up. She'd been a motivating force. As I withdrew to my kids and television work, the idea fell asleep in my notebook.

It woke up at Lord's in 2014 when I was asked to be captain of a Rest of the World team against MCC, captained by Sachin, to celebrate the 200th anniversary of MCC. Twenty-seven thousand tickets sold out in an hour on the back of the two of us committing as captains. My guys were Gilchrist, Sehwag, Tamim Iqbal, Pietersen, Yuvraj Singh, Afridi, Collingwood, Siddle, Warne, Tino Best and Muralitharan. Sachin's were Aaron Finch, who scored 181 not out off 145 balls by the way, Tendulkar, Lara, Dravid, Chanderpaul, Lee, Chris Read, Saeed Ajmal, Tait, Umar Gul and Vettori.

Finchy said he considered throwing his wicket away on about 60 as he reckoned the crowd would prefer to see the other blokes bat! Oh, and another thing, Brett Lee bust my wrist with a beamer. I went out to bat in the last over, against my gut instinct. The guys in the dressing-room said, 'Go on, mate, the crowd would love to see you out there.'

Crash! I don't know why Binga didn't just bowl a nice half-volley outside off-stump and let me smack it for one out to the fence or something, but no, he was trying to rip my pegs out with a thunderbolt yorker and got it wrong. It's a friendly game, Bing!

I didn't bowl a ball, and the Warne/Tendulkar match-up never happened. In fact, I hardly saw any of our innings, because I was getting plastered up in hospital. Not Binga's finest hour. Fancy Binga not reading the play right!

After the general excitement of that day, I knew the Harlem Globetrotters idea could work and that it was exactly what I wanted to pursue. For six months, the idea went around in my head and more notes filled the book, until, on Boxing Day 2014 – at the MCG – I went to see Lloyd Williams, who was in the ground watching the cricket with his grandson Henry and a few mates. I told him about the idea. 'No hesitation,' he said, 'I love it, I'll back you.' That was the moment Cricket All-Stars was born.

'You need Tendulkar,' he added. In no time he had sorted lawyers and they were drafting contracts for the potential signing of players. On the first day of the Sydney Test, I called Sachin.

'I want to recreate that MCC game we played at Lord's in a series of three T20 matches in the US, with a view to going global if it works. My idea is to become cricket's Harlem Globetrotters, taking the game to people who haven't had the opportunity to see their heroes play and show them to their kids; to give free coaching and to help promote and grow the game in territories that don't have cricket on their doorstep. America is jammed full of Indians, Aussies, Poms, South Africans, Pakistanis and Sri Lankans.'

'I love it,' he replied. 'I've been thinking the same sort of thing for a while now and I've already had talks in America, so I know the people we can follow up on.'

'Fantastic,' I said. I told him I'd like to set this up myself with Lloyd, and added that Lloyd insisted on having Sachin on board. 'If we do this together,' I said, 'we'll have a great chance of pulling in the best players and most high-profile sponsors. The key will be getting the right people to run it.'

'Great, let's have a chat,' said Sachin.

We met in London in late January/early February, about a month after our call. Sachin had his guy there, Sanjay, who was very much a mentor and business advisor. I explained my concept and gave them a slide show. They loved it and flew in a guy called Ben Sturner from America. Sachin was adamant that his team of people run the whole thing.

I said, 'Well, it's my idea. I know I can get the best players and I'm prepared to go 50-50 with you. I suggest we pay experienced people to organise it and appoint two from each of our camps.'

Sachin said, 'No, I have to have Sanjay and Ben.'

I was uneasy with that, but remained sure Sachin and I together would make it work, so I agreed. At the next meeting, he brought a couple of other guys along who seemed efficient and on the ball. I figured, 'Okay, I've known Sachin for 25 years and he's done unbelievably well off the field, so he must have the business side of his life well organised. Relax and go with them.'

I ended up regretting that. The organisation was not as it could, or should, have been, which was a real shame. They were decent guys but the event got too big for them. We took it to the ICC – to James Sutherland and Tom Harrison, the CEOs of CA and ECB respectively; Sundar Raman, who'd been Lalit Modi's right-hand man in the IPL, and David Richardson, CEO of ICC. They loved it too, but said we had to have the proposal cleared by the home country's governing body, the USACA. They said that things were tricky in the States at that moment and that the strained relationship, pending potential investigation into USACA governance, needed working through. In other words, they were up for our idea but couldn't guarantee America's warmth towards us.

We felt that we could be a force for good and that maybe our ICC-approved matches would bring the two bodies closer together. We pushed the fact that we could work with the ICC in promoting the game globally, not least in the States, while at the same time being in a position to support such things as disaster funds and spread a bit of cricket's joy. Richardson and the others liked that. As far as we were concerned, all we needed was to retain our brand so that ticket sales, merchandising, coaching clinics, an educational website, interactive games etc would be bracketed solely under the All-Star name, while still being affiliated to the ICC.

It didn't happen like that. In fact, we ended up paying huge money to the ICC, well into six figures, to play each of these games in America. When we got there, the USACA people were surprisingly aggressive towards us and tried to sabotage the event, claiming we had no rights to play in their country and that they'd sue us if we went ahead. We told them to take their grievances to the ICC and went ahead anyway. We never heard another word from them!

The players we'd approached were well up for it. The morning before the first match, Sachin and I rang the bell at the New York Stock Exchange. Matthew Hayden and Wasim Akram were there too, as well as my dad, which was very cool. A few of us went on morning TV shows, we played a mini-exhibition in Central Park – which was sensational, by the way – and, in general, New York welcomed us with open arms.

The only problems were with the pitch, a drop-in that cost us a mind-boggling amount of money, and the refusal of the ground authorities to let us train or practise in the days leading up to the game. They wanted another $250,000 for that – what a joke – which Sachin's people understandably said was a rip-off and wouldn't pay.

The truth is, if you ask me, that they probably didn't do the pitch/ ground deal quite right and fell foul of that old line of the devil being in the detail of the contract. This, along with other small but important aspects of a top-level event – cars from the airport for the guys, for example, kit, schedules for the promo events, corporate hospitality suites and boxes for sponsors etc – was all very last minute, and not slick as I had wanted.

I think it's because Indians leave everything so late, which they can make work at home, but it's not easy to pull off in someone else's country. Each day felt like they were flying by the seat of their pants and I didn't like that at all. Sachin got onto a guy called Raj, who, strangely, I knew a bit from poker, and he came in at the very last moment, saving the day with his organisational skills and, most importantly, paying a heap of outstanding bills that allowed us to go ahead.

So, in the end, Sachin and I walked out to toss the coin, on time, at Citi Field in New York on 7 November 2015, and there were 37,000 people there, screaming and yelling. The noise was insane and I shouted, 'Sachin, I think this was a good idea, mate!'

I'll always argue that the $175 ticket price was too high – which was why we didn't sell out the stadium – and I accept the overheads went beyond budget, which stopped us making the money we should have done. Whatever, 37,000 fans, clearly loving every second, was not to be sniffed at for a first outing.

I forgot to mention how we put the teams together. It was Sachin's bloody good idea to match up two similar players and pull out one each from the jug. It was a genuine draw, in front of a huge press contingent, except that the Indian players kept coming out on Sachin's team and the Aussies on mine! It was uncanny. In went Sachin's hand and out came Sehwag, Ganguly, Laxman. In went my hand and, boom, Hayden, Ponting, Symonds! The draw finished like this:

Warne's Warriors: Hayden, Vaughan, Ponting, Kallis, Jonty Rhodes, Sangakkara, Andrew Symonds, Warne, Saqlain Mushtaq, Vettori, Walsh, Akram, Allan Donald, Agit Agarkar, Shane Bond.

Sachin's Blasters: Sehwag, Tendulkar, Lara, Laxman, Ganguly, Jayawardene, Carl Hooper, Moin Khan, Murali, Graeme Swann, Ambrose, Pollock, McGrath, Klusener, Shoaib Akhtar.

The game was fantastic. Sachin's team came out swinging, and he and Sehwag put on 85 in eight overs before my mediocre attack (joke!) – Akram, Donald, Walsh, Kallis, Warne and Vettori – dragged it back. I got 3/20: Tendulkar, Lara and Laxman. Cool. Shoaib steamed in, hitting Haydos and Jacques Kallis with a couple of thunderbolts, which was really important in the context of the credibility of the series, showing that this thing in America wasn't just exhibition hit and giggle. Ricky and Kumar, with a bit of help from Jonty, knocked them off. We won in Houston and LA too – them competitive juices never stop flowing!

And since this is my book, I'll tell you how the last match finished. The Blasters seemed to have it covered after we collapsed to 5/129, chasing 220. Then Ricky and Jacques pulled us out of trouble until six were needed from the last three balls and Jacques chipped one back to Sehwag. Two balls left, in goes Warne. One ball left, match over. I hit a little Sehwag fizzer over the fence at long-on; the only ball I faced in the whole series!

The crowds were also good in Houston and LA, though not quite like New York, and we were all convinced that All-Stars cricket had legs. I wanted to repeat it the following year, but we needed a month to take a breath and work out what we got right and wrong.

When we eventually met for a debrief, the first thing I said to Sachin was that the size of the events overwhelmed a couple of his guys, Sanjay in particular, and that we'd be better employing others for the event management. He took offence at that, which was fair enough. I suggested we find an independent agent, while at the same time offering my own manager, James Erskine, as an option to broker it all, because he'd had previous success staging events in the entertainment industry.

'At the very least,' I said, 'let's go with the two and two idea I had at the beginning.'

Sachin said, 'No, it has to be my people.'

We went away for a rethink. Time slipped by, so much so that I feared we were missing the chance to make a second year work. In the meantime, I thought I'd confirm some of the key players' ongoing interest, which was when I heard that Sachin had approached some of them directly, saying All-Stars was on again and that he'd told the Indian players not to sign up with me.

I rang him immediately but got nothing. In fact, for a couple of months he wouldn't take my call. I later found out he was under the impression I was trying to do it without him, but my instinct was to give him the benefit of the doubt on that one – there were a lot of jealous people out there, happy to turn us against each other, I thought. For one thing, it was my idea and he certainly wouldn't dispute that; for another, we'd known each other a long time and there was a lot of mutual respect.

When we eventually spoke I adapted my first idea of an independent agent and went harder on the idea of appointing two guys each, answerable to us, to run the All-Stars venture. In the meantime, I said we had to pay the bills. He said he'd take care of things and insisted he hadn't spoken to any players about going it alone. However, I was soon to find out that his people had told him he didn't need me to make the venture work. I can believe that.

We met at Alfred's in London, with James Erskine and one of Sachin's guys, and agreed a route forward. It never materialised. I blame the people around Sachin, not Sachin himself. One of the players told me he was actually signing with Sachin, which caught me off guard. I said, 'That's cool, he has a right to do exactly as he wants, as do you. But it can't be under the All-Stars banner – that's mine.'

I'm really sad about it. I had 30 players lined up and ready to go again. I even had it out there on social media, but the uncertainty became too hard. I always wanted All-Stars to be a legacy created by Sachin and me together but, for a reason that I've never fully understood, he didn't see it that way. No way is there room in the market for us both to do the same thing. It would be stupid to try, anyway, as we'd be spread too thin.

My dream remains the same. I believe cricket can make a difference in parts it doesn't usually reach. I think kids need heroes and us older blokes can be those heroes by going live to the places where the international game doesn't otherwise go. And I don't think it's too late either. As I say, Cricket All-Stars has legs.

London Calling

After starting with Sky in 2009, I spent more and more time in London, eventually living there for almost half the year from 2014 to 2017. It's a great city and in the sense that there is always something happening, the vibe is very like Melbourne. I always enjoyed London, right from the Bristol days in 1989 when a trip to town was, well, like a treat. I know my way around, almost better than Melbourne, and love the vibe. When the sun shines, it's as good a place as anywhere; when it doesn't, when that grey rain sets in for days on end and the summer temperatures drop to 10 degrees, it loses the magic!

Clive Rice, the great South African all-rounder who captained Notts to the county championship in 1981, summed up English weather pretty well: 'Nine months of winter and three months of bad weather.'

He has a point, though when it gets hot, and occasionally it does, it can feel hotter than higher temperatures in other cities. New York is like that too. Blame the lack of space and the massive populations, I guess. I live in St John's Wood, right by Lord's, in a cool little mews house owned by a mate of mine in the music business, Rod MacSween, who manages and promotes rock and heavy metal bands. There is no lovelier bloke on the planet.

Over the years, I've developed so many great friends, really interesting people, mainly from business, sport and music. It's sort of funny when mates come over from Australia and I find myself wanting to show off my London – Wimbledon tickets, Lord's, of course, cool clubs, even great restaurants – though my idea of a great restaurant is not everyone else's!

Favourite Italian? Lucio's on the Fulham Road and Little Italy in Soho, where, midweek, the tables go back, the DJ steps in and the dancing begins! Favourite clubs? Soho House, Annabel's and 5 Hertford Street. Favourite place, full stop? Pizza Pomodoro in Beauchamp Place, particularly Sunday nights when it rocks. The kids love London, Mum and Dad too.

Golf is big for me. I've joined Beaverbrook, a new private club created by some super guys who wanted a top venue – course, clubhouse, hotel, spa, food, staff etc – with a relaxed atmosphere and style. They've managed to create just that. Playing at Queenwood, Sunningdale and Wentworth with good friends is pretty special too. I know I'm lucky, because these are all awesome places, ranking with pretty much anywhere in the world.

Flower of Scotland

I never thought I'd say it, but my flower of Scotland is the Old Course at St Andrews. When you first have a hit, you think, 'What's all the fuss about?' It's not like there are great views or one-off spectacular holes, or impossible challenges, or super-fast greens, or amphitheatres that create excitement or atmosphere. No, none of that, but, well, it's like it's got history. Real history. And that's where the atmosphere comes from. When you've had a few goes at it, the magic begins to seep into your body and the subtleties of the course play with your head. Once you've driven off the first tee and walked up the 18th fairway a few times, you just can't get enough of the place. St Andrews is addictive, simple as that.

Anyone lucky enough to be invited to the Dunhill Links Championship, which is played over four days at St Andrews, Kingsbarns and Carnoustie in late September/early October every year, will know what I mean. There's a bunch of us, all good mates, who sit by our computers from May/June time, hoping and praying that you, Johann – or should I say Mr Rupert or Sir or Father Christmas, whatever you wish to be called; let's say The Boss – sends an invite.

When the inbox on those computers goes 'ker-ching' and that invite flashes up, we press reply before we've read what the email says. Oh man, it's like a huge load off the back because you just don't want to miss it. It's hard to describe but the easiest thing to say is that it's the greatest week of the year, every year. It's the best of everything, with an unbelievable chemistry created by Johann's generosity and enthusiasm and the fun list of guys he asks along, year upon year. There are lots of good pro-ams out there, but there's only one Dunhill. The camaraderie is second to none.

Yes, the top players and a fantastic mix of celebrity sports and showbiz people give it a buzz, but the key thing is that you get to live in another man's world for a week and to play at their level. I don't think there's another sporting event where amateurs can play with pros in genuine tournament mode. For example, I can play an exhibition cricket game or a charity match and lob up some leg-spinners, but I won't be bowling like I'm competing in a tournament. Those sorts of games are fun and very worthwhile, but you don't have to be in the zone. In the Dunhill, if you're not in the zone, it's goodnight.

The pros are playing for huge bucks – the biggest prize money on the European tour – and we walk the fairways as their partner, discussing strategy, hitting shots and holing putts (hopefully, but not often enough!). So it's a unique experience and a real privilege. Which isn't to say that off the course it's not fun, because it is – in fact, it's a riot.

Take the Saturday night party: Huey Lewis leads the band and belts out 'The Power of Love'; Don Felder from the Eagles, Mike Rutherford of Genesis, Ronan Keating, Brian McFadden and Tom Chaplin from Keane all play and/or sing; Andy Garcia does a great job on those bongos, and the mighty Tico Torres from Bon Jovi rips it on the drums. I mean, are you kidding? What a line-up! It's just insane! Kelly Slater might join them for a jam, big Schalk Burger, the larger-than-life (larger than everything, actually) former South African rugby forward, strums the guitar like it's a ukulele with those massive hands of his, and so on and so on. Amazing!

Last year's tournament was special for me, because after 11 years of trying I made the cut. Although the top 60 pros have their own cut mark, the top 20 teams out of the 168 that start out – those that have the lowest amateur/pro best ball score – make the cut too and play on the last day at St Andrews.

My long-term partner had been my great mate Peter O'Malley, or 'Pom', as we all know him, and we've come very close to making the cut on a couple of occasions. Since Pom pulled back from full-time commitment to the tour, I've played with some other Aussies too – Nathan Holman, Wade Ormsby, Brett Rumford. Then last year I was drawn with a Kiwi, Ryan Fox. This guy hits the ball so far, it's a joke. I asked him if he'd played alongside Dustin Johnson and, if so, how much does he give Johnson off the tee. He replied, I have and I don't! Now that's long!

Annoyingly, Ryan missed the cut himself by a whisker but had a chance to make decent money if our team could win the tournament. We were two shots off the lead going into the last day, and at 1 am at the party he was on the dancefloor rocking to Huey and the boys. He turned to me – poleaxed, he was – and said, 'Warney, the driver is coming out everywhere tomorrow and I'm ripping it. I'm looking to drive every green! We're gonna win this thing, mate!' And then he was back to his air guitar!

So, except for the two short holes and the first, the ninth and the 18th, where driver is too much club, he hit it everywhere alright and shot 68. Pretty good. He missed a couple of putts. I missed a couple more. Aaarggghh! In fact, I missed four from inside six feet and I'm a good putter. We all miss the odd little one, but these – four from inside six feet; no way, you have to hole two or three of them. I was *so* disappointed in myself. We finished equal fifth, four shots behind the winners Kieran McManus and Jamie Donaldson. Four shots, that's all. It's what the pros go through every week. It's painful.

I got home to London and thought, 'You know what – you're disappointed because you blew a chance to win something that was among the best experiences of your life. The opportunity to play on that last day in front of those big crowds and compete at a decent level was just incredible – maybe not quite Ashes or the IPL final but not far off.'

The point is that it's right up there and has given me inspiration to improve my golf and to go again. I want to get down to three, four, five handicap. I'm praying for an invite to the next Dunhill and I'm desperate to go low and win it. Never mind the fact that I hardly slept on the Saturday night because I was so nervous, I want that adrenaline rushing through me again! Yes, I loved it – absolutely loved it.

Remember, I began with the AFL dream but didn't make it. Then I had a taste of Test cricket and knew that I wanted more. I drove to Adelaide and, with Terry Jenner by my side, lost nearly 20 kilos and bowled for four to five hours a day until I was good enough to look Test cricket in the eye with confidence. In other words, I'm a determined sort of guy. If I get asked back, I'd love Ryan Fox as my partner again and I'd put a few bucks on us to go all the way!

It's Only Rock and Roll (But I Like It)

The 2001 Australian tour of England and I walked into the lift at the Royal Garden Hotel in London, where we always stayed. I recognised the guy in the back corner, head dipped from the other four or five people in there. I thought, 'Is that . . .? No, don't think so.'

He caught my eye and kind of did a double take. The other people got out on the first floor. He looked at me again, me at him.

'Are you?'

'Err, are you?'

'Shane Warne?'

'Yes, mate.'

'Chris Martin?'

'I am. What are you up to?'

'Nothing much. Fancy a drink?'

'Sure.'

So the Australian leg-spinner and the Coldplay front man got to talking. The sun was coming up by the time we finished. He liked cricket, I like music. 'Yellow' off the *Parachutes* album was already a favourite. We swapped numbers, sent a few messages and we've been mates ever since. We share a lot of stuff, maybe that other mates wouldn't quite get. He's a true friend, very loyal and supportive. I think he'd say the same about me. When you're public property, it sure helps to have someone to talk to who understands the game out there.

I had some good dinners at his house in London – just Chris, Gwyneth and me. She does a mean risotto. It was sad when they split up, she's a really lovely girl. Chris and I walk the hills up above his place in Malibu, and if we don't see each other for a while we keep in touch by text or phone calls. We just click. It's a friendship I value greatly.

I've been on stage with him three times, once to introduce him and John Farnham together at a charity concert in Sydney after the 2009 Black Saturday bushfires in Victoria, and again in Sydney when Coldplay were live to 40,000 people. I was in the crowd and his PA came and grabbed me: 'Chris wants you on stage.'

I said, 'No, no, what are you talking about?'

'It's not a question,' she said, 'it's a fact.'

'Oh right.'

I followed her backstage and then into the wings. Chris came offstage and said, 'You're the fifth member of the band. You need a jacket, you need to wear everything the boys are wearing. Quick!'

So everyone was running around the joint, finding stuff, and suddenly I was out there. The crowd gave me an amazing welcome and the band went straight into 'I'm a Believer' by the Monkees. Chris handed me the maracas and when I had a crack at playing them – so embarrassing – he sort of looked at me, like, 'What the hell sort of an effort is that?!' Well, I hadn't got a clue, had I? So he swapped them for a triangle. I was rubbish at both but the crowd went berserk and loved it, I think. Then he said, 'Thanks, Shane,' and I went back to my seat, rock-star career on hold!

In 2017, the band were in Melbourne and he came to my place for a barbecue with my kids and a couple of their mates. He said he wanted me on stage again.

'Last night's show was unbelievable – the longest we've played for in years – and we want something new for tonight to take it up another notch. Come and play with us again and we'll have some fun.'

I was thinking, 'Take it up? I'll drag it down if I come on!'

'No, mate,' said Chris, 'you're coming on stage with us in your hometown. We'll make a little story out of it, like we've got this guy on work experience, a bright new talent that we picked up on the streets and we're hoping to integrate into the band. "Hey, everyone, please give a massive Melbourne welcome for . . . Shane Warne!"'

The kids were saying, 'Yeah, do it, Dad. You've got to do it!'

So I agreed to do it. I went to the gig with Mum and Dad, Chris' dad was there too, and Michael Slater. The kids were rocking in the mosh pit. About halfway through the show, some security guys came to get me, and as I made my way to the side of the stage I passed Jackson in the crowd but didn't know it. He was shouting out 'Dad, Dad', but I didn't hear him at first and later he said he thought I was going to fresh-air him, but at the last moment I saw him and we had a cuddle and a few high-fives with his mates.

Then the security guys grabbed me and said, 'We seriously gotta go, Warney,' and suddenly I was on the side of the stage, shitting myself. The sound techos handed me a harmonica for 'Don't Panic' but when the band ripped into the song, I thought '*Phew*, Chris has changed his mind.'

But almost as soon as they'd started, they stopped. Chris stuttered, 'Hang on, hang on, we've messed that up. Let's start this again.'

Then he winked at me and began the pre-planned intro. I mouthed, 'You bastard!'

Onto the stage I went, harmonica in hand, with Coldplay.

The crowd went berserk. Melbourne people happy to see one of their own up there, I suppose. The band started on the song again until Chris took over, singing solo, and signalled for me to play. I did my thing with the harmonica, blowing into it like I knew what I was doing, and out came perfect notes.

Chris went, 'Yes yes yes!', and, as we high-fived, the huge crowd – 60 or 70,000, I think – cheered and sang along.

One report of the show said, 'It was a throwback to Australian cricket's most dominant era, a sporting ground in Melbourne chanting, "Warnie, Warnie, Warnie." . . . If we are being honest, he didn't suck. In fact he kind of nailed his little harmonica solo. And the crowd went berserk once again for Shane Warne.'

Later, people said it sounded fantastic and asked how long I'd been playing the harmonica. I said, 'Come on, you idiots!' It was good fun. I mean, let's face it, who gets to go on stage with one of the biggest bands in history?

Music is huge for me. They say it's good for you to sing and I sure sing along, especially in the car, and in the shower. Music reminds you of different times in your life, it can make you think, change your philosophy and improve your mood. It can make you miss people and love people more. It makes you move, dance, and it fills a room with joy and fun. I'm the world's best chair dancer – just ask the owners of Pizza Pomodoro! They only have to crank up 'Volare' by the Gipsy Kings and I'll rock a chair dance like no-one else in the joint.

My go-tos are Coldplay, Ed Sheeran and Bruce Springsteen. Fleetwood Mac would be up there too, along with U2 and some INXS stuff. The first record I bought was 'Cum on Feel the Noize' by Quiet Riot. When I was younger, I'd ride my bike to CC Records with a few bucks worth of pocket money and proudly sprint-cycle home to play a new album at full blast all day, every day for the next week. Dad liked the Rolling Stones, so I got into them too, as well as Neil Diamond and Rod Stewart from that earlier era.

I never liked house or acid music and I'm not much into heavy rock or metal. I'm a softer sort of rocker, leaning to pop. 'Dancing in the Dark' is my favourite Springsteen song, closely followed by 'Glory Days', which sort of reminds me of cricket and football days and all the fun we had with the guys. Bruce came to the Melbourne Showgrounds in 1985 and I lined up overnight to see him send the place crazy in a black-and-white headband: *'Boooooorn in the USA!'*

Right now, Ed Sheeran has got me hooked. That song 'Photograph', oh my God! I love Ed. His songs are great because they bring out emotions in you that others don't. He's such a terrific person and he's become a close friend. The more time I spend with him, the more I see the music as an extension of his personality. I've bowled in the nets with his dad for hours at the MCG, and at Ed at Lord's, and have got to know the family well. They're good people, very humble and kind.

Obviously, meeting these guys is a great thrill. I just hope they feel the same when they meet me! During my enforced lay-off in 2003, the Stones came to Melbourne on their world tour and I managed to get in touch with Mick Jagger for tickets. We met up and got along well. Mick and Charlie Watts love their cricket and Simone and I ended up at a party in his room watching some of the South African World Cup together. What was really nice was that they publicly said to the Australian press something like: 'If Shane Warne is banned for a year for a diuretic, jeez, we'd have been banned for life within a year or two of starting out!' And then, on the back of that comment, Elton John came out and said if he could be anyone else in the world, he'd like to be me. That was pretty cool. Mick and Elton, on my side.

20

Imagine

I WAS VERY LUCKY to play almost all of my career when the summer schedule was made up of Tests and one-day internationals that had regular dates in the calendar and consistently huge crowds. The Sheffield Shield was king of the domestic game and grade cricket was strong. You knew what you were getting, which led to accepted and usually very high standards across the board in two formats of cricket that stood the test of time. The message was pretty clear and the rest of the world was envious. If the foundations are good, the building will stay solid.

The Big Bash has changed that a bit. Different types of cricketer are emerging who appeal to a new audience. Standards of technique and application are less important than thrills and spills. It's a quick fix for an age that doesn't do patience very well. That's fine, because it matches up to the habits of the world today.

Among the things that have needed fixing are the format for Test cricket, so that young people can appreciate the skill level and see its attraction before it's too late; the plan going forward for one-day cricket to bring clarity and relevance to the 50-over format; and the scheduling for all international cricket, which at the moment is confusing for spectators and over-demanding on the players.

Thankfully, in June this year the ICC announced a new future tours program that deals with some of these thoughts.

At international level, I'd stick with just two formats of the game – outside of a T20 World Cup, that is. To me, T20 should be played almost exclusively in the independent leagues that are growing so fast everywhere in the world. These provide the perfect environment for the style of cricket that it is. I can see the commercial value of a T20 World Cup, but every four years, not every two. Cricket is killing itself with so much exposure, and Test cricket, in particular, has no chance of holding its own if T20 is the go-to format for both income and growth at both international and domestic level.

In fact, recently I've begun to wonder if we shouldn't just see Test cricket as a television game. The rights still sell for incredibly high prices, but grounds outside England and Australia are never full, not even in India, and many are actually empty. I'd give away free tickets and organise special events for kids at the Test-match venues, creating interaction with players in the hope of encouraging kids to get to know the players better and see them as their heroes.

Right now, Test cricket needs much smarter marketing. All the messages out there are about T20. In Australia, it's Big Bash, Big Bash, and more Big Bash; in India, it's IPL, IPL and more IPL; in England, it's this new 100-ball idea, as well as a T20 tournament! But T20 already has an enthusiastic and secure audience. Test cricket is losing its audience and no-one seems to care.

It's as if the authorities have their heads in the sand, hoping the five-day game will survive, instead of acting to make sure it does. It needs heavy marketing and advertising, on billboards as well as TV, with the use of current star players selling the Test cricket dream.

So the point is, we need to educate young people about the subtleties of a very long and quite complicated game, which actually brings out the very best in the players and pretty much always sees the better team win. That way, we'll get heroes for the youngsters to relate to.

I'm a big believer in four-day Tests. We need to move the game on. Over rates are ridiculously slow these days; I mean, teams struggle to bowl the minimum 90 in the day and most of the time they don't. I believe it's reasonable to expect 32 overs in a session, especially if you extend the hours of play to include the extra half an hour that the players almost always use up to get somewhere near completing the 90 anyway.

Each session should be two hours 10 minutes, and the two breaks for lunch and tea 30 minutes each. This would work better for day-night Test matches, which should be played in dry climates only – Adelaide, Barbados, Johannesburg, and most of India, for example. The game needs to be more energetic. Too many guys are wandering around like Brown's cows – changing gloves, having drinks etc. It's annoying and painfully boring to watch!

We presently have 450-over Test matches, most of which finish early. I'm proposing 384 overs over four days, with a first-innings limit of 130 overs. That pushes everyone to get on with the game, not drag it out because they can. And, if the overs are not bowled – remember, it's only 16 an hour – the captain misses the next match. Simple, no argument. Believe me, the overs will be bowled then. Obviously, umpires would be sympathetic to the time DRS takes and the other natural stops in play that are unavoidable – sightscreens, injuries and stuff. Consistency is the key, so the players know where they stand.

While I'm going, let's deal with DRS. I'd only allow one review each innings. All the game needs to be worried about is the howler – the kind of umpiring mistake everyone knows has been made. The rest of the time, we can trust the umpires. They're pretty good. I hate it when DRS is used tactically, and I hate it when it's used so often that it slows the game down.

I'd get rid of 'umpire's call'. It's so bloody confusing, especially for the viewer. To me, we need to simplify the game and the easiest way to do that when it comes to LBWs is to say that when a review is requested, the umpire's decision is overruled by the technology. And, effectively, this means getting rid of the umpire's call aspect of the DRS for LBWs.

If 25 per cent or more of the ball is hitting the stumps, that's out. End of story. If it's less than 25 per cent then there is doubt, because no way can you trust the technology, so it's not out. I've seen that many dodgy decisions on LBW reviews and every time I'm more convinced that the technology is not quite foolproof, which is why I feel a 25 per cent margin is needed.

Anyway, we want the umpire's decision to mean something. If a 50-50 call goes against you, so be it, but the howler, well, it can decide a game and maybe ruin it. People at home, sitting on their couch, they can see the howler – like, 'He's effing smashed that!' – and then see it replayed time after time. Damien Martyn, Old Trafford in 2005, massive inside edge, given out LBW at a real crucial point in the game – DRS would have picked that up. Edgbaston, same series, last ball, Kasper caught down the leg-side – DRS would have proved his hand was off the bat.

Let's get back to Test cricket and how to make it appealing for everyone. The most important thing of the lot is the pitches. Good pitches mean every type of cricketer can have a say. The pitches just *cannot* be flat roads, like Melbourne in the Ashes last summer, if you want Test cricket to survive. Pitches must provide a contest between bat and ball and, if anything, slightly favour the ball. If batsmen can't handle a swinging, seaming ball in England, a faster and bouncier pitch in Australia or a turning ball on the subcontinent, they'd better learn to play better. I don't care if it spins, I don't care if it seams, I don't even care if it flattens out. That's okay too, because a game of cricket cannot be predictable if it's to be any good. So four days, 96 overs per day, and you'll get results if the pitches are conducive to the ball doing anything other than going gun-barrel straight at an easy pace.

Moving on, I believe that when we're marketing Test cricket, we should start with a massive financial reward for the winners of matches and series. Think of it like the Race to Dubai in golf. Imagine a two or three-year cycle and $20 million prize pool. Everyone should play each other in three-match series, except for 'icon series' – the Ashes definitely, and India-Pakistan, should the time come when they can play against each other again.

How exciting was it when we were watching Justin Thomas play the final round of the FedEx for $US10 million? How good would it be if it came down to the last Test match of a cycle with the

World Test Championship on the line? I'm not in favour of a final, I'm in favour of a long campaign rewarding the winner. Test-match cricket is seriously demanding and if you've been the most success-ful team over a long period, you deserve the trophy and the cash, not a play-off in which a toss or a freak one-off performance can go against you. Also, a final can be a shocker if the pitch is too flat; though, in theory, limiting the overs of each first innings would take care of that.

What else? I know – the size of the bats. Irrelevant. Make them as big as you want. I have no interest in the size of the bats, because when you've got the right pitch – that balance between bat and ball – no-one mentions bats. The size of bats and flat pitches are joined at the hip. Oh, and the boundaries, they're part of this conversation. Too many grounds bring the rope in five to 15 metres to accommodate television cameras and the health-and-safety offi-cials. Make the grounds as big as they can be! Of course, there are massively different dimensions at different venues – Eden Park and the MCG, for example. That's fine, but don't make Melbourne smaller than it needs to be. A metre space, max two metres, is plenty of room between the rope and the boards. That space should be standard, not a last-minute decision by the groundsman or the home governing body.

Test cricket is unique and has lasted since 1877 because it's a great and beautiful game. It should be at the forefront of cricket thinking and whatever decisions are made for cricket going forward, they should all lead back to protecting and improv-ing the Test-match game. Every country should play a standard number of Test matches and one-day games. The one-day games should count towards qualification and seeding for the World Cup that comes along every four years. This stupid disparity of one country playing, say, six Tests and 27 one-dayers in a year and another playing 13 Tests and 12 one-dayers in no way helps cricket attract an audience to all forms of the game. Well done, ICC, for looking to improve that situation.

I believe that one-day cricket should start every series, like the entrée of a meal if you like, and that Test cricket should be the main course. If there is no avoiding T20 as an international game, then it should follow the Test matches, like dessert at the end of a meal. That should be the pattern of all bilateral series – three matches in all formats; no more, no less. Except, as I say, for five Ashes or India–Pakistan Tests.

One-day cricket would benefit from some changes, from a bit of freshening up. Forty overs per side, maybe? There's no doubt that the middle 10 overs get lost in a sort of Bermuda Triangle. I'd loosen up the field restrictions to encourage the captains to take more initiative and use more imagination. I'd like to see some pilot games with three outside the ring for the first 15 overs and then five for the remainder of the innings.

And I'd like to see more emphasis on quality bowlers, both in 50-over and 20-over cricket. Maybe four bowlers could do the bulk of the work, and not rely on a fifth who, more than likely, is a bit-part performer, anyway. In T20 I want to see four bowlers allowed five overs each. Why should batsmen be able to bat a whole innings and bowlers be so limited?

Bowlers have always got a bad deal from the law-makers. It's a batsman's game! The ball has to do something – I'll keep hammering away at that principle till I drop dead. Why doesn't the new ball swing anymore – red or white? It has to be the way it's manufactured. We should experiment with that process – try weighting the ball or making the seam stand up more proudly, so the rudder effect is more prominent. We like day/night Tests in Australia, partly because of the spectacle, partly because of the hours of play, and mainly because the ball does something under lights and the balance switches back a bit to the bowler. Test cricket needs all the drama it can find.

Finally, some thoughts on the big ICC tournaments. I'd prefer to see a four-year cycle comprising a Test-match championship, a 50-over World Cup, a T20 World Cup and a 50-over Champions Trophy. The two World Cups – 50 over and 20 over – should include at least 14 teams, perhaps 16, and spread the game's message as far as it can go. Two games should be played on the same day of World Cups to speed the thing up – six weeks is too long! The Champions Trophy should be short, sharp and for the elite eight teams only, just as it has been over the years.

If a two-year Test-match cycle is manageable – and we'll see now, because the ICC recently announced its future tours program with exactly that in place for the first time – then let's drop the Champions Trophy and give Test cricket more exposure. In the ICC's new future tours program is a 50-over one-day league, serving as qualification for World Cups. Progress! But the idea of two T20 World Cups in the new four-year cycle is not progress, it's overkill. I love T20 and support domestic leagues enthusiastically. But too much T20 is dangerous. Standards of technique, application and concentration are already slipping. The right balance between all these formats of the game is the key to cricket's wide appeal for old-school fans and new-age audiences. As is the way these formats are marketed.

You don't give your kids sweets just because they ask for them. You have to convince them that a balanced diet is the way to go – protein and carbs; fruit and veg too. Do as I say, guys, not as I always do!

21

In the Year 2018

3 June, St John's Wood, London

IT'S 25 YEARS SINCE the Gatting ball. A quarter of a century – unbelievable. I'm in London for a week, putting finishing thoughts to the book with Mark. We started here, in this room at my house in Little Venice, a year ago. One of the best days was with Mum and Dad, who were over on a holiday and told us the stories about my grandparents and great-grandparents. Family means so, so much to me. We sat here in awe of Dad's knowledge and memories, and of Mum's recollections of her childhood. I hope Brooke, Jackson and Summer find me as interesting in the years to come!

The anniversary of the first ball I bowled in Ashes cricket has made me think back yet again to how it changed my life and the ways in which my life has changed. I was a kid then – a 23-year-old kid, mind you – keen to play sport professionally, but with no real idea of what was involved to be successful.

My nerves on the morning of my first Ashes Test match were the same, I guess, as those of any other young cricketer's as he starts out on that great journey. Mainly, those nerves are driven by the fear of failure, and the fear that you'll make a fool of yourself. You pray you don't drop a catch, make a duck or bowl a shocker first-up. As I've mentioned, if someone had said to me that I'd be voted one of the five cricketers of the century seven years later, I'd have laughed. But it happened, so I must have learnt pretty quick and gone on to get more than a few things right. And I didn't bowl a shocker first-up. I bowled the ball that made me.

Cricket has given me so much – good mates, good times, many privileges and some unbelievable experiences that others aren't so lucky to have had. I'm very thankful for that. On more than a couple of occasions, though, a simple life in sport has become a complicated life. I have at last understood that nothing in this life is predictable – the trick is to ride the waves, live it hard and love every second. The rewards will be all the better for doing so. My mistakes have been my own, my successes too – at least I can say that. There's no-one else behind the stories on these pages, only me.

2018 has been an extraordinary year. I don't know why, but I kind of thought it would pass by without a whisper. Hardly, Warney, hardly. The Aussies got into a terrible mess in Cape Town, a mess that led to a massive fall-out; I was back at the IPL but I wasn't back at Sky; Channel Nine lost the cricket rights and now I've signed with Fox. Brooke had her 21st recently and has become such a beautiful girl, inside and out (remember the baby I first saw!); Jackson, who is thinking about work as a model, is putting in the hard yards in the gym, while doing a variety of jobs to keep himself ticking over, and Summer has almost left school. Mum, amazing Mum, was recently diagnosed with Alzheimer's, which is painful for all of us, but she's coping brilliantly, and Dad is forever by her side. He is the world's best and most loyal man. I love them both, just like I always did. Oh, and I had a hole-in-one at a famous golf course.

17/18 March, Augusta National

The best sporting experience of my life, nearly.

Did I really just say that? I did, but I'm exaggerating. ('Exaggerating?' I hear you say. 'Warney, never!') The truth is that winning

World Cups, Ashes and the IPL was the ultimate in cool. I guess that when you've worked most of your adult life for something, the joy when you achieve special things is pretty hard to beat – especially when it's in a team environment. Having said that, Augusta was pretty cool too. We've all hung on to every televised shot at the Masters since golf first grabbed us. To play there was, well, a tick off the bucket list; another one of those dreams of mine! To do so with two of my best mates made the experience all the more fantastic.

We were told no-one had ever had a hole-in-one to the back right pin position at the 16th hole. In truth my six iron never looked like going anywhere else. The story has to be told, but I'll try not to take up too much of your time!

John Carr, son of the great Irish amateur player, Joe Carr, asked Ric Lewis, Ross Desmond and me to Augusta three weeks before this year's Masters tournament. It didn't take us long to say yes. We tapped into some other contacts and stopped en route in Florida to play Seminole and The Bear's Club – wonderful courses that beat us up easy!

I'd been to Augusta as an on-course reporter for Channel Nine in 1996 but was a hacker back then. Nowadays, I play okay off nine handicap and couldn't wait to get at it. On the Saturday afternoon we played 18 holes off the members' tees, I shot 84 and hit it to two feet to make birdie at the 16th, with the pin bottom left where the ball gathers towards it.

That night we had dinner in the clubhouse and were given a tour of the famous Augusta National wine cellar. John's generosity was extraordinary and the Augusta welcome matched it. We were up early on Sunday to play 36 holes off the back tees – a very different game from there and the scorecard didn't read so good! At the 16th, I skimmed my tee shot across the water and hit the shell on the back of a turtle. The noise was something else and the ball, well, it disappeared into that famous little lake – embarrassing.

In the afternoon, we all hit it pretty well. By the time we reached the 16th, the caddies were in our ear: 'Come on, guys, we need a hole-in-one from one of you real bad!' The tradition at Augusta is that a hole-in-one pays each of the caddies in the group 500 bucks. Mixed feelings then!

Anyway, John, Ross and Ric all hit good shots to the back right pin position from where, as I've mentioned, apparently no-one had *ever* had a hole-in-one. My turn. I felt good. I had 155 yards to the hole – slightly uphill and into the breeze. It seemed like a seven iron to me but the caddie didn't like it and pushed for a six. No worries. Out came the six. Placing the ball on the tee, I wondered if I had too much club but convinced myself no. 'Hit it easy, mate, nice rhythm . . .'

Just before I hit the shot, in a commentator's voice Ross said, 'The last time Shane Warne was seen in the United States of America, he was on the 16th tee at Augusta National. He hit a perfect six iron into the hole, the first man ever to do so with the pin in the back right position. After that, the party took over and Warne just disappeared . . . and was never seen again!!'

The boys loved it. 'C'mon, Warney, you're the man. Do it for all of us, the caddies especially.'

Well, I hit this ball so sweet, just perfect. It felt soft off the club face and it flew dead straight at the flag. 'That's good, very good,' I thought. 'Be the club – be as good as you look!'

Suddenly, we were all shouting at it to be good. It bounced right on line and then disappeared.

Silence.

Three, maybe four, seconds passed.

'Did that just go in?'

'It sure did, man! *Shane, you just got a hole-in-one at Augusta National!*'

Oh my God.

The caddies went nuts. So did we. Ric and JC were chesting each other; Ross and me were high-fiving. It was electric out there at 16! Hugs wherever you looked, laughter, shock, amazement. Everyone was jumping up and down.

'Wow, man, no-one has ever done that before in the history of this club. That's the best shot I've seen at Augusta, man. *Arrrrsome!*'

I was so pumped, I drove it 280 yards down the 17th fairway and made a tidy four. It was much the same story at the 18th. This had to be a dream.

In the pro shop, they'd already heard the news. You're not allowed phones on the course at Augusta, but the caddies have little pocket cameras to record special moments. They were so damn excited that there were more shots of our feet and of the sky than of us. No worries, guys!

Thankfully, there were three good ones that will live with me forever. Meantime, the pro showed me the glass cabinet and photo of the hole that will have the ball mounted and the scene signed by the four of us that, they said, will be sent to me within a few weeks. I was pretty rapt. I mean, are you kidding? I'd just made a hole-in-one at the 16th at Augusta National, home of the Masters! It now sits in pride of place in my office.

24 March, Cape Town

Like most Australians, and many genuine cricket lovers around the world, I was shocked and angered by what we all saw in Cape Town last March. It was embarrassing that the Australian cricket team should cheat and, worse still, in a pre-meditated way. There's no way their actions can be condoned.

At first, it was hard for us to know how to react because no Australian had been accused of tampering with the ball before. The hysteria went worldwide, partly because of 'Sandpaper-gate' but also because, over time, the team had lost popularity through failing to play the game in the true Australian spirit of being hard, uncompromising and fair. There's been a growing arrogance in the attitude of some of the guys, along with too much unpleasantness on the field – both to umpires and opponents – and a whole lot of whingeing off it. Aussies don't bleat about their opponents at press conferences and point their fingers at others in the public domain; Aussies go out and make their point on the field.

I'd say that over the last couple of years, there'd been a build-up of hatred against this group which exaggerated the problems they suddenly faced on that horrible day. In short, everyone, everywhere, was happy to put the boot in.

Let's examine the players' guilt for a minute. Ball-tampering, and therefore bringing the game into disrepute – well, yes, they were guilty of that, for sure. But, and it's a massive but for me, there's a long list of players who've been charged with ball-tampering, some of them big names – Michael Atherton and Sachin Tendulkar for example, though both had the tampering charge dropped to something much more minor. It's not so long ago that South Africa's captain, Faf du Plessis, and his new-ball bowler, Vernon Philander, were done and convicted, but they weren't vilified for it.

It was the pre-meditated bit that got everyone ticking, and the use of sandpaper. So, is use of a mint to shine a ball not pre-meditated? Or the application of sunscreen? And is the impact of a mint or sunscreen not as effective as sandpaper? Who is able to answer that question for certain? Not me, I know. What I do know is that you either tamper with a ball or you don't, and anyone who does is breaking the laws of the game and is as guilty as the Australians were at Newlands.

For that reason, I don't believe the nine and 12-month bans were fair, and were certainly not in line with the punishments previously given to du Plessis or Philander. Yes, the three Australians – Steve Smith, David Warner and Cameron Bancroft – were hammered for breaching the spirit of the game – something that is so important to us all – but they were also hammered for not playing the game in the true Australian way. The fact is, the public had lost faith in them and Cricket Australia decided to take matters beyond the ICC's initial punishments and nail the guys for more than just ball-tampering.

At times, the teams I played in made mistakes – and I would now agree that we pushed behaviour on the field too far on occasions. In truth, the win at all costs attitude in modern sport had made a few of us do stupid things. I think Steve Smith was guilty of a severe error of judgement that day. He was naive to think he'd get away with it and was a victim of the bubble he'd helped to create. Once you think you're indestructible, or above the law, you've lost sight of reality. For all that, however, I don't think Steve Smith is Pablo Escobar – he just made a mistake.

I repeat, being rubbed out for a year was not a punishment that fitted the crime. Their actions were indefensible, but they didn't deserve to be destroyed in the way they were. My punishments would have been for Smith and Warner to be sacked from the captaincy and vice-captaincy; for all three of them to miss the fourth Test match in Johannesburg and then to be hit with a huge fine. After that, and under a new captain, normal service should have been resumed.

We're told that Darren Lehmann didn't know the ball-tampering was happening. I believe it if he says it. Having said that, I understand people's doubts, because in the teams I played in, everyone had to be on the same page to get the ball to reverse-swing. If one player shined it wrong, or got the dry side wet, it just wouldn't swing. Other plans like throwing the ball into the ground or bowling cross-seam would have been set out a long time back, not last minute in the dressing-room at lunch. There-fore, in this example, it's possible that others in the team might not have known what was going on.

I felt for those involved and could imagine what they went through over those dramatic days – especially the three who bore the brunt of it all. It comes at you from all angles and you think there's no way out. You plead from within your heart to win back the trust of your team-mates and the public worldwide.

The Australian people are hard on their sportsmen and quickly judgemental. Only time can heal the relationship. Steve has already won a few hearts and minds with his moving press conference and acceptance of the mistake, alongside the hours he's now putting in for good causes. The key things these three guys can continue to do is to be true to themselves and take responsibility for how they move forward.

I've made a number of mistakes in my own life and will continue to make them. This is what it is to be human. I've always said to young cricketers, 'Don't worry about how many runs you make or how many Tests you play – do the right thing by cricket and it will do the right thing by you.' Our sportsmen and women are held in high regard, that's why this hurt so much. Playing fair might be the most important thing of all.

This group of players needs to find themselves again. What happened in South Africa shook everyone and now, understandably, the guys are reacting to public pressure, to sponsors, and to Cricket Australia by doing the 'right thing' – like shaking hands with the opposition before play starts. Pleeeese! By trying to do the right thing, they're doing the wrong thing. The best way to win back trust and popularity is by playing the Aussie way, and if that means some confrontation in the thick of the battle, so be it. It's an international stage they're playing on, not the village green.

I've read that we should play the New Zealand way. No we shouldn't! We should play our way – I repeat, hard and fair. Cricket is our number-one national sport. Australians want to see us win in style and in the right spirit, and they want us to respect the game and the opposition. Yes, as I've said, I crossed the line a handful of times – moments I'm not proud of – but overall, I played the game true to its traditions and earned respect for that, I think. The teams I played in were popular for the way they went about their cricket and admired for what they achieved.

Let's be honest, Australia has only been marginally above an average side for a while now. Smith and Warner have carried the batting, making just enough runs between them for a quality bowling attack to do some damage. The young batsmen coming through the first-class structure are a worry and I'm amazed to see Graeme Hick as the national batting coach – nice fella, but hardly the mentally strong character that's needed right now.

Justin Langer gets a tick from me but he needs time. JL achieved great things with WA and the Scorchers but international cricket is a whole new ball game. His work ethic is unbeatable and his attention to detail is excellent. I just hope he allows the guys outside the box – flair players who don't necessarily conform – the chance to express themselves freely. That's the challenge for him, to make sure he doesn't run a one-dimensional unit. He's tough and he's smart, so I'm backing him to get things on track.

He needs a good captain. In fact, Australian cricket is crying out for leadership on and off the field. Tim Paine is a very decent bloke but a caretaker captain – an interim choice – and with guys like Alex Carey around, his place is by no means certain. Australian cricket has always picked the best team and then chosen a captain from those 11 players. No way should that principle be changed because of a hiccup in Cape Town.

What matters most now is that the old-fashioned principles of Australian cricket are followed religiously. This group of players needs to stand up as men and represent their country like nothing else on earth matters more. That way, they'll soon be on the right road again and an inspiration to the kids out there who see our cricketers as their heroes.

13 May, Jaipur

Unfortunately, this was my last day with the Rajasthan Royals today as I head back to Australia tomorrow! It's been great fun being back with the IPL as I'd forgotten how intense, wonderful and great this tournament is. What have I learnt? The modern-day batsmen in this form of the game have evolved into terrific, innovative players with tremendous power. The bowlers need a more aggressive mindset and to think, 'How am I getting this batsman out?', rather than think containment first. The ground fielding is super-athletic and has improved out of sight – but the overall catching can improve!

Lastly, a few thoughts looking ahead. Jos Buttler has to play Test match cricket for England as he's a quality player. What a difference he could make to the England Test side! Mr Root should demand he be picked. I've really enjoyed his company as he's a quality person too. Ben Stokes is someone you want in the trenches with you and has a quality work ethic. I'm looking forward to seeing him back playing international cricket – he's a bloody good man! D'Arcy Short will become an awesome all-round cricketer for Australia and will surprise people with his bowling. Sanju Samson will be the next big Indian superstar batsman, along with Rishabh

Pant. Jofra Archer will soon be the best fast bowler in the world! Come on, the Royals . . .

17 May, Melbourne

I'm at Junction Oval in Melbourne doing a photo shoot with Adam Gilchrist. We've both signed for Fox Sports to cover the cricket. After 25 happy years, I didn't want to leave Channel Nine – I'm a loyal kind of guy, sometimes to my detriment – but the deal Fox offered brings exciting opportunities and a pretty decent pay cheque too.

I didn't want to go to Channel Seven, even though they had the free-to-air rights. Over the years, the Seven Network had come hard at me and the final straw was bringing out the wheelchair-bound children and claiming that my Foundation had let them down. No, Seven and me were not friends. Nine still had some bits and pieces of cricket and were keen for me to work on the Australian Open tennis and Masters golf from Augusta, as well as develop other ideas for new shows. I was happy with that, really, and at first I thought that was where I'd stay.

All three networks offered me deals – how flattering is that! I like Steve Crawley, the former Head of Sport at Nine, now the boss at Fox Sports, and he told me about their planned cricket channel and ideas for imaginative programming around it. Better still, he was happy for me to be non-exclusive outside the main part of the cricket season, which allowed me to still do stuff with Nine. So, going with Fox was no wrench. In fact, I'm quite excited by it and just hope that more and more people buy into the great coverage of sport that Fox provide.

15 July, Las Vegas

Disappointing! Got knocked out on the second day of the World Series of Poker Main Event – a bit unlucky but there was a silver lining, because I cashed in on the Wynn Main Event, where I came 70th out of nearly 2500 players. Nearly $10k in my pocket overall, so

I can't complain. I played well and feel good about my game at the moment.

Not many things have grabbed me in the way poker has. In fact, it's gone a long way to replacing the heartbeat of cricket in my life. I heard a stat that cricket has the highest suicide rate of former top-level players in any sport and I'm not surprised. The game provides its players with the buzz of competition, alongside the comfort of a controlled and rewarding 24/7 lifestyle, which means tight friendships that come from long days and nights on the road most of the year round. There's no doubt that it's very hard to replace full-time cricket.

I am a super-competitive guy and I loved the ball in my hand, the individual match-ups, the team ethic and the satisfaction of winning a mind game to win the contest. Cricket was the best part of 25 years of my life: replicating the competitive juices that flow from the biggest occasions is close to impossible. Or so I thought. Though golf is great fun and I love nothing more than playing for plenty of bucks against good mates at great courses, it's poker that has rocked my boat in a way I never thought possible again.

There are three variations: online poker, which is good for learning the game and doesn't have to involve much money; cash-game poker, the T20 equivalent that seduces the guys with the biggest balls and the biggest wallets, but can cost you dear if you get it wrong; and tournament poker, which is the game I love.

Tournament poker is the ultimate test of skill. Everyone puts in the same amount of money and after that the strategy and mind games take over. In cricket, I had to out-think the batsman by reading the play, planning ahead and staying match aware. Poker is very similar.

The question you ask yourself most is: what is my position and where do I stand with other players? There are 10 players at the table, so, simple questions: who can play, really play? Who's the pro? Who's the flashy business guy? Who won his seat online? Who has played a live tournament before and who hasn't? Who's scared? Who's not? And here's the big one . . . who is the worst player at the table? If you can't see him, it's almost certainly you!

Between 7000 and 8000 people enter the WSOP Main Event. It's a $10,600 buy-in, which gives you 50,000 worth of chips. Do the maths – that's upwards of $80 million prize pool before TV and sponsorship. Of that, it's 10 million bucks to the winner, so it's big, real big.

Tournament poker is, I repeat, a game of skill, so you need to be sure of what sort of player you want to be – aggressive or patient, for example – and what image you want to project around the table. First you position yourself, then you weigh up the pot odds and the probabilities, either way. Then you make sure you play your opponent, not the cards, which is why you *have* to work out your opponents.

The best players are one of two types: super-brainy mathematicians who usually play in structured formats based on probability; or the less brainy guys who know the basic maths but run on gut instinct. The first thing I do is look for 'tells' – people who scratch their nose, play with their earlobes, look down, look around, cough nervously, talk too much and too loud or not at all – and try to limit my own tells, or do some on purpose! My table image is loose and super-aggressive and I look to play my hand as if I'm not too bothered how it turns out.

The essentials are (1) how you bet and the amount – you just have to learn to protect your chips without getting too curious elsewhere; (2) the ability to concentrate because of the amount of time you spend at the table – 13 hours a day, over 10 days or more, and therefore it's pretty easy to lose concentration; and (3) the courage not to be afraid to lose. I love the banter and try to mix it with anyone on the table who's ready to get involved. It's the starers who get me – these blokes who stare straight-faced at you for three, four, five minutes at a time. That's daunting. My sort of challenge!

I've played all my life. At home when we were growing up, Friday night was card night, or other games. We played canasta, kalooki, 500 and poker, as well as backgammon. I loved them all.

I've only made money once in 10 attempts at the World Series Main Event, which earns a cheque of about $US30,000. Three times I've bubbled – in other words, just missed out. My best-ever finish in a major tournament was second in a high-rollers event in Melbourne. I was all in with 10s against the other guy's eights (a two outer, only two eights left in the deck) – and he rivered the only card that could beat me, another eight! That was 150K for the winner, 65 for second. And lastly, while I'm blowing smoke up myself, I came 21st in the WSOP Asia Pacific event that features a lot of the world's best players.

The very best of them are Daniel Negreanu and Phil Ivey, who's become a good mate of mine, and is known as the Tiger Woods of poker. Imagine I'm a scratch player . . . and he's Tiger. That's the gulf. My mate from home, Joe Hachem, won the Main Event in 2005 – even back then it was worth 7.5 million bucks! Joe and I play a lot together and I've learnt more from him than anyone. He's been a great mentor in the poker world, and became a great mate.

I hope my new sponsor isn't disappointed with me this week. I'm with Dafabet now, a company out of the UK, having spent a happy 10-year period with 888. After I retired from Test cricket in 2006/07, Crown asked me to play in the Aussie Millions, the world's biggest tournament outside of the US. They paid my buy-in fee and I did pretty well. 888 picked up on that and offered me a deal to captain the 888 team and play around the world – a tough gig but someone has to do it. I aim to please!

I can't emphasise enough how much I love poker and how fortunate I've been to find something that goes a fair bit of the way to replacing the juices that flowed when I walked out at Lord's or the MCG. I'd like to go all the way, to stare down the best at crunch time in the Main Event. Phil Ivey says he's looking forward to the moment we meet. Meantime, we have a few beers together and I'm always reminded of my place in the hierarchy of the game by these great players. But I'm off dreaming again . . .

22

Simply the Best

Mac and Fries, Tiger and Nugget

I'VE HAD A GOOD life and fought hard for most of it. Jason and I didn't come from anything fancy, but our parents made sure we wanted for very little and maintained a price on good manners and good living.

I've tried to tell my stories as honestly as I know them and hope that they've given you something of the life I've led. I'm not a hell-raiser but I like a good time; it's not a rehearsal, after all. The book has allowed me to confront some issues that, before now, might have been misunderstood. Over this past year as Mark and I have worked on the stories, I've looked inside myself more than I have done before.

Mark asked me if I thought I'd changed the game. Maybe, maybe not. It has certainly changed me. The longer we've talked, the more often the Gatting ball moment comes into the picture. In different ways, I became the hunter and the hunted at the same time. The night after that Test, I was walking down the street eating McDonald's and suddenly there were five or six photographers in my way taking pictures of me stuffing my face with a burger and fries.

'What are you blokes doing?' I said naively. 'What the hell are you interested in? Leave me alone!'

It's been pretty much like that ever since. As I've said, there's no school where you can learn how to handle the endless intrusions. Your mistakes are made and you hope you learn how to deal with them. I've tried to be myself but probably should have been a little bit more – what's the word? – responsible, because the consequences of my actions have never been my first thought. Yes, I admit I've made mistakes, but they've shaped who I am today.

At the time, I never thought I was having any significant effect on cricket, but looking back now I can see how perhaps I have. Wrist-spin was dying out, but by performing well I kind of gave it a kick up the backside and made it cool. I suppose I bought a sense of rock and roll to the game – an excitement and flair that wasn't usually associated with something increasingly seen as old-fashioned. It was satisfying to bowl leg-spin – in fact, it was a gas – and I wanted people to be able to see the fun in it. A lot of kids have had a go because of me. I love that.

There's a mystique to sliders, wrong 'uns and flippers that I was happy to exaggerate, and when those balls took wickets, they were bigger news than your average off-break. Add in the fact that the bloke letting them go had dyed hair, an ear-stud and liked a party, I can see that there's a story there.

Of all the compliments people have given me, a couple of short and simple ones from two truly great men of cricket have meant the most. There was Bill O'Reilly's article in the *Sydney Morning Herald* when he said I had a huge future: 'It is fantastic to see leg spin back in the game . . . I hope they stick with his guy,' he wrote, which was really nice. They say he was a brilliant observer of the game.

The other was from Keith Miller who, unfortunately, was in a wheelchair by the time I met him. Ian Chappell has always said how well I'd have got on with 'Nugget' – same sort of blokes, says Chappelli. Anyway, it was soon after one of the controversial tabloid headlines had broken that Keith came into the Aussie change-rooms to meet the guys, the one and only time that I know of.

He shook my hand and said, 'How you going, Shane?'

'I'm good, mate,' I answered.

He kind of smiled before saying, 'Don't let those bastards bring you down, mate. Do it all. I love what you've done on the field and how you're going off the field. Be your own man.'

I thanked him and that was that. Keith Miller, legend.

C'mon, Aussie, C'mon

You'd struggle to leave either of O'Reilly or Miller out of Australia's best-ever team. There'd be a few from my time playing in that side too. Obvious candidates are Hayden, Ponting, Border, Gilchrist, McGrath and maybe even Warne! I've battled with the idea of naming a best-ever Aussie side, but I just don't know enough about the older guys. Instead I'm going to have a crack at the best side from all the players I walked onto the field with.

Haydos opens the batting with Michael Slater, because they set a tone that is exactly as I see cricket – attacking, confrontational and exciting. Ponting is at three, the ultimate start-up man and able to switch between defence and attack quickly; a great player of the short ball, less good against spin on the subcontinent, but we can live with that. In my view, Punter is close to being one of the greats, only a fraction behind Lara and Tendulkar.

Mark Waugh is at four. With the bat, his talent was close to genius, he could bowl a bit of everything and, jeez, he could catch and field. Then Allan Border, because he was all that an Australian cricketer should be. This nonsense about worshipping the baggy green – just watch film of AB and you'll see what playing for Australia means to any proud Australian.

Number six is difficult. At first I had Steve Waugh but decided his style and tempo was too like AB's, so we needed something different – pity Nugget wasn't younger! Other candidates were Dean Jones, Michael Hussey and Michael Clarke, all sensational in their own way and on their day. But, on reflection, I have to go with Steve Waugh for his all-rounder skills. We had our differences, but there's no denying Tugga's strength of character or ability to play at his best under pressure. His best was very good, enough said. His bowling was more than handy too.

Gilly at seven or Heals? Gilly just killed teams with the bat and that is a powerful thing to add to his adequate wicket-keeping. Heals was a genius behind the stumps, especially to me when I bowled round the wicket into the rough to right-handers. Hmmm, let's go with . . . err, don't know! Aarrggghh, sorry Healso, it has to be Gilly – he's just too destructive with the bat.

Tim May is at eight. I've already mentioned what a terrific bowler he was. Then pace and reverse swing with Brett Lee and sheer class with Jason Gillespie, who both just pip Bruce Reid here, I think. Jeez, they're all good bowlers. No, sorry, Binga, I'm changing my mind, you're out – it's 'Chook' and Dizzy (Reid and Gillespie). Chook had everything, but that extra bounce on the awkward angle sways it.

Finally then, the Pigeon, of course – 563 Test wickets. That's 1271 between us! I didn't play with Mitchell Johnson or Ryan Harris. If I had, well, the team might be different because they were magnificent bowlers and great together, even if only for a short time. I've got Merv Hughes as 12th man – no bowler I saw has a bigger heart or greater sense of humour and he was a very skilful cricketer. The ultimate flat-wicket quickie, because he made miracles out of nothing.

So the team is: Hayden, Slater, Ponting, Waugh M., Border, Waugh S., Gilchrist, May, Gillespie, Reid, McGrath. With Hughes the 12th.

I'd pick a World XI from the same era to play against us and still back Australia to win. Pidge would say 5–0! Errr, no, Pidge.

The Boys of Summer

Okay, so that's given me an idea. I can't pick a World XI from when I started out, because guys like Ian Botham and Viv Richards were still playing but past their best. I think the way to go is to only include those I played with or against, including the Aussies, and the period under consideration is January 1991 to January 2007.

I won't pick one XI because any team is dependent on conditions, so I'm going with a touring party of 16 but a first choice XI for the first Test of an imaginary global tour that opens up at the Gabba and goes on to see a SuperTest played in every major full member ICC country.

Haydos is in again, just ridiculously powerful and frightening to bowl to. Then it's one of Slats, Graham Gooch, Saeed Anwar and Virender Sehwag. I'd like a left and righthander, which rules out Anwar – some timer of a cricket ball, that guy – and I only caught Gooch as he was finishing, though as I've said he was still the best English batsman I played against. Sehwag was very good on hard pitches and very brilliant on Indian pitches, so he gets the nod over Slats. He put such pressure on the bowler; in fact, they both did. It's a firecracker start to the innings.

Three candidates stand out for first wicket down – Ricky, the most explosive; Jacques Kallis, the most correct; Kumar Sangakkara, the one with the most natural touch and flexibility. All three will feature in my touring party but I'm going with Ricky at three for his ability to both set games up and close them out.

The next two positions are already pretty clear from previous chapters in this book. The best two batsmen of my time were clearly Tendulkar and Lara, each for the different reasons I've explained a couple of times in these pages. Often, we had no plan for them, other than 'hit the top of off-stump'. They both had slumps in form that we exploited, but in general their batting was ridiculously good – Sachin the better technician, Brian the greater matchwinner.

At number six, I want an all-rounder. I missed the age of Imran Khan, Kapil Dev, Richard Hadlee and Botham – sadly, I never played against any of them. But I didn't miss Kallis. His record is incredible; every opposition had to break him down, piece by piece, otherwise he was still there building a big score, nagging those outswingers around off-stump, or catching everything at slip. He has to play in any team of the past 25 years.

The wicketkeeper thing is the most difficult. There are three ways to go – the best keeper, because we've got plenty of batting; the best middle-order batsman wicketkeeper, which was my pick in the Australian team above; or the best all-round cricketer. So, in order, it's one of Healy, Gilchrist and Sangakkara. Given the six batsmen before him and the ball-strikers who follow, I was committed to Heals because he's the best wicketkeeper I've seen and this team is the best of the best. But Gilly has nicked him out again, for the exact same reasons as earlier.

Next up, Wasim Akram. Incredible bowler. Fast, or very fast, depending on his mood and/or the pitch. Not that the pitch mattered much – he was so quick through the air. He swung the new and old ball, orthodox and reverse, had a bouncer that could cause grievous bodily harm and a yorker that broke feet, toes and stumps. He won matches single-handedly but could also be a perfect foil for Waqar Younis, Mushtaq Ahmed and any of the others. A master of his art, a no-brainer of a selection. Let's make him captain as well.

Then Anil Kumble at nine, for his heart and competitiveness, as much as his skill. Curtly Ambrose and Glenn McGrath come next, marginally ahead of guys like Waqar, Shoaib, Shaun Pollock and Courtney Walsh. Very few bowlers that I've seen can both hold a game and break a game. There's no question that King Curtly and the Pidge are the most accurate, Pollock included. In one spell, Curtly took that 7/1 against us in Perth – that does it for me. And Glenn, well, he's my partner, so he's coming with me wherever I go.

My XI for Brisbane is: Hayden, Sehwag, Ponting, Tendulkar, Lara, Kallis, Gilchrist, Akram, Kumble, Ambrose, McGrath.

Now we're off on tour, so I need cover. Sangakkara is a definite. He bats anywhere from one to six, keeps wicket and fields great. It's interesting how keeping affected his batting – 40.48 in 48 Tests with the gloves; 66.78 in 86 Tests without them. He's still my number-two keeper, whatever the stats!

My other spare batsman would be Kevin Pietersen – I love that flair, that game-changing ability. And I love his positive attitude. Murali is the second spinner, easy. I also need a couple of reserve quicks. Andrew Flintoff is a candidate, because at his best – like in 2005 – he hit the bat horrifically hard at genuine pace and made runs powerfully and quickly. Pollock offers superb all-round skills so is a candidate, but I favour Fred marginally ahead of him. But, but, but, but . . . the choice is simple, it's Waqar Younis. Wow, what a bowler! The best reverse swinger, the best destroyer of a tail and bloody quick.

My final choice is a wildcard but I want him around, ready to be unleashed. Shoaib Akhtar is the man, the fastest bowler I ever faced and with a strike rate of 45.7 in his 46 Tests, which is only bettered in the modern era by Shane Bond (18 Tests), Kagiso Rabada (31), Dale Steyn (87) and Waqar himself. He's a good lad too – we'll have some fun.

My final five are: Sangakkara, Pietersen, Muralitharan, Waqar and Shoaib.

This collection of Warne's Warriors would take some beating. So, who's up for it?

I know, the blokes from the era I first watched as a kid – a fantasy team that we play at the MCG on the Boxing Day of my dreams! Remember, these selections are made from the start of World Series Cricket in 1977 to the day I first played for Australia in January 1992.

Viv was my hero, so he's captain of the Master Blaster's XI. Here's the line-up: Barry Richards, Graham Gooch, Viv Richards, Greg Chappell, Martin Crowe, Ian Botham, Ian Healy, Malcolm Marshall, Jeff Thomson, Dennis Lillee and Abdul Qadir. Joel Garner is 12th man – I loved the 'Big Bird'. Imran Khan, Richard Hadlee and Kapil Dev are a bit unlucky to miss out. So too Gordon Greenidge, Javed Miandad and Chappelli. Graeme Pollock didn't play WSC, so I never saw him. No worries, be a hell of a game whoever is out there.

Wasim tosses with Viv, win it and we bat first. After that, the magic takes over . . .

Epilogue

A Beautiful Noise

Brooke, Jackson, Summer

JACKSON: 'He's a father in the right way, like he's there for us when we need him. For sure, we can rely on him, and through all of our lives he's worked hard to see that we're happy. He's also a friend. We can talk to him and share stuff that matters to us. People say we must be embarrassed by him, but we're not, we love him. Errr, actually, we're sometimes embarrassed by things he does on social media – oh, Dad – but he's learning from his mistakes and has even started to listen to us a bit now. He's good fun to socialise with – I mean, he's pretty cool, isn't he? I don't see him as Shane Warne, Australian cricketer, I see him as my dad.'

BROOKE: 'Yeah, he's always there for us and definitely tries his best on our behalf. You can't ask for much more than that. I know a few families with divorced parents and the dads only see their kids once a month. That's never the case with us, unless he's working on cricket somewhere, which is fair enough. In fact, we all try to see each other as much as we can. He wants us to be happy more than anything else. I hope he's happy – I think he is. Maybe not 100 per cent of the time – who is, I guess?! – but mostly.'

SUMMER/BROOKE: 'He's very funny. We laugh a lot and he's got a mad side that's really fun to be with. In fact, he's not that "wanker Warney" that we've heard people call him, not at all. That's so unfair. He's a very genuine guy and it's not right to say he searches for fame or celebrity. It happened because he's good at cricket and a natural showman. He's entertained people for years, hasn't he? Why criticise him for that?'

BROOKE: 'He's not, like, uptight or strict. He's fun . . .'

SUMMER: 'That depends on the situation. Sometimes he over-reacts but I've got quite good at persuading him to think about things a different way. He can still be strict but he's not so unreasonable as he was.'

BROOKE: 'Maybe that was more when we were young.'

SUMMER: 'I'm still young!'

JACKSON: 'When we were little kids, it was like we didn't have our own name – we were just, like, Shane Warne's son or daughter. I mean, we were sort of labelled. It wasn't like we resented it because I'm proud to be his son, but it got to a point where we wanted to develop our own identity and be recognised for who we were, not who we came from.'

BROOKE: 'That was worse for Jacko, I think, because girls don't care so much about cricket and most of my friends didn't really know who Shane Warne was. I have come to like cricket more and more. Last year I went to the Adelaide Ashes Test and sat on the hill with two mates. I went for one night and stayed for four – loved it! Back at home, I found myself watching the next Test on TV, first time ever!

'The problem for us came when Dad appeared in newspapers and stuff for things outside cricket. That was embarrassing. Like, Dad, what are you doing? But I agree with Jacko – we weren't embarrassed by him, only by the story that appeared. We still felt bad for him and thought, well, people make mistakes and let's hope he's learnt from them. We still love him through all these things.'

SUMMER: 'Yeah, I've never been embarrassed by him. There are times when you think, "Oh no, not another story," and other times when you think, "I wish we found out before the newspapers," but, well, it's bad the way he's followed wherever he goes and stuff. He doesn't have much privacy.'

JACKSON: 'He hasn't fully learnt. He's learning . . .'

BROOKE: 'True! We've had some difficult times, whether it be with girls or the break-up of the marriage with Mum. I guess each of us has dealt with that differently, but over time you sort of get used to it. I think we're stronger people now than we were 10 years ago.'

SUMMER: 'Yes, that's right. We've come a long way in 10 years. For a start, we've got to know him better, to actually understand him. As a kid I didn't have a clue what was going on or know him at all.'

JACKSON: 'We were all kids once, so, like when we were eight, 10, 12 or whatever, we just did as we were told and lived with it. Now we can give our own opinion and he'll listen to us.'

SUMMER: 'That's the big difference. It's a friendship now.'

BROOKE: 'We're so lucky to have everything that we have and do everything we do because of who he is and how hard he's worked in his life, but obviously if we had the choice not to be in the public eye, 100 per cent we would choose not to be, because it impacts everything else. Whichever way you look at it, we're Shane Warne's kids. So, when people say, "Oh, but you hang out with Chris Martin and Ed Sheeran," it's like, yes, but even those advantages have their disadvantages. We never complain, though. Overall, we're very fortunate. Look, sometimes it can be hard, but that's life, isn't it?'

JACKSON: 'Yeah, like we can't go out to dinner and just sit and eat without someone asking Dad for a photo, hitting him on the back, like, "Hey," and then expecting him to talk to them about cricket or whatever. Last year at the Melbourne Cup, it was just me and him watching the horses walking around, having a chilled time, and we went for a hot dog – a walk that usually takes two minutes but it took half an hour because every step someone wants something. Social media kills everything. Everyone thinks they have a right to take a picture and then they tweet it or put it on Facebook. And some of the rubbish people say about him, it's ridiculous.'

BROOKE: 'Yeah, and I hate it that the press, and sometimes even social media, knows things before we do. For example, Dad and Elizabeth got engaged one night in Europe, but he hadn't had the opportunity to tell us and someone on the boat blabbed, and the next thing you know it's in a magazine. We had no idea about it so we obviously jumped down Dad's throat, like, what the hell's going on?! That's unfair on us all.'

SUMMER: 'Or he takes someone out on a date and gets followed at the time. He's over there and we're in Australia and we find out about it from someone else. That really irritates us.'

JACKSON: 'We are proud of him, though, whatever he does. His accomplishments are pretty good – you know, 708 Test wickets, the IPL, commentary, even writing a book. We're always going to be proud of him. Even if this book doesn't sell, I'm pleased that it will have given people a chance to see who he really is.'

SUMMER: 'At the end of the day, life with Dad is what it is. Obviously, things can hurt us, even in the book they might, but you can't change what's happened, so we all just get on with it. He tries his best for us – that's what matters.'

JACKSON: 'Yeah, and he has feelings too. People can say all these things on social media and think, "Oh, he won't see them or they won't affect him," but they all add up. I mean, once everything has been retweeted and re-sent, it's millions of people talking about him. Say, it's one-tenth of Australia, he must think, "If one-tenth of my country is having a crack at me, why should I bother to stop for them and have photos and sign autographs?" But he does, always. He's really good like that. People say he's brought a lot on himself, but that's easy for them to say and then just have a go at him out of spite!'

BROOKE: 'The sort of people who do that can't have met him. I think, with Dad, you're never disappointed when you meet him, because he always smiles and tries to have a chat – most of the time!'

JACKSON: 'He loves his fans, he really appreciates the people who support him and never forgets them. I'm always amazed by who and what he remembers.'

SUMMER: 'We love being with him, especially in Spain where not so many people recognise him.'

JACKSON: 'Spain has brought us closer together. Brooke and me are adults, Summer is 17 – I mean, we can just all go out, have proper conversations, nice dinners and have a great time.'

BROOKE/SUMMER: 'The three of us were talking yesterday. It doesn't matter if we're in Spain, London, Australia or Antarctica – as long as we're all together, we're happy. And he gets on fine with Mum, which is good.'

JACKSON: 'They are very, very, very good friends.'

BROOKE: 'A hundred per cent, he's a great dad. I wouldn't want anyone else in the job! We're lucky to have him and anybody that knows him well would understand why we say that.'

SUMMER/JACKSON: 'We do, we really do. I hope the book sells well. He's achieved a lot. Australia should be proud of him.'

Acknowledgements

WHAT A JOURNEY THIS has been! Writing a book of your own is harder than I imagined and I have been guided through the process during this past year or so by some fantastic people.

First up comes Keith Warne, my dad, who put me straight on the history of our family, both past and present, and spent time with Mark in making sure it appears right on these pages. Then there is Brigitte, my magical mum, who had a bit to say too and, as ever, had me in stitches with her memories of childhood. Thanks, guys.

The team at Penguin Random House have done a great job. At various stages, Alison Urquhart has been quick to make sure I haven't lost sight of my responsibilities, while Patrick Mangan must be the most patient, knowledgeable, detailed and understanding editor of all time. Huge thanks go to them both. Also to Nikki Christer and Karen Reid, whose efforts go unsung but who keep the engine running.

I have been lucky to have great friends alongside me over the years – my first manager, Austin 'Ocker' Robertson; James Erskine, my manager these days (and my art advisor and wine-taster too!); Andrew Neophitou – 'Neo' – who runs the Melbourne arm of James' operation; and the man across the oceans in the UK, Michael Cohen, who wouldn't take no for an answer back in London in 1999.

You are special people to me. I appreciate all the hours you have put in on my behalf.

Richard Isaacs, scorer and statistician for Sky, has been amazing – transcribing every word of the many hours of conversation I had with Mark and then checking fact and figures with patience and a long-acquired knowledge of the greatest game. As if that wasn't enough, Rich then took on the pages of stats that appear at the back of the book here. Thanks a million, Big 'un!

And so to Mark – or Nicko, as Ian Healy christened him – who wrote the whole damn thing. Now that *is* a good effort. We have talked about the game that has dominated our lives for hours on end at both our homes, in both our countries; in cars, in bars, on golf courses and on planes. He has asked me hard questions and I have given honest answers. His enthusiasm and clear-thinking have never wavered. We go back a long way, having both captained a county team we love – and still follow to this day – and we continue to battle from tee to green like our lives depend on it. Thanks, mate, it could never have happened without you – what fun we've had choosing songs, picking teams and telling these stories, and what a brilliant job you've done stitching it all together.

Finally, to all of you out there who have supported me along the way. We share this wonderful game in our blood and hope it lives on for many others to share as well. See you down the tracks.

About the Author

MARK NICHOLAS CAPTAINED HAMPSHIRE for the best part of 12 summers, making 36 first-class hundreds – including two against Australia – and leading the county to four titles. He also captained England A in nine unofficial Test matches.

Mark went on to become a presenter and commentator with Sky TV, Channel 4 (whose coverage won three BAFTA awards) and now Channel 5 in the UK. He was a fixture on Channel Nine's cricket coverage in Australia from the summer of 2003/04 until the television rights moved elsewhere earlier this year. He has twice been named Britain's Sports Presenter of the Year by the Royal Television Society.

For 16 years he was a sports feature writer with the London *Daily Telegraph* before moving to Cricinfo. He has had three spells in radio with talkSPORT and is to broadcast again with the station over the coming months.

Mark has worked as a presenter in other fields of television, including the UK edition of *Survivor* and the cooking show *Britain's Best Dish*.

His first book, *A Beautiful Game*, was published by Allen & Unwin in October 2016 and won both the Cricket Society and MCC book of the year, as well as the Cross Sports Books Cricket Book of the Year.

He has lived in Sydney for much of the Australian summer and otherwise in London, with Kirsten and their 12-year-old daughter, Leila.

SHANE WARNE
TEST MATCH STATISTICS
Compiled by Richard V. Isaacs

TEST CAREER – SERIES BY SERIES

Series	Season	M	Inns	NO	Runs	Avge	Overs	Mdns	Runs	Wkts	Avge
Australia v India	1991/92	2	4	1	28	9.33	68	9	228	1	228.00
Sri Lanka v Australia	1992/93	2	3	0	66	22.00	38.1	8	158	3	52.66
Australia v West Indies	1992/93	4	7	0	42	6.00	108.2	23	313	10	31.30
New Zealand v Australia	1992/93	3	4	2	49	24.50	159	73	256	17	15.05
England v Australia	1993	6	5	2	113	37.66	439.5	178	877	34	25.79
Australia v New Zealand	1993/94	3	2	1	85	85.00	151.3	49	305	18	16.94
Australia v South Africa	1993/94	3	4	1	16	5.33	175.1	63	307	18	17.05
South Africa v Australia	1993/94	3	5	0	41	8.20	190.5	69	336	15	22.40
Pakistan v Australia	1994/95	3	4	0	69	17.25	181.4	50	504	18	28.00
Australia v England	1994/95	5	10	1	60	6.66	256.1	84	549	27	20.33
West Indies v Australia	1994/95	4	5	0	28	5.60	138	35	406	15	27.06
Australia v Pakistan	1995/96	3	4	1	39	13.00	115	52	198	19	10.42
Australia v Sri Lanka	1995/96	3	1	0	33	33.00	164.4	43	433	12	36.08
Australia v West Indies	1996/97	5	7	0	128	18.28	217.1	56	594	22	27.00
South Africa v Australia	1996/97	3	5	0	42	8.40	133	47	282	11	25.63
England v Australia	1997	6	10	0	188	18.80	237.1	69	577	24	24.04
Australia v New Zealand	1997/98	3	3	0	71	23.66	170.4	36	476	19	25.05
Australia v South Africa	1997/98	3	5	1	27	6.75	187.1	51	417	20	20.85
India v Australia	1997/98	3	5	0	105	21.00	167	37	540	10	54.00
Australia v England	1998/99	1	2	1	10	10.00	39	7	110	2	55.00
West Indies v Australia	1998/99	3	6	0	138	23.00	83.5	18	268	2	134.00
Sri Lanka v Australia	1999/00	3	4	0	6	1.50	56.1	20	115	8	14.37
Zimbabwe v Australia	1999/00	1	1	0	6	6.00	53.1	13	137	6	22.83
Australia v Pakistan	1999/00	3	4	1	99	33.00	130	37	370	12	30.83
Australia v India	1999/00	3	3	0	88	29.33	127	35	335	8	41.87
New Zealand v Australia	1999/00	3	4	0	36	9.00	129.2	33	414	15	27.60
India v Australia	2000/01	3	5	0	50	10.00	152.1	31	505	10	50.50
England v Australia	2001	5	4	0	13	3.25	195.2	41	580	31	18.70
Australia v New Zealand	2001/02	3	4	0	201	50.25	124.2	19	430	6	71.66
Australia v South Africa	2001/02	3	4	0	85	21.25	173.3	35	473	17	27.82
South Africa v Australia	2001/02	3	5	1	129	32.25	162	38	442	20	22.10
Pakistan v Australia (in SL/UAE)	2002/03	3	4	0	30	7.50	124	29	342	27	12.66
Australia v England	2002/03	3	3	0	117	39.00	131.1	29	347	14	24.78
Sri Lanka v Australia	2003/04	3	6	0	79	13.16	100.5	24	521	26	20.03
Australia v Sri Lanka	2004	2	4	0	9	2.25	100.5	24	280	10	28.00
India v Australia	2004/05	3	5	0	38	7.60	140	27	421	14	30.07
Australia v New Zealand	2004/05	2	2	1	63	63.00	95.2	17	256	11	23.27
Australia v Pakistan	2004/05	3	3	0	38	12.66	124.3	24	402	14	28.71
New Zealand v Australia	2004/05	3	3	1	53	26.50	131.3	25	374	17	22.00
England v Australia	2005	5	9	0	249	27.66	252.5	37	797	40	19.92
ICC Super Series in Australia	2005/06	1	2	0	12	6.00	31	7	71	6	11.83
Australia v West Indies	2005/06	3	3	0	48	16.00	132.2	27	366	16	22.87
Australia v South Africa	2005/06	3	5	1	38	9.50	172	45	462	14	33.00
South Africa v Australia	2005/06	3	4	0	82	20.50	127.4	19	423	15	28.20
Bangladesh v Australia	2005/06	2	2	0	11	5.50	87.2	12	300	11	27.27
Australia v England	2006/07	5	5	1	196	49.00	241.2	43	698	23	30.34

TEST CAREER – AGAINST EACH OPPONENT

Against	M	Inns	NO	Runs	Avge	Overs	Mdns	Runs	Wkts	Avge
Bangladesh	2	2	0	11	5.50	87.2	12	300	11	27.27
England	36	48	5	946	22.00	1792.5	488	4535	195	23.25
ICC World XI	1	2	0	12	6.00	31	7	71	6	11.83
India	14	22	1	309	14.71	654.1	139	2029	43	47.18
New Zealand	20	22	5	558	32.82	961.4	252	2511	103	24.37
Pakistan	15	19	2	275	16.17	675.1	192	1816	90	20.17
South Africa	24	37	4	460	13.93	1321.2	367	3142	130	24.16
Sri Lanka	13	18	0	193	10.72	527.5	132	1507	59	25.54
West Indies	19	28	0	384	13.71	679.4	159	1947	65	29.95
Zimbabwe	1	1	0	6	6.00	53.1	13	137	6	22.83
CAREER	**145**	**199**	**17**	**3154**	**17.32**	**6784.1**	**1761**	**17995**	**708**	**25.41**

TEST CAREER – ON EACH VENUE AND EACH COUNTRY

Venue	M	Inns	NO	Runs	AvgBat	Overs	Mdns	Runs	Wkts	Avge
Sydney	14	19	3	276	17.25	676.4	164	1800	64	28.12
Adelaide	13	19	3	329	20.56	677.3	177	1705	56	30.44
Perth	12	16	0	329	20.56	475.5	109	1349	37	36.45
Brisbane	11	12	1	365	33.18	553.2	162	1381	68	20.30
Melbourne	11	15	2	113	8.69	523	129	1284	56	22.92
Hobart	6	6	2	112	28.00	229	50	621	28	22.17
Cairns	1	2	0	6	3.00	75	21	199	7	28.42
Darwin	1	2	0	3	1.50	25.5	3	81	3	27.00
in Australia	**69**	**91**	**11**	**1533**	**19.16**	**3236.1**	**815**	**8420**	**319**	**26.39**

Venue	M	Inns	NO	Runs	AvgBat	Overs	Mdns	Runs	Wkts	Avge
Birmingham	4	6	0	147	24.50	190.1	57	544	25	21.76
Lord's	4	4	0	35	8.75	157.2	41	372	19	19.57
Nottingham	4	6	1	100	20.00	215	65	514	29	17.72
The Oval	4	5	0	86	17.20	251.2	60	712	32	22.25
Leeds	3	2	0	0	0.00	119.2	36	268	3	89.33
Manchester	3	5	1	195	48.75	192	66	421	21	20.04
in England	**22**	**28**	**2**	**563**	**21.65**	**1125.1**	**325**	**2831**	**129**	**21.94**

Venue	M	Inns	NO	Runs	AvgBat	Overs	Mdns	Runs	Wkts	Avge
Johannesburg	4	6	0	76	12.66	174.3	52	448	21	21.33
Cape Town	3	4	1	96	32.00	202.5	57	465	17	27.35
Durban	3	5	0	89	17.80	158.5	41	399	18	22.16
Centurion	1	2	0	12	6.00	36	11	89	0	
Port Elizabeth	1	2	0	21	10.50	41.2	12	82	5	16.40
in South Africa	**12**	**19**	**1**	**294**	**16.33**	**613.3**	**173**	**1483**	**61**	**24.31**

Venue	M	Inns	NO	Runs	AvgBat	Overs	Mdns	Runs	Wkts	Avge
Auckland	3	5	1	25	6.25	130.3	38	350	18	19.44
Wellington	3	3	1	79	39.50	142.2	49	351	14	25.07
Christchurch	2	2	1	24	24.00	102	28	237	14	16.92
Hamilton	1	1	0	10	10.00	45	16	106	3	35.33
in New Zealand	**9**	**11**	**3**	**138**	**17.25**	**419.5**	**131**	**1044**	**49**	**21.30**

Venue	M	Inns	NO	Runs	AvgBat	Overs	Mdns	Runs	Wkts	Avge
Chennai	3	6	0	67	11.16	155.3	30	513	13	39.46
Bangalore	2	3	0	65	21.66	120	27	379	9	42.11
Kolkata	2	4	0	20	5.00	96.1	10	364	3	121.33
Mumbai	1	1	0	39	39.00	50	18	107	5	21.40
Nagpur	1	1	0	2	2.00	37.3	10	103	4	25.75
in India	9	15	0	193	12.86	459.1	95	1466	34	43.11

Venue	M	Inns	NO	Runs	AvgBat	Overs	Mdns	Runs	Wkts	Avge
Colombo–SSC	3	5	0	91	18.20	101.1	24	336	9	37.33
Galle	2	3	0	23	7.66	86	26	193	13	14.84
Kandy	2	4	0	30	7.50	64.1	12	225	15	15.00
Colombo–PSS	1	2	0	0	0.00	55	10	188	11	17.09
Moratuwa	1	1	0	7	7.00	11	3	40	0	
in Sri Lanka	9	15	0	151	10.06	317.2	75	982	48	20.45

Venue	M	Inns	NO	Runs	AvgBat	Overs	Mdns	Runs	Wkts	Avge
Bridgetown	2	3	0	51	17.00	78.2	13	260	6	43.33
Kingston	2	3	0	47	15.66	78.4	22	236	7	33.71
Port-of-Spain	2	4	0	57	14.25	29.5	9	77	1	77.00
St John's	1	1	0	11	11.00	35	9	101	3	33.66
in West Indies	7	11	0	166	15.09	221.5	53	674	17	39.64

Venue	M	Inns	NO	Runs	AvgBat	Overs	Mdns	Runs	Wkts	Avge
Karachi	1	2	0	22	11.00	63.1	22	150	8	18.75
Lahore	1	1	0	33	33.00	71.5	14	240	9	26.66
Rawalpindi	1	1	0	14	14.00	46.4	14	114	1	114.00
in Pakistan	3	4	0	69	17.25	181.4	50	504	18	28.00

Venue	M	Inns	NO	Runs	AvgBat	Overs	Mdns	Runs	Wkts	Avge
Sharjah	2	2	0	30	15.00	69	19	154	16	9.62
in UAE	2	2	0	30	15.00	69	19	154	16	9.62

Venue	M	Inns	NO	Runs	AvgBat	Overs	Mdns	Runs	Wkts	Avge
Chittagong-D	1					54.2	7	160	8	20.00
Fatullah	1	2	0	11	5.50	33	5	140	3	46.66
in Bangladesh	2	2	0	11	5.50	87.2	12	300	11	27.27

Venue	M	Inns	NO	Runs	AvgBat	Overs	Mdns	Runs	Wkts	Avge
Harare	1	1	0	6	6.00	53.1	13	137	6	22.83
in Zimbabwe	1	1	0	6	6.00	53.1	13	137	6	22.83

TEST MATCH HALF-CENTURIES

Score	Against	Venue	Season
99	New Zealand	Perth	2001/02
90	England	Manchester	2005
86	Pakistan	Brisbane	1999/00
86	India	Adelaide	1999/00
74*	New Zealand	Brisbane	1993/94
71	England	Sydney	2006/07
70	New Zealand	Hobart	2001/02
63	South Africa	Cape Town	2001/02
57	England	Brisbane	2002/03
53*	New Zealand	Adelaide	2004/05
53	England	Manchester	1997
50*	New Zealand	Wellington	2004/05

BOWLING WICKETS BREAKDOWN

	b	ct	ct+	lbw	st	TOTAL
v Bangladesh	2	5	2	2	0	11
v England	39	82	26	37	11	195
v ICC World XI	0	4	2	0	0	6
v India	7	24	5	6	1	43
v New Zealand	21	50	8	18	6	103
v Pakistan	9	40	6	29	6	90
v South Africa	23	67	7	28	5	130
v Sri Lanka	6	34	8	7	4	59
v West Indies	9	36	8	9	3	65
v Zimbabwe	0	3	1	2	0	6
TOTAL	116	345	73	138	36	708

FIVE WICKETS IN AN INNINGS

Bowling	Against	Venue	Season
7-52	West Indies	Melbourne	1992/93
5-82	England	Birmingham	1993
6-31	New Zealand	Hobart	1993/94
7-56	South Africa	Sydney	1993/94
5-72	South Africa	Sydney	1993/94
5-89	Pakistan	Karachi	1994/95
6-136	Pakistan	Lahore	1994/95
8-71	England	Brisbane	1994/95
6-64	England	Melbourne	1994/95
7-23	Pakistan	Brisbane	1995/96
6-48	England	Manchester	1997
5-88	New Zealand	Hobart	1997/98
5-75	South Africa	Sydney	1997/98
6-34	South Africa	Sydney	1997/98
5-52	Sri Lanka	Kandy	1999/00
5-110	Pakistan	Hobart	1999/00
5-71	England	Birmingham	2001
6-33	England	Nottingham	2001
7-165	England	The Oval	2001
5-113	South Africa	Adelaide	2001/02
6-161	South Africa	Cape Town	2001/02
7-94	Pakistan	Colombo-PSS	2002/03
5-74	Pakistan	Sharjah	2002/03
5-43	Sri Lanka	Galle	2003/04
5-116	Sri Lanka	Galle	2003/04
5-90	Sri Lanka	Kandy	2003/04
5-65	Sri Lanka	Kandy	2003/04
6-125	India	Chennai	2004/05
5-39	New Zealand	Christchurch	2004/05
6-46	England	Birmingham	2005
6-122	England	The Oval	2005
6-124	England	The Oval	2005
5-48	West Indies	Brisbane	2005/06
6-80	West Indies	Adelaide	2005/06
6-86	South Africa	Durban	2005/06
5-113	Bangladesh	Chittagong-D	2005/06
5-39	England	Melbourne	2006/07

TEN WICKETS IN A MATCH

Bowling	Against	Venue	Season
12-128	South Africa	Sydney	1993/94
11-110	England	Brisbane	1994/95
11-77	Pakistan	Brisbane	1995/96
11-109	South Africa	Sydney	1997/98
11-229	England	The Oval	2001
11-188	Pakistan	Colombo-PSS	2002/03
10-159	Sri Lanka	Galle	2003/04
10-155	Sri Lanka	Kandy	2003/04
10-162	England	Birmingham	2005
12-246	England	The Oval	2005

TEST MATCH WICKET TAKING MILESTONES

1st wicket	RJ Shastri	c DM Jones	206	v India	Sydney	1991/92
50th wicket	N Hussain	c DC Boon	71	v England	Nottingham	1993
100th wicket	BM McMillan	lbw	4	v South Africa	Adelaide	1993/94
150th wicket	SJ Rhodes	c ME Waugh	0	v England	Melbourne	1994/95
200th wicket	HP Tillakaratne	c RT Ponting	119	v Sri Lanka	Perth	1995/96
250th wicket	AJ Stewart	b	1	v England	Manchester	1997
300th wicket	DJ Richardson	c and b	0	v South Africa	Sydney	1997/98
350th wicket	HH Kanitkar	lbw	11	v India	Melbourne	1999/00
400th wicket	AJ Stewart	c AC Gilchrist	29	v England	The Oval	2001
450th wicket	AG Prince	c ME Waugh	48	v South Africa	Durban	2001/02
500th wicket	HP Tillakaratne	c A Symonds	25	v Sri Lanka	Galle	2003/04
533rd wicket (World Record)	IK Pathan	c ML Hayden	14	v India	Chennai	2004/05
550th wicket	JEC Franklin	lbw	7	v New Zealand	Adelaide	2004/05
600th wicket	ME Trescothick	c AC Gilchrist	63	v England	Manchester	2005
650th wicket	AG Prince	lbw	8	v South Africa	Perth	2005/06
700th wicket	AJ Strauss	b	50	v England	Melbourne	2006/07
Final wicket	A Flintoff	st AC Gilchrist	7	v England	Sydney	2006/07

LEADING BATSMEN DISMISSED

	b	ct	ct+	lbw	st	TOTAL
AJ Stewart	4	5	3	2	0	14
AG Prince	1	7	0	3	0	11
N Hussain	1	5	4	1	0	11
MA Atherton	3	3	2	2	0	10
AF Giles	1	4	1	3	0	9
MV Boucher	1	7	1	0	0	9
SJ Harmison	1	3	0	4	1	9
GP Thorpe	1	5	1	0	2	9

FIELDERS WHO ASSISTED IN DISMISSALS

	M	Ct	St	TOTAL
AC Gilchrist	70	39	20	59
MA Taylor	66	51	0	51
IA Healy	74	34	15	49
ME Waugh	103	39	0	39
ML Hayden	69	39	0	39
RT Ponting	85	36	0	36

TEST MATCH HAT-TRICKS – 1

v England at Melbourne 1994/95 – dismissed PAJ deFreitas, D Gough and DE Malcolm

MAN OF THE MATCH AWARDS

Runs	Bowling	Ct	Opponent	Venue	Year
6	8/117	0	v West Indies	Melbourne	1992/93
22	7/86	0	v New Zealand	Christchurch	1992/93
15	8/137	1	v England	Manchester	1993
74	8/125	2	v New Zealand	Brisbane	1993/94
22	8/150	1	v Pakistan	Karachi	1994/95
2	11/110	1	v England	Brisbane	1994/95
5	11/77	0	v Pakistan	Brisbane	1995/96
12	11/109	1	v South Africa	Sydney	1997/98
0	8/70	0	v England	Nottingham	2001
dnb	11/229	2	v England	The Oval	2001
47	8/170	2	v South Africa	Adelaide	2001/02
78	8/231	1	v South Africa	Cape Town	2001/02
0	11/188	0	v Pakistan	Colombo (PSS)	2002/03
11	8/130	0	v Pakistan	Sharjah	2002/03
24	10/155	1	v Sri Lanka	Kandy	2003/04
36	8/166	1	v South Africa	Durban	2005/06
40	7/85	1	v England	Melbourne	2006/07

MAN OF THE SERIES AWARDS

Runs	Wkts	Ct	Opponent	Series	Year
113	34	4	England (A)	The Ashes	1993
85	18	4	New Zealand (H)	Trans-Tasman Trophy	1993/94
69	18	2	Pakistan (A)	Australia in Pakistan	1994/95
39	19	0	Pakistan (H)	Pakistan in Australia	1995/96
27	20	5	South Africa (H)	South Africa in Australia	1997/98
30	27	2	Pakistan (N)	Aus v Pak in UAE & SL	2002/03
79	26	3	Sri Lanka (A)	Australia in Sri Lanka	2003/04
249	40	5	England (A)	The Ashes	2005

FIRST-CLASS RECORD – FOR TEAMS PLAYED FOR

Against	M	Inns	NO	Runs	HS	Avge	Overs	Mdns	Runs	Wkts	Avge
Australia(ns)	185	249	26	3947	99	17.69	7916.4	2060	21349	859	24.85
Australia B	2	3	2	53	35*	53.00	97.4	28	207	11	18.81
Australian XI	2	2	1	7	6	7.00	70.5	16	240	12	20.00
Hampshire	66	92	12	2040	107*	25.50	2411	479	7062	276	25.58
Victoria	46	58	7	872	75	17.09	1975.4	446	5591	161	34.72
F-C CAREER	**301**	**404**	**48**	**6919**	**107***	**19.43**	**12471.4**	**3029**	**34449**	**1319**	**26.11**

FIRST-CLASS CENTURIES

Score	Team	Against	Venue	Season
107*	Hampshire	Kent	Canterbury	2005
101	Hampshire	Middlesex	Southgate	2005

ONE-DAY INTERNATIONAL,
LIST A and TWENTY20 STATISTICS

Shane Warne Career Statistics

ONE-DAY INTERNATIONAL – SERIES BY SERIES

Series	Season	M	Inns	Runs	AvgBat	S/R	Overs	Mdns	Runs	Wkts	Avge	Econ	S/R
New Zealand v Australia	1992/93	1	1	3	3.00	100.00	10	0	40	2	20.00	4.00	30.0
B & H World Series in Australia	1993/94	10	6	15	3.00	41.66	90	5	301	22	13.68	3.34	24.5
South Africa v Australia	1993/94	8	3	87	29.00	88.77	69	3	285	11	25.90	4.13	37.6
Austral-Asia Cup in Sharjah	1993/94	3	1	4	4.00	30.76	29	1	103	9	11.44	3.55	19.3
Singer World Series in Sri Lanka	1994/95	3	2	31	15.50	68.88	28	1	109	7	15.57	3.89	24.0
Wills Triangular Series in Pakistan	1994/95	6	3	39	39.00	114.70	58.2	4	238	6	39.66	4.08	58.3
B & H World Series In Australia	1994/95	4	2	26	13.00	78.78	39	1	133	6	22.16	3.41	39.0
NZ Centenary Series	1994/95	4	2	7		63.63	40	6	140	5	28.00	3.50	48.0
West Indies v Australia	1994/95	4	3	22	22.00	91.66	39.1	5	204	4	51.00	5.20	58.7
B & H World Series in Australia	1995/96	9	2	6	6.00	75.00	80.1	7	317	15	21.13	3.95	32.0
ICC World Cup in Ind/Pak/SL	1995/96	7	5	32	10.66	110.34	68.3	3	263	12	21.91	3.83	34.2
Carlton & United Series in Australia	1996/97	8	5	38	9.50	73.07	75.4	6	325	19	17.10	4.29	23.8
South Africa v Australia	1996/97	6	5	45	11.25	80.35	54.1	2	272	10	27.20	5.02	32.5
Texaco Trophy in England	1997	3	3	20	10.00	57.14	29	0	129	1	129.00	4.44	174.0
Carlton & United Series in Australia	1997/98	10	6	35	7.00	58.33	93.3	3	405	12	33.75	4.33	46.7
Pepsi Triangular Series in India	1997/98	5	4	27	9.00	81.81	49	0	219	5	43.80	4.46	58.8
Coca-Cola Cup in Sharjah	1997/98	5	3	32	32.00	139.13	47	2	221	4	55.25	4.70	70.5
Carlton & United Series in Australia	1998/99	12	8	43	7.16	74.13	112.5	2	532	19	28.00	4.71	35.6
West Indies v Australia	1998/99	7	5	84	28.00	67.20	63	10	254	13	19.53	4.03	29.0
ICC World Cup in Europe	1999	10	4	34	11.33	79.06	94.2	13	361	20	18.05	3.82	28.3
Aiwa Cup in Sri Lanka	1999/00	5	4	43	10.75	61.42	40	1	214	6	35.66	5.35	40.0
Zimbabwe v Australia	1999/00	3					19	1	82	4	20.50	4.31	28.5
Carlton & United Series in Australia	1999/00	4	3	29	29.00	67.44	36	4	170	4	42.50	4.72	54.0

Series	Season	M	Inns	Runs	AvgBat	S/R	Overs	Mdns	Runs	Wkts	Avge	Econ	S/R
New Zealand v Australia	1999/00	6	2	19	9.50	90.47	49	4	194	9	21.55	3.95	32.6
South Africa v Australia	1999/00	3	2	32	16.00	69.56	28	3	98	3	32.66	3.50	56.0
Australia v South Africa	2000	3	2	16	16.00	94.11	30	2	101	2	50.50	3.36	90.0
Carlton Series in Australia	2000/01	9	1	7	7.00	53.84	84.5	5	377	18	20.94	4.44	28.2
India v Australia	2000/01	4	2	31	15.50	62.00	38	0	222	4	55.50	5.84	57.0
NatWest Series in England	2001	5	2	28	28.00	73.68	45	3	232	10	23.20	5.15	27.0
VB Series in Australia	2001/02	8	6	72	12.00	56.69	75	4	324	6	54.00	4.32	75.0
South Africa v Australia	2001/02	3	2	7	7.00	87.50	25	0	154	5	30.80	6.16	30.0
Australia v Pakistan	2002	3	2	32	16.00	52.45	30	2	118	5	23.60	3.93	36.0
PSO Triangular in Kenya	2002	5	1	15	15.00	107.14	39	3	150	4	37.50	3.84	58.5
ICC Champions Trophy in Sri Lanka	2002/03	3	2	36	18.00	51.42	20.2	4	60	3	20.00	2.95	40.6
VB Series in Australia	2002/03	4	2	19	19.00	118.75	37.5	0	167	6	27.83	4.41	37.8
Tsunami Relief Fund in Australia	2004/05	1	1	2		100.00	7	0	27	2	13.50	3.85	21.0

ONE-DAY INTERNATIONAL CAREER – AGAINST EACH OPPONENT

Against	M	Inns	NO	Runs	Avge	S/R	Balls	Mdns	Runs	Wkts	Avge
Asia	1	1	1	2		100.00	7	0	27	2	13.50
Bangladesh	2						20	4	51	2	25.50
England	18	11	4	108	15.42	82.44	168.4	2	729	22	33.13
India	18	15	5	109	10.90	78.98	162.2	2	844	15	56.26
Kenya	3	2	1	15	15.00	93.75	22	0	76	3	25.33
New Zealand	27	13	1	143	11.91	75.66	242.4	16	943	49	19.24
Pakistan	22	12	2	129	12.90	58.37	208.1	20	879	37	23.75
Scotland	1						10	0	39	3	13.00
South Africa	45	29	6	275	11.95	75.34	410.4	23	1718	60	28.63
Sri Lanka	18	10	2	89	11.12	56.32	166	9	746	29	25.72
West Indies	27	12	6	132	22.00	74.57	250.4	29	1045	50	20.90
Zimbabwe	12	2	1	16	16.00	88.88	105.3	5	444	21	21.14
CAREER – Australia	**193**	**106**	**28**	**1016**	**13.02**	**72.00**	**1766.4**	**110**	**7514**	**291**	**25.82**
CAREER – ICC World XI	**1**	**1**	**1**	**2**		**100.00**	**7**	**0**	**27**	**2**	**13.50**

ONE-DAY INTERNATIONAL CAREER – ON EACH VENUE AND EACH COUNTRY

Venue	M	Inns	NO	Runs	Avge	S/R	Overs	Mdns	Runs	Wkts	Avge	Econ	S/R
Melbourne (MCG)	28	14	3	95	8.63	53.67	264.3	18	1040	46	22.60	3.93	34.5
Sydney	26	12	4	81	10.12	69.23	230.1	11	978	43	22.74	4.24	32.1
Adelaide	8	5	0	49	9.80	87.50	73.5	5	308	16	19.25	4.17	27.6
Brisbane	7	4	0	56	14.00	53.84	69	2	323	7	46.14	4.68	59.1
Perth	7	6	3	33	11.00	106.45	69	2	317	11	28.81	4.59	37.6
Melbourne (Docklands)	5	3	1	17	8.50	70.83	50	3	177	5	35.40	3.54	60.0
Hobart	4	2	0	9	4.50	52.94	35.2	0	154	8	19.25	4.35	26.5
in Australia	85	46	11	340	9.71	65.00	791.5	41	3297	136	24.24	4.16	34.9

Venue	M	Inns	NO	Runs	Avge	S/R	Overs	Mdns	Runs	Wkts	Avge	Econ	S/R
Lord's	4	1	0	5	5.00	62.50	37	1	188	8	23.50	5.08	27.7
Leeds	3	2	0	5	2.50	20.00	30	1	129	3	43.00	4.30	60.0
Cardiff	2	1	0	15	15.00	107.14	20	1	96	4	24.00	4.80	30.0
Manchester	2	1	1	14		107.69	17	6	27	5	5.40	1.58	20.4
The Oval	2	2	2	11		137.50	16.2	0	88	1	88.00	5.38	98.0
Birmingham	1	1	0	18	18.00	78.26	10	4	29	4	7.25	2.90	15.0
Bristol	1						9	0	48	0		5.33	–
Chester-le-Street	1						10	2	18	1	18.00	1.80	60.0
Nottingham	1	1	0	14	14.00	56.00	9	1	60	2	30.00	6.66	27.0
Worcester	1						10	0	39	3	13.00	3.90	20.0
in England	18	9	3	82	13.66	70.68	168.2	16	722	31	23.29	4.28	32.5

Venue	M	Inns	NO	Runs	Avge	S/R	Overs	Mdns	Runs	Wkts	Avge	Econ	S/R
Delhi	2	1	0	14	14.00	100.00	20	0	89	2	44.50	4.45	60.0
Visakhapatnam	2	1	1	0		0.00	20	0	63	4	15.75	3.15	30.0
Ahmedabad	1	1	1	11		110.00	10	0	45	2	22.50	4.50	30.0
Bangalore	1	1	0	13	13.00	72.22	10	0	58	1	58.00	5.80	60.0
Chennai	1	1	0	24	24.00	171.42	10	0	52	2	26.00	5.20	30.0
Indore	1	1	0	18	18.00	56.25	10	0	64	0		6.40	–
Jaipur	1						10	1	30	0		3.00	–
Kanpur	1	1	0	2	2.00	66.66	9	0	43	1	43.00	4.77	54.0
Kochi	1	1	0	0	0.00	0.00	10	0	42	0		4.20	–
Margao	1						8	0	62	0		7.75	–
Mohali	1	1	1	6		100.00	9	0	36	4	9.00	4.00	13.5
Mumbai	1	1	0	0	0.00	0.00	10	1	28	1	28.00	2.80	60.0
Nagpur	1						9.3	1	34	4	8.50	3.57	14.2
in India	15	10	3	88	12.57	83.01	145.3	3	646	21	30.76	4.43	41.5

Venue	M	Inns	NO	Runs	Avge	S/R	Overs	Mdns	Runs	Wkts	Avge	Econ	S/R
Nairobi	5	1	0	15	15.00	107.14	39	3	150	4	37.50	3.84	234
in Kenya	5	1	0	15	15.00	107.14	39	3	150	4	37.50	3.84	58.5

No Spin

Venue	M	Inns	NO	Runs	Avge	S/R	Overs	Mdns	Runs	Wkts	Avge	Econ	S/R
Auckland	4	1	0	7	7.00	63.63	40	4	121	6	20.16	3.02	40.0
Dunedin	2	1	1	5		71.42	20	1	111	2	55.50	5.55	60.0
Wellington (Basin Reserve)	2	2	1	5	5.00	71.42	20	3	58	4	14.50	2.90	30.0
Christchurch	1						9	0	50	3	16.66	5.55	18.0
Napier	1	1	0	12	12.00	120.00	10	2	34	1	34.00	3.40	60.0
Wellington (Westpac)	1												
in New Zealand	11	5	2	29	9.66	82.85	99	10	374	16	23.37	3.77	37.1

Venue	M	Inns	NO	Runs	Avge	S/R	Overs	Mdns	Runs	Wkts	Avge	Econ	S/R
Lahore	3	1	0	2	2.00	33.33	30	2	129	0		4.30	-
Faisalabad	1	1	1	15		100.00	9.2	0	40	4	10.00	4.28	14.0
Multan (Ibn-e-Qasim)	1						10	1	29	1	29.00	2.90	60.0
Peshawar	1	1	0	13	13.00	118.18	10	0	51	1	51.00	5.10	60.0
Rawalpindi	1	1	1	11		137.50	9	1	47	0		5.22	-
in Pakistan	7	4	2	41	20.50	105.12	68.2	4	296	6	49.33	4.33	68.3

Venue	M	Inns	NO	Runs	Avge	S/R	Overs	Mdns	Runs	Wkts	Avge	Econ	S/R
Cape Town	4	2	0	26	13.00	83.87	38	1	168	8	21.00	4.42	28.5
Durban	4	3	0	35	11.66	67.30	34.1	3	159	5	31.80	4.65	41.0
Port Elizabeth	4	3	1	59	29.50	98.33	26	0	151	6	25.16	5.80	26.0
Johannesburg	3	2	1	38	38.00	76.00	30	2	131	3	43.66	4.36	60.0
Centurion	2	1	0	9	9.00	90.00	18	2	93	3	31.00	5.16	36.0
East London	2	1	0	4	4.00	80.00	20	0	70	3	23.33	3.50	40.0
Bloemfontein	1						10	0	37	1	37.00	3.70	60.0
in South Africa	20	12	2	171	17.10	81.42	176.1	8	809	29	27.89	4.59	36.4

Venue	M	Inns	NO	Runs	Avge	S/R	Overs	Mdns	Runs	Wkts	Avge	Econ	S/R
Colombo (RPS)	4	4	0	73	18.25	56.15	37	2	176	5	35.20	4.75	44.4
Colombo (SSC)	4	3	0	34	11.33	72.34	27.2	3	105	5	21.00	3.84	32.8
Galle	2	1	0	3	3.00	37.50	16	1	75	4	18.75	4.68	24.0
Colombo (PSS)	1						8	0	27	2	13.50	3.37	24.0
in Sri Lanka	11	8	0	110	13.75	59.45	88.2	6	383	16	23.93	4.33	33.1

Venue	M	Inns	NO	Runs	Avge	S/R	Overs	Mdns	Runs	Wkts	Avge	Econ	S/R
Sharjah	8	4	2	36	18.00	100.00	76	3	324	13	24.92	4.26	35.0
in United Arab Emirates	8	4	2	36	18.00	100.00	76	3	324	13	24.92	4.26	35.0

Venue	M	Inns	NO	Runs	Avge	S/R	Overs	Mdns	Runs	Wkts	Avge	Econ	S/R
Port-of-Spain	4	4	2	50	25.00	66.66	37	2	209	4	52.25	5.35	44.4
Bridgetown	3	1	0	20	20.00	117.64	28	5	112	4	28.00	4.00	42.0
Arnos Vale	2	2	1	17	17.00	42.50	19.1	6	63	4	15.75	3.28	28.7
Georgetown	1	1	1	19		111.76	6	0	35	2	17.50	5.83	18.0
St George's	1						10	2	39	3	13.00	3.90	20.0
in West Indies	11	8	4	106	26.50	71.14	102.1	15	458	17	26.94	4.48	36.0

Venue	M	Inns	NO	Runs	Avge	S/R	Overs	Mdns	Runs	Wkts	Avge	Econ	S/R
Harare	2						10	0	42	2	21.00	4.20	30.0
Bulawayo	1						9	1	40	2	20.00	4.44	27.0
In Zimbabwe	3						19	1	82	4	20.50	4.31	28.5

ODI BEST SCORES

Score	Against	Venue	Season
55 (58b)	South Africa	Port Elizabeth	1993/94
36 (69b)	Sri Lanka	Colombo-RPS	2002/03
32 (44b)	South Africa	Johannesburg	1999/00
31 (54b)	Pakistan	Brisbane	2002
30 (40b)	Pakistan	Colombo-SSC	1994/95

BOWLING WICKETS BREAKDOWN

	b	ct	ct+	hw	lbw	st	TOTAL
v Asia XI	0	2	0	0	0	0	2
v Bangladesh	2	0	0	0	0	0	2
v England	4	10	1	0	4	3	22
v India	1	10	1	0	0	3	15
v Kenya	0	0	0	0	1	2	3
v New Zealand	5	24	2	0	10	8	49
v Pakistan	7	11	5	0	7	7	37
v Scotland	1	1	0	0	0	1	3
v South Africa	10	23	4	0	11	12	60
v Sri Lanka	6	15	2	0	2	4	29
v West Indies	10	19	4	0	11	6	50
v Zimbabwe	4	8	3	1	1	4	21
TOTAL	**50**	**123**	**22**	**1**	**47**	**50**	**293**

FOUR WICKETS IN AN INNINGS

Bowling	Against	Venue	Season
5-33	West Indies	Sydney	1996/97
4-19	New Zealand	Melbourne	1993/94
4-25	New Zealand	Adelaide	1993/94
4-29	South Africa	Birmingham	1999
4-33	Pakistan	Lord's	1999
4-34	New Zealand	Sharjah	1993/94
4-34	Zimbabwe	Nagpur	1995/96
4-36	South Africa	Port Elizabeth	1993/94
4-36	West Indies	Mohali	1995/96
4-37	Pakistan	Sydney	1996/97
4-40	South Africa	Faisalabad	1994/95
4-48	West Indies	Melbourne	2000/01
4-52	Pakistan	Adelaide	1996/97

ONE DAY INTERNATIONAL WICKET TAKING MILESTONES

1st wicket	AH Jones	st IA Healy	29	v New Zealand	Wellington	1992/93
50th wicket	RS Mahanama	b	20	v Sri Lanka	Colombo (PSS)	1994/95
100th wicket	JR Murray	c GS Blewett	24	v West Indies	Melbourne	1996/97
150th wicket	CL Cairns	st AC Gilchrist	56	v New Zealand	Sharjah	1997/98
200th wicket	Moin Khan	c AC Gilchrist	6	v Pakistan	Lord's	1999
250th wicket	VVS Laxman	st AC Gilchrist	11	v India	Visakhapatnam	2000/01
Final wicket	Mohammad Yousuf	st RT Ponting	4	v Asia XI	Melbourne	2004/05

LEADING BATSMEN DISMISSED

	b	ct	ct+	lbw	st	TOTAL
DJ Cullinan	3	3	0	0	2	**8**
WJ Cronje	0	4	0	1	2	**7**
CD McMillan	0	0	0	6	0	**6**
Inzamam-ul-Haq	1	0	0	3	2	**6**
JN Rhodes	0	3	1	1	1	**6**

FIELDERS WHO ASSISTED IN DISMISSALS

	M	Ct	St	TOTAL
IA Healy	68	13	21	**34**
AC Gilchrist	123	8	25	**33**
ME Waugh	61	17	0	**17**
MG Bevan	159	11	0	**11**
DR Martyn	84	10	0	**10**

MAN OF THE MATCH AWARDS

Runs	Bowling	Ct	Opponent	Venue	Year
dnb	4/25	1	v New Zealand	Adelaide	1993/94
dnb	4/19	0	v New Zealand	Melbourne	1993/94
dnb	4/34	1	v New Zealand	Sharjah	1993/94
30	3/29	1	v Pakistan	Colombo (SSC)	1994/95
5	2/27	1	v Zimbabwe	Perth	1994/95
dnb	4/34	0	v Zimbabwe	Nagpur	1995/96
6*	4/36	1	v West Indies	Mohali	1995/96
dnb	5/33	0	v West Indies	Sydney	1996/97
11	4/37	1	v Pakistan	Sydney	1996/97
29	3/35	0	v West Indies	Port of Spain	1998/99
18	4/29	0	v South Africa	Birmingham	1999
dnb	4/33	0	v Pakistan	Lord's	1999

MAN OF THE SERIES AWARDS

Runs	Wkts	Ct	Opponent	Series	Year
15	22	4	NZ and SA	B&H World Series	1993/94
6	15	3	SL and WI	B&H World Series	1995/96

MATCHES AS ONE DAY INTERNATIONAL CAPTAIN

Date	Against	Venue	Result
14/01/1998	New Zealand	Sydney	Won
10/01/1999	England	Brisbane	Lost
13/01/1999	Sri Lanka	Sydney	Won
15/01/1999	England	Melbourne	Won
24/01/1999	Sri Lanka	Adelaide	Won
26/01/1999	England	Adelaide	Won
31/01/1999	Sri Lanka	Perth	Won
05/02/1999	England	Sydney	Won
07/02/1999	Sri Lanka	Melbourne	Won
10/02/1999	England	Sydney	Won
13/02/1999	England	Melbourne	Won

LIST A CAREER RECORD – FOR TEAMS PLAYED FOR

Team	M	Inns	NO	Runs	Avge	Overs	Mdns	Runs	Wkts	Avge
Australia(ns)	203	112	29	1056	12.72	1850.4	119	7875	305	25.81
Australia A	3	3	2	17	17.00	26	3	102	2	51.00
Hampshire	71	60	8	568	10.92	571.4	36	2367	120	19.72
Victoria	30	22	1	210	10.00	268.1	18	1201	43	27.93
World XI	4	3	1	28	14.00	20	0	97	3	32.33
LIST A CAREER	311	200	41	1879	11.81	2736.3	176	11642	473	24.61

TWENTY20 CAREER RECORD – FOR TEAMS PLAYED FOR

Team	M	Inns	NO	Runs	Avge	Overs	Mdns	Runs	Wkts	Avge
Hampshire	2	2	0	12	6.00	8	0	51	1	51.00
Melbourne Stars	15	1	1	0	–	47	0	341	11	31.00
Rajasthan Royals	56	29	9	198	9.90	203	1	1471	58	25.36
T20 CAREER	73	32	10	210	9.54	258	1	1863	70	26.61

CAREER HONOURS

Wisden Cricketer of the Year 1994
Wisden Cricketer of the Century 2000
Wisden Leading Cricketer of the Year 2004
World Cup Winner 1999
World Cup Runner-up 1995/96
Man of the Match in World Cup Final 1999 v Pakistan
7-time Ashes Winner (1993, 1994/95, 1997, 1998/99, 2001, 2002/03, 2006/07)
Friends Provident Trophy Runner-up with Hampshire 2007
County Championship Division 2 Runners-up (promoted) with Hampshire 2004
County Championship Division 1 Runners-up with Hampshire 2005
Indian Premier League Winner with Rajasthan Royals 2008

Index

Index

Index

Index

Index

Index

Index